THE WORLD HAD GONE CRAZY!

Vahn, the Aerenarch's Marine bodyguard, appeared and without warning slammed Jaim against the landing rail. "Where is the Aerenarch?"

Jaim shook his head, his long braids splattering water on Vahn's immaculate uniform. "I don't know," he said.

For a moment it looked like Vahn would gut the Rifter right there, and Jaim just stood, chest heaving, making no effort to defend himself.

Vahn turned away then, addressing the Marines in a short voice, but he stopped when one of the guards ran down the path.

"He's just been inside," the man gasped. "And he's gone."

"Don't read this book in the bathtub, or you'll turn into a prune!"

—Debra Doyle,
co-author of
THE PRICE OF THE STARS

Tor books by Sherwood Smith and Dave Trowbridge

The Phoenix in Flight
Ruler of Naught
A Prison Unsought

A PRISON UNSOUGHT

EXORDIUM: BOOK 3

SHERWOOD SMITH AND
DAVE TROWBRIDGE

A TOM DOHERTY ASSOCIATES BOOK
NEW YORK

A PRISON UNSOUGHT

Cover art by Jim Burns

A Tor Book
Published by Tom Doherty Associates, Inc.
175 Fifth Avenue
New York, N.Y. 10010

Tor® is a registered trademark of Tom Doherty Associates, Inc.

ISBN: 0-812-52026-2

First edition: August 1994

Printed in the United States of America

0 9 8 7 6 5 4 3 2 1

Our thanks to James David Audlin—teacher and shaman—for the gift of Tate Kaga; to Lisa Merkin, whose taste for low dives inspired bluff billiards; and to Jan and Rachel Ewell, Leigh Kimmel, Lynn Maudlin, Paula Kate Marmor, Alice Morigi, Jan Clark, and John Hopfner for cheering us on.

PROLOGUE

Imagine, if you will, an ocean, the life-layered aqueous skin of a planet. Above, where life burgeons in the sunlight striking through the shallows, racked by wind and wave, every creature is either predator or prey. It is a world of eternal struggle: the sudden slash of tooth, the lazy diaphanous drift of blood that triggers the predator's frenzy. But deep beneath the surface, undisturbed by any storm, is unchanging calm; there vast schools swim in peace. Death still strikes, but few are the victims compared to the whole.

Now turn your eyes to the world in which we live, the vast ocean of night with its widely scattered islands of life: the planets and Highdwellings of the Thousand Suns. It, too, has its shallows, their sun the power flowing from the Mandala, in whose light, and for whose favor, the Douloi struggle endlessly among themselves. As well its depths, wherein the Polloi work and play and live and love, billions passing their entire lives in freedom.

True, suffering and strife still linger in the Thousand Suns and can never be eliminated, for strife is coaeval with humanity. We have long sought ways to limit its extent, with varying degrees of success. It was the genius of Jaspar Arkad, and those who followed him, to strike the bargain which has since then upheld the Panarchy: that in exchange for power and privilege the Douloi should forever surrender peace.

Magister Lemel sho-Harris
Gnostor of Gnomic Universals
Akademia Elaion, Hellas Prime, 879 A.A..

Court is a place where joys are visible but false, and sorrow hidden but real.

Madame de Maintenon
ca. 500 B.E.

The Bori pushed the deposed Panarch through the opening into darkness, and with a hissed admonition—"Be silent!"—closed the door. Gelasaar heard the lock engage and stood with his back to the door, waiting for his eyes to adjust to the gloom.

The thick, coarse-woven cloth of the *dzirkash-juluth*—the Dol'jharian penance robe that the Bori had disguised him in—did little to ward off the chill of the room. As a dim shape took form at the end of the chamber across from him, he shuffled cautiously forward. Although the plates sewn into the robe were merely dyplast foam, instead of the heavy iridium ordained for Dol'jharians who incurred their superiors' displeasure, the 1.5 standard gees maintained on board the *Fist of Dol'jhar* constrained his movements just as effectively. It was a realistic disguise for one accustomed to standard acceleration, perhaps the only one that would have worked among a people accustomed to the brutal gravitation of Dol'jhar.

But if he was already feeling the effects, after less than a week, how would he feel by the time they finally reached Gehenna? The Panarch smiled ironically. It hardly mattered. The Isolates his justice had exiled there would see to that.

He stopped short as a skull smiled back at him with the humorless grimace of the fleshless dead. It hung above a long, high carven table, flanked by two massive candles that emanated a faint sweet-carrion odor. The shock of recognition was immediate: he was in the Chamber of the Mysteries.

As he puzzled at the significance of this, the Dol'jharian name of the chamber came to him unbidden: *Hurreachu i-Dol*. It meant something like "the Unknowable-Presence-Indwelling of Dol," although the first word was essentially untranslatable. His mere presence here was a death sentence, as it would be for any non-Dol'jharian found in this cultic center of the Avatar's power. But the Bori was Anaris' secretary. Did Anaris intend his death here and now, rather than on Gehenna as his father had decreed?

Behind him the door hissed open, then closed. Before him stood Anaris rahal'Jerrodi, son of Eusabian of Dol'jhar.

Gelasaar pushed the cowl of the robe back and let it drop. He sensed an odd amalgam of emotions in the young man; his stance was easy, but his gaze wary in its appraisal.

Anaris said, "I see you've met Grandfather."

The Panarch nodded. *Is that how it's to be?* Irony had, at the end, become one of Anaris' strongest defenses during his fosterage in the Mandala. He wondered briefly if the young man's choice of this room for their meeting revealed the final victory of his Dol'jharian nature, or a fear of the resurgence of his Panarchist nurture.

"We didn't have much to say to each other," he replied.

Anaris let a short bark of laughter escape him and stepped forward to place his hands on the altar, looking up at the skull of his father's father.

"He has no words for anyone, but most fear his voice nonetheless." The irony was more distinct in Anaris' voice. "Even my father avoids this chamber except in execution of his ritual obligations, especially now that he has formally accepted me as heir."

Ah. Not death, then, but secrecy enforced by religious fear. And now Anaris was heir! No longer rahal'Jerrodi, but achreash-Eusabian, indicating a sharing of the ancestral spirit. Gelasaar knew what that meant: danger and opportunity both.

Anaris stepped away from the altar, tension apparent in the set of his shoulders, the decisive strike of his boots on the inlaid stone of the floor. He wheeled about and faced Gelasaar.

"But I needn't speak to you about the efficacy of ritual, empty though it be. We share that habit, Panarchists and Dol'jharians alike: using ritual as a tool of statecraft."

Gelasaar heard bitterness in the young man's voice, almost accusation. His lessons from the College of Archetype and Ritual had shown him the political necessity of symbolism and ritual, and other factors in his fosterage on Arthelion had emptied him of Dol'jharian superstition. *But we somehow failed to put anything in the place of the void that was left.*

Anaris approached him again.

"This journey itself is the final ritual of power. Only at its end, after I have dealt with the guardians of Gehenna and delivered you to your fate, will authority finally pass from Arthelion to Dol'jhar."

So they don't *know about the Knot!* As had so many others, Anaris and his father had assumed that Gehenna was secured by force of arms, rather than the anomaly that had claimed so many ships before its secret was unraveled, over seven hundred years before. That was not altogether surprising: the Knot was one of the best-kept secrets of the Panarch's government. So he had the option of delivering the exile ship to sudden death, if he so desired.

But Anaris had said "I," not "we," implying that he alone would escort him to Gehenna. If so, his death would do nothing to shake Eusabian's hold on the Thousand Suns; and the tone of Anaris' voice had made his final statement almost a question. *He seeks something from me, but what? What can I give him?*

There was silence between them for a time. Suddenly the Panarch knew what Anaris was asking for, and what he could give him. But was this inspiration merely a cowardly clutching at survival for a few days longer?

No, Gelasaar decided. He knew Anaris. He had raised him almost as one of his own heirs. So he did have one last task as Panarch of the Thousand Suns. He had no doubt that the fusion of Dol'jharian savagery and Panarchist subtlety that his fosterage of Anaris had created would be more than Eusabian could deal with in the end. So if it was to be that Anaris would rule the Thousand Suns, this conversation, and the ones that might follow, would be his final, necessary lessons in statecraft. For Anaris could not rule the Thousand Suns as a Dol'jharian—that kind of brutality would smash the polity beyond repair, if it were not already. He had to learn patience, and compromise, and respect.

And there was hope that Anaris would listen, and hear, and even understand. *He did tell me that Brandon was alive, when there was no need to do so.* So, he could do no less than to be equally open, and more so.

And if, when they reached Gehenna, he had seen no signs of understanding, or if Eusabian were indeed still with them—the decision for death would still be his.

Gelasaar smiled at his foster son.

* * *

Anaris was astonished at the reaction Gelasaar's smile engendered in him. He ruthlessly expunged the feeling, realizing as he did so that nothing his father had done or ever would do could ever evince any such emotion from him. But it was a weakness he could ill afford.

"You know that is not so," said the Panarch. He held up his hand, forestalling Anaris' objection. "Oh, certainly the transfer of authority will appear valid to your fellow Dol'jharians, but they are naught but an atom in the void against the trillions you intend to rule."

He still hopes the paliach will fail.

"No," continued Gelasaar, "you cannot hope to succeed without adopting and adapting the rituals of power, as you term them, that we have evolved over the past millennium. They are too deeply ingrained in the people of the Thousand Suns." He smiled again. "But you, at least, can see this, and grasp the necessity, I think. Your father cannot."

"Agreed," Anaris replied. "He cannot and will not." He could sense control of the conversation passing to the Panarch, as had always been the case on Arthelion during his fosterage there. It was time to assert his authority.

"But neither, I fear, could your son Brandon."

Anaris saw only a hint of pain flicker across the Panarch's face, and knew he would not have seen even that much had the deposed ruler not admitted to himself the truth of the statement. Brandon had utterly abandoned his responsibilities by avoiding his Enkainion—no matter that the act had saved his life.

"I am grateful to you for telling me he lives," the Panarch said mildly. "What have you heard of him?"

It pleased Anaris that Gelasaar asked simply, without any hint of either demand or plea. For now he would tell him the bare minimum. Perhaps later he would describe the humiliation Brandon had inflicted on the Avatar in the Mandala.

"He was taken on board the battlecruiser *Mbwa Kali* near Rifthaven, in the company of a group of Rifters. By now he is no doubt safe on Ares."

"Safe?" the Panarch repeated. "No more than you, I should say. Do you remember so little of your lessons in the Mandala?"

Chagrined, Anaris realized that he'd let control slip away from him again, but he forbore to interrupt. There was an odd comfort in resuming the old relationship, overlaid with the newer comfort of knowing that now he held authority.

"My eldest son was fond of saying that politics is the continuation of war by other means," the Panarch continued. "I'm not sure if he knew that for the misquotation of an ancient theorist of Lost Earth that it was, but it was and is true of the Panarchy. Suspicion, intrigue, treachery, and violence—both subtle and overt—are the price we Douloi pay for our privilege, so that, at least ideally, under us the Polloi may live in freedom."

The Panarch's gaze was distant with the intensity of his thoughts. Never on Arthelion had Gelasaar spoken so frankly. It was as if the loss of power had liberated him.

"Think, Anaris! Ares must now be the last bastion of my government, for its location is unknown to your father. There will be concentrated all the millennial subtlety of the surviving Douloi, with Brandon at the focus of all their hopes and fears.

"You know your opponent, Anaris—there is only one, your father, and the terms of your engagement are fixed by ancient tradition and religious force. On Ares my son can be sure of neither his friends nor his enemies, nor can he be sure that one will not become the other at a moment's notice."

Gelasaar was silent for a moment, then shook his head. "I did not know him as well as I should have. There is no more that I can do. I can only hope that he will, in the end, prove to be a true scion of Jaspar Arkad."

The Panarch looked up at the Dol'jharian heir. "But your task is simpler. And even though I feel sure your father's plans will fail, though I know not how, I would have you . . ."

Gelasaar stopped, looking through Anaris—past him, to some vision of the future.

After a time Anaris broke the silence. "What, Gelasaar? What of me?"

The Panarch's focus returned to Anaris' face, and he sighed. "I would have you on the Emerald Throne rather than your father, if we are defeated."

The deposed ruler turned away and looked up at the skull grinning down at them. "And I'm sure we have very little time. Both of us."

Anaris couldn't decide who he meant: himself and Anaris, or himself and Brandon.

The Panarch turned back to him.

"So let us make the best use of it."

Part One

One

❋

ARES

The tailor's deft fingers twitched at sleeves and hem, making certain the tunic's lines were straight, the fit flawless. Aerenarch Brandon vlith-Arkad stood patiently, his eyes distracted, under the man's ministrations.

No one spoke, or moved, but still the tailor exhibited signs of increasing nervousness. At last he glanced one last time at his finger-chrono and muttered, "It'll have to do . . . time is short . . . it might suffice."

Brandon glanced sideways into the mirror just once. Watching from across the room, the Aerenarch's personal guard, Jaim, saw blue eyes meet blue eyes in the mirror, then scan briefly down the slim figure in mourning white. The cloth was the best available, and the cut of tunic and trousers perfect—as one would expect from Archon Srivashti's own personal tailor—but Jaim had never seen plainer civilian formal wear. The Aerenarch wore no decorations, and his only ornament was the signet with the dark-faced charioteer that Jaim had seen on his hand since their first meeting.

He also wore a boswell, whose plain face gave no hint that

it was one of the most powerful kinds made. The Aerenarch checked it, his eyes still distracted, then he looked up at Jaim.

"Ready?"

Jaim had been ready for an hour. He glanced in the mirror at his new livery. The color he had chosen was gray—the gray of stone, of steel, of compromise between light and darkness.

Jaim nodded.

"Then let's go," the Aerenarch said.

After several days of intense tutoring, Jaim had a fair understanding of the externals of Douloi protocol. Instead of speaking, he bowed, the low bow of servant to sovereign.

The gesture was a kind of question. Brandon stopped with a look of mild inquiry, and then he bowed to Jaim, the same bow, to the precise degree. It was a wordless answer, but it was the right answer.

Jaim smiled as he walked behind Brandon to the transtube.

In the central house on the other side of the lake, Vannis Scefi-Cartano, Aerenarch-Consort to Brandon's eldest brother (now deceased), faced the biggest crisis of her life, and she had nothing to wear.

She cursed steadily as she ripped gown after gown from the closet and flung them onto the floor. Her maid stood helplessly in the background, her eyes a silent reproach. They both knew who would have to pick up the mess after Vannis was done.

Vannis bit her lip, halted by memory of her mother's soft voice in rebuke: *There is never a time, or an excuse, for bad manners*, followed by her governess' practical tones: *Treat your servants like human beings, and they will be loyal; treat them like machines and they will plot against you.*

Vannis stared hopelessly at the last of her clothes, then pressed her fingers against her eyes. "That chatzing blungekisser Corbiat, she *knows* what this means to me," Vannis muttered into her palms.

What to do?

Resolutely she lowered her hands. Yenef stood there still, watching. Alarm kindled in Vannis: another of her mother's lessons warned of letting servants find out too much about one's private goals and losses. Each secret learned was another weapon to be used against one.

"Go to the front, see if the Aerenarch has left yet," Vannis said. "Come to me as soon as he leaves."

Yenef bowed, hands together, and left silently.

Vannis sighed, sinking down onto a couch. What to do? It was all very well for the *novosti* to keep talking of daring and heroism and hair's-breadth escapes. Vannis had enjoyed the aura of danger and desperation that being a refugee had surrounded her with on her arrival—but that kind of thing did not last.

When it all started, Vannis had cursed the accident that disabled the fiveskip on Rista's yacht, preventing her from being on Arthelion for Brandon's Enkainion. She'd raged futilely as time wore on, knowing how angry Semion would be; he had interfered rarely in her life, but when her husband bestirred himself to make a request of her, she had taken care to see that it was done. He had wanted her to be at that Enkainion.

When they were finally able to skip to Arthelion's middle system, it was to horrifying news: the Panarchy was at war; Arthelion had fallen to the Panarch's old enemy from Dol'jhar; the Panarch was a prisoner. Vannis still did not know how the yacht's captain obtained the code for Ares, but she had, and Rista and Vannis were among the first refugees.

During that first few weeks it had been fun, the handful of Douloi among the military elite on Ares. Protocol had even been relaxed to a degree, military and civilian, Downsider and Highdweller, Douloi and Polloi mixing freely. But that was before the number of refugees increased, and the best habitations of the civilian portion of the huge station became crowded with the Service Families of the Panarchy of the Thousand Suns.

Now everyone was a refugee, and with the known universe so shattered, the old rules seemed to bind tighter than before.

Vannis had traveled with just enough clothing for a short stay, and had not brought much in white, which was the color of death, or of youth. The awful symbolism haunted her dreams: the fraction of her once vast wardrobe that she now possessed was a tangible reminder of the fraction of position that she now held.

Semion was dead, and she had been his consort, but she was not an Arkad. That was according to ancient law: unlike other Douloi marriages, when spousal adoption was negotiated at the marriage contract, an outsider married to an Arkad was only adopted into the ruling Family on the accession of his or her spouse, the Panarch or Kyriarch directly descended from Jaspar Arkad a millennium ago.

Now that Semion was dead, her position as the foremost person in social circles had shifted to ambiguity. And though she had been on the fringes of political power, she had not—*yet!*—crossed over.

As soon as the news about Semion became known, Vannis had gone to mourning white, which was entirely correct, just as it was correct for people to use her titles. And they had automatically accorded her social preference, but that would last just until she stopped wearing mourning. For the truth was, she no longer had any real position beyond her own family's. The high titles, without political clout, were mere air.

And if that weren't problem enough, she no longer had the highest title among the refugees; there was a new Aerenarch.

Somehow, the Panarch's youngest son had miraculously escaped the mass murder at his own Enkainion, and he was now recently arrived on Ares. He would take his place among them at tonight's reception.

Vannis' future depended on this reception—and she had nothing new to wear: everyone had seen these half dozen white gowns, despite her attempts to vary them with her jewels and artful drapings of exotic fabrics.

She kicked viciously at the filmy lengths of shanta-silk and mothgauze lying on the floor. She'd seen a bleak hint of her future role in the fact that the four tailors that a low-ranking woman named Corbiat had managed to bring in her retinue had been busy working for someone else; everyone else, it seemed, had priority.

For the Aerenarch-Consort who had set fashions for over a decade to appear at this reception in an old, much-worn garden-party white gown would be humiliating. Should she thumb her ear at the universe and wear *all* her jewels?

"Damnation!" Only effort of will kept her from weeping; she would not, even if she was flayed, betray herself with red, puffy eyes.

"Your Highness," Yenef spoke from the doorway. "The Aerenarch is just leaving the Enclave."

Vannis turned. "Who's he with, and what is he wearing?"

"Just one other man, Highness," Yenef said. "I don't know him; in gray, no device or insignia. The Aerenarch is in white. Looked like a uniform at first," she added.

"He can't be wearing a naval uniform," Vannis exclaimed, thinking: *Wasn't he thrown out of the Navy? The Academy, anyway.*

Yenef shook her head. "Plain, Highness." Unasked, she

dropped a chip into the console slot and Vannis saw two male figures walking across the grass toward the central pavilion. The colors were hard to discern because of the darkness; the imager apparently had poor light enhancers.

Vannis hit the enlarge key and studied the flattened figures. The tall one in gray could be dismissed—he walked in the place of a bodyguard. Brandon . . .

Vannis chewed her underlip. His tunic was indeed utterly plain; he didn't even wear any jewels. What did it mean?

Doesn't matter what it means.

Killing the image with a sweep of her hand, she scanned the riot of colorful cloth on the floor. "Ah." She grabbed at the shimmering folds of a white shanta-silk gown and ripped away the jeweled lace trim and the overskirt of fine-spun gossamer.

"Put my jewels away," she snapped over her shoulder. "And find my white slippers. No, not those, the *morning* slippers—"

Yenef sent her an eloquent look as she turned to obey, and Vannis laughed. The maid probably thought she'd gone crazy. *And maybe I have, a little*, she thought.

Sitting down at her dressing table, she tore the jewels out of her high-dressed hair, and laughed again.

⁂ ⁂ ⁂

Jaim sniffed the air as he followed Brandon down the curving path toward the huge, golden-lit pavilion. Under the oneill's false night the air was cool and soft, laden with the scents of loam and blossoms and fresh water. Jaim could almost believe he was on a planet: high overhead, the patterns of light created by the dwellings on the far side, nine kilometers away, simulated the constellations of a planetary sky. He stopped, staring upward, as the intricate design of Ares suddenly became apparent to him. Now, as never before, the awesome wealth and subtlety of Douloi culture gripped him viscerally. The dwellings in the Ares oneill were arranged not only to appeal to people in their proximity but also with an eye to their appearance in the night sky of the opposite surface.

Ahead, Brandon was silhouetted against a gentle incline at the edge of the lake, staring off across the water and the distant lights on its far side. For a moment Jaim had the sense that all the constellations of Ares were revolving around that single feature.

And then Jaim remembered the echoing spaces of New Glastonbury on Desrien, and the shock on Brandon's face as the

Dreamtime released him. He shook off the mood and joined Brandon at the water's edge.

They stood a moment in silence. Water lapped at the shore, and unseen frogs croaked a curious rhythm. In the distance the light of the dwellings overhead outlined rolling hills. Jaim heard the rush of a waterfall; beyond them the path veered between a graceful line of trees. Before them was the spectacular pavilion, a big building of graceful lines that could never have withstood real weather.

He looked over at the Aerenarch, trying to assess his mood. Anticipation? He had spoken rarely since their debarkation from Nukiel's cruiser, except to address practical concerns.

They had not left the Arkadic Enclave since their arrival. Officially it was so that Brandon could recover—and the fading bruises on his face from the fight on Rifthaven had been mute testimony to the truth of that—but actually the time had been spent in hidden preparations. Security had been first, at Commander Nyberg's orders. Brandon had not questioned it, had not made any demands, but somehow the Marine solarch that Brandon had befriended aboard Nukiel's cruiser had been attached to them. It was Vahn who had given Jaim his lessons in Douloi usage.

And it was Vahn who awaited them at the pavilion, as part of the honor guard—from an unseen vantage, he would watch the reception and provide Jaim with information he might need via boswell.

But there had also been a staff to assemble, and clothing to order—all the trappings of the last free Royal of the vast collection of planets and Highdwellings called the Panarchy of the Thousand Suns. Brandon had submitted to all without demur, not asserting any demands of his own until this evening when he insisted on that white tunic without any ornamentation at all, to the dismay of Archon Srivashti's little tailor, who had no doubt labored for days on the resplendent formal mourning tunic that Brandon had rejected.

Jaim had watched, confused; the rejected tunic was handsome with a kind of barbaric splendor, and it certainly suited Brandon's trim body to perfection. It looked like something a king in a serial chip would wear, but that was probably the way that the nicks dressed—they certainly had the wealth. The tailor had been aghast at Brandon's polite but insistent refusal to wear it, and no one had spoken at all when the Aerenarch changed.

Jaim's eyes went beyond the straight shoulders in the plain

tunic to the dwellings across the lake, no more than an uneven line on the horizon and a string of twinkling lights. Large as the oneill was, he did not think it was large enough to house both the civilian portion of the naval population and the influx of refugees, not while maintaining the agricultural portions of the interior that made the station largely self-sufficient. Had those lesser in rank been moved somewhere—into the cap portion of the station, perhaps?

Vahn might know, he realized. Though as newly arrived as Jaim, he was in constant contact with the military authorities. Using the boswell's privacy mode so as not to disturb Brandon, he queried: *(Where are the naval dependents?)*

Vahn's reply was prompt: *(Military quarters. The Cap.)* The neural link somehow conveyed a fine shade of irony as Vahn added, *(A retreat, you might say, but not a rout.)*

It was the first sign, Jaim realized later, of trouble.

⁂ ⁂ ⁂

"Vannis, do hurry, the reception has begun," Rista said from the hallway. She appeared a moment later and gasped. "Vannis? Are you *ill?*"

Vannis turned away from her mirror and smiled. Rista's round, pleasing figure was enhanced by a glittering gown of pale lavender, sprinkled across by diamonds, kauch-pearls, and deep violet *tizti* stones, her pale hair dressed high, circled by a coronet of faceted tizti. When she moved, reddish fires seemed to flicker in the hearts of the stones. Fine filigree bracelets encircled her plump arms and her neck, which still had the smoothness of youth.

Vannis turned away and laughed as she faced her own reflection. The plainness of her white unadorned gown, and the simple sweep of her heavy brown hair, bound up only with a thin strand of pearls, was quite a contrast. She'd had to dismiss Yenef while she redid her hair; the reproach in the woman's eyes as she undid what had taken her maid the better part of two hours to achieve had been distracting.

"What have you done?" Rista demanded, her jeweled shoes clattering on the parquet floor. Then she gasped, and clutched at her neck. "You haven't heard something—that is, they haven't gotten word from the Panarch? About court mourning?"

"Of course not," Vannis said soothingly. "You are entirely

correct, I think: since the Panarch is alive, but is not here, you mourn for his heir as is customary on your planet."

Rista sighed, plumping down onto a chair. "That's what Matir Masaud said, but it could always have been a mislead, to make trouble." She blinked at Vannis. "Really, there's never *been* anything like this before, has there? You have it simple—you mourn a spouse—but for the rest of us . . . no one knows what to do!" She frowned. "But what you're wearing!" She gestured, her rings flashing. "What does it *mean?*"

"We are at war," Vannis said. "Is it not time to retrench?"

Rista's round mouth opened, then closed again. She bit her underlip, then breathed a soft laugh. "If you carry this off, NorSothu will be furious. I hear she's brought out some embroidered thing she had made for their Archon's funeral, and she's got a Hopfneriad wig—complete with butterflies." Rista's hands fluttered about her head. "But, Vannis, we're *late*."

Vannis smiled. This was, she reflected, another evidence of the distance between the consort of an Aerenarch and someone whose ambitions went no higher than a Chivalate. Vannis had watched Brandon's progress along the lakeside to the pavilion, waiting in case he might alter his course and come to escort her.

He had not, of course. She had no doubt he knew where she was housed. But he had not contacted her at all since his arrival; she had found through some discreet checking that he initiated no contact save only one, an inquiry after a Rifter boy from his rescue ship, who had gotten somehow mixed up with the Kelly.

It could mean anything, and eventually she would find out. Right now, though, it meant that he would arrive alone. She had no desire to arrive at the same time unless they were together.

The women stepped out onto the lamplit slidewalk. An aromatic breeze riffled through their hair and clothing as the slide whispered its way toward the pavilion halfway around the lake.

Rista gossiped on about how that hideous Lady Risiena Ghettierus had refused to take her husband into her quarters, and the poor gnostor had been forced to take a room with the administrative functionaries. She laughed about it.

Vannis laughed as well and did not mention that the news was already old. Her contacts had reported just hours ago that the gnostor Omilov, Brandon's old tutor, had been invited to take up residence with the High Phanist—he was to move the next morning. A social blow for Risiena, she thought, and then dismissed the woman from her mind as she glanced across the lake at the splendid building built to house the Panarch's family.

The Arkadic Enclave, an elegantly rambling enlargement of the manor of the Temenarch Illyahin, who had willed her oneill to the Navy eight hundred years before, was large enough for a sizable family and all the attendant staff—although it was unoccupied except during the occasional visits of Panarchs and Kyriarchs. Brandon had no family, and his staff, from all reports, was minimal. No one else had moved in with him. Why had Brandon not invited his brother's wife to occupy one of the empty suites?

I wish I'd bedded him, Vannis thought suddenly. It was not for lack of interest that she had refrained—an interest that had gone both ways, she was certain, at least upon their initial meeting.

But Semion had been very clear on the subject. *You will stay away from my youngest brother,* he'd said in that cold, dispassionate voice. He'd added with faint distaste, *He's stupid and lazy, and what's worse, a drunken sot. I will not have the Family made a target for the coarse-minded.*

A drunk could not be trusted to keep quiet, and anyway the idea that that handsome face had no wit behind it had killed her interest. Some might have a taste for beautiful dolls, but that was not one of her vices.

As well; raised by an utterly permissive family, she had been bemused to find out that the general taboo against incest had extended, among the Panarchy's oldest families, to inlaws. *Not for genetic considerations, but for reasons of power.*

The slidewalk stopped and they stepped off. Ahead were the huge arches of the pavilion. The graceful intricacies of a melody drifted out, amid laughter and the tinkling of crystal. *The sounds of impending battle,* Vannis thought, smiling in the darkness. Circumstance had denied her political power, but she had been trained from birth in all the social arts. The ballroom was her theater of war.

As they walked up the wide, shallow marble steps, Vannis thought about how carefully she had behaved since her arrival, always mentally assessing what Semion's ubiquitous spies would report of her conduct.

She gritted her teeth. Semion was gone. It was time for her to recoup on her own. The campaign would begin here and now.

They crossed the main antechamber in silence, Rista fingering her hair with nervous gestures. The steward waiting at the huge carved doors bowed to them; as the lackeys sprang to the doors, he grounded his mace, and over the chimes he called, "Her Highness Vannis Scefi-Cartano and the Chival Rista Litsu-Frazhien."

"Her Highness"—no mention of "Aerenarch-Consort." So the battle begins, Vannis thought, straightening her back as faces turned in their direction.

A quick scan singled out Brandon's slim figure across the room. He looked up, smiling, his blue eyes quizzical.

Vannis stepped into the ballroom.

⁂ ⁂ ⁂

For the first few minutes, Jaim was mesmerized by the spectacular panoply before him. The ballroom was a vision of elegance, all marble and costly draperies, glittering chandeliers floating above the guests, and a low, faux balustrade behind which was an immense, realtime vid of Ares seen from space. The illusion was nearly perfect, as though the back of the immense hall was open to space, the massive Cap with its scattered ship bays—each capable of half swallowing a seven-kilometer-long battlecruiser—looming over the slowly rotating oneill which was attached to its underside like the stem of a mushroom, the whole surrounded by a glittering cloud of ships.

But it was the people who held Jaim's attention. Although he had been raised on crowded Rifthaven, among people who valued individualism above almost anything else, nothing could ever have prepared him for the vision of a gathering of the High Douloi. It was an onslaught to the senses that rendered him almost giddy until he was able to begin separating out individuals from the whole.

Luckily his position required him to be merely present; the Douloi moved around him as if he were utterly invisible, just as Vahn had warned him. Jaim was grateful for the respite.

Their movements reminded him at first of the ripple of the breezes through the reeds at the lakeside. How did such a crowd know when to sidestep, when to come forward, and when to defer? They did it with those graceful, stylized gestures that reminded him of some kind of dance, the smiling faces with their watchful eyes just like masks.

From time to time, Vahn provided names as the faces passed.

Jaim knew he ought to listen, and perhaps he would later recall them. Now it was enough to concentrate on being invisible—and impalpable. He must not step directly into anyone's path, yet he had to scan them all for weapons, for intent to attack.

Brandon never faltered as the Douloi flowed around him. He seemed to know when to turn, and whom to address first as he received obeisance after obeisance, touching lightly the open hands sometimes with his palms, sometimes just his fingers.

Jaim began to notice details, eddies of collusion and avoidance in the graceful movements of the Douloi. There were undercurrents of tension dividing the guests. The most noticeable was the segregation of Downsiders from Highdwellers. Jaim's Ulanshu training soon elucidated a reason for this that had nothing to do with politics: Downsiders required more interpersonal distance than Highdwellers, so that mixed groups naturally tended to break up. He also noted that only Highdwellers were to be found along the low balustrade fronting the vid of Ares—the Downsiders were apparently less comfortable with the illusion.

Jaim sighed. It seemed so futile. Even were there not the grievances between Downsiders and Highdwellers that, according to Vahn, the late Aerenarch Semion had encouraged for political gain, something so simple as a psychological preference could divide people.

Those who see naught but a single road have no choice in where it takes them, Jaim's dead mate, Reth Silverknife, had once said.

Jaim brought his mind firmly back to the present, concentrating on the other eddies in the movements of the guests: younger naval officers standing apart from the two civilian groups, while older naval figures could be seen among both. Nyberg stood carefully neutral.

But the focus of all was the Aerenarch. Jaim noted the flash and glitter of the signet on Brandon's finger, and how eyes watched it, then lifted away quickly to meet other gazes. Jaim could not read those looks, but he sensed a question spreading among them.

Once the crowd parted. Jaim observed no signal, but somehow they knew. The man who knelt before Brandon had silver hair and a pointed beard, and his handsome face was lined. His spare frame, clothed in dark blue velvet, somehow gave the impression of great physical strength, just as the sheath of a rapier implies its edge; Jaim knew here was another Ulanshu master.

This time he heard Vahn's info.

(Archon Srivashti. Head of one of the most powerful Downsider Families.) Vahn's flat voice hinted at danger—as if Jaim could not sense it on his own.

"Welcome, Highness," the Archon said, his voice a husky murmur just above a whisper. "After weeks of grim tidings, your restoration to the living has been welcomed as a miracle."

"Thank you, Your Grace," Brandon said, just touching the offered palms.

(Used the honorific for Archon, not his territorial name,) came Vahn's voice. *(Lost control of his planet Timberwell, forced to withdraw to the Highdwellings.)*

Srivashti had risen. He was taller than the Aerenarch. His light eyes, a curious color midway between brown and gray, narrowed slightly, and Brandon said, "Thank you for the loan of your tailor."

"He did not please you?"

Brandon smiled. "He nearly killed himself in his efforts to finish a truly memorable design—" Jaim wondered if the hesitation he heard before the word "memorable" was really there, or only his imagination. Brandon gestured deprecatingly down his length and added, "But without word from my father . . ."

"Ah." Srivashti bowed low. "Entirely correct."

Again a bow, and Brandon also bowed, and then the Archon disappeared in the crowd.

Jaim found that he'd been holding his breath. What had just happened here?

Vahn must have sensed something, for his voice came: *(The Aerenarch is in private mourning. He probably could speak for his father and order official mourning for the Court—appearing in it would be an indirect order—but he chose not.)*

The flat tones carried no hints of meaning, but Jaim was certain he'd missed something important. Resolving to examine it later, he then became aware that once again the figures moved smoothly back, this time with a susurrus of whispers.

Brandon looked down the long length of the room toward two newly arrived women. The one who commanded the eye was small and straight, gowned in unrelieved white. The contrast was startling; framed by the splashes and glitter of complicated color around her, the simplicity of her garments seemed to enhance the smooth lines of her body.

(Vannis Scefi-Cartano, the former Aerenarch's consort.)

So this was the woman whose smiling adroitness had done the officers' dependents out of their housing. She paused in the center of the doorway, a figure so light and graceful she seemed to be a holo rather than real, and then she moved forward with the control of a trained dancer. Reth Silverknife had moved just so. Jaim felt another pang of grief and could not look away. Jaim heard the rustle of Vannis' gown about her feet before she spoke.

"Brandon!" Her voice was clear and musical. Then she sank into a profound bow, her body expressive of sorrow but her eyes joyful.

"Vannis," Brandon said, raising her to her feet. His grip shifted, and he carried her fingers to his lips, where they lingered, the woman smiling brilliantly up into his eyes, before both dropped their hands.

She looked around as if breaking a reverie, then gestured, a quick fluttering movement. "There will be time for talk. I hear music; let us dance."

Brandon bowed and held out his arm.

Jaim moved back, observing narrowed eyes and thin smiles.

The unseen orchestra skillfully turned the background music into a waltz, and around Jaim the Douloi paired off, whirling with practiced ease about the gleaming floor. In the center Brandon and Vannis turned and stepped, their plain clothing marking them out from the bejeweled whites and grays and blacks and lavenders around them.

Jaim watched with interest, until he sensed someone at his shoulder. He looked into a familiar face.

It was Osri Omilov, the gnostor's son. The dark eyes that had been so hateful during the long adventures aboard the *Telvarna* were now perplexed.

Jaim belatedly remembered his role, and bowed, the correct degree for the heir of a Chival.

To his surprise, Osri looked confused for a moment, then he acknowledged with a curt nod. "Have you—" He broke off, watching another surge in the crowd.

This time the susurration conveyed excitement—even alarm. The crowd parted rather more quickly, and Jaim saw the familiar tiny white-furred Eya'a, their blue mouths open, faceted eyes throwing back the light from the wall sconces. They walked quickly, without looking directly at any of the humans, their gossamer-light robes fluttering. Behind them, tall, straight, and forbidding, was Vi'ya, her ubiquitous plain black flight suit so out of place in this environment that Jaim grinned.

Her head turned then, her long, glossy tail of space-black hair swinging past her hips, and her black eyes caught Jaim's gaze. Unsmiling, she gave a slight nod of recognition, and then shock burned through Jaim when he saw two fingers just brush against her clothing as she walked on. *Meeting: ASAP.*

Beside him, Osri drew a breath. "What is she doing here?"

"Has to be as interpreter," Jaim said. "Only one who can communicate with the Eya'a."

"I should have said, what are *they* doing here?" Osri muttered.

Jaim grinned again. He was used to the Eya'a, who, despite their fearsome reputation for psi powers, had never harmed anyone aboard the *Telvarna.*

"They have ambassadorial status," Jaim said. "Though nobody knows if they know it." *Vi'ya must have got them to come just so she could signal me.* Alarm accelerated his heartbeat.

* * *

Vannis had danced once with Brandon some years before. She had forgotten how good he was. For a time it took all her attention to match her movements to his, making them seem effortless; he seemed to like speed, and she had to focus to keep vertigo from blurring the edges of her vision.

But she got her bearings and swiftly assessed the situation. She knew that every pair of eyes was on them, questions circulating. She could almost hear her light words to Rista being repeated from tongue to ear:—*Time to retrench*—and knew that once again, she'd managed to pull off a social coup.

But what was Brandon's reason? It couldn't be the same—she ought to find out. Turning her focus on him, she was aware of his attention just over her shoulder, and his clasp was light and impersonal.

She flicked a glance, just to see a pair of small sentients moving through the humans, their twiggy feet brushing over the marble floor in a way that gave her shudders. These were supposedly the ones who could fry brains from a distance. She was vaguely aware of the tall, dark-eyed unsmiling woman behind them, but dismissed her from consciousness with the scarcely acknowledged label: servant.

More interesting was why Brandon watched their progress.

Surely he was not afraid of the Eya'a's psi powers? Then she remembered someone saying that these sentients had also been on the ship that had rescued him. Strange: she'd have to ask him about that. But right now, she had to make certain of his attitude toward her.

He'd acknowledged her right to the first dance; that was an unlooked-for boon. It assured—for the moment, anyway—her social supremacy. Now to assess, if she could, what it meant to him. *Simplicity—real mourning, by any chance?*

"I'm sorry about your brothers," she said.

He glanced down, and she met his eyes directly. There was nothing to be read in his gaze beyond polite inquiry.

"I'm sorry about your husband," he said.

How to interpret that?

She tried again, this time taking a small risk. "It seems the time for the family to draw together."

Brandon spun them suddenly into a tight turn, and Vannis caught a flash of rainbow color as they veered between two converging couples.

"We all need to draw together," he replied.

Was he really as stupid as Semion had said? Their social interactions hitherto had been so damned limited! She cast about mentally for some kind of opener to give her a hint of what—if anything—went on behind those blue eyes.

But then he spoke, with a sudden, serious look, "Did they tell you my father lives?"

She nodded. "I heard. It's true, then?"

"I hope it is still true," he murmured.

"What should be done?"

He smiled. "Get him back."

The dance ended; more time had passed than she'd assumed. He bowed, relinquishing her to the first hand that reached.

She smiled, bowed back, and forced herself not to look after him as he moved away.

Two

"I thought," Anaris said, "that you valued truth."

"So I do," Gelasaar replied.

"Then why did your advisers not warn you about Semion?"

"There are layers to truth," the Panarch began.

"Sophistry," Anaris remarked.

The Panarch's eyes narrowed with mild amusment. "Let me rephrase, then: there are layers to perception."

"They either told you about Semion's excesses, or they did not."

The Panarch seemed to slip into reverie, his brow clear and untroubled. Anaris waited in silence, the dirazh'u quiescent in his hands.

At last Gelasaar looked up. "They did, but obliquely."

"They have not been so oblique since?"

"No," said the Panarch. "We have the leisure—one might call it the luxury—to be direct."

"Ah," Anaris said, "one would expect the opposite. When you were in power, since you say you valued truth from those around you, directness would be deemed a virtue."

The Panarch inclined his head. "When we were in power, time and the weight—measured in consequences—of one's words combined in exponential pressure. To function at all under those circumstances, one learns the language of compromise."

⁂ ⁂ ⁂

Eloatri paced the perimeter of the Cloister, entertaining herself with speculations about the mind and motives of the unknown person who had designed this area. She had located, so far, two hidden accesses to private transtubes, making her wonder what connection the religious enclave here on Ares had had with Panarchist government in the past.

I am too new to my position, she thought. No doubt somewhere on Desrien were writings destined only for the eyes of the High Phanist. But the Digrammaton had come to her so recently, and she was still recovering from the spectacularly unconventional method of the transfer of power.

She rubbed her palm, wincing; she would never be entirely free of the pain of the burn inflicted on her by the Digrammaton in its mysterious leap across the light-years separating Arthelion and Desrien. Her time since then had been spent in learning a radically new religious tradition—and in finding the persons the Dreamtime bade her follow. Except one, still unidentified, all had come to Desrien, had been seized by the Dreamtime, and now were here, with her, on Ares.

Now what?

The com chimed, and she welcomed the distraction gratefully. At her acknowledgment the screen windowed up the image of Admiral Nyberg. She'd only met him once, upon her arrival here, and had come away with an impression of a careful, calculating, yet utterly honest man. *The perfect choice to command Ares.*

"Numen," he began without preamble, "forgive me for not making this call in person."

She waved her hand in negation and he continued.

"Since this line is not secure, I will be brief, and somewhat oracular." To her astonishment, evanescent humor eased the lines in Nyberg's austere, craggy face. "Captain Nukiel said you would understand. I've been told you are the only human other than the Dol'jharian woman to whom the Eya'a have responded; and we have learned from Lieutenant Omilov that they are capable of detecting, at some distance, the presence of

Urian machinery. Therefore, you will understand our eagerness to learn more about these sentients. Can you help us?"

The hyperwave. When she arrived on Ares she had been surprised that the Navy would choose to inform her of the existence of the captured hyperwave; now she was beginning to realize that the position of High Phanist carried more weight than she had assumed.

She nodded, choosing her words carefully. "I doubt that I myself can be of much assistance. Our communication, such as it is, is highly abstract—more a recognition of archetypal energies than anything else." She noted respectful incomprehension in his expression. "However, there is someone who may be able to assist."

She overrode his thanks with an upraised hand and spoke with the full authority of her office. "But know you, Admiral, that Telos moves in these people and those sentients: they are a hinge of Time. I will do nothing to imperil the opening of that door."

He nodded once, acknowledging her concern. "I understand, Numen. My concern is the safety of Ares and the prosecution of the war against Dol'jhar. I hope our paths will run parallel."

"I'm sure they will," she replied. "I will always be available to you."

"And I to you, Numen. Thank you."

His image flickered out. Eloatri shook her head and sighed, wondering yet again why it was *she* who had been chosen. *I do not like politics, and I know so little of these Douloi.* But Tomiko had made it clear her wishes were the least of priorities: she saw again the vision of the cup and its terrible liquid, and what the dying Tomiko said to her: *Surely you did not suppose you drank that for yourself?*

She shuddered. *The taste of blood.*

Reminded of the urgency of her task, she turned her focus from the past to the present.

The Cloister was a square building around a central private garden. Someone had told her it mirrored the Arkadic Enclave, but was not as large. She wondered how many secret egresses that other Enclave boasted—and if that smiling, blue-eyed Aerenarch had found any of them yet.

Passing an open window, she glanced across a leg of the lake at the Arkadic Enclave, which was partially visible a kilometer or so away. The gnostor Sebastian Omilov had accepted her invitation to make his abode with her, and his few belongings had been sent over, but he himself had yet to appear.

Probably still asleep, she thought. He, too, had stayed up until the small hours, and she had seen in his slightly breathless voice and his pale face the physical evidence of the heart condition Captain Nukiel had hinted at during their first conversation aboard the *Mbwa Kali* on their way to Ares.

It had seemed mere impulse to offer him space when she overheard a report that he had been denied lodging with his family, but she had long ago learned that coincidences were seldom that.

Her prompting had come from the consciousness that the gnostor had been on board the Rifter ship that carried most of the people the Dreamtime had bade her follow. Last night she'd had an immediate reward as he stood by her and gave a running account of who she was seeing and wherefrom they came as the Douloi twirled by in their interminable waltzes and quadrilles.

She stopped before a long window and considered the human being at the center of this magnificent construct: Brandon vlith-Arkad, the only one of his family to escape the vengeance of Jerrode Eusabian of Dol'jhar, and now heir to the Panarchy of the Thousand Suns. So far she had had only short encounters with him, always in the presence of others. Except for once, very briefly on Desrien, he seemed to be as slippery as glass and about as deep.

There in the New Glastonbury Cathedral she had seen underneath his shock a flash of intent, the same kind of high-energy focus that seemed to reach out from old vids of his ancestor Jaspar Arkad.

Last night he had surprised her yet again, when he abandoned the mask of Douloi politesse to communicate with a dancing trinity of Kelly in their own sign language. He had seemed genuinely pleased to see them, and there was no mistaking the trills and hoots of delight that they had exhibited.

The Kelly. She remembered, suddenly, the boy into whose flesh had been impressed the genome of the Kelly Archon. *They are going to remove it today*—she glanced at her chrono—*in less than an hour*. Moving again, she thought: *Time to try one of those little private transtubes.*

⁂ ⁂ ⁂

Vannis Scefi-Cartano sat, bored, at the elegant breakfast party, wondering when she could check her mail.

"Another ship came in last night." That was Charidhe ban-Masaud, who always had to be first with any rumor.

Some polite expressions of pleasure, then a very young woman with looped and bejeweled rainbow braids drawled, "Anyone on it?"

Charidhe sent a spiked smile across the room to the young woman. The *of course, or why would I bring it up?* was all the more potent for being unspoken. Charidhe transferred her gaze to their hostess before saying, "They report that the last of the refugees from the Mandala have been located by Captain KepSingh. One of them is a laergist who was supposedly assigned to the Aerenarch's Enkainion."

Vannis happened to be watching Tau Srivashti at that moment, and saw him go still, so still the smooth fit of his wine velvet tunic did not alter for breathing. Her interest sharpened: why would Tau find that news so interesting?

Then the rainbow spoke, her drawl pronounced, "That's Ranor. My mother had him trained."

Tau's gaze rested on the young woman's face, and Vannis felt a spurt of amusement. It wasn't the speech, it was the speaker that interested him. He had a taste for inexperienced young people, she recalled.

"Will we be seeing him among us?" Rista asked. "I'd like to find out who else is still alive."

"Not yet," Charidhe said, sounding bored. "Apparently someone—they did not name who—was not able to travel yet, so they'll be sent later, special courier. But as for last night's new arrivals, some Kitharee were aboard, and there's talk about whether they will establish a chantry here. . . ."

Vannis repressed a yawn and moved her wrist in the folds of her gown. Making certain no one was observing her, she touched her boswell and tapped the code to check her e-mail. Four drops.

She gauged the talk: entertainment. Rising to her feet, she smoothed the folds of her gown and then moved with leisurely steps to the buffet a few meters away.

Those in her path drew feet or garment folds aside, and she smiled graciously. Preference her title assured her, but last night's coup netted her deference.

She chose something cold to drink, and while waiting, coded for the mail IDs and felt a sharp stab of disappointment. Still nothing from Brandon.

A moment later she sensed proximity and looked up into Tau's smiling gray-gold eyes. Had he seen her bozzing? *Probably.* Hoping he mistook the gesture for a privacy with some other guest, she smothered another yawn and reached for her drink.

His cold amusement deepened. "I can offer you something better afterward." His hand indicated her waiting drink, but his tone was ambiguous, causing a complex reaction with alarm and interest foremost.

She signified assent, then turned; a stir of air and a whisper of silk indicated general movement in the room. She saw her hostess leading the way to the refreshments, and Vannis recognized by the slight fixity to her smile her inner chagrin.

She thought I was bored. Vannis found this misperception on Caroly ban-Noguchi's part interesting; she had indeed recouped.

A polite clamor of voices eddied around Vannis as she made her way to Caroly's side. It took only a few moments to soothe her hostess' feelings. Then, setting out on a carefully calculated circle, Vannis exchanged a few words with every single guest. At some point on her circuit Srivashti disappeared. Vannis did not see his departure, but she saw its effect in the sudden pout on the face of the rainbow lady.

⁂ ⁂ ⁂

Osri Omilov sat up in bed, fighting a massive headache. The room his mother had put him in had no wake-up tech on the bed, so he'd slept with his boswell on. The neural bloom behind his eyes flourished in a counterpoint to the throb in his temples. Two hours of sleep, and he had less than an hour before his leave ended, requiring him to report for duty in the military portion of Ares Station, known as the Cap.

The good thing was that he'd be given quarters among the rest of the naval personnel. Reminded of the prospect of quitting his mother's space, he found the energy to get into his uniform and pack his few belongings.

Finishing, he noticed the mail light on the desk console blinking. He tapped the key to window it up, saw that it was coded specifically to him, so he entered his personal code.

It was only a line: *Need a favor. Meet me at 07:45? B.*

Osri blinked, reading it again, then realized it had to be from Brandon vlith-Arkad. His heart thumped painfully.

Erasing the message, he picked up his duffel and tiptoed

down the hall toward the entrance. The other bedroom doors were shut; his half siblings were still asleep. Good.

But exit was not to be achieved so easily. A servant in Ghettierus livery hovered just before the door. On seeing Osri, she bowed and said, "Her Grace desires speech with your honor."

Osri tried to hide his annoyance as he retraced his steps, entering his mother's room. She sat up in a huge bed draped with embroidered silk. At least she was alone.

"Osri," she said, her dark eyes, so like his own, narrowed. "Who was that message from? How rude it was to key it to your code only."

Only Mother could think that. Osri fought an impulse to laugh. He hesitated, hating to lie, but he was not going to tell her about any message from Brandon; it would start the hideous arguments all over again.

Unexpectedly she relieved him. "It was *your father,* I suppose," she said in a nasty voice. "Gloating, no doubt, about his trick with the High Phanist. If he had simply told me that he and the Aerenarch were on intimate terms again—"

Osri had been hearing about it for three days. "My father congratulates me on my new duties," he said largely, glancing at the chrono. "Which begin in just a few minutes."

Brandon had not mentioned a rendezvous, so Osri guessed he had to meet him at the Arkadic Enclave. If he reached the tube in about two minutes, he might just make it in time.

"You'll be here when I entertain." It was not a question.

"As my duties permit," he promised.

His mother proffered her cheek, and Osri bent to salute it. Then he effaced himself, leaving the apartment with a great sense of relief.

Though Risiena Ghettierus was absolute ruler of her moon, her position among the thousand-year-old Service Families was relatively low. She had been relegated to the housing for the low-ranking naval employees and dependents. Looking around, Osri found little to complain about in the pleasingly designed buildings set against hills, with farmland visible from all the windows.

But the houses that had belonged to the officers' dependents were far more resplendent, and even more important was their relative proximity to the Arkadic Enclave and the sites for large and grand entertainments. Most of the High Douloi refugees were housed there, those who had not claimed space on one of the luxurious yachts attached to the station.

Osri punched in his destination, then sank gratefully onto the tube seat, relieved to find that he was alone. He leaned against the window with his eyes closed.

He had been detained at that damn party not just by fellow Navy officers who wanted to hear about his adventures since the attack on Charvann, but by a number of Douloi as well. Despite their smiling questions and open admiration, and despite the liquor offered as lubrication, Osri had kept his answers short and vague. Though his father seldom gave directives (unlike his mother), one of the lessons Osri had recently learned was to listen to his father's occasional mild suggestions. Just before the party Sebastian had murmured, "I say as little as possible at these things. Less to defend later." Osri heard it as advice, and took it.

The tube came smoothly to a stop. Osri debarked and walked quickly across the grass to the Arkadic Enclave gate.

A Marine honor guard saluted him as he passed; he heard one murmur into her pin mike as he entered the garden. The door stood open, and he saw Brandon, his father, and Jaim sitting on a low, circular couch before a dyplast table so transparent their porcelain breakfast dishes appeared to hover in midair. Osri's heart constricted at how old and worn his father looked. Jaim's long face was somber. Only Brandon showed no evidence of lack of sleep or excess of liquor—his eyes were clear.

It was a testimony to Brandon's practice at dissipation during the last ten years of his life, a fact that had angered Osri once. Now he set the thought aside: too many things had changed, too much had been lost.

They all looked up at his entrance. Jaim turned to Brandon and said, "It takes twelve minutes to get to the Cap."

Brandon swallowed his coffee and stood up. "Let's go."

Osri hesitated, uneasy about using proper protocol when no one else was.

A shadow lurking on the edge of his vision made him look up quickly. His headache pounded, but through it he recognized the grizzled face of Montrose, ship's cook and surgeon aboard the *Telvarna*.

Montrose squinted at Osri and reached for something on a sideboard. "Here," he growled, holding out a glass of milky white liquid. "I made up plenty." He jerked his finger at Brandon and Sebastian: "Thought they'd need it."

Osri took the glass and quickly drank off the thick liquid.

His stomach gave one lurch, then settled into quiescence. A cool, cottony sensation soothed the inside of his head.

With his headache diminishing rapidly, the ability to think reestablished itself. Before he could voice a question, Montrose spoke once again.

"You'll pee it out in half an hour, and it'll leave you thirsty." When Osri nodded his thanks, Montrose turned to the Aerenarch. "Listen, Arkad," he said, waving a huge paw. "I still think it a mistake not to make more whoopee over this. Why you didn't summon him and do it last night, in front of all those damn nicks—"

Brandon shook his head. "Better this way," he said.

"What?" Osri said, looking from one to the other.

"This," Brandon said, holding up his hand. Osri saw the gleam of ruby and once again felt a pang when he remembered Tanri Faseult. "Anton vlith-Faseult goes off duty in . . . fourteen minutes."

"Go," Sebastian said. "If he wishes to talk to me—" He gestured, indicating reluctance and regret.

Brandon said, "I will convey your offer." He smiled. "Get some sleep."

As Brandon started out, Jaim rose, but Brandon motioned him back down again. "Take a seat. Vahn can run shadow."

Jaim nodded wordlessly and sipped at his coffee, his dark eyes bemused. The lack of protocol, echoing their treatment aboard the *Telvarna,* made Osri feel peculiar.

But he said nothing as he followed Brandon outside. Self-consciously Osri returned the Marines' salute—they were back in the world of hierarchy and protocol again. Brandon did not salute, but he greeted both Marines by name, as Solarch Vahn appeared and fell in at precisely the correct distance behind them.

The tube was empty again. Brandon keyed in the destination, then dropped into a seat, rubbing his eyes with one hand.

"You wanted a favor?" Osri asked, conscious of the listening ears behind them. But a surreptitious glance showed the Marine several seats back, busy with his boswell; he seemed beyond earshot.

Brandon glanced up, and this time his tiredness was evident. "Two, actually. One: will you witness my handing off the Archon's ring? I believe your father wanted you to be there. . . ." He gestured, indicating a violent end.

Osri nodded. "I don't think he really wants to have to retail the manner of Tanri's death. And your other request?"

Brandon leaned his head back. "I'd like you to get me some study chips—the course on realtime tactical vector analysis and maybe the advanced course on tactical semiotic matrices."

Osri did not even try to hide his surprise. "Why? Won't you be busy enough?"

"Even a figurehead has some free time," Brandon said, giving a soundless laugh. "And I'd like to brush up on my old studies. But if I make it an Official Request—"

"I see, then Nyberg is obliged to take notice. I'll get them for you. It should be simple enough," Osri said, "since it seems part of my duties will be teaching the subjects I'd taught at the Academy to the cadets brought in on the various ships."

"Thanks," Brandon said.

They did not talk again until they reached the debarkation point inside the Cap. The Marine solarch was scarcely more familiar with the complex than Osri or the Aerenarch, as yet, but inset consoles at accessways windowed up directions, and they proceeded via another tube and then down a long hallway.

Osri looked about him with interest, and was jarred a little to see that the Cap had been designed along Archaeo-Moderne lines, a style familiar from his enforced stay on the *Telvarna*. The utilitarian corridors and storage accesses had been set into walls with clean, pleasing lines—just enough curves to diminish what might otherwise have been a sterile atmosphere.

They reached the security node just as the chrono indicated shift change. A door slid open and several men and women came out, passing by with a casual salute to Osri.

Startled, he glanced behind him, to see Brandon's head down as he studied one of the access consoles with apparent intensity. His dark head was bare, and his anonymous tunic and trousers marked him as merely a civilian.

Then a tall man with ebony skin walked out, and Brandon was suddenly at his side. "Commander Faseult?"

The Commander stopped. His eyes went from Brandon to Osri and back to Brandon again, as slow—but unbelieving—recognition transformed his features. Then he bowed, the elegant and correct bow from military to Aerenarch.

"May we be private?" Brandon asked, his voice so light it could not have carried to the Marine solarch, who stood at a respectful distance down the hall, his eyes averted.

Faseult silently indicated a small anteroom a few meters away. They went in, the Marine stationing himself outside the door. Then Brandon held up his hand with the signet ring.

The commander's face changed again, and Osri glimpsed grief, all the more terrible for its soundlessness, before the man exerted tight control.

"It was my promise to your brother to carry this to you, and to give it, from my hand to yours," Brandon said. His voice had taken on a curious cadence. "The Archon Tanri died in honor, and that honor passes to the next Faseult Archon whose family motto is *Volo, rideo.*"

" 'I will, I laugh,' " Osri whispered to himself as the familiar ache of grief gripped him again. His father's friend for most of two decades, Tanri Faseult had been a larger-than-life figure, a hero. The laughter had given him a sense of balance, he'd often said: he who could laugh at himself could laugh at the world, and not fear it.

Osri had learned that lesson too late. His eyelids burned as he watched Anton drop to one knee, his palms out in the ancient noble-to-royalty mode. Osri saw the signet stone flash: a smiling charioteer drawn by the two sphinxes. And then the ring was on the commander's finger, and Brandon was raising him to his feet.

"You are Anton hai-Faseult now," he said. "When my father is free, he will confirm the succession to the Archonate."

The commander made a quick, convulsive gesture, but as if to forestall formal expressions of gratitude, Brandon said, "Later we can tell you more of the battle over Charvann. Your brother got in some priceless zings at Hreem the Faithless." He glanced toward Osri and added gently, "The gnostor Sebastian Omilov, father to Lieutenant Omilov here, was there at the end." Brandon glanced up at Osri, who saw strain in the light blue eyes. Had Brandon ever slept at all?

He recognized his part. "Your Highness," he said, "I have to report for duty."

Brandon nodded, hit the door control, and they went out, leaving the commander in privacy.

✻ ✻ ✻

Jaim watched Brandon and Osri walk through the garden toward the gate, then he studied the coffee swirling in his cup, trying not to betray his impatience. *It has to be now.*

In his cup was real coffee, brewed from beans grown and roasted right there in the station. Another sign of the limitless wealth and power available here; not that everyone at Ares Station could get coffee anytime they wanted. Vast as the place was, there was a limit on how much space could be given over to the production of luxuries. Perhaps there were people on Ares who never tasted coffee, and some who got it rarely. For the Arkadic Enclave, though, there was an unending supply.

Jaim looked up from the brew to Montrose, who met his eyes, then moved closer to Sebastian Omilov. The gnostor was still sitting on the plush couch, gazing through the branches of the silver-leaved tree growing up from the floor.

Montrose sat down and helped himself from the silver pot. Then, indicating the splendid console set discreetly into a sideboard, he spoke jovially: "Look at that thing. He's got a hundred and forty-nine drops waiting—three of those just since we began talking. Which of us is supposed to deal with those?"

"His problem," Jaim said. "Never told me to answer his mail."

The byplay broke Omilov's reverie, but still he was silent, looking from one to the other of them.

"Well?" Montrose turned to him, hands propped on his knees. "You've got something to say—spit it out. And then your medico advises you to get started on that rest."

"One of Brandon's reasons for taking that signet ring to the Faseult heir instead of summoning him to a formal function," the gnostor said slowly. "If he made it into a pageant, on whom would the focus be?"

"On them both," Montrose said with a shrug.

But Jaim saw the point. "On Brandon Arkad."

Omilov smiled briefly. "On the Aerenarch—you have to remember that 'the Aerenarch,' besides being his correct title, is a persona. To resume: the way he has chosen will permit Anton Faseult his grief in privacy, and it will not force him into a statement of public gratitude."

Montrose gave a gusty sigh. "Idiocy!"

Thinking back over the reception, and the careful patterns of avoidance and confluence he'd sensed, Jaim said, "Do they lie, these high-end nicks?"

Omilov gave a rueful smile. "You mean the High Douloi? No, for to lie outright is a sign of vulgarity—of stupidity to some—carrying with it the risk of being caught. But you must always remember that they don't always tell the truth, either. They never say what they think, only what they want you to think they think. And the deep ones will say something that may mean one thing to you and another to your neighbor, and something else again to both of you a week later."

Recalling a pair of metal-cold gold eyes, Jaim murmured, "Srivashti and his tailor . . ."

Montrose's eyes narrowed. But he said nothing.

Omilov looked up in mild inquiry. "One of our oldest, and most powerful, families, the Srivashti. They were Jaspar Arkad's backbone, in action and in materiel, a millennium ago. Tau, the present Archon, is a very . . . complicated individual."

"Ruined Timberwell," Jaim said with another glance at Montrose's hard, angry face.

Omilov nodded soberly. "As was his right, so far as the government was concerned: they could not interfere." He sighed, and got to his feet. "A subtle man, Srivashti," he said. "He was a loyal and powerful ally to the former Aerenarch. I hope devoutly he will be a friend to the present one." He paused, inclining his head courteously. "Speaking of whom, I believe I will take his advice—and yours—before I make the official move to the domicile of the High Phanist."

"Get a good rest," Montrose said gruffly.

They both watched him leave, then walked quickly out of the Enclave. Jaim half expected the guards to stop them—question them, at least—but they only gave him a polite nod, which he returned, and ignored Montrose.

Out of earshot of anyone, Jaim said, "You're going to duff Srivashti." It wasn't even a question.

Montrose gave him a piratical grin. "Justice, my boy, justice. You heard my friend Sebastian: the nicks won't do anything about him. According to their rules, they can't. This is why I am now a Rifter."

Jaim said, "Did you ever talk like high-end nicks during your days on Timberwell? Say one thing and mean another?"

Montrose laughed as they got into the transtube. Then he looked around the empty compartment and said, "You have to remember there are nearly as many kinds of nicks as there are Rifters. We were a Service Family—several generations of service. But not high enough in rank to attract the attention of the likes of Tau hai-Srivashti."

Jaim nodded, thinking through the implications behind

Montrose's words. He said, "If you jump him while we're here—"

Montrose snorted. "Jump." His grizzled face twisted in scorn. "Just because I never learned that sneaking, lying way of talk doesn't mean I do not know how to wait."

"You took the job Brandon offered you."

"With pleasure and pride," Montrose said, sweeping a bow. "I shall enjoy being house chef and surgeon to the illustrious Aerenarch." Montrose turned to look out the window. For him the conversation had ended.

For a moment, Jaim followed his gaze. The transtube was now about halfway to north spin axis and the access to the Cap, where the *Telvarna*'s crew was housed. Below them a distance-softened patchwork of greenery and water stretched into hazy distance below hook-shaped clouds, curving up on either side to become a verdigris sky until it was lost from sight behind the sun-bright diffuser just below the spin axis high above. The brilliant filament of a stream, threaded with the shimmering pearls of a chain of ponds, winked at them from antispinwise.

Jaim wondered if Montrose regretted having mentioned his intentions toward Srivashti. But Jaim did not care what happened to any Archon. "Arkad said we're equals inside his house. You don't believe it?"

"It is not a question of belief, it is a question of convenience." Montrose paused and rubbed his jaw. "I like that boy," he said. "But consider this: when we were on the *Telvarna,* he was ready to do his best to recruit us into going after his father on a suicidal rescue mission. And he was in a fair way to making us like him enough to get us to do it. But since we've come here, the game has changed, and so have the rules. He's no longer our prisoner, we're his."

"Prisoner—" Jaim repeated.

"You don't-like the term? Then let me ask you: we will not even consider poor Lokri, who seems to have gotten himself tangled up in a murder charge. But you know we cannot leave this station. And did you not feel we were sneaking off just now? Do you think it is possible we are not under someone's surveillance even so? And we are the lucky members of the crew. Do you think Brandon has gotten even this measure of freedom for the others?"

"He was surprised to see Vi'ya and the Eya'a at the party last night," Jaim murmured. He remembered the sharp angle to

Brandon's face as he watched the progress of the three unlikely figures cutting their swath straight through the whirling Douloi. "He didn't expect to see her there."

"And I'll stake my life she didn't want to be there." Montrose laughed. "Except it was the only way for her to get the word to us. Wonder what she wants! Feels like the old days. . . ." Montrose laughed reminiscently.

Jaim saw again the vivid image of Vi'ya, her tall figure stark against the flowing colors of the dancing Douloi. She was never easy to read, but no, she hadn't wanted to be there.

Jaim abandoned speech when a blot of color bloomed behind his eyes. The relay system on Ares gave the boswells of those authorized to use it considerable reach; Brandon could call him anywhere. Jaim touched the accept code.

(Duties almost executed. Want to sleep, or join me in a visit?)

Jaim rubbed his eyes as the transtube stopped. *(Visit?)*

(Strictly unofficial—I'm ditching Vahn after the official tour. Meet me in half an hour?)

Jaim tabbed the accept again and followed Montrose out of the transtube. They paused to look out once more over the interior of the oneill from their lofty vantage at the north spin axis. Up here the air was cool, thin, and refreshing. Then they turned and entered the Cap access.

Jaim looked around curiously. Here was the antithesis of the elegance of the Ares oneill: dyplast and metal predominated, but, he noted, with the inevitable touches of elegance that were characteristic of Panarchist architecture. He felt a twinge as he recognized the similarity to the remod of *Telvarna* that Markham had done when he took over as captain.

Quick glimpses at guide consoles oriented them when necessary, and they proceeded quickly, garnering only brief incurious glances from others in the accessways and corridors they traversed. Jaim repressed the urge to look around him. He knew that any surveillance would be unseen, anyway.

Montrose was uncharacteristically quiet. Jaim wondered if he, too, was reminded of Markham.

They nodded at the guard outside of Detention Five, and went in.

Three

The living space assigned to the *Telvarna*'s crew was functional by Ares standards, certainly no worse than being on shipboard: a main room, fitted with a console (heavily filtered, Jaim knew) with access to an artfully designed garden beyond that gave a convincing simulation of being outdoors. Around the main room were small sleeping rooms, each with a tiny bain.

Jaim and Montrose found Vi'ya and Marim eating breakfast. Ivard was asleep on a low couch. His skin had a pale green undertone, shading to an almost emerald cast on the arm to which the Kelly ribbon had bonded. Jaim felt his stomach clench. Despite the fact that since Desrien the boy had seemed on the mend, the ribbon was still apparently dominating his metabolism.

Vi'ya said, "We must talk quickly. The medtechs will come for him soon—the healing will be at the Kelly enclave." She turned to Montrose, making a gesture including him and Jaim. "You both have mixed freely with the nicks. Have they said anything of Eusabian's fleet possessing hyperwave capabilities?"

Jaim felt a slight shock going through him. In truth, he had forgotten Marim's startling news, mentioned so quickly before the *Telvarna* was captured by the cruiser *Mbwa Kali*. He'd half discounted it as mere gossip.

As if reading his mind—which Jaim knew she couldn't—Vi'ya said, "I believe it is real enough for us to consider the consequences if we talk about it."

Marim looked up sharply, then hitched one small foot up onto the table so she could scratch at the black microfilaments that genetic alteration had caused her to be born with. She grinned. "I start work today on a refit crew." And she brandished a pair of mocs before pulling them over her feet: the Panarchists did not approve of gennation, so Jaim figured Vi'ya had prevailed on Marim to hide her feet while out among them.

Jaim felt a tug of longing. He was an engineer by choice, and he knew that refit would be badly needed, with the glut of ships coming in each day. "Engine repair?"

Marim laughed and shook her head. "No chance! Told us that every civ ship coming in gets its fiveskip disabled and sealed, and the Navy blits do that. We're gonna patch up the ones Eusabian's chatzers couldn't blow out of space." To Vi'ya she said, "I'm mum."

Jaim watched her merry face with its fringe of blond curls. *She'd sell us all if she thought there was high enough pay—and she could get away with it,* he thought dispassionately. He'd known Marim a long time. Above all things she prized her personal freedom, but she was also a pragmatist. She'd be working every angle, Jaim knew, to escape from Ares: if she managed to get herself locked up, she'd never be free unless the nicks chose to let her out.

"We speak of it, even in hints, and we join Lokri in their security facility," Vi'ya said. "I do not know if the nicks have found out or not: either way, we say nothing. Agreed?"

Marim shrugged, returning promptly to her breakfast. Montrose and Jaim assented, and Jaim looked over at Ivard.

"I will impress it upon him," Vi'ya promised. "You are still guarding the Arkad?"

Jaim nodded.

Vi'ya said, "Then you will have a certain amount of freedom of movement. Will you visit Lokri?"

"Soon as I have free time," Jaim said. *Whenever that might be,* he thought, remembering he was expected to meet Brandon again very soon.

Montrose yawned. "Well, that's settled, then. I'm back to our palatial quarters and for bed."

Jaim followed him to the door, hesitated, then turned to Vi'ya. She was watching him. "Having a job will occupy the time," he said.

She shook her head. "Perhaps. But I will not permit them to monitor my movements."

Marim waved her fork. "Montrose! Sneak us some real coffee, would you?"

Montrose snorted. "As if you can taste the difference, nullrat."

They left on the sound of her merry laugh.

* * *

(Hyperwave?) Vahn could hear his partner's disbelief over the boswell link. He understood her tone; "hyperwave" had always been the technological equivalent of a word like "unicorn": denoting something mythical, impossible, yet eternally sought. And Eusabian had it? A chill trickled down his back, and Ares suddenly seemed very small and fragile.

Vahn gazed at the back of the Aerenarch's dark head three seats ahead of him, wondering how much of this he knew. He cursed mentally: too many hours without sleep, Rifters to guard (one of whom had only minutes before announced his intention to assassinate an Archon) as well as an Arkad famed for indiscretions, and now this. *(I haven't heard anything about it from anyone. But if they just agreed to keep it quiet, we can sit on it as well, and wait.)*

(Right. Let Nyberg and Faseult worry about it.) Roget gave a soft laugh, then she reverted to business: *(Montrose and Jaim are now exiting the A-3 adit: over to you.)*

* * *

Jaim found the Aerenarch just leaving the transtube outside the Enclave with Vahn and a thin, mild-faced young man wearing the robes of an Oblate.

"This is Ki," Brandon said. "A former student of Sebastian's. He will be taking on the comtasks, which, I understand, have backed up to a formidable degree." He gestured to Vahn, who bowed and led the way toward the Enclave. "Find him a room, then let him get at it."

Jaim caught a glance of muted curiosity from the Marine, but

Vahn said nothing as he and the Oblate walked up the gravel pathway toward the house.

A former student of Sebastian's. Jaim had come to the conclusion recently that Brandon seldom said anything that was not to a purpose, even if he did not state the purpose. *Oblate, student of an honest man: probably this Ki can be trusted not to be reporting our every movement to someone else.* Would that, in turn, be an oblique warning to Vahn? Jaim grinned sourly down at the worn path, deciding he'd already spent too much time among the Douloi: even the simplest action was beginning to take on complexities and conflicting meanings.

So he abandoned Ki and looked over at Brandon, who was scanning the distant line of dwellings. He seemed intent on something. Jaim walked in silence, waiting; presently Brandon spoke. "So give me your impressions of last night."

Jaim thought for a time, noting the Aerenarch's gaze moving restlessly across the lake waters. A small knot of people appeared on a distant grassy hill; Brandon chose a pathway that would avoid a meeting.

"Tension," Jaim said at last. "Patterns of avoidance and coherence. A sorting out, not complete." *Whispering—about you. Is it time to say that?* He paused. "Or did you want individuals?"

Though Brandon had not looked his way, he was listening carefully, it seemed. "Speak."

"That business with the tunic, and Archon Srivashti," Jaim said. "Why did you refuse to wear the flash one? Would have looked all right in that crowd."

"Would it have?" Brandon walked sideways, his blue eyes amused.

Jaim considered the costumes of the Douloi, some of which (he guessed) might cost half as much as a ship. "One degree more flash," he said finally.

Brandon grinned. "A little test."

Remembering the Archon's husky voice, and the slight emphasis on "miracle" when referring to Brandon's escape from the Enkainion, Jaim wondered how many tests he hadn't discerned.

He said, "Did you pass it?"

"I . . . postponed it. What did you think of Vannis?"

Jaim drew in a deep breath. "Diamond."

Brandon laughed. "I've heard that before. I don't know her

at all—she's always avoided me. I suppose my duty now is to find out why."

They had been steadily approaching a grove of low-sweeping trees. Just as they passed among them, without warning Brandon whipped his arm around in a lethal strike. "Attack!"

Jaim snorted a laugh, blocked the blow, then grabbed at Brandon's arm to spin him around. Just barely the Aerenarch avoided his fingers, whirling to kick up at Jaim's face.

It was the Ulanshu Kay-To, wherein either partner can attack the other at any time. It was an ancient form of training—the origin of its name had been lost in the Exile, but it was a fundamental aspect of the Ulanshu disciplines. Vi'ya had insisted on it from time to time, when the gang was on either base for more than a few days.

The outcome was inevitable, but it did take Jaim somewhat longer than before to get Brandon pinned down on the mossy ground, one arm twisted up behind his back. "Give?" Jaim asked soulfully.

Brandon was laughing too hard to reply, his breath wheezing. Jaim lifted his hands and they stood up, Brandon spitting out bits of green plant matter. He brushed absently at his clothes, which, Jaim noted, were much the worse for grass and mud stains now. He suspected he, too, was streaked with mud.

He thought they would return to the Enclave directly, and was surprised when Brandon resumed walking in a westward direction. Soon they would arrive at the front row of splendid villas, once the home of the high officers' dependents, and now the quarters of the high-end nicks.

Brandon scanned them, his face thoughtful. "Looks like most of 'em are asleep, or gone, doesn't it?"

"We have business here?"

"Of a sort," Brandon said, eyes narrowed in amusement. "While things are still relatively peaceful."

Jaim thought this over, and remembering the Aerenarch's injunction, said, "What?"

His reward was a quick, mildly startled look; the Aerenarch, it seemed, was already light-years ahead in whatever plans he was evolving. He gestured at the houses. "The ones who have nothing to prove or to pursue are sound asleep. The others are glaring at one another over coffee at one of three parties. Long odds," he added under his breath, "on Her Highness."

They walked up a gravel pathway, and Jaim felt viscerally

some kind of security scan, though nothing was visible. Then Brandon turned up a flower-lined path and tapped at a door in a pleasant, low-roofed villa set around a shrub-framed pool. Within mere seconds the door was opened by a woman in a subdued livery. Jaim recognized the former Aerenarch's personal colors.

The woman's eyes widened, then she bowed.

"Morning," Brandon said. "Is Vannis here for visitors?"

Jaim saw the woman's eyes go from Brandon's messy clothes to his own face, then to the ground. "She is out, Your Highness. Would you like to leave a message?" She opened the door wider and indicated a console inset in the foyer.

"We'll meet up eventually," Brandon said with a casual wave of his hand. "Bid her good morning." He turned away, and the woman bowed in silence.

Now Brandon led the way to the closest transtube. When they were near it, he said, "Nice timing, what?"

Jaim was about to question this when they were joined by a group of Douloi, who pressed forward with graceful but deliberate movements, each making a grand obeisance. Brandon was soon the center of a swarm of questions and comments, leaving Jaim to reflect on the ambiguity of that "timing."

⁂ ⁂ ⁂

In the peristyle of the Kelly enclave Eloatri found herself welcomed by three dancing Kelly, their headstalks twirling, their pseudopods patting gently over her body. They smelled of cinnamon and burned cork; their voices reminded her of the living wind-harps on the peaks of the Hazard Mountains of Donya-Alann.

"Welcome, Numen," the Intermittor of the trinity fluted, as all three twisted their headstalks into a sinuous interpretation of a formal deference.

She bowed in return, smiling at the delight the Kelly showed in imitating human gestures, while adding their own inimitable tripled grace. Yet behind their authentic enthusiasm she sensed, as never before, the emanations of a very alien people, ancient with a weight of ancestral memories that in humans were accessible only in dreams, if then.

Even as she replied, and continued the formal exchange of greetings, Eloatri wondered if the presence here of their Archon's genome, welded somehow to the flesh of the Rifter boy, was responsible for this feeling. For the Kelly, the memories of those passed into the embrace of Telos were vividly present and immediate. And their Archon, murdered on Arthelion by Eusabian, was the repository of their most ancient knowledge: only that Kelly trinity remembered the awakening of the race to sentience, a million years past and more.

The Kelly ushered her into the warm interior of the building, humid and redolent of the spicy atmosphere of the Kelly homeworld. Inside the large single room they brought her to, the gawky boy Ivard gangled to his feet, his flaming-red hair vivid against the lush greens of Kelly foliage. He blushed as he put down the serial chip he'd been engrossed in. Eloatri suppressed a start of revulsion: the sudden rush of blood to his thin skin, tainted green by the Kelly genome, made him look like a badly embalmed corpse. Behind him, silent, stood the tall black-clad Dol'jharian woman, near the two small sentients with the ice-white fur.

Eloatri's eyes were drawn back to the green ribbon embedded in Ivard's wrist, its color leaching into the flesh of his arm all the way up under the short sleeve of his shirt. There, replicated by the strange biology of the Kelly ribbons, which were both sexual and neural tissue, resided the last trace of the Archon and their memories.

"Ivard," she said, "how are you feeling?"

The Rifter boy bobbed his head. "I'm all right," he replied. "Uh, Numen."

The Kelly swarmed around him, honking and hooting, and Ivard replied. Eloatri blinked. She hadn't known a human throat could make such noises. Nor could it, comfortably, she decided as Ivard broke off and started coughing. The Kelly pressed him down into a drift of pillows near the center of the room, and at their urging, Eloatri seated herself nearby.

As his spasm subsided, Ivard looked up at Vi'ya.

"Soon, Firehead," Vi'ya said. She did not touch him; her hands were behind her back. Something in her manner seemed to reassure the boy, though, because he relaxed against his pillows.

"They're gonna take my ribbon," he said to Eloatri with a fair show of bravado, holding up a skinny wrist. His other hand gripped tightly on something small—she saw a tuft of silk protruding beyond his little finger.

"We can only take from you the genome," the Intermittor

said in her reedy voice. "The Archon now is part of you, and you of threm. That was accomplished far from here, and not by any art we know." The other two blatted agreement, their pseudopods writhing in a mesmerizing pattern.

On Desrien, in the Dreamtime. She did not know the details of Ivard's encounter with the central Mystery of New Glastonbury—he had never spoken of it. But before it he was dying, his immune system overwhelmed by the Kelly ribbon.

The Eya'a abruptly moved closer, their eyes not on the Kelly, but on Eloatri. When she met the faceted eyes, the beings chittered softly: recognition?

Vi'ya said, "They remember you, Phanist."

"Thank you," Eloatri said. "Will you be a part of this procedure?"

Vi'ya nodded.

Ivard sat up on his elbows, and asked in the half-cocky, half-frightened manner of adolescents across systems: "Will it hurt?"

The Kelly trilled laughter. "Not at all, O small seeker." The Intermittor pranced over behind Ivard while the other two Kelly disposed themselves in front of the boy, making the three apices of an equilateral triangle around him. Vi'ya knelt between the two in front, facing the young Rifter. The Eya'a remained behind her, their faceted eyes glinting in the suddenly subdued lighting.

There was silence for a time. Slowly Eloatri became aware of a low hum. As it intensified, the voices blended and separated in hypnotic harmonics. Now the headstalks of the three Kelly were twisting slowly, the fleshy lilies of their mouths oriented always on Ivard, who began to blink, as if fighting sleep. His eyes closed and Eloatri saw the tension leave his body.

The alien threnody grew louder, resonating in Eloatri's chest, subtle rhythms beating against each other within the polyphonic drone. The light in the room faded further and she saw that the ribbons of the Intermittor were glowing with a faint phosphorescence that fluctuated in synchrony with the crooning of the Kelly. The sound was haunting, laden with emotions that corresponded to nothing human.

Now the ribbon in the boy's wrist glowed too, fluctuating in the same rhythm as the sound grew ever louder, catching Eloatri up in a dizzying rush of feelings. The palm of her hand tingled, the burn inflicted by the Digrammaton pulsing with the ever-stronger rhythms. The music was impossibly complex; it sounded like an entire choir of Kelly. Eloatri's vision blurred and she found herself swaying. She let go of fear, let go of self, and watched, feeling herself on the edge of a million-year precipice, peering back into the natal history of a people civilized before humankind achieved speech.

Ivard opened his mouth and his high tenor joined the song of the Kelly. His body remained utterly relaxed while his arm, girdled by the green, glowing ribbon, snaked up into the air and swayed gently. Vi'ya, too, was swaying, her body eloquent of a terrible tension.

Eloatri thought at first it was the blurring of her vision; but no, the ribbon on Ivard's wrist had twinned, a new loop twisting up from the greenish flesh. Suddenly Ivard's back arched and a terrible cry broke from the boy's lips, but Vi'ya's voice rose with it, wordlessly matching it and then, somehow, forcing it back into the music of the Kelly. Twice more the boy cried out; pain lanced through the image of the Digrammaton embedded in Eloatri's palm, then vanished as the headstalk of the Intermittor darted forward like a snake striking, thrust through the twinned loop writhing up from Ivard's wrist, and pulled it free.

The alien song rose to a shout of triumph and joy as the green ring rotated slowly down the Intermittor's headstalk and disappeared amongst its ribbons, now fluffed out as if by a huge charge of static electricity. Bands and splotches of color chased across the Intermittor's body, accompanied by wafts of complex scents. Eloatri's eyes watered.

Then there was silence. The Kelly did not move, their headstalks frozen. Suddenly the Eya'a keened shrilly, their heads twitching with inhuman speed from side to side, and Vi'ya's body jerked in a clonic spasm. The Kelly hooted, their headstalks swiveling to watch while their bodies remained still. Eloatri sensed deep surprise. The image of the Digrammaton in her palm tingled, almost painfully this time.

The small sentients pushed past Vi'ya as her head bowed, her arms slipping off her thighs onto the floor as if attempting to support a terrible weight descending on her shoulders. The Eya'a's twiggy hands danced gently across Ivard's slowly relaxing body, finally freezing momentarily in a lacy cradle around his head.

Slowly the terrible tension left Vi'ya's body. Ivard emitted a whistling snore, his body completely slack in deep sleep.

Something rolled from his hand and hit the floor with a muted clink. Vi'ya moved quickly, her fingers trembling, to pick it up. Eloatri glimpsed the silver of a coin and a crumpled bit of silk before the woman tucked the objects into a pocket on the boy's unresisting body. At the sight of the coin, Eloatri's palm gave a last, valedictory pang, then subsided.

The Eya'a stepped back. All movement ceased.

This tableau held until the door suddenly opened and two men came in. Distracted, Eloatri glanced at the newcomers, and when she recognized the Aerenarch, her attention splintered and she turned to look again. It seemed he had just come from some kind of accident or fight—his clothes were smeared with mud and grass stains, and mud streaked one cheek. His guard, too, the Rifter Ulanshu master, was so marked.

The Aerenarch stopped and looked at the Kelly, frozen around the sleeping boy, and then at Vi'ya's back. There was no change in his expression; Eloatri sensed something evanescent flitting across her inner senses, but it was gone before she grasped it.

Vi'ya's face was marked by fatigue, and something else, a certain tension. She met Eloatri's eyes and her expression smoothed into unreadability. Behind her the Kelly flowed toward the Aerenarch. He greeted them, again using their sign, but very quickly, then he said, "Will he be all right?"

The question was addressed to Vi'ya. She looked at him just once, giving him an unreadable regard, then never looked his way again. "Yes," she said. "He will recover."

The Intermittor danced over and guided the Aerenarch further into the room, away from the sleeping boy. The trinity commenced a complex sign conversation with him.

Eloatri used the moment to address the silent Dol'jharian: "You have a telepathic link to Ivard?"

Vi'ya's dense black eyes touched briefly on Eloatri's, then moved away. Eloatri felt a curious inner tingle, as if she'd been through a security scan.

"It is the Eya'a," the young woman said. Her voice was low and soft. "Through them I can link with anyone, it seems. Even you." She smiled slightly.

Which explains the scan.

"Though there is a cost, am I right?" Eloatri said. "A sense of dislocation—vertigo—and a terrible draining of energy?"

Vi'ya shrugged, but did not deny it.

Eloatri said, "I ask because I believe I can help you."

Vi'ya looked up quickly, her smooth face betraying a muted surprise—and great distrust.

Eloatri smiled, doing her best to project reassurance. "Telepathy is indeed rare among humans, though it apparently wasn't always so. Certainly it was not rare among your own people of the island—the Chorei—before they were annihilated by the mainlanders." Eloatri paused. Vi'ya said nothing, but Eloatri knew she had her attention. "Among the refugees arrived at Ares are some of my own colleagues, from the College of Synchronistic Perceptions and Practice. For a number of reasons, they are still living aboard their escape ship. One of their number is a Dol'jharian, a descendant from your Chorei. I can ask if he would be willing to work with you."

Vi'ya still said nothing.

She has not refused. Eloatri knew when retreat was the best tactic.

"I'll be in contact," she said, and went out. She was inclined to smile, but then she remembered that one look sent the Aerenarch's way. *I shall have to be very careful.*

The excitement of the Eya'a still seared across her mind as Vi'ya watched the High Phanist depart. Their thoughts were incomprehensible, the images reminiscent of their excitement back on Dis when the Arkad had arrived bearing the Heart of Kronos, now lost to Eusabian. But their import was clear; now the Battle of Arthelion made sense. Somehow the growing linkage between Ivard, the Kelly, and the Eya'a had triggered an awareness of the presence of an Urian mechanism, less powerful than the Heart and thus previously unsensed by them, here on Ares. The Eya'a, who did not build machines, had no idea what it was they'd sensed, but Vi'ya the ship captain did.

The Panarchists had somehow gotten one of Eusabian's hyperwaves.

If they find out I know, I will never escape, if they even let me live.

She glanced at the Kelly, still dancing their conversation with the Arkad. Did they know she knew? Would they tell him? And how much had the High Phanist understood of those last moments, after the genome had twinned off of Ivard?

The images from Desrien welled up from memory, pushing past barriers weakened by the onset of a staggering headache, and she pushed them back viciously. Eloatri had no psychic talents, Vi'ya was sure, but she saw far more than most. Behind her slight figure loomed the unknown powers of the Magisterium; after Desrien and the vision of the Chorei she had experienced there, and had discussed with no one, Vi'ya could no more discount the reality of those powers than that of her own heartbeat.

But she's right. The link with the Eya'a is becoming more than I can handle. The realization grated on her, but what was, was. She would do what she had to do: a greater mastery of their link, and the new strengths lent by Ivard and the Kelly, could only advance her plans. The nicks would not hold her long.

Jaim watched the Kelly and Brandon in the dance-like conversation. He used the opportunity to step closer to Vi'ya.

She looked up at him, her dark eyes unblinking; Jaim felt her regard as an almost palpable blow. *Is she angry with me? Why?* There had been no trace of anger when they'd met the preceding hour.

Her first question took him by surprise. "Why is he here?" She lifted her chin slightly in Brandon's direction.

"Wanted to check on Ivard."

"Why?"

"I don't know. I came at his command."

She did not look away, but somehow it was easier to return her regard. Jaim felt as if a vise had eased from his brain; either he was more tired than he'd thought, or else her talents were gaining in magnitude.

"Are you then his creature?" Once again the slight lift of the chin toward Brandon.

That's the cause of the anger. "I am no one's creature," Jaim said. "The Fourfold Path leads me this way: for a time I must be his shadow."

She understood—it was the Ulanshu way. She said, "I wish you would train Ivard."

Jaim glanced at the sleeping boy. "Forgetting how to live in his body?"

"Exactly."

Jaim hesitated.

"Why don't you train him?" he asked.

Her face did not change, but he knew very suddenly that she

did not like the question. Old memories made fear prickle down his arms, but he stood his ground, forced himself not to react.

She said only, "The Eya'a occupy most of my time." She smiled a little, a wintry change of expression. "And you know how heavy my kind are. I might slip and crush him."

Jaim grinned. *It might even be true.* "I'll teach him."

Vi'ya lifted a hand. "Fighting?"

"Just movement control at first," Jaim said. "Until he regains his strength. No hurry; there's certainly no danger here—" He stopped when he saw her eyes narrow. "Is there?"

She hesitated a long time, and when she spoke, it seemed to Jaim she was reluctant. "The Eya'a heard it last night, when we passed through that room of chaos," she said finally. "There is no identity—they still cannot sort humans unless they know them—but there are those who want your Arkad dead."

My Arkad?

He started to speak, aware of Brandon's approach. Vi'ya turned away abruptly and walked across the room to the Eya'a, who chittered on a high, ear-torturing note. On the pillows, Ivard muttered something, and the Kelly added their voices in a weird counterpoint.

What's going on?

No one was going to tell him, obviously. Brandon watched after for a moment, staring at Vi'ya's back, and then he said, "Let's go."

Vannis sank into the plush chair and smiled up at Tau's face. His yellowish eyes were tender and appreciative; her smile did not diminish, but wariness made her careful in the way she arranged her draperies and posed her hands. Until today he had adroitly avoided any personal contact with her here on Ares, which rather proved what she had suspected: that Tau had considered her finished in the social arena. Her coup had proven that wrong, but if he'd wished to reestablish social contact, their conversation at the breakfast would have been enough.

This private meeting smacked of political overtones, which set her heart racing. Was this her chance? If so, why had he suddenly decided it was time to include her?

Do not underestimate him, she reminded herself, sipping at the exotic hot drink he handed her, and watching him over the delicate rim of the chinois cup.

He saluted her, still standing, then went with leisurely steps to look down at his console. He tapped a quick code—probably denying his servants access to the room—and then came back, sitting down right next to her.

She'd thought he would choose the chair, and fought the chill that gripped her upper arms. His sudden proximity forced memory—as, she sensed, he was very well aware.

"What is this?" she asked, indicating her drink.

"Cambrian tea," he answered. "Apparently the Shiidra find it intoxicating."

She almost dropped her cup, but kept control. He'd done that deliberately, to put her off balance. *After all, it can't be so very poisonous to humans, since Shiidra can—and do—eat humans,* she told herself. She then swallowed off the spicy drink and held her cup out for more.

The yellow eyes narrowed in amusement—and a deeper appreciation. "Now," he said, "to business. I propose that we join forces, you and I."

"Join forces?"

He gestured largely, his signet ring glittering bloodred. "The leaders of the two most powerful families in what remains of our polity—either of us"—he raised his brows—"eligible heirs, should we lose our two remaining Arkads."

"It has its advantages," she said slowly.

"Of course it does. Even if it is only temporary, each of us can help the other—and if we were to find it to our advantage to ally, ah, permanently . . . who is there to gainsay us?"

The idea was astonishing, and very sudden. Warning tingled through her. "Well," she said, "let us consider it. But you must have something more immediate in mind."

If he felt the sting, he gave no sign. "Immediately—we will jointly give a reception for the conquering hero."

"Brandon?"

He shook his head. "I refer to the hero of the Arthelion battle, Captain Margot Ng. But of course we must invite Brandon as well. He will need friends."

This response sent questions clamoring through her mind, but she resolutely stilled them, following one train of thought at a time. "We can," she said slowly, sifting through the social implications. "But . . . wouldn't that be Brandon's right?"

"We can't know that His Highness will do it—and if he does, whether it will be private or not," Tau said. "Several of our friends have already tried, and Ng has refused them all. If you and I throw in together, I believe our combined, ah, status might obtain a different answer."

"I'll do it, of course," Vannis said slowly. "But will you forgive my stupidity today and tell me why it is so important? If you want to hear about the Battle of Arthelion, they'll have something on the novosti channels before long—"

"They'll have everything but the objective and the outcome," Tau cut in. He got to his feet and walked slowly across the room. She watched the muted glimmer in gold threads in the dark cloth that fitted his shoulders so nicely—and then, with another shiver, she banished the thought. "Tomorrow Nyberg is holding a briefing," he said, turning to face her. "They will be going over the vid records from the battle."

How did he know that? If they really were going to be allies, she hoped he'd give her access to his contacts.

"I shall be honest," he said with a rueful gesture.

She laughed. *Is this really pax?* Almost immediately she remembered those amber eyes, and the merciless smile, aboard this very ship ten years ago. *Don't trust him.*

"I tried to obtain an invitation. I used every method I could contrive. But the Navy—so simple with their black and white judgments—cannot forget that Timberwell was lost to the insurgents. They were polite enough to avoid trouble, but firm enough that I still remain determined."

You will avoid intimacy with Tau hai-Srivashti, Semion had said shortly after their marriage. *His family holds great influence, and he purports to be my ally, but he has earned the Navy's distrust through his actions on his own planet.*

The Covenant of Anarchy was pervasive enough to make it very bad taste to ask rulers about the way they governed their own territories. Vannis could have found out what the truth was on Timberwell, but she had not been interested. Tau . . . had been interesting. Once again she forced her mind to the present.

There had been an edge in his voice when he mentioned the Navy, and Vannis suddenly remembered what the captain of Rista's ship had said, when they arrived at Ares and were greeted by a contingent of naval officers and techs. *"They're coming on board to disable the fiveskip—no one leaves Ares while the emergency lasts."* She was sure even Tau's ship had been so treated. *Which must gall him terribly.*

She said, "So you think a gentle hint—purely within the pleasant boundaries of social interaction—might remind our naval friends that they, after all, defend what is ours . . . but that we, as the Panarch's sworn servants, must have access to information that concerns our government?"

"Correct, my dear."

She pretended not to see the hint of condescension. She was aware by now that she had made a tactical error in acceding so quickly to his request for an interview. He'd beckoned; she'd come. It put her in the weak position, the needy position. *Though it's true, I never should have admitted it in deed.* He regarded her as weak; let him continue to do so. There was no more exquisite way to undermine the strong than through their own underestimation of their rivals.

"It sounds delightful. And I do want to know what happened," she added, smiling. She reached for the pot to pour out a third cup of the tea, no more than a gesture. She had no intention of drinking it; already she felt a dangerous fuzzing of her awareness. At least he had drunk it as well.

Forcing her mind to clear, she sat back, cradling her cup. "Another question," she said. "Why will Brandon need friends? From my—admittedly little—experience of him, that was the one thing he had no dearth of."

"True," Srivashti said softly. "And I hope he will always retain them, for I hold no grudge against him—really, a very charming, pleasant young man. But there are some rumors, among those handicapped with a narrower vision, that might harm him."

"I've heard nothing."

"Consider your position," Tau reminded her, still with that irritating air of condescension. "Surely no one will wish to lacerate the grieving widow with hints about why her one remaining relation by marriage was the only one who escaped the disaster at his Enkainion?"

Her breath caught. She had not thought that far. It had been a shock to find out that Brandon was alive, and all her energy had gone into considering how to retrieve her own position with respect to his reappearance.

She looked up. "But surely it was not through his contrivance. If his bodyguards found out about the plot, they would have bundled him aboard a ship so fast he would not have had any choice."

"Except"—Srivashti tapped the rim of his cup with his nail—"none of his bodyguards lived. From what little news we've obtained from Arthelion, very few people made it out of the Palace Minor after the bomb went off. And none of them were the Panarch's guard."

"There's got to be an explanation," she said.

"Of course," he agreed, spreading his hands. "And we will see that it gets disseminated when he does tell us. For he is one of us, isn't he? And we protect our own."

Warning made her head throb. There was definitely something going on underneath his words, but she could not ferret it out, not with that damn tea clouding her mind, and her tiredness accelerating the effect.

He set his cup down and took his place beside her once again. This time she could not repress the shiver, and his smile increased. "Cold, my dear? Shall I adjust the tianqi?"

"Just fatigue," she said. "The relentless pace of our celebrations."

"You can rest here, if you like," he said, reaching out to stroke his finger along the inside of her wrist.

She gritted her teeth, fighting the sensation—fighting memory. "I'd better go."

He sat back, just long enough to remind her that here again, she'd managed to put herself within his power. But surely he would not do anything here, on Ares. He wouldn't be that stupid.

And he wasn't. "Sleep well." He raised her hand and kissed her palm. "We will discuss our reception when you feel refreshed." He leaned back and touched his console, and the door slid open. "Felton will show you out. Unless you remember the way?"

If she didn't get out, *now*, she would be sick.

"Good day," she said.

She exited, knowing he was watching.

The silent man waiting in the corridor took her directly to the lock, and somehow she got herself into the shuttle and keyed her destination. By now the effects of the tea made her head swim unpleasantly.

Why did he tell me that about Brandon? It could be he was hoping she would not try to ally with him. *And if he's dis-*

graced himself, I won't. He'd disgraced himself once before—it was conceivable he would again.

But she would not move until she knew. Despite all Tau's talk of power, and of the end of the Thousand Suns as a polity, there was still allure in the Arkad name.

Get back . . . check my mail. . . . She managed to get from the shuttle to her door, and from the door inside.

And there was Yenef, bending over her. Vannis stared blurrily up into the revolving face, trying to make sense of the words, until at last they penetrated:

"The Aerenarch called in person while you were gone—"

Vannis made it to the bain just in time.

FOUR

"I tried to kill Brandon," Anaris said, smiling. "Several times." Obliquely he watched Gelasaar for reactions, and saw nothing but his own amusement mirrored back.

Of course he won't react, whether he knew about it or not.

And then Gelasaar did speak. "As a lesson in manners?"

Surprised, Anaris gave a laugh. So he must have known, at least at the end. Which means it was not an accident that Brandon was sent off to school. Except . . . why was he sent, while I was the one to remain in Gelasaar's house? *"At first, it was anger, but after that, I guess you could call my efforts an attempt at intimidation."*

"With what result?" Gelasaar asked mildly, his oblique blue eyes on the row of double knots Anaris looped with the dirazh'u in his hands.

Gelasaar knew the what of it: where did his question really lead? To oblige him, Anaris gave the obvious answer. "With no discernible result. He continued to harass me with practical jokes exactly as much as ever."

Gelasaar shook his head slowly, the silver beard, even untrimmed and unbrushed, neat and composed. "You were short-

sighted, then," he said mildly. "I expect your attempts . . . inspired . . . him to fresh efforts. Probably long after he would ordinarily have cried truce."

❋ ❋ ❋

Margot Ng watched as the gallery high above the Situation Room slowly filled. It was not a large room—perhaps a hundred seats, each with its own analysis console, arranged in ranks rising steeply above the bank of presentation consoles at the front where she sat. She could see most of the seats without turning her head.

On the control rostrum with her were Lieutenant Commander Rom-Sanchez and Sub-lieutenant Warrigal from the *Grozniy*, and the tactical officers from the *Babur Khan* and other ships that had fought at Arthelion. Next to her sat Admiral Trungpa Nyberg, commander of Ares Station.

There were two double doors into the gallery. Ng noted with a frown that with a few exceptions, the ship captains and other space officers invited entered through one, and the civilian analysts and station officers, the latter mostly older men, through the other—the lingering influence of the late Aerenarch's attempts to politicize the Navy. Then the elegant severity of a Douloi tunic among the blue and white of naval uniforms drew her eye. The wearer was an older man followed closely by a young naval lieutenant, who ushered him to a console and seated himself next to him. Their similarity of features told her they were father and son—their fleshy earlobes triggered her memory.

The Omilovs. An interesting story: the elder Omilov tortured by Eusabian in the Mandala where that Dol'jharian autocrat had usurped a thousand years of Arkadic rule, the younger credited with rescuing the last Arkad heir from the siege of Charvann.

Next to her, Admiral Nyberg stirred restlessly, then swiveled around past Ng to look out over the Situation Room. He left his chair angled slightly toward her; accepting the tacit invitation, she followed suit.

Before them a thick dyplast window revealed a huge three-dimensional projection of the Thousand Suns hovering over the bustle of activity among the banks of consoles far below. A multitude of colored lights and ideograms glittered coldly among the holographic stars, representing the data laboriously culled out of the Rifter chatter from the hyperwave Ng had captured in the Battle of Arthelion, and the less timely reports from the Navy couriers and various civilian craft reaching Ares. She recognized some of the symbols as versions of the Tenno battle glyphs—tactical ideograms—that had been modified and extended by her tactical officers on the *Grozniy* to deal with the apparently instantaneous communications enjoyed by Dol'jhar and its Rifter allies. Wherever Eusabian had obtained the hyperwave devices, they had rendered centuries of strategic and tactical experience useless. *Much as if Nelson and the British Admiralty had faced a French Navy equipped with radio.*

Admiral Nyberg squinted at the projection. "I understand you've organized a seminar on the new Tenno?" His tenor voice, surprising in a man of his bulk, was mellow, resonant with the concealing singsong of the High Douloi.

"Yes, sir. It begins right after this briefing."

He glanced at her, his face revealing nothing of his thoughts. "I wish I could attend. But the Tenno are of little use to me here on Ares."

It was a warning, but Ng could not tell how it was intended. She knew that the huge station, the last center of power remaining to the Panarchist government, would inevitably become the site of a battle whose intensity would rival the action in the Arthelion system that had nearly battered her ship into scrap. But the battle of Ares—whose combatants would all be nominally on the same side—would be fought with words, and gestures, and all the mannered subtlety of a millennial aristocracy.

Nyberg had turned back to watch the ever-changing holograph. She studied his profile briefly, wondering if they would find themselves allies. With the death or capture of High Admiral Carr, who had been with the Panarch on Lao Tse, Nyberg was de facto head of the Navy. He was Downsider, old-line, but unlike many of that background he did not owe his appointment to the late Aerenarch Semion.

And that's exactly as one would expect of the commander of one of the Panarchy's poles of power. Arthelion, Desrien, Ares: the Arkads, the Magisterium, and the Navy: these were the legs of the tripod that had given the Thousand Suns a thousand years of peace.

Until Dol'jhar struck.

A sudden flurry of activity from the rear of the gallery drew their attention away from the holograph. As Ng turned back, she saw a cloud of older station officers through the wide doorway, surrounding a slim, dark-haired young man in a plain blue tunic. With him were two other men, one in the uniform of a Solarch of the Arkadic Marines, the other wearing gray. Ng recognized in the latter the easy readiness of a Ulanshu master. An officer stepped in front of the man in gray and held up his hand, evidently forbidding him entrance, then yielded at a few words from the young man in blue.

The Aerenarch Brandon vlith-Arkad and his Rifter bodyguard. Ng felt a spurt of anger, which she tried to dismiss. *I will suspend judgment until rumor is confirmed as truth or denied.* She transferred her gaze to the Rifter bodyguard at his side. She knew that only a small percentage of Rifters were allied with Eusabian of Dol'jhar, but her back still prickled with reflexive wariness at the sight of one here, at this briefing. The government's possession of the hyperwave, won at great cost, was the most closely guarded secret on Ares.

Then her wariness altered to reflection as the implications of the Rifter's garb became clear. He was not wearing the livery of the Phoenix House, yet his presence here made it certain he was a sworn man—otherwise even the Aerenarch could not have prevailed against Ares security regs. *So he's sworn to Brandon vlith-Arkad, but not to the Aerenarch.* A personal oath, leaving his Rifter identity intact. Interesting.

As the Aerenarch made his way down the center aisle, the two men with him somehow isolated him from the crowd of hangers-on, so expertly that Ng could not see how it was done. He seated himself, with the Marine behind him and the Rifter to his right.

Another blow at precedence, she thought. The attendant officers seated themselves nearby, reluctantly leaving space free around him in response to subtle but unmistakable signals from the two bodyguards.

Ng glanced at Nyberg. His face gave no hint of his thoughts, but he did not stand. She noted Warrigal and the other tactical officers on the rostrum watching the admiral. *He didn't escort the Aerenarch here.*

That confirmed the anomalous nature of the Aerenarch's position on Ares. On the civilian side, he was heir apparent of the Phoenix House, and with his father imprisoned or dead, the leader de jure of the Panarchist government. But rumors of treason echoed around his unexplained escape from the nuclear atrocity that had wiped out the highest levels of the government at his Enkainion on Arthelion, and his reputation as a scapegrace and a drunkard left him with no base of power.

On the military side, he had no standing at all, having been withdrawn from the Minerva Academy ten years ago. It was inevitable that he would be the vortex of a storm of gossip, but she had been surprised at the vehement polarization of her officers. The majority ranged between anger and a sense of betrayal at the unexplained escape from the Ivory Hall atrocity; the half dozen or so who had known him during his brief time at the Minerva Academy maintained steadfastly that rumor had to be false, or only partly true.

Ng watched the Aerenarch as he set up his console, surprised at the sureness of his movements. His face, a pleasant echo of the austerity of his father and the severity of his late brother Semion, was composed and utterly controlled. Even the sudden smile that flashed in response to a comment from his Rifter bodyguard obviously revealed nothing except what the Aerenarch wanted the outside world to see.

Beside Ng, Admiral Nyberg stood. Two pairs of Marines drew both double doors closed and the murmuring of conversation ceased. She sensed the tianqi shifting to a different mode, the hint of a complex, faintly pungent scent she knew was designed to promote alertness and analytical thought.

The Admiral began without preamble. "This briefing falls under the protocols of secrecy as outlined in the Articles of War and under the Silence of Fealty." Ng detected heightened alertness from everyone in the room: Nyberg had formally given notice that disclosure of the matters discussed here to anyone not present would constitute a capital crime for both military and civilian personnel.

"All of you are aware of the general state of affairs, but to focus us, I will restate them. Eusabian of Dol'jhar, having armed a large number of Rifter vessels with weapons of unprecedented power, and equipped with apparently instantaneous communications, has overthrown His Majesty's government and now occupies the Mandala. This station, and the Fleet, are likely the only remaining centers of resistance.

"We will consider two topics during this briefing. First, the provenance of Eusabian's advanced technology, and what can be done about it, and second, the effect of this technology on strategy and tactics."

Ng was startled by the intense blue gaze of the Aerenarch, suddenly focused on Nyberg. The reason for it escaped her for a moment, then she remembered. There was to have been a third topic at this briefing: the fate of the Panarch Gelasaar, captured by Eusabian on Lao Tse and now, according to Sebastian Omilov's report, destined for delivery into the hands of the Isolates of Gehenna.

In the absence of a constituted Privy Council, there was no one who could order the Navy on a rescue mission to the planet of exile. Nyberg could not promote himself to high admiral—he was de facto but not de jure head of the Navy. No one save Brandon vlith-Arkad could make appointments, but without a power base he lacked authority.

Nyberg continued without pausing, although Ng was sure the Aerenarch's reaction had not escaped him.

"But before all this I have some good news to leaven an otherwise disastrous situation. Scarcely three weeks ago forces under the command of Captain Margot O'Reilly Ng fought a desperate action in the Arthelion system. Many of you will have heard that the object of this battle was an attack on the Mandala and the usurper, Eusabian of Dol'jhar.

"If that were true, Captain Ng would not now be sitting beside me."

Nyberg paused and looked down at her. She kept her face impassive.

"She would have been shot," he continued, a hint of a smile at the corners of his mouth.

There was a hushed buzz of comment, quickly stilled.

"Captain Ng lost two battlecruisers, three destroyers, nine frigates, and a number of attached ships. Casualties amounted to almost ten thousand killed or missing, and another fifteen hundred wounded. Despite that, the judges at her court-martial commended her for a brilliant success. In fact, she was decorated for her efforts, but the decoration, and the very fact of its award, are classified. The judgment of the court is sealed."

Ng noticed Captain Nukiel smiling at her from the space officers' side of the gallery, his expression echoed by some of the others around him, not all of whom she recognized. On the other side she saw only puzzlement or guarded looks of consideration. A pang of memory brought to mind the face she didn't see among them; she pushed it down and forced herself firmly into the present moment.

"What the court knew that you do not know," the admiral continued, "was that the Battle of Arthelion ended, as had been intended from the start, in the capture of one of the enemy's hyperwaves, the instantaneous communicators that, in combination with some unknown power source, are the key to Dol'jhar's success in overthrowing His Majesty's government."

Now the whispered comments crescendoed to a hum of speech, which Admiral Nyberg overrode without raising his voice. "It is now feeding data to our analysts, all of whom have been sequestered in high-security quarters for the duration." He gestured at the holograph behind him. "You see some of the data represented here.

"Although communications between Dol'jhar and the Rifter ships equipped with a hyperwave are encoded, and have so far resisted cryptographic efforts, there is an ever-increasing volume of transmissions—both en clair and in Brotherhood codes that we can read—between Rifter ships."

The admiral allowed a wintry smile to reach his lips. "The undisciplined proclivities of Eusabian's Rifter allies are a major weakness in his strategy, which the hyperwave will permit us to exploit. The content of these messages enables us to position their ships with some accuracy. In addition, correlation of ship-movements data obtained from these messages with the encrypted communications will eventually enable us to decode the Dol'jharian message headers, revealing what ship each message is addressed to for an increasingly clearer apprehension of the enemy's strategy. All this information is fully worth what Captain Ng and her detachment paid for it.

"Needless to say, these messages will continue only so long as our possession of the hyperwave is unknown to Dol'jhar. So far, there is every indication that they do not know we are listening."

Nyberg paused and looked around the room. Everyone became very still at the intensity of his gaze. "Thus, I reiterate: there will be no mercy for anyone discussing these matters with anyone not authorized. It is unlikely that any communication can pass from this station to the enemy, but we are determined to take no chances."

The admiral let the silence that followed this announcement build for a time. Ng saw the Aerenarch studying Nyberg, but his reaction was impossible to read.

"Now, before we move on to the Battle of Arthelion, I would

like to introduce a man who deserves your utmost attention and respect. He maintained his Oath of Fealty in the face of the worst torture that Eusabian could inflict on him, to conceal information that, in our hands, may yet doom the usurper to failure and death. Gnostor Sebastian Omilov, Chival of the Phoenix Gate."

Startled by the sound of his name, and the unexpected formality of his title, Sebastian Omilov stood, feeling all eyes upon him. Then Admiral Nyberg placed his left hand over his heart and began striking it rhythmically with his right, in the measured cadence of the salute normally rendered only to fellow officers wounded in the Panarch's service. The shock of emotion was almost physical; Omilov struggled to control himself, knowing that he was failing in the face of this stunning, almost unprecedented encomium.

Moments later Captain Ng and her officers at the presentation consoles stood and joined in, followed by the space officers present, then, hesitantly, by the station officers.

Taking refuge in analysis, Omilov noted that the civilians around him stood respectfully, as did the Aerenarch, but quite properly did not join the salute—that was the prerogative of the Navy.

Omilov bowed in gratitude and began speaking. He heard the hoarseness of emotion in his voice, but he quickly gained control by imagining himself in the comfortable surroundings of a lecture hall.

"Thank you, Admiral Nyberg, all of you. I only wish I had more to tell you—Eusabian probably would have learned nothing from me he did not already know. But I have hopes, thanks to Captain Ng and the many men and women of the Navy who fought at Arthelion, that we may solve the riddle of Eusabian's power and win through at last."

"We." For a moment he was distracted, wondering whom Nyberg had appointed to pursue what little was known of the Urian artifact and its center of power. He repressed his longing to be part of that team and forced himself to go on.

"What little I do know is this. Ten million years ago the race we call the Ur vanished from the galaxy after a war that lasted for millennia. They left behind those astronomical works of art known as the Doomed Worlds, various artifacts resembling each other only in their degree of incomprehensibility, and the selfsame legend among the few races not exterminated by the energies unleashed in the death throes of the Ur. Humankind calls it the Suneater—and its reputed powers are described fully by its name."

Omilov stopped, looking at the hologram behind Ng and the others. Perhaps it was the impact of Nyberg's salute, shaking him loose from the comfortable groove of Douloi formality, and thus from other comfortable assumptions, but suddenly he saw in that flattened ovoid of stars, distorted by the chaotic emptiness of the Rift, an implication—no, an utter certainty, he realized—that shook him to the depths of his being, a frightening glimpse of a power beyond anything that humankind was ready for. A force now in the hands of the Avatar of Dol, a man unconstrained by any moral imperative save that of power.

Omilov swallowed, sensing puzzlement in those around him at the unexpected hiatus in his speech. "In fact, it's my belief that this device created the Rift, that anomalous frontier of the Thousand Suns that has conditioned so much of our history in Exile."

Shock silenced them; no one spoke, or keyed, or even seemed to breathe. Then he noticed one of the nearby space officers look down at her console and touch its tabs lightly, as if wondering what human technology could do in the face of such power.

"I will not go into details now, except to say that I believe Eusabian has discovered the Suneater and, moreover, now possesses the key to its full potential. Our only hope is that the full use of this key will evade him until we, too, can find the Suneater and destroy it. If it can be destroyed."

He paused again, looking at the hologram of the Thousand Suns, feeling an odd, complex dissonance of emotions. It was as though he were seeing it for the first time, and yet with a sense of familiarity. And, overlaying it all, there was a poignant sense of impending loss. A sudden stab of memory opened a wound in him that had never healed. *Ilara.* He'd watched her leave the Mandala, twenty years gone, on her doomed mission to Dol'jhar. The feeling was the same.

No. This time Dol'jhar will not win.

The silence of the gallery recalled him to the present. They were waiting for him to go on, but there was little more he could say now.

"I am a xenoarchaeologist, accustomed to casting my vision

back into the distant past to decipher the nature of races long vanished and little known. You are warriors, accustomed to gazing into the furnace of the present moment in battle, and into the fog of the future created by your actions and the response of the foe.

"I know little of the art of war, or of those functions you professionals call SigInt. So I cannot guess how much you will learn from the hyperwave that Captain Ng has brought us. But I am sure that by synthesizing these two branches of knowledge that perhaps have never before been combined, the heart of our enemy's power can be located and wrested from his grasp."

As the gnostor concluded his peroration and began to answer questions, Margot Ng's mind raced ahead, assessing this revelation of what they faced. No satisfactory hypothesis explaining the creation of that chaotic abyss of sundered stars and fivespace anomalies had ever been advanced by the gnostors of the College of Ontological Physics.

She shrugged slightly. It didn't really matter. What was important was that the Suneater gave the usurper's forces an offensive weapon an order of magnitude beyond anything the Navy could field, and vastly superior communications. And as far as she was concerned, the latter was the more important.

With growing excitement, she realized that the Suneater's power was both a strength and a weakness for the enemy. Eusabian would have to sacrifice anything, any plan, to protect it. The Fleet would have to be redeployed in any case—most of it mustered here at Ares for the attack on the Suneater when it was finally found. That movement would inevitably be detected by Dol'jhar, and in combination with carefully crafted intelligence leaks implying that the Navy had *already* located the Suneater. . . .

Margot Ng smiled. If they timed it right, after they had broken the message header codes so they could track ship deployments, the motions of the enemy's ships as he shifted them to counter the coming attack on the Suneater would inevitably point right at its hiding place, if specialized knowledge from those like Omilov didn't lead them to it even sooner.

She looked thoughtfully at the portly gnostor as he reseated himself and Admiral Nyberg took over again. Sebastian Omilov had retired from Court quite suddenly ten years ago; her patrons had implied that he'd been a peripheral victim of the L'Ranja affair. She didn't know enough about him otherwise to assess the reliability of his professional judgment, but there was no doubt he had Nyberg's respect. Did he have his backing? Who would Nyberg put in charge of the research project? If one were to consider the scene that had taken place from a purely political point of view, Omilov would be in a perfect position to head that project.

She sighed quietly. Politics. One's oath could lead one on some strange paths, but if the Navy did end up dependent on Sebastian Omilov's expertise, then she must know if he could be trusted. She would use any source of knowledge to that end.

". . . Margot O'Reilly Ng, who will guide our exploration of the battles of Treymontaigne and Arthelion, with the goal of understanding the new tactical reality imposed upon us by the enemy's weapons and communications."

She'd been following Nyberg's voice with a portion of her attention; now she allowed her political train of thought to lapse as the admiral turned to her. "Captain Ng."

As she stood up she was astonished to see the admiral step down from the rostrum and take his place in the audience, and she could see that the significance of this act was not lost on the officers and analysts present. She would have their full attention.

"Thank you, sir. What you will see here is a compilation of the actions at Treymontaigne and Arthelion, assembled from multiple ships' records. We'll run through a unified view of each, then each of you may access the segments of interest to you via your consoles during the multiple-replay sessions. Each of us here on the control rostrum is available to you for questioning and interpretation via the adapted tabs at the top of your consoles.

"I will stress several considerations that we all need to keep uppermost in our minds, that this data may be most useful. First, and most obvious, what you are seeing here is not the raw data, but a selection of it by those of us who experienced it. We may be too close to it; I encourage all of you to investigate the full records on the secure consoles that will be made available to you later. You may well detect subtleties that evaded us, during the battles and later.

"I'd also like to remind you that while there have been many secret weapons in the history of human warfare, and many have been decisive in one or more battles, none has ever decided a war. Sometimes the impact of the weapon has been overestimated; other times—and I believe these battles are an example—the side possessing the weapon has not trained enough with it to integrate it sufficiently into tactical doctrine. Dol'jhar's need to keep the powers of the Suneater secret during his preparation for war crippled the tactical knowledge of his Rifter allies by preventing them from exercising sufficiently with the new weapons and communications.

"I also believe that what you are about to see reveals that Dol'jhar's tactician, Kyvernat Juvaszt, whose style is known to many of you, has made a fundamental mistake. His tactics appear to be patterned after what the Urian technology can do. Rather should he have discovered what it cannot do and found a way to accomplish his mission despite that. We can exploit this.

"Thirdly, a philosophical consideration. It was pointed out long before the Exile that the unity of control exercised by totalitarian regimes such as Dol'jhar is a recipe for overwhelming technological mistakes. Only the freedom of discussion—and the confusion that sometimes results—found in a liberal society can prevent that. I do not know if this will be the case with what faces us now, but it is a possibility. The specialists in moral sabotage among you will need to consider this."

She reached down and tabbed her console. The dyplast behind her clouded, then shimmered into a view of space, and the wreckage of the *Prabhu Shiva* swam into view, echoed on her console. Within minutes, compressed by careful selection and editing, the Battle of Treymontaigne raged again. She was soon grateful for the distraction of manifold summons from the audience consoles for interpretation as the emotions of that day also replayed themselves, heightened by the time compression of the recording.

The replay of Arthelion was even worse. She struggled with the wash of grief triggered by the raking attack of the *Falcomare* on the *Fist of Dol'jhar,* attempting to distract herself by sequencing through the audience consoles to get a sense of what the officers and analysts were focusing on. A rapid-fire flicker of Tenno caught her eye, in an unusual configuration, and she paused, astonished. It was coming from the Aerenarch's console.

She looked up. The young man's fingers tapped unerringly

across his console, his face intent, almost severe. She looked back at the echo of his actions on her console and watched in fascination, her unconscious judgments of him dissolving in the face of his obvious competence. Some of his configurations were naive, yes, but with an edge that held great promise, needing only the honing of the simulator and finally the stress of battle to bring him to tactical maturity.

And more, she realized. Brandon vlith-Arkad was applying the data strategically as well. He'd moved many of his more complex Tenno configurations to a holding matrix where they were evolving through a series of differentiations apparently patterned on the classic *tsushima* strategic semiotics. The ten years since his dismissal had obviously not been spent in mere carousing and drunkenness, as rumor had it.

Without warning, he looked up and met her gaze. She felt transfixed by the blue intensity of his regard, but he didn't appear to really see her. His gaze fell away, releasing her, but her mind remained in turmoil, all her political calculations upset. She now had even more to probe the younger Omilov for; what had he seen in those weeks in the company of the heir?

Her console clamored for attention, and she plunged back into the task at hand; but now, like the soundless thunder of a distant storm, the presence of the young man in the plain blue tunic loomed on the horizons of her mind.

* * *

Admiral Trungpa Nyberg was not a happy man.

The war had transformed Ares Station from a smoothly functioning starbase into an aristocratic madhouse, an overcrowded maelstrom of political infighting, intrigue, and venom. The population had swelled from under fifty thousand to nearly double that, and the influx showed no signs of slowing. Every day, it seemed, brought new refugees, with a whole new set of problems.

Worst of all, with no constituted government, there was no one for him to share the burden with. The machinery of Douloi governance had been wrenched awry by the Dol'jharian onslaught. The new Aerenarch was an unknown quantity, virtually powerless; Telos alone knew how long it would be before a new Privy Council emerged from the wreckage. And there were some on Ares now who he would prefer never grasped the reins of power.

Nyberg stared moodily out the wall-sized dyplast port behind his desk, taking little comfort from the sweeping view it afforded of the top of the Cap. The massive plain of metal, scattered with refit pits, glinted crimson in the light of the red giant whose gravitational field protected the station from skipmissile attack. In the foreground the battered form of the *Grozniy* loomed, flares of light swarming around it as the crews labored to undo the tremendous damage inflicted on it in the Battle of Arthelion.

He smiled sourly. That was one bright spot: the arrival of the *Grozniy* had brought Captain Margot O'Reilly Ng to Ares. He'd put her on open assignment, for from their brief meetings so far, he judged that she could become a valuable ally in his effort to maintain the Navy against the erosive effects of Douloi infighting.

That was his goal and his duty: to present whoever eventually assumed power with a functioning Navy. It was not for him to judge who that would be, for all that he had his preferences.

The annunciator chimed and Nyberg slowly crossed his office to the door, the thick carpet underfoot muffling his footsteps. This would be Sebastian Omilov, another possible ally, and one with far more influence in the Douloi world, despite his having retired from politics ten years ago. That in itself was indicative of the man's potential trustworthiness: that he had given up an influential position at the Panarch's side rather than, as Nyberg understood it, compromise with the harsh expediency of the former Aerenarch Semion.

And what was his relationship to the new Aerenarch? Former tutor, rescued victim, and now? That, too, needed probing.

Nyberg tabbed the door open. "Welcome, Gnostor Omilov. Thank you for making time for me."

"Entirely my pleasure," Omilov replied, grasping his proffered hands briefly in a semiformal deference, Douloi-to-Douloi in the context of business.

Nyberg ushered him over to a tête-à-tête of overstuffed chairs and a low table, where a coffee service had been laid out. They chatted of inconsequentials, until the admiral judged sufficient time had passed—just enough to satisfy custom, not so much as to mitigate the urgency of the meeting.

"I was sorry to have to spring that introduction on you at the briefing, Gnostor, but I judged it best to give no one advance warning of my intentions." Nyberg stressed the words "no one" slightly, and saw in the lift of an eyebrow that the message had been understood.

"I quite understand, Admiral. If your purpose is to place me on the project team—"

Nyberg bowed, hands apart, and Omilov stopped, mild inquiry on his face at the interruptive gesture. Nyberg said, "I want you to head it."

Nyberg saw his blunt statement impact the man before him. Joy, then assessment, and then muted pleasure were clear from Omilov's countenance: he was now sifting the reasons for the unorthodox approach to appointment.

Retired he might be, but his political instincts were still sharp. He knew, as did Nyberg, that lacking advance notice, there was no possibility that any of the more powerful Douloi on Ares could have promoted their own candidate for head of the Suneater project over Omilov.

Not that there really is anyone here on Ares as knowledgeable about the Ur as Omilov. But Nyberg knew that wouldn't stop some from promoting a more controllable person masquerading as a scholar.

Nyberg continued. "As far as I am concerned, you have absolute discretion. I expect regular reports, but I will not interfere. I've already arranged the highest security clearance for you, and you have the ability to extend a similar clearance, one level lower, to whomever you choose." He paused. "Do you need quarters? I understand you recently accepted the invitation of the High Phanist to take up residence at the Cloister."

Omilov nodded gravely. "Yes, I judged it best to let the Aerenarch maintain his own household, without the need to concern himself with my foibles."

"Splendid," Nyberg said. "Then the demands of social obligation will be fewer."

He saw comprehension in Omilov's eyes: for "social" both men knew "political" was meant.

"The High Phanist has her own concerns. I will be able to devote myself full-time to this project," Omilov said.

Nyberg nodded, well pleased. His hint that political involvement be kept minimal had been met with ready compliance, and Nyberg thought he detected relief. He wondered again whether the L'Ranja Archon's suicide, and the then-Krysarch Brandon's expulsion from the Academy, had been caused by

Semion's machinations as had been whispered—and if these events had really forced the gnostor into retirement ten years ago. Then he gave himself a quick mental shake. It didn't matter now. Enough that the man was falling in quite willingly with his plans.

Omilov frowned slightly, then added, "In any case, Brandon vlith-Arkad must make his own way for his position to take on any real meaning, as I am sure he will." His tone of voice indicated that further probing would meet with bland generalities.

If he knows what happened at that Enkainion, he's not going to talk.

Nyberg's focus returned to his original thread of inquiry. Whatever Omilov thought of the new Aerenarch, it apparently was not disapprobation—which was enough for now.

Deciding that he'd learned as much as he could for the moment, and that the gnostor would not allow himself to be distracted by politics, he guided the talk into specifics about the project, which Omilov suggested be code-named Jupiter, the ancient name for the god who had overthrown Kronos. The general shape of the project rapidly took form, and after a last request that his son, Osri, be made liaison between the project and the Navy, Omilov took his leave with the promise of a report within forty-eight hours.

Nyberg returned to the port and looked out, feeling better than he had in days. Omilov was another he could trust, as far as trust could be extended consonant with duty. And he'd gained another grain of information about the anomalous new Aerenarch. It had been a profitable half hour.

The glow of satisfaction lasted until the con chimed again, and his aide's voice said urgently: "Sir. Two sector-level emergencies, first at . . ."

Nyberg returned to work.

FIVE

Ivard sat up in bed and stretched. Energy sang through his veins and pulsed in his brain. He felt strong and happy—for the first time in a very great while, he felt *good.*

He looked around at the suite the Kelly had assigned him while he recuperated. It was luxurious, but he'd rejoin Vi'ya as soon as the Kelly let him. He wanted to be with his shipmates.

He jumped up and pushed open the window to the garden. The heavy door made his arm twinge—he'd gotten weak during his long journey. The Kelly ribbon still marked his wrist, but now it felt like part of him. It was like wearing a piece of jewelry, just like all the nicks. *Only none of them have a bracelet like this.*

He looked up, gaze caught by a flight of birds riding high on an invisible air current. Here it felt like being outdoors, if one ignored the horizon curling up to either side and merging into the sky. A chuckling sound came from his left and he saw someone's pet wattle lump its way up a tree trunk, its furry dangles puffed with excitement. He watched it settle on a branch and start chittering at the birds.

The garden smells were redolent of blossoms and herbs, and

he took long, deep sniffs, sorting the scents until the inevitable: his sinuses clogged and his eyes teared.

Wiping his eyes impatiently, he observed his own white, freckled hand, and regretted anew the cursed pale skin and the bad eyes and sensitivity to all airborne motes that he and his sister had inherited.

Reminded of Greywing, he lifted the neat little pouch that hung on a long chain about his neck. Vi'ya had given it to him when she visited him last, and it now housed the ancient coin that Greywing had taken from the Arkad's palace just before she was killed, and the flight medal that the Arkad's friend Markham had awarded Ivard after a rough encounter with some other Rifters. The two people Ivard had loved most, now dead, and this was all that was left of them. Ivard had vowed never to remove the chain from his neck.

He fingered the coin, thinking of Greywing, and how she, too, had railed against their ugly, atavistic skin and bad eyes.

Why can't we pick our genes? he thought as he tucked the coin away and let the pouch fall against his bare chest.

Then a familiar presence stirred within him. He shut his eyes; blue fire danced against the velvet darkness, voiceless echoes shouted along his nerves. But no longer was it smothering, hazing his thoughts as it had before . . . Desrien.

Ivard opened his eyes, his thoughts shying away from what he had seen at New Glastonbury. That was real, but he could never talk to any of the others about it.

The sight of the flowers and trees around him calmed him, and he closed his eyes again. His mind cast back to what the Kelly had said to him after they recovered the Archon's genome from him, leaving the ribbon embedded in his wrist. *Only the Archon thremselves can remove that, and threir rebirth is yet to come. You must go to* ******. His throat spasmed at the memory of the impossible whistle that named the Kelly homeworld.

But that meant the Kelly Archon was still with him!

The blue fire surged, gratified. Ivard struggled to understand: it was not like a separate mind, or something foreign within him, as it had been before. Now it felt more like a part of himself he hadn't known about, like finding an extra eye or hand.

Ivard laughed, delighted with the image; delighted also by the sudden surge of satisfaction—tinged with humor—from the blue fire at the image of himself with three arms. Then he sneezed four times in rapid succession.

The blue fire danced impatiently against his inner vision, then whirled away in a direction he couldn't follow. He opened his eyes, frustrated. The movements of the blue fire echoed what the Kelly doctors had done to him. He'd seen so clearly then, why not now?

Ivard sat down cross-legged in the middle of the garden, ignoring the itch-burn from the grasses on his bare skin, and shut his eyes.

His breathing slowed as the blue fire returned, then retreated again, more slowly this time. Ivard followed, sinking deeper into the myriad processes of his body: the steady *thrum-thrum* of his heartbeat, the flex of his diaphragm pulling air deep into the complexities of his lungs, oxygen slipping across the membranes of his alveoli and whirling away captive in red blood cells, the slow fire of metabolism repeated trillions of times in the mitochondrial furnaces of his cells.

He dove deeper within, deep, deep, guided by the blue fire dancing on ahead. He swooped and soared, watching the glorious interworkings of the cells, and within the cells the molecules.

He stopped when he saw before him a curving ladder to heaven, the double helix. Blue fire lanced up and down it like heat lightning, making the patterns within the helix glow like gems. Patterns within patterns, all with the same fourfold foundation. It was like music, like the carvings of the cathedral of New Glastonbury, it was like nothing he had ever seen, and yet partook of everything he'd ever known.

The blue fire coalesced into a sort of hard buzzing point, dimensionless yet potent, and he began to sort the patterns, reading the facets of each, and searching deep within one then another. And each time he touched the double helix, like an instrument of unparalleled complexity it responded to him with bursts of memory, snatches of experience, pulses ranging the spectrum from suffering to ecstasy.

Ivard hesitated, confused. None of this was him, and yet . . . The blue fire swelled into a sphere of meaning momentarily. It knew, and so he knew, and he stood a moment, looking back down the long years of experience preserved in his germ plasm, and those who'd gone before greeted him who they had become.

Then Ivard sensed, far in the distance, the slow booming of his heart, and knew that it ought not to be so slow for long. He must not linger here.

So he found the string of facets that controlled the working of his eyes, and using the new-taught abilities flowing from the point of blue fire dancing deep within, he grasped the critical gem and shifted it over and over, sorting the facets until he found a better pattern, and set it into place. Turning his awareness away from the helix for a moment, he felt the changes slowly radiating outward into his body, cell by cell; he wondered how long it would take before he saw the difference.

Next his mucous membranes, quelling their sensitivity to air changes, and then his sinuses and larynx, adding the resonance and flexibility demanded by the Kelly language that came so easily to him now.

Then he located the gene that had cursed him with the easily burned pale skin. Changing that, he delighted in the melanin released, which would slowly suffuse his skin with protective color. A last alteration, to help his muscle structure learn more quickly, and he rose back to consciousness, looked around, and discovered that he was profoundly hungry—but he was also too tired to move.

So he sat in the light for a time as the itching faded, his eyes closed and upturned to the brightness of the diffuser far above, enjoying the evolving patterns in the darkness behind his eyelids. A gentle breeze caressed his skin. Welcome at first, it strengthened steadily, and then Ivard realized that it was blowing, not across his body, but down on his head. A faint pungent scent, like herbs and smoke, tickled his nose.

Then a subtle change in the sound of the open space around him snapped his eyes open, and he looked up into the hideously deformed face of some horrible alien creature, brown and deeply wrinkled with a rubbery sphincter gaping in a ghastly frown above dark brown eyes in deep sockets. . . .

After a moment of utter terror his mind grasped the scene properly and the face resolved into that of an incredibly ancient human hanging upside down in front of him within a faintly shimmering bubble of energy. The wind was coming from the bubble, and the ancient was smiling at him. Ivard stared back doubtfully, wishing he had his clothes on.

"Ho there, Little Egg," said the man, his voice somehow identifying his gender. "You are the one the Kelly are hatching, no?"

As he spoke, the bubble slowly rotated, bringing him right side up, and Ivard realized that the man was a nuller, like Granny Chang, enclosed in a gee-bubble to insulate him from the acceleration of Ares. The geeplane drive of the bubble was generating the downdraft.

"I'm Ivard," he managed.

"More or less, yes," the nuller replied, laughing. "Rather more now, I'd say."

Ivard shook his head, confused. He sensed no sarcasm; the man was not laughing at him. His amusement, in fact, seemed approving. Ivard thought briefly of Greywing, there on Desrien—it was almost the same feeling.

"The Kelly asked me to assist your hatching," the nuller continued.

"Hunh?" Ignoring his own nakedness, Ivard stood up slowly, bringing his face more on a level with the nuller's. The man's body, wrapped in some brightly striped cloth, was shrunken, with stick-like arms and legs protruding from his garment, but his wrists and hands were almost full-sized, gnarled but strong-looking. His ankles, too, were larger than one would expect, and his feet quite strangely shaped, as though all of their strength was in the toes.

"Breaking out of your shell, Little Egg. Don't you feel it? The Kelly said you would about now."

Ivard stared at the man. Did the nuller really know what he had done within his body, guided by the Archon's fire?

The nuller merely waited, smiling.

"Who are you?" Ivard demanded, feeling heat creep up his neck.

"Ho! Six hundred fifty years I've seen, and the answer to that question would take as long. But nobody has the breath for that, so I answer to Tate Kaga, and other names as well, which you may discover. Or not."

Perhaps because of the man's strangeness, Ivard suddenly felt comfortable with him. The nuller's gaze seemed to see him as a whole, without judging him. Like Eloatri.

"Why do you call me Little Egg?"

"It's more descriptive than 'Ivard,' which is just a noise your parents dubbed you with when you had no choice in the matter. A name should tell your story, and you'll have to find your real one for yourself, and soon, but for now it's Little Egg."

Ivard shrugged. Truth was, he didn't feel like just Ivard any more. "What story does Tahtay Kahgah tell?" he asked, saying the name carefully the first time.

"Tate Kaga is my name, Makes the Wind, and that tells

many stories. Two I'll tell you now, a third you must discover, more you will find if you live long enough."

"Your bubble!" exclaimed Ivard. "It makes wind."

"Ho!" exclaimed the nuller, sounding surprised. "This egg is swift, but is it wise? What's the second?"

Ivard shook his head. "I don't know."

"Wise it is. Few among my fellow Douloi would admit *their* ignorance so readily." The nuller cackled loudly. "Beans!"

"Beans?"

Tate Kaga pursed his lips and made a rude, wet noise. "Beans. They make me fart. And I love 'em."

Ivard laughed.

Tate Kaga laughed too and his bubble spun around, end over end, making Ivard dizzy. "Only damned physical pleasure left to me after nearly seven hundred years—that and a good dump, but that name'd tell a different story, and not mine, thank you very much. I leave that to my fellow Douloi."

The young Rifter laughed harder, remembering some of the nicks he'd seen here on Ares. When he finally caught his breath he asked, "And what's the third?"

Tate Kaga stopped smiling, and his bubble halted its rotation, leaving him upside down. "That you must discover." His bubble began to accelerate upward. "Come visit me."

Ivard stared up as Tate Kaga's gee-bubble disappeared into the soft dazzle of the diffuser, then a wave of dizziness warned him of his depleted state and he walked back into the suite.

Ivard dialed some nourishing food and ate it almost without noticing the taste. As soon as he had eaten, he dropped onto his bed and closed his eyes.

Ivard no longer dreamed alone. Bypassing the long necklace of interconnected memories that the Kelly Archon's genome had bequeathed him, he sank into more familiar dreamscapes, pursued by the whispering voices he now knew were the Eya'a.

One-who-hears-three has emended herself?

I'm a he, Ivard corrected sleepily, looking for a likely dream pattern to leap into. He was learning how to control his dreaming, but sometimes it didn't work. He hated some of the things he saw sometimes. . . .

Then a distinctive voice came in, cool and soft-toned: Vi'ya. *Don't try, Firehead. They'll never get it straight.* Her amusement was like a thin stream of golden light.

How come I can hear you like this? Ivard asked. *I'm not a tempath. And you're all the way up in the Cap.* As he sent the thought, memory flickered: Vi'ya and Lokri, locked together in rage-fueled passion.

Perhaps she could catch his words, but—relief—not his images. She returned the answer he'd already figured out: *Your connection with the Kelly and mine with the Eya'a seems to have brought us into contact this way. And the Eya'a are impatient for you to add your focus to a project of theirs—but not yet. Not until you are stronger.*

What is it?

We have to locate the Heart of Kronos. But do not think about it now, and do not, ever, discuss it with the nicks. Sleep, regain your strength. When you awaken, Jaim will visit you. We will talk about this later.

Ivard sent his wordless compliance, and Vi'ya's presence vanished. But behind his obedience, somewhat to his surprise, an obdurate bit of self complained: *But Tate Kaga is a nick.* Why that came to mind he didn't really know. Then memory supplied an acid comment from Greywing: *You can't trust someone just because they talk nice,* but the blue fire added its weight of experience with the observation that the ancient nuller tasted good.

Oh, shut up, all of you. Interior silence fell, but the good feeling he'd gotten from Tate Kaga lingered, and Ivard slid gratefully into a pleasant memory-dream of the good days a year ago—when Greywing was alive, and Markham, and they were all together on board the *Telvarna*, and free. . . .

⁂ ⁂ ⁂

"Two duels?"

Vannis turned away from her mirror and looked down at the woman lying across her bed.

The corners of Besthan's smile deepened into sardonicism. "You did not know, child? Where have you been hiding?"

Vannis laughed. "I was puking up my guts for one day, and sleeping off the effects of that the next." She would not admit to anyone that she had used an admittedly bad reaction to whatever chemicals were in Srivashti's accursed Shiidra tea to wait for Brandon vlith-Arkad to repeat his visit.

"Were I coarse-minded," Besthan said in that same dry tone, "and were we on home ground, I would recommend a stroll through the Whispering Gallery some evening."

"I'll be spending days making amends to those I offended yesterday," Vannis said with a sigh.

"You shouldn't have had your maid tell them you were ill," came the imperturbable answer.

"But I was." Vannis still felt enervated, which made her petulant. And it was a luxury rare enough to be cherished to actually be able to vent her emotions.

Besthan laughed. "But no one is *ever* sick, not unless there's a damn good reason."

"Tau gave me a horrid tea, some Shiidran hellbrew. Which, of course, he identified after I'd drunk it. Would you want the medtechs spreading that all over—even if they have a remedy, which they probably don't?"

Besthan wrinkled her nose. "No. No one needs a reputation for deviance at this moment."

Vannis closed her eyes, rubbing her temples. "Tau would probably love just that."

"Anything but vulgarity, which is merely dull, for that one," Besthan said. "What does he want?"

Vannis sighed. "Mother used to say, 'When people profess honesty, you may be sure they are hiding something more important than the issue at hand.' He wants to know what the Navy attacked Arthelion for, and he wants to know how Brandon found out about the plot against his life. More than that I can't yet guess."

Besthan considered a mote in the air, one thin hand rubbing gently at her lower belly. Vannis watched, distracted by the gestures. She'd grown up loving Besthan as the "aunt" her own blood relations never had been, but she did not really understand the woman. Why, for instance, had she suddenly decided to birth an heir at seventy years of age—and insisted on incubating it herself? The baby had been due just before Eusabian's Rifters arrived, and Besthan, her spouse, and family had hastily fled in an old merchant vessel, the only one still working after the surprise attack. There'd been no real med equipment on board that ship. *She's lucky she made it to Ares in time.* Vannis felt a chill.

"I miss your mother," Besthan said suddenly. "Has the High Phanist said aught of her?"

"No, and I haven't asked. People disappear on Desrien all the time—and she might not have even used her real name."

"Fifteen years is a long time for a religious pilgrimage, especially for a woman who had no religion," Besthan mused.

Vannis nodded, beset by the old, familiar conflict of emotions. Alone of all her powerful relations she loved her mother, and she still missed her, a sentiment that warred with her resentment of her peculiar upbringing.

For reasons Vannis would never fathom unless she found her mother to ask, all her early training had been in the social arts, from personal to architectural. When her mother disappeared, the family business had gone to Vannis' uncle—but Vannis' nascent ambitions had been satisfied. What she'd learned about politics and economics had been indirectly—and very much despite Semion's wishes.

She reached over and tapped her console to life. "I know. I'll have an intimate breakfast. For just those I supposedly snubbed yesterday."

Besthan nodded, rising to her feet. Then she leaned against the bed table and swore softly, pressing her hand against her middle. "Childbirth!" she muttered, so low Vannis had to strain to hear her. For a moment, the elegant, polished woman looked old. Then she looked up, the amusement back, despite the circles under her eyes. "Time for me to go visit the little heir."

Vannis kissed her and saw her to the door. Then she turned around and rubbed her palms down her skirt. *And it is time for me,* she vowed, *to go visit the great heir.*

* * *

Sleepless under the weight of the lives she had spent at Arthelion, Margot Ng dressed and made her way to the Situation Room. Installed there was the officially justified reason for her decision. It remained only for her to justify it to herself.

The guard saluted and triggered the door open for her. She stood for a moment, looking around at the strange dichotomy of light and darkness at the heart of Ares.

As always, the floor of the Situation Room knew nothing of the ancient diurnal rhythm of its makers. Here was always the high noon of artificial light and the exhilarating tension of well-trained minds pitted against the straightforward constraints of spacetime and the devious designs of the enemy.

But above this bright activity, wrapped in a gloomy darkness born of cunning optics, hung a misty, glittering hologram of the Thousand Suns, responding with ceaseless ripples of change to the data flowing from the consoles beneath. The heavy inversion of it, dark over light, oppressed her, and she looked down again. It was too much like the regret that gnawed at her.

Unnoticed by the officers and analysts at their consoles, Ng crossed to a small door, guarded by two Marines. After the brief flicker of a retinal scan, they stepped aside and the door slid open. There, against a wall in bizarre contrast to the clean geometry of humankind's machinery, crouched the red-glowing form of the Urian hyperwave, its alien lines looking half-melted, almost organic.

Ng clasped her hands tightly behind her back. She wouldn't touch it again willingly, not since her first encounter with it in the hangar bay of the battered *Grozniy* following the Battle of Arthelion. She clenched her jaw against the ache of memory: the warmth of firm human flesh somehow incarnate in a machine that knew nothing of humanity, recalling to her Metellus Hayashi, her beloved. Lost in battle—at her command.

This now was her penance, for a decision she knew was right but would always regret. She'd always known, even as a cadet, that violent death was a possibility for any who chose a naval career. But now she knew her own death was nothing to be feared, compared to the pain of the necessary deaths of others in obedience to her orders.

Almost blindly, Margot Ng turned away and left the room, seeking the bustle of the Situation Room as an anodyne. She wandered from console to console, looking over the shoulders of various analysts, asking a question from time to time, gathering a sense of the data flowing from the hyperwave that was slowly building a picture of Dol'jhar's strategy, despite the fact that most of the traffic was coded and still indecipherable. Enough of the traffic was en clair, the undisciplined rantings and boastings of Dol'jhar's Rifter allies, to build a clear picture of their movements, and, as expected, the message headers of the coded Dol'jharian communications were yielding to cryptanalysis, generating even more information.

Around the edges of the Situation Room were a number of small bays, each holding a single console. Clustered around one of these was a knot of young naval officers, a couple of civilian analysts, and the diminutive form of the Rifter comtech the Marines had rescued from the Rifter destroyer *Deathstorm* along with the hyperwave. She had been crucial to understanding the operation of the Urian communicator.

Aziza. The Rifter's name sifted through Ng's mind, and she started to turn away when a snigger from one of the analysts drew her attention back. She drifted closer, suddenly recognizing the nature of the expressions on the faces watching the flickering console. As she entered the bay proper, coming within the influence of its acoustic dampers, the noise of the Situation Room diminished, allowing her to hear clearly the panting moans coming from the console.

What are they watching? She refused to believe that naval officers would amuse themselves with a mindless sexchip in the midst of the most critical area on Ares.

One of the officers, a lieutenant, looked up at that moment and the smile on her face froze as she saw Ng. She jerked to attention. "Officer on deck!"

The other officers sprang to attention, while the two civilian analysts looked up in mild confusion. Only the Rifter paid no attention, grinning at the action on the screen.

Ng stalked around to the other side of the console, the young officers melting out of her path. She looked at the console screen, blinked. It *was* a sexchip. Anger started to burn through her, but was suddenly arrested by the overlay in one corner of the screen.

REALTIME.

"What is this?" She made no attempt to disguise her anger.

"Sir," replied the lieutenant, correctly assuming responsibility as senior officer of the group. Her name tag identified her as Abrayan. "It's a realtime feed from two Rifter ships, about five hundred light-years apart."

The little Rifter woman giggled suddenly, a light, infectious sound. "It's a first, Captain."

Ng looked back at the screen, which was split into two windows. In one floated a man, in the other a woman. Both were obviously in free-fall, and both were clad from head to foot in a slick, formfitting dyplast bodysuit. Clutching a life-size doll of the same substance, each was writhing in the throes of extreme sexual excitement.

"They're wearing telegasms," said one of the civilian analysts helpfully, his moon-like face shining with sweat.

"Ohh, lower, ahh, in there, ohh!" said the woman on-screen. Ng suddenly noticed that her doll was rather more formidably endowed than her distant partner.

"The gasms transmit the sensations of the simulacra to the

other partner," said the other analyst. He had oversized, badly chapped lips in a long, bony face.

"The captain knows what a gasm is, you blit," snapped one of the officers; then his eyes bulged and he blushed furiously.

"Unnh! Unnnh! Unnnnh!" said the man. The dyplast doll squeaked furiously in his impassioned grip.

Ng's anger collapsed abruptly at the piteous expression on the officer's young face. His naval pride had tripped him up. *Let him wriggle for a while, it'll do him good.*

"It's a first," Aziza repeated, giggling again.

Ng raised an eyebrow.

"They're the first people to bunny while being on opposite ends of the Thousand Suns."

"Umm." Ng let the silence stretch the officers on the rack of their anxiety for a moment.

"We've verified that the communication is instantaneous by comparing their responses," volunteered the moon-faced analyst.

"At least within the reflex-response limits of human norms," said the other analyst.

"Harder! Faster!" shrieked the woman.

"Unnnnh! Unnnnnnh! Ooooooogh!" bellowed the man.

"Squeakasqueakasqueaka," went both the dyplast dolls.

"I see," said Ng.

There was a sudden blip from the console.

"There's another channel coming on line," Moon Face exclaimed. He tapped at the keypads, and another window popped up. A narrow, pale face stared out, disdain in its dark eyes.

"Oh, blunge," said Aziza. "That's Barrodagh, the Avatar's voice. What's he doing?"

The analyst tapped again at the console, expanding the window. The Bori sat at a desk on which was a pair of miniature dolls like the full-sized ones now writhing in squeaky passion in the grips of the two distant Rifters.

"He's overriding the gasm channels!" Chapped Lips shouted.

Barrodagh picked up one of the dolls and tweaked it viciously. The man on-screen suddenly screamed, flung his doll from him, and clutched his groin. Then Barrodagh picked up the other doll. Ng felt her insides twist at what he did next; the female Rifter shrieked and curled up like a crushed insect.

Then the Bori began to play the two hapless Rifters like an organ in hell, whose pipes are the screams of the damned. They tried frantically to reach their consoles and disconnect, but

Barrodagh gave them no chance. The expression on his face made Ng nauseous.

"He's gonna play this back to every ship, as a warning not to chatz around on the hyperwave," said Aziza. "He's been screaming about that since the attack began—this'll shut them down for sure."

"Stop him," said Ng. "We need that chatter to continue."

"We can't," Abrayan protested. "The consoles are locked; incoming only."

"We can do it without detection," Moon Face put in. "We're sure now that the broadcast nature of the hyperwave makes it impossible to know where a signal is coming from."

Ng tapped her boswell, signaling the duty officer.

(Cuatemoc here.)

(This is Ng. I need Console 28 unlocked. Emergency Command Override.)

(I'll have to clear that with Admiral Nyberg.) She heard the click of disconnection; she'd put her reputation on the line with the override, which would ensure that Nyberg would be interrupted no matter what he was doing or where he was.

A particularly gruesome scream clenched at her gut. "Cut the sound on that," she ordered, noting heads turning outside the bay despite the dampers.

An endless moment passed, then a window swelled on the console, revealing the heavy features of Admiral Nyberg, tight with distaste. She could see a reflection of the same realtime feed from his console in his eyes.

"What is this?" he snapped.

She explained the situation tersely. "If we don't stop him, the en clair hyperwave traffic may diminish dramatically."

"Do it." His image vanished.

A red light above the keypad on the console turned green. Aziza bent forward, tapped at the keys. The two analysts crowded in next to her; the three of them muttered back and forth in disconnected sentences that Ng couldn't follow.

"I think . . ." said Moon Face.

"Grab that channel, heterodyne them. . . ." said Chapped Lips.

"Got it," said Aziza, and, shoving the two analysts out of the way, seated herself and started tapping at the keypads.

The screams ceased abruptly. The two Rifters drifted weakly over to their consoles and slapped at them, and their windows vanished, leaving only Barrodagh's image, which expanded to fill the screen. He looked surprised and disappointed.

The Bori put the dolls down and reached for his console, but the dolls stuck to his hands. A moist sucking noise came from the screen, and a look of panic crossed Barrodagh's face. He shook his hands frantically; the sucking noise got louder and the two dolls flowed up over his hands, up to his wrists.

The two analysts shouted with laughter. "She's put their sphincters in reverse!"

The rhythmic sucking increased in tempo, now combined with a ripe fruity sound.

"Sounds like the Thismian Bloat," one of the officers murmured, not quite sotto voce.

Ng watched, fascinated, as the two dolls began to swell up, growing larger and larger as they sucked in air in response to Aziza's commands from her console. Barrodagh flailed at his console, but the dolls were swollen into great bladders larger than his head and he couldn't reach the keys. Suddenly, with a deafening pair of reports, the dolls burst, tipping Barrodagh over backward in his chair.

There was silence for a moment. Then, slowly, a hand dripping with iridescent fluid groped its way over the edge of the desk and tapped the console. The screen went dark. Moments later the console locked again—Cuatemoc had been watching.

For a moment there was silence in the bay, then Ng heard a small choked gasp; one of the lieutenants was valiantly trying to control pent-up laughter.

Grinning, Ng gave vent to her own chuckle, and at once the mirthful release of the officers filled the tiny space. Ng waited a few moments, noticing looks from outside the bay. She knew what would be secretly circulating among the young (and not so young) officers for days.

Let them, she thought. *We've little enough to laugh about recently.*

Moving toward the door, she said, "Carry on."

Except for a sniff here and a squawking chuckle there, the officers controlled themselves admirably as they saluted and stepped out of her way.

Barrodagh. I will have to remember that name. She was still smiling when she left the Situation Room.

Six

❋

Nyberg motioned at his screen. "It seems," he said with a sardonic smile, "that our enemies are striking a blow for order."

Ng watched as Barrodagh's face appeared, with the Fist of Dol'jhar*'s ship blazon on a wall behind him.*

"A message to the entire fleet," he said. "You will desist shooting the courier ships. Confine your target practice to Navy ships and Panarchist civilians." He cut the connection.

"Tidy," Ng commented. "No threats, no reasons."

"Anyone with half a brain knows the reason," Nyberg said. "The Datanet is already unraveling—Barrodagh has to need it as badly as we do. As for threats, he knows where his ships are, and he can shut down that damned Urian power relay."

Ng nodded; by the time a Rifter could start up their cold engines, Barrodagh could have someone find and shoot them.

She shrugged the thought away. "He knows where his ships are." Yes, Barrodagh, you do, don't you? Just keep talking. . . .

❋ ❋ ❋

The first two Ulanshu training sessions took place in the Kelly enclave. The third time, Ivard was back at the detention quarters in the Cap. When Jaim arrived he found his shipmates' quarters empty, and passed through the anteroom into the faux garden. There he found Lucifur, the big white Faustian cliffcat that Vi'ya had rescued on one of their runs years ago, prowling restlessly along.

Ice-blue eyes glowed at Jaim, reflecting the muted lighting that indicated a late hour. The big wedge-shaped head butted Jaim's thigh, and when he reached to scratch between the battered, notched ears, Luce's low, racheting purr rumbled.

Suddenly the cat looked up, still and alert, and with a graceful bound, disappeared over a low, ivy-covered wall.

Jaim turned around: Vi'ya was there.

"Ivard's away, but he will return shortly," she said.

Jaim shrugged, relieved. "Tomorrow, then." He was tired.

Vi'ya nodded. "As you will."

She could read him, of course. Jaim realized she would not offer any more information, unless he asked. "Will he be disappointed if I don't wait?"

"Probably," she said. "But he will live."

Jaim hesitated, then moved inside the domicile.

Vi'ya's expression did not change, but he had not crewed for her for years without learning to read certain subtle signs: she was pleased.

"Where is he? Oh. Of course—with the Kelly."

"Actually I believe he is visiting his nuller friend."

Vahn had filled Jaim in on Tate Kaga; when asked what interest the ancient Douloi had in Ivard, the Marine had shrugged. *He's a nuller* and *a Prophetae, and he's over six hundred years old. Who can tell what interests him, and why?*

Vi'ya punched up something to drink. A moment later Jaim smelled caf. After a week of real coffee, the synth drink smelled sharp and unappetizing, but he said nothing.

Two cups appeared in the waiter. She took one, leaving one for Jaim, then she left the room, the door closing behind her.

Surprised, Jaim considered her action, and the possible reasons, and then followed. The door slid open at his approach. He saw her sitting at a console, her fingers moving with assurance over the keys. It was such a familiar sight that he started to back away lest he disturb the captain at her work, but then he remembered that she was no longer captain; she could not be monitoring supplies, or planning a run, or anything else: the *Telvarna* had been impounded somewhere deep within the military compound, and she had nothing, in fact, to do. He wondered briefly why she even bothered with the console, so heavily filtered it must be—perhaps the challenge of bypassing its limitations appealed to her. But that could only be a game.

Which meant she was avoiding him.

Why?

He studied her, considering the question. Knowing that if she had not shut him out, she would sense his mood of abstraction. The key to his answer would come, he thought, in how she reacted.

For a time there was silence. She sat at her console, her long brown fingers moving steadily. Her profile was somber, its planes and curves clear-cut, her blue-black, glossy hair pulled back in the uncompromising tail Jaim had always seen her wear. In eight years it had only gotten longer.

She has beauty, but it is irrelevant to her, Reth Silverknife had said once. And it was true. Vi'ya hid the graceful lines of her tall, strong body in the regulation flightsuit. She had never worn jewels or ornaments, though she liked to look at them; it was only possible to see the generous curve of eyelid and brow, enhanced by the dramatic sweep of dark lashes, when her attention was otherwhere, for when she looked straight at you, you noticed only the density of her pupils in an uncompromising gaze that usually made people uncomfortable.

You can take the Dol'jharian out of Dol'jhar, but you can't take Dol'jhar out of the Dol'jharian, Lokri had joked.

Jaim had been there when Markham found her. She had been plain about her utter rejection of her native planet, and she had learned Uni with the rapidity that indicated a fierce concentration, her accent being—except at times of great stress—Markham's pure Arthelion cadence.

She worked steadily, her eyes on the keypads.

What can she be doing? A sudden conviction grabbed him, that she was trying to break into the station system, that she had found out, somehow, about the captured hyperwave.

No. Though she was a tempath, not a telepath, he wouldn't even let himself think about what he had heard in that briefing: too dangerous.

He forced his thoughts back to the immediate, scanning her. No reaction at all, yet she had to feel the intensity of his contemplation, if not its direction.

That is in itself a reaction, he thought, remembering that in all the years she and Markham were mates, they had never once touched one another, or displayed any kind of affection, in front of the others. Yet each had spoken for the other with an effortlessness that comes of intimate knowledge—and trust.

"You're here!"

Ivard's glad cry caught Jaim by surprise, and old habit spun him around, hands stiff. Behind him, he heard a snort of amusement from Vi'ya.

Unheeding, Ivard rushed forward, his freckled face shining with sweat as if he'd run a long way. Jaim studied the unprepossessing boy, noting certain subtle changes.

"I hoped you'd wait," Ivard said. "I was up at the spin axis in Tate Kaga's palace. It's nacky! And then I visited the Kelly. We lost track of time, doing the—" He trilled and honked, making noises Jaim would have thought impossible from a human throat. Ivard didn't seem to notice his change to Kelly-language. "Goes so *quick*."

"Let's get started," he said.

Ivard nodded, closing his eyes as he concentrated on his breathing. Vi'ya moved quietly to help Jaim push back the sparse furnishings to the edges of the room. Then she took up a station at the archway into the garden, the angle of her head intent.

"Falls," Jaim said to Ivard, who obediently dived forward, rolling in an awkward tangle of adolescent arms and legs.

Jaim watched for a moment, then his eyes strayed to Vi'ya. *Watching the Marine guard again,* he thought. Why? This, also, puzzled him.

But he would get no answer if he asked, so he turned his attention back to Ivard, working the boy through various falls.

This time Vi'ya stayed to watch the lesson, though she neither moved nor spoke until Ivard, frustrated with his mistakes in a certain exercise, called to her for a demonstration.

Expecting her to refuse, Jaim was surprised when she silently left her post by the window and took up a stance facing Jaim, just out of arm's reach. Looking up, he saw a faint glimmer of humor, no more than a narrowing of the curved eyelids above the night-dark eyes.

"Hah!" she breathed, and attacked.

Jaim's body reacted before his brain did. After a lightning-fast exchange of light-handed blows, Vi'ya picked Jaim up bodily, with only a soft grunt of effort, and threw him. Jaim twisted, landing in a perfect roll-to-crouch, hands ready.

"That was great!" Ivard enthused. "Do it again!"

They did. Now Ivard was ready to try, putting his foot into Jaim's cupped hands and permitting himself to be tossed a meter into the air. His landing was awkward but not dangerous; he completed his roll and scrambled to his feet.

"You'll need to practice that," Jaim said, hands on hips. "Dive off that chair."

Ivard nodded, swiping back the sweat-dark red hair. Jaim studied him; the boy had been seriously ill until recently. Ivard did not seem to notice his own rasping breath, but Jaim motioned for him to sit down.

"Do a bout," Ivard said. "Show me. You'd never let us watch you before." His voice ended on a faintly interrogative note, his eyes on Jaim, not Vi'ya.

He got to know her as well, within his own perceptive limitations, Jaim thought wryly.

Then he abandoned thought as Vi'ya reached for him. They feinted and attacked, engaged and retreated. Jaim had always found her proximity disturbing: memory-images, no more than echoes, flickered through his mind. The scent of sweat mixed with a subtle spice; the sight of the long-fingered hands, their nails closely trimmed; the soft sigh of midnight-black hair against his cheek or his arm when she spun out of his grip.

A difficult blend of emotions accompanied that memory: humiliation and excitement, fear and anger. He had laughed most of any of them at Lokri's tired old joke because until recently he of all of them knew best that she was, after all, a Dol'jharian: she had attacked him, with rape the intent, one terrifying night not long after her arrival on Dis, and he'd ended up fighting for his life.

His gaze brushed her dark gaze. Was she remembering as well? Or had it so little meaning to one of her culture she had long since forgotten? She had never again referred to it, and after she had forced onto the hapless Lokri a similar encounter not long ago, she had behaved as though nothing had happened.

When they finished, Ivard was disappointed. He went off to his room, feinting and jabbing before him at imagined enemies.

Jaim said to Vi'ya, "Back tomorrow, if circumstances permit."

She did not query the circumstances, just nodded and went into her own room, leaving Jaim to escort himself out.

The guard lifted his hand in a casual salute, which Jaim returned. Jaim retraced his steps through the corridors to the transtube and leaned against the door, waiting for the next pod. He sniffed the air. It was "morning"; the lighting had been altered subtly to resemble morning light on one of the planets that claimed to be most Earth-like.

The transtube arrived, a quiet rumble under his feet. He stepped in, found a seat behind a number of people going off to work. The transtube pulled forward with a jerk, and Jaim felt the smooth acceleration in his midsection. Moments later the pod burst out of the Cap and began its descent to the surface of the oneill. He watched the patchwork of greenery evolve detail as they fell, with the raw scars of newly constructed refugee camps scattered across them.

Unlike Rifthaven, there was no ugly place on this habitat. Even the new camps, prefab though they might be, were pleasant to see, albeit crowded. But the surface space of the oneill was limited, since much of it was given over to food crops, and now quarters were being established in the Cap, and these were much less pleasant.

He smiled as he thought of the anger expressed by the civilians at their displacement, smiled even more at the thought that for a few of them, those sequestered in the Cap for their work with the captured hyperwave, that anger was feigned.

Jaim suddenly remembered the dispassionate gaze of Admiral Nyberg at the briefing. Obviously even so small a detail as exploiting the infighting for living space to cover the sequestration of critical personnel had not escaped his attention. Jaim knew nothing of the station's commander, but was beginning to understand that the man was as much a master of the political arts as he, Jaim, was of the Ulanshu. *And he'll need every bit of that talent to deal with the likes of these doll-faced Douloi.*

He looked out the window, but the lake near the Arkadic Enclave was invisible in hazy distance. That was where the Douloi competition for high-status living space was most intense, but he wondered if Vannis Scefi-Cartano and her friends even looked once out their windows at the lake. *No; they look across to see what those next higher on the rungs are doing.* And for Vannis, that meant Brandon.

Some of his earlier urgency returned: when Jaim had asked about Vannis, Brandon had said, "We'll leave the door open once. I owe that much to my brother, I think." What had he meant?

I don't have to understand it. Jaim leaned his head back on the seat, too tired to think.

⁂ ⁂ ⁂

Marine Solarch Artorus Vahn stood beside the window with his hands behind his back, watching the children play.

From his standpoint he could see both the room—which was empty save only for himself and Aerenarch Brandon, busy at his console—and beyond the window the grassy sward which rolled gently down to the lakeside, softlit in "morning" color.

The window stood wide. Vahn could hear, faint as insects in the garden, the voices of the children. He fancied he recognized the environment each had come from: that clump near the trees, their bodies stiff, their peeks at the sky tentative, were Downsiders. They did not trust the ground-becoming-sky that is an oneill's substitute for a horizon.

Those who'd raced straight out to play were Highdwellers. The ones who ran the longest, as if joy-crazed by the wide horizons, were from smaller habitats, or even ships. And those who set up a game in a business-like fashion had probably been born and raised on a standard oneill, like the civilian portion of Ares, whose size and maximum population were prescribed by one of the statutes known as the Jaspran Unalterables.

The games reminded him of his own young days, playing in the gardens of Arthelion. Vahn liked watching the children.

Soon enough they'll be hidden away. Ares' apparent peace was only on the surface.

The grim reminder turned him around again. No change. Brandon sat leaning slightly forward, the posture of one utterly focused. Vahn tipped his head, saw what seemed to be a multiple vector problem on the screen. The Aerenarch's hands moved with swift assurance over the keypads, and the screen rippled, adapting to his input and then altering the problem.

Superficials again—on the surface his actions made no sense. He'd been kicked out of the Academy, and now that he was heir, he would never be commissioned in the Navy. Yet he spent all his free time—sometimes late into the night, if the increasing demands of social engagements used up his day—poring over navchips. Vahn sensed he was looking on long habit. *In fact, the only reason I'm seeing him at it is that Semion is dead.*

This was not the Aerenarch's only secret that caused Vahn to speculate. Though ostensibly the telltale inside of Jaim was for Brandon's own protection, Vahn knew the real reason was somewhat more complicated.

Faseult's orders had been succinct on this point: "When he is alone with the Rifter, you and only you will listen. Do not record anything except details concerning his experiences, from the time he left his Enkainion until he was rescued by Nukiel."

Vahn suspected it was the mystery concerning the Enkainion that concerned his superiors most.

Why did the Dol'jharians spare him from the attack on Arthelion? Or had they? If they hadn't, what could have caused him to skip out on his own Enkainion, an act so unprecedented that no one dared discuss it with him? *Yet.*

A rose bloomed behind his eyes. Flexing a wrist muscle, he activated the accept on his boswell.

His partner, Roget, said: *(Jaim's back.)*

(Report?)

(Detention Five, the Rifter captain and the boy. Very brief chat, no consequence. Silence for a time; one of them was working the comp. Want me to have ComSec run a scan?)

Vahn hesitated. It was still a jolt to remember that the Rifters had known about the hyperwave's existence before the Navy. But then Eusabian had armed Rifters as part of his fleet, and maybe some of them talked. Anyway, he knew that Jaim had not mentioned the captured hyperwave to anybody—had not even discussed it with Brandon. He reached a decision: *(Not necessary.)*

(AyKay. The boy arrived, the three of them trained. That's it.) He acknowledged and cut the link.

Vahn activated another signal and waited until Keveth on the outside post had moved to the garden where he could see inside the room. Vahn watched Brandon, and when he was focused on the left side of his screen, jeeved noiselessly from the room.

He was there to intercept Jaim, but in his hands were two coffee mugs, and he was moving. "You've been up all night," he greeted the Rifter. "Coffee?"

Jaim veered and followed, as Vahn had intended.

The kitchen was empty; Montrose did not favor early hours. *Another Rifter.* As Vahn moved to the urn, he cursed mentally the difficult position the Aerenarch had put them in, with this whim of his, a Rifter bodyguard and another—a survivor of Timberwell with a cordial hatred for the Archon Srivashti, perhaps the most powerful Douloi on Ares—as his chef.

Jaim sat down at the table, his long face tired, his attitude one of patient waiting.

He knows this is an interrogation. Jaim's willingness to comply might mean anything, but his falling in with the fiction of a couple of guards taking a coffee break came down heavily in the credit side.

Jaim said, "Has he been studying nav all night?"

Vahn nodded, poured fresh coffee, carried two mugs to the table, sitting down opposite Jaim. "Seems to be enjoying it."

It was an opportunity to enlarge on what reasons Jaim saw behind it, but Jaim just shook his head, the chimes woven into the long mourning braids hanging down his back tinkling on a minor key.

"Get some R&R?" Vahn asked.

Jaim smiled a little. "Visited my shipmates."

"How's the boy recovering?"

"Looks good, sounds good." He hesitated, shrugged slightly, then offered a piece of information unasked: "Vi'ya asked me to train him Ulanshu."

"Expect to ship out together after we finish with Eusabian?"

Jaim's brows lifted and he stared into his coffee as if seeking an answer there. "No," he said presently. "I don't know why she asked."

"But you do it, anyway?"

Jaim smiled a little. "She was the captain. It's a habit."

Vahn said, "Two masters? That's a lot of work."

Jaim seemed vaguely surprised, then rubbed his eyes. "Vi'ya is probably looking out for Firehead's welfare," he said. Holding out his hand flat just above the tabletop, he added, "Ivard was that small when his sister Greywing brought him to Dis. Greywing died on our Arthelion run. I think Vi'ya sees herself responsible for him."

Vahn nodded. Sipped. Said, "I understand they offered her employment, and she refused."

Jaim shrugged, cradling his mug. "Won't wear telltales."

Vahn thought about Detention Five, the official name for the nondescript quarters in the Cap that had formerly housed low-ranking clerical workers who didn't rate space in the oneill. Now the detritus of the great refugee influx was kept there. People not classifiable as either citizens or capital-crime criminals, who the higher-ups deemed could not be let loose without monitoring. *Especially now.*

Vahn dismissed the grim reminder and got back to task. "Those telltales are simply that, to monitor where one goes. For most it will be a temporary measure, a necessary one given the circumstances."

Jaim flicked his fingers up. "Understood." He hesitated, then said, "You'd have to know her background."

That wasn't what he wanted to say. Vahn wondered what he would say if he found out that he had a far more subtle—and more powerful—transmitter planted in him.

"She's Dol'jharian," Vahn prompted. "Escaped from the planet in '57, is what Nukiel's techs found out under the noetic questioning. There's a relation?"

Jaim grinned mirthlessly. "If you knew much about Dol'jhar, you'd see it. Slaves have old-fashioned trackers planted in their shoulder blades, soon's they're sold. Big metal lump, like this." He indicated a knuckle. "Her first act when she escaped the quarry—she wasn't much older than Firehead—was to dig it out of her own back with a stolen table knife. Said she'd never bear another, and she keeps her word."

Vahn winced in sympathy. Instinct prompted him to trust this man, but he held back from the decision. Too much was at stake: Jaim could either be a plotter or a dupe, and either could be quite lethal.

I can't trust you wholly, but I can let you know that it would be best if we were on the same side.

"You'll need to get some sleep," he said, finishing his coffee and getting to his feet. He put his cup in the recycler, then turned back. "Unfortunately I have some news that might make it hard to rack up the Zs. Want it now, or wait?"

"Let me guess—someone wants our guts for a trophy?"

Vahn shook his head once. "Already tried. Found it just before you two got in from that Archonei's this evening."

"It?"

"Helix. On a personal invitation. Clone cells in the tianqi monitors caught it."

Vahn was gratified by Jaim's reaction of unequivocal revulsion. He hadn't been sure if Rifters shared the civilized abhorrence of the Voudun genetic poison, cultivated from cloned cells taken from the intended victim and affecting only that person. Rare as it was, only the death of the sensitized clone cells in the tianqi substrates—an expensive precaution that Vahn had ordered as part of his security measure—had revealed the presence of the poison.

Jaim's face became thoughtful. "Hard to pin down the poisoner, then, or the accomplices. Anyone from Srivashti's tailor, to any of Brandon's dance partners at the ball, or later." It only took a few cells, from under a fingernail brushed lightly against the victim's skin, or a couple of hairs, to supply enough of the victim's genome to clone the poison.

So he understands. The invitation might have passed through many hands on its way to the Arkadic Enclave. Like Vahn, Jaim had immediately dismissed the issuer of the invitation from his suspicions. No one would be that stupid. *Of course, that might be just what we're intended to think.*

"Right," the Marine replied.

Jaim grunted and rubbed his fingers from eye sockets to jaw. "Dol'jhar?"

Vahn smiled ruefully. "I'd like to think so, but it's just as likely to be plotters in the government with an eye to their own advantage should the heir die or, better, be disabled. Forensics hasn't analyzed the poison yet, so we don't know which was intended."

The Rifter didn't speak for a moment, his eyes downcast. Vahn wondered if he understood just how complicated the situation really was. Finally Jaim said merely, "Arkad know?"

The name, bare of titles, jarred Vahn; his reaction was mixed. During his days under the former Aerenarch Semion, one could have been flogged for relaxing protocols even in one's sleep. But the new Aerenarch's orders had been clear: no protocol enforcement when they were alone in the enclave. "Not yet," he said.

Jaim smiled, that mirthless smile again. "My job, right?"

Vahn opened his hands.

Jaim swallowed his coffee, got up, and went out.

Vahn remained where he was, and with a distinct feeling of distaste that grew each time he did it, activated Jaim's monitor.

"*. . . interrupt you?*" Jaim sounded loud, god-like.

The Aerenarch's voice came, flattened slightly. "*What, dawn already? Can't we arrange to slow the chrono?*"

Jaim sighed. "*Vahn says there was an assassination attempt. Last night. Helix. Found it before our return.*"

After a pause, Brandon's reaction surprised Vahn: "*Do you believe him?*"

"*I don't see the utility in a lie.*"

"There might be several reasons, but none of them likely. Well, then, there was an attempt. Events are moving with a speed I hadn't anticipated. It's time, I think, to—"

Vahn had seen the visitor code, but ignored it; now the others heard the chime through the house system. As Vahn cursed to himself at the interruption, Keveth's voice came over the boswell: *(Former Aerenarch-Consort Lady Vannis.)*

Over the link, Jaim said, *"You want to be alone for this?"*

The Aerenarch replied, *"Why?"*

Vannis had dressed with careful simplicity. She had abandoned mourning white—indicating, she hoped, sincerity—and only wore two jewels, one to catch up her hair and the other a clasp on her gown. Her hands were bare, because she'd noticed that Brandon wore no rings, and she dared it because she had been told that she had beautiful hands.

The guards at the gate bowed, and no one came forward to stop her. Was Brandon always as accessible as this? Or was his position so ambiguous no one tried?

The thought made her steps falter, but she dismissed that idea. Whatever they were whispering about Brandon, he was still who he was. The weight of a millennium's power imbued everything he did with interest and possible affect.

She lifted a hand to put aside a huge frond and found Brandon standing just beyond, leaning in the doorway. Without speaking she bowed, not the bow of family but of peers one degree removed; it was for Brandon to make any acknowledgment of relationship. She smiled at the last, just a little, hoping that the time—early morning—would impel him to drop formality, so that gallantry could inspire him to the familial response.

He touched her hand, smiled, gestured her inside. Informal but impersonal. "Morning, Vannis," he said. "Want some breakfast?"

His clothes were rumpled, as if he'd been up all night, and his hair, too long for the latest court fashion, lay tousled on his neck.

She stepped inside the room, casting a quick glance around; would he, with a freezing urbanity, introduce her to some lover, relaxed on a sofa in borrowed robes and smiling with pride of possession?

Then her eyes found the tall Rifter in gray. His long face was marked with exhaustion. *Is that it, then?*

"Coffee, certainly, Your Highness," she said. "I take it you have an unlimited supply?"

"Comes with the location." He made an apologetic gesture. "And in here, we can dispense with the titles." Which dispensed entirely with formality—leaving the way for intimacy.

The Rifter moved with soundless steps to the wall console and worked there. Glancing at him, Vannis thought, *But we're not alone.*

Approaching the question obliquely, she commented as she sat on a low chair and arranged her skirts about her, "Semion preferred the amenities observed whatever the hour or place." *"Even in private?" he can say, and I can hint that we're not private.*

"He would." Brandon sat down opposite her and smiled. His eyes, unlike Semion's steel-gray ones, were very blue. "I've always wanted to know something. Did you ever set foot in his fortress on Narbon?"

He had not followed her lead, but his unexpected reply still left the way open for intimacy.

She gave her head a shake, conscious of her loosened hair spilling about her shoulders. Tiny golden chimes on the gemstone in her hair tinkled merrily. "Not once. But you can't think Semion would permit his spouse to be in the same orbit as an Official Mistress." She gave a soft laugh. "He *didn't* have a suite for me . . . ?"

Brandon nodded, his smile wry. "Brought me out there once. To teach me discipline, I think. I evaded his watchhounds long enough to take a tour. His suite was enormous, and right next to it another, twin to his, complete down to the clothing in the closet and, I realize now, the scents in the tianqi. All yours."

She put her chin on her hand. "How do you know which scents I like?"

"Distinctive blend of blossoms and spice," he said. "I noticed them when we were dancing."

Have I got him so quickly, then? But he made no move, and behind him, the Rifter was busy; there came the ringing of crystal, the clink of silver on porcelain. Had she misjudged?

Vannis idly ran her thumb over the silken edge of a pillow. *A general question, then. If he wants to be personal he'll bring the subject back.* "He *didn't* keep the singer in the servants' quarters?"

"No. Her own wing. I don't think she was ever in his suite,

either." Brandon's light voice was very hard to interpret. *He can't be angry. Did he want her?*

"Semion did like everything in its proper place." The sting was not aimed at Sara Darmara—Vannis had never resented the woman who'd presided over Semion's private life. Again, she was probing at Brandon's own walls.

But his eyes were otherwhere, distracted, as he said, "Did you know that Galen wanted to marry Sara?"

Vannis stared. "What? I knew that she had been with Galen first, but word in Arthelion was that Semion had seduced her away. Which surprised people—"

She let the sentence drift.

Brandon's sardonic smile recalled his eldest brother to mind for a brief unsettling moment. "Though I never met her, she was probably the most beautiful woman I have ever seen in holo or person, and her voice made one forget her face. I'm sure Semion found that added inducement."

"She was with him for years, and certainly no other name was whispered around Court on Arthelion."

Brandon grinned. "Eight. Eight years. Semion was not known for his romantic conquests, was he?"

The subject was of little interest to Vannis; what she reached for was the undersubject. "I do recall that Semion was furious when Galen refused to marry the Masaud heir as Semion had arranged."

Brandon nodded. "My dreamy brother didn't even seem to be a part of the same universe. Political boundaries were nothing to him, and he usually acquiesced in Semion's plans out of a desire for peace, which Semion took for docility. Until he found Sara and fell in love with her—apparently Galen had inherited my father's predilection for monogamy."

Vannis watched the long hands, the distracted smile. He turned to her, seemed to be waiting for something. She said, "And so Semion swooped down and grabbed her, and took her off to Narbon. I am not surprised."

Brandon nodded. "It was a lethally simple way to ensure Galen's obedience for the next eight years—half of which I spent trying to concoct some way of springing her." His face was still abstracted, his voice so light it was hard to hear.

It was a strange way to offer intimacy, but then his brother had been far stranger—and much more dangerous to cross.

She said, matching his light-over-serious tone exactly, "You wanted to rescue Galen's singer and I wanted to rescue my mother."

As a transition from the distant affairs of three dead or missing people to the present, it was peerless. He could now stretch out his hand, whether out of pity, or lust, or sympathy, or shared grief, and make the first move—or what he could think of as the first move, if making the first move was important to him—and thereafter the subject would be Brandon and Vannis.

She was pleased with her wording and tone, for these transitions were an art—a gift—and had never failed her.

But as soon as she saw his face, she knew that it was the wrong answer.

Not that he said, or did, anything overt. He smiled, but the politesse was back, the Douloi mask that shielded thoughts and motives, and it did not leave again.

Gesturing at the trays the Rifter—whom Vannis had momentarily forgotten—brought forward, he said, "Breakfast?"

As she leaned forward to choose among the gently steaming delicacies, she acknowledged her disappointment, refusing to regard this as defeat. But though she strove mightily during the rest of the interview, using smiles, charm, and even—just briefly—a return to the subject of the dead singer whom Galen had loved, the promise of intimacy had been withdrawn.

It was subtle but ineluctable. The rest of the visit was pleasant as they conversed over a number of topics. She exerted herself to be entertaining, and found that his interests ranged wide indeed, that in fact he had not wasted all of the ten years since his expulsion from the Naval Academy in drink, smoke, and sex, as it had appeared from the outside. She had often professed a fondness for history, but she was hard put to recognize names and quotations that came so easily to his tongue, and twice she sensed he would have initiated a debate but she had not the facts or the background to rebut, and she floundered, laughing out loud against the early hour—against her own laziness—but inside she railed against her own ignorance.

In truth, though she had not gotten what she came for, she was not bored; in fact, the visit ended well before she was ready. And again there was nothing overt, no sign or signal that she could point to, but suddenly she was aware of the Rifter again—he had never gone—and Brandon's patient but tired face, and she found herself rising to leave, protesting that the day was advancing and she would be late for promised appointments.

Brandon also rose, which he did not have to do (and Semion had never done), and he smiled—but he let her go.

As she trod back down the garden path, she breathed deeply of the misty air, looking about her at the splendid gardens without really seeing them. Her mind was back an hour, sorting, sifting, refusing to acknowledge the regret, almost a sense of loss, that hovered at the back of her consciousness.

I love a challenge, she thought as she turned away from the slidewalk and chose a secluded garden path. *If he'd come to me when I beckoned, it would not have been half so fun. And I've learned much this first visit, for it is only the first.* And she counted up the things she'd learned: she knew that he was not stupid. She knew that he had detested Semion as well, but he'd loved the middle brother. She knew he read history, that he was familiar with the writings of his forebears, that he loved music—they had come back, time and again, to music.

She knew that rescuing his brother's lover had been important to him and that she had missed a cue in not perceiving why.

And when she had steadied herself with this internal accounting, she could at last face the regret, and note that it was the very first time she had felt this particular response.

She stopped on a little rise. A breeze ruffled the folds of her gown. Clasping her fingers about her bare arms just above her elbows, she remembered his words about the tianqi on Narbon: *a distinctive blend of blossoms and spice.*

She wished, suddenly, that she had identified the tianqi scents in the Enclave, then remembered there weren't any, that the doors stood open to the garden and the air moving over the lake. As for Brandon's personal scents, she had not gotten close enough to identify them.

Her hands slid up her arms to her shoulders, and she stood there hugging them close, her chin pressed hard against her wrist. She fought an urge to turn around and look back toward the Enclave, to see if the tall, slim, dark-haired figure would be lounging in the doorway again.

He won't be.

This, too, she acknowledged, and then walked on with brisk steps.

SEVEN

Anaris laid aside his dirazh'u and sat back. "Do you believe your prophecy?"

The alteration in the Panarch's countenance was subtle, no more than a change of the light in his eyes. Anaris was at a loss to interpret the emotion behind it.

"My predictions to your father?" he asked, then smiled. "One of the first topics of discussion when my advisers and I were reunited was the end of that interview."

"You don't remember it?"

"Not that portion. From my perspective, the shock collar was effective." His neck was marked with the still-healing purple scars. "But to answer your question: I don't know. I think I told you, did I not once?, that my mother twice dreamed about war just before an incursion by the Shiidran Hordes. Yet she admitted once that she'd also dreamed, before she implemented my conception, that she would bear a daughter." His eyes narrowed with amusement. "What do you think?"

Anaris picked up his dirazh'u again and toyed with its ends. "I think . . . that I will enjoy watching to see who is right."

* * *

Vi'ya felt the flicker of vertigo that presaged a contact from the Eya'a. Closing down her console with a quick gesture, she leaned forward, shut her eyes, and put her head in her hands.

The Eya'a's excitement seared along her nerves, making the contact almost painful, like a neural-induction boswell set too high.

Eya'a can hear the sleeper's-listenstone, but the walls around admit no passage.

The captured hyperwave, she thought. They haven't been this intense since the Arkad brought the Heart of Kronos.

Can you hear human-words from the sleeper's-listenstone?

Eya'a hear the current of words but not the words. Eya'a need touch.

What words did Eya'a hear concerning Eya'a and the sleeper's-listenstone?

We hear fear, we hear chaos. And then a shock ran through them, searing her mind: *We hear the eye-of-the-distant-sleeper.*

Where?

Distant, distant, and moves . . . Their anxiety level rose abruptly, and she was aware of the high, chilling chatter of their speech, used only at times of great stress or ceremony.

Bad sign, Vi'ya thought, fighting a pang in her head from the mental feedback of their speech and thought patterns. To give them another direction, she formed an inquiry: *Do you hear the ones you call Telvarna-hive?*

We hear. We celebrate recognition of Telvarna-hive ones among the many. We hear one-with-three—

Ivard. Thanks to the mysterious bond between the Kelly and the Eya'a, Vi'ya also heard Ivard's thoughts—and she knew he often heard hers, though he did not seem to identify them as yet, except when she consciously tried to reach him.

They described Ivard's dreams through their own perception, then went through the rest of her crew, not by name. Except for their calling her Vi'ya, the One-Who-Hears, they did not use humans' names, but identified them by description.

We hear the moth-one, who contemplates cessation-in-hive, in anger. . . .

Lokri. Locked away by the Panarchists in the maximum-security Detention One, under a charge of murder. So far, only Jaim and Marim had seen him, for very short visits.

We hear the one-making-music-and-food, who contemplates the danger of cessation of the one-who-gives-firestone. . . .

So Montrose had somehow uncovered the plotting against Brandon Arkad, eh? She was not surprised.

She hesitated, sensing the edge of a precipice. But the danger in this method of inquiry about the Arkad's mental state was only to herself, so she persisted:

And the one-who-gives-firestone?

The one-who-gives-firestone contemplates the patterns that move the metal hives between worlds—

And far away, barely a distant echo, she could just hear a whisper of thought, carried over the familiar high-energy emotional signature: she could, if she concentrated, hear him.

She forced her attention away.

The one-in-flight moves in a small metal hive. . . .

The Eya'a abruptly abandoned Marim.

Comes Nivi'ya.

"Another-One-Who-Hears."

Vi'ya had only moments to fight off the vertigo of psi-contact, before the annunciator emitted its flat chime. This was the man who had visited the Eya'a at Eloatri's request, the first human to communicate with them other than herself. She had had to wrench her mind away from their excitement at the time—even now, days later, their interest was still intense. Glad that they were not present just now, Vi'ya rose and tabbed the door open.

It was a shock to see another Dol'jharian, even in the robes of one of the Panarchist Colleges. Tall for one of her people, the old man ducked his head under the door frame as he entered. He was broad in shoulders and chest, and dark of hair and visage, and his long beard did not quite mask the distinctive hawk nose and strong cheekbones and eye sockets common to mainland Dol'jharians. The difference, besides the robes, was the incongruously gentle expression in his seamed face.

"I was sent by the High Phanist," he said in greeting, and then in Dol'jharian, "and I, too, am a descendant of the Chorei who fled the Children of Dol."

Meeting another tempath was always difficult, but the reference to the Chorei, so soon after a contact with the Eya'a, made it especially so. *Desrien.* Intense memory flooded her mind, and she felt a shock of emotion, indecipherable, from the Eya'a. With a wrenching effort she fought down the memory, returning her attention to the tall Dol'jharian waiting patiently before her.

She could feel the strength of his focus, a rarity that made her hackles stir. The instinct to fight or flee was sharp, but she controlled it, and forced herself to use her senses to listen, to evaluate.

The reward was a steadying sense of personal identity. His emotional signature was powerful—had to be, as she knew her own was—and baffling in its complexity. But she did not find the skin-crawling twist that characterized Hreem's pet tempath Norio, or the invasive caresses given off by a certain prominent clubowner on Rifthaven, whose dedication to the pleasures of the senses were famed.

In fact, though she could feel the strength of his focus, it did not trigger her danger sense, any more than she felt danger when the deckplates beneath her feet vibrated with power during the shift to fiveskip.

Her eyes, which had remained on his face, *saw* again—and she realized that a lengthy silence had built. Yet her guest seemed content to wait for her to finish her assessment.

It was a gesture more potent than mere words. She said, "I am Vi'ya, in Eya'a-speech One-Who-Hears. Before my escape, my quarry-mates called me Death-Eyes." In the distance of her mind, she heard a faint ripple of fear-reaction from the Eya'a, which distracted her momentarily. They disliked the emotions that came with her memories of childhood.

His head inclined, equal-to-equal. "I was before my own escape Manderian rahal'Khesteli, of the House of Nojhrian."

"Nojhrian . . . shipbuilders," she said, her mind ranging back.

He nodded. "I was content enough to work with ship design, and hide my talents from my mother's *pesz mas'hadni*, until my sister decided it was time to begin the war for the succession." He smiled. "My talents saved me, and my knowledge of ships bought my freedom from the planet." He shook his head. "It is a bankrupt culture, and there are more of us than the overlords realize. Do you know aught of the history of the Chorei? Not," he added, "the karra-cursed lies they taught us as children, but the truth?"

She hesitated. There were histories, untainted by the lies of the Children of Dol; she'd accessed them here on Ares. But the intent of his question went beyond that. The vision from her stay on Desrien loomed again, with near-paralyzing clarity: the asteroid glow descending so slowly over the eastern sea, heralding the destruction of the island-dwelling Chorei at the hands of the mainland Dol'jharians—but that memory would not be spoken. "Enough," she said.

Once again he inclined his head. "There will be changes one day." The soft-spoken words had all the resonance of foreknowledge. "For now time speeds, and we have much to do. You must know that I have been successful in establishing a kind of communication with the Eya'a."

And from their distant vantage, they sent the thought: *This one makes hand-before-the-face words for Eya'a, for the ones-among-many. We celebrate new word-nexi.*

"Nivi'ya," she murmured.

"Another who hears. Does this mean they accept me as a kind of pet? Their reactions are difficult to interpret." He paused, smiling, as if offering behind the joke a chance for her to elucidate on Eya'a psychology, but she remained silent. Then he went on, "I have devised a signal-language to enable them to communicate necessities to the humans around them as they move about the station."

He did not ask her why she had not attempted anything of the sort herself, during the time she had had them by her, nor did he query the depth of their communication level. She sensed that just as she was, he was concealing some things from her. She could hardly complain. "I shall do my best," she said.

"Good." He switched to Uni. "Then here's where we begin. . . ."

✻ ✻ ✻

Eloatri finished her meditation, took three cleansing breaths, then unfolded her legs with the ease of decades of habit and got to her feet.

Behind her, she could feel her secretary, Tuaan, still deep in meditation. The atmosphere of tension that was slowly gripping Ares had affected them all.

She decided to take a walk in the garden, but first she checked her drops. Among the many messages was one at which she gazed for quite some time: an invitation to a party, at the Ascha Gardens, from Tate Kaga. What was the old nuller up to now? The image of the Digrammaton burned into her palm tingled.

Prophetae, shaman, trickster—he was utterly unpredictable. He'd been a longtime friend to Tomiko; and when they had met, at the formal ball celebrating the arrival of the Aerenarch, he'd looked at her in silence, then said only, "He chose well."

Eloatri decided: this was one function she wouldn't miss for anything, despite the disorienting effects of the Gardens' layout. She tabbed her acceptance, then stored the other messages for Tuaan to deal with and went into the garden.

There she stood for a time listening to the waterfall and the sweet tang of hidden wind chimes, until the signal of her boswell indicated she had a visitor.

Eloatri crossed the tiled courtyard to the reception chamber and saw the huge Dol'jharian gnostor from Synchronistic Perceptions and Practice waiting. Manderian bowed silently.

"How did it go?" she asked.

"We have much to discuss," he replied, and at her gesture of invitation followed her back to the garden. He did not speak again until they were seated on a low bench. A breeze carried wafts of coolness to them from the waterfall, and the busy chitter of unseen creatures.

"I attempted to communicate with the Eya'a," Manderian began, "as you requested."

"And?" she prompted gently.

He looked up, the memory of pain in his eyes. "Forgive me, Numen. It was . . . almost overwhelming. I was only the second human with whom they have exchanged . . . concepts." He shook his head. "It is difficult to describe. They do not, even now, fully understand that each of us is a monad."

"What did they say?"

"Nothing, and too much."

He fell silent again, staring at the ground, his hands, palms flat against each other, pressed between his knees. Presently he looked up again. "I understood enough to devise some very simple gestural semiotics for them to use with other humans—you will have found an explanation among your drops."

Eloatri nodded.

"But for the most part, their communication was a maelstrom of images and emotions with only the most tenuous connection to anything I could understand. I wonder, almost fear, what the years of association with them have done—are doing—to Vi'ya."

"You think she is in danger?"

"Perhaps. I cannot judge. The woman and the aliens are an authentic Primal Contact, a nexus in the collision of two noospheres. Their association is the classic meeting of the

Archetypes being researched by the Joint Conference of the Colleges of Xenology and Archetype and Ritual."

He must have seen something of her confusion at his terminology. "I have heard you speak of a 'Hinge of Time.' That is much the same idea. The psychic energies of the two races are blending; and more, perhaps. I received the impression that the Kelly are somehow involved, and the red-haired atavism as well."

That was confirmation of the impressions she received when the Kelly physician-trinity had retrieved their Archon's genome from Ivard's flesh.

"And one more thing," Manderian said, "one image that repeated: a small silver sphere, with an impression of great power."

Eloatri nodded, unsurprised; but the Dol'jharian's next words stunned her. "The Eya'a seem to believe that it, or perhaps more likely, some component of it, is here, on Ares. They are trying to reach it."

She swallowed, her mouth suddenly dry. "Then they know about the captured hyperwave."

"I believe so. I do not know what they want with it."

She took a deep breath. The Dreamtime had bade her follow these people, a spiritual quest that was drawing her ever deeper into the politics of Ares and the prosecution of a desperate war. Nyberg and Omilov would have to be told.

For now, though, she put the thought aside. She still had her own concerns, and, in the balance of Telos, the fate of one sentient being weighed as heavily as that of an entire polity.

"You met with Vi'ya. How did that go?"

"Well enough," he said. "She does not trust us, but has little enough reason to do so. She is willing to help me with the semiotics we devised for the Eya'a."

"Will she learn from you how to shield the effects of these encounters?"

"Perhaps in time. I wish we could test her," he said suddenly. "But it would be a mistake now to try. For the moment, I can tell you this: I am reasonably certain that she is very strong for a tempath—stronger, indeed, than I ever was, and in fact her talents border on telepathy."

"Then . . . ?"

Manderian nodded. "She does not seem to require proximity to communicate with the Eya'a, as I do."

It was a kind of warning. Eloatri sorted rapidly through the immediate implications, reaching for the conclusions. At last she looked up, surprised. "Then *she* knows about the hyperwave?"

Manderian nodded.

"Well." Eloatri considered, and for a moment relived the dreamtime visions that had shown her Vi'ya and the others. She rubbed absently at the burn scar on her palm, then dropped her hand. "For now, tell no one of this. I will pursue it in my own fashion. You must see if you can win her trust—and teach her as much as possible."

Manderian took this for his dismissal and withdrew.

Eloatri sat where she was for a time after he had left, thinking. She would see Omilov first. For all that she had given him living space here in the Cloister, she saw little of him, as the Jupiter Project drew more and more of his attention and time. She was not sure he realized that he, too, was a hinge of sorts, a critical one in the destiny of Brandon vlith-Arkad. This would be a good opportunity to probe the extent of his awareness, under cover of an official visit.

Her decision made, she rose and made her way to the transtube portal.

* * *

The Situation Room was utterly silent.

Commander Sedry Thetris clasped her hands tightly behind her, careful to keep her sweaty palms away from the wall. At her left and right, a captain and another commander scarcely breathed, their tension nearly palpable.

Before them all a holographic view of the Emerald Throne Room on Arthelion appeared, familiar to just about every citizen. But instead of a small, dapper man seated in the huge, tree-like throne, a tall, broadly built man with a grim, hard-boned face sat, every line of his body glorying in triumph.

The unknown Dol'jharian with the *ajna* swept the view away from the throne to the long approach leading down from the huge double doors. Small at first, but instantly recognizable, the Panarch—dressed in prison garb and wearing a shock collar—was brought forward by a smirking Bori.

Sedry, who had spent fifty of her sixty years working actively for revolution, felt her hand twitch; she would have loved to rip that Bori's lips off his gloating, snively face.

"Kneel," the Bori said to the Panarch, and a moment later

the ajna showed the Panarch kneeling obediently at the left of the throne.

Eusabian is broadcasting this for a purpose, Nyberg had said when they first filed in. *We cannot be certain that anything we see really happened the way it appears.*

The Bori stood forth and addressed a long line of Privy Councilors and other exalted Panarchists, all prisoners. Sedry expected to feel triumph at their downfall, but felt nothing. She was still angry that the imminent revolution, so long needed to rid the Tetrad Centrum Inner Planets of the rule of debauched aristocrats and get power back into the hands of the people, the imminent revolution that had superseded her own group's careful plans, had turned out to be a blind: what she had helped contrive, so willingly and high-heartedly, was this Dol'jharian betrayal.

As the Bori's speech went on, something about fealty, she covertly studied the ring of silent viewers in the Situation Room.

Foremost was the new Aerenarch, whose reputation hinted at stupidity and cowardice. Would he pretend outrage, while hiding relief that he was not there with them? Or would he hide behind the Telos-cursed Douloi wall of politeness, a wall that masked corruption and rot at least as lethal as this Dol'jharian seated on the throne?

A gasp from nearby brought Sedry's attention back on the holograph. "Bring the beasts first," Eusabian said as black-clad soldiers herded a Kelly trinity forward.

Sedry felt a flash of interest on hearing the enemy's voice for the first time, then shock radiated through her as Eusabian held up a ball with something fluttering in it and said, "This is all that remains of your Archon," and dashed it to the floor.

Tarkans with serrated swords then strode forward and cut the unmoving Kelly down.

A jolt of reaction spasmed the viewers around Sedry, who felt sorrow and rage, but under it, fear.

Everyone else in her cell had died after the Dol'jharians swept in; she was the only one highly placed enough to win free, and she had turned and fought with renewed passion against the conquerors.

Nights she had worked the computers, removing every trace of her plans, old and new, and every reference even to the dead. Haunted by how they had been so successfully used . . . no . . . that was not it. . . . Her thoughts jolted as shocking images seized her attention.

She saw eight or ten men and women die under the Dol'jharian swords, until the floor pooled with blackly congealing blood.

I am haunted by how easily Dol'jhar identified us to trick us. Had our government known about us as well?

She had fought without regard to personal consequences, to cauterize betrayal. It had taken rescue, removal, and rest to assess how her position had altered: having subsequently received rank points and two decorations for bravery, she had the respect of her peers that had never seemed possible while caught fast in administration in Shelani.

In those first few heady weeks after rescue, it had seemed as if the revolution had happened, after all: everyone, Downsider and Highdweller, Douloi and Polloi, felt the freedom and exhilaration of change. They had only the Dol'jharians to defeat, and government would begin anew. And with the Aerenarch Semion and his chokehold on preferment gone, anyone could be a part of it.

Or so it had seemed.

She sustained another shock. The tenth person she recognized: it was old Zhach Stefapnas, Demarch of the community of Highdwellings in which Sedry had grown up. She was not surprised to see him shake badly, hesitate, then prostrate himself before the Dol'jharian monster.

A voice which did not belong to him said, "I swear loyalty to you, O Lord Eusabian. . . ."

With a wince of distaste, Sedry blocked out the false litany. She wondered if his horrible sister, Charité-Pius, probably now dancing or drinking with those damned Douloi in the Ares pavilion, had any notion of what had happened to her brother, and wished viciously that she could see this.

After the Demarch, the rest of the Panarchists responded with a similar cowardly refrain: Sedry knew that for a few of them it was expedience, and a desire to fight against the supposed new masters, that prompted them. Her interest wandered, probing at her own fears, like probing an open wound.

Her attention sharpened when the line reached the instantly recognizable remainder of the Panarch's Privy Council: all venerable with age and experience, the tallest of them Padraic Carr, the High Admiral of the Fleet. Bile clawed at her throat at the way he moved. What had they done to him? Somehow it was worse that no marks showed.

With a gesture of contempt the Dol'jharian motioned them away, and he spoke, but it seemed to be more rhetoric about power, and her mind went right back to the startling whisper that came out of the gloom late after a shift: *Sedry Thetris, of the Seven-Eyes Cell. Wasn't your password "When the bough breaks"?*

She felt her sweaty palms turn cold, and memory of the tall, gold-eyed man was replaced in reality by the Panarch, brought to stand before Eusabian.

"It seems," Eusabian said coldly, "neither your prayers nor your priorities did you much good." He waved a hand, indicating the dead and the living, now herded along by the sword-bearing soldiers. "Nor your loyal subordinates."

"What will you do when the Fleet arrives?" The Panarch's voice sounded weak in the vast room. Only Dol'jhar's could be heard clearly, from his position of command.

"Your concern for my travails is touching, Arkad, but your grasp of my power is faulty. . . ." He went on to brag about the Urian missiles to the unbelieving Panarch.

Old news. Why would Dol'jhar broadcast this? *He must be having trouble controlling his Rifters,* Sedry thought.

And her mind reverted at once to her own problem: the former Archon of Timberwell, who had somehow found out about her betrayal, and now threatened to reveal her.

I admire you, the suave voice had whispered, husky with amusement. *You've done well for yourself in the shambles. There will be a place for you in the new government if you are intelligent enough to recognize when to fight and when to defer to those with greater experience. . . .*

Anger licked at her. The Douloi did not lie—he did have the power. It didn't matter how she'd managed to slip up in covering her tracks. He knew, so she either got him what he wanted—or died. The decision was to be made here, right now.

I want to know what Nyberg is hiding, he'd said.

She tightened her grip on her hands, her boswell still recording. At any moment she could turn it off.

But if she did do the noble thing and die, he'd just find another more willing tool—someone who might not work against him should it be necessary. . . .

"So, Arkad," the Bori's gloating voice broke into her thoughts, "are you curious to know your fate?"

Sedry's eyes went to the new Aerenarch, standing so still before the holo. Rumor whispered of expedience, and of cowardice, in his own survival. Was that true? His actions since were puzzling: he had not, for instance, had his father declared dead and started up another government. If he was waiting, was it for this?

Her eyes went to his face, and saw clearly, for anyone to read, his emotions. Pale, sickened, his eyes dark with anger, he watched unblinking as the Bori brought forward two boxes and set them down.

"I'm sure you've spent twenty years devising something bloody, and nothing will stop you now. . . ." the Panarch said, still in that weak voice.

Eusabian smiled. "I need not exert myself to kill you—not when the denizens of Gehenna will do it for me."

A murmur, quickly stilled, rose up from the ring of watching officers. Sedry saw the Aerenarch's hands flex once, then drop to his sides.

The Bori said something gloating, and the Dol'jharian responded. Sedry felt poised on the brink of her own precipice, and suspended thought, watching.

The Bori made a flourish and lit the boxes: inside them, plainly to be seen, were the heads of the former heirs. The Dol'jharian spoke, but the words went past Sedry. It was all meaningless ritual now, the triumphant conqueror parading his prize prisoner in order to ensure obedience in his lower-ranked new subjects.

What struck her to the heart was the grief in the Panarch's face, twinned, amplified, in the Aerenarch's before her. But where the Panarch managed to smooth his features, assuming once again the detestable Douloi superiority, the light in Brandon Arkad's eyes gathered, brimmed, and with an impatient hand he dashed away the tears before they could fall.

"Has your famous wit deserted you?" Eusabian sneered. "You, who have lost your Fleet, your heirs? You, who were never able to penetrate the secrets of the Ur? I have, and I control the powers of the Ur as easily as that controls you." And the Bori triggered the shock collar, forcing the Panarch to drop to his knees, then after an agonizing time, prone, at the feet of his conqueror.

The holograph faded out, replaced by another scene entirely: the Navy's planet Minerva under fire.

Nyberg gestured, and the holograph ended.

"Thank you," the Aerenarch said, and went out, followed by his guard.

For a moment the silence still reigned, then at once the room was filled with voices: angry voices, excited ones, voices filled with bravado as oaths of vengeance were sworn.

Sedry cut off her recording and straightened out her sleeve before letting her arms drop to her sides.

You'll get your secret, Tau Srivashti, Sedry thought grimly, memory of the grief in the Panarch's face, and in his one living son's, still before her eyes. *Perhaps you are strong enough to defeat this monster. And then . . . and then . . .*

The image of grief-stricken Arkad faces blocked out the hallway as she followed her fellow officers out. Convinced that she had seen her own death warrant in there, she felt a strange sense of release. Eventually she would be brought to justice, either by Timberwell or by herself.

But first, she would exert herself to bring about justice for those who had died before her.

❋ ❋ ❋

Augmented priority, future imperfect, threat level two, deferred linkage to . . .

The Tenno glyphs flickered out, and Osri cursed mentally as the tenuous web of understanding he'd laboriously discerned vanished with them. He'd had no reason to go beyond the Academy basics in tactical semiotics—the addition of the new nonrelativistic symbolism slowed him to near imbecility. It was fortunate that as his father's liaison to the Navy for the Jupiter Project he wouldn't be called upon to interpret them in realtime.

He glanced over at the young sublieutenant in the chair next to him. Her shoulders were relaxed, her blunt, dark features in repose as she watched Captain Ng resume her stance in the front of the seminar room. The Tenno were obviously no strain for her. Not surprising, since Nefalani nyr-Warrigal had invented them as her Academy thesis long before the Dol'jharian attack that forced their adoption by the Navy.

In the front of the room, Ng addressed the assembled officers. "That will be all for today. The simulators are set up for you; you'll need to eat, sleep, and breathe these new Tenno to master them in whatever little time Dol'jhar leaves us."

She smiled. "Dismissed."

Osri stood up to leave, but to his surprise Captain Ng approached him, accompanied by a very tall, thin lieutenant commander. His nametag read "Nilotis"; his attenuated frame, ebony skin, golden-red hair, and green eyes identified him as a member of one of the *bomas* of Nyangathanka.

"Lieutenant Omilov," said Ng. "What do you think of Lieutenant Warrigal's hyper-Tenno?"

A sudden impulse moved him to blunt honesty. "They give me a headache, sir. I'm a navigator, not a tactician—I'm glad I don't have to deal with them in realtime."

Ng smiled; it had been the right response. Then she surprised him again. "Will you join us for lunch? I believe you have a couple of hours before your next class." Her phrasing made it not quite an order.

"Of course." The Tenno seminars were the only ones where he was a student. His next class was in fivespace navigation, which he could teach in his sleep.

Ng led the way to the mess, introducing him to the others and chatting of inconsequentials, followed by a comet tail of junior officers. She moved like a dancer; Osri suddenly remembered the young woman who'd seduced him after they'd liberated Granny Chang's habitat from the jackers, and suppressed the memory forcibly. This was Margot O'Reilly Ng, hero of Acheront and Arthelion, a Polloi who'd blasted her way to the top of the captains' list on sheer ability—aided by the quiet patronage of the Nesselryns.

And Nesselryn is cousin to Zhigel. Was this invitation political in nature? Osri felt a surge of disgust. That was a silly question—everything on Ares was political. At least the connection was on his father's side. Inwardly he winced at the thought of his mother descending on Captain Ng, demanding preference for him "for the Family."

As they reached the door to the mess, Ng suddenly slowed and Osri almost ran into her. Tension, gleeful in nature, radiated from the other officers, especially Warrigal and Nilotis.

The walls of the commissary were full-depth holos: a dizzying depiction of space, with a pitted asteroid in the foreground. Nearby a battered battlecruiser with the Sun and Phoenix emblazoned on it was frozen in the act of launching a sorty of lances at a point of light gleaming against the stars. Behind the lances a frigate veered past the asteroid, its radiants flaring, fluorescing gases spewing from a deep gash in its bow.

Warrigal nudged him. "Archeront," she whispered. "That's the *Flammarion*, sortying against the *Blood of Dol.*"

Then the frigate was the *Tirane*, Osri realized, captained by the young ensign Margot Ng, the only officer left alive on the bridge after the ship had been ripped by the edge of a ruptor bolt from the Dol'jharian flagship. She'd shepherded the lances to the crippled battlecruiser, fending off its missiles while betting that its ruptors wouldn't come back on-line too soon.

She'd won her bet, a promotion, and the Karelian Star—the youngest officer ever so decorated.

Ng laughed and turned to Nilotis and Warrigal. "I wondered what you were up to."

"Broadside O'Reilly," the tall lieutenant commander said with a laugh, as they found a table. "Scourge of Dol'jhar."

The edges of Ng's smile turned grim. "It wasn't as easy, the second time."

Nilotis and Warrigal revealed their Douloi origins in their lack of overt reaction, but Orsi saw in one's suddenly blank smile and in the other's tight shoulders a disconcertedness indicating awareness of personal trespass.

Ng lives in uniform. Osri felt his interest in the captain sharpen: he was inclined that way himself.

Then the captain touched Nilotis' arm. "Forgive me, Mdeino. There's no call for you to share my ghosts. You, too, Nefalani. Here, sit with me."

Her use of their given names was an indirect apology, which put the conversation on a more comfortable basis—not personal, maybe, but informal. She guided them to sit on either side of her and motioned Osri to sit across from them. The other officers found places to either side, watching Ng curiously. Osri noticed officers at the other tables glancing at them.

Ng indicated the holo surrounding the mess. "It was a wild ride, and you've done a great job reconstructing it." She laughed. "At least it looks like you have. I sure didn't see it that way!" Then she looked across the table at Osri. "But, from what I've heard, it can't have been as wild as your flight from Charvann. You outran a Rifter destroyer and burned two ablatives to bring a courier in with insufficient delta-V?"

Osri paused while the steward took their orders. "I actually had very little to do with it. The Aerenarch was piloting." He hesitated, sensing something missing. Anger, he realized—it had been a while since he reacted with anger whenever he thought of those terrible experiences only weeks (but feeling like decades) ago. Aware of the splintering of his thoughts, he marshaled them, sensing an intensifying interest in the officers around him. Every other conversation had stopped.

He went on. "My suit's med circuit oranged me out about halfway through the flight, anyway." He smiled. "Probably for the best. I don't know that the suit cache could have handled it, otherwise, when we made that last skip just outside of the gas giant's radius."

Several people hooted with laughter, then they all began plying him with questions. Very soon he had laid before them the entire story of their flight from Charvann, and more. Their questions started general, but as the talk went on they focused more and more closely on the role of the Aerenarch.

Osri realized that, insulated by his certainty at the time about Semion, he'd never really understood the full impact of the Lusor affair and its aftermath on the Navy.

But then the questions veered from "Did you see . . . ?" to "Did you hear about . . . ?" At first, the questions ranged back to Brandon's activities after the Academy expulsion, but they quickly moved toward the present.

They want to know what Brandon did before he came to my father's—what happened at that Enkainion. That question had obsessed Osri a great deal during the early part of his adventures. Though he still had no idea what had happened, he was not at all certain anymore that he wanted to know. What could the truth do but cause more chaos?

The others eventually sensed his reticence, if not his ambivalence, for slowly they broke off into little conversations, gradually returning to their own tables. Ng sat silently the entire time, her narrowed eyes going from Osri's face to her officers'.

Is that what this lunch is about? Of course, it was unlikely that Ng had only one purpose in mind; though born a Polloi, she could not have risen as high as she had without subtlety to equal and exceed that of most Douloi. Osri sensed that she was garnering as much information from the reactions and questions of the younger officers as from his story, but there was more. He could see it, he just couldn't tell what it was.

EIGHT

"Your son rescued a prisoner from the Palace," Anaris said. "A Praerogate."

Gelasaar raised his eyebrows.

"My father's pesz mas'hadni extracted the codes from a woman in your council."

A shadow of pain flickered behind the Panarch's eyes.

"That institution does not make sense to me," Anaris continued, toying with his dirazh'u. "Do you truly impose no limits on their power?"

"None but those enjoined by their oath and their moral sense."

"I cannot believe that."

Gelasaar smiled faintly. "Do you suppose the Bori in your service always tell the truth?"

"No. Of course not."

"No more do the infinitely deeper layers of bureaucracy that run the Thousand Suns. I could not be everywhere, nor could I rely on those below me to transmit the truth. Thus, the Praerogates, my surrogates."

"But without limits?"

"I did not say there were no limits, only that I imposed none. A Praerogate cannot act in a vacuum. There must be an egregious wrong to set right, a fulcrum for the lever of their power. And they only get one chance."

Anaris shook his head. "One has power, one acts."

"True power lies in choosing when, and where, to act. Lacking a proper target, the greatest blow yields only wind."

* * *

Throughout the lunch conversation, Nefalani Warrigal listened with growing astonishment as the last of her assumptions about the events ten years ago crumbled under the impact of Lieutenant Omilov's diffident words.

It was a process that had begun with the Aerenarch's competence with the Tenno in the briefing two days ago. That she had dismissed, feeling some outrage that such a talent was wasted on the youngest Arkad. Now, sifting the tones underlining Omilov's laconic tale, she sensed an admission that he, too, had once felt the same. But what came through more clearly was his reluctant admiration for a man who'd been portrayed as a wastrel, a drunkard, and a sexual athlete without a shred of responsibility. No such person could have piloted a ship with such skill. *Not just skill—panache.*

Really unsettling was the link to the Lusor affair of ten years past. If what Omilov was saying was true, Aerenarch Semion had cold-bloodedly destroyed the L'Ranja Family just to keep his own brother firmly under control. Which raised the question: if Brandon were truly such a sot and a scapegrace, why had Semion gone to such lengths?

As the steward cleared away the remnants of their food, she glanced over at Mdeino ban-Nilotis. From the tenor of his questions during the meal, she knew he hadn't shared her assumptions. And he'd known the Aerenarch at the Academy.

"The L'Ranja what?" Sublieutenant Ul-Derak asked.

"The L'Ranja Whoopee," Osri repeated. "They said that Markham and Vi'ya"—Warrigal heard a faint tension in his pronunciation of the Dol'jharian captain's name—"had figured it out several years before."

"So they used the ship's teslas to hold them just off the S'lift cable while they accelerated to orbit, so's the Dol'jharians wouldn't zap them?"

"Right. Only they did—I mean, they tried."

Ng nodded. "The Node was gone when we got to Arthelion. There was a lot of speculation about what might have happened."

Osri nodded. "The *Fist* used its ruptors. We skipped out right then, but when the ruptor hit the hohmann launch cable, it must have yanked the Node right out of orbit and shredded it at the same time."

"Just to pick off one ship?" Nilotis asked.

Osri shrugged. "Hard to tell. Up until then, it looked like they'd let us go."

Ul-Derak shook his head. "Hard to believe that even Dol'jharians'd blow up the Arthelion Node just to zap one ship."

"Then you must make some time for study of your enemies," Ng remarked. "Vengeance is the key to Dol'jharian thought. This whole war is a direct result of that action." She waved a hand at the wall holos. "But none of us saw the inevitability of it until it was too late."

Warrigal noted a tightness to Omilov's face, and remembered then that part of the little ship's actions on Arthelion had been the rescue of his father, who was being tortured by the Dol'jharians.

"If you'll excuse me, I've some business to attend to," Ng said, gesturing to Omilov. "Lieutenant, I need to talk to your father about something. Would you accompany me to the project room and introduce me?"

As the two left, Warrigal turned to Nilotis. "What do you think that was about? Can't be Navy; don't need an introduction for that."

He shrugged. "No telling." He hesitated, looked around briefly. "But I hear that some of the cruiser-weight Douloi civs are hot on her radiants for something."

"Battle of Arthelion," said Lieutenant Tang. "They may be civs, but they aren't stupid. They'll want to know what we fought for."

"Officially it was to save the Panarch," Nilotis said. "Most of them know little enough of strategy to swallow that."

"Or seem to," Warrigal put in soberly. Several highly placed Douloi had tried to exercise their influence to attend Nyberg's briefing. They'd been excluded, but from hints she'd picked up from Ng, one or two of them had since been exerting every effort to find out what the Navy was hiding. However, that was not a subject for open discussion.

"Some of them were allies of the late Aerenarch, weren't they?" Warrigal looked over at Tang. She was probing some topics that, until recently, had been spoken of only in whispers, among close friends.

Nilotis nodded. "Spheres of influence, I think. And all Downsiders." He waved a hand apologetically. "Deference to present company."

No one followed up on that: the tension between Downsiders and Highdwellers was a constant of Panarchic politics, but Warrigal was sure that everyone at their table, even the Downsiders, would agree that Semion had exploited it beyond the bounds of propriety. But no one had dared say anything.

"Lusor raised his son as a Highdweller," Tang commented.

"High Politics, in more ways than one," Nilotis agreed. The others groaned at the pun. "However, that—thank Telos—is probably behind us. I shouldn't say this, but with Semion gone, the politics won't be as bad, and promotions will probably be more fairly distributed."

The others nodded in agreement, except Warrigal, who shook her head in negation. "No."

The rest of the officers at the table looked at her, arrested by her tone of voice. She felt their deference to her—they were all Douloi, but her Family was oldest. That carried weight, even in the Navy, especially in a noncommand situation such as this.

"No," she repeated, feeling a frisson of almost psychic certainty as she continued. "Quite the contrary. I don't mean about promotions," she added hurriedly, seeing their expressions. "That's undoubtedly true. At least I hope so. But as for politics, it's only going to get worse."

She waved her hand around, encompassing Ares with the motion. "This station is all that's left of the Panarchy's government, all that's left for the play of cunning and calculation that has sufficed to rule the Thousand Suns for a thousand years. All squeezed into a few hundred cubic kilometers."

Again she remembered the blue-eyed Aerenarch at his console in the briefing. "All focused on the last Arkad."

"But his father's still alive," Tang protested.

Next to Warrigal, Nilotis nodded. "Right. Alive, but a captive. While his son is equally a captive—and we Douloi are even less merciful than Dol'jharians when it comes to High Politics. Just ask the L'Ranjas."

He pushed himself away from the table. "And with that thought, genz, I bid you farewell."

❋ ❋ ❋

The pod slowed to a halt, and as the transtube hatch hissed open, Eloatri found herself in another world. There'd been no occasion for her to come to the Cap since her arrival on Ares. Her first impression was that she was glad of it.

But as she made her way down the metal and dyplast corridors with their cool, faintly scented air, she reminded herself that her father, a career Navy man, would have felt right at home. And, in truth, she began to notice the touches of elegance that were the hallmark of Douloi design, even in such a utilitarian setting: the smooth, almost organic transition from the pragmatic form of conduits and cables to flowing ornament. In its own way, it was almost soothing, a reminder that, after all, this was but another expression of the human mind, as valid in its way as the beauty of the cloister gardens of New Glastonbury, on Desrien.

The corridors grew more crowded as she approached the laboratories housing the Jupiter Project. Several times she passed through security cordons; each time the brief flicker of a retinal scan and the bone-deep tingle of a security sweep underlined the importance of the captured hyperwave.

The people she passed, mostly naval personnel in uniform, eyed her curiously. She looked down at her black soutane with its archaic neck-to-hem row of buttons. *They're probably wondering how long it takes to get it on and off.* She smiled at the memory of her first experience with the garment, after her sudden elevation to the *cathedra* of New Glastonbury. Tuaan had hooted with laughter when he realized she actually undid all the buttons. It had never occurred to her just to undo the top few and pull it over her head.

The sight of two Marines in battle armor put her memories to flight. They were standing to either side of the hatch that gave access to the project facilities. After yet another scan, one of them tabbed the hatch open while the other handed her a follow-me and motioned her through.

The green wisp dancing under the dyplast cover of the little device led her quickly to another, anonymous hatch. She keyed the annunciator; after a bit of a delay, the gnostor Omilov's voice came back, a hint of irritation in it. "Just a moment."

But the hatch slid open immediately, and she stepped through into interstellar space.

The impact was visceral and overwhelming. For a moment she couldn't breathe, and a deeply buried, animal part of her brain cringed and gibbered in terror. There was no floor, no walls, just space, the stars slowly wheeling around her, and standing astride a wisp of nebula the figure of a man.

The man reached up, and a flourish of stars dripped new-minted from his fingers, dancing outward to take their place among the panoply of glory he was constructing.

"Let there be lights in the firmaments of the heavens. . . ."

Eloatri shivered with awe, momentarily forgetting where she was. Then the man reached out and grasped a red star, which flared up brightly for a moment, then guttered out.

"Aaargh!" he exclaimed in disgust. Tilting his head back, he spoke to the darkness looming above. "It still isn't working right. Give me some light."

Eloatri choked on a laugh and the man spun around. "What?"

"I'm sorry, Gnostor," she said unsteadily as the lights came up and the stars faded. "You make a singularly inept Creator."

He stared at her, blinking in confusion, then smiled. "Ah. Yes, I think I know what you mean. The seven days of Creation are part of your tradition." He looked around, then chuckled. "Give me some light, indeed."

A woman's head suddenly poked out of a rift in the stars above them. "It'll be a few minutes, Gnostor. A whole bank of projectors just blunged out. We're reprogramming."

"Thank you, Ensign. I can use a short break." He turned back to Eloatri. "There's so much information to winnow through, trying to find the Suneater, or just some clues to its whereabouts, that this kind of direct perception and manipulation of the stellar topography is necessary."

"I'm sure it's better than a pile of printouts, or flicking through countless display screens," said Eloatri. "And a lot more fun," she couldn't resist adding.

"Yes, well, there's that," Omilov admitted. Eloatri sensed a slight embarrassment in his manner. "But I'm surprised to see you here. Are the briefings keeping you sufficiently up to date?"

His tone seemed slightly defensive to her; she decided to probe a bit. "No, they're fine. But I haven't seen much of you lately. Not everything of importance is happening here, you know."

The Douloi mask smoothed his features into unreadability. Eloatri almost smiled. *Are you that much a fool, Sebastian Omilov? Have you forgotten what Desrien is like?* He must have, to think that she couldn't read past the shielded politeness of an aristocrat.

"The project is taking a great deal of my time," he replied neutrally. "And I retired from politics ten years ago."

"The same time our present Aerenarch was pulled from his own path and forced on another's?"

Omilov's eyes were somber. If he said anything about Brandon, she could lead the topic to the mystery surrounding Brandon's escape from the terrible weapon that had claimed Tomiko—and placed her here, now, in this damnable position.

"Ten years of seclusion has vouchsafed me little knowledge of anything outside of xenoarchaeology," Omilov murmured, making an apologetic gesture.

The guilty man flees when no one pursues. He understood very well her thrust and, for whatever reason, felt it necessary to deflect.

"Then I can see why you spend so much time here," she said in a pacific tone. "It is perhaps the only place on Ares that is apolitical." She continued before he could speak; she'd learned what she needed to know, for now. There was no sense in antagonizing him further. "I don't want to keep you from your researches—I do understand how critical they are to the war. But I have a bit of information that may be useful. I've just learned that Vi'ya and the Eya'a know about the hyperwave."

Omilov snorted impatiently. "Of course they do. Didn't the briefings make that clear? They undoubtedly learned about it on Rifthaven. The devices monitoring the Rifters' conversations told us that."

Eloatri gestured at the walls, now visible through a faint holographic fog of stars. "This hyperwave. The Eya'a can feel the hyperwave here on Ares. They are trying to get to it. There is even the possibility that through it, they are still linked to the Heart of Kronos."

Omilov stared at her. Then a flood of questions spilled out of him. How did she know this? Did the Eya'a have a sense of direction about the Heart of Kronos? Why didn't she know? Who did?

She was explaining about Manderian, the Dol'jharian gnostor, when the annunciator chimed again and the hatch hissed open.

Eloatri recognized Omilov's son, Osri, at once; she was struck immediately by the lack of anger—once seemingly a constant in his personality—in his demeanor. The woman with him, in the uniform of a naval captain, took a moment longer. Margot Ng, the hero of Arthelion.

"I know you didn't summon me, Father. Is this a bad time?"

Eloatri forestalled Omilov's reply. "There's nothing more I can tell you," she said to the gnostor. "You must speak to Manderian. I will arrange a meeting at the Cloister."

He nodded. "Very well, but please stay. I have a few more questions you may be able to answer." He turned back to his son and the captain. "No, Osri, it's no problem. The simulation is down. You really couldn't have picked a better time."

"Father," Osri said, "this is Captain Margot Ng. You'll remember I told you about the Tenno seminars she organized—I'm attending them to help you with the hyperwave data."

Captain Ng stepped forward. Eloatri was intrigued: a Navy captain who moved with the grace of a dancer. What was this woman's past?

"Gnostor Omilov, Yevgeny ban-Zhigel requested that I bring you his greeting if the opportunity ever presented itself, so I prevailed upon your son to make the introduction."

Eloatri watched as the intricate ritual of introduction proceeded, establishing, through mutual requests for information about related third parties not present, the web of obligation that existed between Ng and Omilov. *She is Polloi, but she plays the game as well as any Douloi.*

Then the gnostor drew her smoothly into the ritual, with an introduction, and Eloatri found herself the focus of a pair of warm brown eyes behind which shone a lively intelligence.

"Numen," said Captain Ng, "I'm honored to make your acquaintance."

"The honor is mine, Captain Ng. But if this is a personal matter, I can withdraw. I hope, however, that you will find time to visit me at the Cloister sometime soon."

Captain Ng gestured, the Douloi turn of wrist and fingers including them all. "I only intrude for a moment, and on an entirely civilian matter." She inclined her head toward Omilov. "At least, it is my intention to keep it civilian. You are acquainted with the Archon of Timberwell, gnostor?"

Omilov bowed his agreement, his bushy brows betraying faint surprise. Then suddenly, perhaps unwillingly, he smiled. "Yes, and I've been invited, and I'd intended to turn it down in favor of my work here."

Ng's amusement was blended with just the right amount of sympathy. "I, alas, do not claim acquaintance with the Archon, and would very much like an escort to help me avoid the worst social blunders."

A civilian escort, which will make very clear to Srivashti and his High Douloi guests that her presence is a social one only, Eloatri thought. And, with deeper appreciation: *She is a realist, and a skilled one at that—she must know that the gnostor was once tutor to the Panarchist heirs.*

Omilov bowed, an elaborate acknowledgment of social obligation, with something implied in the cant of his head, and the placement of his hands, that made the captain's smile hover on the border of laughter. Nothing was said, but they had all, with artistic finesse, conveyed to one another their thoughts about the prospective entertainment.

⁂ ⁂ ⁂

Dandenus vlith-Harkatsus stepped off the shuttle beside his father. He was actually on board the Archon Srivashti's famous glittership. His father stood impassively, looking neither right nor left, and Dandenus took his cue from that and kept his head still, though his eyes flickered side to side, up and down, taking in everything possible.

The lock slid open, and they walked down a corridor that made Dandenus breathe in ecstasy: one side open over a drop of fifty meters, the other a long mosaic featuring mythological figures from Lost Earth. Underfoot, the living carpet of mosses silenced their footfalls.

The yacht was certainly bigger than any of the Harkatsus trade vessels, and, Dandenus reflected in delight, probably faster and better armed than any Navy frigate its size.

But he was careful to keep his reaction strictly to himself. The other Harkatsus relatives distrusted the Srivashtis, with all the resentment (so Dandenus had discovered since he started delving into the records) reserved for someone who bests you in your own area of expertise. His father, however, loathed the Archon with a depth that hinted at some other kind of defeat.

But they were here. As relatives by marriage, they had been included among the select numbers chosen to attend this party, and his father had said that to turn down the invitation would be political suicide.

Dandenus wondered briefly if he would see his mother here. Though she'd spent the two months a year required by the marriage adoption treaty at the Harkatsus family Highdwelling, Dandenus scarcely knew her.

They rounded a corner, stepping under the leaves of a gnarled argan tree. The silvery hand-shaped leaves were open toward the light below, wraith-like and curiously supplicating. In the distance, soft twelve-tone music played, so soft Dandenus could feel the bass notes more than hear them, but the combined effect of this and the unidentifiable scents in the soundless tianqi made his neck hairs stir. Anything could happen here—and, he remembered rumors whispered about his infamous relation-by-marriage that had circulated around school, probably had.

Without warning the Archon himself was before them. Though Dandenus had never actually met Tau Srivashti, he'd seen plenty of holos, and recognized immediately the tall, handsome man, now splendidly dressed in forest green and gold.

"Kestian," the Archon said, holding both hands out to Dandenus' father. His voice was soft but rough-edged, like a predator cat's growl.

Dandenus' father touched his hands briefly and made a formal bow, which the Archon returned with grace and a gesture of welcome that was disarmingly deferential. Then the man turned immediately to Dandenus, and for a moment eyes that seemed golden in the muted lighting bored into his. Then the Archon smiled. "Dandenus," he said. "I am delighted at last to meet my young nephew. My sister has much to say in your praise."

The words were the usual politesse you expected to hear, but the soft voice conveyed a sincerity that warmed Dandenus despite all the careful coaching and warnings he'd listened to since the invitation came.

He bowed, the correct bow to one of superior age and social

standing, his hands at his sides, which would make claims of kinship ambiguous; that much he'd been told, but at the end he could not prevent a return smile.

This seemed to delight the Archon, who could then have turned back to his father, ignoring him, but instead addressed him again: "Charis tells me you are now the heir—that you will soon make your Enkainion?"

Gratification suffused Dandenus, though he endeavored not to show it. "I was to go to Arthelion."

His brief response seemed to please the tall man, who asked a few questions, still in that soft voice, about his studies. Dandenus was careful to keep his answers brief and his tones neutral, and he sensed his father's approval.

Then the Archon—his uncle, Dandenus realized with an odd stirring inside—turned at last to his father and touched his sleeve, the gesture of intimates. "Let the boy wander about. He'll find compatriots his own age. Permit me to introduce you to our guest, Captain Ng. You will have much in common."

Dandenus looked in the direction of the Archon's gesture and saw a trim, dark-haired woman with a dancer's grace, wearing a flowing, flame-colored gown. If that was Captain Ng, why was she wearing civilian dress? Was there some significance to this?

More significant, seeing that he'd been instructed straitly to stay at his father's side while aboard the ship, was the fact that Kestian's eyes were not angry—more bemused and wary. After the briefest hesitation, he said, "Enjoy yourself, son."

Dandenus heard the warning underneath the permission, bowed to the Archon first, then to his father, and descended the stairway by himself, his heart pounding. The hated Archon had chosen to mark his father out as a special guest by his promised personal introduction to Ng, and had even added in the compliment about Kestian's Navy years.

Looking about the spectacular ballroom, whose design hinted at vast spaces impossible on a mere yacht, Dandenus found himself reviewing his first meeting with the Archon and reassessing their roles. *He wants Father as an ally*. And then, remembering the smile, the words: *He wants me as an ally.*

Feeling himself safe from watching eyes as he descended the last of the curved stairway, Dandenus gave in at last to impulse, and grinned.

⁂ ⁂ ⁂

How long it's been, Margot O'Reilly Ng thought as she sipped at the liquor a silent servant had just poured.

All around her the light Douloi voices, their cadence a curious singsong, blended pleasantly with the musical plash of a fountain.

The party reminded her of her early days under Nesselryn tutelage—one or two of the faces here even seemed familiar from those days. And though none of the Nesselryns were on Ares (nor had she expected them to be—a Family as old as that had its own well-guarded hidey-holes against trouble), their presence managed to make itself felt.

The most obvious connection was in the unprepossessing figure at her side. Sebastian Omilov not only knew everyone, but judging from the genuine deference in these smiling faces, had managed despite his decade of seclusion to gain, if not their esteem, certainly their respect.

And the best of it was, he deflected every single sally on the part of Tau Srivashti, Vannis Scefi-Cartano, and their guests to lead the conversation into military country, ably assisted—whether by accident or design she could not tell—by the Aerenarch, who managed, whenever attention turned his way, to turn every superficial utterance of Sebastian's into a joke.

It underscored the relationship they shared, which made it the more easy for them to lead the talk. And, Ng saw, just once, in a glance they exchanged when Sebastian paused to refill his glass, that he was thoroughly enjoying it.

This made her relax. She'd recognized the moment she asked him for his escort that he had not wanted to come, but now that he was here he entered into the sport with an air of pleasure.

We will solve this problem of the Ur and their mysterious power base, she thought, her eyes straying to the Aerenarch, in whose flushed face and brilliant eyes were plainly seen the effects of alcohol.

What *did* happen on Arthelion? Who would get the courage to ask him—and would he answer?

When Omilov does solve the Urian question, I just hope we have a government left to see the project through.

"That's Ng." Dandenus pointed down at the woman in the flame-colored gown, currently the center of a knot of Douloi headed by the Archon himself. "She's not wearing dress whites." He made the statement almost a question.

"When my grandmother didn't want to be bothered with Navy blunge at a gathering, she'd go in civ dress," his companion said. Her eyes narrowed critically. "She even looks like my grandmother." Then she smiled. "I mean, Grandmère is almost as pretty—but somehow I expected someone with more . . . presence." She gestured, indicating stature.

Dandenus blinked away the fog of too much liquor and dreamsmoke, admiring the shape of Ami's hands. Once again she turned to smile at him, her face framed by a cloud of light blue curly hair that exactly matched her eyes, her rounded chin resting on her bare shoulder. Her gown had slipped down one perfect arm, and her smile held promise. Desire kindled in Dandenus.

But then Ami turned back to the railing, leaning out at a precarious angle. "I want to see the Aerenarch. He's supposed to be here."

Dandenus stared obediently down at the crowded floor, his eyesight blurring, and his attempts to focus distracted by the flashes of jewels and decorative metals on wrists, ears, clothing, hair.

"There," she said. "He looks *just* like an Arkad."

Dandenus almost asked if she'd actually met one, but resisted. To ask would be callow; she would have worded her remark differently had she met any of them.

Instead, Dandenus tried to focus his swimming vision. He saw a slim male figure in blue, dark-haired, who might be the Arkad, but his eyes were drawn back to Uncle Tau (so he had decided to name him privately), so resplendent in green and gold, especially against the fabulous mosaics behind him. Tau himself was the center of attention below, not the Aerenarch as might be expected, he could see that much clearly.

Dandenus leaned out next to Ami, scarcely noticing his own precariousness. His father was a part of that group. Not relaxed—his folded arms indicated that—but nodding and smiling, and Dandenus rather thought he saw pride in the cant of his father's head. Certainly there was no hostility in the way he sat, body angled toward his hated brother-by-marriage.

"That's the Aerenarch-Consort, next to him. I saw her once. She's asking the Aerenarch to dance. I wish I dared! Huh. Her hair is *still* brown. How dull!"

"Last time I saw my mother, she told me that court fashion is to appear as nature made you."

"Court." Ami repeated the word, but Dandenus had sensed her interest sharpening when he mentioned his mother.

My mother is a Srivashti, he thought. Somehow this justified his own pride in his uncle's splendid ship. Clearly Ami had just decided he was a part of this.

Ami leaned further, a slight frown between her brows as she listened to the talk below. What could she hear? Half-dizzy with drink and smoke, Dandenus couldn't hear anything, nor did he want to. He studied his partner, wondering how to get her attention from the adults to himself.

"Lusor," she said suddenly, and turned, her gown slipping further down one shoulder. "I've heard that before."

"Lusor, Caerdhre IV," Dandenus said automatically, going on to name the principal attributes of the system and its location in his own octant. "My father made me memorize all the Tetrad Centrum systems when I was first chosen heir," he added, trying to impress her further. "Why?"

Ami nodded below. "Why should it cause that old man, the one with the big ears, to freeze up?" she murmured.

Dandenus squinted down at the circle, seeing subtle changes in the adults. The man with Ng was indeed quiet, but Dandenus was relieved to see his father leaning forward, talking to Tau.

"L'Ranja Family," Dandenus said, and then he remembered. "There was some kind of scandal. Someone else is there now." Looking down at the man with the big earlobes, he said dismissively, "He's a gnostor, and a Chival—Phoenix Gate, I think. Omilov, a cadet branch of the Zhigels."

Ami tapped her thumbnail on her teeth. "Strange."

"What's strange?" Dandenus said, crushing some of the fragile blooms along the rail in his impatience.

"How just a name could act like a kind of warning."

Dandenus had lost interest in politics. He deliberately broke more of the blossoms hanging over the rail. Aromatic petals drifted down, resting on the hair and arms of the adults below. None of them noticed. Ami giggled.

"Want to wager who beds whom tonight?" Dandenus whispered, leaning against Ami. Her hair tickled his ear, and her breath was warm and redolent of spiced smoke.

"I can think of more fun than that," she whispered back.

Dandenus' desire warmed into urgency, but not unpleasantly.

Before he could frame an answer, Ami was gone, twirling about to beckon to two or three more people their own age. Dandenus did not know any of them: he knew Ami from school, and though she had kept a distance before, today she had been friendly.

Because I'm my family's heir now, he thought. *Because it's my uncle giving this party.*

The realization was not a disappointment. This, then, was what power was all about. He smiled to himself as the others chattered about the Ascha Gardens and the incredible free-fall gym there, better even than the one in—their voices fell to whispers—the forbidden naval territory, where the young dependents had all the best free-fall sports going. The Gardens had been recently renovated, and someone—a Prophetae—was going to hold a party there. They would go as a group to scout it out, so they could commandeer the best jump pads on the big night.

Dandenus found himself agreeing to whatever was proposed, without really hearing anything. It didn't matter. What he reveled in was the easy acceptance of the others, and in Ami's fingers twined in his.

* * *

Sebastian Omilov bowed a last time to his escort, then sank back in the transtube seat and shut his eyes.

With the disappearance of Margot Ng, all his energy seemed to drain out of him. He breathed deeply, fighting claustrophobia, knowing it was mere stress. The tianqi in the transtube emitted the same flat, odor-free air of precisely the correct chemical composition found in transtubes all over the Panarchy. There was no malfunction, but still, he longed for the freedom of Charvann—the night sky overhead and the cold breezes bearing scents of loam and garden.

My home is gone. He pressed the heels of his hands into his eye sockets, trying to force the desolation back.

But it would not stay. He heard again the suave voice of Archon Srivashti at that damnable party: . . . *shortly before Tared L'Ranja and I were confirmed to the Archonate—I to Timberwell and he to Lusor . . .*

The subject had been memory, so the comment could have been random; nonetheless it had sunk like a barb into Sebastian's heart. *Might have been random, but probably wasn't.* Tau knew Sebastian had also been there; had led the toasts to his best friend, Tared, on his triumphal night. *What was the purpose? To warn me off of political involvement? I'm too old for politics, Tau. Too old and too disillusioned.*

For a few painful moments Sebastian fought memory—Tared's face, so alive in laughter, alight with honesty and intelligence. The formality swiftly dissolving into hilarity, as often occurred when Ilara was there.

Ilara, Ilara. That grief would never die, but joining now the ever-living image of her beloved face were those of his comrades, all of them young together, so full of promise and high plans, now so many dead.

Nahomi. Tared. Ilara. Tanri . . .

The transtube stopped, and Sebastian hauled himself to his feet. He felt old of a sudden, old and tired and an utter failure.

He could not even help his old charge; when Brandon snapped his fingers in the face of the entire government by skipping out on his own Enkainion, leaving them all to Eusabian's bomb, he, too, had moved beyond Sebastian's aid.

The door hissed open, but he stood, fighting for composure, for balance. His aching eyes studied the lights curving overhead. Stars . . .

Stars. He remembered his work and felt a vestige of the old energy stir. He was not a total failure, he told himself as he walked down the ramp toward the Cloister. The Jupiter Project, the secrets of the Ur, waited to be unlocked.

Politics were for the young. The Ur . . .

Leave the ancients to the ancients, he thought, smiling grimly. He would bury himself in work and exorcise the ghosts at last.

Nine

Admiral Trungpa Nyberg shut his eyes, waiting for the first sip of coffee to perform its magic. Warmth spread through him, but the miraculous regeneration of energy was absent.

Anton Faseult smiled tiredly at him, then tapped the console. "This one came through last night; I hate to spoil your breakfast, but I thought you ought to see it."

Nyberg turned his eyes to the console. An unfamiliar banner flashed across the screen, evocative of power and wealth.

"The Syndics of Rifthaven," Faseult supplied from the background.

Then, without warning, a stomach-twisting sight appeared: a gutted ship spinning with lazy slowness in space, against the backdrop of a scattering of stars. In one corner, the bruise-colored limb of a red dwarf sun identified the place, not far outside of Rifthaven.

The ship, still glowing with heat, and so twisted and seared it was difficult to recognize the make, moved with inexorable slowness toward the viewer, until details appeared. What appeared to be blobs resolved into human beings, all exhibiting the ghastly bloat of death by vacuum. They were all tied to the hull by a line clamped to arm or leg.

Nyberg felt his stomach clench. Someone had been to a great deal of trouble here to make this as vicious as possible.

Abruptly the picture blanked, replaced by a view of a room, dark-paneled and rich. Three people sat in a row: a skeletal man with red, filed teeth bared in a feral grin; an enormous woman, bizarrely decorated with jewels, a gloating smile, and little else; an old man, dark of visage, with cruel cold eyes.

"The three most powerful Syndics on Rifthaven," Faseult said. "Xibl Banth, Oli Pormagat, Jep Houmanopoulis."

The Draco spoke, in a hissing voice calculated for the maximum negative effect: "That ship was the Sword of Ariman, *captained by Teliu Diamond. You saw her floating right near the bridge viewport."*

Pormagat spoke next, her voice an insinuating whine. "Diamond had just returned from her raid on Torigan, which apparently was quite successful."

"So much so," Houmanopoulis grated, "that she ignored our new limitations on entry. Anyone else who wishes to trade with us will find the new statutes continually posted on the Brotherhood channel."

All three smiled. It was not a pleasant sight. "We look forward to doing business with you."

The window blanked out.

Nyberg looked up at Faseult, who looked back, brows raised. "It would appear that Rifthaven is holding its own despite chaos everywhere else."

"Isn't it a law of nature," Faseult returned with a rueful smile, "that trash will always rise to the surface?"

❋ ❋ ❋

Despite careful planning, Tate Kaga's party was not a success.

Or so it was said by some, mostly Downsiders, who claimed that the regrettable episode that terminated the gathering was almost inevitable, given the ancient nuller's choice of the Ascha Gardens as the locale. Others, among them Highdwellers, seemed to prefer the term "amusing" to "regrettable."

"Like a small boy with a stick and nest of *psando,*" one of these latter murmured, a comment judged in bad taste by certain

Douloi who resented the comparison to those industrious insects whose individuality is subsumed into the collective whole.

When that simile was relayed to him, Tate Kaga cackled loudly and said, "Ho! I wish I'd had a bigger stick!"

❋ ❋ ❋

"Tate Kaga said I could invite anyone," Ivard said.

Vi'ya sat at the window, looking out. Ivard sensed her annoyance. Why she should be annoyed to be invited to a nick party—probably the best nick party ever—escaped him.

"You'll like Tate Kaga," Ivard said. "He's a nick but he doesn't talk nick. He's old—old as Granny Chang, and you like her. Maybe he's even older. And he's *funny.*"

"I have work to do."

"But you can't work all the time, and I don't want to go alone—" Ivard paused as a complex image flickered like blue lightning through his mind, too quick to follow. It was the Kelly Archon, that's all he knew, but he was used to that happening. "We'll bring the Eya'a" he said. "They will like the Ascha Gardens, they ought to see it once. That's what Tate Kaga said."

Vi'ya sat silent for a long time, entirely ignoring the Marine guard—who usually stood outside Detention Five—waiting quietly, somehow almost invisibly, just inside the entrance. Ivard could no longer tell what Vi'ya heard over the mental connection with the Eya'a, and what she didn't. In any case, he was not going to say out loud that he wouldn't ask Marim.

Pain briefly squeezed him inside when he thought of Marim. He knew that people bunked other people out all the time, but did she have to talk about her new lovers over meals, as if Ivard had turned into a plant or something?

Ivard's nose twitched, responding to a scent too faint to identify, and the blue fire leapt inside his head again. The image this time was more complete, and he sensed the proximity of the Kelly healer trinity—the Archon's images were always clearer when Portus-Dartinus-Atos were nearby.

Then the Eya'a appeared in the doorway to their chamber, their faceted eyes glittering. Ivard realized then that the Kelly had somehow let them know about the party—though he wondered if they even knew what a party was. They moved to the outside door and stood with eerie stillness.

Vi'ya raised a hand. "You win. Let us go, then."

* * *

The Kelly joined them at the transtube portal. When they debarked at the entrance to the Ascha Gardens, Vi'ya hesitated, and Ivard stood transfixed by wonder. What he saw here was impossible, frivolous, magnificent, revealing a kind of elegant humor that Ivard, through the multiplicity of new experiences, was just beginning to discern, and hadn't thought a part of the Douloi world.

But Tate Kaga is a nick, and this is his party. The blue fire flared up inside his mind with the Kelly equivalent of a chuckle, and Ivard suddenly realized that the nicks were as complicated and different from each other as Rifters—and that the Ascha Gardens was just as much a part of the nick world as the blank-faced politeness he'd always associated with the Douloi.

Stretching away from them was a formal garden under the faux night sky of Ares, looking at first glance like any Downsider garden cradled in the safety of planetary gravity. Its measured stateliness lulled the mind into an expectation of deadly symmetry, framed by gravel pathways and marble stairways, with sinuous balustrades along terraces rising up in gradual steps toward the fragile construct at the Gardens' center. But then, impossibly, the stairways continued rising until they attained impossible angles, some vertical, sideways, even upside down, framing in a disorienting tangle a bubble of free-fall at the center.

The immense central edifice was an improbable snarl of walkways, balconies, platforms, and portals, and everywhere there were people, adults and children alike, walking, gesticulating, drinking, eating, dancing, running. Their heads pointed in all directions; Ivard saw two Douloi talking to each other from different staircases, each upside down with respect to the other. Nearby, a gang of children raced about in a demented game of tag, jumping from wall to floor to ceiling. Ivard realized that there must be gravitors everywhere to maintain local gravity at all angles within the Gardens. It was even more disorienting than Granny Chang's, for here there was, not free-fall, but multiple gravitational planes.

Then he was distracted as, far above, from one of the landings at right angles to the surface of Ares, he saw someone launch into the free-fall zone. For a painful moment the null-gee grace of the diver seemed familiar, then he saw that this woman was younger than Marim, his own age in fact. He watched her as she joined a crowd of others on a platform in one corner of the free-fall section of the Gardens.

A sudden breeze ruffled his hair and the Eya'a looked up at something over his head, then Ivard smelled the welcome scent of pungent herbs and smoke.

"Tate Kaga!" Ivard spun around.

The nuller brought his bubble to rest at head level, right side up for once. "Ho! Little Egg. I see you brought the Listener."

Ivard caught a hint of something—a scent?—from Vi'ya. She regarded Tate Kaga, her face as ungiving as always.

"Welcome, Vi'ya," he said to the Dol'jharian, and for the first time Ivard heard the voiceless "th" in her name from someone else's lips. "Welcome, I say again. Convey the same to your alien friends. May you hear only what you need to."

This time Ivard was sure of it. Tate Kaga's comment had startled and irritated her. Her demeanor gave no hint of this, but he could somehow *smell* her reaction. The blue fire whirled briefly behind his eyes, and Portus, the Intermittor of the Kelly trinity standing nearby, honked a brief confirmation. *That's using your nose,* was the sense of it.

Behind them the transtube hissed open again, discharging a swarm of new people. After greeting their host, they joined the crowd making its way toward the gardens. Ivard noticed that they split into two groups as they approached the central tangle. Not Polloi and Douloi, as one might expect; Ivard had learned to tell them apart at a glance, here on Ares.

Instead, one group—they had to be Downsiders—shied away from the improbable geometries of the fragile edifice, eddying in small sets around the periphery, their shoulders tight and elbows drawn in close. The others, Highdwellers no doubt, strode without hesitation toward the gravitic maze.

Another pod arrived, and Ivard saw the High Phanist among its Polloi passengers. She looked up at the maze, a trace of nausea crossing her face.

"Ah!" Tate Kaga brought his bubble to rest over her head, upside down. "Need something for your stomach, Numen?"

Eloatri looked up and laughed. "I'll be just fine, as long as you don't sling me into that gravitational obscenity over there."

The nuller cackled. "Mudfoot, eh? You need to come flying with me someday, like Little Egg over there." He motioned toward Ivard, who felt himself blushing.

Ivard did not see Eloatri's reaction to this invitation. His attention was caught by the arrival of another group, Douloi this time, centering on a tall man with strange yellow eyes. Something about his stance and the way he moved reminded Ivard of Jaim, but he was dressed like a high-end nick, and everybody else in the group seemed to move around him, as though he were the sun and they the planets.

The breeze coming from Tate Kaga's gee-bubble changed subtly; Ivard's new Kelly sense of smell suddenly told him that the nuller didn't like this new arrival, didn't like him at all. Another waft told him the feeling was mutual. But there was more. He sensed a . . . link between the two. The blue fire pulsed within, a whisper on the edge of intelligibility.

The man's indifferent gaze swept across Ivard, and he shivered; the man's eyes were death-cold, yet keenly aware.

A sudden movement from Vi'ya drew his attention back to the transtube platform. She was watching the tall man, whom Tate Kaga had addressed as Tau; no, she was watching the thin, neutrally dressed man with long black hair who followed at the gold-eyed man's left shoulder, like a bodyguard. Ivard sensed deep unease in her. He looked closer, opened his mouth, and drew in a breath in the funny way he was learning made his nose work better. Then he snorted all the air out, trying to expel the scent. There was something deeply wrong with Tau's bodyguard. The Kelly honked agreement. *Death breathes through his nostrils.*

Tau finally moved into the Gardens. Ivard could tell from his haughty countenance that he was a Downsider and didn't like the distorted parts, but he didn't avoid them.

The transtube opened once more, and Ivard felt the attention of everyone nearby sharpen as it revealed the slim figure of Brandon vlith-Arkad, accompanied by Jaim. Vahn left their group and took Jaim aside as Tate Kaga spun over to the Aerenarch.

"Hau! Now my party is a success!" He sketched a formal deference within his bubble. The fact that he was hanging sideways made Ivard snicker.

Brandon smiled. "You don't need me to make your parties a success, Old One. And I'm certainly not the first Arkad you've hosted."

"No!" Tate Kaga cackled. "Old Burgess was a wild one. Ha! Never missed my parties." The nuller's face assumed a thoughtful mien. "Until Desrien took him."

Ivard sensed discomfort in the Aerenarch, although his countenance showed nothing. "No more would I," Brandon replied, ignoring the last comment.

Behind him a number of liveried servants filed out of the pod bearing numerous wooden objects, ornate and bizarrely twisted. Ivard saw Jaim, and was going to ask him about the objects, but then the blue fire surged up with almost blinding intensity, and Portus-Dartinus-Atos swarmed forward, honking so fast that Ivard couldn't follow their speech. The Aerenarch greeted them with Kelly-sign, and the voice of Portus, the Intermittor, now speaking Uni, rose above the melodious blatting of the other two, who began patting and stroking the wooden things.

"A *trinat!* Your Highness, this is threesomely unexpected. Two-thirds three threes of years on Ares we've been, and haven't seen one."

"It was in the Enclave, buried in a storeroom. The comp indicated the room hadn't been accessed for over a hundred years."

"What's a trinat?" Ivard asked Jaim.

"I think it's a musical instrument," he replied. "It's in pieces and still has to be put together—the computer didn't know how." He looked around. "Where's Vi'ya? Vahn said she came with you."

Ivard looked first at Vi'ya's Marine guard, but he was alone, waiting patiently at the Gardens' single entrance. Vi'ya was gone— "There!" he said, pointing.

But Jaim wasn't looking. Instead, Ivard saw the Aerenarch gazing out into the Gardens, his blue eyes unblinking, watching a straight, dark-haired figure, accompanied by the Eya'a, moving in an invisible bubble of careful space among the other guests.

Vahn jeeved as their host ushered the Aerenarch toward the center of the Gardens and then began to mingle with the guests. Watching him move from group to group, the Marine wondered if Tate Kaga was as oblivious to the effect that his setting was having on his party as he seemed. There were more than a few tight angles to elbows and jaws, and ferret-glances at parts of the edifice that refused the firm identity of floor or ceiling. Drifts of music echoed from every surface, adding to the disorientation; the presence of various shrubs and trees, some of them obviously quite old, growing at impossible angles, made it even worse.

Anywhere else, any other time, Vahn might find it amusing. But the Aerenarch had decided to come, despite (or maybe because of, Roget had pointed out) the nonexclusivity of the guest list. It was a gigantic party, in a weird setting. A perfect place, Vahn reflected grimly, for the unknown poisoner to try a little personal mayhem.

Brandon very soon took up a position under the central free-fall space, in a well-lit, open area with plenty of room. Several openings led onto it, including one that gave a view of a long concourse that jutted off upward at an acute angle.

He was very soon surrounded by a group of social highflyers. Vahn noted several naval officers appear, pay their respects, then disappear into another area, but some younger officers lingered, the group swelling by twos and threes until the Aerenarch was the center of laughter and high-animation chatter that nearly drowned out the drifting music.

Vahn caught sight of Commander Faseult watching from an adjacent walkway, his black eyes appraising, then did a quick check with his security team.

(The youths in the free-fall area are hyper—a bit of the High/Down tension, I think), Hamun said. Everyone else reported status quo.

Nyberg and several high brass appeared. The lesser officers gave way, and after a short, polite exchange, the brass moved on, leaving the way clear for the civilian flatterers to close in again. Brandon showed no reaction to the comings and goings; he seemed content to sit and let people come to him, which made Vahn's task the easier.

Signaling Roget, Vahn jeeved back into the shadows of a huge argan tree and set out on a deliberate circuit.

Ivard was drawn toward the free-fall zone as if pulled by an electrical current.

There, in a breathtakingly large space, broken here and there by jump pads linked by grab cables, one or two brave figures sailed happily back and forth, using the strange structures to propel themselves. There was even a bubble of water, suspended like a living jewel, its surface rippling quietly in the vagrant air currents generated by the surrounding structures.

Nearby, on a platform jutting from a bulging wall into the huge space, the Kelly were busying themselves with the trinat, assembling its complex curves into a graceful, organic, almost tree-like structure. Thrums and squeaks emanated from it, piercing through the soft honking of the trinity. Portus' headstalk wove in his direction for a moment and blatted a brief greeting before returning to the instrument. In the distance Ivard could hear some nick music playing.

On other platforms on the periphery, knots of nicks and civs his own age stood around, the nicks in fancy party clothes, the civs in less flamboyant garb. They didn't mix: each platform held either nicks or civs; and Ivard noticed that the two groups were divided further, into groups whose body language identified them clearly. *Downsiders and Highdwellers.*

Though they talked a lot and stole glances at other groups, none seemed willing to make the first move outward. He remembered some of the things Tate Kaga had told him, up in his strange dwelling at the spin axis, and realized that the civs wouldn't move before the nicks did, and that the nicks were probably afraid of looking awkward in front of each other.

That wouldn't stop Rifters. But the brash thought rebounded with a sudden scorch of embarrassment as he realized that wasn't true. He was the only Rifter up here in the free-fall zone, and he wasn't doing anything.

But he couldn't approach the nicks—he'd long ago learned that it wasn't a good idea to speak to them until spoken to, unless you liked being stiffed. He made an abortive motion toward one of the groups of civs, until a glimpse of a smile and a cloud of blond hair from a girl in the group recalled the pain of being bunked out by Marim.

What if they didn't like him? Or laughed? Or just ignored him?

He hung there, aching with the years of rejection he'd endured, with only his sister, now dead, to soften it. Slowly some of the civs moved into the free-fall zone and began dancing, flinging themselves from pad to cable to pad with increasing abandon, but Ivard didn't move.

Finally a sudden flash of black and white caught his attention, launching with practiced grace from one access to another. It was Vi'ya and the Eya'a and, not letting himself think the word "coward," he left the free-fall area and followed them.

❋ ❋ ❋

Artorus Vahn jeeved through the crowds, watching the movement of the guests and listening to drifts of conversation. He visioned a structure over the whole: despite the erratic decor, the sense-mesmerizing jumble of lights and angles and colors, he saw Brandon at the eye of a social hurricane.

Maybe it is because of this setting, he thought, springing over a balustrade onto another gravitational plane at ninety degrees to the one he'd just left. Although the Gardens were modeled on similar amusements on other Highdwellings, only a nuller could be entirely comfortable in such a place. Indeed, that was part of the attraction they held for Highdwellers, giving them a way to be free, if only for a few hours, from the powerful—and necessary—social constraints characteristic of oneills. Downsiders found it almost impossible to assimilate. And to neither did it admit of control.

It was almost, Vahn thought, what he'd imagined the infamous Whispering Gallery on Montecielo to be like. As he moved through the background, silent and unseen as a shadow, some of the conversations connected in a surreal blend that suited the setting. Vahn found it intriguing and, finally, unsettling.

At first he did not realize how the disorienting background and constant undercurrents of music seemed to free tongues; the further he got away from the central dais under the free-fall area, where Brandon sat with his crowd of highborn sycophants, the more sibilant whispers he overheard.

". . . Regency . . ."

". . . Isolates . . ."

". . . disgrace . . ."

"Arthelion . . . Enkainion . . . Regency . . ."

"Gehenna . . . Isolates . . . suicide mission . . ."

And than again: *"Regency."*

Curious, Vahn identified some of the speakers. The Harkatsus Aegios was the one whose lips seemed to shape the word "regency" most often, but he was not alone, and his auditors did not seem to disagree.

The continuous music drowned out most of the discourse, even with his enhancers turned up; Vahn did not dare to get closer lest his presence be discovered.

And he did not need to hear every word, he thought soberly as he made his way down a long, madly twisting stairway toward that central pit where the Aerenarch held court. Those fragments were enough to indicate that though he had the name and the title, Brandon did not even remotely have the government: and more seriously, the remains of the old government—at least some of the civilian portions—seemed reluctant to make the rescue run that might free his father.

Who, then, would try to take over? Common sense pointed to Archon Srivashti—but he was not among the whisperers. He was seen, when seen at all, forming part of Brandon's smiling court, exchanging lighthearted chatter and laughter.

As Vahn returned to the dais, he caught the tail end of a fast exchange. Brandon quoted a dialogue from a satirical play, to have his quotations capped by Lady Vannis. For a few moments they played at dueling, each saying a line faster and faster, until it broke up in laughter and commentary from the appreciative auditors. Puns, obscure political allusions, wit flowed like the sparkling pale yellow wine. They were all having a good time, oblivious, it seemed, to mutterings and machinations scurrying through the shadows.

Vahn stepped up next to Jaim, whose long face was merely patient. He obviously caught little if any of the references, and cared less. His eyes drifted more than once toward one of the exits, as if his salvation lay there.

Though he stood a scarce two meters behind the Aerenarch, he seemed by his manner utterly divorced from the proceedings. Most of the guests ignored him as well, except for Brandon, who addressed him from time to time, once raising a slight smile, other times merely requesting this or that delicacy from the table.

Brandon's attention seemed equally divided among everyone there. Lady Vannis Scefi-Cartano, the former Aerenarch-Consort, was equally skilled in social byplay. But Vahn was an experienced observer, and after a time he noted how her eyes returned again and again to Brandon's face, gauging his reactions to the talk. She seemed to watch with special interest his interplay with the naval officers present—most of them near his own age; and once, during a flurry of movement among the guests to help themselves to a new course of delicacies, Vahn saw her studying Jaim, her profile reflective.

Brandon's attention, like Jaim's, strayed most often to the concourse with its many adits and exits. Bored, Vahn thought, wondering when he would prove true to rumor and retire, drunken but graceful, with one of the obviously eager sycophants on his arm.

Once Vahn caught a flicker of white across the edge of his peripheral vision, but when he turned, no one was at the entrance. Brandon glanced up, then back, and rose to help himself from the table.

Making his way to Jaim's side, he murmured something, and then went back, talking over his shoulder to a small group as he leaned against the table and swirled a new liquor idly in his glass.

The sycophants seemed to take that as a signal to refresh their own drinks, and for a few brief seconds there was a whirl of movement. Through it all, stolid as stone, Jaim made his way to Vahn. "Wants to leave in an hour," Jaim said.

Wondering why he did not use his boswell for that, Vahn nodded, and Jaim retreated, weaving his way back through the crowd. *Doesn't seem to be the one to care about the niceties of privacies,* Vahn thought, watching. But then adrenaline boosted his heartbeat when Jaim stopped and looked down at Brandon's empty chair.

A fast scan—no sign of him. Somehow he'd disappeared. Angry, he looked at Jaim, to catch surprise and alarm in his face.

"Where is he?"

Jaim spread his hands. "Said he wanted to leave. Said to tell you."

(FIND HIM.) Vahn activated the wide-spectrum call on his boswell.

* * *

"Come on, Vi'ya, you have to see this." Ivard's voice, however much he had effected physiological change, still managed the plangent note of youth. "You'll *never* see a free-fall gym anything like it—better than the one on Rifthaven."

He reached for her wrist, as if to pull her. Standing in order to avoid his touch, she assented. "I will see it," she said. "On my way to an exit."

Ivard sighed. "I can't believe you don't want to stay here. Hey, even the Eya'a are having fun."

She could not disagree; the pair continually looked this way and that, their necks stretching at impossible angles as they chittered on a high note. Their mental exchange was too fast to follow, but she could read the emotional tone: excitement, curiosity.

She thought about leaving them. It was either that or drink: so many lives, faces, voices she did not know, would not know, did not want to know, forming a tidal wave of emotional intent—and at its center, like sunlight on water, the familiar signature. . . .

"I leave," she said. "Now."

Ivard's eyes were bright and inquisitive. "Kelly think you ought to stay."

She said nothing.

Ivard sighed. "All right. Here's the way out. But just a peek at the dancing first, all right? We'll be fast."

He led her to a doorway and shot off down a long concourse, whose walls were all floors to crowds of people. He dodged past a chattering group of civs, probably techs from the Cap. She lost sight of him, but followed his emotional signature until a sudden void caught at her, and she turned to find the Eya'a gone as well. She could still sense them, but their attention was turned elsewhere.

Vi'ya shrugged. With Manderian's hand signs, they could make their needs known. She would not wait.

She pushed her way through the crowds, avoiding contact, noting dispassionately that no one moved aside for her when she walked without the Eya'a.

Slowly, even through the high-energy emotional output of the people around her, she became aware that someone was matching pace with her. She hastened her steps, ever turning away from the densest clots of people toward relative quiet; but this strategy, born of growing distress, betrayed her as she found herself at a dead end.

She turned.

The other manifested into a male silhouette. A latticework of light and shadow masked clothing and face, but not the angle of a cheekbone or the familiar hands. Or the near-blinding focus of his emotional spectrum.

It seemed that Brandon Arkad had somehow shed his vanguard and had strayed along the same path. She started to pass him, cursing the maliciousness of circumstance.

"Vi'ya," the Arkad said, raising a hand.

Perforce she halted.

"I have a question," he said.

❋ ❋ ❋

Only when he finally reached the free-fall area again did Ivard realize that Vi'ya wasn't behind him. Instead, he turned to find the Eya'a regarding him silently, their huge faceted eyes reflecting the distorted architecture around them in even more fragmented form. The space around them echoed to the compelling rhythms of the Kelly trinat; most of the civs were dancing to its sound, or trying to. They were handicapped by having limbs that didn't work in threes.

Ivard looked on longingly. Going to get Vi'ya hadn't changed anything—wouldn't have even if she'd come.

The Eya'a chittered softly. One reached out and stroked his face with its long twiggy fingers. *One-in-three fears the unity-in-many?*

The blue fire surged within, with a half-realized image of a single Kelly trying to manipulate something complex, and failing, lacking the help of the rest of its trinity.

The Eya'a looked up, past him, then withdrew. Ivard turned around to see a group of Douloi staring at him. A young woman with a cloud of blue hair stepped forward.

"Aren't you afraid?" she asked. Her soft voice with the singsong accent of the Douloi gave Ivard a funny feeling in the pit of his stomach, which intensified as he noticed how well her gown modeled her figure, and how her hair matched her eyes.

"Afraid?" he replied, relieved that his voice hadn't cracked. "Oh, you mean the Eya'a? No, I've been around them for a long time." He hesitated. "I can even sort of talk to them."

A young man standing just behind the lady snorted derisively. "I'm sure," he drawled. "Most interesting discussions, no doubt." He turned to the blue-haired Douloi. "Can you imagine the poetry recitals they must have?"

She frowned at him, but the others laughed, and Ivard felt himself reddening. The blue fire surged, and suddenly he realized that blushing wasn't something he had to put up with anymore—he knew how his body worked. He constricted the blood vessels at the surface of his skin and relaxed as he felt the warmth ebb away.

The sarcastic young man squinted at him, and Ivard sensed his sudden unease. "Come on," he said to the others, "it's just one of the jumped-up Polloi infesting the station. You can find more interesting sport."

A faint breeze and the scent of herbs drew Ivard's gaze up briefly, to find Tate Kaga watching from behind the Douloi. They were unaware of him. The old nuller winked at him.

Ivard laughed suddenly and reveled in the surge of almost-fright from the pugnacious boy before him.

"I'm not one of your tame Polloi," he said. "I'm a Rifter." Overhead, Tate Kaga's bubble whirled end over end, the nuller grinning broadly.

Ivard pulled back the sleeve of his tunic to display the Kelly ribbon. "Ivard Firehead, bonded in the phratry of the Archon of *****"—with no little gratification he scented the girl's surge of interest as he whistle-honked the name of the Kelly homeworld flawlessly—"wounded in battle with the Avatar's personal guards on the Mandala, haji of Desrien . . ." He paused, feeling the blush threatening to break through all over again, then went for broke, "and I'd very much like to free-fall dance with you."

"I'd love it," she breathed, and, taking his hand in hers, stepped to the edge of the platform and launched them both into space.

⁂ ⁂ ⁂

"I don't know where he is, but I know who can find him," Jaim promised. He looked up, and Vahn followed his gaze. Far above he saw a familiar red-haired figure soaring through the immense free-fall gym.

Jaim made his way to an exit and Vahn followed, Roget staying behind and their backup moving to the exit and other key points.

A short time later they emerged onto a platform jutting into the upper portion of the vast free-fall area, where youths shrieked their delight as they swooped through the air.

Jaim launched himself across the space to one of the jump pads in the high-middle, where the redhead Ivard was seated with a pretty Douloi girl, talking earnestly. He held a short talk with him. Vahn watched curiously as Ivard slid his hands over his eyes for a long beat, two, and then suddenly spoke. Jaim nodded shortly, came back.

"This way," he said.

TEN

Vi'ya did not immediately respond to Brandon; his voice could have been lost in the rise and fall of the strangely compelling Kelly music now echoing from far below them.

The pathway would only admit one. She moved toward it with deliberate step, counting on the ingrained habit of nick courtesy to force him to withdraw. But he did not, only looked up.

She was near enough to see the patient expectation in his face. Stopping short of physical contact, she said, "What?"

He did not answer at once; his attention was otherwhere, his breathing still. The Kelly had stopped, and other music now dominated the space around them. She recognized then a familiar melody, running up the chromatic scale, dancing in and out of dissonance to harmony, like the laughter of children. *KetzenLach, Markham's favorite. But of course the Arkad would have listened to him as well.* She pulled her attention back and assumed a waiting stance.

When he spoke, once again the subject took her by surprise. "What kind of person was Jakarr?"

"Jakarr?" she repeated the name as though it were unfamiliar, which it was—but only in this setting, this context.

"Yes. Your weapons tech on the *Telvarna*." Now his voice was amused.

She knew that the Arkad had never met Jakarr, except as a target in a swift firefight that had ended with Jakarr's death, just moments after Brandon and Osri Omilov were first brought into the Dis base.

A strange subject, but a safe enough distraction. She put back her head, looking past the Arkad through a disorienting tangle of stairways leading nowhere. Most of the rest of the gathering were just visible, not as individuals, but as insect-figures moving about in meaningless patterns.

And then she turned to glance at her still-waiting companion, his blue-eyed steady regard the lens of his familiar high-intensity emotional signature.

Proximity was toxic; the buffer of distance must be regained, and soon. "Good shot," she said. "Bad temper."

"That's all?" he asked. "That's all you can say about a man you crewed with, and then commanded, for eight years?"

Her pulse drummed in her forehead with the effort it took to shut him out, yet even so she sensed a complexity of reactions, foremost being regret. Regret?

She forced her attention back to memory, summoning up the unlovely vision of Jakarr's narrow, suspicious face. "He was a liar. Cheat. Liked games with risk. His humor required a butt, a scapegoat. Enough?" An oblique glance, nothing more than a noting of position, so she could move away—as if a meter would afford much protection.

"Did he have any other name? A family? Did anyone love him, call him friend?"

His regret had sharpened into remorse.

"Never mentioned any family. Temper kept friends at a distance. Names . . ." Somewhere, the Eya'a picked up her own increasing regret, and they sang to her mind: *One-who-gives-firestone seeks to amend ceased ones.*

None of it made sense. She clung to self-control, her answers random. "Just the insulting tagnames earned by the unliked. Greywing was his bunk-partner for a time—was he who brought her and Firehead in. Then she bunked him out."

Talking made her sick—she needed to control her breathing. "Enough?" she asked again, no longer hiding the hostility.

Now he stood beside her, hands clasped behind him—still between her and the pathway out. "Is it enough?" he repeated. "I want to know something of the man I killed."

With difficulty she forced her mind back to Jakarr's abortive attempt to take over Dis. A few vivid images flickered across her inner eye: the Arkad's courier ship crashing so spectacularly on the hydrocarbon ice; the crew's shock when the Arkad was identified—alive—after that landing; Jakarr's short-lived triumph when he tried to take the Arkad and his entourage hostage—and his attempt to kill them all when his plan failed.

The Arkad, bent over his dying liegeman, turning and firing at the rock overhead; the slow, lethal fall of stone on Jakarr.

A final image: the Arkad's face as he held them all off, threatening to bring the entire cave down on them—himself included—just so he could listen to a dying man's last speech.

He would have done it too: even then she could read him without difficulty. She had kept them all away until the liegeman was dead, until the Arkad's adrenal-shock had metamorphosed into something unreadable except to the Eya'a—and it had frightened them.

Memory brought her back to the present. She had to end this interview, in any way she could.

* * *

Ivard sat back down on the edge of the jump pad, clasping his hands in front of his knees. Next to him he could feel the heat of Ami's body, could smell the scent of her perfume, of her flesh and her hair. It made him dizzy, exultant. Not far away, the Eya'a swayed in front of the Kelly playing their trinat, piping and keening while people, mixed civs and nicks, hung from cables and jump pads nearby, watching in fascination. Ivard had never seen the Eya'a do anything like this before; their thoughts, what he could sense of them, were utterly incomprehensible. He wished he could ask Vi'ya about it. But when he'd tried to reach her for Jaim, he felt a blackness that he shied away from.

"What did you do just then?" Ami asked. "And who is Vi'ya?"

"She's the captain of our ship. Jaim thinks the Aerenarch might be with her."

They looked down at the floor far below, where Douloi drifted aimlessly, the center of their attention now absent.

"The Dol'jharian? The woman with the aliens?"

"Mmmm. The Archon's ribbon links me to her and them, somehow. I can hear them, sort of."

Ami stretched out her hand and ran a finger over the Kelly band in his wrist, leaving her hand on his arm. He felt a tingle that made him weak.

"It must be very strange," she said, leaning toward him.

Their lips met, and Ivard lost all sense of his surroundings for a moment. Then the jump pad rocked under them and Ami pulled back. Ivard looked up to see the drink-bleared gaze of the boy who'd mocked him earlier.

"Dandenus," Ami said reproachfully.

The boy's face was cold, alcohol strong on his breath. Ivard sniffed more delicately: the boy's emotions whiffed of hurt and affront. He was clutching an unopened bottle of the sparkling wine and two glasses.

He gave Ivard one haughty sneer, then looked away toward the girl. "Never had a Rifter, huh?"

Ami colored, and Ivard felt his stomach sink. Was that why she was with him, because he was a Rifter, an exotic toy? Marim had used him for the loot from the Mandala. Was Ami no better?

Then she looked back at him, not with that nick blankness, but with curiosity and tentative friendship and a kind of light-hearted attraction all breathing through her skin.

She touched his arm, then rounded on Dandenus with a fierce movement. "If it hadn't been for this Rifter, and his friends, we'd be mourning all three of the Panarch's sons." She gestured at the floor far below where earlier the Aerenarch had held court. "He earned personal access to the Aerenarch—which of *your* exalted Family can say the same?"

"The Aerenarch!" The boy snorted, swaying slightly. "He's not so important. There are others who . . ." He broke off, as if suddenly aware of having gone too far.

Ivard stood up slowly, conscious of Ami's regard. "Others who what?" He knew the Douloi made a big thing about honor and obligations; was time they learned that Rifters knew it too, only they didn't waste time with big words about it.

"If you have to ask, you couldn't understand the answer," replied Dandenus, but he seemed to hear the lameness of his own reply and turned to the girl. "Come, Ami, you're better than this no-family chatzer." He put the glasses on a little pedestal at the edge of the jump pad and held up his bottle, working at the release tab. "Here, I brought this for you and me."

Ivard suddenly realized that Dandenus was too drunk to know what he was doing. He heard the beginning of a hiss from the bottle, and then he lunged forward and pushed Ami aside.

There was a loud bang, and something punched him cruelly in the temple, sending a shower of stars across his vision. He fell to his knees as pain shot through his head.

Ami shrieked his name: "Ivard!" Then his vision cleared.

✻ ✻ ✻

"Too late for regret," Vi'ya said to the Aerenarch in her hardest voice.

She felt rather than saw him look at her. "Is that Dol'jharian practicality?" His light voice almost blended with the singing of the distant choir, but the humor was still there. "Yet your mythology is more ghost-ridden than any I've encountered. I wonder," he said, "if Eusabian sleeps easy at night. I know Anaris never did. Though he didn't manage to kill anyone on Arthelion—not for lack of trying."

Behind the musing voice was a temporary easing of intent.

She drew a breath in, let one out. Said: "Tried to kill the Panarch?" The idea, later, somewhere else, would be amusing.

"No—he and my father seemed to get along quite well. It was me he was after, with a single-minded focus that I never could explain. My brother Galen came in for a few shots as well, probably because of proximity."

I wish he'd succeeded, she thought viciously, and from far off came the Eya'a: *Shall we amend one-who-gives-firestone with* fi? Something like panic lent force to her *No!* And far in the distance she heard the Kelly echo her negative.

The exchange accelerted her vertigo, made her breathing short. Nausea clawed its way up inside her.

"Am I boring you?" Now he was in front of her, the blue eyes on a level with her own, searching. She took refuge in the knowledge that the nicks saw her face as unreadable Dol'jharian stone. "You knew Markham," he went on quickly, with disarmingly apologetic sincerity in voice and face. "You knew him after he left the confines of Panarchic society. Here our violence is circumscribed, most of it diverted into word, tone, gesture." He spread his hands palms-up. "Did he kill anyone? How"—he faced her again—"did he live with the regrets once the danger was over, and time permitted the endless reviewing of one's actions?"

"Every man's death diminishes me." It was something Markham had said to her after their very first meeting.

Again memory claimed precedence, though it was no longer a refuge. The parallels in her meeting with the Arkad and his friend were an ironic counterpoint: both times, a firefight first, both times centered around her. Only with Markham it had been his chivalric rescue of one chased by many as she made her last desperate attempt to win freedom by sprinting for the Rifter ship that had just raided the asteroid's mineral storage.

Afterward, Markham's questions, wanting to know who they were, why they chased her. When at last he said that about diminishment, she thought they were his words, and the very alienness of the concept had caught her interest.

She looked up, knowing what was coming just before it came: " 'Every man's death diminishes me,' " the Arkad said. "I found that in an old book when I was a boy, and we used to debate its meaning, Markham and I, before we had any idea of its real significance. Did he—"

"Yes," she said, stepping back. Looking away.

The interruption surprised him, and his intent stilled, pooled into question.

Time to thrust back. Now. "But only until the reality of survival stripped away the futility of sentiment." A deep breath. "He changed, Arkad. He wasn't a nick, mouthing philosophy and ordering servants to do his killing for him." She unleashed some of her anger, hearing it color her voice, sharpen her words. Knowing how her anger made others afraid of her.

It had taken time to accustom to that, but the fear had proved to be useful: it bought her distance.

Using the anger as a shield, she turned to gaze straight into his eyes, standing close enough to hear his breathing, to see the pulse in his temple just beneath the soft fall of hair. He returned the gaze, his pupils so wide his eyes darkened. All his attention was on her now, a danger she'd risked once before. All his focus, the entire spectrum of emotion—except fear.

"But he didn't survive," the Arkad said gently.

Ivard gasped.

Propelled by the violence of the sparkling wine escaping from the bottle, Dandenus staggered off the edge of the platform into full free-fall and shot away like a comet, trailing a fizzy tail of yellow wine, straight for the bubble of water, just as the ear-torturing keening of the Eya'a rose to a climax above the frightened shrieks of the youths diving away from the Kelly platform in all directions. The sound was like knives in Ivard's ears. Ami buried her head in her arms and screamed.

A series of loud detonations, each accompanied by a shower of sparks, erupted from parts of the structure around them as the ultrasonics from the aliens disrupted the delicate electronics of the Gardens. The water bubble distorted, then as Dandenus impacted its center, still clutching the now-empty bottle, it exploded into a nova of tiny wildly gyrating jewels.

Below them the dark circles of open mouths blossomed in suddenly upturned faces as the Douloi stared up uncomprehending. A whooping siren added to the chaos as the failsafes engaged; a forest of reddish beams erupted from the walls, spearing the human figures flailing in space and bearing them to safety. Ivard saw Dandenus carried off upside down, his eyes manic.

But the overload had left no spare capacity in the safety devices. With awful slowness, the countless globs of water, writhing like demented slugs, accelerated toward the distant floor. The ant-like figures underneath suddenly scurried in all directions, but too late, as thousands of gallons of water deluged the floor of the gardens, upending tables and washing the Douloi and all their elegance into tangled heaps of sodden splendor among the ruins of the landscaping.

The Eya'a were silent now. They stood completely unmoving, their white fur fluffed up.

Ivard tore his gaze away from the disaster far below and looked up at Ami. She met his eyes, hers wide. Then her mouth twitched, Ivard snorted, and a tide of hysterical laughter overwhelmed them both. And when that died away, a very different passion took its place, to the utter satisfaction of them both.

But he didn't survive. Vi'ya's anger flared.

The Arkad released her gaze one moment before she would

have struck, to smash that face, feel bone splinter and brain spurt, closing those eyes forever.

"Vi'ya." A moment to realize that the voice had spoken twice. Jaim's voice. "Vi'ya. You better come. Some blit wrecked the free-fall gym. People are panicking and the Eya'a are acting strange." And then, "You all right?"

Nausea was acrid at the back of her tongue, but she swallowed it down. Spoke. "I'll come." Brushed past Jaim's assessing gaze, felt him flinch. The fallout continued, magnified: The Eya'a, probing for meaning, their thoughts resonant with fear. Ivard's dizzying mélange of emotions: triumph, desire, remorse at her anger. And the Kelly, a remote, compassionate presence, their question unspoken.

She longed for removal, to be alone. But she would not be alone, until she could get away from Ares—or unless she died.

"I'll come," she said again. "It's nothing."

Vahn followed Jaim, scanning ahead with practiced speed. The Aerenarch and the Dol'jharian woman appeared to have been alone, though neither betrayed even remotely the aspect of lovers; Brandon's blue eyes were distracted, his countenance amiable yet wary. The woman, however, walked with feline tension, and the black eyes that brushed past his as she went by were cold and hard as volcanic rock.

"Liquor," the Aerenarch said plaintively. "I got lost."

The Marine seethed. So the Aerenarch had gotten bored and wandered off, had he? *He knows the dangers—is he a simpleton?*

"Burgess liked the juice too," came a voice from overhead. Vahn whirled, his hand going to his jac and then falling away as he saw Tate Kaga in his bubble. The aged nuller moved over Brandon's head, facing down, forcing the Aerenarch to look up at a sharp angle.

"Caused no little talk during his Regency," the Prophetae continued.

"Our livers are justly famous," the Aerenarch replied, still with his head forced back.

"On Lost Earth some thought it the seat of the soul," said the nuller. "Where's yours?"

"Where's what, my seat or my soul?" The Aerenarch's voice

was light, his smile easy. "My liver will serve both functions, filtering and discarding poisons."

Although Vahn never ceased his careful surveillance of the surroundings, the conversation now dominated his attention.

"Too much of that and it turns to stone," the old man said. He brought his bubble down in front of Brandon. "Will you be a man or a memorial?"

"The Phoenix Antechamber is lined with my ancestors." Brandon made a graceful gesture with one hand. "All carved in marble. None of them," he added, "are likely to move."

Although he'd seen it only once, Vahn had a sudden vivid image of the long hall in the Palace Minor in the Mandala, lined with the busts of former Panarchs and Kyriarchs.

Tate Kaga's bubble suddenly snapped upside down, making his expression unreadable. "There are many opinions about that."

" 'A plague of opinion,' " the Aerenarch replied. " 'A man may wear it on both sides.' " Vahn heard the quotation in his voice but didn't recognize it.

"Ho! A plague! Life and death: more the latter, no?"

Instead of answering, Brandon made a profound bow.

Tate Kaga's bubble snapped upright. "Washte! It is good. Be careful, Arkad Pup—check carefully which side is out before you put it on!" A rush of wind stirred their clothing as the nuller vanished, the motion of his gee-bubble almost too fast to follow.

Brandon turned to Vahn. "Lead the way."

Vahn indicated the direction, his earlier anger changing to perplexity. He did not understand the conversation he had just witnessed, but sensed that both participants did—that they both possessed some key he'd not yet grasped. As if a moment of decision had been reached, though what it was he could not say.

Bleak humor steadied him as they progressed along another weird stairway. *With any luck he's decided it's time to call this disaster a night.*

SOUTH CAP ALPHA SHUTTLE BAY

The assassin stood midway in the crowd of people awaiting the debarkation of the last refugees from Arthelion, listening to the conversations at either side. A holiday atmosphere prevailed, as a number of them gossiped about the spectacular disaster at the Ascha Gardens the night before.

Most of the crowd seemed to be relatives awaiting loved ones. No one took notice of a nondescript person in tech clothing.

The assassin waited patiently, neither speaking nor being spoken to.

New voices joined, from the back: the assassin did not turn around, but recognized one in particular.

Your target is a laergist, *of Archetype and Ritual,* this voice had said in yesterday's interview. *Tall, thin, angular, may be in mourning if not in the robes of his College. He is the only laergist aboard the courier, so you will not mistake him. You are to strike quickly, without being seen, and if you can manage it with a minimum of violence, all the better. Do not touch the body. He is carrying something I require, and if it is not with him, you will not live past the lock doors. If you are successful, and if I get what I want, there will be other jobs. And, soon, I hope, a position of great power in the new government.*

The assassin smiled.

* * *

Fierin vlith-Kendrian heard the annunciator and paused in her preparations, surprised that anyone would wish to visit now. The ship was about to dock.

A trace of impatience flashed through her: it was so very important to look her best when she debarked. *If it's that drunken Gabunder again, I think this time I will be rude.*

Tabbing the door open, she felt her face settle into a mask of remote politeness, and was surprised to find, instead of Gabunder, the man who had rescued her from the old sot's attentions.

"Ranor," she said.

Her surprise turned to alarm when the man touched her wrist, his bony face serious. "I must talk to you. Please, Aegios."

"I haven't been confirmed yet," she began, the words automatic. She no longer added *"until my brother has been found."*

Ranor gave a quick shake of his head, as if dashing aside her words. It was the first time he had ever used her putative title—or exhibited rudeness.

"Come in," she said, and locked the door behind them.

"I've come to request—beg—your aid," Ranor said.

"Would you like to sit down?"

He did not seem to hear her, striding the few short steps to one wall, then turning to face her. He thrust one hand through his disordered hair; she noted trembling fingers, and the alarm inside her sharpened.

"What is it?" she said.

"I'm not sure where to begin," he said quickly. "I . . . find . . . myself in a . . . strange position." His breathing was quick and shallow, the words almost inaudible, as if they were being wrung out of him.

"You've never mentioned any trouble," she said.

"I . . ." He took another quick turn about the cabin, his steps too fast for the small space. He radiated tension; Fierin felt suddenly claustrophobic.

"Ranor, we are about to dock. Speak, please!"

He stared at her. "I believe I can trust you," he breathed. "My . . . instincts were always good for that, anyway."

Fierin felt, and fought, the revealing flush mounting in her cheeks: fourteen years of a stained name, and more recently, the fallout resulting from her first liaison, had sensitized her to innuendo.

But Ranor did not notice. "Will you hold something for me?" he asked. "Just for a time, after we debark?"

She had expected anything from a sordid confession to a declaration of passion. Numb, she nodded.

"Understand, I believe I am in . . . danger," he said. "Though I do not think that any suspicion would fall on you," he added quickly. "If you do not mention my . . . item to anyone. *Anyone.*" He repeated the word with sudden vehemence, his dark eyes wild.

Fierin felt a chill prickle its way down her back. Fifteen years ago, the possibility of danger, of people acting irrationally, had been remote—the stuff of wiredreams. She had learned, at the cost of her family, that violence could lurk behind a smile, that death was an eyeblink away.

"Why?" she said.

"Because it . . . because," he said, breathing heavily. "I can't say anything—I guess the years of conditioning are too hard to overcome. But I . . . I vow to you that my cause is justice . . . and so . . ." He paused, reached inside his robe to a hidden pocket, and withdrew an ordinary datachip. "If you would just hold this for me. For a time. I will claim it from you . . . if . . . I feel it is safe. You needn't do anything or say anything."

"But what if—" She stopped, shaking her head.

He took another deep breath. "What if something happens to me?" He gave her a crooked smile. "This *is* why I'm asking you to hold this chip for me. If something happens, then you must deliver it into the hands of Admiral Nyberg. Do not tell anyone else, or permit it to pass through the hands of intermediaries, for then . . . the danger will befall you." He held out the chip, then snatched it back as a deep thump reverberated through the ship. They were docked.

She bit her lip. "I—do have a connection, with a highly placed Archon—"

"No," Ranor said quickly. "Nyberg. Or his replacement. Will you do it?"

She held out her hand. "I'll do it."

He placed the chip on her palm. It was warm and slightly moist. Grasping her hand between his for a moment, he said, "Please don't run it: no system is safe."

She smiled. "I realize that," she said.

He withdrew his hands, then went to the door. "Thank you," he said, and he bowed, the deep bow of obligation to a superior.

Something in his manner made the chill increase. Before she could say anything, he keyed the lock open and went out.

Ranor walked quickly away from the young Aegios' cabin, lifelong habit smoothing his face.

When he reached his own cabin, he sank onto the bed, covering his face with his hands.

Shock had closed him in its vise the day of Krysarch Brandon nyr-Arkad's Enkainion, when he had watched, helpless to intervene, a bomb destroy everyone who had gathered in the Palace's great Ivory Hall to see Brandon take the vows of Service. Brandon had not appeared, for reasons no one ever did explain.

Afterward, those few who escaped the bomb in the Ivory Hall were angry that Brandon's unknown guardians had not seen fit to warn the guests, much less whisk them to safety. Ranor knew it was not that simple: for the last report he'd received before the coms went down completely were that all of the Krysarch's guardians on duty at that time had been found dead in some sublevel of the Palace.

But Ranor had been beyond speculation, for with the titled guests and the unknown guards and servitors had died his mate, Leseuer gen Altamon of Ansonia, and their unborn child.

Much later the tall, muscular Navy captain who sneaked in under the guns of the Dol'jharians in order to rescue the last remaining fugitives complimented him on his selflessness and presence of mind, compliments which bemused Ranor. Numb with grief, Ranor had seen no further reason for living: it had been habit to calm hysterical people after the bomb, and to lead to safety through the labyrinthine Palace those few who were willing to follow.

The Dol'jharians had been quick and brutally efficient in taking control of the planet, and depressingly few Panarchist survivors gathered at hiding places here and there, hoping to contact someone off-planet.

Ranor had been one of the last to leave, after working steadily at communications. And all that time, he had carried with him, next to his flesh, his last link with his beloved Leseuer: the chip containing the images she recorded through the ajnalens on her forehead, recorded right up until the moment of her death.

He'd viewed the chip repeatedly, despite the almost unbearable pain: it was, he realized, an act of penance as much as grief. *I should have been there with you!*

But it was not until he transferred aboard this Navy courier that the implications of the images that Leseuer gave him detonated in his skull like the bomb that had killed his beloved.

Still reeling from grief, Ranor had racked himself over the decision he faced: destroy the chip and permit the shattered government to re-form, most probably around high figures who—if the images were to be trusted—were implicated in the Dol'jharian plot? Or speak, and watch them fall?

The benefit of silence, he'd thought, would be the healing of the remnants of the Thousand Suns, but would it heal if even the Panarch's own family were somehow implicated? Ingrained in his psyche were the impulses, and later the training, to fix, smooth, ease . . . to *hide* the fissures in a creaking structure. Social harmony had been his calling: his talents had been honed by years of explaining high-powered people to one another, making them appear amenable so that the diplomatic process might carry on under the guise of pleasant discourse.

Dissonance was anathema to him. His belief in the system had been clawed into blood-drenched shreds by that bomb: the grinning death's-head of chaos, so unthinkable until the day the Krysarch deliberately shunned his Enkainion, now was inescapable fact.

At the end it was personal loyalty that made the decision for him. Leseuer, newest citizen of the Thousand Suns, had entrusted him with this last testament—had died in the process of handing it on. Though his reason for living had died with her, it was his duty to see that her death was not completely pointless.

He got up and threw his few possessions into his valise. Last was the original chip, which he briefly considered hiding among his clothes.

A waste of time.

He shut his eyes, reconsidering yet again the process that had led him to his decision. He had used the long flight to Ares to think through the consequences of all that had happened.

Couriers had gone both ways. At about the same time he and the passengers had been given the news about Ares, those on Ares would hear about them—including the laergist who had lived through the Enkainion disaster. The laergist whose mate was a novosti, albeit from a planet not yet part of the Panarchy.

People far more experienced in the lethal byways of political infighting would assume—would *know*—that a chip, just like what lay on his bed now, existed.

The thing to do had been to make a copy—and then to gauge, as best as he was able, his fellow passengers, to find the right one to entrust the copy to.

At that he was adept. He circulated among the passengers, serving as the good listener he was trained to be. The person he chose had to be Douloi first of all. It took only moments of consideration before reaching that conclusion; Nyberg had to be faced with numbers tripled beyond the station's normal capacity. He'd therefore be busy at all hours. No one else but a Douloi would be able to force a personal interview—and it had to be personal, he would impress on his carrier. Beyond that. . .

No Navy, he'd decided. Most of them were loyal—to the Panarch. He did not believe that an officer would heed his exhortation not to view the chip, whereas another civilian, one born to the ties of politesse and one's word of honor, might.

Most likely I'll never know if she betrays me, he thought, an image of Fierin vlith-Kendrian's beautiful face in mind.

It had been instinct, not logic, that made him select her. Logic would have ruled her out early and put someone else—even that drunken sot Gabunder—ahead of her. Gabunder's brains were so sodden he'd do anything to guarantee a liquor supply so that he could drink himself to death. The man had lost family, place, home, and status when the Dol'jharians blew the Node out of Arthelion's sky.

The young Kendrian woman had managed to accrue an incrustation of gossip in a very short life. The Kendrian name was tarnished; murder had disposed of her parents and their chief executives, the blame laid on the shoulders of the brother who had run off to the Rifters and lived under an assumed name.

Fierin had directed the family business as soon as she was able to take the reins, but she refused to take the title. *My brother is not a murderer,* she'd maintained—although not to Ranor. They had never discussed anything so serious. Gossip followed her, whispers like the train of a robe on marble. *I will not make my own Enkainion until we know the truth, and Jesimar takes his place,* she'd said. Such altruism was remarkably rare.

To offset that was the rest of the gossip: that she had become linked with the Archon Tau Srivashti, a man infamous for his political machinations.

A slight trembling through the ship broke his thoughts. The locks were open.

It was done now. He had only to debark and witness, as well as he might, the events he had set into motion.

He picked up his valise. A sense of relief lifted the tension from his mind, from his soul. Leseuer seemed near; tenderness breathed through him as he looked beyond the narrow causeway leading to the forward lock, and contemplated the question of infinity.

Fierin kept her fingers steady as the ship trembled. The com light went on, and she flicked it:

"We are docked. All passengers come forward for debarkation. Those who require living space proceed to . . ."

Fierin flicked it off again. Tau would have space for her, she knew that much.

She sat back, studying the effect of the diamonds she'd woven into her hair. Pale silver-gray eyes stared back at her, wide and slanting under dark lashes and winged brows. She shared those same eyes with her brother: so startling framed by faces of coffee-colored flesh and blue-black hair.

Her hands dropped to her tight bodice, the embroidery and draped lace hiding the outline of Ranor's chip. It had been a quirk of humor that inspired her to put it there—in keeping with the poor man's obsession with secrecy.

She thought about telling Tau, letting him secrete it for her until Ranor came for it. He'd certainly have the wherewithal, far more than she. *And he loves secrets. Just like a small boy.*

It would be fun to surprise him with the chip.

Or would it? It was difficult to predict his reactions. He was kind to her, most of the time, and when he wasn't he was extravagant with presents afterward: a fascinating but utterly unpredictable partner both in bed and out of it. He exuded power and grace, and she had reveled in the admiration and envy of his friends. Yet separation from his orbit had brought to her ears ugly rumors and glances of hatred. Tau was not universally loved, she had recently found out.

Ambivalence made her hesitate. She did love him, but who exactly was the man she loved?

He promised me he would use all his connections to find my brother and clear his name. Well, Jesimar had been found: she'd discovered that when going through a newsbase in the computer of the ship that had shuttled them to Ares from a refugee staging point in a system not yet overrun by Dol'jhar's Rifter allies. But according to that, he was in detention.

She touched the trunk, moving it forward into the corridor. *Tau has the power to get Jes free, and if he has spoken true to me, he will have exerted that power already. If Jes is free, then I'll believe in Tau, because I'll know he believes in me. If Jes is free, then I can entrust Tau with Ranor's chip.*

She rounded a corner just in time to see Ranor's tall head above a crowd moving into the lock. Hurrying her steps a little, she decided it might be a nice gesture to debark with him.

She was the last one through, held behind Ranor by an eager

group of techs who kept bobbing about and jumping to see over heads. From her few meters' distance Fierin saw that Ranor looked pale but calm. She wanted to catch up to him, press his arm to reassure him.

The concourse thronged with people, who surged forward when they saw the passengers. Fieren scanned the crowd, felt her heart speed up when she spotted Tau's familiar hawkface. So he had come, and had not just sent Felton, as she'd told herself to expect.

A very good sign, she thought happily, searching for Jes' head nearby. What a great surprise that would be!

The first of the passengers reached the greeters, and hugs and cries of gladness rang out. Ranor walked alone.

No one is here to meet him.

Thinking of the man's dead mate, Fierin felt a wave of compassion. At least he could walk with a friend! And, her mind rushed on, maybe Tau could find space for him too, aboard that huge yacht of his.

She hurried forward, just as Ranor reached the front of the crowd.

Another surge in the press of humanity almost swallowed him up. Fierin cleared her throat to call, but then stopped when she saw Ranor jerk aside, then spin around, his eyes wide.

Pain and shock flashed through her, reflected in Ranor's face. Their eyes met for a long instant: the crowd's roar seemed curiously distant, and time suspended. The dark eyes seemed to plead with her: *Remember. Remember.*

Then they turned up and he crumbled into the crowd.

Shrieks and shouts surrounded her as she ran forward. Concerned people bent over Ranor's recumbent form; Fierin rushed forward, saw Tau use his authority to force the crowd back. Then he bent over Ranor, his long hands competent as they checked for pulse, then slid into the laergist's robe to seek a heartbeat.

Ranor was right. He was in danger, Fierin thought, and the chill inside her turned to the ice of terror. She resisted the urge to touch the chip in her bodice: whoever had done it might be watching the other passengers, looking for anyone who might have been an accomplice.

Still bent over Ranor, Tau looked up. "Call the medics, fast," he said to the people standing frozen near the wall console, and then he met Fierin's eyes.

A smile of welcome transformed the tension in his face. He straightened up slowly. "Guard him, will you?" he said to the rest of the concerned helpers gathered around Ranor, and two or three assents came back.

"Fierin." Tau made her name a caress as he held out his arm.

She took it, feeling the strength latent there under the smooth fabric of his tunic.

"There's nothing to be done for the man," Tau murmured. "We're better out of the way."

She almost said, "Poor Ranor," except the fear kept his name from her lips. Glad to get away, she matched her steps to Tau's long strides as somehow the crowd parted to make way for them.

Suddenly she couldn't bear it anymore; sophistication deserted her, and she said, "Is Jes free?"

Tau's golden eyes narrowed just for the briefest of moments, then his expression brightened to the tender amusement she was used to from him. "I wish I could tell you that he was, my dear," he said. "But there are . . . complications."

"What complications? He did not kill our parents, I told you that. He wouldn't have."

Tau laid his hand over hers, and his fingers tightened, just enough to bring her words to a halt.

"The Justicials," he said, "will require proof. Right now, they maintain that the proof indicates that he did. I've checked, you see, and I'll continue to move on his behalf. But . . . my child"—he smiled down into her eyes—"shouting it along the corridors here is not going to make my task the easier."

She searched his face. So handsome, yet he was impossible to read. Could he be trusted? Again she saw Ranor fall, knew she would dream forever of the pain and pleading in those eyes before death claimed him.

"Very well," she said, forcing her lips to smile. "I'll wait."

And Ranor's chip will wait, as well.

Part Two

ELEVEN

"You, and most of my tutors on Arthelion, quoted many times from the Polarities of your ancestor," said Anaris. "But I never understood exactly how Jaspar Arkad intended them."

Gelasaar smiled. "What do you think?"

"My father thinks the first one is a prophecy," Anaris replied. " 'Ruler of all, ruler of naught, power unlimited, a prison unsought.' From one to the other: your rule is shattered, and in a few hours we embark on the last leg of your journey. Gehenna awaits you."

The Panarch laughed, a light, almost carefree sound. "The Polarities were not prophecy, but your father will understand their true meaning soon enough."

"I think the Polarities are a meditation on the limits of power," Anaris said, toying with his dirazh'u.

"A very un-Dol'jharian concept," the Panarch interjected. "We taught you well."

"Your ancestor grasped an interstellar imperium and found himself trammeled by relativity. With the Heart of Kronos in our hands, those limits no longer apply."

The Panarch shook his head. "Your father will never understand, Anaris, but you should know better."

Anaris said nothing; with a twist the dirazh'u pulled free of its knots and stretched between his hands, humming with tension.

"The greatest limitation on our power has always been the human heart in its infinite diversity," the Panarch continued. "And against that, no device, no matter what its powers, can give you any lever."

Anaris shook his head. "The Urian device that my father now holds lay within your grasp for seven hundred years, and you denied it." He leaned forward. "With that force, all that was yours will be but the smallest part of my inheritance."

"I was ever the ruler of naught," Gelasaar said quietly. "If your time on Arthelion did not teach you that, your portion shall be even smaller."

PHOENIX SUD OCTANT
FIST OF DOL'JHAR

The cavernous interior of the forward second landing bay was cold and drafty. Morrighon shivered.

Ahead of him Anaris stood easily, flanked by his Tarkan honor guard, all of them silhouetted against the view of space afforded by the wide-open bay door. Beyond, only slightly distorted by the energies of the lock field, the waspish shape of a destroyer hung unmoving, so close the blazon on its hull was clear to Morrighon's eyes: a strange, round-topped, narrow-brimmed hat impaled on the upright of a cruciform, the whole enclosed in an inverted star and pentacle.

Samedi. God of the dead on Lost Earth. Morrighon wished he hadn't looked it up. His fundamental rationalism had been eroded by life among the demon-haunted Dol'jharians; he didn't like the omen.

At the rear of the bay Morrighon heard the muffled whirr of a transtube pod arriving. As he looked around, the hatch hissed open, disgorging a squad of Tarkans. They took up position to either side of the hatch as a group of elderly men and women in prison garb stepped out. Morrighon noted a subtle change in the Tarkans, an increase in wariness and tension, as the last of the Panarchists debarked into the bay: the slight, upright figure of Gelasaar hai-Arkad demanded and received respect even in defeat.

They moved slowly, fettered by the heavy gravity, the shuffling of their feet echoing. The Tarkans did not hurry them.

The Panarchists halted on the other side of the bay from Anaris and his escort. A flare of light curved up over the hull of the *Samedi,* dimming into the angular form of a shuttle as it came about to begin its approach to the *Fist of Dol'jhar*. Anaris watching unmoving, not glancing at the prisoners.

Subtle movement drew Morrighon's eye; though the Panarchists' countenances were wholly unreadable, some of them had altered their stances. A kind of drawing in, Morrighon decided, resolving to consider later this instinctive motion to act in concert. He noted, though, that their leader, like Anaris, remained unmoving as he watched the approaching shuttle.

Again the transtube whirred, and Morrighon did not need to look to know who was arriving this time: the atmosphere of the landing bay changed, somehow colder, charged with power as the hatch hissed open.

Out of the corner of his eye the Bori saw Eusabian stride forward to stand between Anaris and the Panarchists, Barrodagh his ever-present shadow. Barrodagh's eyes flickered to one side; following his gaze, Morrighon saw the cold, faceted glint of an imager complex, recording everything within the bay.

Another propaganda piece for the hyperwave. Morrighon knew that Barrodagh had placed the imager in what he had hoped would be the right position: to draw the maximum attention to his lord.

Even while he despises the Panarchists, he is using their predilection for symbol to increase Eusabian's power. Morrighon wondered if he ought to be thinking along the same lines, then turned his attention to the shuttle, which seemed to hover outside the bay for a moment as the deep hum of a tractor beam resonated through his bones. Then the craft eased through the lock field, rings of light fleeing outward from its hull, and settled to the deck with the characteristic spray of coronal discharge.

After a long moment, during which conquered and conquerors stood together in utter silence, the ramp of the shuttle swung jerkily down and clanged onto the deck. A tall, sour-faced man appeared at the top of the ramp, dressed in a gaudy captain's uniform, and clutching in bony hands a small box.

Emmet Fasthand, captain of the Samedi. His appearance didn't inspire confidence; it was just as well, thought Morrighon, that most of the Tarkan and service personnel that would accompany Anaris when he escorted the Panarch to Gehenna were already on the Rifter destroyer, thoroughly inspecting it and installing the data locks and other control systems that he, Morrighon, had specified.

The Rifter started to descend the ramp, his head jerking one way then the other then back again as he stared from Eusabian to the Panarch. Fasthand obviously had forgotten the heavier gravitation—he stumbled on the ramp, flailed helplessly, went sprawling, only barely managing to convert his fall into a roll.

The Avatar's face showed no reaction as he watched the box in Fasthand's clutch spring open. Barrodagh's intake of breath was Morrighon's first clue that the small silver sphere that flew out was of any importance.

The sphere fell with blurring speed to the ramp. Something about its motion bothered Morrighon: when the sphere landed, it didn't bounce; indeed, its impact made no sound. Instead, it rolled down the ramp and then, curiously, stopped instantly as soon as it hit the level deck, less than a meter from where Anaris stood.

The Heart of Kronos, he realized, feeling unnerved.

Barrodagh motioned toward the sphere but subsided as Anaris bent down and picked it up. Anaris paused for a moment. It was only an instant, but Morrighon, used by now to observing the most subtle signs in his lord, saw Anaris' muscles contract, as if he'd received an electric shock.

But then he straightened up, moving the sphere about on his hand. All eyes were drawn to its weird behavior—as if it were both weightless and massive at the same time. Morrighon dragged his eyes from the sphere to Anaris' face and saw tiny beads of sweat just under his hairline.

What happened? Was it merely the sphere's properties? Morrighon didn't think so. Anaris bowed to his father, dropped the sphere into his hand, then retreated to his former place. His eyes were somber, and wary, forcing Morrighon to remember the eve of his rise to the heirship, when Morrighon caught Anaris performing psi experiments. The Dol'jharians were ruthless in trying to expunge any traces of the talents of the

Chorei from their offspring; though Anaris was now the only heir, Morrighon knew that Eusabian would have no hesitation in having Anaris executed if he knew about those talents emerging in his own son.

There must be some kind of psi resonance in that sphere, Morrighon thought, forcing his gaze to return to the Avatar, who hefted the sphere, seeming wholly absorbed in its strange motion. Barrodagh watched in fascination, his gaze flickering only once to the luckless Rifter captain, who rose painfully to his feet. Morrighon let out a breath of relief a trickle at a time; he was glad they would not be anywhere near that damned sphere until it had been taken to the Suneater and put to whatever task awaited it.

The Rifter limped down the ramp, rubbing his shoulder. He looked uncertainly at Barrodagh, who moved forward and spoke in an urgent undertone.

With one look eloquent of fear and mistrust, Fasthand turned and limped back up the ramp again. Barrodagh sidled a glance at Eusabian, who appeared to be entirely absorbed with the sphere.

The Panarch is already dead in the Avatar's mind, Morrighon thought. *A lesser man might gloat, but Eusabian lost interest in the Panarch as soon as his enemy proved too weak to stand against him. Now he is just a means to end a ritual.*

As if in confirmation Barrodagh motioned for the Tarkan guards to herd the Panarchists up the ramp behind the Rifter.

Certain now that Anaris' reaction had not been noted, Morrighon watched the Panarch closely. Gelasaar looked up at last, but not at Eusabian; to all appearances each man was unaware of the other.

Where Gelasaar's light-colored eyes seemed to linger was on Eusabian's son. His gaze was reflective, but betrayed no thoughts beyond that. Then he turned, mounted the ramp at an unhurried pace, and disappeared within the shuttle.

Morrighon released the breath he hadn't known he was holding. Now the huge bay was filled only with Dol'jharians and those who served them.

Eusabian looked up from the sphere to his son. "Anaris achreash-Eusabian, of the lineage of Dol," he said, his voice resonant in the chilly bay, "complete my paliach, and return to my right hand."

Anaris bowed deeply. "As my father commands, so it is done." He turned and walked up the ramp, and Morrighon hurried after, feeling Barrodagh's gaze bore into his back.

* * *

ARES

The shuttle lifted off the deck and eased through the lock field in a spray of coruscant light, dwindling rapidly toward the Rifter destroyer. Then the screen blanked.

Admiral Nyberg turned away from the display, his face grim. Commander Anton Faseult felt the admiral's tension with a visceral pang.

"Do we have enough information to set a deadline?"

Vice-admiral Damana Willsones, head of Ares Communications, nodded. "The cryptography section has completely deciphered the message headers on the Dol'jharian hyperwave transmissions. With your permission?"

Nyberg flipped his hand toward the console, a gesture of informality he used only with those he'd worked with for decades—and trusted.

Willsones got up with the care of age and walked to the console. The subdued lighting of the admiral's office evoked subtle highlights from her white hair as she tapped it into life.

Faseult felt a draft on his neck. Nyberg had the tianqi in the Downsider Summer's End mode: cool, almost wintry, carrying a faint trace of burning leaves. It was the customary setting for the three of them; but there was now a fourth person in the room.

"Our information put the *Samedi* here, at the Rouge Sud edge of the Phoenix Sud octant." Willsones worked at the console; in response to her input, lines of light speared across the display. "Gehenna, of course, is here, high in Phoenix Sud toward the Rift, and the *Fist of Dol'jhar* was coming from Arthelion."

She paused, looking over at the fourth person. "Your strategy is working perfectly, Captain Ng. Ship movements in response to our feints indicated that the Suneater must be somewhere in the Rift off Phoenix Sud, and the ship locations revealed by this transmission confirm that."

Captain Ng nodded. If she had any idea just how rare it was for Nyberg to include a ship captain in one of these planning sessions, her composure vouchsafed no hint. "But that still leaves us with close to half a million cubic light-years to search. Gnostor Omilov still doesn't feel he has enough information available to narrow it down any more than that."

"In any case," Willsones continued, "given Ares' position here"—another line lanced through the starmap on the display—"our best guess is that we have no more than ten days to launch a rescue effort."

"And if not?" the admiral asked, his mouth tight.

"After that, we would arrive at Gehenna after His Majesty had landed, and since the Dol'jharians will doubtless destroy the orbital monitors, and we know absolutely nothing of the planet, we might never find him."

Nyberg turned away to face the port again. He said nothing.

"Even if the Isolates didn't first." Ng's voice was flat.

"Meanwhile," said Willsones, "we know that at least some on the Privy Council are still alive: Banqtu, Ho, Kree, Paerakles, and Admiral Carr."

All the more reasons to mount a rescue, thought Faseult, *and all the more reason why the Navy, by itself, can't.* With the High Admiral still alive, Nyberg could no more assume command of the Navy than, with the Panarch still alive, the Aerenarch could of the government.

"Ten days," Nyberg repeated, his gaze bleak.

Faseult felt tension pulling at the back of his neck. He assessed their fighting power—a lamentably simple task. Another battlecruiser had joined the *Grozniy* in the refit pits on the Cap: the *Malabor,* badly damaged in action in the Hellas system. That made three new cruisers, when one counted the *Mbwa Kali,* now doing picket duty in-system. Three cruisers, a handful of destroyers, and a host of lesser craft—all they had to propagate a war against Eusabian's superarmed fleet. *Unless we can recall the Fleet.* Which was the prerogative of the government—or the high admiral, both of whom were on their way to Gehenna.

"Do you see any signs that a government will have coalesced by then?" Nyberg didn't turn around as he spoke.

Faseult spoke up. "There are several factions, sir, among prominent Service Families. Though speculation and social competition are intense, our reports indicate nothing definite beyond that." *Which is as neutral a description of the claws and teeth behind those smiling Douloi masks as I can manage.*

Now the admiral did turn around, and Faseult felt the impact of his gaze. "What about the Aerenarch?"

The commander felt a pang of memory and looked down at the signet ring on his hand. The ruby eyes of the sphinxes winked in the subdued lighting of the admiral's office. "I don't know. He is active socially, but . . ."

"You have learned nothing more about his leaving Arthelion?"

Faseult shook his head. "Nothing."

"We're running the discriminators full-time on the data from incoming ships," added Willsones, "and that's one of the top priorities in the search pattern. We've turned up nothing beyond what we already know." She rubbed her eyes, looking tired.

Nyberg gazed across the room at the official portrait of Gelasaar hai-Arkad, forty-seventh on the Emerald Throne. Even as the admiral's head of security, Faseult knew there was much that Nyberg didn't share with him; he was a very private man. But he was sure that this uncertainty weighed heavily on the admiral.

"And someone wants it kept that way," he added. "The murder yesterday, in the South Cap alpha shuttle bay."

"The laergist?" asked Nyberg.

"Yes. He was on Arthelion, assigned to assist one Leseuer gen Altamon, an artist from Ansonia reporting on the progress of that planet's petition for admission to the Panarchy. She died at the Enkainion."

"And?"

Faseult motioned to Willsones, who returned to her seat.

"As I indicated, there was nothing new in the ship's datanodes," she replied, "but a search of the records here turned up a vid about her from the Stella Novostu organization, done a month before the Enkainion. It shows her equipped with an ajna."

Nyberg turned to Faseult, who shook his head. "We found nothing on the body, nor in his cabin on the ship that brought him here. We are questioning the other passengers, but only as a matter of course: he was killed with a neurojac, which usually implies a professional assassination. Which might," he added, "be related to the badly mangled body we found only hours later in one of the subtransits off of Alpha. This one had died of a neurotoxin, one of the slow and painful ones."

Nyberg sighed and sat down again behind his desk. He put his elbows on its surface and rubbed his forehead with the fingertips of both hands.

"I think we can assume the existence—up until then, at least—of a recording of the Enkainion," he said finally. He sat up. "But that does us no good now." He turned to Ng. "Captain, have you anything to add?"

"Nothing," she replied. "Except . . . an intuition, if you like: the Aerenarch may surprise us all."

Nyberg merely bowed politely, and Willsones exchanged glances with Faseult. Alone, they would have commented; before Ng, who was largely an unknown quantity, they maintained the safe shield of strict protocol.

So why is she here? Despite his admiration of Ng and her record, it had taken him aback when Nyberg attached her directly to his staff, and it surprised him again when she was invited to this session. Nyberg had hitherto had little use for the fiercely independent cruiser captains, who—entirely within the wide-ranging limitations of their standing orders—were notorious for disregard of the careful infrastructure of Central Command.

"There is little time," Nyberg said. "We'll have to force the issue so that a decision can be made, one way or the other." He turned to Willsones. "Admiral, can you monkey up a communication conveying that deadline, and link it to one of the most recently arrived couriers? I want to announce it without revealing its true source."

Willsones nodded, apparently unsurprised. "Not hard at all. You don't want an image, then?"

He shook his head. "Too hard to explain, don't you think?" He smiled grimly, his eyes taking in both Ng and Willsones. "And there's another reason. Commander Faseult believes there may be a leak in the Jupiter Project. If we put just the right amount of information in this communication, whoever is at the other end of the leak may just reveal a bit too much knowledge."

Nyberg turned to Faseult without waiting for a reply. "Commander, I want you to monitor social affairs in the oneill. Your man Vahn is doing an excellent job with the Aerenarch, but we'll need a lot more intelligence about the people he sees."

Faseult nodded, resigned.

"Captain," continued the admiral, turning to Ng, "I'd like you to sound out your officers and crew, and others, if you like, concerning a mission to Gehenna. But don't even hint that it's being considered—I don't want to tip our hand."

Ng said, "Begging your pardon, sir, but I've already begun."

Some of the tension in Nyberg's face eased. "I thought as much." Then it was back again, more focused. "But remember, it may never come to pass. We cannot defy whatever government may form here—that could shatter what remains of the Panarchy."

And suddenly Faseult knew the reason she was there. Whatever government the civilians managed to put forward could very well be short-lived if any of Semion's former cadre of captains showed up. *There's no room for gloating at the way the civs are ripping at one another for position,* Faseult thought as Nyberg dismissed them. *Their ballroom and bedroom skirmishes would be nothing to the infighting we'd face if Koestler or sho-Bostian or Imry skip in.*

Faseult paused at the door and looked back. Nyberg had not moved; he gazed up at the picture of the Panarch, his thoughts obviously thousands of light-years distant.

Was any of that man's strength of purpose and visionary skill in the one remaining son? Faseult shook his head and walked out.

"He may surprise us all." I hope for all our sakes that Ng is right.

* * *

Lokri looked down from his ceiling holograph of the black void of space. The visitor chime—again? Had he dreamed it?

No, the annunciator light was on.

He got to his feet, waited for the visitor door to slide open. When it did, he looked through, surprised to find, instead of Marim's insouciant grin or his sister's half-remembered face, the grizzled, ugly visage of Montrose. Lokri dropped into the pod on his side of the dyplast, not hiding his lack of enthusiasm.

Montrose's smile was grim. "So Marim's been here, helpfully told you the good news?"

Surprise broke through the tight band of anger and pain that had gripped Lokri since he'd found out that his sister was alive, and on Ares. Not even being arrested had hit him this hard; that ghost had ridden him since he first escaped from Torigan.

"Yes," he said.

"But she hasn't been down to visit you, has she?"

Lokri half rose. "Is there a point?"

Montrose looked impatient. "No. I'm wasting my time, and yours, because two jobs don't keep me busy enough."

Lokri expelled his breath, feeling suddenly tired to death. "Your pardon. Speak, I'm listening."

"Apology accepted." Montrose planted his hands on his knees and leaned forward. "She's living on board Tau Srivashti's glittership. Mean anything to you?"

Lokri shrugged. "Archon of what, Timberwell? Interesting rep. I don't remember anything else." He laughed. "It has been a while since nick politics was an interest of mine."

"Well, it'd better be one now," Montrose said soberly. "I came down here to tell you that I don't think your sister is going to be visiting you, but not for the reasons you may think."

"I'm grateful for your interest, but please don't play games," Lokri murmured.

Montrose grunted. "No games, but no truth, either—yet. Only a lot of guesses. Main one is that your sister won't be down here in order to protect her life. And yours, although you're probably a whole lot safer." He grinned.

Lokri snorted. "Safe? Here?" Lokri's gesture included the entirety of Detention One, the maximum-security facility on Ares.

"No one can get to *you,*" Montrose said.

"Who'd want to kill Fierin?"

"Who wanted to kill your parents?"

"I did," Lokri said with a bitter laugh. "Ask the nicks."

Montrose snorted dismissively. "My job cooking for the Arkad doesn't take me but a couple of hours a day—until he starts entertaining. If he does. So I lend a hand at the general infirmary, where I hear things." He paused.

"I'm listening."

Montrose nodded. "May be no connection at all, but one of the people on the courier your sister came in with was killed when he walked out of the lock. Another one just got challenged to a duel. Two more have shown up with a mysterious rash—one that appears as a side effect of a highly illegal truth serum."

Anger flooded Lokri again. At the man before him, at his sister, at his parents, at himself. Especially at himself and his total helplessness. "My parents were killed in '51—fourteen years ago. I don't see how there could be any connection between that and any of this—including any problems Fierin might have gotten herself into."

Montrose shrugged. "All I'm telling you is what I've seen. That sister of yours is walking soft, walking soft indeed. She's seen everywhere on Srivashti's arm, but the rare times she's alone she's been talking to some odd choices. Jaim. Ivard . . ."

"Crew of *Telvarna*." Lokri felt a sharp stab of hope.

"I'll know more if she manages to sit down next to me in a transtube," Montrose said with a laugh.

Lokri shook his head, the hope dissipating in the cold glare of logic. "Why would she waste time with you? If she knows who my crewfellows were, she knows the damned Arkad was with us. If anyone can help her, or me, if she's even remembered who I am, it's your Aerenarch."

"Wrong," Montrose said. "You must have been listening to that rockwit Marim. You *know* she's got no interest in anything that doesn't directly involve her, and even less understanding."

"You can't be telling me that the Arkad doesn't have any power," Lokri protested.

Montrose pursed his mouth. "That's a difficult question. On one hand, there's this: Every time he pisses, they hear the splash on every com from the brig to the bridge. He can't scratch his ass without Vahn's security team running scan first."

"So he can't do anything?"

Montrose shrugged. "There's no government, and there can't be one until they either try to get the Panarch off Gehenna or else declare him officially dead. If the Arkad won't, then it has to be done by the Privy Council, but they're all dead, or with the Panarch, so who's going to name their successors?"

For the first time in what seemed a century Lokri thought past his immediate problems. "Arkad said at Granny Chang's that he wanted to run a rescue. That wasn't just gas?"

Montrose shook his head. "He doesn't talk about it at all. Nor"—his black brows slanted sardonically—"does he talk about how he escaped that hellspawn bomb in his Palace, though the rest of these chatzing honey-voiced nicks sure whisper about it. Whether because of that or for some other reason, he hasn't declared his father dead." He sat back in his pod. "Let's leave him aside for now. As to your sister, and whatever else may be going on, I will be listening." His eyes narrowed, his familiar, heavy-boned face menacing. "I have my own reasons. Meantime, what I want from you is what happened on Torigan."

Lokri shook his head. "For whose entertainment?"

Montrose snorted. "You think we're wired here?" He laughed. "What an irony—delicious. You're probably in the only place that *is* deadwalled."

"Don't you carry some kind of device?"

"Locator," Montrose said, touching his wrist. "Simple location signal. They don't have enough staff to listen to the chatter of all the riffraff they've got gathered here." He laughed again, but it was not humorous this time.

Lokri rubbed his jaw. "All right." He sighed. "I'll give it to you, if you'll see that it gets to her. If she asks. But first, about the Arkad. You said he can't do anything. But—?"

"But the potential is there. Or someone must think so, anyway." Montrose's smile was grim. "Because someone has tried three times to kill him. Now, then, let's have that story. Every detail you can remember."

* * *

Jaim slid Vahn's palm-jac into his wristband and then picked up the chip he'd designed himself. He tilted it slightly from side to side, watching the subdued lighting of his room glint off the ID holo on it, its simple pattern indicating a custom burn. Then he slipped it into his tool pouch and picked up the new boswell Vahn had issued him. Bulkier than usual, it was fitted with a clone-cell monitor attuned to the Aerenarch's genome, able to detect any type of poison, including Helix. He winced as he slipped the boswell onto his wrist, and with a final look around the room, went out.

He found Brandon in the garden room, standing behind Ki at the central console. Brandon looked the part of the Aerenarch, wearing a tunic of severe cut, with no decoration—the richness was in the fabric. Dark trousers and single-seam boots, gotten from somewhere, completed the sartorial catalog; as accessories Brandon added only a superb bone structure, excellent posture, and a simmering blue gaze.

Jaim wondered what Vi'ya might make of the energy that he could feel clear across the room. Though Brandon had not said anything about the impending visit to Archon Srivashti, the signals were there: this was more important than an afternoon of food, liquor, and games of chance.

"Shall we go?"

They walked in silence down the pathway to the transtube portal. Halfway there, in a spot Jaim had already chosen, he waited until Brandon, who walked a little ahead, turned, and then reached for him just out of peripheral vision.

If he had trained the Aerenarch properly, Brandon should be subliminally aware of the change in Jaim's breathing, the shift of cloth—

And Brandon whirled around, one hand out, body moving to one side. Even prepared, Jaim found his balance thrown off; he stumbled, reflecting as he recovered that Brandon's speed, his high-voltage defense, was another indication just how much the impending visit had keyed him up.

They exchange a flurry of light blows, both with a care to their clothing. It would not do to arrive sweaty and disheveled at Tau Srivashti's glittership.

The transtube took them to the lock. Jaim checked everything, then they stepped inside the gig that awaited them.

A glance at the console showed a bank of peaceful green lights. Still, Jaim inserted his chip, and a cold trickle of acid runneled along his spine when the console overlay showed a blinking red light deep within the engine system.

Brandon's lips parted, then he touched his boswell. *(Request another gig, and we advertise this.)*

(I can disable it,) Jaim returned. He tapped at the console for a while. *(But it's locked out; I'll have to do it manually.)*

(Is it set on a timer?)

Jaim entered a different code, said, *(No. It's set to blow the hull when we are a certain distance from either ship or station.)*

(So we don't take anyone with us. Tidy.)

Jaim expelled his breath, reaching into his pocket for the microtools he rarely was without.

(Want help?)

Jaim shook his head. *(You've never been in the engine of one of these things. Marim would find it a tight fit.)*

Jaim lifted the hatch and squeezed his way down into the bowels of the gig. He took a deep breath, calming the animal part of his mind that yammered in terror at the terribly cramped quarters, trying not to think about the tremendous energies constrained all around him by a few centimeters of metal and complex twists of energy. Once he reached the tampered node, he squirmed around uncomfortably to reach his tool pouch and set to work. His hands labored automatically, his mind moving fast.

Four times. Five, counting that damn Helix. His guts tightened at the thought of the Helix. Somehow the attempts to kill Brandon seemed cleaner than that; upon analysis, the genetic poison turned out to have been intended to disable the Aerenarch with a rather nasty form of dementia, but not otherwise harm him. He might well have lived out his natural span—the perfect setup for anyone aiming at a Regency, Montrose said when Jaim told him about it. Brandon hadn't said anything at all.

Tau Srivashti seemed too obvious a suspect. The bomb on his gig was so blatant, Jaim wondered if it put the Archon beyond suspicion. Srivashti had a rep for deviousness, and this was mere crudery.

And maybe we're to think just that, Jaim thought.

* * *

Nothing untoward occurred on the short journey to the glittership. They made it in silence, Brandon looking out in open appreciation at the long length of the fabulous yacht. Jaim eyed the weapons nacelles, both the blatant ones and those disguised, and reflected on the utility of visual communication.

I'll know more when I can see this Archon without the usual crowd of heel-licking blungesuckers around.

The gig nestled up against the forward lock of the yacht. A muted boom and clank, a hiss of air, and the doors slid open.

The Archon waited there himself. If he was surprised to see them alive and unharmed, there was utterly no sign of it in his coin-colored eyes. Jaim looked past him at the servant hovering behind, a long-faced man who wore patience as a shield, his clothing designed for unobtrusiveness. This was Felton, Srivashti's personal servant. Jaim remembered what Vahn had said about him: *He's a mute the Archon found and rescued from a hellhole somewhere when they were both hardly old enough to shave. No one knows anything about Felton except that he's an expert in the Kelestri numathanat—the breath that kills—and other neurotoxins.*

Srivashti welcomed Brandon with a profound bow, then gestured the way inside. Jaim missed the first few exchanges as he scanned the environment, the stances of the Archon and his servant. Slowly the light cadences of Douloi talk penetrated his consciousness: first sound, then sense.

". . . demands on your time," the Archon was saying. His voice was husky and low, not unpleasant. "I trust that we can keep you tolerably entertained."

"Entertainment," Brandon returned, lifting his hands, "has been my goal in life."

"And a worthy one it is," Srivashti said, smiling. "Come this way. Felton! Is the table laid?"

The liegeman bowed, his lank dark hair swinging close to his face. Then he motioned Jaim ahead, and they descended a spiral stair into what appeared to be a garden—complete with waterfall.

The gesture was benevolent; by permitting Jaim to go first, the Archon was acknowledging the necessity of his having to check things over. The Archon could have forced a trust issue, making Jaim's job more difficult.

Heady scents filled the air: arrissa, jumari, swensoom. Tranquillity seemed to be the keynote, Jaim thought, as they approached a low, inlaid table set under a sheltering tree. On silver platters were cleverly arranged a variety of delicacies. Jaim recognized some of the many-layered pastries, and a surreptitious sniff promised mouth-watering complexities of taste: the Archon had a Golgol chef on his unseen staff.

Jaim moved from dish to dish, glancing at his boswell unobtrusively. The clone monitor remained quiescent.

A little behind them came Brandon and Srivashti; the Archon approached the table just as Jaim, satisfied, moved to the background. It was adroitly done, and suddenly Jaim knew that he would find nothing amiss anywhere here.

But he would go through the motions, anyway.

"Please, Highness. We've a variety of things to offer. I can particularly recommend the crespec. It was an especially fine blend, laid down by my grandmother."

Brandon gestured compliance. Srivashti picked up a bottle and poured out yellow liquor into two fragile shells grown naturally in the shape of flutes.

"Aerenarch Semion was my close associate," he said, handing Brandon one glass, "and I like to think my friend." Srivashti lifted his glass. "In honor of that friendship, you behold me exerting myself to continue that alliance."

Brandon's slight bow was polite, his hands graceful in deference. Jaim knew enough to recognize it as an answer, but not what it signified.

Srivashti smiled, and they drank. "Come, Highness," he said suddenly. "Shall we speak plainly?"

"Plain speaking," said Brandon, his smiling blue eyes guileless, "is a gift."

Srivashti laughed. "Let us talk, then, as we play."

He led the way down a mosaic-blazed corridor, to a round room carpeted with living moss. Their footfalls were silent; the tianqi diffused the cool air with a trace of astringent herbs.

Matte-black walls were lined with rare plants from several systems, indirectly lit. The ceiling opened to space, or appeared to; through the window an edge of the huge station loomed, glinting redly in the light of the giant sun it orbited.

In the center of the room a billiards table waited, set on legs carved of paak-wood, the metal-rich soil of its world of origin showing up as subtle colorations in the dark wood's grain.

Felton came last, bearing an ancient silver tray, so it was the Archon who moved to a discreet console and caused part of a wall to slide noiselessly aside, revealing a rack of cues.

"Bluff billiards," Brandon murmured, looking intrigued. "My brothers used to play that."

"I had many a good game with His Highness," Srivashti said, "which made the tiresome necessities easier to dispose of."

Brandon was silent as he selected, with care, a cue. These, too, were carved from paak-wood, tipped with gilded metal.

Felton set the tray on a sideboard, refilled the shells.

"Will you break, Highness?" the Archon asked, bowing.

Brandon again made the gesture of deference and sipped at the liquor. Crespec, Jaim recalled, was a liquor distilled several times from a plant found only on a world far outside the boundaries of the Thousand Suns. Extremely expensive, it tasted beguilingly of blended wood and smoke, and it didn't take much to hit the human system hard; Jaim thought he could scent the alcohol fumes from where he stood.

The Archon tabbed his console once again, and a subliminal hum signaled the activation of gravitic fields. Across the smooth green surface of the table colorful billiard balls rolled, both holographic and real, to assemble into a perfect triangle. The computer brought the white ball out last, positioning it at the other end of the table from the triangle's apex.

The Archon stepped around the table, lined up his cue, and with a sudden forceful thrust knocked the white ball directly into the triangle.

Both players watched the random scattering of the balls. Jaim watched as well, trying to note in the veering trajectories of the balls where they passed through gravitic fluctuations, and at the same time keeping the white ball in sight, in case it touched any of the real balls or passed through a holoball.

One of the solid-colored balls thunked into a pocket.

"Low balls to me, Highness," the Archon said with elaborate politesse. "A cosmically appropriate disposition of affairs, no?"

Brandon smiled as he sipped at his drink.

Srivashti stepped around the table, his eyes roaming over the setup as he said, "Most regrettable are what appear to be growing tensions between the Navy and your civilians in Service. One wishes they would perceive how facilitating cooperation would benefit everyone, don't you find, Highness?" The title was added just after the Archon bent to line up a shot.

"I do," Brandon said, sipping again.

Smack! The white curved around the one obvious anomaly and ticked against a solid ball near a pocket. As Srivashti straightened up, the ball dropped out of sight.

The Archon looked up, good-humored. "Details," he said, tapping his cue lightly, "must stay within bounds, of course, but: has Nyberg taken you into his briefings?"

"Just as much as he is required by law," Brandon said.

Snick! Once again the white ball wound its way between the others, not touching any but its target, but this time the ball rolled gently to a stop.

Dead zone? thought Jaim. Or just not strong enough a hit?

With another of those bows, the Archon stepped back.

And once again Brandon returned his deference, courtesy for courtesy. He cocked his head, bent, shot.

It was a bad shot by anyone's standards. The white caromed into a cluster of balls, scattering them fanwise. Two of them rolled swiftly to a stop: he'd found the dead zone, or one of them, at least. The other three ran merrily through—holoballs, despite the *tick* as they rebounded off the side. Three of them were the Archon's, and only two his.

The Archon stepped up to the table. "You are, Your Highness," he said slowly, as if his mind were not at all on the game, "in probably the most difficult position any of your illustrious House have ever found themselves." He looked back over his shoulder.

Brandon saluted him with his glass, but said nothing.

The Archon bowed, then continued studying the table. Two balls were easy shots, but were they real or not? Only a player's ball could move a holo; the white passed right through them.

He paused to line up a hard shot, then sent a rueful smile back at the Aerenarch, who drank again. "One endeavors to avoid the tactlessness of the obvious simile."

Simile? Jaim thought, watching the Archon's cue strike, swift and sure, sending the white toward a blue—and through it.

Srivashti drank deeply, then said, "Sympathetic as I am, that is not the crux of our dilemma. Until we know, we have merely the ashes of the former government."

He means the Phoenix—the Panarch—dead.

Brandon made a random shot. Again he sent the balls scattering; Jaim tried to watch them all, and thought he saw the white pass through the edge of one high ball. Three others passed through, or near the edge of the dead zone—then the timer chimed, which indicated another change in the gravitic flux.

"But my father is still alive," he said.

TWELVE

"Another message header directed to Barrodagh," the ensign at the hyperwave console declared.

Ng broke off her conversation with Y'Mandev and looked over.

Aziza laughed, pointing at the screen. "That's Anderic, captain of the Satansclaw. *Was at Arthelion, same's* Deathstorm.*"*

The word "Arthelion" affected Ng, as it always did, with a powerful combination of grief, triumph, regret, pride. The memory of her battle would always carry that impact, she suspected. But Aziza had been there as well; she'd been captured off the Deathstorm *along with the hyperwave, the only person to survive from her crew. Yet nothing of this seemed to affect her as she laughed. Contemplating the little Rifter tech, Ng wondered if her apparent resilience was a gift or a curse.*

Anderic, a long, saturnine man, faced the screen, his pose so stiff and rehearsed Ng knew immediately he was afraid, very afraid, of Barrodagh.

"Orders received," he said. "Requesting permission to stop at Rifthaven for a refit before we proceed to the Suneater."

A female voice out of view of the imager called, "Tell him we can't be sure of the fiveskip until we can go cold."

Anderic threw an impatient look over his shoulder. "Shut up, Lennart. He doesn't need—"

A secondary screen windowed up, and there was Barrodagh, looking tired and grim, his dark eyes like pits in his thin face. "Permission granted, Satansclaw. *You will have five days to stop over. I am sending a priority rating to the Rifthaven Syndics." And his window abruptly went dark.*

Anderic opened his mouth, then made an impatient chopping motion to his unseen comtech. That screen, too, went dark.

"Suneater." Y'Mandev turned to Ng, his brows raised. "Another one on its way, Captain." His tone was congratulatory—she had predicted this movement.

She nodded, but inside felt the chill of certainty: before too much more time had passed, she, too, would be seeing the Suneater—if only as a target.

⁂ ⁂ ⁂

"We'll know, if a rescue mission goes to Gehenna," Brandon murmured, watching the Archon sink another ball.

Srivashti moved around the table. "The prospect of battle," he said, lining up another shot, "is the only subject I've heard more frequently than battle reminiscenses."

Brandon said nothing.

"The risks are very real, Your Highness, as I am sure you are aware." Srivashti looked back, his smile reflective, then said, "And the reminiscences hint at a disturbing possibility."

Brandon said, "The Dol'jharians possessing hyperwave capabilities."

The Archon's smile widened—he was not at all surprised to hear the word "hyperwave." "So that was the subject of Nyberg's secret briefing?" He tapped the white ball delicately and stood back to watch its slow progress, bent by a flux.

"Ng and a few of her officers put together a hypothesis after analyzing battle data," Brandon said.

The white brushed Brandon's two real balls, making them roll inward slightly.

And I'll just bet that's the dead zone, Jaim thought.

"And nothing more concrete than that?" Srivashti said, stepping aside with a graceful gesture.

Jaim knew what his air of surprise meant; anyone with any

kind of connection knew to the minute how long the briefing had been.

Brandon said with a slight shrug, "Those not involved in the pertinent battles found it difficult to believe. Wouldn't you?"

"Did you, Your Highness?"

"I believe nothing without evidence," Brandon replied.

The Archon laughed softly. "The assurance of youth. I, however, am older, and I have come to give credence to persistent rumors—even the inconvenient ones."

"Such as?" With great care, Brandon shot, and sank one of his balls. He made a second shot, which seemed to go wide.

"Such as the belief, held by many, that a government in suspension is more dangerous even than the enemy."

"There is the question of authority," Brandon said.

"True." The Archon bowed, then scanned the table. "But where one is limited, several can carry a point."

"Belief," Brandon said, "requires evidence."

The Archon laughed as he made his shot, and the ball rolled just short of the pocket. "Belief, if Your Highness will honor me with permission to contradict"—again, the deferences, sustained as a dance—"requires faith. Those who made their Vows of Service swear to a person, but only insofar as that person symbolizes the polity as a whole."

Brandon's look was utterly blank, then he bent and made three shots in succession. *Brandon doesn't need to be told what the vows—* Belatedly Jaim remembered that Brandon had not made his own vows, had skipped out on the ceremony.

His mind churning furiously, Jaim tried to focus on the game—and realized that Brandon was, very suddenly, ahead.

"Well done, Highness," the Archon said. "You were quite helpless: I really thought I had you."

His tone was congratulation on being a worthy opponent, then the Archon bent to shoot, his shoulders and arms lined with a new tension. He took a long minute, during which no one spoke, to line up his shot, and when he made it, even Jaim could see that it was brilliant. The balls moved in a complex pattern, some dropped—and he was only one shot behind.

"Good," Brandon murmured. "Very good."

The Archon bowed, his deference the one of gratitude, then he said, "You see, there are some things an old man such as myself could teach you."

Now it was Brandon's turn to make the deference, but with

a trick with his fingers, a gesture of airy grace that somehow indicated humor. "I've so many interested in my welfare," he said. "Nearly half a dozen tutorials offered since my arrival."

What the hell does he mean by that? He can't be about to tell this chatzer about the Navy lessons?

But Srivashti did not query it. His eyes narrowed, and he shot, a convulsive movement that unaccountably missed by a thread's breadth. He had one ball left. As he stood back, Jaim sensed his reluctance—the man had to win.

The Aerenarch flexed his hands, paused to drink off his liquor, then he blinked his eyes, bent, and lined up his shot. He grunted when the white ball veered, making a lazy run that slingshot past a slow zone and caromed off the Archon's ball before homing straight for his own.

It could have been the best shot of the game, for the white smacked Brandon's last two balls right in a line. But the white was too slow, and the Archon's ball had been hit too hard; all three reached pockets, the solid one, quite clearly, first.

The Archon had won by default. Brandon winced and rubbed his jaw. Srivashti's mouth stretched out in a smile of triumph but smoothed when Brandon looked up, his blue eyes cloudy.

"Another game, Highness?"

"As you wish," Brandon said. "I'd like to recover my honor."

It was said in the grand style, and the Archon laughed. "But there is no dishonor in losing to me, Highness," he said expansively. Now Jaim heard the genuine note of pleasure in his voice. "Even your brother lost to me, and he was one of the most formidable players I ever faced."

"My brother," Brandon said. His light voice betrayed the faintest slur. "I've a question for you."

"Please, Highness." The Archon bowed, and indicated for Brandon to shoot first, which he did, a random shot that sent the balls everywhere.

Brandon hardly seemed to notice them. He made several more random shots, sinking one ball each time, then he said, "You were my brother's ally, you must have had mutual contacts before Eusabian's fleet blew everything to fragments." He shot and missed.

Srivashti winced, bending to line up his cue. "I know very little," he admitted, "but what I do know I will place at your disposal if you wish, Highness."

"Please." Brandon stood back, watching the Archon make another careful, calculated shot that downed a pair of balls. "I was given to understand that my brother's body was found in the singer's bedroom. But did your sources happen to note what happened to the singer?"

"Suicide, Highness," the Archon said, bending once more to tap the white. "Her body was found in the bain. A time-honored neurotoxin often employed in suicides and mercy killings: quite painless." Snick! One, then two balls dropped into pockets, and the Archon smiled.

"Damn," Brandon said congenially. "You've won again."

"Another game?"

Regret informed Brandon's deference. "If there were time," he said. "But I promised to be an official presence at another gala event this evening."

They exchanged politenesses as they progressed back through the huge ship to the lock. Then, just before they reached it, the Archon said, straightening up from bowing over Brandon's upturned palms, "You enjoy these official appearances, it is to be hoped, Your Highness?"

Brandon's brows lifted just slightly. "They're a habit."

Srivashti inclined his head. "I was going to say—if you will do me the honor of bearing with my obtuseness—that it does people good to see you in the social arena. The chaos we decried earlier creates added tensions; your presence indicates at least an appearance of things resuming their natural courses."

"Thank you," the Aerenarch said, "for the reminder."

They took their leave then, seen off by the silent Felton. Jaim's last sight before the lock closed was the man's unwinking gaze, blank as a holographic statue.

And as soon as they were on the gig, Brandon walked straight through to the bain. Jaim touched his boswell; there were no words in response, but the connection conveyed the unmistakable sounds of someone being thoroughly sick.

Jaim guided the gig away from the huge ship, thinking rapidly.

On the surface, the visit had been pleasant and agreeable. Brandon's reaction was mute evidence that Jaim's instincts were correct: some kind of battle of wills had just taken place, though who had won was impossible to say.

It was the first indication Jaim had that Brandon was not, after all, steering his tranquil course wide of the maelstrom of reforming government.

Indication but not evidence.

Yet Jaim had learned to listen and to evaluate not just what was said, but what was left unsaid.

Jaim had assumed that Brandon, in finding himself back within Panarchic governance, merely made the best of it with his habitual grace, contenting himself with convivial company, a continual round of parties, and in quiet hours a resumption of his old studies.

To him, Brandon talked freely about food or drink, about games, navigation, archaic forms of music, the difficulties of retuning a drive cavity when the fiveskip has gone down; all the minutiae of daily life, even—with an objective moderation that rarely failed to entertain—the people he met during a day's course in that life, but never about those whose energies were expended primarily in shaping, guiding, or destroying the destinies of whole planets. He never confided in anyone, never talked of the things that mattered.

Once he did confide in a person, in Markham vlith-L'Ranja, Jaim reminded himself. *Then Markham was taken away, and by the time Brandon caught up with him, Markham was dead.*

Jaim's mind went back through the conversation, and he counted up what had been said and what had not been said.

The Vows of Service: the Archon had made them, that was said, and what was not said: Brandon had not. Implied: he'd run away.

Said: the government is falling to pieces, needs authority. Not said: the Panarch must be declared dead before Brandon can be that authority.

"Until we know . . ." With a sudden shock Jaim realized he'd missed the second meaning of that comment: not just knowing about the Panarch, but about the truth of his last remaining son's escape from the mass murder at his Enkainion.

But that just accentuated the point of the whole conversation, summed up in its last part.

Said: that Brandon ought to make more social appearances. *Not said: Brandon ought to stay out of government.*

Jaim turned around, saw the Aerenarch lying back in a chair, his forehead sweat-lined, eyes closed, his face drawn. Jaim realized that two separate conversations had taken place, and wondered, suddenly, if Brandon had lost both games deliberately. He rubbed his jaw, wishing he could recall the exact sequence of shots in the first game; he was convinced now that the apparently random shots—sometimes at real balls, sometimes at the faux—had even conveyed some kind of meaning.

It wasn't a conversation, it was a duel.

The reference to the "half dozen tutorials" drifted through Jaim's mind, and with his new clarity he understood what they had referred to: the murder attempts. *Tutorials? But what more effective way to force conformity onto a foolish drunkard?*

Whether Srivashti had initiated those attempts or not, his reaction made Jaim fairly sure he knew about them. Which didn't prove complicity: he also had found out about the hyperwave.

The gig bumped up gently next to the station lock then, and Brandon opened his eyes. "Let's go," he said.

When they reached the Enclave, Brandon seemed to have recovered his energy. He summoned Ki and Montrose, and kept Jaim there. "It is time, the Archon Srivashti reminded me, to spread goodwill through social pleasures," Brandon said, his hands wide. "Ki, run the list of invitations we've received."

"Here they are," came Ki's quiet voice.

The Aerenarch stared down, his arms crossed and his head askance, then he reached past Ki's shoulder and tapped once.

"Again, along this axis," he said.

Ki nodded, worked, then sat back.

"I think, comrades, it is time for the Enclave to return the hospitality of our outside friends."

Surprised at this turn of events, Jaim waited as Brandon stared distractedly out into the garden. Then he snapped his fingers. "I know: a concert." He smiled around, his gaze landing last on Montrose, who had just returned from some errands outside. "Don't you think?"

Montrose shrugged his massive shoulders. "What I think is, are we feeding any of them?"

"Just refreshment. And in keeping with the, ah, spirit of Lady Vannis' new fashion for abstinence, let us keep it simple."

"Simple but memorable," Montrose said.

"I leave it in your capable hands," Brandon said.

Montrose shut his eyes, then smiled. "Capable indeed. Well, let us see what your ancestors laid down in those storerooms. . . ."

"And," Brandon added, raising a finger, "I would request your musical talents as well, to open and close the affair."

"Ah?" Montrose turned to him, his heavy brows raised.

"Yes." The Aerenarch smiled; there was an edge of anticipation to it. " 'The dead shall live, the living die, and Music shall untune the sky.' "

Brandon turned to Ki as Montrose nodded, smiling broadly, and pointed at the screen. "Invite them all."

"All?"

"Yes. With an addition or two of my own."

Ki blinked, his high brow faintly puckered. "I think that's too many to fit comfortably into your hall here—"

"Exactly." Brandon gestured toward the lake. "We'll use the pavilion. But"—his smile showed teeth—"we will make it seem like home."

Montrose rubbed his hands and motioned to Ki. While they talked, Brandon stepped up to Jaim, who expected anything but what came next: "I understand," he said, "you are taking Ivard and the *Telvarna* crew to the splatball tournament. I'd like to tag along."

⁂ ⁂ ⁂

With delicate twists of her tool, Marim finished wiring the underside of the console. "There," she called. "Try that, Ozip."

She waited, contemplating with mild appreciation the shape of Ozip's legs as seen from below, as he tested the console above. Shortly thereafter the legs shifted, and a dark, handsome face with merry eyes appeared upside down. "Up and running green," Ozip said. "We're done!"

"And in plenty of time," Marim said, scrambling out. "Shall I meet you there? I have to change and get my roommate."

Ozip blinked. "Your mysterious Dol'jharian is actually stepping out of that hole? I didn't know Dol'jharians had a taste for splatball—is it violent enough?"

Marim just grinned. *A taste for escape, chatzhead.*

"I can walk partway with you," Ozip offered.

"You live closer; get there ahead and save some good seats," Marim said, shoving her bare feet into her mocs.

Ozip hesitated, then got to his point. "And after?"

Marim laughed, leaning against the console of the ship they were in the midst of repairing. "After comes after!"

Ozip echoed her laugh, not trying to hide his desire. Marim

made a slow business of putting her gear together, waiting until he was gone.

Then she moved quickly, sliding a small chip from a concealed pocket. This she kept pressed against her palm as she hefted her bag of tools and started out. One last admiring glance around the ship, which was a well-designed old Guildenfire, popular among traders. Its unknown owner had taken a terrible beating in some battle; Marim wondered what the story was as she slapped the lockplate, then forgot all about the ship as she sprinted down the tube to the relay desk.

A tired-looking young Navy midshipman logged her in. Her heart sped up: this was her boy.

"Long shift," Marim said agreeably. "But we seem to be getting somewhere."

"Until we get another fleet of refugees," the midshipman answered, sitting back. He seemed glad to be distracted.

"More refugees?" Marim asked. "Where'll they put 'em? No more room in the oneill; and up here, D-5's already crammed to the max, and they just doubled up all those 'dwellers from Cincinnatus in D-4—"

"I don't know," the young man said, fighting a yawn. "I hear they're thinking of opening up a couple of areas in the oneill and shifting over to hydroponics for some of the crops. But for now, they'll just jam them somewhere in the Cap."

She leaned against his console. "Going to the tourney?"

"Not off duty until twenty-two hundred," came the reply. Another yawn, which he tried to suppress until his eyes watered, then he smiled apologetically. "Four on, four off, until further notice. But at least it's getting our ships finished."

"Someone said that the *Grozniy*'s almost ready." Marim leaned over his console, grinning.

The midshipman grinned back. "Sure is. I'm *Grozniy*—we're moving back on board tomorrow. Not too soon! You *know* it's crowded when shipboard seems spacious."

"Poor blits," Marim said, watching his eyes track quickly down her body, then away. "Too bad you can't go to the tourney. Everyone is going to be there. Civ, Navy—even us Rifters!"

He looked wistful. "They were all talking about it in the barracks. But once we get *Grozniy* back, maybe we can host one."

"That'd be fun." She yawned and stretched her arms over

her head, feeling her suit mold against her flesh. "Think they'll have this one on the net?"

"Probably." He sounded distracted. "But when we're on duty—"

"Blunge!" she cried as her bag of tools spilled across his console, bounced off his lap, and clunked unmusically on the floor about his feet. She made a futile dive, one of her breasts pressing inadvertently against his nose.

The midshipman jerked back, a crimson tide suffusing his neck. "Here. I'll get them," he said, ducking hastily down.

"Oh, dear, how disgusting," Marim crooned. "I'm *sooo* tired, I just don't *know* what I'm doing anymore. . . . You're so nice. . . ." She went on in this manner as her fingers moved swiftly over his keypads: first killing audio, then entering a code. Last she slid her chip in, hit the execute-program key, then with one hand pulled it out as the other retoggled the audio—just as the youth began to straighten up, both fists full of tools.

She held out her bag to receive her tools. "I must be more tired than I thought," she said, smiling directly into his eyes. "I'm *so* sorry."

"I think we're all tired," he said. "No trouble."

She waved jauntily, slinging her bag over her shoulder. "See you!" And she left, holding her breath.

Vi'ya seemed to have pulled it off again: no alarm rang, no shouts chased her. When Marim reached the transtube, she leaned against the wall, dizzy with relief, and with laughter. If she were caught, it would mean death—unless, of course, she could lie or cheat her way out.

Which was a challenge with its own attractions. But for now she'd stay strictly on the path Vi'ya had outlined, for with Vi'ya, Marim knew, lay real escape. Marim couldn't get off this chatzing station on her own.

She reached Detention Five and greeted the bored guard by name, winning back an answering smile but no relaxation of vigilance. This, too, she'd noted: on Rifthaven, one could often get past watchflash by money or other methods. These nick Marines seemed—so far—hard to get around.

Leave that, too, to Vi'ya. She was in a thoughtful mood when she hit the doorpad and found Vi'ya, as always, hard at work.

"Did it!" she announced, posing.

Vi'ya did not even look up. "I know."

Marim sighed. "Oh. Well, of course: you're now into the system. I guess you *would* know. But—"

Vi'ya looked up, her mouth smiling faintly but her black eyes steady. "Well done, Marim."

Marim evaded that stone-cold gaze and draped herself across the back of a chair, which tried unsuccessfully to mold itself to her weight, then gave up with a disaffected whine. "Ozip said he'd save us space at the tourney. When's Jaim due?"

"He's overdue," Vi'ya said. "But he will be here."

Marim sighed, straightening up. "I wish you'd reconsider. I don't mind jetting Montrose, but I like Jaim, and Telos knows he'd get the fiveskip up and running a lot faster than I will working alone."

"No. He is to know nothing of our plans. Not even a hint."

Marim winced. Lokri was beyond their reach, and though Ivard might be brought in at the last moment, he was more a liability than not. Marim had always found the tall, somber-faced drivetech attractive, but he'd been mated with Reth Silverknife. Now that Reth was dead . . .

Marim got up to go shower and change. *No harm in sounding him out,* she thought.

And a hand gripped her shoulder, not to crush, but with utterly no give. Off balance, Marim staggered. She righted herself and twisted to look up into Vi'ya's face. Her heart bounded. Damn that tempathy! What had she picked up? "I *like* Jaim," she protested.

"So do I," Vi'ya said. "But he stays."

Marim tried once to free herself, and when Vi'ya's grip did not shift or loosen, she crossed her arms. "Then tell me why."

The silence attenuated beyond the length of Marim's nerve. "I've always been a good crew member," she said, hating to have to point it out. That and knowing that Vi'ya could read her real emotions put her in shifting gravity.

"When it suited you," Vi'ya said, her soft voice completely without inflection. "I'll tell you, but I will need a promise from you first," she added.

Marim slid a glance upward into the smooth, impervious face, touched the drilling black eyes. *And you'll know if I lie.* She struggled silently with her desire to know and her unwillingness not to use knowledge that might serve as a weapon.

She tried just once to test the knowledge while sidestepping the question: "You don't want him anymore because he's sworn to be the Arkad's man."

"False," Vi'ya said. And again: "Your promise."

"All right," Marim said flatly, letting Vi'ya feel her annoyance. Not, of course, that it would matter a whit. Dol'jharians, she'd figured long ago, didn't have emotions. They occasionally had appetites: for blood, for rape, for power. Luckily Dol'jharians were rare outside their own planet, and if they weren't allies, you left them strictly alone. "No hints, no word to Jaim. But why?"

"Because he has a telltale in him, and the nicks hear every word that he does," Vi'ya said calmly.

Marim stared. "Sanctus Hicura," she breathed. And then her thoughts splintered; fear propelling her backward through memory, trying to recover what she might have said in Jaim's hearing, and curiosity verging on outright laughter considering what this might mean now—or in the future.

She hiccuped on a laugh. "Did he tell you?"

"He does not know," was the dispassionate reply.

Marim gasped. "But . . . the Arkad—does he know?"

"Of course not." Now Vi'ya sounded slightly impatient.

"But—then—how do *you* know?"

Vi'ya released her shoulder at last, and Marim flopped into the chair.

"Because within an hour of our conversation about the hyperwave, the Eya'a heard the word passing along among the Arkad's watchbeasts." Vi'ya's smile was grim.

Marim's mouth dropped open. Shock quickly gave way to anger. "But . . . but . . . if you knew he was monitored—why, we could have *all* been locked away."

"It was a risk," Vi'ya said calmly, "but I figured they would prefer to keep Jaim's monitor secret. This is why I was so very clear about our keeping our knowledge secret."

Marim shook her head, thoroughly unsettled by a power play that she hadn't known about—yet had come too close to involving her. "How did you know about the monitor in the first place?"

"Markham," Vi'ya said. "How do you think he and the Arkad were betrayed, those years ago in their Naval Academy? Markham put it together with certain things he was told just before the nicks exiled him. That bodyguard, the one who died on Dis, carried the telltale in him, and everything he witnessed was eventually heard by the brother on Narbon. I thought they would be using the same methods, perhaps for different reasons, against the Arkad now."

Fascinated by all the implications, Marim gave in at last to laughter. "So . . . any plots poor old Brandon tries . . . or even when he bunnies?"

Vi'ya shrugged faintly. "If Jaim is there."

Marim got up slowly, still snickering at vivid mental images of secret depravities and passions. Her active instinct for self-preservation was still at work; she whirled around. "What if they find out how the Eya'a spy for you? That old blit—"

"They know." Vi'ya nodded once. "It was inevitable that Manderian would find out. Did you notice how much more frequently the Eya'a are going into hibernation? The nicks have mindblurs set up in their command areas now."

"So it's a trade off." Marim whistled, her mind veering back to Brandon's situation. "So *anything* the Arkad does . . ."

"The Arkad," Vi'ya said, "can look to his own problems. Jaim is observant: conceal your reactions, for he will be here s—"

The annunciator interrupted her.

Marim gulped, slapping her hand across her face. "I'm for the shower," she whispered, choking down laughter. "When I come out I'll be fine—I promise."

Vi'ya smiled a little then. "Hurry. I want to see the concourse before it gets too crowded."

Marim took just long enough to get control of her imagination. She had little interest in hypothetical hyperwaves. What consumed her imagination was the news about Jaim's telltale. The problem, she thought as she faced into the streaming water, was that she found the Arkad even more attractive than she found Jaim. Purely for personal entertainment, she decided she'd have to find out what—if anything—the Arkad was doing with his time.

But not when Vi'ya was around.

When she went out, she was under control. Which was as well, because not just Jaim but the Arkad was along. Ivard had appeared from somewhere and was babbling eagerly, his nose twitching and sniffing like some kind of rodent.

Marim looked past him, to meet Brandon's smiling blue gaze. She grinned at him, but before either could say a word, Vi'ya hit the doorpad. "Let us go."

Mindful of listening ears, Marim stayed silent on the walk. The time it took to get downstairs and to the transtube steadied her; Vi'ya, of course, scarcely spoke at all, and Ivard blathered on about what fun he was having with that crazy old nuller up at the spin axis. Fear was soon replaced by the strong urge to create mischief, but she controlled it (she thought) admirably, only permitting herself to add an interesting variety of adjectival opprobrium to any reference to the Navy or Panarchy.

Obedient to Vi'ya's wishes, she led them the long way down the concourse so that Vi'ya could see for herself the ways to the ships, and the obstacles that would have to be planned for.

When they reached the null-gym the game was already in progress, the huge space echoing to the eponymic impact of the thirty-centimeter balls on the fine repel mesh surrounding the playing area. As yet, very few of the players in the cavernous space had balls adhering to them. The two teams were still maneuvering for position among the jump pads and vector cables that permitted the contestants to change direction in free-fall. The balls stuck only to each other or the uniforms of the players; they were dispensed automatically by machines within the goal spheres of each team. Eventually the arena would be adrift with floating shoals of balls, posing a serious hazard to any player pushed or deflected into them by an opponent.

Marim sneered mentally as they made their way toward some seats near the boundary mesh of the arena, their feet firmly making contact with the floor at one standard gee. It was typical of nicks to balance out the gravitors only inside the arena, leaving the spectators under acceleration. Half the fun of splatball, in her opinion, was having the spectators jetting around in free-fall too, trying for the best vantage point as the focus of the two teams shifted. Sometimes the action outside was even more exciting than the game.

She had decided it might be amusing to just flirt a little with the Arkad, and make those listening ears wish they knew something about Rifter fun. When Ivard saw a friend and dashed off, she was pleased.

But somehow—she wasn't sure how—she and Jaim ended up together, stationed behind the Arkad and Vi'ya. A crowd of enthusiastic spectators separated them: Navy and civilian and noncitizen, packed together in friendly chaos as the cadence of the game accelerated.

The crowd bellowed with delight as a muscular young woman grabbed an opponent in midflight and, pulling him briefly against her body to accelerate their spin through conservation of angular momentum, kissed him mockingly and then whipped him sprawling into a clump of splatballs, converting him into an ungainly lump of mass that spun helplessly up against the boundary mesh.

The young woman blew kisses at the spectators, then grabbed a vector cable and spun around to support her teammates' drive on the opposing team's goal. Her flight took her across the arena in front of Vi'ya and Brandon, the two of them, both of a height, silhouetted against the increasingly frenzied action in the arena.

Marim tried to edge Jaim closer so she could overhear their conversation, but Jaim didn't move, his eyes staying on the entertainment.

So Marim watched. Vi'ya stood very still, her hands behind her back and her face bent toward the arena. Marim could only see the hard edge of her cheekbone and the long fall of glossy black hair.

But she could see the Arkad, the lights playing across his sculpted face, the wide blue eyes intent. What was he talking about so earnestly?

She nudged Jaim. "Does he have lovers?"

"Who?"

"The Arkad."

Jaim's gray eyes were remote. "Ask him," he said.

Marim pursed her lips, studying him: the blank face, the unconscious poise that was not at all characteristic. This was not the old stooped, shambling Jaim, who had deferred to Reth Silverknife in everything and hid his lethal training behind a lazy front. He looked, she realized, like a bodyguard. *He might not count himself a nick, but he is changing. I wonder if he knows it?*

What was he seeing and hearing, living all day with those mask-eyed Douloi? She wouldn't find out, but someone knew. The change in her perspective was dizzying.

She chewed a thumb as she went back to watching Vi'ya and the Arkad. Something had happened in the brief time she'd looked away. Vi'ya's stance had not changed, but Brandon had stepped closer, and he gestured once, the tendons in one long hand highlighted by a pouring of golden light from the arena.

His face was the same as always: smiling, open, tolerant, but the intensity was still there, in the half-lifted hand, and in compressed breathing.

He was waiting for something, but Marim could not see what it was, and finally she gave up, and sank back, watching the splatball players. A rasping honk filled the null-gym as the young woman who'd so competently disposed of her opponent speared the goal with her outstretched fist.

When Marim looked again, the Arkad was lounging gracefully against a chair, talking to a small circle of naval officers, who, from their attitudes, seemed to know him.

From his days at the nick Academy, she thought, regarding the Arkad with renewed interest. She'd never seen him among friends before; it was astonishing how much he reminded her of Markham, yet they had not looked even remotely alike.

She felt the urge to comment, then realized Jaim was gone from her side. Standing on tiptoe, she spotted him just behind the Arkad, stolid as stone, just like a bodyguard.

Marim realized Vi'ya had vanished—and a moment later a soft voice said at her shoulder: "Let us go."

Marim held her tongue all the way back.

Inside their suite, she flung her arms wide. "So?"

Vi'ya turned, unsmiling. Her stance was a warning, but Marim, crazy with frustrated conjecture, almost yelled: "If you don't tell me what the Arkad was on about, I'll . . ."

Vi'ya was still a long, sickening moment, then shrugged faintly. "Escape," she said. "He offered me anything I wanted if I'd get him off this station and take him to Gehenna."

Marim breathed out, sagging like a collapsed bellows. "*Damn* that logos-chatzing telltale," she groaned. "Can you imagine the money we just lost? Not, of course, that we'd actually do something as idiotic as go to Gehenna, but . . ."

Vi'ya went to her room and shut the door.

Marim turned to the wall and slammed her fist against it repeatedly in slow motion, leaning forward until the cool dyplast stopped her forehead. As far as craziness went, she decided, there was little to choose from between nicks and Dol'jharians.

They deserve each other, she thought as she pushed away from the wall; then shrugged. There wasn't anything she could do. Maybe Ozip was still free. That was one way to stop thinking about what you couldn't change.

THIRTEEN

"I learned skepticism from you Panarchists," Anaris said. "I experienced the spectrum of passion without the relative safety of rage as motivation. I learned to laugh."

"Yet?" the Panarch prompted.

"Yet there remain two concepts, both of which I observed with interest, without divining their purpose. The first was your custom of marriage."

"That is simple enough to explain," Gelasaar said. "It is a custom retained from the days of Lost Earth. It provides a venue for continuity both materially and genealogically, for those families who desire it. It has a stabilizing influence on the social fabric."

"Yet you yourself stepped outside of the conventions when you made your own marriage: your wife was from an obscure family who—at least on record—refused closer involvement with your network of social alliances. Yet I found that your marriage included vows of monogamy."

"All true," the Panarch said. "And the exchange of rings, both of which are very old customs from Lost Earth." He held up his hands, and on the ring finger of each could be seen

pinkish worn skin: one from his wedding ring, and the other from his personal signet.

"So you did not, in fact, make an alliance for the good of society in general."

"No, I chose to please myself."

"Why a marriage, then, if there was no advantage to your social infrastructure? Why not a mate match, as is common at all levels in your society?"

The Panarch's eyes lifted contemplatively, then he said, "If you had known Ilara, you would not need to ask. In your researches, did you discover any criticism of my choice of Kyriarch?"

"No," Anaris said, his dirazh'u lying quiescent in his hands.

The Panarch inclined his head. "It is not completely true to say that I chose to please myself. I hoped that some measure of her brilliance would invest our offspring."

"And?" Anaris asked, amused.

"And there was nothing of her in my oldest son, who is a mirror for my grandfather. There was too much of my reclusiveness in my second son, leaving room only for Ilara's humor, her acute sensitivity to the arts. But in Brandon"—he lifted his hands—"the one who never really knew her, the best of us both is blended."

* * *

Vannis moved across the spectacular backdrop of stars, the hush of her silken skirts as soft as vapor. She leaned on the balustrade. To either side of her a white-capped expanse of water spilled over an invisible edge, disappearing into the infinite void below. The room appeared open to space; the circular black couch, sunk into the floor between two streams of running water with the tianqi generating a salt-tinged ruffling breeze, created the fantasy of a boat sailing under the stars at the edge of the ancients' flat world-disc. She watched with distracted pleasure the aesthetic advantage of the gown she'd chosen—how the reflected starlight runneled down the intricate silver embroidery over her shoulder, around wrists, along hem.

Spiritually reinforced, she looked down into the circle and listened.

On the surface, this was merely a dinner for friends, but Tau Srivashti never exerted himself to entertain unless it was to a purpose. The location, a central room on the yacht seldom seen by any but Tau's intimates, increased its importance: only here could he feel certain of not being overheard, not even by his own staff.

"There's very little to tell you about his visit," Tau said, his husky voice mild. "The Aerenarch is an intriguing young man. Very pleasant, really. His manner reminds one occasionally of his mother." He gestured. "Joking with the hands."

Tau's tense. No, he's angry, Vannis thought. *I wonder what he asked for? Whatever it was, he did not get it.*

"I think the Aerenarch's attractive." Fierin smiled, toying with Tau's fingers.

"A cogent reminder," Tau said, lifting her palms up to kiss them, one then the other. "Even those without tangible ambition can charm followers when they choose."

Amusement flickered through Vannis at Tau's rare show of weakness. Did he really see subtlety in Fierin's callow statement? *Is he smitten, then?* His relationships were usually chosen with some political end in view, but Fierin vlith-Kendrian had no political clout whatever. Superficial but not stupid, Vannis had decided on meeting her; at first it had seemed foolish for Fierin not to take over her family's title and assume legal custody of their considerable holdings. After observation, Vannis had come to the conclusion that Fierin knew very well what she was doing—she got a great deal further on the sympathy engendered by her unorthodox handling of her faintly sordid past.

It amused Vannis that Tau should exhibit a sentimental streak at this late date. Unless, of course, there was more to the Kendrian situation than met the eye.

The Harkatsus Aegios spoke for the first time. "He seems remarkably reclusive."

The rider, unspoken, was clear: *despite what one has heard.*

"But he's giving this concert," Fierin said. "I was told that he's managed to get the Kitharee to perform with that consortium from the Akademia Musika. Don't the Kitharee have some religious ban on making music with outsiders? I don't believe they've ever done that before."

"They will this time," Tau said gently. Then he looked round at the others. "I understand that His Highness has recruited the Navy Band as well. And that the program will be music of his choosing."

"Charm indeed," Fierin said, smiling brightly all around.

"It's the title," Kestian Harkatsus put in with a trace of impatience. "Who will gainsay him?"

"The Kitharee could," Tau said. "They forswear loyalties to anyone outside their Jephat when they join. And even an Aerenarch has little authority over the Navy unless commissioned first."

"So he has bestirred himself at last, for purposes of entertainment," Stulafi Y'Talob said. "The question is: has this anything to do with the deadline?" The Archon of Torigan's voice was harsh. "We found out only because we have sources. Would they tell him?"

"We should assume as much," Tau murmured. "As for his entertainment, will you honor me with your forbearance if I invite you to consider the point again?"

Y'Talob bowed a deference, but his heavy face and folded hands conveyed his disdain. "I suppose it is possible he will propose a Privy Council in between concerti and rastanda on the program."

It's how *he did it, fool,* Vannis thought, watching Tau.

Then the old Archonei from Cincinnatus squinted round the faces, her voice cracking, "A successfully arranged concert is not necessarily a sign of leadership ability. However, the timing gives one pause. How many of us know this young man well?"

Gestures of deferential disavowal presaged exchanges of glances, a few of which turned thence toward Vannis.

Vannis knew that her removal from the circle had signified her boredom with the subject. In reality, she did not want Tau's shrewd yellow eyes discerning the truth of her ambivalence.

But the question pulled her in again; she was, they all knew, the only one among them who had lived at the Palace on Arthelion with the then-Krysarch. Vannis shrugged faintly. "We had so little contact," she said, informing her pose with polite regret.

Her manner effectively invoked Semion. The power of the late Aerenarch's memory, and his known opinions, spoke for her. She did not have to explain herself—or risk exposure.

Tau sat back, his countenance benign. "Semion vlith-Arkad was a strong leader, and in the normal course of events would have been a strong Panarch. It is to be expected that an heir twice removed would find it difficult to learn, in days, the vision necessary to one who assumes authority. The new Aerenarch needs allies who are lessoned in command."

Vannis' heart thumped her ribs, then raced. *This is it.*

The Archonei pursed her lips and rattled the iced liquid in her glass. "He talks of the Panarch and the rescue."

"His heart is there, with his father." That whisper came from Hesthar al-Gessinav, the sinister woman who was praecentor of the Alannat Infonetics Comb at the heart of the Rouge Nord octant. "But one does not govern trillions of people with one's heart."

"Guidance." Tau's hands opened. "Can we agree?"

"I'd like to help," Fierin said, bright appeal in her face. "I'll make friends with him, or try, if he'll have me."

Tau touched her hand, almost a pat, as the others exchanged murmurs of assent. It served as a kind of signal; they rose and moved to the outer room, where Felton stood, patiently awaiting them, in order to serve the meal.

Tau's eyes reached Vannis over the heads of the others. He paused, his question unspoken. For a moment they seemed alone, just the two of them in Tau's private room, and Vannis felt the force of his will.

Coldness gripped her insides, though long years of self-command maintained her surface attitude of repose. The seeds of a new government were to be sown this night, then. And she was to be a part of it.

Triumph and ambition realized blocked the image of a blue-eyed face. She smiled back, stepped down off the little bridge, and laid her fingers on his arm. "Tell me how I am to help you?"

❋ ❋ ❋

Ivard altered his walk so that his footfalls were soundless, the better to listen to the lisping step of the Eya'a.

They all stopped, and the Eya'a's faceted indigo eyes lifted upward. Then both heads turned to Ivard, in unison as always, and the hands shaped the semaphores Manderian had taught them: *We hear the pain-maker. We will not go near.*

He'd lived aboard the same ship as the Eya'a for some time, but until Manderian gave them the hand signs to communicate with, they'd always been utterly opaque to him. They still were reluctant to use the semaphores with any humans they did not know. The Eya'a seemed to like following Ivard around, practicing their hand signs.

Sometimes he could even hear their thoughts, but most of the time that was only when he was with the Kelly. The Archon's genome in him brought the whispering voices and multiple images only when the Eya'a were under great stress.

A flicker of memory, the blood-smeared cabin walls and two long bodies gripped in a struggle that veered between death and passion, made his insides squirm. He shoved that memory away.

The Eya'a turned to him suddenly, keening on a high note: despite their desire to gain proximity to the hyperwave, the mindblurs kept them at a distance. If Ivard concentrated, he could even sense them himself, a faint subsonic whine, slightly unpleasant. He wondered what it was like for the Eya'a. He frowned, concentrating . . .

Weird energies scraped along Ivard's bones. No way to know what they were thinking, so he raised his hands: *We go.*

And the Eya'a mirrored his movement: *We go.*

It was communication, the beginnings, he thought happily as they started the long way home to Detention Five.

What could he distract them with? If they went back they'd probably withdraw into their freezing room and hibernate for days again. Of course, he could look at their weavings. Those were incredible. He didn't know where they even found the microfilaments they put together in fascinating patterns; they probably pulled them out of regular stuff, he thought, glancing at the needly ends of their twisty long fingers.

Five fingers. They had five fingers, just like humans. He contemplated that in wonder. Were they somehow connected with humans, then? Might they be evidence that the first wave of humans through the Vortex were sent way, *way* back in time?

Now he wanted to get at the computer and look at a history chip again, about humans leaving Lost Earth, and how the Vortex had acted to spread them out across time as well as space. He'd talked to Manderian about that, and the old Dol'jharian had said that his people were almost certainly from that first wave, somehow propelled back through time as they hurtled the distance toward the heavy, terrible planet they eventually settled on.

Ivard thought about Manderian and again wondered why Vi'ya didn't like talking to him. Wouldn't she be glad to find another person who spoke her language? Especially one who didn't do all the rotten things she'd escaped Dol'jhar to get away from?

Ivard liked Manderian, and he enjoyed talking to Tate Kaga. The old nuller had shown him things that echoed the strangeness Ivard found on Desrien. And even more he loved the Kelly. They told him things that others did not know, could not smell, or hear or see. Including thoughts, which they somehow heard from the Eya'a.

Thoughts not spoken in his presence. Like Vi'ya's escape plan. Reminded, he felt chilled again.

He thought about Vi'ya as he and the Eya'a entered the transtube. His first memory of her was just this tall, dark figure standing silently with light-haired Markham. She was different in those days; he remembered how she used to laugh, how it changed her face so suddenly. No sound, just the brilliant smile, the dark-fringed eyes catching light from somewhere.

She never laughed anymore.

Remembering that she was planning escape made him feel slightly sick inside. He could take care of himself—Greywing had seen to that—but it hurt that she and Marim had these secret plans, and they hadn't told him. *Don't they trust me?*

He could hear Lokri's sarcastic laughter echoing in his mind. He'd overheard Greywing and Lokri arguing about trust, just once. Lokri had scorned Ivard's sister for even using such a word. She'd never brought it up in Lokri's presence again, but she certainly had with Ivard.

You find a captain you can trust, and you act trustworthy, and you'll live longer, she'd told Ivard. *Let Lokri laugh. He'll never pilot his own ship even if he stays with the Dis gang his whole life. You watch.*

Though Greywing herself had not lived very long after she said that, the part about trust seemed to be true. After the Arthelion raid, the talk had been about using some of the loot for a third ship for the Dis fleet, and Jaim and Reth Silverknife to run it, and Ivard to run nav and train as backup pilot. Even though Lokri knew piloting at least as well as Jaim or Reth.

Ivard's dream had always been to pilot his own ship—and Vi'ya had seemed to be preparing him for just that.

Not now, though. *She doesn't want any of us anymore, ever since the Arkad came. Why?*

They reached Detention Five, and he followed the Eya'a, who raced up to their cabins. He knew they'd want to communicate to Vi'ya their distress at the mindblurs hiding access to that hyperwave. He would follow along and see what he could sniff out about these other things.

The Eya'a went straight to Vi'ya's room, and there she was, at the console. As soon as she saw the three of them, she saved her work with a quick gesture. The Eya'a stood near her knees. Vi'ya bowed her head, supporting it with her fingers, as if she had a headache. She did that frequently now, though he didn't remember seeing her do it in the old days.

Abruptly the Eya'a turned and went into their own room. Ivard briefly heard the hum of the refrigeration unit as the door opened and closed.

Then Vi'ya looked up at Ivard. Her eyes were marked with tiredness, and there was a trace of something in her expression that made him stumble into speech: "Jaim says that the whole crew—except Lokri—is going to the Arkad's concert. You gotta come."

Vi'ya didn't smile, but that look eased a little. "Montrose was just here. Rather than cause comment, I will go with you."

"Why don't you want to?" Ivard asked carefully. "You always liked music when we played it, when Markham was captain."

"Possibly this nick music will not be as good as ours was."

Caught by surprise, Ivard laughed. *She hasn't made jokes since the old days, either,* he realized.

Her eyes narrowed suddenly, and she touched the console. Behind Ivard the door closed. "You must remember," she said, "that when you walk with the Eya'a, they hear all your thoughts. Even the ones you thought were private."

Ivard felt his face burn. "All right. I know you and Marim are working out some kind of escape plan. Why won't you take me?"

"Do you really wish to go?" she countered.

He opened his mouth to say *Of course* but then he considered leaving the Kelly, Tate Kaga, and his new friends—which brought to mind another thing that had bothered him. His attention splintered for a moment, causing the Archon's genome to fill his mind with vivid imagery. He was learning to cope with it, though; with an effort he found his way back to the issues at hand and said, "I guess I'd like to have the choice."

"Fair enough." She gave a nod. "But it would be best not to

mention knowledge of these things to Marim until the time comes."

He felt that betraying heat in his cheeks again. By now he'd figured out that Marim'd only taken him as a lover in order to get her fingers on his part of the Arthelion loot. He'd been severely tempted to say something about that, like to the woman Marim was seeing now. But he hadn't: Greywing had told him over and over, long before he had any interest in sex, that lust had no permanence, and certainly no loyalty, and that if he expected nothing he wouldn't be disappointed.

And to be fair, Marim tried to tell me too, in her own way, he thought, studying his hands. Then he looked up, to find Vi'ya waiting. It was possible she was hearing some of his thoughts even now, through the Eya'a, which was kind of sickening. Except she had never once used anyone's insides against them.

"I'll be mum," he said.

"Very well." Her expression eased a fraction more.

Now the earlier problem resurfaced, and he blurted: "Is a Regency Council bad?"

Vi'ya was very still, a slight frown in her eyes. "What?"

"A nick thing," Ivard said. "I looked it up in the chips, and it just says it's a 'governing body advising a ruler during his or her minority,' which sounds like nothing. But this blit Dandenus—"

"Say nothing to no one," Vi'ya said.

Ivard stared at her. "Then it is bad. But why? And shouldn't we tell the Arkad? The Kelly—they read it in Dandenus, who sneaked on a boz from his father—said it's a secret against him."

"Then let the Kelly talk." Her smile was wintry.

"They won't. Said they will not meddle in human affairs."

"They are wise," she returned. "The Arkad can take care of himself. Or his many guardians can do it for him. But you have no guardians, and to these nicks politics is not a game, it's a death hunt. Promise me you will say nothing to the Arkad."

"Can I tell Jaim?"

"No." She hesitated, then said: "It would place him in danger."

"Blunge." Ivard sighed. Maybe Vi'ya could hear his thoughts, but she did care what happened to him—or she wouldn't have warned him about the nick thing. "I promise," he said.

She gestured, and he stepped closer to her console. "Here is the beginning of my plan," she said.

⁂ ⁂ ⁂

Anton Faseult stepped forward in line, and listened, with a private wince, to the Masaud boy's badly mumbled congratulations. Hating to feel someone's humiliation, he looked away, focusing on the murmur of chat around him.

The boy lunged in an awkward bow, his furtive gaze on his mother's rigid smile making it clear he knew how badly he'd done.

Then he stumbled away, and Anton saw relief in the faces of Besthan nyr-Haesterfeldt and her spouse, the Aegios Colm Yskandir, standing at either side of their brand-new baby.

Faseult's tongue provided with automatic ease the pleasant words of Name Day Ritual; his eyes assessed the couple, both of whom seemed proud of the small scrap of humanity lying on its velvet bedding, utterly insensible to its surroundings.

He bowed; they bowed; he moved on, to join his escort. "She nearly lost that baby," Cath Y'Mandev murmured. "Started the birth process while in transit."

Anton hid a wince. The mysteries of family propagation were beyond him; he'd always been glad that Tanri held the heirship.

Except. A pang of grief seized him, and disbelief that Tanri could really be dead. But it had to be true. The Aerenarch himself had traveled light-years to give him Tanri's ring, and Anton had seen corroboration in Sebastian Omilov's eyes when they'd met at a party: Tanri was dead and his dying could not have been easy. *I wonder if Bikara is still alive,* he thought. But he wouldn't ask Omilov. The fact that the information was not volunteered meant that Sebastian did know—and that this news, as well, was not good. *If she died, I hope at least they were together.*

Faseult made his way to the refreshment table, and the ring seemed to drag on his hand, an unfamiliar weight. There was no heir beyond Anton, so either the ancient Faseult line died out or else Anton took up a duty he'd thought would never be his.

He looked back at the little family. What drew his attention was not newborn Ilara, but the involvement of the man and woman, indicating more than just a marriage contract between them.

He shifted his gaze away to his companion, who hovered over a choice between some strange-looking pastries and a creamed something. She'd been happily mated with a colleague for decades, but she loved socializing as much as Enre Y'Mandev despised it. She served often as escort to various members of Nyberg's staff when an escort was needed.

"Try these, Anton. Besthan's cook knows some of the Golgol tricks with pastry."

"Mmmm," he said, piling a few things onto a plate.

Cath grinned with her customary good humor, then tipped her head. "Now that the receiving line is done, I'm going to catch up with Besthan. She's been out of circulation since the birth."

Faseult watched her make her way between the guests. Then, shoving away thoughts of his personal life, he turned his mind to duty and started circulating, grimly focusing on each conversation he passed.

Very soon he ascertained that the general chat was nothing that required official attention—in fact, any kind of attention at all—so he stood in the background and watched. It was somewhat of a relief to note that Haesterfeldt and Yskandir did not seem to command the presence of the cruiserweights in the social arena. The highest rank present was Charidhe Masaud, and it was easy to see why she had condescended to attend a party with so many dowdy folk present: she was trying to force young Geof Masaud to gain a little polish. But it was equally obvious that Geof's worst enemy was not his clumsy body and preternatural sensitivity so much as his mother's angry hovering. Almost anything the boy did earned a dark look or a hissed reproof.

Before long, Geof had retreated to the far end of the room, half-hidden by a bank of nodding blooms, his untouched plate lying in his lap. His mother held pride of place near the hostess and led the conversation, punctuating it with titters of angry laughter.

But then the steward appeared at the door and announced in a deadpan voice that did not hide his disbelief: "His Highness the Aerenarch."

Exclamations were almost smothered by the rustle of costly

materials as everyone rose; Faseult almost dropped his plate. Though he was certain Brandon was invited to every single party on Ares, no one had expected him to show up at this one.

But there he was, dressed for the role in indigo and silver, apparently unaware of the sudden heightening of energy in the little room. His reason for coming was soon apparent; the genuine delight in Besthan Haesterfeldt's eyes reminded Anton that the woman had been a friend of the Kyriarch's.

But once his respects were paid, he did not leave, as might someone with a lesser title. He looked about, greeted several by name, and sat down with a drink in hand.

"We were talking," Charidhe Masaud said, "of the new historical play by Elisa Benet; we were agreed that though court tastes might find it backward, those of us used to frontier entertainments found it well worth attending."

Several shots there, Faseult thought, entertained despite himself. He liked young Brandon, and he did not like any of the Masauds he'd met.

But Brandon seemed impervious to veiled insult. He said agreeably, "The part that made me laugh was the young lady's description of the dream-demon, and the eavesdropping prince thinking it a description of himself."

Murmurs of appreciation sounded round the circle, and they dissected the play enthusiastically, laying its strengths and weaknesses out as a target for frequently barbed wit. After a brief bombardment of innuendo from Charidhe aimed at Brandon (who defused the attack by agreeing with everything she said) the conversation ranged to whom in court circles Benet was digging her quill into.

Midway into this discussion Brandon rose and made his way at a leisurely pace to the refreshment table. Faseult watched, at first with idle interest, how he paused to exchange brief words with everyone.

The general conversation had switched to the latest names in kinetic art when Brandon finished loading a plate, but instead of making his way back to the favored side of the room, he chose a bench a meter away from Geof Masaud.

Every room had its central point, but if the highest in rank did not choose that prerogative, it often unhinged conversation.

Not at once. Charidhe Masaud had gripped leadership again, delivering a stinging opinion of the fall in public taste as more and more people favored holographic accompaniments to music. Defenders and attackers spoke up; more than one glance was sent Brandon's way, but he had fallen into converse with Geof.

Faseult gulped down his last pastry, and with his empty plate as his shield, made his way to the table. As he stood poring over the cakes, he heard an adolescent snicker, followed by Brandon's voice: "No, we really did use the mechwaiters."

Faseult took a step nearer. Brandon went on. "Picture this. The Tarkans in their servo-armor . . ." He mimed heavy mechanized steps. "The mechs load up . . . clang . . . whizz . . . splat! A helmet full of glop that none of the gauntlet gear can remove. Two of them move blindly toward each other, and . . ." He pinched a pastry, causing filling to squirt out.

Geof snickered again. "That's the way the Rifter told it, at the f-free-fall gym," he stuttered. "Some s-said he made it up."

"Truth," Brandon said, hand high.

"I heard that story." It was another youngster, a tall weedy girl who'd sat on the fringes at the other end of the room. "But"—she looked serious—"did you really let the Rifters loot the Palace Major, Your Highness?"

"Only the Ivory Antechamber," Brandon said. "And every one of those items is cataloged. I'll buy them back someday."

Geof mumbled something.

Brandon laughed. "Yes, my plan exactly. And what better use for Eusabian's treasury?"

Two new voices joined in the laughter from behind Faseult.

"So who else has a good escape story?" Brandon asked, looking up at the little group now gathered.

And Faseult watched as, too gradually for it to be perceived as a social coup, the conversational matrix shifted to center around Brandon and Geof Masaud. Reminiscences—comedic and tragic—gave way to talk of what had been left behind. The exchange was cathartic as Douloi, so adept at hiding, talked frankly of what they had lost.

The subject stayed with material things, but the emotional undertone was loss as well—losses shared, pointing the way to unity. Anton Faseult felt a disturbing tug at his memory, too fleeting to identify. So he watched, and listened, discovering with astonishment that the lumpish Masaud boy harbored a burning desire to pilot. Brandon's sympathy, his subtle encouragement, seemed to go right past the mother, who hovered nearby, her thin cheeks flushed. Was she angry at being supplanted? Or pleased to find her son for once at the center of a social circle?

Perhaps Charidhe herself did not know—for when Brandon left, some little time later, it was on her arm, the boy walking close by his other side, and the last sound was their mingled laughter.

Faseult stayed a while longer, contemplating how all the energy and light seemed to have gone out of the room.

* * *

Though embroiled deeply within the secret plottings of the Regency cabal, still Vannis watched, when she could, the Enclave from the privacy of her house. It seemed that Brandon was seldom at home anymore—but he was right now.

There would be no chance whatever for private converse at any of the increasing number of social gatherings that he now attended, unless Brandon desired it (and she'd watched, amused, Fierin's attempts at the Akbani ball the night before).

Indeed, her own situation was not without its amusing aspects. More and more frequently since they all found themselves thrown together in this nightmarish proximity, she felt she was acting out her part in a farce. That everyone else seemed to believe that the old realities still ruled them, and that their actions would have permanent meaning, amused her even more.

She could right now be queening it over yet another social gathering, with everyone desperately observing the minutiae of court etiquette, but instead she raced back here to spy on someone she'd regarded mere weeks ago as beneath contempt.

She considered her ambivalence, intrigued by the endless possibilities. *The first order will be for the Fleet to stay here, to gather for an attack, and to go into official mourning for the Panarch. Brandon has made only one wish clear: that he wants to rescue his father.*

Yet he had done nothing about it. Was he then as politically naive as Vannis had been when she first came to Court?

Her thoughts splintered when she caught a glimpse of somebody emerging from the transtube access near the Enclave.

"Omilov," she murmured, recognizing the straight back and the big ears. What business had a mere lieutenant with Brandon? Osri Omilov had been there twice in as many days.

Of course he'd been on the Rifter escape vessel along with

Brandon; some had tried, without success, to milk him for information and for connections. But if Omilov knew anything about the mystery of Brandon's escape from the Enkainion holocaust, he wouldn't talk, and he never attended any but the most general functions—and then he stood with the Navy brass.

She slapped her enhancer into its case and opened the garden door. Time to think.

She looked down at the path and saw her hands clutching at her elbows. Truth was, under the pose of amusement, there was fear.

Damn Tau, anyway, for telling her the manner of Semion's death. The headless figure of a man haunted her dreams now. Besthan, who pursued interests in arcanities such as dream symbolism, told her it signified the headless government, which was partly true.

But Vannis knew her feelings were more complex than that: much as she had detested Semion, she would welcome him back now. What they desperately needed was someone who wielded power, who could command ships to go this way and that, defeat the Dol'jharian devils, and restore life to normal—*restore me to my old position.*

Except she had grown beyond mere social ambitions; they held no real power. What she wanted was access to true power, the political arena.

But even if we manage to reestablish ourselves . . .

Things still wouldn't be normal, and that was her worst fear. Before Santos Daimonaskos walked out of a lock into space on hearing from Hesthar al-Gessinav that his metals refinery in the middle space of the Konigvalt system had been blown apart by Rifters acting for Eusabian of Dol'jhar, Vannis had not thought about the second, bloodless war that had been triggered by the first: the economic one. Hesthar undoubtedly had clever agents in place, who would protect those of her interests not destroyed by the enemy fleet, but some people had come to realize that even if their homes might not be touched, their industries might. And the Panarchy, when restored, would do nothing to help them.

Did Brandon know all of this? Ought she to tell him?

On impulse she touched her boswell and sent a message to Brandon, who was, after all, within range.

The irony of that required contemplation; she didn't realize she'd sat down on a bench and was staring sightlessly into a stream until the neural bloom behind her eyes startled her.

(Brandon?)

(You bozzed me?) She could hear laughter hoving behind his words.

She forced a matching tone, knew it would come through acid-tinged: *(Forgive me: Danaerik brooking over the ruins. It was an impulse, a need for converse free of the bindings of Court.)*

It didn't matter, she told herself, what he said, this do-nothing third son of Gelasaar-who-might-still-live, but still her heart rate accelerated and she did not breathe until, after an endless pause, his answer came back.

(Why don't I come over?)

He arrived not long after, and Vannis, having dismissed Yenef on an errand likely to take hours, opened the door herself. She was relieved to see the Marine with him instead of the long-faced Rifter. The Marine's empty eyes were easily ignored; he knew the rules, and stayed unobtrusively at a proper distance. The Rifter with his tinkling Serapisti mourning braids . . . watched.

"Morning, Vannis." Brandon stepped through the garden door.

She smiled and held both hands out, the pose one of deference but her manner inviting—daring—intimacy. Brandon pressed her hands together between his and brought them up to kiss her fingers. Not with Tau's lingering possessiveness, but lightly.

"Something to drink?" Vannis asked. One had to say something while the Marine made his circuit of the room.

"Thanks, no," he said, waiting politely for her to invite him to sit.

Unwanted, an image of Semion crossed her inner vision, so she laid her hand on the door latch. "Let's walk," she said.

Politesse in Semion, and Tau, was a weapon; in Brandon it seemed innate. There was no hint of irony in this wordless gesture of deference. As she led the way outside, she wondered if it was a habit of those in power to use manners as a hiltless knife. *But Gelasaar never did. And Brandon never had any power.*

She reached the little bridge over a tumbling stream. The

sound of the water was soothing. She realized her neck was tight with a stress she could not easily define.

She cast a sidewise glance. She had been near him so seldom; he was taller than she remembered, and the blue gaze, so oblique on the ballroom floor, was acute now.

Thrown into random speech, she waved at the flickering silver fish below. "Are they real or mere holos, do you think?"

His gaze shifted to the stream, and she could think again. But her own focus seemed to sharpen, her observations both subtle and far-reaching: how his lashes, seen just this way, hid the entire iris; the diffuse light outlining the curve of his cheek; his light breathing.

"They're real," he said. "At least, the ones at our side of the lake are. Ducks too." He grinned, a quick, merry grin without a shadow of intent. "Jaim and I sometimes throw bread to 'em. They like it."

"Brandon . . ." His name was out before she thought, but if he noticed the lack of title, he betrayed no sign. She felt her throat tighten. "About the government . . . we cannot live long with chaos," she said quickly.

The oblique look was back, thought how he did it escaped her observations: merely, one moment his face was smiling and boyish, the next smiling and impervious as steel.

But he said nothing, so, with a distracted glance around for the Marine—who was, quite properly, not in sight—she went on, "There are whispers of some kind of intercepted com from the Dol'jharians. I fear there might not be time to rescue your father if something is not done soon." *Will you act? Or must we act for you?*

She realized as she studied his face that she wanted him to act, wanted him to take control. Ambition placed her in Tau's group, but emotion, so ill-defined and difficult to control, wished for them to fail. For Brandon to indicate he would take his rightful place—with her by his side.

Blood sang in her ears; she did not breathe, waiting for him to speak.

Finally he did, in the light voice of the ballroom floor. "I have great faith in our ability to rescue him."

He really believes his father can be rescued—he's a political innocent, she thought, and her dilemma was decided. He could never withstand a Regency. Ambition was satisfied: she would keep silent about the cabal, and let events take their natural course.

Which left the way open for pure emotion.

"I'm sorry," she said. "I—hope he'll be rescued, of course." And turned to face him.

But now that the time had come, she was beset by a different sent of doubt-impelled images: Tau, never consenting to sleep in any bed but his own; the Arkad name; Semion's sneering face.

Premeditation fled into the void; her palms sweated, and tingling kindled in her midriff. "Stay," she said voicelessly.

The shuttered look had not gone from his face, but in the angle of his head, and the one half-lifted hand, there was caution.

"No one need know," she said quickly. "Or if they do, you can cut me dead tomorrow, for I will never ask you again." She reached to pull the jeweled clasp from her hair, which fell down about her shoulders as she opened her hand with a quick gesture. The jewels glittered, then splashed into the stream. "Today, just you and I."

He looked down at the frightened fish, and she read faint regret in his movements, and fighting desolation, she said, "You're not thinking of Semion. . . ."

It was a wild thought, from nowhere, but as soon as she said his name, the quick flicker of Brandon's eyelids told her she had guessed right.

"Though he haunts me everywhere else," she said in a low, quick voice, "there is no ghost in my bedroom. Semion never slept with me. Ever."

Then shock silenced her, for she had told no one that, not even Besthan. Not even—

But he smiled, a sweet smile she had never seen, and took her hand, and his clasp was warm. "Just you and I," he said, and walked inside with her and shut the door.

FOURTEEN

Ng stood in the background, watching with appreciation the polite pas de deux *as Nyberg welcomed the Aerenarch to his office.*

"Thank you for taking the time to visit, Your Highness," the admiral said. "We recently decoded this communication from the Mandala, sent over the hyperwave, and I wondered if you might be able to clarify it."

They turned to the screen, where an unidentified Bori in Dol'jharian service gray appeared. He bowed profoundly to the imager, then said in an obsequious voice, in accented Uni: "Senz lo'Barrodagh, I regret having to report increasing difficulties here with the Tarkan units. The . . . the incidents"—he pronounced the word carefully—"are increasing. And Dektasz Jesserian insists I contact you on behalf of the Avatar's forces. They insist that the Palace is haunted. What are your orders?"

The Aerenarch surprised them all by his sudden laughter.

"You are almost as selfish as your father, Osri," Lady Risiena Ghettierus snarled, her black eyes slitted.

Osri stood silently under the harangue, his mind distracted by a commotion outside on the green. Finding the distraction more welcome than the noise being aimed at him, he tried, at first without success, to identify it.

"He won't answer coms, he won't come visit—now that he's lodged with the highmuck blungekissers. . . ."

Osri felt, and suppressed, an urge to laugh at the description of Eloatri as a blungekisser. Instead, he shifted, angling himself so he could see past his mother's shoulder out the window. The disturbance resolved into the shouts of the young, playing a game.

"Who is that out there?" Lady Risiena interrupted herself, looking impatiently outside. "Disgusting brats! As I was saying, Osri, I've tried again and again to get just the barest modicum of cooperation from your father, and I must add . . ."

Osri stood patiently, mentally reviewing his list of things to be done as he waited for the earliest opportunity to throw down his flag and run.

Belatedly he heard the rise in pitch that indicated question, and he forced his attention back on her. ". . . but of course *you* see him every day!"

Him? *My father.* "Well, yes," Osri said, looking past his mother at his oldest half sister, who lounged on a couch, watching. It was jolting to see a face so like his own on a person he did not know. Pomalythe gazed straight back at him with sulky dislike. He turned back to his mother. "But the truth is, he never has time for anything not directly bearing on the assignment he received from Commander Nyberg." And as Lady Risiena opened her mouth again, he added hastily, "It's classified. And of course," taking a step toward escape, "I have my own duties to keep me busy. . . ."

His mother slapped her hand against the door, the rings hooked through her long nails clattering against the wood. He backed away from them, repelled as always by her proclivity for fashions that ripped and tore.

It brought him near the window, and he looked out again. This time he saw them: a mixture of Douloi and Polloi youths playing some kind of game with hand paddles and darting pods. One of them moved deliberately into view, a short redhead.

Ivard. But the boy looked different somehow.

He motioned to Osri to come out.

Lady Risiena said, "Poma! Tell Kuld to run that rabble off."

"Oh, Mother," Pomalythe whined. "He won't. It's a public green, that's what those Marines said when I tried to get rid of those religious nullwits, with that hellish chanting."

"Osri," Lady Risiena said, showing her teeth. A wink of golden enamel embroidery gleamed off a canine. "You *can* manage to pay attention. You're worse than Sebastian, who . . ."

His mother was now launched onto Osri's rotten upbringing, a topic (he knew) that could consume hours—unless one surrendered and gave her what she wanted. So what did she want?

Gathering his splintering thoughts, he thought back for clues, noticing as he did that Lady Risiena and Pomalythe were gowned as if for a formal garden party. *Did she try to force her way into some titled person's house?*

". . . dreadful old woman who calls herself Numen, but who'd do better in life, I should think, as a doorstop. My legal spouse, and I cannot even exchange so much as a word. . . ."

She's trying to get Father's attention—and has had even less luck than I've had.

". . . even *see* the musicians, much less properly hear them. And you *know* that your sister is musically sensitive, much more than most people on this station, and would in fact have been a master performer had she had the time to take lessons—"

Brandon's concert. Osri glanced overtly at his boswell. "Mother, it desolates me to go, but I have an appointment with the Aerenarch and I will be late if I don't leave at once. While I am there, shall I ask him to include you in his party?"

His mother's mouth opened, showing some very exotic dental art. Behind her, Poma smirked.

Lady Risiena was, if possible, even more frightening when gracious. "Well, dear boy, for such exalted company, even a mother must give way. As for your offer: do. Not, you understand, for myself, but for your sister, who . . ."

A step back, another, a few more assurances that he was serious, and he was out the door, breathing deeply. *Let Brandon handle her. It'll be good practice,* he thought, walking around the side of the game just as Ivard ran flat out toward a knot of players. The pod darted near him, and with a mighty swing of his paddle, he sent it across the sward to tangle in Osri's feet.

He might have recovered his balance, but the velocity carried him over; he fell into a thick shrub, the pod caught under him, its gravitor whining as it tried to rise.

Cursing, Osri pushed aside leafy fronds, hoping none of them would stain his uniform. A small, square hand appeared; he grabbed it, and with surprising strength Ivard pulled him to his feet. Osri opened his mouth to blast the boy, but the words withered when he saw the intent look in Ivard's eyes. This was no longer the half-crazed, sickly youth Osri had seen aboard the *Telvarna*. Even the ugly freckles and pale skin had somehow blended into a more normal pigmentation.

"Promised Vi'ya I wouldn't tell Jaim or the Arkad, because she said it would put them in more danger, but the Kelly overheard someone talking about a Regency Council. You tell them?" The boy raced through the words, the pitch barely audible, as he helped Osri brush leaves and dirt from his uniform.

Osri's head buzzed; he could not return an immediate answer.

With one straight look Ivard picked up his pod and bounded away, launching himself into the game as though nothing had happened.

Osri puzzled over this during the transit to the Enclave. Ought he to mention it—or would he merely be making a fool of himself, to repeat the gossip of a Rifter boy?

Wouldn't Vahn and the others know? Osri finally decided, as he trod up the path to the door, he'd mention it only if it seemed there was an opportunity.

Though Brandon greeted Osri in much his usual manner, Osri sensed his excitement. It surprised him a little, and at first he was inclined to attribute it to the impending concert. It certainly couldn't be the prospect of toughing his way through the Naval Academy exams, which were difficult even for those who had completed their course of study. Though Osri had been sent specifically to administer the tests, he couldn't believe that Brandon was actually going to go through with them.

Brandon was alone; Jaim was nowhere in sight, and Vahn sat in the main room, doing something at one of the consoles.

Osri performed a bow, which Brandon acknowledged absently, and Osri said, "Before we start, I have a favor to ask."

He watched Brandon withdraw behind the mask of politesse, and he hastened into speech: "I should say I feel constrained to ask." Brandon evinced faint interest, and when Osri was done retailing his mother's desire, in the driest, flattest voice he could contrive, it was with a laugh that Brandon agreed.

That would have been the chance to bring up that gossip, but then Brandon said, "Can we get started?"

"I'm ready," Osri replied. *He really does want to take the tests. Why don't I just leave the political gossip to those who earn their pay filtering such stuff?* Relieved, he made a check of Brandon's console. He cleared it, then inserted his chip, calling up the first test.

"These are timed," he said.

"I remember the routine." Brandon's smile was wry as he sat down and flexed his hands.

Why the nerves? Two weeks of review even from a genius does not give one mastery of these courses. Why did he decide on this whim now, here, at Ares?

A sudden regret for ten years of sybaritic sloth would not score well—and there was no place for titles or names on the tests. The Aerenarch's scores would be compared to the scores of the year's cadets, and not just those of the small group of cadets up in the Cap who had taken the same tests the day before.

"Begin," Osri said, moving out of Brandon's field of vision so that he could concentrate.

Osri stood at the garden door looking out, deciding that the better part of wisdom was to dismiss what Ivard had said. What did Vi'ya know about dangers surrounding Brandon—or anyone?

Of course she has those cursed white-furred brainburners reading minds, he thought grimly. *I just hope Nyberg's security forces are watching her.*

A quiet step some meters away brought Osri's attention back. Vahn stood at the inner doorway, out of Brandon's vision. He held two mugs, his eyebrows telegraphing a silent query.

Osri hit his boswell. *(Whatever it is, I'll have some. Thanks.)*

He stepped soundlessly to the doorway.

Vahn handed him a warm mug. The welcome pungency of real coffee met Osri's nostrils, and he breathed deeply before sipping.

"Standard Series?" Vahn murmured, tipping his chin in Brandon's direction.

Does everyone know? Probably. He'd forgotten what an impact the Arkad name had—and just how fast gossip traveled.

A last flicker of uneasiness ran through his mind when he recalled Ivard's words. Should he mention it to Vahn? A horror of overstepping the safety of his bounds into another's kept him silent. Surely Vahn knew whatever was going on as soon as it happened; that was his job.

So he just nodded, and both of them glanced over at Brandon, who was utterly absorbed in what he was doing. Osri suspected he wouldn't notice if a bomb went off right under his chair.

"Heard it's a tough one," Vahn said.

Osri nodded. "I can attest to that."

Vahn hefted his own coffee. "Here's to his success."

Was there an edge to the man's voice? Osri considered Vahn, whose face was utterly bland as he turned away and retreated back down the hall.

With a mental shrug, Osri moved to one of the side consoles, brought it to life. It was time to see to his own job, he thought, and slotted one of his personal chips in.

The time passed swiftly. While Brandon silently took test after test, Osri scanned the assigned work of one of his classes, and got three responsive lectures roughed out.

The Aerenarch never spoke once, not even to ask a question. At the end, he got up from the console and moved straight to the dumbwaiter. As he drank down some dark liquid, Osri shut down his work and retrieved the test chip. "I'll send your standing in the mail," he said. "It won't take long."

"Thanks." Strain shadowed Brandon's eyes, and once again Osri wondered why he had put himself through this.

Hopefully he won't humiliate himself with a total failure, but even if he managed to do a creditable job, where will it get him? There is no possibility Nyberg would commission him now.

* * *

Up in the Cap, Osri was surprised to find a number of senior officers in the wardroom. A party atmosphere prevailed, but as soon as he walked in, conversation stopped, and he knew why they were gathered.

Captain Ng got up from her chair and held out her hand. "I've been officially appointed stand-in for Y'Mandev. Not even an Aerenarch could keep him from the rack," she said.

A ripple of laughter went around the room, but it did not abate the air of expectancy.

Ng cast a wry glance at the other officers, then motioned for Osri to go into the console cubicle adjacent to the wardroom. In silence Osri stood at the back while Ng started up the console. She keyed in the codes for the test evaluations, then took the chip from Osri.

The evaluation did not take long. Quite properly Osri waited at the back, out of sight of the screen. Instead, he watched Ng's face, his heart rate unaccountably accelerating. The woman's fine brows arched and her lips pursed. Some of the silky short hair swung forward, hiding her eyes. She reached for a printout and scanned the sheets as they came out.

"Well," she said at last. "Well, well, well." She looked up at Osri and held out the top sheet.

Osri took it, his eyes moving so rapidly over the page, he had to go back and start again. The scores were high, the top percentile in every field.

"He ranks second for the year, Omilov," Ng said. "Not just our group here on Ares, but for the Academy—three tenths of a point behind Tessa Chang." Osri remembered the exceptionally gifted midshipman who had been commissioned very young—and who had died aboard the *Korion.*

And he could not hide his astonishment. He flipped through the pages, looking through Brandon's work. Even at a glance he could see elegant solutions to justly infamous problems in the math section, and as for the tactical section, it was obvious he had not just gotten lucky; he had drawn on a vast store of knowledge.

Finally he looked up at Ng, who sat on the edge of a chair, her smile acid. "I wondered," she said, "when he took to the new Tenno glyphs as if Warrigal had trained him. He's got talent—probably a lot more than his brother ever had."

"He must, if he could master all this in two weeks!"

Ng laughed. "He's talented, but not a computer."

"I don't understand."

A slim finger tapped the flimsies. "What this shows, incontestably, is that—somehow—during those ten years of peaceful social pursuits he never stopped his studies."

Which must have been damned difficult, watched as he was by Semion, Osri thought. And—slowly—the implications started settling in.

That Brandon, after all, had had a goal. Had pursued it without pause, without discussing it with any living soul.

And then the night of his Enkainion, when he was to step into the political arena as a player, he threw it all away and disappeared.

Why?

Osri looked up to meet Ng's knowledgeable eyes. "This is classified," she said. "Until Nyberg decides what to release, and when. And how."

"But I promised him a notification, by mail. . . ."

Ng shrugged, smiling. "You have a social engagement to prepare for. And he has one to host. This will wait."

Osri thought of his mother and winced. "But I'll be right with him, the entire evening."

Ng dropped the flimsies into the disposer and stored the files under a high-level code. "My opinion of that young man has undergone some serious revision in the last few days, and will again, I suspect," she said slowly. "But I'll hazard a guess on this much: he won't ask you. He might not even remember it." She took the chip out and pocketed it.

"What do you mean by that?" Osri asked. "Sir."

Ng shook her head. "Go. Watch. Listen to his music. I have an idea he's giving us a message, in the way he's most adept. A message, or a warning."

She turned and went out.

Osri followed, not hearing the questions and comments of the other officers. Ng stayed and fielded the comments; the last thing Osri was aware of was her laugh, high and silvery.

He glanced at his boswell. An hour and a half to go.

⁕ ⁕ ⁕

Fierin vlith-Kendrian matched her steps to Tau Srivashti's as they ascended the shallow stairway to the pavilion, her hand light on his silken sleeve. She had every nerve under strict control, so the first sign that something out of the ordinary was going to happen was Tau's short intake of breath.

Marines in formal uniform lined the wide hall, an honor guard for a ruler's son. But there was no mace-bearing grand steward standing at the door to announce the visitors. The Aerenarch was there himself, dressed in a blaze of white and gold and cobalt blue, his dress resplendent to the edge of vulgarity, but he carried it off with an air.

He's on display, and he knows it, she thought, admiring his slender form, from the perfectly barbered hair to the glossy boots. Jewels glinted about his person, mostly diamonds.

Where had he gotten them? Hadn't he arrived with nothing but Charvann's family signet?

Then she heard Vannis, just behind her, laugh softly. "That's Charidhe Masaud's blue diamond in his ear. How in Haruban's Hell did he get it from her?"

Without turning her head, Fierin glanced around, saw the exquisite Charidhe, who always reminded her of a poisonous flower, standing in the background with the already arrived guests, a smile of pride on her thin lips.

Borrowed jewels, Fierin thought. *An Arkad wearing borrowed jewels. And from a family that hates his.* She heard runnels of excited talk extending behind as the reception line made its way up the steps. There was no doubt that he'd carried it off.

Now they were close enough to hear snatches of conversation. He was greeting everyone by name. Of course there was some laergist concealed in the background somewhere, bozzing him the IDs when he needed them, but still it was impressive.

Fierin had tried, so far without success, to get close enough to him to speak with him about Jes. It seemed utterly impossible to engage him in any kind of conversation, and she had expended a great deal of energy in attempts to contrive it.

She had managed to speak, briefly, to each of the *Telvarna*'s crew, except for the captain, who she found out seldom left Detention. None of them could do a thing for Jes. It looked like it would be up to this new Aerenarch. Was he really a beautifully trained fool, full of empty politenesses and no substance, as Tau and his friends hinted?

She was glad of the line, for it gave her time to assemble some kind of question to gain his attention, and test that perfect facade. Tau was engaged in talk with Vannis and Kestian. Fierin smiled, seeming to listen, but she thought furiously.

Music. It had to mention that, and it had to seem a joke in case Tau was listening. And it had to be quick, for she would only have him to herself for a few seconds.

Then it was their turn, and Tau went first, as the highest of rank in their party.

Tau's obeisance was perfect: severely formal, more suitable for the ballroom floor than a concert, except for a trick of the hands and a smile that made it amusing.

Brandon matched it, with a very grand air, his hand arching wide to include the entire pavilion. "You see, Your Grace. I took your advice. I hope you will be pleased."

"I am delighted you deemed my counsel worthy of notice," Tau said, smiling as he passed on.

The Aerenarch kissed Vannis' hands, one then the other, but said nothing. She smiled slightly, her eyes cool. Did she dislike him, then? Fierin was puzzled; at parties, when they both were present, Vannis watched his progress through the room.

Kestian was next, their exchange nothing but politenesses. And then the blue eyes gazed directly into hers, and he touched her outstretched palms and called her by name.

Was his mind already going right past to the next one in line? She rose from her curtsey and said, "Thank you for inviting me. Any clues on what we'll be hearing?"

"Can you wait, and let it surprise you?" he murmured.

Was that a hint—or not? The others had already moved on, but then Tau looked back, question in his raised brows.

She licked her lips. "I just wish everyone could come." And then, in a rush, so low no one could possibly overhear: "I always believed that music—like justice—has eternal appeal."

His eyes, so very blue, gazed directly into hers, and though his smile remained exactly as pleasant as before, she felt the cold tingle of warning. But all he said was, "I hope the music will please you." And a bow.

The other three were ranged there, smiling at passersby, waiting.

Tau took her arm. "Converse in a receiving line, Fierin?"

It was considered a gaucherie to make the line stop. She needed another gaucherie, and fast. Flipping a lock of hair back, she said, "Oh, I tried to prise the program out of him. Music, you know, was my study before Jes left." She admitted ruefully, "I guess I was hoping to show off my knowledge. What else can I use it for?"

The two men laughed, and Vannis smiled. To Fierin's surprise, there was just a hint of real color staining the former Aerenarch-Consort's flawless cheeks.

Fierin turned to scan the entrance to the concert hall. She'd heard that the Ares theater had one of the most extensive adaptech installations in the Thousand Suns, able to evoke, if not actually imitate, almost any kind of entertainment facility.

She was not disappointed. When they reached the hall,

Vannis drew in her breath. Tau glanced at her, saying nothing, but Fierin saw a slight line between his eyes.

The hall was a swirl of color; concentric circles around a low pit, wherein stood a single keyboard and a chair. Above, a carillon of crystal sconces refracted light in a glory of rainbow patterns. It was beautiful, but not so much that it should have such an effect on Vannis and Tau, Fierin thought, glancing at their faces.

He's making some kind of statement, she realized. *And it must be aimed at them.*

She wondered then if she really had been gauche; if he had given her a message—a warning—and she'd missed it. A memory niggled at her, but she couldn't recall it.

Raised brows and sustained politesse on either side indicated that some point had been made in a wordless but altogether effective manner.

They took their seats, ordering drinks, but no holo display to beguile the music. Other circles might blend laser art with the music, but Tau and Vannis, so recently at Arthelion's Court, would not disgrace live musicians that way. As they settled in, Fierin finally brought the elusive memory to consciousness—from a chip she'd viewed once—and she saw the hall before her with fresh eyes, knowing what the Aerenarch had done that had upset her companions. The Ares theater was adapted to evoke the Halle Concertum in the Palace Minor on the Mandala.

Tau's eyes were ceaseless in their movement as he talked, low-voiced, to Kestian. Vannis, too, watched, but her gaze seemed drawn toward the royal balcony. What other surprises was she expecting from the Aerenarch?

A hum of comment rose above the general susurration in the theater as a single figure emerged onto the stage, a large, rather ugly man, dressed in a plain gray tunic and trousers that were, nonetheless, finely tailored. As he reached the keyboard he stopped and looked up; his eyes, dark under heavy brows, seemed to sear directly into her with a startling intensity, and she recognized him: Montrose, the cook from the crew of the *Telvarna*—Jes' ship.

Montrose seated himself and without further hesitation began to play a somber, wandering melody, more like an introspective improvisation than a performance piece.

Fierin tore her glance away and looked up at the royal box,

where two women were being seated by a naval officer. There was no sign of the Aerenarch; this must be merely incidental music. As she watched, one of the women made a comment in an unpleasant voice that caught at her ears, reminiscent of tearing metal. ". . . Rifter outlaws?" was all she heard for certain, then a susurrus of whispers ran about the room.

Rifters? Who else from the Telvarna *is here, and what does it mean?*

"Who?" Kestian said, and Fierin remained silent, trying to radiate unconcern.

"The crew from that Rifter ship, the one he was on before *Mbwa Kali* found them," Vannis said, her tone indifferent. "The musician is one, a former member of a minor Service Family. And see that tall woman in black, with the white-furred sentients? I'd thought her some kind of translator, but apparently she's the captain."

"Dol'jharian, I've been told," Tau murmured, looking very amused.

Fierin looked down into the first level, easily picking out the straight-limbed black-haired woman flanked by the two exotic-looking beings. "She's not at all bad-looking. In fact, with a decent gown and something done with that hair, she'd turn every head," she remarked.

Vannis' smile was a shade condescending. "Of course. Dol'jharians kill their ugly babies."

"I've always found that curiously compelling," Tau said. "A race that concerns itself entirely with power, pain, and death, yet requires its progeny to be pleasing to the eye."

Suddenly the music changed, taking on form and substance, and Fierin shivered. She didn't recognize it, but the measured tones now tolling from the synthesizer irresistibly evoked age and awe and the depths of time that sundered all of them from Lost Earth.

A rustle of silk nearby drew her attention. Vannis was sitting stiffly upright, staring at the musician, her cheeks pale, while Tau watched her, his features tight. They both looked stunned; then Tau's eyes met Fierin's and his face smoothed out.

She wanted desperately to know what had so affected him, and was still casting about for an approach when the music ceased and the musician withdrew. A moment later the Aerenarch entered the royal box.

They rose as the Phoenix fanfaronade pealed out.

The audience made its obeisance, then the Aerenarch his, the ancient ritual as stylized and graceful as ballet. Then came the rustle of expensive fabrics as all were reseated, the whispering of expectation.

"And so it begins," Vannis murmured, so softly Fierin nearly missed it.

But Tau didn't. He showed his teeth in a soundless laugh.

* * *

Eloatri gazed about the theater, reveling in the bright attire and graceful motions of the Douloi in attendance upon this, the Aerenarch's concert. Next to her the tall Dol'jharian woman sat erect, and beside her the two small white-furred sentients that seemingly never left her side. They noted the direction of Eloatri's gaze and chittered softly in response, their immense eyes glittering in the fulgent light of the hall, their twiggy hands briefly forming a simple pattern. It was one of Manderian's semiotics: *We see you.* She nodded in response.

Vi'ya glanced at her, briefly, expressionless, then turned back to the front as a man emerged onto the stage. Eloatri recognized him.

"That is one of your crew, is it not?" Montrose was his name; she had already enjoyed a meal prepared by him at a private dinner in the Arkadic Enclave—there had been no hint that he was also a musician.

"He was." Vi'ya's voice was soft, giving no hint of her emotions, but Eloatri sensed a tension in her. No doubt the emotional radiation of the many in attendance was taking its toll on her; Manderian had reported that she was gaining control only slowly, struggling with the enhanced sensitivity engendered in her by her association with the Eya'a.

Montrose played a slow, introspective improvisation, then the music changed, slowing even more, deeply evocative. Eloatri stiffened, shock flooding through her; she knew that piece. *Dangerous. Oh, so dangerous.* An almost subliminal movement swept through the assembled guests: many of them had recognized it as well.

She looked up at the royal box, but the Aerenarch had not yet arrived. This, then, was a warning and a challenge to his enemies on Ares. *Perhaps you are your father's son.*

Beside her, Vi'ya rubbed her temples; the Eya'a emitted a brief soft pulse of almost ultrasonic chatter.

"It's the *Manya Cadena*," said Eloatri. Vi'ya looked over at her. "It commemorates the great chain of lives that links all of us to Lost Earth through two thousand years of Exile."

Seeing incomprehension in the Dol'jharian's face, she added, "It would have been played at the Aerenarch's Enkainion during the Three Summons."

Vi'ya stared at her a moment, then turned back. The knuckles on her strong hands showed white for a moment, then relaxed.

After the entrance of the Aerenarch the concert proper began, with a medley of ancient music performed by members of the Akademia Musika. Eloatri was impressed; had the Aerenarch chosen these pieces himself? If so, it betokened an encyclopedic knowledge of musical history.

Then a familiar melody caught her ear, born on the haunting plainsong voiced by a single musician, and her throat thickened. *Veni Creator Spiritus*. She had first heard that tune at her forced assumption of the *cathedra* at New Glastonbury. But then it had merely been a pleasant sound; now she knew what it meant.

With irresistible force the music caught her up beyond herself, drenching the theater with a numinous aura. Beside her for a moment sat no human woman, but a luminous flame so bright her eyes watered. Two smaller flames attended her; beyond, like the radiation of an unquenchable furnace, the royal box vanished in supernal light. And in the audience another flaming spirit, red-haired, double-imaged with an impression of a triune presence. Eloatri trembled. These were all linked, yet lacking some vital presence that would complete the hinge of time which they comprised.

Then the musicians moved on, climbing the years from the Exile toward the present, and the Dreamtime released her.

Eloatri looked up at the royal box where the Aerenarch sat, merely human now, his Douloi mask impervious. *Are there messages here of equal import for others in the audience?*

No matter, she decided; the general impact was plain enough, evoking the deeply praeterite feelings of the Exiles, engaging their dependence on tradition and continuity. *They have all suffered loss—none of them know what is to come. He has offered them the familiar haven of their collective memories of Lost Earth.* And he was the last of the Arkads, a tradition in itself, the family that had ruled the Thousand Suns for a thousand years.

The Akademia withdrew from the stage during a brief intermission. The audience was quiet; bursts of comment, quickly stilled, were the only sign of the music's impact. Then the Kitharee glided onstage playing a variety of strange instruments, no two alike, their costumes just as varied. There was no beginning to their performance: it seemed as though they were continuing an act that had never been interrupted. The music was strange, wild, compelling, utterly itself, uncompromising.

The Kitharee sect was famous throughout the Thousand Suns. For them, music was worship, a ritualistic combination of dance, chant, song, and instruments. Each Kitharee made his or her own instruments, which were burned with the musician at death.

Their performance was a different statement by the Aerenarch, for the Kitharee had never before performed in a secular setting—doubtless many here had never heard their music. Even an Arkad could not have ordered it. Persuasion only would have sufficed. Despite Brandon Arkad's ambiguous status, the cloud of suspicion that hung over him after his solo escape from the annihilation of his Enkainion, that was a statement of a power no one else on Ares could match.

And then, after another brief intermission, the third part of the program commenced, and hearing it, Eloatri bowed her head and gave thanks. Danger there was still, and even the possibility of failure, but she now had no doubt that whatever the nature of the grace that Telos had bestowed upon the Arkads, it inhered as strongly in the forty-eighth of that lineage as in the blood and bones of Jaspar Arkad himself.

* * *

The concert's final third forced the doors of memory.

Jaim looked up at Brandon, who sat motionless in his balcony seat, his head inclined, his expression pensive. Why? What was he looking at? Did he not know that the concert was a success, that the musicians were superlative, and the choice of music—his own—inspired general approbation?

A new melody pealed, a concerto for brass, tugging at images buried within Jaim. He gave up scanning the audience and faced the memories unlocked by the familiar music.

Light, dark, dancing brightness like sunbeams on water, deep and slow as molten rock beneath a planet's crust; all the music was from the years he crewed *Telvarna,* and it freed, like no drug or mantra ever could, all the emotions of the past. Jaim listened, fought at first, then at last recognized the futility of resistance and sank into the beckoning images, saluting his surrender as a lesson to be learned.

Symphony, melody, rastanda, twelve-tone, eight-tone, and syncopated, polyphonic: the pieces ranged all over the known universe, but a single theme bound them, stitched by the genius of a musician named KetzenLach. His greatness had lain in taking ancient art forms, forgotten arias and melodic lines, and weaving them anew for modern audiences, infusing them somehow with modern experience. As a child a brilliant mimic of great artists, KetzenLach had written only one original melody, his last—his gift was in reforming the old.

And KetzenLach had been Markham's favorite composer.

Every piece of music chosen evoked Markham vlith-L'Ranja; all had been his favorites, heard time and again aboard the *Telvarna,* and on Dis, and even in concert halls on distant planets, when—Telos knew how—Markham found out that this or that famous artist was to perform, and he took his crew lightyears beyond their immediate goal, just to hear music.

Some of the music Jaim did not know, but he guessed it was from the childhood that Brandon and Markham had shared; for this was a memorial, a tribute, though out of the audience of glittering aristocrats from many planets, probably fewer than half a dozen people knew it. And the fact that it was the Navy Band playing it gave the tribute a razor's edge, for Markham had been a brilliant cadet before he was cashiered.

Jaim looked aside, saw Omilov and Montrose sitting near one another. Montrose's eyes were shut, his ugly face relaxed in enjoyment. Omilov sat with his fingers steepled, his brow thoughtful, his eyes on the performers.

Jaim turned his head: yes, Vi'ya was there as well, with the Eya'a, whose eerie stillness was impossible to interpret. Vi'ya sat with very near the same stillness. Her face was like carved rock, her eyes in shadow. Dol'jharians were never very expressive even at their most relaxed, but Jaim had learned to read her: she was not, even remotely, enjoying the music.

Music feeds the soul, Reth Silverknife said once. *For those who deny the soul it is a weapon without defense.*

* * *

Vi'ya focused on the musicians before her, studying the forms of the instruments, the motions made by the players, the modification of sound. Anything to fend off the onslaught of the familiar grief—and of something deeper, more dangerous, than grief.

She glanced down at the Eya'a, fighting hard to maintain her shield. It was a new lesson, and one that taxed her to the utmost: to guard her thoughts—to protect her privacy.

Her eyes burned and her jaw ached with the effort she was expending and still the music fell around her, invisible knives to flay her outer shell and expose raw nerves to the air.

She would not raise her eyes to the balcony where Brandon Arkad sat, though she could feel his presence, like sunrads through an opaqued port.

Possibly he was watching her, trying to ascertain her reaction—for she knew that this entire concert, every piece of music, even the order in which they were played, was aimed at her. *I refused to talk to him about Markham, so here is the result.*

It was a kind of communication she could not ignore, but she knew it was not meant in malice, for that was not in his nature. The Arkad intended this as a tribute, a gift. He was giving her to know, as clearly as if he spoke, his feelings for his dead friend, for Brandon had loved and trusted Markham vlith-L'Ranja. The music was a gift to the one other person who had loved and trusted him and in turn had earned Markham's love and trust, a wordless acknowledgment of the bond of loss they shared.

She would not close her burning eyes. The musicians' heads bobbed, each with a smearing aura of light surrounding it.

He could not know—and would not—that she would rather be anywhere, even the torture pits of Dol'jhar, than here, seeing in Markham's music what Brandon Arkad could not.

There was no original music tonight, did he not perceive the terrible parallel? That KetzenLach was, after all, only a clever mimic—and so, too, had been Markham?

And that . . . and that . . .

She forced the thought away, with a violence that caused an answering pang in one temple. A tremor went through the small white-furred figures at her side, and she felt their question inside her aching skull. She sent a reassurance, even as the insidious melodic line whipped monothread tendrils through layer after layer of buried memory, stirring up images and emotions she had labored to banish.

The Masque of the Red Death . . . A long face, drifting blond hair, a lazy, lopsided smile, all unreal, all a mask, for the poses, the cadence of the words, and deeper, deeper, the gaze of humorous compassion on an unforgiving universe, the delight in finding beauty in the most unexpected places and the urge to share it, those things were not characteristic, but had been consciously modeled after another.

> *"The other two, slight air and purging fire;*
> *Are both with thee, wherever I abide;*
> *The first my thought, the other my desire . . ."*

The pure voice of the young singer carried KetzenLach's plainsong note through the swooping, fluttering melodies fashioned by the musical instruments. Vi'ya did not have to close her eyes; she could not see the singer now.

For she was a tempath—a telepath now—and to deny nature, to shutter the instinctive urge to touch that other mind, the one that, after all, she had really been attuned to all these years, caused a terrible mental feedback that made her head reel with pain, muting sound and sight. Each breath rasped her dry throat, and the need to remain still took every vestige of her energy.

But she welcomed it. Pain was immediate, it required no risk, it was merely there to be endured: it was the anodyne to passion.

FIFTEEN

"You said before that there were two things you did not understand. Marriage was one, and the second?"

"The second," said Anaris, "is regret."

"Ah."

"It seems an utterly futile emotion," Anaris said. "Why think at all about that which cannot be changed?"

"One cannot mend the past," the Panarch said, "but regret is a motivator for shaping the future."

"I do not see that," Anaris said. "I formulate my plans, I carry them through. In this way, the future becomes today, exactly as I would have it."

The Panarch looked down at his folded hands for a time, then at last said, "In so doing, you merely perpetuate the mistakes of your forebears. If this is the extent of your goal, then so be it. But I do not think it is."

"Say, then, that it is not, for purposes of explanation."

"I would direct you to read the words of Sanctus Gabriel, in his discourses on the teaching stones. He calls regret, remorse, mercy, compassion, patience, and humility the rocks that one carries in one's rucksack on the uphill journey."

"And then . . . presumably one sets them down at some point?" Anaris asked, still amused.

The Panarch smiled. "Never. But one becomes strong enough to bear them, and eventually to replace them with the burdens of one's accrued responsibilities."

"You describe a servant, not a leader," Anaris said, making a dismissive gesture with his dirazh'u.

"The best leader serves," Gelasaar replied. "If you want to lead people, you must learn how to follow them."

Anaris extended a hand, encompassing them both, there in the hold of the commandeered Rifter ship, he in his family's accustomed black, and the Panarch stripped of all insignia of rank, garbed in prison gray. "A leader leads," Anaris corrected gently, setting aside the dirazh'u to summon the guards. "Next time, let us discuss our perceptions of the word 'strength.' "

⁂ ⁂ ⁂

Light-headed with pride, Kestian Harkatsus stood back against the wall and surveyed his salon. The room, too small by Douloi Highdweller standards, and set with furniture he would not give his servants, gained in significance what it never had in grace by virtue of its occupants: the most powerful people in what remained of the Panarchy of the Thousand Suns.

His pleasure was too boundless to rein, so he stood in the background, watching as they arrived one by one and settled into the plain Navy-issue chairs, ordered food or drink from Tau Srivashti's silent liegeman Felton, who had come early to aid Kestian's servant in vetting the place for intrusive devices.

Tau and Stulafi Y'Talob had enjoined everyone to secrecy, to which Kestian had agreed, but still, unknown to them, Kestian was recording it all in his boswell for posterity.

Future generations will remember this day, he thought, wishing he had an ajna so he could record visuals, and not just audio.

"We just await Hesthar," a husky male voice rose above the rest: Tau Srivasthi.

Passionless? Memory tweaked at Kestian, and old anger and humiliation stirred, like black mud in a stream, but he forced it to settle again. He must rise above his twenty-year-old grudge; pettiness was not for those who guide the destinies of planets.

Besides, he had learned by patient listening and the occasional oblique question that he was not, in fact, the only newly titled youth that Tau had romanced and then—quite suddenly—dropped.

Tau has a taste for the young, he'd overheard the former Aerenarch-Consort saying to someone at a party, while all of them watched Srivashti dancing with that little Kendrian heir. *But there's nothing of the chatz-house for him: his toys are always inexperienced, handsome, and of course well born. And he always makes them fall in love with him, then he marries them off into some alliance he'd arranged before the very first meeting.*

Painful as it was to have his own experience described—and so baldly!—as a caprice, Kestian gave no sign of remembering those days, taking his cue from Tau.

His gaze was still on Tau's bent head, so he saw the signal that went from him to Felton. It was no more than the flicker of an eye, but Kestian had learned to be observant. Very smoothly, Felton stepped forward and poured more of a curious thick black liqueur into the Archon of Torigan's cup.

Stulafi Y'Talob drank deeply of the dark liquid, then rubbed his fleshy face and snorted. "Damned inconvenient."

"Inconvenient?" said little Fierin, who was settled quite close to Tau. How long would she enjoy Tau's capricious benevolence? Kestian suddenly pitied her and wondered, briefly, whether she ought to be considered for his son. *Find out her holdings first—and if this scandal of hers is really settled. Someone said the brother is not dead, after all, but is here on Ares.*

Y'Talob did not answer; his one glance in Fierin's direction made clear his scorn for her youth and inexperience.

"Inconvenient?" The old Archonei of Cincinnatus keened her high monkey-laugh. "I'd say he threw that Lusor rizz right into your teeth." She glared around, her eyes reminding Kestian of a reptile. "Who noised that foolery about again?"

Hands reached for drinks or beckoned for servants to bring more: everyone remembered Torigan's little speech after Tau's dinner the other night. *Our Aerenarch's tentative status might take harm,* he'd sneered, *if people remember that he has no commission because he was thrown out of the Academy ten year ago—he and Lusor's adopted son, Markham vlith-L'Ranja.*

"NorSothu nyr-Kaddes was babbling on about it in front of a dozen people," Hesthar al-Gessinav said from the back of the room, her whispery voice somehow carrying. "KetzenLach was a favorite of both Lusor and his son, and the *Memoria Lucis*—played by a Rifter follower of L'Ranja, no less—at the end made it fairly clear that the concert was a tribute."

She came slowly forward, taking her place with the self-assurance of one who knew that even important meetings would await her presence.

Kestian watched her thin hands reaching for a goblet. The edge of her emerald sleeves did not completely obscure some kind of complicated tattoo on her smooth gold-brown skin; he couldn't make it out exactly, but something in the indistinct shape made the hairs on the back of his neck prickle.

Tau said, "It would appear that the incident is redounding to Aerenarch Semion's discredit, and not to our present Aerenarch's. You must remember that His Highness is remarkably adept at expressing himself through the social medium, if I may employ so inept a term."

The old Archon of the ice planet Boyar spoke up, a very rare occurrence: "Evoked the Mandala as well."

"Which we may take as a challenge," Hesthar said.

"What kind of challenge?" Y'Talob grunted, thrusting a finger toward al-Gessinav. "Defense of his favorite's family, or—?"

"A threat? To us?" Kestian put in, and heads swung briefly in his direction.

Kestian did not see a movement, but a privacy came promptly from Tau: *(Let us endeavor to remain positive. Stulafi is with us now, but his loyalties are notoriously flexible. And I fear we have a limited amount of time.)*

A pang of alarm mixed with excitement seized Kestian. Tau had discovered something. Would he tell them all? Or only selected persons?

Then Tau lifted his hands, and everyone's focus followed the movement. "Friends," he said, "you talk as if we were gathered together to plot something dire. Far from it: we are here to form a council of advisers for His Highness. If he wishes to restore the memory of the House of L'Ranja to its former honor, why should we not help him as much as we are able?"

From his vantage, Kestian saw Fierin make a small, nervous gesture. What was the Lusor affair to her? *Except it was a scandal that removed her own from the public arena.* A smirk on Y'Talob's face reminded Kestian that her scandal had taken place on that Archon's own planet.

There was no time to consider the importance of this, for Tau smiled across the room at Kestian. "A more constructive topic would be how, since the machinery of government has been effectively destroyed, to achieve our transition as smoothly as possible."

"We must stay secret until we have control," Y'Talob said.

"Permit me to disagree," Tau said, giving Y'Talob a profound bow. "And honor me with your pardon: remember, we've four days."

"Inertia might keep any rescue from going out," Cincinnatus added. "No one gives the Navy the command, the deadline passes."

"But *Grozniy* has been repaired with a speed that hints at purpose," Hesthar said. "Please, Tau. Finish your thought."

Tau bowed. "As time is so short, and we do not know what the Navy might be planning, it is time for us to gain the support of the Service Families, which means we must emerge into the open."

It was Y'Talob's choice, as the challenged one, to demur or to concede. He bowed from his seat on the couch, a perfunctory rippling of his massive frame, but it was a concession.

Tau did not appear to notice how the man's face purpled with annoyance. "I thank you, Stulafi, for your forbearance." Tau's respectful deference was an exercise in grace; when Y'Talob did not respond, he continued. "His Highness appears to be taking his expected place in the social hierarchy, and I believe it ought to be there that our gesture of unity begins. Kestian: it falls to you to give a few stirring words concerning our goals."

Kestian bowed, not trusting himself to speech. Tau's gold eyes gleamed with triumph, and Kestian realized that the man knew something that he was not telling.

"We'll have to neutralize the Masauds." Cincinnatus sighed. "They've all gone insane over that *pas* with the diamonds."

"It was a splendid gesture," Vannis said, smiling. "And the Masauds are notoriously heart-driven."

Tau looked amused. "Exactly. You are both correct, Vannis, Cassir."

"The Masaud masquerade," the Archonei said. "It must be there."

Y'Talob lifted a hand, closed it into a fist. "As hosts, they're immobilized. Now, how do we neutralize the Navy?"

"They exist to serve," Tau said, his voice gentle. "We have no need: when the time comes, our united voices will give them the directive that the Panarch's regrettably absent leadership cannot. But they must be distracted long enough to prevent preemptive action, should any desire such."

Hesthar looked sidelong at Tau. "You may leave that to me. An intimate gathering for Nyberg and his staff will suffice."

Tau bowed to her. "Then we need have no further concern in that direction. There are, however, other interests we must consider. We will have to be vigilant, but I think we can convince the greater portion of those sworn to Service to see our way." Tau's voice was bland, but Kestian noted subtle indicators of a strictly repressed tension, an excitement. *He does know something. Will he tell us when Y'Talob is not present?*

Hrishnamrutis of Boyar spoke once more: "Aerenarch."

Silence fell, and Kestian watched Hesthar, then Tau, then Cincinnatus move slightly: *Privacies.*

Annoyed at being left out, Kestian said: "What about the Enkainion? Is that what we use to gain his cooperation?"

No one moved or spoke, but Kestian felt a sudden, visceral conviction that that had been the subject of the privacies. "Our problem with that," Hesthar said with a slight smile, "is that none of us were there. Regrettable: I was to have represented our family, as my cousin was on Lao Tse, but my yacht would not cooperate." Kestian was distracted by a glitter at the edge of his vision—but it was only Vannis lifting her head, and the light catching in the gemstones in her hair. "We've only hearsay," Hesthar finished, "which does not constitute proof."

Y'Talob grunted. "What matter? Whether out of cowardice or expedience, he left, and we can hold him to an investigation if it's necessary. Legal, perfectly legal . . ."

"And if he submits, it will ruin him," Cincinnatus whispered.

Tau gestured reluctance, his expression one of faint distaste. "One regrets any gesture of disrespect to the thousand years of Arkadic rule."

"No finesse," Hesthar said, still smiling. "What is much better is to secure our position while he is busy elsewhere."

Y'Talob drank deeply of his dark liquid again. "Which means he can't be at the Masaud ball," he stated over the rim of his cup. "How do we contrive that?"

Tau, stroking his fingers over Fierin's wrist, said nothing.

It was Hesthar who turned her smile up at Vannis. "We will leave the Aerenarch," she said, "to you."

Vannis was so still her jewels gleamed steadily. Then she bowed, a graceful gesture of profound irony.

Admiral Nyberg stood and lifted his glass; the other three rose with him. The rich wine within their goblets glinted redly above the snowy-white linen on the table. "His Majesty Gelasaar III," he intoned, and emptied his glass with a defiant toss.

The wine hit the pit of Margot Ng's stomach with a rush of warmth, reminding her that she hadn't eaten breakfast or lunch. She noted a glitter in Anton Faseult's eyes as he lowered his glass, and Damana Willsones drained her goblet with an air of relief. They were all working too hard. But they had no choice.

As they seated themselves, the steward lifted the silver dome off the platter in front of Admiral Nyberg with a flourish, releasing a puff of richly scented steam. On the platter lay a roast encased in flaky pastry. Ng's mouth watered, and she resolved to spend more time at the salon, as Ares actually had a competitive fencing team; being a de facto part of Nyberg's staff was hard on the waistline.

During dinner the conversation was light, leaping from subject to subject but never touching on the present. Nyberg's dislike of "working meals" was well known and not even Vice-admiral Willsones, with the crusty fearlessness lent by age and long, distinguished service, tested that. But Ng sensed in their tension and occasional lapses into reverie that both Security and Communications had news of import to impart.

And so did she. Her hand strayed to the chip in her breast pocket, with the Aerenarch's test result encoded in it. *I wonder how their news will fit with this?*

When they finished the last course, the steward brought them after-dinner cordials with coffee—Ng was the only one who had to specify her choice—and Nyberg dismissed him. They sat in companionable silence for a few minutes; some of Ng's own tension had leached out of her during dinner, but now it was time to get back to business. Or nearly time.

She enjoyed the last moments of tranquillity, sipping at her Algar Sisters brandy. The candles flickered in an occasional draft from the tianqi, now making the transition from the neutral dining setting to a crisp, slightly cooler phase, filling the room with a faintly bitter herbal scent.

Finally Nyberg set down his glass and looked around the table. "You all seem to have news, and I hope it's good—or as good as it gets around here these days."

Vice-admiral Willsones laughed. "Here we are," she said. "The masters of Ares, slaves to duty."

Commander Faseult snorted. "Not for long, if the Harkatsus cabal has any say in it."

Nyberg cocked his head, picked up his glass, and sipped.

"Scefi-Cartano, Srivashti, Torigan, Harkatsus, al-Gessinav, Cincinnatus, and Boyar met again yesterday evening, comaccess denied."

"Srivashti yacht again?" Nyberg murmured, his smile fading. Now he just looked tired.

Anton Faseult shook his head. "Harkatsus' dwelling. But the ubiquitous Felton was in command of security, which meant we did not get an ear in."

"Don't need to," Nyberg said, sitting back. He flicked a finger over a slim sheaf of papers and printouts at his side. "With us invited to the al-Gessinav dinner and all the rest of the Douloi going to the Masaud ball, they'd be fools not to move: they're aware as we are that time has run out." He leaned forward. "My question is, where will the Aerenarch be?"

The commander sat back, hands spread.

Willsones startled them all with a laugh. "I think I can tell you that. My news is a delightful bit of gossip."

Nyberg's lips quirked. "You're incurable, Damana."

"When you get to be as old as I am," she retorted, "you realize that people are really the only surprising things in this universe. But it's gossip to the point: you'll never guess who came to me—herself, no intermediaries—to rent (at a smacking good fee, I should add) that old lovers' barge I inherited."

Faseult's eyes gleamed with amusement over the rim of his crystal, which contained some fuming concoction that Ng didn't recognize; the tang of it caught at her throat even across the table. "Why you ever held on to that thing," he said, "let alone shipped it out here . . ."

"You never know, Anton. You just never know." Laughing, she poked with one gnarled finger at the ice in her drink, a thick green liquid that Ng thought might be Shiidra Tears—

appropriate in a decorated veteran of the last war against those dog-like aliens. She'd given them more than enough reasons to weep. "And it has paid off at last. Vannis Scefi-Cartano!"

"Ah," Nyberg sighed, sitting back. "So that places the Aerenarch."

"My question is, has she planned this as a countermove, or is she acting on the part of the cabal?" Faseult mused.

Willsones shrugged. "Either way, the end is the same."

Ng tapped her nail on the edge of her snifter, listening to the *tink*. The sense of well-being imparted by the meal had almost dissipated, leaving a curious sense of unreality. "My experience of court coups being limited," she said, "bear with me, I beg. The cabal comes out into the open tomorrow, at this ball, right?"

Nyberg nodded once. "If they can get the majority of the Douloi behind them, they'll march straight to me and start handing out orders. And if everyone complies"—he lifted his fingers away from his glass—"a government is born."

"And the Aerenarch?"

"He's kept out of the way until it's too late," Anton said.

"So while he's bunnying with Vannis on the barge—"

"Exactly." Willsones nodded. "He wakes up to find a new Privy Council ready to serve him."

Faseult said, eyes narrowed, "If it really is Harkatsus in charge, that's the likeliest plan. If Tau Srivashti is the backbone, he'll make certain of the Aerenarch first."

Ng considered this. "How? Threats? Do you think they've been behind the murder attempts?"

Anton shook his head. "At this point it hardly matters. But they'll use whatever works, whether promises, blandishments, or . . . threats."

"I can't believe they'll use violence," Ng exclaimed. "They'd never get away with it."

"Agreed," Nyberg said, setting his glass down. "Srivashti would not be so crude if he could possibly avoid it. Hesthar al-Gessinav even less so. Why, when a more effective threat would be the release of information?"

Faseult nodded, his black eyes sober. "The dead laergist and his missing recording of the Enkainion. There could be a connection."

Damana sighed. "What could be on it? What did he do?"

Nyberg gestured, a graceful turn of wrist that chilled Ng with its fatalism. "It hardly matters, does it? If Brandon vlith-Arkad can't seize control despite whatever he's done, he's lost. All that remains is the matter of what sort of justice the cabal will demand, or will use to force him into compliance."

Ng made herself breathe slowly, releasing what she recognized as prebattle tension. *No, this is worse: there is no enemy to shoot at. Supposedly we are all on the same side.* She looked up. "Do you believe he will comply?"

"I don't know," Nyberg said lightly. "Though a pleasant young man, he is completely opaque to me. I cannot gauge him at all." He turned to the commander. "What say you, Anton?"

Faseult sighed. "If you will honor me with your forbearance while I digress into irrelevance?"

Nyberg deferred with a stately gesture, and Willsones grunted, her eyes keen. Ng smiled into her cup, entertained, despite her tiredness and the tense situation, with the ineradicable ritual of Douloi interactions. *Will the Panarch be as polite on Gehenna?* The random thought jolted her.

"Did any of you ever meet the Kyriarch Ilara?" Faseult asked.

Surprised, Ng nodded. Willsones shook her head, and Nyberg murmured, "I saw her once, but it was at a huge court function. We were never closer than fifty meters."

Anton turned to Ng. "Your impressions, Margot?"

Ng closed her eyes, calling up the vivid image of clear blue-gray eyes. "It was right after Acheront," she said. "When I received the Karelian Star. We spoke briefly. . . ." She paused, reliving the intensity of that day: herself a young ensign, about to be decorated and promoted, still grieving over the losses of good comrades; the occasion her only visit to the Palace Major, for a dauntingly formal ceremony that would be broadcast to the furthest reaches of the Panarchy; her conflicting emotions overridden by her fear that she would fumble and disgrace herself.

"They both spoke to me. The Panarch was grave and kind, but I was dry-mouthed with terror." She paused for a murmur of laughter from the others. "But then the Kyriarch spoke to me, and . . . it was as if we were alone in the room together, just for those seconds." She lost the image and turned her gaze to the three pairs of eyes watching her now. "She asked just a couple of questions, nothing I hadn't been asked a hundred times since the battle. But . . . she really *listened.* When I walked away, I *knew* she would remember me forever, that I carried her pride and trust with me as my special charge."

"Ah," Nyberg said. "Go on, Anton."

Faseult inclined his head toward Ng. "Are you aware of the circumstances of the Kyriarch's marriage?"

"I was told by my patrons that she sprang from a frontier family and that the marriage had taken everyone by surprise."

"It was a scandal," Anton said. "My mother told me the whole story before she took me to Court. This was before I was old enough to go to the Academy; Gelasaar had just succeeded his mother. Since his birth everyone had expected an alliance with the Cartanos—it was their turn, and these things had come to follow a certain pattern of rotation, which kept the most powerful families happy. But Gelasaar broke it, risking the enmity of the Cartano faction."

Nyberg whistled. "I vaguely recall hearing several officers discussing that once, when I was a middy doing slub duty in the wardroom. Though it was old news then. Not much else to talk about, patrolling the fringes for Shiidra."

Faseult smiled a little. "My mother told me that the actual marriage ceremony was quite memorable: wars nearly broke out that day. But." He paused to drink. "Within half a year, Ilara had managed to win them all over. Every one of them. The Cartano candidate had even become her staunchest supporter in Court: she never had an enemy. Until the end."

Willsones sighed, and Ng winced, remembering the doomed peace mission to Dol'jhar. *She was Eusabian's first victim.*

"Whatever it was about her, it was innate: one only had to meet her to fall in love. I certainly did," Anton added with a wry smile. "Case-hardened fourteen-year-old that I was. To a certain measure, her second son, Galen, inherited that ability, though he was seldom seen at Court." He paused again, looking around at them, last at Nyberg. "At your request, I have attended as many of these interminable civilian entertainments as duty allows, and I've watched the Aerenarch."

"Does he exhibit this remarkable trait?" Ng asked, rapidly reviewing her own brief observations of the young man.

"When he wants to," Anton said. "I don't know whether to be frightened or impressed, but he seems able to cloak it at will. When he first arrived, he moved through the crowds making all the correct gestures and responses, but leaving no more impression than a knife through water. After that concert, he suddenly invoked the whatever-it-is and has been winning partisans ever since. Social, always within a purely social context. There's been no hint of political maneuvering, and I have been on the watch for just that."

"Leaving aside the question of his conduct at his Enkainion," Nyberg said, "one is left with his reputation."

"Ah, yes," Ng said, withdrawing the chip from her inner pocket. "The drunken sot who lives only for pleasure."

The others turned her way.

"I also have my bit of news, but it can wait for a moment. I've been doing my own investigations. It will not surprise you that one of the hot topics of gossip in our own wardrooms is the truth behind the Aerenarch's expulsion from the Academy ten years ago. There's inevitably more speculation than fact, but this much seems clear: everyone on Minerva, or almost everyone, knew why the Krysarch was expelled for irresponsibility and insubordination, but no one dared talk openly. The death of Aerenarch Semion," she said dryly, "seems to have had a remarkable effect on freeing tongues."

"Perhaps the former Aerenarch did contrive his brother's expulsion," Anton put in, "but—if I may be permitted to speak freely—Brandon vlith-Arkad's subsequent record seems to underscore the unsavory reputation."

"Yes," Ng said. "So explain this."

Receiving a nod of permission from Nyberg, she tapped at a console, throwing up the results of Brandon's tests onto the screen. Then she sat back and watched comprehension work its way into the others' faces.

"In addition to a gifted individual," Ng said as Willsones shook her head slowly, "which is entirely to be expected, we are seeing the results of a single-minded focus on one goal. Despite what probably had to be a lethally close watch, if anything I know of Semion is true, young brother Brandon managed to stay with his studies."

"To what end?" Nyberg breathed, drumming his fingers on the edge of the table. "To what end?"

"I can't begin to guess," Ng said, "but I'll wager that Karelian Star his father hung on me that it's all connected with the events at the Enkainion. His mother gave the impression that she believed in everyone she met and trusted them completely. I suspect that our new Aerenarch might have retained his belief in human potential, but he does not trust anyone."

Nyberg's brows lifted; Faseult's face could have been carved from stone.

She turned to Willsones. "Back to the Enkainion. Anything on civ or naval vessels?"

The communications chief shook her head. "Gigas and teras from incoming ships, and not one clue to what really happened on the Mandala that night."

Ng turned to the security chief. "If I had a charge that important and he appeared with a Rifter in tow, I'd plant a telltale," she said, smiling.

Faseult exchanged a glance with Nyberg, who nodded fractionally. "We did," Faseult said.

Ng said, "And I'll bet you've had nothing from that, either."

"A raconteur's delight, according to Vahn," Faseult replied. "Airs and humoresques, but no substance. He and Jaim talk about everything—music, history, dress, Rifters and Highdwellers and Downsiders—everything but politics."

"Which leaves us exactly where we were before," Nyberg said wryly, "only at a substantially advanced hour. I suggest we adjourn and get what rest we can: tomorrow should be interesting."

"So we fall in with the plan," Damana said. "We all appear at Hesthar's dinner?"

"With your permission," Ng said, "I'd prefer not to."

Willsones looked mildly surprised, Faseult saturnine. Nyberg's face was unreadable as he inclined his head.

"*Grozniy* is almost finished," Ng said smoothly. "I should like to be there for the final status run-through."

"Yes," Nyberg said, standing up. His smile widened, then he laughed. "Do that, Margot. I'd like to know that *Grozniy* is ready for orders."

❋ ❋ ❋

The tianqi shifted into evening mode as the light outside slowly dimmed. Eloatri sighed and put the chip viewer down; she missed the comfort of the leather-and-paper volumes in the library of New Glastonbury Cathedral on Desrien. She looked out the window of her study and frowned slightly. She also missed planetary sunsets—a Downsider born and bred, she felt uncomfortable with the gradual dimming of the habitat's diffusers, unaccompanied as it was by any further change in the angle of the light.

At least there was weather. Through the north-facing window she could see the strange hook-topped clouds of the oneill gathering, enwrapped on either side by the upcurving surface, herded by gravitic fields toward an evening rain shower. There might even be lightning—Eloatri knew she could check the habitat schedule to find out, but that would make it seem less like weather and more like theater.

It's a wonder Highdwellers aren't even more different than they are, she thought.

A crooked arc of light traced its way spinward to the surface from the clouds, confirming her speculation. A few seconds later the sound reached her, strangely hollow compared to planetary thunder. A splatter of rain beat against the slightly opened window, bringing the scent of dampness to her.

She wondered if the weather techs knew how appropriate their efforts were. But no storm could match the fury building among the Douloi factions immured here on Ares. She had no idea just exactly what was happening, but the tension was palpable, reaching even into her dreams.

The book viewer blinked as, sensing inactivity, it shifted into cover mode. Eloatri stood up and looked down at the title.

Bearing a Sword: The Christian Church and Politics on Lost Earth.

Well, now she knew one more reason why the hand of Telos had ripped her out of her comfortable journey along the Eightfold Path and chivvied her toward New Glastonbury, to assume the burden of an alien faith. No religion had a deeper tradition of meddling in the affairs of state. She shook her head in wonder at the depth to which her predecessors in that tradition on Lost Earth had lost themselves in politics, ofttimes to the detriment of their faith. *But sometimes, even despite themselves, they accomplished good rather than evil.*

When the time came, would she do as well? Could she? Somehow, despite the desperate struggle building among the Douloi on Ares, she rather thought her role lay elsewhere, but she also knew that Telos rarely used a tool for one purpose only.

The com chimed at her.

"Gnostor Omilov to see you," came Tuaan's voice.

At her bidding her secretary ushered the gnostor in. He refused refreshments; she sensed excitement and tension in him. Perhaps she'd been wrong about him, thinking that the Jupiter

Project had consumed him utterly. Was he here to ask her help for the Aerenarch, the center of the coming storm?

As required by courtesy, their conversation began with generalities, but quickly Omilov steered it to the round of gatherings that had signaled, to her at least, the onset of decision among the Douloi.

"It's my understanding," she said, "that the Aerenarch will be at the Masaud ball, while Hesthar al-Gessinav has obtained the attendance of Admiral Nyberg and his staff at a soiree. I have my suspicions about that arrangement. I imagine that like me, you also have been invited to both."

"Yes," replied Omilov. "And since the Masaud and the Gessinav hate each other cordially, they will each assume we are attending the other's gathering."

"You don't intend to go to either of them?" she asked carefully. Had he, then, truly abandoned politics?

Omilov blinked. "I'm sorry, Numen, I'm getting ahead of myself. But it's a perfect opportunity to introduce the Eya'a to the hyperwave and test their reactions. All eyes will be elsewhere."

Shock stopped Eloatri's breath for a moment. Was this instead what she had sensed, what the disorder of her dreams was pointing to? Or was it all related somehow? Was that why her visions linked the Dol'jharian to the Aerenarch, despite his utter lack of psychic powers? Was this, too, part of the political endgame? All her conjectures crashed in ruin as she struggled to adjust to this new possibility.

"Numen?" A wash of acid light from the storm outside silhouetted his figure.

"Your pardon, Gnostor. You're right." She paused, trying to marshal her thoughts while the thunder rumbled overhead. Evidently Omilov had bowed out of the political game—but there was no doubt this was equally important. Well, then, she would have to make sure it served a larger purpose than the gnostor might otherwise arrange, and the Aerenarch would have to take care of himself: it did not seem she could contrive to help him.

"But you'll need time to prepare. Perhaps I could assist you by bringing them all to the hyperwave?"

Omilov nodded, then suspicion sharpened his features. " 'Them all'? Just Vi'ya and the Eya'a—and Gnostor Manderian."

She stood up. "No, Sebastian. Not just Vi'ya and the Eya'a.

We must also have Ivard and the Kelly—they, too, are part of it."

The gnostor frowned, all his Douloi assurance momentarily swept away by the strangeness of her request. Then he gathered himself visibly and stood to face her.

"I'm sorry, Numen, but I can't countenance that. It will make things too complex."

"Have you spoken to Gnostor Manderian about this?"

He had not, and Eloatri touched the com tab, requesting Tuaan to connect her to the Dol'jharian scholar and tempath.

Moments later a landscape on the wall shimmered and became a window into Manderian's quarters on the ship he shared with others of his College—like him, most of them were sensitives of one sort or another and preferred isolation from the simmering noetic energies of the crowded souls on Ares. The room was starkly somber. "Yes, Numen?"

"Gnostor Omilov has suggested introducing Vi'ya and the Eya'a to the hyperwave while the attentions of the rest of the Ares are bent upon the social activities coming up."

"An excellent idea."

"But he objects to the presence of Ivard and the Kelly."

"I feel it would complicate the experiment too much," Omilov interjected with polite firmness.

"Experiment." Manderian's voice was flat, conveying a hint of distaste at Omilov's choice of words. "Say rather a stage in a process that we are privileged to witness. It would be a grave mistake to exclude the boy and the Kelly—they are an integral part of the noetic unity whose perceptions you wish to test. Are you aware that Ivard has often been seen in the company of the Eya'a—without Vi'ya—in the Cap, on the periphery of the project security cordon?"

"Ah." Omilov looked discomfited. "I see. Well, Gnostor, I defer to your specialized knowledge."

And not to me, the High Phanist. She couldn't know what the Dreamtime had shown Omilov on Desrien, but it was obvious to her that Omilov had barricaded himself against the memory and would yield nothing to her on religious grounds. Well, it didn't matter now.

Omilov and Manderian then discussed the protocols for the procedure at some length. After the Dol'jharian agreed to meet them at the entrance to the Cap, Omilov withdrew with a formal deference that underlined his psychological intransigence.

He must have been very deeply hurt, to build such a formidable wall, thought Eloatri.

The High Phanist turned to the window and stood there for a few minutes, watching the storm move away antispinward. A last flash of lightning illuminated the garden outside, freezing its afterimage in her vision as darkness hid it once again. Then she turned away.

There was much to do.

Sixteen

Vahn's private signal bloomed, and Keveth reported a visitor—Vannis Scefi-Cartano. He waved Keveth off and walked silently along the pathway adjacent to the garden entrance to the Enclave. From behind the drooping leaves of the swensoom tree he watched, his augmented hearing picked up Vannis' soft footfalls.

He saw her just before Jaim opened the door; her hands flexed once, then buried themselves among the folds of her skirts.

Vahn's interest sharpened.

At four that morning Faseult had summoned him for a briefing. They expected a coup that night, and it was possible that Vannis would appear to sidetrack the Aerenarch. *That much we know,* Faseult had said. Then he added: *You will not disseminate any of this information to anyone at the Enclave. That includes the Aerenarch. Understood?*

Vahn understood the orders, but not the reasons why. But he'd placed his best coverts at that Masaud ball, in case they were needed.

Jaim silently opened the door, then jeeved back into the

shadows of the garden room as the Aerenarch came forward. He was dressed for the ball, the candles gilding with rich light the golden leaves embroidered on his night-black tunic. "Vannis?" he said, his light voice merely inquiring. "Good evening."

Behind her back, her hands tightened on the fragile silks of her gown. "A surprise," she said, smiling, her head back. "Now, don't be angry. The Masaud ball will be a hideous crush, so I arranged a little diversion. Of course you have only to say the word, and you can be restored to the crowd. . . ."

She stepped back and waved toward the lake. A barge sat near the platform, colored lanterns strung along its railing just above the water. Vahn could see a table and musicians waiting.

She had obviously gone to a lot of trouble, and it was possible within the complicated patterns of Douloi etiquette to accept a private invitation from someone of higher rank than the original host, even at the last minute—though it carried implications.

But it's a trap. Don't walk into it. . . .

"Well, then," the Aerenarch said, holding out his arm. "Let us divert."

Biting on a curse, Vahn bozzed Roget. *(Pull teams two and three from the Masaud ball. I want them down at the lake perimeter—fast.)*

(You going?) Roget bozzed.

Vahn sent her the negative signal, bozzed Jaim, careful to make his order sound like a request. He had come to like the laconic Rifter, for his cooperative spirit if nothing else.

(They wouldn't dare try anything violent. The timing would hang them.) Roget, his partner for over a year now, knew where his thoughts were headed.

(I've sent Jaim. If they do try anything, it'll be after these two debark. Whatever happens, I can't be stuck in the middle of the lake on a logos-loving barge. Now. Keveth is to proceed. . . .)

With part of his mind he went on issuing orders for the deployment of his people, as he watched Vannis and Brandon tread down the grassy path toward the landing. She was still nervous; Vahn saw that in the sudden shimmer of the string of gemstones wound through her hair. *Poised and tense as a duelist . . .*

He sent Jaim a carefully framed warning, ending with the request that he stick close to the Aerenarch. Vahn was going to need to listen to every damn word.

* * *

Ordinarily Ivard would have enjoyed looking out over the interior of the oneill from the broad ring-promenade that fronted the entrance to the Cap. Up here at the spin axis the view was unmatched anywhere else on Ares, except for Tate Kaga's palace at the other pole. But he could feel Gnostor Omilov's impatience, like the lightning stabbing at the curving landscape far below, and it made him nervous.

The gnostor was talking low-voiced to Manderian, who stood quietly, his hands hidden in the robes of his College, but now Ivard could smell Omilov's impatience.

The blue fire of the Kelly Archon suddenly bubbled up inside, bearing with it a sudden, clear communication from Portus-Dartinus-Atos: *"Wethree are making haste as slowly as possible."* The accompanying image, of the trinity pirouetting in a complex dance that moved them sideways as often as forward, made him snicker. He swallowed it at the harassed look the gnostor shot him from underneath his heavy brows.

Ivard glanced over at Vi'ya, standing silently with the Eya'a, but she didn't look at him. Her gaze seemed turned inward. He could smell her tension, as though she were balancing something almost too heavy to hold; and he felt a searingly focused, unintelligible emotion from the aliens. Ivard felt his fear intensify. When they actually touched the Urian thing inside, what would it be like?

He looked out along the spin axis, hoping to see the bubble of his nuller friend and teacher. Where was Tate Kaga? A sour knot of panic welled up in his stomach. He didn't want to face the gnostor's experiment without Tate Kaga there.

The transtube portal hissed open, and out stepped the Kelly and the High Phanist. Ivard caught a glimpse of a broad smile on Eloatri's face as he ran forward, honking a greeting at the trinity, which was returned threefold. Manderian walked over and greeted them as well.

"Ah," Omilov said. "Now that we're all here, let's move on before something else happens to slow us down." He turned toward the two Marine guards at the entrance to the Cap.

His arms intertwined with the headstalks of the trinity, Ivard looked helplessly at the High Phanist. She made a slight movement with her hands that said as clearly as words: "It's your responsibility."

"Uh, gnostor?" Ivard began, but his words were drowned out by a sudden thunderclap as Tate Kaga's bubble blurred into view and stopped just outside the dyplast window overlooking the interior of the oneill. The Marines jerked their jacs up reflexively, then relaxed as the nuller maneuvered his gee-bubble through a hatch. For once, he was right side up.

"Ho, Little Egg! Are you ready to lose your self to find it?" Then he pivoted upside down and darted over to the High Phanist, whose eyebrows had lifted at his comment. "Eh, Numen! Did you think you had a monopoly on that idea?"

"No, indeed, Tate Kaga," Eloatri replied, then laughed. Next to her Manderian smiled slightly, his black eyes regarding the nuller with open interest. "In fact, if two or more—"

Their exchange was interrupted by Omilov's approach. "Your pardon, Prophetae," he said, sketching a bow to the nuller. Then he turned to Ivard and the High Phanist, his face distracted. "We really must hurry."

Ivard felt both Tate Kaga and Eloatri look at him, and then the gnostor frowned. "Ivard?"

"I want Tate Kage there too," Ivard blurted. "He's been teaching me things, things I'll need."

Omilov threw his hands wide in a gesture eloquent of frustration. "Isn't it enough of a circus already?" he said to the High Phanist. "Perhaps we should invite the Kitharee to furnish us with incidental music."

"He has to be there," Ivard said.

He could feel himself blushing with embarrassment; he controlled the reaction, but he couldn't do anything about the awful shrinking feeling that grabbed him when the gnostor turned to him, tiredness, tension, and impatience clear in his face.

"Enough, young man. You've already committed a major breach of security; don't make it worse. Just come along." He turned back to Tate Kaga. "I'm sorry if Ivard brought you all this way for nothing, but there's really no place for you in this experiment. He shouldn't even have told you."

The gnostor turned away and began to walk to the Cap portal.

"No," said Ivard, his voice cracking. Even with the physical control the Kelly ribbon had conferred on him his body felt alternately hot and cold. "I won't do it without Tate Kaga."

Omilov rounded on him, astonished.

"You don't know what I'm like now," Ivard said desperately. He could smell the gnostor's impatience turning into anger, and, behind it, a dull pain he didn't understand. "You don't know how I think, or how I hear Vi'ya and the Eya'a and the Kelly, or anything about how it works. How can you decide that Tate Kaga can't help? I say he can. He will. Or I won't."

For a moment Omilov seemed poised to react in anger; Ivard scented it and felt weak-kneed in reaction. Then Eloatri stepped forward and laid a hand on the gnostor's arm. "You cannot force the boy."

As if to emphasize her words, the Eya'a chittered softly.

The gnostor tossed his hands up slightly in defeat. "Very well. Rather than waste any more time." He walked past the Marines into the Cap, followed by the others. "Let's go."

It did not take much discernment to perceive that Aerenarch Brandon vlith-Arkad was annoyed.

Vannis Scefi-Cartano, many years his sister-by-marriage and just once, here on Ares, his lover, could appreciate this: she was furious.

Tired and tense from contemplating, unsuccessfully, all through the long watches of the previous night the exquisite irony of her position, she had risen determined to somehow pull inclination and ambition together.

We will leave the Aerenarch to you. Vannis gripped her lower lip between her teeth as she trod down the grassy path toward the lakeside, her slippers damp from the recent rain. High overhead the diffusers shed a silvery light, simulating a full moon; reflections danced on the rippling surface of the lake. At her side Brandon walked. His voice gave no thoughts away, but his arm beneath the smooth fabric of his sleeve was merely there, as a prop for politeness. It forced on her a memory, those arms around her, the blend of strength and tenderness which—

She jabbed her teeth further into her lip, and as they paused for the Rifter bodyguard to go ahead onto the barge and scan it, she faced her choices, each unbearable: either she hand Brandon over to the cabal at the appointed time, and thus lose him forever, or she tell him about the coup and join him in defeat.

She should have known that Hesthar and Tau would somehow ferret out knowledge of Brandon's single visit to her rooms, so she could have planned to sidestep this particular trap.

She could even see their point of view. It made logical sense that a person might surprise a lover with an entertainment tête-à-tête. She was even sure that Tau wished her well of the affair; his unspoken message was that personal inclination could not be involved with the exercise of power. By being the one to take Brandon away from the ball, she had removed herself from the political arena: she would not be there when they spontaneously nominated one another as the new council. And the fact that this had been accomplished without a word being spoken functioned as a warning: she was not yet adept to compete in the political arena.

Which left her the personal connection—except that by betraying Brandon to the cabal, she would lose him as a lover, which would keep her loyalties clear. That, she knew, was Hesthar's notion.

Damn! She had to reign, even better to rule. Her training had designated her all her life for the first, and as for the second, it was her deepest desire.

Not the deepest, not the deepest . . .

Damn, damn, damn. Wasn't there some way to ensure that Brandon win? Then she could have both.

Only three days left.

She resisted the impulse to touch her boswell. Strange, how she had misjudged Fierin vlith-Kendrian. Because she was decades younger than most of the cabal, it had been easy to assume she was a fool. "I'll sidetrack Brandon, if you prefer," she'd said. "I don't mind: there's nothing more for me to lose."

And she'd handled the offer so skillfully, the timing perfectly managed, in transit between one party and another, when no one else was looking their way.

Vannis had been severely tempted at first, but she had not taken the easy way out. *Tau would only find some other way to bind me to them.* And she did not like to think of what he might do to the well-meaning young woman to indicate his displeasure at the contravention of the plans.

It was time to put regret behind her and face the present. There might still be some way out. If only there was some way to slow things down!

Three days, she thought, feeling tension grip her head in its invisible vise. *In three days the Panarch is beyond us. Either the cabal gains enough power to forbid any rescue missions, or else it and its opponents mire one another in three days of squabbling, and then it will be too late. . . . Either way, the cabal wins—and I lose.*

"Checks fine, Highness," the Rifter said.

Vannis' attention was caught by the Rifter's flat voice, his long, curiously attractive face that reminded her of a hound. Though he moved softly enough, he did not affect the selfless blank stare of the trained servant. He met one's eyes straight on, his stance correctly deferential but his gaze intelligent and dispassionately assessing.

Brandon turned to Vannis, smiling, but his attitude was clear: Your move.

He *couldn't* know, could he? They walked aboard the barge, Vannis stepping carefully. Part of her mind was busy with light chatter about the disaster at the Ascha Gardens party, and about the Masaud ball later this evening—to which, she promised, they could go at any time he wished.

It was up to her to make sure that the barge landed only after she had received her signal from Tau.

A quick glance around showed that the barge, at least, was everything the owner, that rude, battered old vice-admiral, had promised. She had further made clear her dislike of the frivolous Douloi civilians by charging a stinging price, way beyond Vannis' present means—but like the other gambles, she hoped this would be paid back through events.

The vessel was a relic of a bygone era, when sneaking off for stolen time with one's adored was in fashion. The design fostered intimacy; the details, from brocaded couches to the graceful pattern of dancing dolphins carved into the low rail—a pattern that never repeated, yet still evoked the yin and yang—were perfect. In keeping with its air of fantasy, it even had a geeplane drive, making it capable of slow and dreamy flight if the lovers' impulses so demanded. For tonight, though, Vannis had engaged a steersman to pole the barge along the lake; the techs had set the geeplane to merely stabilize the barge.

"I borrowed a chef—" she said. No need to mention that this chef was Tau's. "Shall we see what she has to offer us?"

Brandon cast a look over the beautifully arranged delicacies. As Vannis followed, mouth-watering drifts of spices and herbs blended with cream pastry tickled her nostrils. She had not eaten all day, but when Brandon passed by the food and walked to the rail, she, too, turned away.

"Something to drink?" she asked.

Brandon rested against the rail as the barge gently moved away from the landing. "Please."

Vannis moved to the monneplat, busying her fingers with the list of available wines. These, too, had been provided by Tau; more gentle hints of the bonds of political bedfellows. Leading the list was an exceptionally old year of crespec, the strange, costly liquor that Tau was known for serving to honored guests.

Running her eyes down the list, she said, "I have two respectably old Charvannese reds and a promising Locke."

"Whatever you prefer," Brandon said courteously.

My move, yes. Well, how will I move?

Though Yenef stood by, silent and ready to serve, and she knew that the Rifter could order and pour wine, she decided to do it herself, her thoughts accelerating.

And ambivalence nearly paralyzed her.

Aware of the lengthening of the silence, but suddenly unable to think of entertaining talk, she brought the wine to Jaim, who opened it, glancing momentarily at his boswell; then she poured out two glasses.

As she joined Brandon at the rail, the barge began its slow circuit of the lake, and on prearranged signal the quartet—two strings, two winds—concealed behind a finely carved set of antique Rhidari panels in the draped pavilion at the stern, began playing KetzenLach's "Variations on a Theme by Dè Blukerln."

She stood at his shoulder. "So tell me," she said, touching her glass to his, "how did you get that diamond from Charidhe?"

His smile was slightly preoccupied. What was he thinking? As tension increased its vise grip on her skull, she cast a quick look over the lake, and was startled to see a head just above the shrub in front of a well-lit gazebo on the shore—but then the barge moved further along, and it was only a tall young woman, absorbed in feeding some ducks.

"I admired it," Brandon responded, shrugging slightly as he watched the woman with the quacking, waddling ducks. "And then I asked her if I could borrow it."

"So simple!" Vannis laughed. "I guess it serves as another indication how things have changed."

"How is that?" he replied.

"To borrow jewels would have caused a scandal not so long ago," she said, humoring him with the obvious. At least he was talking.

He bowed slightly, smiling, and she realized that he would have borrowed those jewels, anyway, careless of the results, back in the old days. . . . *And he's an Arkad, so he would have gotten away with it,* she thought belatedly.

It made her look up at his eyes, which were watchful above the polite smile. His gaze was almost a palpable blow. *He does know something's amiss,* and she felt, and repressed, the urge to start chattering like a child.

What held her back? The visceral thrill she felt at the oblique reminder of the weight of his background was almost as strong as her own physical response to Brandon himself: she acknowledged that. But the Arkad name was not enough. He would soon be relegated to mere figurehead—her old status—and she could not bear that again.

What shook her was the strength of her regret; it was the first time, ever, that she had had such thoughts, that she would even consider throwing away power and position just for a person.

The bustle of activity in the Situation Room faltered and died as Sebastian Omilov led his unlikely troupe through the hatch. They'd turned off the mindblurs, which seemed to have functioned as a signal that something was about to happen.

First the Eya'a went inside, then Vi'ya, then Ivard and the Kelly, Eloatri, Manderian, and finally Tate Kaga, his bubble squeezed down to minimum size. With each succeeding entrance the room became quieter, and Omilov felt himself the focus of several dozen pairs of eyes under the vast hologram of the Thousand Suns glimmering overhead.

"Wait here," he said tersely; an unnecessary instruction. During their passage through the heavy security surrounding the project, he had told them all the procedure he and Manderian had worked out. All of the participants would wait outside until called; Vi'ya and the Eya'a, as the psychic focus of the experiment, would enter last.

"Once they see the hyperwave, their actions will be unpredictable, and perhaps uncontrollable. Attempting to restrain them at that point could be fatal," Manderian had said.

That thought, and its corollaries, weighed heavily on Sebastian as he approached the hatch with the Marine guards to either side, beyond which lay the Urian hyperwave. He barely noticed the security scan, wondering briefly if it could read the knot of fear curdling in his stomach. He'd reviewed the interrogation chip from the *Mbwa Kali,* with the descriptions, by the Rifters who'd rescued him, of the carnage the Eya'a had left behind in Eusabian's torture chamber underneath the Mandala. And his own College of Xenology had similar data in its records, replicated here on Ares.

The door to the hyperwave room slid shut behind him, cutting off the stares of the officers and technicians in the Situation Room, but not before Ysabet, his head technician, slipped through behind him, a sympathetic look on her face.

She jerked a thumb over her shoulder. "What in the Nine Shiidran Hells is that exhibition all about? I thought this was to test the Dol'jharian and the aliens? Isn't that Tate Kaga?"

Omilov sighed heavily. "It's very . . . complicated. But Ivard, the boy bonded to the Kelly, is evidently part of the polymental complex that is sensitive to Urian artifacts, and he will not cooperate without the Prophetae."

She snorted derisively, looking around at the small room, with the red-glowing lump of the hyperwave wired into the wall opposite the door, and the various instruments now ranked along the other walls for the experiment. "Gonna be crowded—hope those little brain-boilers aren't claustrophobic."

Omilov nodded, and Ysabet reviewed their preparations. Save for Omilov himself, all the technicians would monitor remotely, to avoid biasing the noetic and mental potentials of the participants, and for their own safety, should the Eya'a react negatively. He glanced at the ceiling, where neatly installed nozzles now protruded, ready to flood the room with a complex of gases that, based on the best guesses from the scanty biological data they had on the aliens, might immobilize them. Might; it might also kill them or, perhaps worse, have no effect at all. He had a brief, chilling vision of a Situation Room filled with corpses, blood and neural tissue leaking from eyes and noses.

"Gnostor? Are you all right?"

He tried to shake off the mood. "I'm sorry, Ysabet; too much work, too little sleep. You've done a fine job here. Why don't you send in the first group of participants?"

She departed with a final, indecipherable look at him. Moments later he sensed the tianqi shifting into a new mode, one he recognized as intended to subdue anxiety, but it had little effect on him.

Omilov looked around the room, at the gleaming instruments blinking their messages of logic and mathematics, the polished floor reflecting the banks of lights and the mysterious artifact of the Ur. Here, at least, for a time he'd felt in control, in contrast to life outside. It had compensated, in a way, for his inability to help Brandon, who he feared was slowly drowning in the maelstrom of Douloi intrigue focused on him.

But now that control was slipping away; the clean symmetry of science pushed out by the amorphous pressure of mysticism, and there was nothing he could do about it. Old memories pushed up from the silence of the past, triggering the dull ache of regret that was never far away. Then the door slid open, admitting Ivard, the Kelly, Eloatri, and finally Tate Kaga.

"We'd better hurry," sald the High Phanist. "Manderian says the Eya'a may not wait much longer."

But then, to his utter astonishment, Tate Kaga floated over to the hyperwave and commenced a guttural chant in an archaic language that resembled nothing Omilov had ever heard before, and Ivard echoed it. The Kelly swarmed over to the boy and moaned in counterpoint, their headstalks pattlng and stroking both him and the Urian artifact. On the walls, the lenses of the imagers reflected the scene in miniature as they recorded it all.

The nuller handed something through the gee-bubble's field to the boy—some sort of burning herb, which Ivard flourished at the hyperwave and then at himself, breathing deeply. A sharp fragrance filled the air.

Tate Kaga handed the boy more herbs, black and sweet-smelling, then a reddish bark, but Omilov strode angrily over to the High Phanist. "What are they doing? What is this nonsense?"

"Tate Kaga is a shaman of the Shanungpa tradition; he is helping Ivard to prepare. . . ."

Really angry now, Omilov cut her off. "I suppose they'll sacrifice some small animal next." He raised his voice. "That's enough of that. This is a scientific experiment. . . ."

But the High Phanist grabbed his arm and swung him back to face her with surprising strength.

"Be silent, Sebastian Omilov! Your ignorance is willful and unforgivable." She raised her hand, revealing the image of the Digrammaton burned into it in its leap across the light-years from Arthelion, where her predecessor had died in the atrocity aimed at Brandon. "Have you so soon forgotten Desrien?"

A chill possessed him, and he fought desperately as the Dreamtime stirred within the vaults of memory, bringing with it an image of a man in archaic dress, facing a snarling leopard in a dark forest.

At that moment the hatch hissed open and the Eya'a raced through, followed more slowly by Vi'ya. She moved as if exhausted, her eyes wide and unseeing, the muscles in her neck rigid. Next to her, Manderian watched closely, not touching her but apparently prepared for anything, his face echoing her agonized concentration.

The keening of the Eya'a mounted above the chanting and the alien threnody of the Kelly, as they ran their twiggy hands over the hyperwave. Then, abruptly, they stood still, their white fur fluffed out. Omilov felt a pressure in his head, heard Manderian's breath hiss. Ivard's voice ceased.

As one, Ivard, Vi'ya and the Eya'a all pivoted to face in the same direction.

Omilov's ring finger tingled, rising to an ache up his left arm. He took a step forward, another, fighting off a buzzing tide of blackness. He heard Vi'ya gasp a name: "Arkad!"

Then she, Ivard, and the Eya'a crumpled to the floor.

The Kelly bent over the prone boy and the little white-furred sentients; they made space for Eloatri, who knelt next to the boy's head. Omilov looked from one to the other, helpless to act or to intervene; the last thing he saw was the limp body of the Dol'jharian woman borne up into the air below Tate Kaga's bubble, her dark hair like a banner in the wind as the nuller sped out through the door.

Then the mystery of Desrien claimed him once again, and he fell into the Dreamtime.

❋ ❋ ❋

Omilov awoke, knowing for a moment he was dreaming. Then the knowledge fled and he found himself standing in a street in Merryn, on Charvann.

Above, the light vanished from the sky over the city, taking with it the last traces of his sense of direction. Around him the buildings were mere slabs of darker night; no windows glowed. The streetlights and lumenpanels were powerless to pierce the darkness; they cast no illumination beyond the puddles of light directly beneath them. A restless wind scourged the street around him; the air bore the tang of dust and ozone.

Omilov heard a confused roaring in the distance: a crowd, he thought, in that uneasy state between excitement and riot. He walked toward the sound, but it receded from him.

Finally he entered the great square before the Archonic Enclave, just in time to see the crowd pushing madly through its gates, pursuing some sort of banner or guerdon—it was too dark to see the device emblazoned on it—that twisted in the air in front of them, ever just out of reach. Douloi and Polloi alike, in finery or in rags, they scrambled through the towering doors and vanished from his sight.

Omilov made to follow them, seeking some refuge from the strange emptiness of the streets, but the solid darkness within repelled him. He could still hear them, deep within the Enclave, their shouts and cries sounding like the growl of some vast beast lying in wait.

"There is no safety in there for you, Sebastian. You must take another path."

He turned, startled. At his side stood Nahomi il-Ngari, his superior in the Praerogacy, her gaunt features somehow clear to his eyes despite the darkness. Something was different about her. Omilov frowned, then he had it: missing was the blason d'solei that had been the sole adornment of her sober garb.

Her hand strayed to her breast for a moment, then dropped to her side. "My aegicy issues from another now. Come."

She turned and walked away. The set of her shoulders forbade speech. Omilov followed in silence, the only sound the grit of their shoes in the dust underfoot.

She led him out of the city. They encountered no other people; slowly the buildings dwindled, giving way to open fields, the restless breeze carrying a sour tang.

The sky still flickered from time to time, less frequently. After a time measured only in heartbeats and the solemn tread of their feet, an angular form took shape against the horizon, now glowing with the light of first moonrise. Then Tira bulged over the distant mountains, and Omilov gasped as its magenta orb, swollen by the horizon effect, silhouetted the archaic, terrible form of a gallows. There was a body suspended from it.

As they came closer, he saw that the gallows was guarded by two Marines in battle armor, as unmoving as the deadly framework above them, their visors closed, reflective.

Nahomi stopped at the foot of the gallows. Omilov perforce stopped too and looked up at its gruesome burden, swaying slightly in the wind.

"No!" The word was impelled from him as if by a fist in the stomach. Despite the corpse's swollen face, its blackened, protruding tongue and glaring eyes, he recognized it: Tared hai-L'Ranja, Archon of Lusor.

Omilov ran to the foot of the gallows, where a ladder lay on the ground. He bent and grasped its rungs, trying to heave it up against the upright; a foot pinned it to the ground, bruising his fingers. He looked up into Nahomi's face.

"You cannot help him now."

"Why? He was the most loyal of men!"

There was no reply. Rage seized him; he pounded his fists against the unyielding surface of the Marine's battle armor, shouting wordlessly. Then he stumbled back, terrified, as the Marine's visor popped open. The armor was empty; the taint of carrion wafted out.

Omilov began to run. He heard a harsh cry behind him, a creaking, inhuman sound, and the beat of vast wings.

He left the fields behind, fleeing into the closeness of a dense forest of twisted trees. His breath came white now: it was cold, bitterly cold, and around him he heard the trees cry out in the crackling speech of branches split by freezing sap.

Finally he emerged into double moonlight to the welcome sight of home: The Hollows, its marble walls and high-peaked roofs gleaming. Omilov slowed to a walk, his breathing eased.

And stopped, as a coldness deeper than the frigid air settled in his heart. The windows of The Hollows gaped empty, lightless; the doors hung askew, and the gardens were brittle, not with the natural sleep of winter's rest, but with the blighted death of an aborted spring.

Omilov stumbled into the sculpture garden outside his library. Thick rime coated the limbs of the stone figures, furring their outlines into distortions of their former grace.

And then he saw the other figures, sitting here and there on the benches he'd had placed for the ease of guests. He approached one and found a man encased in ice, unmoving. He bent over, peering through the blurry armor frozen on his face, and hissed in surprise. It was the Archon Srivashti, whose betrayal of the norms of power had ruined Timberwell. Omilov straightened abruptly and backed away when, suddenly, Srivashti's eyes moved and focused on him, his gaze a mix of mute appeal and madness.

Something cold touched his back, stopping his retreat. He spun around, recognizing another frozen form: Semion vlith-Arkad. The ice around his body was even thicker, but his eyes, too, tracked Omilov as he moved away.

Omilov fled toward the library, ever his refuge, and ran headlong into a third figure. The impact cracked the ice on it, thinner than the layer on the others, and the figure's head turned.

"Sebastian, I didn't know," whispered Brandon; but as the older man watched, horrified, the ice grew back over his face and neck, crystallizing in patterns like frost on a window, immobilizing all but his eyes.

Weeping, Omilov climbed the steps to the library and pushed open the doors, seeking safety, security, the familiar.

The roof had fallen in, leaving the room open to the sky. The two moons peered over the jagged edges of the walls, brightly lighting the ruin within. Books littered the floor, their bindings torn, pages scattered; daggers of ice hung from every shelf, like the teeth of dragons.

But in the center of the room, miraculously spared the destruction all around, his carven reading stand still stood, an opened book upon it. He moved forward, looked down. It was no book he'd ever known, the pages brown with age, printed in a font he'd never seen before, the edges of the letters ragged. They were, he realized, hand-cut—it was a relic of Lost Earth.

He bent forward, angling his head to cast the double shadow from the moons elsewhere than on the page. The words sprang out at him.

> "Where are you damned?"
> "In hell."
> "How comes it then that thou art out of hell?"
> "Why this is hell, nor am I out of it:
> Thinkst thou that I who saw the face of God,
> And tasted the eternal joys of heaven,

Am not tormented with ten thousand hells,
In being deprived of everlasting bliss?"

Omilov jerked backward, trying to retreat, but the only result was a grating, almost musical crunch as his legs refused to move. He looked down, horrified, to see the ice creeping up his torso: he was already encased in ice from his hips down.

He looked back at the book, as if the answer might lie there. A shadow fell across it and he looked up into Ilara's eyes, soft blue-gray and understanding. She closed the book firmly with one slim hand and smiled at him. He drank in the sight of her hungrily, forgetting his desperation for a moment; but then the cold settled in him even deeper as he saw the gaping wound blooming like an evil rose in the center of her chest. The ice mounted to his throat, across his chin, sealed his mouth, and finally blurred his vision of her face.

And then Ilara touched her wound and, reaching forward, touched him in the center of his chest. Warmth flared, ice shattered and fell away in musical relief.

And she vanished, was taken up in a motion so swift his eyes refused all but the direction.

He looked up. High in the southern sky, the bright ring of Highdwellings arched up into the sunlight still denied the surface of Charvann as night retreated westward. He had the dizzying sense of the heavens wheeling about him, or him about the heavens, all about all, center about center, in the ceaseless dance of intention and delight that is Totality. Somewhere a voice spoke, declaiming:

"High phantasy lost power and here broke off;
Yet, as a wheel moves smoothly, free from jars,
My will and my desire were turned by love,
The love that moves the sun and the other stars."

Sebastian Omilov awoke, knowing he was no longer dreaming, knowing he would never lose the dream again. Slowly the lights suspended over the hyperwave room came into focus, framing Ysabet's anxious face.

He sat up. "I'm fine," he said in response to Ysabet's questions. "Never better." Something cold tickled his palm; reflexively he wiped his hand against his thigh before wonder stopped him. Ice? Sweat? It didn't matter, he realized; the Dreamtime was real beyond all calculation.

He looked up to meet the calm eyes of the High Phanist from where she crouched across the room, cradling Ivard's head, with the Kelly crowded near, crooning softly. Nearby, the Eya'a lay, their bodies limp, their chests rising and falling slowly.

Ivard opened his eyes. "We saw it. Vi'ya's thing, the Heart of Kronos." He twisted around and pointed. "It's there. I can feel it. It's moving." Then he closed his eyes.

"It's there. It's moving!" Joy and excitement infused Omilov with energy. His path was clear.

Ignoring Ysabet's protests, he gave instructions for the care of the Eya'a and the others, and left the room. Now to report to Nyberg that the Suneater could be found; then to find Brandon and give him whatever he needed.

Telos grant I'm not too late.

Seventeen

The tired, stressed techs deserved their triumph, Ng thought, watching them exchange insults and compliments. Nyberg had placed any communications from Hreem the Faithless on the priority decoding list. So far, they still had not cracked Barrodagh's codes, or Juvaszt's, but they'd just sent word that Hreem's had been unraveled.

On her way back to the Grozniy, Ng stopped at the Situation Room to see for herself.

"Most of this appears to be his comtech's idea of serial vids," the head tech explained, waving a hand toward the screen. "He's been sending to new recruits edited versions of the Dol'jharian fleet's. But this one is the real thing."

On the screen, a dark face appeared, cruelty lines etched into it. A thick mane of hair and a gaudy uniform of gold-trimmed red, worn half-tabbed over a grizzled chest, completed the picture of one of the most infamous Rifter pirates on the naval bonus chips.

"Senz lo'Barrodagh," Hreem said, "I will be happy to proceed to the Suneater, but I have a suggestion first. We're conveniently near to the Barcan system. Lord Eusabian might like

production of their Ogre battle androids secured for his own use, by someone who knows how to take orders."

A tap windowed up Barrodagh, who pursed his lips in thought, and then nodded. "You are right, Hreem," the Bori said. "The Lord of Vengeance could use the Barcan matériel to effect, and he also has use for those who follow orders." He smiled thinly. "But the Barcans might have taken more precautions than we know of, and I fear for your safety. I will dispatch Neyvla-khan and his fleet to join you; they have just finished—an admirable job—securing the Minervan Tetrad."

Hreem's mouth tightened, but he shrugged, affecting nonchalance. "Sure. We'll be waiting for 'em."

Both screens blanked.

Neyvla-khan. Where have I heard that before?

Someone behind whistled. "Now, that," she said, "will be interesting. I wonder which of them has the longer record for uninterrupted villainy?" And as several people turned to face the speaker, she went on, "The Neyvla clan has been terrorizing the Rouge Sud octant since before I was born."

The little Rifter tech spoke up from the back. "And long before they swore a blood oath to Eusabian they swore a death vendetta on Hreem."

⁂ ⁂ ⁂

At first, Osri Omilov was amused by the differences in his reception. *It seems to be true,* he thought, returning the sketchy bow that Aristide Masaud gave him. *Leave off the uniform and there goes your identity.*

Aristide Masaud was only a cousin of the line currently holding titles and directorships of the family businesses, and he was a minor cousin at that, but his disinterest was noticeable as he bowed to Pomalythe and Kenzit.

A walk between the polished metal panels of the doors threw back distorted reflections of four dark-haired people, all with heavy brows and angular jaws. Startled, Osri recognized himself among them.

Masaud thinks I'm another Ghettierus.

It was also clear, he realized as he trailed after their mother, who bullied her way through the guests on the ballroom floor, just how unpopular the Ghettierus family was.

"Oh, Telos," Poma whined. "They've called up Highdweller decor. I *hate* Highdweller taste."

"Feel like my next breath will be vacuum," Kenzit grumped. "Or else we'll be puking from nullgrav."

Osri, who enjoyed Highdweller life despite his Downsider upbringing, appreciated as much of the ambience of the salon as he could despite his siblings' complaints. It was hard, he decided, to point out just what distinguished the architecture of the Highdweller overculture. It was less any one detail than an accumulation of details: the slight exaggeration of vertical scale, paradoxically combined with a feeling of closeness and enclosure; the fact that the focus of accents and flourishes tended to be up and inward, rather than down and outward; and a more three-dimensional feeling to the masses and spaces created by the furnishings.

His mother did not seem to notice. She plowed on, pushing her way past people, until a sudden stop meant that she had attained her goal: a circle of seats along a main concourse.

Bickering halfheartedly, Kenzit and Poma squeezed in beside Osri. Their mother settled into the seat with the best view, then activated the table console to order for everyone.

Osri sat back, resigning himself to a tedious stay. At least his mother hadn't brought one of her light-accursed lovers—but then she wouldn't, unless she could manage to snare one who was better born than she. *And if she did have one, she'd want him as escort, not me.*

Amusement at his mother's predictability shaded into annoyance at Sebastian's refusal to come. *Why was he so obdurate? He at least knows the hosts of these never-ending parties.* But despite a daily bombardment of abusive messages from Lady Risiena, Sebastian had remained adamant: he was too busy.

So Lady Risiena had promptly turned her fire onto her son, and to escape her tireless harassments, Osri had given in. He had, however, refused to wear his uniform. It was not his duty to go, so he would attend as a civilian.

The difference in his reception was immediately obvious to him. It was not long, however, before the difference became obvious to his mother.

"Don't you know *anyone?*" Kenzit whined presently.

Guests were still arriving, and Osri had only seen one familiar face, but he'd managed not to catch the person's eye.

"I told you I don't," Osri replied. "I've been too busy on Minerva. Civilian Douloi don't visit Minerva."

"But there's bound to be an officer passing by," Lady

Risiena muttered, jabbing her finger into Osri's shoulder. "Whether you know the person or not, salute."

"I can't," Osri said. "I am not in uniform." He saw then his mother's plan: anyone who stopped to salute or return his salute could be dragooned into introductions, and from there bullied into partnership with one of his half sisters for one of the infernal dances.

An overwhelming desire to laugh had to be hidden in his cup. Lady Risiena started tapping her nails on the table. Poma and Kenzit promptly began bickering with her about it; Osri turned his attention away, wondering how long it would take his mother to figure out that she'd been foiled, so they could leave.

Because they had an excellent view of the ballroom, Osri could watch, with ease, the patterns of spectacularly dressed Douloi. Why did people go to these things, anyway? Who wanted to be squashed into too small a space with too many of just the people one least wished to see?

Glaring down at the ballroom floor, Osri realized that he did not see anyone he would talk to: in fact, he did not see anyone in uniform at all.

Curious, he turned in his chair so he could see better, and scanned the room. No: not one uniform. *How did this happen?* Had the Navy and the civilians polarized that much? No one would have bothered telling him: he never paid any heed to talk of social functions, and everyone who knew him knew he avoided them whenever possible.

As his gaze wandered over the assembled people, he noticed that fewer than usual were dancing, though the music was very well played. Small clumps of people stood along the sides, talking. Here and there excited gestures indicated subjects of great interest. And around the Harkatsus Aegios was a crowd. . . .

Tall, grim-faced Kestian Harkatsus speaking animatedly to a crowd. Images connected in Osri's mind: red-haired Ivard, talking to a young Douloi who was pointed out as the Harkatsus heir; Ivard's whisper, "Regency Council."

"At least you can smile," a hard voice said in his ear.

He looked up, startled, to see his mother frowning at him. "Do you see anyone you know?"

Osri shook his head. Speculations raced through his head.

". . . I *said*, why don't you and Poma go out and dance?"

Distracted, he turned to his mother. "I know. Why don't I

take a quick walk through the crowd, and if I see a friend, I'll bring him over."

"Two friends," Kenzit said, with a glare at her sister.

Osri was already on his feet by the time his mother thought of extra instructions for him, and he backed away so that her words melded into the sound of other voices. Smiling, he made the sign for *I'll be back,* then escaped with a sense of freedom that swiftly cooled into urgency.

As he made his way down the graceful curve of the rampway, he recalled his dismissal of the Regency Council talk, after he'd had the leisure to think it through. After all, he'd thought, how could anyone pull a coup over the Navy? For that was what any group would have to do in order to establish its claim. The thought was absurd.

But what if there was another way?

He arrived at the back of the crowd around the Aegios, who was talking, his hands spread, his smile wide.

"That's exactly what I mean," Harkatsus was saying. "It is time—right now—to throw our support behind the new Aerenarch. He will learn swiftly the ways of government, and meanwhile, those of us who have had experience can guide him."

A murmur of approval went through the crowd, then a woman said, "But the Aerenarch wishes to rescue the Panarch."

Harkatsus bowed acknowledgment. "Thus providing his Family loyalty—and his inexperience. Think! How can we recover a man who is probably guarded by the biggest fleet Eusabian of Dol'jhar can field, when we were not able to stand against his forces when we had the superior numbers? Do not forget their skipmissiles. They are real."

"That's true," someone muttered. "I saw what one did to the *Korion*. One shot."

The murmurs had changed. Alarm mounted in Osri, which peaked when Harkatsus spoke next: "Meanwhile, the Navy—which exists to serve—can do nothing in a power vacuum. The Aerenarch awaits his father; the Panarch is beyond reach, and nothing is done. It is up to us, those who serve, to proclaim our wishes, to help guide the new Panarch. . . ."

Osri backed away slowly, his mind already reviewing the crowds he'd seen from above. He knew he had not seen Brandon.

The Aerenarch isn't here, either.

And: *They are going to betray him.*

For an endless moment he stood alone in the press of jeweled and scented Douloi, his loyalties pulled in two directions.

He could stay put and do nothing, which in one sense would be just. He'd once sworn to see to it that Brandon was given over to justice for his reprehensible abandonment of duty and honor at his own Enkainion.

Except Osri had since learned that duty and honor were not as simple to define as he'd once thought. The facts were unchanged, but the reasons behind the facts were still a mystery—and, as sudden urgency moved him smoothly through the crowd, he acknowledged that his faith had not been betrayed, it had only changed form.

I believe Brandon wants his father back; so I must believe he had a reason for what he did.

Osri took two or three quick steps, and with a sense of relief found the door to the disposers. He wasn't one of those persons who were remarkably adept at keeping privacies private.

As the door shut behind him, he hit Brandon's private code, and was rewarded with an instant response.

* * *

Low clouds drifted over the lake; now it was time for a nurturing rain. Vannis saw a couple sitting on a secluded sandspit put up an umbrella, and on a rise just above the water, a man with a sketchpad backed under a tree.

A cool breeze ruffled through Vannis' hair and skirts, and she gestured to Yenef, who touched the console.

A brightly bannered awning slid silently overhead just as the first droplets stung cheeks and arms. Brandon looked down at the ruffling lakewater and the droplets sending out quick rings that blended and disappeared. He was very still, his gaze on the dark water. Vannis watched him, her mind running rapidly through possible gambits to catch his interest, make him want to stay. He did not seem to notice the music, and he obviously did not want to talk.

Without warning he drained his glass and turned to face her, leaning companionably on the railing. "Am I poor company?" he asked with a quirky smile. And lifting a hand in a gesture of appeal, "Ought I to do my duty by the Masauds?"

Vannis' gaze went from the long fingers so close to her own

hand, up to his expectant blue gaze. Again she felt an almost unbearable urge to blather out the truth, to eradicate the distance between them, to inspire gratitude, which might ignite into passion—

Except passion's rewards were ephemeral. She could not throw away her ambitions just to please one man.

"Stay," she said. "Am I so dull?"

"Never." He caught her hand up and kissed it, with that mocking grand air that always made her want to laugh. She curtseyed in the same manner, thinking, *I'll keep to the plan, but I will not go back along the pathway Tau wants.* Despite Tau's talk of safety, Vannis sensed that Felton lay in wait on that path—probably with several of the yacht's well-trained servants. At least she could keep Brandon free of their "escort" and twitter some excuse or other later.

Brandon spoke then, his back to the railing. "Why don't we make this a real party?"

Vannis laughed, relieved and intrigued with his sudden change of mood. "Of course," she said. "This is for your pleasure."

He bowed. Was there irony in the flourish of his hand? "Jaim," he said. "You haven't eaten yet, have you? Come on, don't let this spread go to waste."

And the Rifter promptly came forward, and without any hesitation, picked up one of the fine porcelain plates and loaded it judiciously.

Brandon nodded, then surprised Vannis further by walking across the barge to the concealing Rhidari panels. Pulling them aside, he addressed the musicians, who looked up in fourfold shock: "The music is splendid, but I can hardly hear you for the rain. Come out and eat something with us."

Wordlessly they laid down their instruments and bowed, then filed out in a row. Brandon held the panel open until the last of them had passed, then let it pivot shut. He turned to Yenef. "Dear lady," he said, giving her a polite bow. "Please. Will you honor us with your company as well?"

Yenef's face remained wooden, as a proper servant's always must, and even as she made her reverence, her eyes sought Vannis'. Vannis rather helplessly signed back that she was free to do what she liked. Though she still retained control of the timing, control of the party itself had passed out of her hands.

She followed, smiling left and right as the musicians helped themselves to the food, but she wondered if her moment had slipped by and found her wanting, exactly as she'd felt after that first conversation, when he so unaccountably brought up the fate of his brother's mistress.

She occupied her hands by placing delicacies on a plate, then stood against the rail watching as Brandon went from one to the other of the unlikely guests, asking names, making jokes, commenting on their profession as if it were a main interest of his. Thus he bound them together into a party of sorts, with the musicians laughing freely, and even the Rifter cracking a smile from time to time.

She watched Jaim as he ate. What *was* this Rifter to Brandon? The Aerenarch had not talked about his experiences with the Rifters except in the most general way. Yet there was some kind of bond: he had taken this one as his personal liegeman, and another as his cook, and visited a third, the boy who had somehow annexed the Kelly genome. The only ones he seemed to avoid were the stone-faced Dol'jharian captain and those hideous white-furred sentients that everybody said could kill with psi, and he had not visited the one in prison, brother to Fierin vlith-Kendrian.

Jaim looked up from time to time as the talk progressed. He seldom added to it, until the subject veered to music, and then the breadth of his knowledge of arcane musical forms was surprising.

Brandon laughed and talked, looking out now and then at the lakeside. Distracted, Vannis also looked out at where three or four young men strolled, one of them tossing a glowing nullball into the air meditatively, each time walking several meters while it ever so slowly drifted back to his hands.

Then Brandon moved to the pavilion, clapping loudly.

"Well, put," he said to the musicians. "You are right; I see the influence now. And I thank you, most profoundly." He looked to the right and left, then bowed, the formal bow of admirer to artist. "Jaim!" he called, his voice bright with laughter. "Help me remember: when we do return to Arthelion, I'll want these players there. . . ." He backed up, his gestures wide and mock solemn, as if he were drunk.

One of the musicians snickered; the others watched, in fascination, as he clowned, describing in increasingly silly terms his coronation. ". . . and we can issue Ysselian roaring flutes to all the children in the procession, and Foneli nose-trumpets to each temenarch . . ."

Brandon mimicked the sound of the ritual flutes of the Yssel clans with a hideous droning noise through his nose, alternated with demented tweets, backing up as he did so. The poler turned to watch as the Aerenarch climbed up on the rail, his arms waving.

"And you"—he gestured grandly to the lead musician—"perhaps can compose a divertissement for strings, winds, and Karelian Mace."

He bent and grabbed the pole from the steersman, tossing it into the air and catching it with a wide two-handed grip, miming with exaggerated care the actions of the mace bearer, swaying from side to side while banging the ends of the pole on the deck.

Jaim snorted with laughter and ducked out of the way as the pole narrowly missed his skull. Then, as the other end came down, Brandon seemed to lose his balance. Jaim was fast, moving swiftly to his side, but somehow Brandon escaped his grasp, falling outward and flailing helplessly with the pole.

And then—Vannis watched it unfold with drama-like slowness, helpess to intervene—the end of the pole swept around and smashed into the control console, which erupted with a flare of light. A wave of nausea swept through her as, with a buzzing screech, the little geeplane used to stabilize the barge overloaded and the entire barge slowly upended, dishes sliding down to crash with musical tinklings against the rail as it tilted with majestic grace toward the spin axis far overhead. The deck became steeper and steeper, provoking inharmonious bumps and thumps as the musical instruments slid over the side and splashed into the water.

Two of the musicians screamed and dived after; the geeplane gave a final despairing screech and the barge lurched up to a near-vertical stance and then toppled over, flinging them all, with a mighty splash, into the cold lake.

Vannis caught her breath just before the water closed over her, and she found herself entangled in the ripped awning. She fought free of that and then ripped away her skirts, which clung to her legs. Kicking free of her gown, she swam toward the bobbing, cursing heads.

Screams, high and hysterical, turned out to be Yenef, who insisted some creature had bitten her. A confusion of agitatedly swinging lights and voices converged on them, and suddenly they were surrounded by the young picnickers, who seemed to have found long rowboats and lights.

A woman gripped Vannis under her armpits and pulled her smoothly from the water. Vannis let her head drop back against the edge of the boat as the picnickers helped fish the others out of the water. She let her eyes roam over the distant lights, hovering between tears and laughter; it was such a spectacular disaster! How would she explain bringing a soggy wet Aerenarch to the Masaud ball for their damned coup?

What a historic moment! she thought, and then: *But where is Brandon?*

She lifted her head, ignoring the heavy dripping mass of her hair, and scanned the soaked figures for Brandon's familiar person. As she sobered, she noted what had escaped her before: weapons at the sides of the purposeful men and women, and the short, trained exchanges indicating not civilians at all, but Marines.

And they had noted the Aerenarch's absence as well.

Vannis sat upright, clawing her hair out of her eyes. Curse the darkness, anyway! Her heart thumped painfully as she squinted over the churned-up waters, looking for a floating body.

"Might have swum to the shore, sir," a man said.

Another answered in a clipped murmur, too low to catch. Then one of them turned to her, sketched a salute, and said, "Your Grace: with your permission, we will return to the shore."

She lifted a hand. "Whatever is best."

Tau will blame me if he's dead, she thought, and then with a kind of desolate certainty: *Not as badly as I will blame myself.*

Other noises crowded her attention. Yenef sobbing; one of the musicians bemoaning the loss of his instrument.

"I'll replace it," Vannis said automatically, then wondered how she would pay for it.

The world had gone crazy—almost enough to make that strange, desperate laughter return. That was, until they reached the shore, and Vahn, the Aerenarch's Marine bodyguard, appeared and without warning slammed Jaim against the landing rail. "Where is he?"

Jaim shook his head, his long braids splattering water on Vahn's immaculate uniform. "I don't know," he said.

For a moment it looked like Vahn would gut the Rifter right

there, and Jaim just stood, chest heaving, making no effort to defend himself.

Vahn turned away then, addressing the Marines in a short voice: he never once looked Vannis' way. They established that everyone else was accounted for, and then they started the short walk toward the Enclave.

But Vahn stopped when one of the guards ran down the path. "He's just been inside," the man gasped. "And he's gone."

* * *

Brandon's voice infused Osri with a curious elation.

The conversation had been short. Osri told him briefly what he'd witnessed, and Brandon replied, *(Something of the sort was inevitable; I figured when, and even where, but until now I did not know what my part was to be. Thank you.)*

He'd signed off before Osri could ask for clarification, but Osri did not boz him back: he didn't need to know. The conviction that he had acted right cleared Osri's head like a week of sleep during better times. He touched his boswell again, this time activating the direct link Captain Ng had given him.

Again the response was immediate. *(Lieutenant Omilov?)*

Osri swiftly outlined everything Harkatsus had said.

There was a momentary silence, then, sounding grim even through the limited bandwidth of the neural link, Ng said: *(Who else have you contacted?)*

(Only the Aerenarch.)

(Well done, Lieutenant. I'll take it from here. Keep an eye on developments there and boz me if anything changes.)

Osri sighed in relief, running the water in the disposer to cover the sound. Anything could happen now—it was even possible that Srivashti, or Harkatsus, or whoever had someone planted in communications would hear of this conversation shortly.

But it was out of his hands: he had done his duty.

Now to go back and listen. And wait.

* * *

Admiral Nyberg's voice was clear and cool and expressionless over the neural link. *(Thank you, Margot. We'll leave this dinner—the exigencies of duty—and I'll return to the Cap to await events.)*

Margot Ng tapped her boswell off and stretched in the command pod of the *Grozniy*. Around her, a few techs and officers ran through the last checks of the bridge systems, but her mind was no longer on the ship. Instead, she saw again the laughing face of the Aerenarch at the Archon Srivashti's party, effortlessly playing the complex game of Douloi social maneuvering.

Social and political maneuvering, she thought. At the time he had given utterly no sign that he was aware of the intent beneath the verbal feints and parries, but she had since been convinced that he had indeed known very well. What had then seemed a teasing game of "Do you remember?" with his old tutor had provided a shield for Sebastian; she was not certain that the gnostor—distracted as he was by his Jupiter Project—was aware of just how effectively he'd been shielded from the political questions that, Ng was sure, had been one intent of the party.

It's now up to him: the time for feints and parries is past. Either the direct thrust—or the game is forever lost.

She rubbed her tired eyes. Should she interfere? *Could* she interfere?

Instinct was definite: Yes, and *yes*.

She leaned forward and touched, lightly, the General Address tab. Clearly one faction had decided that the time for ambivalence was past; so, too, must she.

And so it begins, she thought. No, she realized, it had begun ten years ago, when the overweening ambitions of the then-Aerenarch, Brandon's eldest brother, Semion, had ruined a blameless family to cut short his youngest brother's career. All for fear of Brandon's capabilities.

Fears well founded, it would appear. The Navy had given up on Brandon, his reputation carefully besmirched by Semion; but Brandon had not given up on the Navy. It was time for the Navy to repay his faithfulness.

"This is the captain speaking. I need volunteers for a mission." She paused, looking up into the startled gazes of the bridge crew. Commander Krajno turned in his pod, while Lieutenant Commander Ruiz Sanchez jerked upward from his consultation with a tech underneath a console, uttering a muffled oath as his head banged into the open panel. She smiled at them, and then, still connected to every corner of the massive ship, continued:

"I'm afraid this mission will set back the exchequer for danger pay. . . ."

⁂ ⁂ ⁂

Kestian Harkatsus noticed the young man with the heavy brows, large ears, and angular jaw only because his movements took him against the flow of the guests in the Masaud ballroom. Then the man disappeared around a corner and Kestian forgot him, reveling in the rapt attention of the growing circle of Douloi as he expatiated on Cooperation, Order, and Service.

". . . and when we have once again established a competent government, aligned behind the Aerenarch, giving him the benefit of our many years of service and experience, then it will be time to strike back at the usurper."

He caught the eye of the old Archonei of Cincinnatus among them. It was going just as they had planned—in the absence of any naval personnel, there was no potential center of opposition. Social opposition had already been defeated; no one of any importance danced now, despite Charidhe Masaud's personal invitation to do so.

Kestian saw Aristide Masaud standing on the fringes of his group and smiled. Hesthar, it seemed, was right about that family: ambition always outweighed the caprices of personal loyalty. "Without a strong government," he continued, "the Navy, burdened with the task of managing Ares and the refugee population, cannot effectively prosecute the war."

Kestian paused and looked up, while several of his listeners agreed. He saw Tau Srivashti across the room; but the Archon did not return his gaze. His face was abstracted as he bent to listen more closely to the Kendrian heir, Fierin, and unease chilled Kestian as he saw that Tau was not really listening to her, either.

Has he received a privacy he hasn't shared? Kestian knew that Tau was monitoring the actions of the others, especially Vannis and the Aerenarch. But then, so was he.

(Father?) As if summoned by the thought, Dandenus' voice came through his boswell. He nodded a deferential agreement to the woman who was speaking even as he answered the privacy.

(What is it?)

(There's something wrong with the barge. It . . .)

(What?) Alarm burned in Kestian at the worry in his son's voice. Since the boy had disgraced himself at the Ascha Gardens party he had forbidden him to attend any but the smallest

social functions, a fact well known. Which had turned out to be a perfect cover—he'd dispatched Dandenus to watch Vannis and the Aerenarch from a distance.

(It blew up! No, it . . . I can't tell, it's tipped over, everybody is splashing around. There are people running toward it on the shore from all over. I think they're Marines in civ clothing. I can't see the Aerenarch.)

(Get out of there. You mustn't be seen. Don't call me again until you are safe.)

Kestian realized that the woman was looking at him, expecting a reply, and that he had no idea what she had said. He bowed to her. "You make your point very cogently," he said, glancing at Tau, who regarded him without expression. Out of the corner of his eye he saw Cincinnatus frown in mute question.

Why hasn't Tau alerted me? The alarm cooled into anger. He was the head of the group, they'd chosen him. Why was Srivashti concealing information from him?

Another of the people in his group was now speaking, his hands gesturing with excitement, but Kestian was unable to concentrate. Were events slipping away from him? He bowed to the Archonei, yielding the focus of attention to her even as Tau's voice came to him via boswell.

(Hesthar couldn't hold Nyberg. She does not think he is on his way here.)

As the Archonei began speaking in her high, crackling voice, Kestian excused himself from the group with a general deference, modulating it with a humorous lift to his brows to indicate a summons of nature, and made his way to the disposers. He nearly collided with the big-eared young man he'd noticed earlier—something about him tickled his memory, but he didn't have time to pursue it.

Privacy assured, he signaled Srivashti. *(What is going on?)* He was glad of the emotional cloaking effect of boswell communication; he was sure he could have concealed his anger or his anxiety otherwise.

(No doubt you already know of the problem at the lake.) Kestian sensed a worrisome implication in that statement, but events were moving too fast now to give him the luxury of reflection. *(I cannot reach Vannis. She is no longer wearing her boswell.)*

Kestian clutched his head, trying to think as Tau continued.

(We must assume that Nyberg is returning to his office in the Cap to await developments. He will not act on his own.)

(And the Aerenarch?) asked Kestian.

(I do not know), replied Tau. There was a long pause. Why had Vannis removed her boswell? Had she been hurt in the barge disaster? Too bad to be so clumsy; Kestian dismissed her from his mind.

(Well, it doesn't matter, does it? We are ready here, and the Douloi are behind us. The Aerenarch can't stop us now, and if Nyberg will not come to us, we must go to him and present him with the newly formed council.)

(You appear to have that well in hand. I will follow your lead. As for the Aerenarch—Felton has a knack for finding those who lose themselves.)

Somewhat mollified, Kestian left the disposer, just in time to see the thin, lank-haired servitor in green livery depart through an unobtrusive door. Kestian had not even noticed Felton's presence.

Shrugging, he rejoined the group, where Y'Talob was now holding forth, his earlier reluctance evidently erased by the apparently solid consensus now apparent among the guests. With satisfaction, he noted the relative positions of the various players: all of their group were in dominant stances, deference apparent in the postures of the others around them. Even Charidhe Masaud had been drawn in.

His confidence returned, bringing with it his earlier euphoria. History was in the making, and he was a part of it. Y'Talob saw him, and deferred.

"If we are in agreement, my friends," Kestian said, "let us discuss the formation of a Privy Council. I will lead off by nominating my esteemed neighbor, the Archon of Torigan, whose grasp of trade issues is scarcely equaled."

Murmurs of polite compliance wreathed Y'Talob as he bowed profoundly, then spoke: "If I may serve the polity that has given me birth, and gifted my Family for eight generations, I can ask no higher. May I in turn nominate the excellent Aegios of Boyar, whose abilities with respect to economics are renowned?"

One by one they pulled each other in, applauded by an ever-growing circle. Even the absent Hesthar was nominated, in a superbly passionate speech by the elderly Cincinnatus: her age guaranteed preference. And last was Tau Srivashti, who closed the circle by proposing Kestian as their chief.

His head rang with glory, and a childish flush of pride suffused his neck and cheeks as Charidhe Masaud bowed, smiling, and music began.

He missed the signal that returned the party to her governance, but she made her desires clear as she extended her hand to him to lead off in the Masque-Verdant Quadrille. A subtle movement of the nominees converted them into a circle apart; the rest of the guests withdrew slightly, indicating acceptance of the decision, and soon the ballroom was filled with people dancing.

At the end of the quadrille, the new Privy Council left the Masaud salon, departing for the Cap via transtube. The atmosphere in the pod was electric, but no one spoke. Kestian studied them all, committing each moment to memory: these people, then, would guide the destiny of the Thousand Suns. Personal inclination had to be set aside: he must exert himself to bind them into a cohesive body.

Unless . . . Reminded of the barge disaster, of the disappearance of the Aerenarch, Kestian felt control slipping once again. His eyes sought Tau's face for reassurance, but the Archon gazed out at the glory of lights.

Where was the Aerenarch? What was he doing? What could he do?

Nothing, Kestian decided, nothing. Really, a pleasant young man, but clearly not suited to the demands of government. They would find him presently, and he'd have no choice but to fall in with the desires of his people.

Kestian sat back and considered how to win the last of the Arkads to supportive cooperation—and obedience.

EIGHTEEN

Brandon waited until the door slid shut behind him, melding seamlessly into the wall. He scanned the bedroom: bed neatly made; bedside console dark. The bain was empty, and the wardrobe. He had already found and disabled ancient imagers set into the walls; a touch to his boswell, and he was satisfied they were still dead.

He moved to the wardrobe, stripping off his wet, dank-smelling clothing, then hesitated before the shower; using anything might signal Vahn's guard in the kitchen alcove.

Grinning, he pulled out fresh shirt and trousers. Whatever was to come next, he would go to it smelling like a swamp.

His boswell flashed, an unfamiliar ID. He tabbed the accept.

(*Young Seeker, look you for a bolthole?*) Though he'd only heard it twice, he recognized the laughing voice immediately: the ancient Prophetae, Tate Kaga.

(*No,*) Brandon said.

The oldster's laughter echoed weirdly through Brandon's bones. (*So! You have chosen to end your long sleep, eh? But first there's one here to waken. Will you come?*)

Brandon pulled on his last boot and ghost-stepped back

through the bedroom, pausing before the pile of sodden clothing.

(*You'll have to tell me more than that, Old One. I've just skipped one trap, and am probably on my way into a bigger one.*)

Once again Tate Kaga laughed. (*Makes-the-Wind never sets bars, but breaks them! I have here the body of* Telvarna*'s captain; her spirit is elsewhere. Come! Summon her back. Her last word was "Arkad."*) And the communication ended.

Brandon paused before a window, looking up at the lights that hid the Cap. It seemed he had one last chance to bridge that gulf, and he knew he had to take it.

So he turned his back on the Cap, rummaged in a drawer beside the bed, then signaled the hidden transtube access open.

A small portal opened in the mosaic-decorated wall before him. Looking around the tiny pod with its still air probably unchanged for generations, Brandon wondered which of his trusting ancestors had had these private egresses built into the Enclave—and why. Making a mental note to search the archives more thoroughly when he had time, he sat down and keyed the destination for the spin axis. All those years exploring the Palace Major had taught Brandon and Galen that ancestors inclined to secret passages were also fond of secret records.

If I lose, there might be nothing but time.

He had known from the moment he told Lenic Deralze that he would go through with his escape from Arthelion that the consequences would eventually catch up with him, but the reasons had outweighed the risks.

The problem was, by the time he had reached Charvann, the reasons, and the risks, had changed forever. Yet the action would still exact its price—as it had from Deralze.

He felt the pod shift as the transtube curved up vertically, carrying him up the south pole of the Ares oneill toward Tate Kaga's palace. Brandon suddenly realized he had no idea what the nuller's residence looked like; brief speculations raced through his mind and died as his train of thought resumed.

He'd play out the consequences, whatever they were, but afterward he would go after his father. Either with the Navy behind him, or . . .

His thoughts splintered, images of Dis, of Markham, of the *Telvarna,* of Vi'ya flickering through his mind.

Vi'ya . . .

It was probably outright stupidity to leave, right now, at the height of crisis, just to pay one last visit to a woman who went to such lengths to avoid him that she had alienated most of her crew and had walked into a Dol'jharian trap. But he had to know what it was in her that had caused the laughing, freedom-loving Markham to live with her as his mate—and he had to know what he had done to make her utterly despise him.

His ears popped as the transtube approached its destination 4.5 kilometers above the interior surface of Ares. The pod slowed, the interior suddenly flooded with a yellow wash of light warning of null-gee conditions, and his stomach lurched as weight diminished. Brandon grabbed the hold-ons as the pod stopped, and he swung himself out, pausing only momentarily to apply the affinity dyplast to his feet at one of the dispensers just outside the portal.

Then he looked up.

The shock was even greater than his first sight of the interior of Granny Chang's. He was looking along the spin axis, between the massive trefoil of girders and cables supporting the diffusers, a complex tracery of alloy and dyplast with the nuller's palace—a confusion of vitrine bubbles glinting polychrome in the dim light of the diffusers—perched dead center like a spider in its web. A small, swiftly moving blot resolved into the form of a brightly decorated gee-flat, like one of the legendary flying carpets of Lost Earth.

He stepped onto it and it accelerated back toward Tate Kaga's palace with the characteristic motionless feel of all geeplane devices. Far below he thought he saw the lake, a dark blot gleaming with mirror reflections of the lights above it.

He sent a silent apology to Vannis. It was a cowardly thing to do, leaving her to cope with the mess of her crashed barge and ruined plans. *And Vahn will probably try to hold her against my return*, he thought, *but that will protect her from the cabal's wrath if she just takes the time to see it.*

Poor Vannis! How clearly she'd hated the position she'd been thrust into. But she'd chosen her bars; pity would not make him join her there.

The gee-flat slowed and stopped. He grabbed a cable, propelling himself into Tate Kaga's domicile.

The interior matched the exterior: a confusion of bubbles and cables and platforms at all angles, more disorienting even than the Ascha Gardens. Plants and objets d'art were everywhere. He heard a sudden peeping as a cloud of brightly colored, bullet-shaped creatures suddenly swirled around the edge of a bubble and danced around his head. He stared in amazement: they were tiny birds, in colors from across the spectrum, their wings flickering out only to change direction, then folding back against their bodies until the next maneuver. Their motions were angular, almost insect-like, completely unlike the flight of the birds he knew from home.

The nuller appeared a moment later, descending at a dizzying angle from somewhere overhead, his colorful robes fluttering. He braked to a stop by slapping at the cables along his path as he approached, his oversized hands and feet evoking a series of plangent tones from them that echoed weirdly off the complex surfaces all around. He brought with him a scent of wood-smoke and tangy herbs.

Tate Kaga was no longer in his bubble. In its absence, his movements had a natural grace that underscored his centuries of life in free-fall and made him seem both alien and human at once. The birds swirled across the space in a breathtaking complexity of patterns and surrounded Tate Kaga in a halo of chirping life and color as he stopped right before Brandon, upside down, his wrinkled face evocative of soundless amusement.

"Ho! It is the Young Arkad," the ancient wheezed. "You know that someone among your Wicked Douloi is about to tweak your tail." He pointed up at his crotch.

"I know," Brandon said, suppressing a laugh. "You said in your privacy that Vi'ya asked for me?"

"She did not ask for you, she mentioned your name. Or was it the name of your grandfathers?"

Tate Kaga spun himself around, orienting at last in the same direction Brandon stood. Brandon knew it was not belated politeness, but an oblique challenge: he was being assessed.

He was used to being assessed, usually as a possible pawn in everyone else's game, occasionally as a guess at when he might initiate his own game. *And that will be very soon indeed: if not within the law, then without it.*

"So why did you send for me?" he asked.

"Why did you come?"

"Curiosity."

Tate Kaga laughed, calling forth another series of tones from the cables nearby as he slapped himself into a sideways spin.

"Hau! And curiosity is why I called you!" The nuller suddenly launched himself away. "She lies here. Come."

Brandon pushed off, diving after the old man.

They came to another opening, and Brandon grabbed a cable and stopped, looking in at the woman floating so still in the center of a spherical room, amidst a wrack of small bubbles hanging motionless at random intervals throughout the space. Below, near the bottom of the room, was a long, wide platform, carpeted in living moss spangled with small yellow flowers. Scattered around, set into the walls, were polygonal viewscreens of various sizes and shapes, showing a variety of ever-changing scenes: deep space, deep-colored skies with swiftly moving clouds, forests, barren dunes, and twisted rock formations.

Vi'ya's long hands were loose, and her night-black hair, usually smoothed back and controlled, floated in a silken cloud about her head and shoulders. As Brandon watched, her eyelids lifted. She gazed without comprehension into the space above her.

Markham's mate. Why?

He looked over at the nuller. Tate Kaga was gone. Grabbing the door frame, Brandon pushed himself through—and though he touched no controls, the door slid shut behind him.

* * *

Vi'ya had only a moment's warning.

Like the first brilliant rays glowing past the viewports before the ship turns toward a sun, she felt Brandon's emotional signature.

She had just enough warning to tighten the shields against the full force of radiation before she turned to face him.

"We have a few minutes," he said, "without an audience loud in its partisanship, or outrage, so . . ." He pushed off slowly from the wall and withdrew one of his hands from his tunic pocket. " . . . I wanted to return this to you."

In his fingers was the large tear-shaped gem—the Stone of Prometheus—from the Ivory Hall in Arthelion's Palace Major.

"It was a gift," he said, when she did not take it.

And when she still did not move, he grabbed one of the little bubbles. She saw surprise in his face as it did not move; then he used it to change his own direction, and moved still closer. Now she could hear his breathing, the rustle of cloth as he reached to lay the stone in her hand.

She kept her palm flat, but his sleeve brushed lightly against the inside of her wrist. She closed her fist around the stone as its armor of light crept up her arm, and turned away, her wrist falling to scour against the rough weave of her clothing, the movement strong enough to set her to spinning.

Pain lanced through her head; an afterimage of the damned hyperwave spun through her mind, echoed from far away by Ivard and the Kelly. Of the Eya'a there was no trace. She forced the image away—and grabbed hold of a bubble to steady herself so she could find an exit.

"Wait."

Her head turned, not to hear what he said so much as to avoid a second physical trespass.

"Did you enjoy the concert?" he asked.

One had to look somewhere. She opened her hand, and watched the remarkable transformations taking place as the colors bloomed out of the stone, fluorescing as the polychrome armor reached toward her shoulder.

"It seemed to accomplish its purpose," she said.

It was impossible to close him out completely. The warmth in the light voice had said: *Did you enjoy my gift?*

Now the warmth withdrew, his face closing behind the mask of polite blandness that one so easily misconstrued. The emotions, unfortunately, did not barrier themselves, shifting instead into a mesmerizing blend with question overriding.

"What purpose?" he asked.

She lifted the stone, its chain writhing like a snake through the air, holding it up against a hexagonal view of the cold stars of space. The colors in the stone swiftly altered through blue, then indigo, and then faded, leaving diamond clarity. "You used Markham to slap the faces of your nick lords," she said. "And it seems to have worked."

He made a gesture of denial, his emotions altering with a complexity dizzying in its intensity. "No," he said. "They designed that message themselves, because they arrived looking for it. I gave them Markham's music, which evoked in each what was most important to him. Or her," he added softly. "Am I right?"

The urge to strike out in defense was very nearly overwhelming. "If you wish to be thanked, then I thank you." If surliness would not end this interview, perhaps pettiness would.

He did not move, or speak, but she felt his recoil—and it still left question. He would not go away, she realized through the haze in her mind. He would not go away, and this time there would be no interruptions to save her.

"Why"—he spread his hands—"won't you talk me?"

She altered her position, all her Dol'jharian instincts awakening. It was time to flee—

Or to fight.

"You're afraid," he said, hearing the shock of discovery in his tone.

She looked up once, briefly, a flicker from night-black eyes.

He felt her anger like a blow and went on. "Not the clean fear of battle. I've seen you deliberately shoot people down, and just as coldly risk being shot at. But that's an admirable trait in a Dol'jharian, isn't it? To deal death without emotion?"

She was silent.

"No answer?" He slung himself nearer, slapping at bubbles to circle around her. "Afraid to answer?"

She looked away, toward what might be the exit. Before the fine black hair floated in a swooping drift to shadow her face he saw a line of tension across her brow.

"Why?" he asked, and then fired a shot at a venture. "What could Markham have said about me to provoke such a response?"

A sharp lift to her chin, one hand flexing: his shot had struck home.

"Nothing," she said. Looking away, "Where is the old—"

"You're afraid," he repeated, and the amusement gathered into a breathless laugh. "You're afraid of my title?" He spread his hands, laughter now making his voice break. "Of all the people on this station, *you*. The tough nihilist Dol'jharian escaped slave, cringing away from a crown like any fawning sycophant begging for a place in the train—"

Her hand cut through the air, straight-edged as a knife, toward his face.

To block her would probably break his arm; he pulled himself aside, using a high-level kinesic to deflect the blow. Force spun her around, and she struck again, still with an open hand, but with all her considerable strength.

"Why?" he asked again, still laughing.

But she was beyond talk. He read, clearly, death in the wide black eyes, as once more she struck at his face.

This time he moved close and used her own weight against her, whirling her around. She flung out arms and legs, no stranger to fighting in free-fall, waiting until she had drifted against a wall, and gathered herself for a launch.

Over the years, enforced leisure had engendered in him a habit of self-appraisal. He recognized, with dispassionate amusement, the twist in his psyche that made seduction a game: allurement, for him, usually came out of indifference, or scorn, and now out of hatred.

Quick as a moth to the flame, he launched first, and buried his fingers in Markham's lover's hair, and kissed her.

It was the first time they had touched, and the effect was terrifying in its intensity. Lightning shot across his vision as her hand crashed across his mouth, and then again when his head hit a wall. She bounced against the opposite wall, and finding a console by her hand, she struck the gravs with a fist.

They both slammed onto the moss-covered platform, Brandon first, the sharp herbal scent of crushed greenery rising around them. Then she dropped on him, her strength as paralyzing as the electric bombardment of rage-hot desire. His vision cleared and he looked up into her teeth-bared feral grin, the killing focus of her eyes, framed by the black velvet fall of her hair.

Her fingers closed on his neck, but he lay unmoving, making no effort to defend himself. The palpable danger ignited his own desire; he saw its effect in the sweat beads across her forehead, and as her fingers found his pulse and slowly, slowly, deepened their pressure, he smiled right up into her hell-hot gaze.

"Tell me," he gasped through rapidly numbing lips, his voice unsteady with hilarity, "after they bunny do Dol'jharians gift their lovers with a new set of teeth?"

Her eyes widened, then she threw her head back and laughed, the wheezing, abandoned laugh of someone who is beyond calculation or endeavor, who has only self-irony left.

It was a transformation that took the last of his breath away: released at last from the mask of cold control and its repelling overlay of anger, her beauty was all the more stunning for being totally free of artifice.

He lifted his hands then, his fingers spread, and ran them through the long black hair, warm next to her skin, cool at the ends. She shuddered, her strong hands still around his throat, but still and tense, and when he gripped her shoulders and pulled her to him, the shock of unleashed passion radiated through him from skull to heels.

Neither spoke: words, her armor, she abandoned in challenge; language, his camouflage, he deliberately stripped away, leaving them both exposed to the intensifying scale of sensory harmonics.

They were exactly of a size. Knee, hip, breast, mouth, fit like bone into socket. Experienced in the arts of passion, he played upon the senses while the antiphonal descant—her pleasure amplified by his, his echoing in hers—beat at them both until the crescendo, prolonged and prolonged, encompassed them both.

The intensity obliterated suns and stars, then spiraled them down into existence once again. It was he, the nonpsychic, who regained first the here and now, and all its attendant dynamics.

Still, it did not come at once, and for a short time, as he gazed down into her fathomless black eyes, he felt the universe wheel.

The first reaction was physical, as it had always been: his hand tightened its grip on hers, as if to steady the station gravitors. Then he realized that Tate Kaga's room had not lost its grav, that they had not moved.

There was no time to consider it further. He remembered the coup, and he remembered Jerrode Eusabian's boast about his father. It was time to go—now.

But he lingered for just a moment, his gaze blending with hers. Sex had always been something he could indulge, then let go with perfect freedom. But Vi'ya was not Douloi; she had been, in a sense, an enemy: she did not play the game of passion by the same rules.

There will be consequences, he realized. But the thought—invested with the last traces of radiance—beckoned, instead of warned.

"Why is it," he said, "you would not talk to me about Markham?"

"Because . . . the man he was, and the man we knew, were not the same." Her voice was low, almost a whisper. "Where is the profit?"

He could not look away from her eyes, the curved lids, the iris so black it could not be distinguished from pupil. Again he felt the dissonance of grav-failure and breathed deeply to steady himself. "The profit would be in prolonging his life by adding to memory," he said. "Yours to mine—and mine to yours."

Her eyes seemed to darken; he realized her lashes had lowered, blocking the reflection of distant starlight. And he watched, off balance, as she drew about her once again the invisible armor.

"One day," she said. "But it cannot be now: they search for you." She turned her head, nodding in one direction. "The Kelly relay great agitation."

"The coup," he said, touching his aching mouth. And laughed, and saw his laugh echoed in her eyes. "Shall I be as lucky in my next battle?"

* * *

Vahn's fury had cooled into relentless purpose. He held them all in the Enclave, even the haughty Aerenarch-Consort, still wearing the night robe that Roget had brought her. Even in this robe, with her jewels at the bottom of the lake and her hair hanging in damp-smelling hanks on her shoulders, she retained her dignity.

Dignity . . . but not innocence. A trace of guilt in the oblique glances and hesitant vowels prompted Vahn to try to hold her, and his sense of her guilt was confirmed when she had not appeared to question his authority to do so, not protesting even when he demanded the surrender of her boswell, rendering her incommunicado.

The musicians were probably innocent, but as Vannis' hirelings they had to be held, the maid and the barge techs as well. Jaim sat alone, under guard; they had not spoken to one another since Vahn had lost his temper at the landing.

He had questioned them all, Vannis first, as her rank required. Jaim he left for last, sifting the others' words against the flow of constant reports spoken into his aural nerves from points across the station.

At least the cabal did not have the Aerenarch; that they'd established right away. The cabalists, except for al-Gessinav, were apparently on their way to the Cap—Vahn had a tail on them, with orders to report their goal as soon as it was known—and Srivashti's sinister liegeman was skulking his way across the darkened grounds adjacent to the lake. Vahn had Hamun on Felton's tail, but he wasn't worried: Felton wouldn't find the Aerenarch. The Aerenarch had really disappeared—

vanished, without leaving a trace, and Vahn, glaring at the preternaturally patient Rifter sitting still in his wet clothing, did not believe he could have contrived it without assistance.

If that was true, the Rifter would shortly find out just how unpleasant the soft, rule-constrained nicks he so despised could be when they were crossed.

"What was his last communication with you?" Vahn asked without preliminary.

Jaim looked up, then aside, and his eyes widened.

Vahn became aware of utter silence behind him; he turned, and stared in shock at Brandon vlith-Arkad, who appeared in the far doorway as if by magic.

The Aerenarch scanned the tableau before him, then moved at a leisurely pace into the room.

"It's not his fault," he said to Vahn. "You should know from the records that I used to be somewhat adept at ditching Semion's guards for the occasional piece of business that required conducting without extra eyes and ears."

The words stung; another shock was the blood dotting the Aerenarch's cuff, and the purpling bruise on his mouth. Had there been an attempt on him, then?

If there had, he'd won.

The rage flared up again, just once, prompting Vahn to the first insubordinate remark he'd ever made: "The punishments inflicted on Semion's guards were for negligence," he said.

Brandon smiled, a hard smile that unexpectedly called Semion to mind. "They chose his service," he responded, crossing the room toward Vannis. "The consequences of his caprice were their responsibility, not mine."

Vahn's emotions veered as Brandon crossed the room and held out his hands to Vannis. "I'm sorry," he said, and then he bent and murmured into her ear, and even Vahn's enhancers could not pick out the words.

Whatever he said was not reflected in her face; she rose, bowed, and walked out, still dressed in the night robe, as if she were going to a ball. Her maid slipped from her chair and followed.

The Aerenarch then turned to the musicians. "You will be compensated," he said. "Be sure to specify the exact requirements for replacement of your instruments."

As a group they rose and bowed.

He turned then, his eyes bright and steady. Energy radiated

from him like electricity, and Vahn felt command of the situation pass once, and forever, from him to Brandon vlith-Arkad.

"Jaim. Get on something dry. Vahn: full dress, and you too, Roget, or whoever is on duty and wants to cross the stage."

"Stage?" It was Roget. "Your Highness," she added quickly.

The Aerenarch laughed. "The music is there, waiting, and the instruments have been chosen. It is time"—he looked around at them all—"past time, for us to go and play."

NINETEEN

"Let us return to the concept of strength," said Anaris, "and its corollary, command."

"Yes." The Panarch nodded. "How do you see them linked?"

"The two blades of a scissors. Without strength, one cannot command. Without commanding, one cannot exert one's strength."

"So power consists of the exercise of strength through command?" The Panarch's tone was mild, but Anaris heard a hint of challenge in it.

"Yes. Which is why I do not understand your endless rituals of government. You waste so much time with symbolism."

Gelasaar was silent for a time, his gaze as if by accident resting on the dirazh'u in Anaris' hands. Anaris resisted the temptation to put it away, and smiled at his own impulse.

Then the Panarch spoke. "Tell me, Anaris, what is the opposite of a dance?"

Anaris made a gesture of impatience. "That is a senseless question. A dance has no opposite."

"Precisely. Yet a command does."

Anaris slowly threaded his dirazh'u, the sense of the Panarch's words quivering at the edge of his mind.

"The art of government is to give as few commands as possible," the Panarch explained, "for a command always brings with it the possibility of disobedience. One cannot disobey a ritual—being nonverbal, it has no contrary."

"But in the end," Anaris protested, "a command must be issued, ambiguity cleared away."

"Oh, yes." The Panarch's distant-seeming gaze held a trace of amusement. "But so often, by the time the ritual is finished, one finds the decision already made."

* * *

". . . and they request an interview, Admiral."

Still gazing out the wall port at the vista of the Cap, Nyberg spoke to the com: "Very well. Bring them up."

"AyKay, sir." The connection terminated, and Admiral Nyberg swiveled around in his chair to face his security chief.

"Now we know," Faseult commented. "Harkatsus, Cincinnatus, Boyar, Torigan, Srivashti. Pretty much as expected."

Nyberg rubbed his forehead with the fingertips of both hands, then looked up. "Still don't know where the Aerenarch is?"

Faseult frowned. "No, sir. There's evidence of tampering—a high-level code—with the security systems in the Arkadic Enclave."

Nyberg nodded. "We shall see, then." He straightened up. "I'll handle this alone, Commander."

"Sir!" Faseult was too professional to allow his face to show more than a faint echo of the protest compressed into that single syllable.

Nyberg smiled, feeling the ache of fatigue behind his eyes, augmented by the haze of al-Gessinav's wine from the dinner—though he'd scarcely drunk any. "I don't expect there will be any violence, Anton, but I'd feel better if I knew you were in Security, ready to lock down Ares if anything did blow up."

After a moment's hesitation, Faseult stood up and saluted. "AyKay, sir. I'll let you know instantly when we find His Highness." He walked out briskly.

Nyberg sighed and turned back to the port. There were no more lights swarming around the *Grozniy,* but the *Malabor* still showed flares of energy at numerous points on its hull. Nearby, the attenuated forms of two destroyers hung above the surface of the Cap, also undergoing refitting.

The com chimed again.

"Yes?"

"Gnostor Omilov to see you. He says it's urgent."

Nyberg turned back to his desk. Was Omilov a part of this? "Send him in."

He rose to his feet as Omilov entered; the grasp of the gnostor's hand in the brief greeting conveyed tension and excitement. "We've found it," Omilov said without preamble.

It took Nyberg a moment to change the context of his thoughts. "The Suneater?" He motioned Omilov to take a seat as he sat down, but the gnostor's excitement was evidently too great, and he remained standing.

"Yes. We tried the experiment I told you about."

"With the Dol'jharian woman and the aliens."

"And the boy with the Kelly genome, and the Kelly themselves. They are apparently a polymental unity, and they gave us a vector on the Suneater. We should have a search space narrowed down within a few minutes." Omilov paced across the room, his face animated. "If we take them on the search mission, we should be able to locate the Suneater within days."

The com chimed again. "They're here, Admiral."

"Very well. Have them wait. I'm in a briefing."

He turned back to Omilov. "That is wonderful news, Gnostor. Is there anything more?"

Omilov stopped his pacing. "I'm sorry, Admiral, am I keeping you from something?" His delight altered to politeness.

"No, Sebastian, I wish you could. I'm just putting off the inevitable."

Omilov cocked his head, indicating with a slight movement of his hand polite inquiry.

"A group which I believe will claim to be the new Privy Council is waiting outside. Their first act will probably be to declare the Panarch dead."

He named them: Omilov's eyes darkened, and he rubbed distractedly at his left wrist. *Thrown back into the middle of High Politics after ten years of peace.* "If you'd like to disappear, there's another exit you may use," Nyberg offered. "You needn't face them."

"No . . ." said Omilov slowly, then: "Where is Bran . . . the Aerenarch?"

"We don't know."

"Then I don't suppose there's much point in my remaining."

"Thank you for your efforts, Sebastian," said Nyberg. "You've done more for the war effort than just about anyone."

A red rose bloomed in his vision.

(The Aerenarch returned to the Enclave.) Faseult's excitement was clear even through the limited bandwidth of neural induction. *(Vahn is bringing him to your office.)*

(Thank you, Commander.) Nyberg moved to his desk and touched the com tab. "Lieutenant, tender my apologies for the extended briefing. Bring them in when the Aerenarch arrives—use both antechambers." He paused. "Find Captain Ng and ask her to come here as soon as possible." He tabbed off the com.

Omilov stopped, turned expectantly. Nyberg nodded. "It appears he has decided his course at last."

Resolution informed Omilov's features. "Then I'd like to stay, even if only to offer moral support." He moved over to a chair to one side of Nyberg's desk, near a data console in the wall. Its position was one which in Douloi terms would automatically be subordinate. "But, if I may ask, what has Captain Ng to do with this?"

"The Aerenarch wishes to rescue his father. She is captain of the only ship available for that."

"There is still time?" Omilov's voice was hoarse with sudden hope.

"Time, yes." He looked over at the portrait of Gelasaar III. "But is there the will?"

* * *

The door to Nyberg's office slid open.

His function was now honor guard, so Vahn matched his step with Jaim and followed behind the Aerenarch.

He'd never been into the sanctum before. Scanning past Brandon's shoulder, the glory of space met his eyes, dwarfing the silhouetted figures standing before the huge window.

As they entered the office, subtle changes in the lighting resolved the figures into Nyberg and—Sebastian Omilov.

No time for speculation; the door opposite opened with a muted hiss, and in walked a cluster of resplendently dressed Douloi, straight from the ballroom floor.

Their battle gear, Vahn thought. But the tension in the cool air drained the thought of any humor.

Brandon took up a position directly below the portrait of his father. He had changed into a simple blue tunic; the eye was drawn to his face, and thence to the face above. The resemblance was striking.

Harkatsus' gaze slid past the Aerenarch as he bowed, then he moved further into the room, his group behind him. A tall, handsome man in his fifth or sixth decade, the Aegios wore scarlet and gold, with rubies in his gold-streaked black hair. His stance, the angle of his head as he performed his bows, his hands, all radiated the euphoria of self-importance.

Grouped behind him in spacing that seemed rehearsed were Stulafi Y'Talob, Archon of Torigan, his chest thrust out and elbows at aggressive angles; next to him, slightly behind, Vahn saw the smooth ebony features of Hrishnamrutis, the Archon of Boyar; the Archonei of Cincinnatus took up a position on the other side of Torigan.

But it was Tau Srivashti, next to her, that caught at Vahn's attention, making him miss the opening salvos: when the golden eyes saw Brandon, they lingered on his bruised face, and the man tensed as if struck. Light Douloi voices murmured, the ritual of formal greeting nearly a thousand years old. Harkatsus drew it out; Vahn wondered if Harkatsus was aware of the semblance of stability imbued by ancient forms.

Whether he was or not, Srivashti used the movement of the others to slip back to a rearguard position, his hands hidden by Torigan's bulk. Vahn watched him, saw his tension ease.

Privacy. Of course, but who? Ah, yes, Felton. *Knows he's safe. Was Brandon's bruise from Felton, after all?*

". . . my privilege and my honor," Harkatsus was saying, his mellifluous voice ringing with sincerity and conviction, "to offer us as a counseling body, to help you, as heir, serve what remains of our Panarchy of the Thousand Suns."

The elderly Archonei of Cincinnatus spoke then, before Brandon could; his rank guaranteed him preference, but her age won her deference: "We realize, of course, that you, Gelasaar's loyal son, will point out that a governing body already exists, as does His Majesty."

"But we cannot communicate with them, nor they with us," Harkatsus finished, the words flowing with such clarity and swiftness it sustained the image of ritual, of ancient incantations against evil. "We cannot even guarantee that they yet live. Meanwhile, chaos threatens not only those few of us fortunate enough to have attained safety. Think of the planets left undefended, the countless Highdwellings established by your ancestors and ours, the Infonetic Nodes, the trade nexi—all left to be exploited by Eusabian's fleet of barbarians, the citizens to be annihilated, or enslaved, at their will."

He paused then, with a bow toward Brandon, though his attention, his focus, was on Nyberg. *He knows the admiral constitutes whatever authority still exists; to him Brandon is merely a figurehead, an empty crown. But why doesn't Brandon answer them?*

Nyberg's gaze went to the Aerenarch, then Harkatsus hastened into speech, his timing just headlong enough to convey a remainder, however small, of uncertainty.

"It is your steadfast loyalty to His Majesty your father that wins universal commendation," Harkatsus said with a generous wave of hand toward the portrait, and the stars. Conviction was back. "We are come fresh from the biggest gathering of Service Families this station has hosted since we first celebrated your safe arrival. Voices raised in praise: these people stand ready to devote hearts, hands, and minds to you, the last living representative of a Thousand Years of Peace."

He glanced from Nyberg to Brandon: neither had moved. In the background, Sebastian Omilov stood, his face worn and even pained; Vahn was startled to note that Captain Ng had slipped in, unnoticed, beside him. "The occasion was a social one, but the question of unity, of direction, has so consumed people as the days wear on, and grim data floods in at exponential rates, that a consensus was formed. Something must be done, and the time is now. We offer ourselves to you, as representatives of various areas of expertise, to advise . . . and to guide you."

Harkatsus paused, performing another deference.

Brandon still did not answer him.

Harkatsus smiled and went on, his voice a shade louder, no longer suggesting, but judging. "If you will honor me with permission for personal trespass, it is a truth self-evident that you are young, that you never dreamed you would be called upon to serve in place of your esteemed brother Semion vlith-Arkad, that therefore you could not have received the training he devoted his entire life to absorbing. We beg the honor of your forbearance, when we note that even such formal education as you received was interrupted by events regrettable but understandable in a youth raised in a purely social arena. . . ."

In other words, "You're ignorant and untrustworthy." Vahn kept his face rigid, but anger sparked. *Why doesn't he deny it?*

"But it is in this context that you excel, presiding with skill and brilliance over the civilized gatherings of peers that are so necessary in these dark times—"

Which is as much as saying you're merely a social mime, that that defines your function in life. And they'll see to that, if you don't act. Defend yourself!

But Brandon did not answer.

Harkatsus' smile became a little fixed, and Vahn noted, with sour satisfaction, the sheen of sweat lining his high brow. Faint acid tinged the noble voice now: "—and the times *are* dark, requiring us, as our ancestors did nearly a thousand years ago, to lead our forces to the very jaws of death if that is what victory exacts. But that faith is not won by those who, in better times, and with fine but shortsighted intentions, contravened what customs, and laws, we still retain. . . ."

The Enkainion. It was inevitable; Brandon doesn't speak, which means there can be no defense. If he grovels in exculpation he will lose even the status of figurehead. This must be why he doesn't answer their charges. Vahn's anger cooled into a kind of despairing conviction. Semion had been right, after all, it seemed: the assumption of command was at the cost of humanity. Seen in terms of power, "humane" meant weak.

"It is with these facts in mind, Your Highness, that we beseech you to accept our guidance."

With a last, sustained bow, Harkatsus turned to Nyberg, and this time his entire focus was on the admiral, as if the Aerenarch had spoken his submission to the popular will.

But then Brandon moved, and Vahn's breath caught. There was no hint of defeat about him, or of apology or guilt. Polite in his deference, everything about him was controlled, from the degree of his bow to the inclusion of every person in the room in his intense blue gaze.

Charged air seemed to spark them all; a profound silence fell, as at last, Brandon spoke.

Margot Ng felt a tingle of awe as Brandon moved.

The motion somehow distilled something of the forcefulness

of his father's portrait on the wall nearby and focused all eyes on him. She found herself holding her breath.

"I thank you, Aegios, and those for whom you speak, for your concern, which befits the devotion to Service which brought you through war and danger to Ares, the last outpost of my father's government."

Fire one! Right across the bow—they're alive and safe while others suffer. Torigan frowned; Harkatsus' face tightened.

"These are indeed desperate times, requiring the ultimate in effort from all of us. Requiring, moreover, the careful consideration of the roles that all of us can play in preserving what my ancestors and yours so built and maintained in the Thousand-Year Peace."

Ng watched the Aegios. She could tell that Brandon's refusal to answer directly his veiled accusations was unsettling him; his attitude indicated uncertainty.

The Aerenarch bowed to Harkatsus. "As you so eloquently insist, we must put forward our bravest leaders, those who have demonstrated the ability to win the faith of their followers and lead them through great difficulties to victory."

Ng fought a smile; now she could see where this was going, and so, from their sudden, subtle shifts of stance, could the faction behind Harkatsus. *He is of the Mandala, has walked all his life among the symbols you are appealing to. He has never lost sight of the fact that they are people too.*

"And these leaders are still within reach." He turned to Admiral Nyberg. "Is it not true, Admiral, that there is still time to mount a rescue operation to Gehenna?" He gestured out the immense port. "And that the *Grozniy* is now fully operational?"

"Yes, Your Highness." Nyberg's demeanor was rigidly correct.

"Then," said Brandon, turning back to the others, "I suggest that, as the best is still within our reach, we stretch out our hands and take it—we owe it to the trillion-plus citizens of the Thousand Suns to spare no effort."

There was a moment's silence. The Douloi facing Brandon stirred slightly, eyes flickering back and forth. Harkatsus glanced to one side; to Ng it seemed he was looking at Srivashti. Then Y'Talob thrust his bulk forward. "Is it not also true, Admiral," he asked, his voice grating, "that such a mission would leave only the *Mbwa Kali* on patrol?" Before

Nyberg could reply Y'Talob raised his voice and asked "Can you guarantee the safety of Ares in that situation?"

The admiral answered with flat reluctance. "No, I cannot."

Y'Talob turned to Brandon with a faint, triumphant sneer on his heavy features, while next to him Harkatsus gracefully spread his hands and cocked his head slightly to one side, his expression intimating regret at his associate's crudity while acknowledging the force of his argument.

"You see, Your Highness, it really is not possible for the admiral to take upon himself that responsibility."

"I am not suggesting that," replied Brandon. His features were taut, increasing to an uncanny degree his resemblance to his father. Only the blue eyes were different, lambent. "As my father's representative and heir to the Emerald Throne, I take upon myself that responsibility, judging it the best hope, not just for the inhabitants of Ares, but for all the peoples of the Thousand Suns." He turned to Nyberg.

"Admiral, make ready the *Grozniy* for a mission to Gehenna."

He had committed himself. If Admiral Nyberg did not obey this, his first order, the Aerenarch was ruined, doomed to life as a powerless figurehead. The tension in the room became palpable; to Ng it felt almost as though the air had coalesced into the charged center of a sun.

"Admiral, you will not," said Harkatsus, his voice crackling with tension. He turned back to the Aerenarch, the mask of politesse slipping to reveal the harsh certainty of triumph. "It ill becomes you, who abandoned to death those gathered to honor you in the Hall of Ivory, to ask the loyal men and women of the Navy to spend *their* lives as well in a suicidal mission."

Shock lanced through Ng, and she couldn't stop herself from looking over at Nyberg. He had foreseen exactly this! She had seen only the possibility of the mission. The admiral, steeped in intrigue, had seen beyond that: had seen, in fact, that this would be the fulcrum over which the balance of power would hinge.

Her thoughts flickered like lightning. How fitting this was, that she, who had not balked at spending the life of her lover and countless others in pursuit of a higher good at Arthelion, should find herself spent in the same way!

For it was up to her. She had always thought it would be the smash of a skipmissile or the growl of a ruptor that ended her career; she'd almost prefer that to the living death of civilian disgrace that awaited her if the Aerenarch failed in his bid for power. But she'd sworn an oath.

Captain Margot O'Reilly Ng stepped forward, felt the impact of all eyes in the room. "He doesn't have to ask," she said, proud of how steady her voice was. "The entire complement of the *Grozniy* has volunteered. Without exception. We can be ready within forty hours."

In defying the Aerenarch, Kestian Harkatsus knew that he had won. The Aerenarch's face was utterly blank, which Kestian knew had to hide despair. The gnostor gazed over at the data console in the wall, evidently unwilling to watch the humiliation of the last of the Arkads, his onetime student. Admiral Nyberg did not meet his eyes: he would obey him, not the Aerenarch; he could not order the cruiser into danger, leaving the civilian population of Ares behind to possible reprisal from Eusabian's fleet. Even the Marine guard accompanying the Aerenarch showed, by the angle of his shoulders, that he knew Nyberg must accede to the new council.

Then his glow of triumph heated into rage as the cruiser captain stepped forward and defied him. He had just reached the pinnacle of power, given his first order as de facto ruler of a trillion people, and this jumped-up Polloi was defying him!

". . . ready in forty hours." She spoke with none of the deference proper from a Polloi to one of the High Douloi; her patrons, whoever they were, should be ashamed.

Would be ashamed. He would crush her, just as he had crushed the Aerenarch, whose weakness had revealed his unfitness to lead the Panarchy against the usurper.

But for now, a simple dismissal would do. He bent the full force of his gaze upon her, feeling the pressure of his followers' support. "Captain," he said, when he had judged the silence had become painful to those awaiting his next order, "you are treading at the edge of insubordination. You may leave."

But she returned his gaze without flinching, and he suddenly remembered that this woman had faced the skipmissiles of Eusabian's fleet at Arthelion, had spent ten thousand lives in what she saw as fulfillment of her oath of fealty. A part of him felt near-regret at the necessity of her destruction. "No, Aegios, I will not," she replied, "until so ordered by *my* superior officer. The Aerenarch is right: if there is any chance we can rescue the Panarch, we must do so—our oaths demand it."

She dares remind me of my oath! Kestian felt his lips draw back from his teeth as fierce anger suffused him, burning away the regret and stiffening his resolve. Now to end it.

"The Panarch is dead, and with him your career, Captain." He turned to the Marine standing near the Aerenarch.

"Solarch, I order you to arrest Captain Ng for defiance of the duly constituted order of government."

The Marine's gaze flickered to the Aerenarch, who watched Nyberg, his eyes dark with a complexity of emotion that sent a spurt of fear through Kestian. *Forget him: he can do nothing more.*

He saw hopeless reluctance in the solarch's eyes, saw his hand stray to his side arm and lift it from the holster, saw the beginning of tension in his leg that would carry him forward. . . .

And then an interruption startled them all: it was the old gnostor with the big ears, standing forgotten at the back of the room by the console.

"No," Omilov said hoarsely. And in a stronger voice, "I forbid it."

Kestian Harkatsus swung around, astonished. Was the man mad? Utter silence prevailed as Omilov tapped at the keys. Then Harkatsus gathered his splintered thoughts.

"You forbid it? Professor, you will do nothing!" Kestian's anger forced him to abandon all semblances of subtlety; by using a title one degree less than the man was entitled to, he tried to force Omilov from inclusion in the power struggle.

Omilov smiled at him, the smile of a man suddenly young again. " 'It is within the capacity of anyone to do nothing,' " he quoted, and slapped the accept tab.

The brief flicker of a retinal scan danced across the gnostor's face, and the dispassionate voice of the computer announced, "Identity confirmed: Sebastian Omilov, Praerogate Prime by the grace of His Majesty Gelasaar III."

Kestian's breath caught in his throat as the brightly driving trumpets of the Phoenix Fanfare pealed out, galvanizing all those present and pulling them physically around to face the console, like puppets on a string.

And suddenly Gelasaar was there, the force of his personality reaching out from the recorded image on the screen like the tsunami, which, lifted from the body of the sea by the massive shifting of a planetary crust, sweeps all the works of humankind away before its irresistible force.

"Hear my words, all those within sound and sight: obey this my servant as you would me, or be forfeit in your oath." His eyes seemed to take them all in a single sweep, and then the recording terminated.

"Command functions initiated," the dispassionate computer voice stated. "Local computing authority terminated, control established of all station nodes. Awaiting input."

The silence that followed rang in Harkatsus' ears. The Praerogacy Worm, which had been running in the DataNet for more than eight hundred years, had once again executed its function: Sebastian Omilov was now master of Ares. There were no failsafes against a Praerogate; if he desired, he could open the station to space, or detonate its reactors, and no one could stop him.

Omilov took a step forward. "His Majesty has placed the high justice and the low within my hands, and here I grasp it. Upon pain of disgrace, dechoukaj, and death, I command that you lend all your efforts to the rescue of His Majesty."

A last, faint pulse of hope lanced through Kestian: Omilov had not ordered them to obey the Aerenarch—he had merely confirmed his order. *There might still be a chance. . . .*

Kestian had not moved, but someone was watching. Before he could draw breath to speak, a privacy came from Tau: *(Don't be a fool. He couldn't put Brandon Arkad on the throne, but he can help him hold it.)*

The warning carried all the ring of command, and Harkatsus' fury boiled over. *(I am the appointed leader of this council, not you.)* Rage made him reckless, and he spoke quickly, without considering his words: "Your power, Praerogate, comes through the Panarch during his lifetime. But he is beyond communication, beyond reach. He is for all purposes dead." He raised his voice, ending on a shout: "You spoke for the old government, but I speak for the new. *That ship stays here to guard us!*"

The words rang against the dyplast walls, then dwindled into silence. But it was not the same kind of silence; the balance of power was no longer counterpoised, it had shifted, forever. In amazement, and sick despair, he saw the Marine replace his jac in the holster and turn to the Aerenarch for orders.

"Captain Ng," the Aerenarch said, his voice mild, "prepare

for departure as soon as possible." And as the captain saluted and left the room, he indicated the remaining people with a lift of his hand: "Genz, let us discuss plans."

Hope died then, as Kestian watched the young man wield the power that he himself should have had.

Kestian Harkatsus stood as if rooted to the floor, and knew himself a fool, a facade for the power lust of others, as Tau Srivashti stepped forward and knelt in a graceful obeisance of surrender to Brandon vlith-Arkad. As one by one the others around him moved to follow suit, Kestian knew that this was not an out for him. His role in the theater of power that was Panarchic politics had been taken. Life, possessions, family—all these would remain, but their proper use was now to him forever lost.

After a moment, he turned and left the room, and no one stopped him.

Part Three

TWENTY

※

GEHENNA

"The Rouge aegios on the Ivory temenarch," said Lazoro.

Londri Ironqueen slapped the dwarf's hand away from the ancient dyplast cards. "Don't touch them, you snarky blot. You'll get them all greasy."

Her chancellor cackled and ripped another strip of flesh off the roasted joint he clutched in one misshapen hand, chewing noisily. Londri's stomach lurched; early in her fifth pregnancy nothing was appetizing, but roast meat was especially nauseating.

Overhead, the sconces crackled as an errant draft toyed with the oil wicks; the thick shutters were drawn back from the deep, narrow windows, admitting the predawn breeze, heavy with the scent of the night-blooming bloodflowers that twined the tower of Annrai the Mad. Londri's stomach roiled again at their overly sweet, almost carrion scent.

Lazoro looked more closely at her. "How long this time?"

"Two courses."

The dwarf said nothing for a moment; the only sound was the slap of the cards on the low table between them. All her other pregnancies had ended in miscarriages by the third month.

Then Lazoro poked at the cards with his free hand. "Now uncover the Phoenix singularity and move it to the bar, which will free up . . ."

"I can see that better than you can, lump. They call this solitaire for a reason, you know."

Lazoro stood up, which made little difference in his height, and performed an exaggerated bow, whacking his head into the low table between them. "Your pardon, O Great Queen," he intoned.

When he straightened up, one of the cards was stuck to his high forehead, the starburst pattern on its back like a strange caste mark above his brilliant gray eyes. He peeled it off and peered at it owlishly as Londri snorted a laugh.

"The Nine of Phoenix," Lazoro pronounced, flipping the card around to show its face: nine heraldic birds enwrapped in flames. "Opportunity and strife."

"Opportunity and strife," echoed a booming voice, startling them both. "What else is new, O farsighted one?"

The bulky figure of Anya Steelhand filled the doorway, shoving aside the hanging with one brawny, spark-scarred arm. The forgemaster pushed her way into the room and dropped into a chair, which creaked warningly under her weight.

"My passion for you, sweet flower of the forge," replied Lazoro, grinning broadly, "renewed as always by the sight of your lissome frame."

"Bah!" Anya snorted, and grabbed a flagon, pouring it full of thick, fresh-brewed beer from the pitcher on the table, and sat down, staring into the drink.

Londri snatched the card from the dwarf's hands and slapped it back on the table. He sat down again, his face suddenly serious. "You really do have to decide about the Isolate woman at Szuri pastures. Aztlan and Comori won't wait much longer, and if they tangle, the Tasuroi will move through: they're stronger than they've been in seventeen years."

Londri felt a sudden, unreasoning rage and fought it down, along with a surge of bile as the scent of the meat wrenched at her again. The woman, an Isolate from the Panarchy, had been landed on the disputed border between Aztlan and Comori. When it was found that her fertility suppression was temporary, the two houses had nearly gone to war. Londri's mother had imposed a compromise: when the treatment wore off, Comori should have her firstborn, Aztlan the next child, then House Ferric the third.

"The Telos-damned bitch would have twins," said Anya without looking up. Londri rubbed her stomach, grimacing, noting from the corner of her vision Lazoro's concerned glance at her. Fertility was rare enough for those born on Gehenna, and child mortality was high—she was the only survivor of fifteen siblings, none of whom had lived beyond three years. Twins were unheard-of. Now Comori claimed both children, while Aztlan claimed the second from the womb.

The Ironqueen sighed and walked over to the tall window. Outside, the stars were paling, and fingers of actinic light reached hungrily over the distant Surimasi Mountains, announcing the onslaught of another day under the searing light of Shaitan, Gehenna's primary.

Behind her came the shuffle of irregular footsteps. She knew it was Stepan, the exiled gnostor who'd joined the Isolates in her mother's reign; a sapperwyrm had chewed half his foot away, six years ago.

But she didn't turn around, looking down instead, past the tangled stone and timber complexity of House Ferric and over its surrounding wall. Beyond, the growing light from the sky threw into bold relief the awesome symmetry of the Crater, a perfectly circular gouge in the high, flat plain that sloped up slowly to the brooding mountains beyond. The foundation of her kingdom, and the center of human life on Gehenna, the Crater was the creation of the hated Panarchists, their jailers, who had steered a metallic asteroid into the planet some 230 years before. The metallic remnants at its center—the treasured iron so rare elsewhere on Gehenna—were the source of House Ferric's supremacy; the rest of the asteroid, vaporized and wide-scattered by the impact, rich in the trace elements necessary to the human body, had created the Splash.

According to Stepan, it was a wickedly clever prison. "They could have dusted the planet to add the trace elements we need," he had explained. "But this way, there's just enough metal to ensure that we won't try to build a civilization without it—just enough to keep us fighting over it, and so never a threat to them."

She turned back to the others. "Why couldn't it have been a man? They're so much easier to share."

"They'd probably fight just as hard over a stud that threw twins—no love lost there," said Stepan, his precise Douloi accent grating on her ears.

"Easy for you to say. They're both staunch supporters of our house, and they're both right, in a way."

"Right!" Lazoro cackled, waving his haunch of roast *jaspar*. "Right? Since when does *that* have anything to do with it?"

Suddenly the hanging was pushed aside again, revealing the seven-foot bulk of her general, Gath-Boru. Moving with unlikely grace, he took his place at the table.

"You know what I mean," she said finally.

The dwarf had been her mother's chancellor until her untimely death twenty-five months before; without him, Londri doubted that the Lodestone Siege would still be hers. He was almost twenty, the same age as Stepan.

But Stepan would say sixty, and call it the prime of life.

However you reckoned it, she thought, twenty—what they called sixty standard years in the Thousand Suns—was old on Gehenna. Deprived in his youth of the supplements delivered from orbit by the hated Panarchists, he'd fallen victim to one of the numerous deficiency diseases that were the lot of so many on this strange planet. But it hadn't affected his mind.

Lazoro smiled at her affectionately, suddenly serious again. "Of course I know. You're just like your mother. But she learned, and so will you, if Telos gives you time, that right and might are uneasy partners at best."

"And as long as I am here," said Gath-Boru, his voice deep and resonant from his massive chest, "you needn't worry about that." He reached over and filled a flagon with beer. "There's only one real question here," he continued. "Which one of them do we want to fight? Whichever one of them you decide against will ally with the Tasuroi. Your army is ready, whatever the decision."

"You cannot hope to make everyone happy with your decision," said Stepan, spreading his long pale hands on the table in front of him. "The best you can do is minimize their unhappiness."

"As well to say 'water's wet' or 'iron is rare,' " Lazoro commented irritably. "That's a tautology of government."

The chancellor used his short legs to push his tall chair back onto its two rear legs, bouncing precariously with his toes against the table's edge. It was a habit of his when he was vexed; Londri had been waiting for him to tip over backward since she was a little girl. He never had.

She said nothing as the two bickered. A yawn cracked her jaws open, intensifying the ache behind her eyes; the onset of dawn signaled the usual end of the waking day for the inhabitants of Gehenna, and she had had little sleep in the past few days. Her stomach churned, threatening a return of the nausea that was never far away.

Underneath the table a hound commenced the rhythmic whimper of a dream, its legs scrabbling in the rushes.

"There, there, bitling, not to worry." Londri smiled at the incongruous gentleness in Anya Steelhand's husky alto. The muscles in the forgemaster's arm flexed as she reached down to stroke the animal's head. The whimpering stopped and the thumping racket of the big dog's tail took its place.

The big woman straightened up and glared at the two men across the table from her, her pale eyes lent even more intensity by the contrast with her glossy black skin. She slammed a big fist down on the table and heaved herself to her feet; the candlesticks danced and the mugs rattled.

"You two would argue over the Last Skyfall itself!"

Lazoro's chair fell forward with a crash as the dwarf threw up his hands to cover his head in mock terror. Stepan merely looked at Anya, unblinking, his round, plump face blank.

"House Ferric has the right to the third child," said Anya. "We get that all the sooner if we decide in favor of House Aztlan and divide the twins, but that will leave us facing Comori and the Tasuroi—a larger force than if we decide against Aztlan."

She peered closer at Londri. "That's the decision, Your Majesty: is getting our hands on a fertile woman that much sooner worth the risk?"

"Our spies say she is in fragile health," said Lazoro. "We can't risk waiting."

Twins. A wave of nausea welled up in Londri's guts, and that decided her, but before she could speak, the attention of everyone at the table was riveted by a sound from the corridor outside.

THUMP, drag, THUMP, drag . . . As the noise grew louder, it was accompanied by a hoarse grunting in synchrony with its rhythm.

The hanging in the doorway bellied out at its base and fell

back over a naked figure, albino-white and epicene, that leapt clumsily on all fours toward the table like a child-sized toad. It was human, but no one could have guessed its sex, if it even had one. Its face was blank of meaning, somehow even less expressive than a corpse.

It stopped behind Londri's chair; she twisted around, not wanting to look, but afraid that if she didn't, it would touch her.

"Oracle . . . Oracle . . . Oracle," it piped in a high, thin voice, thick strings of spittle hanging from its blubbery purple lips. Its eyes were pink and crusted with rheum. "Szuri . . . Szuri . . . Szuri."

Londri shrank back in her chair as it humped closer, repeating its mindless litany. Suddenly Anya was beside her, one big hand on the Ironqueen's neck, its horny weight comforting. The forgemaster kicked the creature away, her voice hoarse with rage.

"Go away, you wretched abortion!" She bit off the last word—the vilest curse on Gehenna—with disgusted precision. "Go tell your master we will come, and not to send you again."

The creature retreated, thump-dragging itself out the door, trailing behind it a wailing cry: "Hurt . . . hurt . . . hurt."

Londri caught a glimpse of Stepan's face. The only Isolate among them, his expression was one of horror—the others, born and raised on Gehenna, merely looked uncomfortable or angry.

They don't have things like that in the Thousand Suns. They don't have to.

"Are you all right?" Anya asked. "We can put him off."

Londri shook her head. "Yes. No." Her voice shook. Her mother had never discussed this with her; her sudden death had prevented Londri from learning the true nature of the link between House Ferric and the exiled Phanist who dwelt in the lowest levels of the castle. She only knew that every time he called, her mother went, and so must she.

She stood up. "This just confirms that the Szuri Pastures are important. Let's get it over with."

❋ ❋ ❋

SAMEDI

"Ow ow ow! R-run it again!"

Kedr Five's voice, a squeal of laughter, was nearly drowned by the guffaws of the others on the bridge of the *Samedi*.

"I can't watch it again," Sundiver cried, her slanted green eyes running with tears. "Send it over the hyperwave—Brotherhood's gonna love this one." She bent over her console, still whooping, her thick mane of silver hair hiding her face.

"Got an idea. Don't sent it yet," Moob put in, red-filed teeth bared in a fleering grin. She hunched over her console, keying quickly.

Hestik clumped his fist on his own console, running the com back. Tat Ombric turned her gaze to the viewscreen overhead, her emotions a strange mixture of laughter and guilt.

Once again they all watched the Panarch and his advisers, all of them old, dressed in the grimy gray prison garb that Emmet Fasthand, captain of *Samedi*, wouldn't let them wash. They were sitting at their barren table eating. Tat sat forward slightly, trying to catch the conversation. They talked so quick, in those musicky voices, it was hard to follow.

Without warning the gravs went off, and anyone in motion floated right off their benches, some of them reaching hastily for anchor. Food on lifting spoons or in glasses about to be drunk from splashed out in messy globules, which several of them swam to catch.

A couple of them bumped into each other, gnarled old arms and legs pumping for purchase, and when most of them were in midair, Sundiver had hit the gravs again, and the prisoners thumped down hard, their food on top of them—that which hadn't splattered on walls and bulkheads.

"Look at that old bald one," Hestik sobbed. "On top of the ugly one with the squint! 'Wanna chatz?' " He parodied a quivering, senile voice.

The bridge crew whooped again, all except Moob, who still worked—and Tat, who smiled reluctantly.

Tat looked away from the tiny old woman on the floor cradling a broken arm. She tried to suppress the discomfort, figuring that these nicks were shortly going to be duffed, anyway. Moob and Hestik had decided to belay needling that despicable Morrighon; at some point his Dol'jharian master might find out what they were doing, and no one was certain how he'd react. This was, of course, Fasthand's ship . . . but Tat didn't think even Fasthand was ready to hand out commands to Anaris achreash-Eusabian, Jerrode, Eusabian's son and heir.

Tat looked down at her hands, small and square on her console. Moob and Hestik loved perpetrating jokes while Fasthand was on his Z-watch, the crueler the jokes the better, and if they hadn't realized that those nicks were theirs to play with, they might have turned on the rest of the crew—like Tat herself—who were too weak to defend themselves, or to get a clique to defend them. The smallest on the crew, Tat felt anew the ambivalence of being posted to the bridge: her cousins couldn't help her here.

"Let's watch this," Moob said, baring her Draco teeth.

The viewscreen flickered to what the imagers in the prisoners' cabin were recording right then.

The nicks had picked themselves up and straightened some of the mess as best they could, with the sparse linen Fasthand allowed them. A big old nick crouched over the tiny woman, trying to wrap her arm with strips torn from a sheet.

Suddenly they all looked in one direction, their bodies tight with alarm, their faces varying from disgust to blank. Moob reached over to Sundiver's console and hit the gravs again, and moments later a nasty brownish cloud of matter rolled into the room.

Kedr Five wheezed, pounding the back of his pod. "You backed . . . up . . . the . . . disposer!" he squealed.

Renewed shrieks of mirth made the walls ring. Tat wondered if the damned Dol'jharians were watching and laughing as well. No one knew for certain if they had the imagers programmed to send to their quarters; they all assumed that Morrighon was spying on them, but no one knew to what extent. Almost his first action after coming on board was to designate a huge block in the ship's computers for his own use, and as yet no one could break his codes. Tat kept trying, on Fasthand's orders; he wanted to know how much of the ship's functions the Dol'jharians had interfered with.

"You're a Bori," Fasthand had snarled at Tat. "You been twisty with systems for years. Get around that ugly popeyed zhinworm."

Tat had just nodded, not pointing out that Morrighon was a Last Generation Bori. Any of those who had survived cullings, purges, and the terrible training one must endure in order to serve the Dol'jharian lords had to be exponentially much twistier.

She glanced once again at the viewscreen, then let her eyes unfocus. Bile tickled at the back of her throat; it was too easy to imagine what that room smelled like.

Behind, she heard Hestik choke. Sundiver wiped her eyes, but Kedr Five and Moob avidly drank in every disgusting detail, gibbering with such delighted abandon they missed the hiss of the door opening behind, and those first thumping steps.

Heart pounding, Tat scrunched low; though her father had skipped off Bori when she was small, just before the Panarchists defeated Eusabian's forces, she still felt terror whenever she sighted a Dol'jharian, and this time it was two of the big black-clad Tarkans, Anaris' personal guard, who strode in.

Silence suddenly fell, Kedr Five hiccuping, as the Tarkans made their way to Moob.

She was up at once, teeth bared and her knife out, but the Tarkan swatted her arm aside and grabbed the front of her tunic. Big as she was, he lifted her right off her feet, as the second one grabbed Sundiver's arm.

"I'm coming," she said, getting up fast. "What's the problem?"

Neither of the Tarkans spoke; Tat wondered if they even understood Uni. They just walked out, their boots clunking on the deckplates, the one carrying a choking, cursing Moob, and Sundiver hurrying in the grasp of the other with rather more speed than she usually displayed.

The door hissed shut behind them. Meanwhile, overhead, the viewscreen showed that the gravs had come on again, and Tat saw a corresponding green light on Sundiver's console: *Interesting,* she thought. *I was right, they do have access to ship's functions.* She watched, her thoughts speeding, as several gray-clad Dol'jharians efficiently herded the nicks out of the disgusting room.

A moment later the Tarkans showed up; Moob hung limply, blood running from her mouth. Sundiver's hair stood out around her face, which was still beautiful even in anger. She managed a defiant stance as without warning Anaris himself appeared, taller even than the Tarkans, with a face like some carving of a warrior king out of the long-lost past. Tat hunched down further in her pod, even though he was just on the screen.

"The prisoners are to arrive at Gehenna alive, and unharmed," he said, in his incongruously accent-free Uni. If anything, he sounded like the nicks. He smiled just slightly, then indicated cleaning gear being dumped on the floor by another of the silent gray soldiers. "When this chamber is habitable again, we'll discuss this further."

The Tarkans let go of the two women and went out. The door shut on them; Sundiver bent over, retching. Moob leaned on a table, unheeding the brown-green slime she sat in.

Hestik tried to kill the viewscreen—and failed.

Tat saw the remainder of the bridge crew exchange looks, and in utter silence they watched the women painfully begin to clean up—or busied themselves at their consoles, trying not to watch.

* * *

Morrighon tabbed the volume down on the communicator tuned to the bridge, laughing as he set it neatly in its place on the row. Leaning back, he watched on his personal screen the pleasant sight of the Draco and her companion scrubbing bilge off the walls, contemplating whether he ought to insert a worm into the ship system, that would cause the tianqi to waft an occasional breath of fetor—a little reminder—into their cabins.

Reluctantly he abandoned the idea and logged the entire scrubbing session under his personal code. Enjoyable as it would be once, he knew they'd just force some other luckless slub into those cabins, and while all the Rifter trash crewing this ship deserved being spaced, some of them were much worse than others.

He had not gotten as far as he had by being unsubtle. Enough for them to find this coded log in the system—they would know that he had the session recorded, and could send it over the hyperwave at any time. That at least would clip the Draco's wings: to be shamed publicly was worse than death for Draco.

As for the silver-haired blunge-eater . . . He tapped his nails on the edge of his console, thinking with renewed fury of the disgusting things the Rifters had done to torment him. He knew that she had been the one to spray the clearmet on the wall above his bed and tap it into ship's power. He flexed his feet within his shoes: the burns still hurt. And it was she and that boil-faced blit at the nav console, Hestik, who had released the plasphage into his tianqi vents, so that his bed linens had dissolved into a disgusting pink slime.

They were not united, Morrighon knew. He smiled, getting up to pace about his cabin. Of course he could never tell Anaris about this silent war going on: the assumption that he could not defend himself against a pack of Rifters would destroy his future as Anaris' right hand. Instead, he would use his subtlety to divide them against themselves. . . .

The com at his waist vibrated: Anaris' personal signal. Morrighon activated the new security locks on his cabin; the next intruders would encounter a nasty surprise, which they might, if particularly unlucky, even survive.

He hastened down the narrow corridor, wondering if Anaris had decoded some new data from over the hyperwave—or if he had decided to hold another private converse with the Panarch.

Morrighon gnawed his lip, finding the idea of discourse between those two strange and unsettling. He longed to discuss the meetings with Anaris, but as yet Anaris had not indicated to him that they were a topic of discussion. Further, he wanted them utterly private, so it was Morrighon and not one of the Tarkans who brought the old man when Anaris wanted him, and waited outside until they were done.

Morrighon's step quickened, and he turned his thoughts back to the best ways to strew a little sabotage in Fasthand's crew, and to amuse himself while doing it.

❋ ❋ ❋

Caleb Banqtu drank deeply of his mug of caf, then sat back, enjoying the burn on his tongue and in his throat and stomach. Across from him, Gelasaar sipped at a steaming mug. Next to the Panarch, tiny Matilde Ho cradled hers in her one good hand, the broken arm now secured in a proper cast.

Caleb had ceased to feel surprise at anything. Torment by the Rifters had been predictable. Unforeseen, though perhaps more sinister, was the rescue by the Tarkans followed by the dramatic improvement in their maintenance.

No one spoke, but he read their intent clearly.

The Panarch, by his pose, invited discussion, and the others moved a little in order to see and hear. Padraic Carr limped over to the bench and sat down on Matilde's other side, moving easier since the visit to the medic; before, pain was almost palpable in every shift, every step, though his long, craggy face had shown nothing. The admiral had not told any of them what the Tarkans did to him that first terrible week after they were captured, but Caleb knew they had exacted their own kind of vengeance for the defeat at Acheront twenty years before.

Separated suddenly and without warning; imprisoned alone for unknowable periods of time; always, always spied upon, they had learned to read one another's thoughts in subtle movement, and in oblique references. And rare, but treasured, were those few seconds of whispered exchange usually while in transit: mostly the exchanges were confined to hasty inquiries about one's health, sometimes—if they were lucky—quickly explained symbols and semaphores, devised by one of them and then passed on.

At first the semaphores were mere signs, meant to cheer one another during those rare encounters. Heightened awareness, the need to communicate, to reassure and be reassured, invested a whispered word, a glance, with a weight of meaning.

Those first signs were simple: a fist for interrogations, a sniff for drugs used; lifted fingers for times compatriots had been seen, and later, their positioning indicated levels of well-being. A brush against one's side meant hunger; a scratch on the ass signified Barrodagh. And a nod meant news, whether real or not they had no way to discern.

Many backsides itched in those early days. Caleb wondered if all Barrodagh's recreational time was spent in dreaming up new torments for the prisoners in his charge.

Caleb himself had to endure vids of the rape of Charvann, and the use of his island home as target practice by a squad of Rifters. He told himself that it was not real—why would Eusabian bother with Charvann at all, which had no vestige of strategic importance?

But his sense of reality had become unhinged until waking and sleeping seemed alternate forms of a dream state. Rage, sorrow, grief, anger again, despair, all haunted him like a pack of howling specters. But specters were unreal; reality intruded just once, in the Ivory Hall, when he was forced to watch his mate die just after the Kelly Archon. The floor ran with red before a halt was called: Eusabian made it clear enough that Caleb and seven Privy Councilors were spared not because of any merit, but because they were deemed too old to be worthy prey.

After that: solitary confinement once again, interspersed with

Barrodagh's vile persecutions. Caleb endured it all by rebuilding his windskimmer, one stick at a time, in the sunny refuge of his imagination.

He had nearly finished stitching seams on the broadcloth sails, between the sessions with Barrodagh's minions, when they were abruptly transported aboard the *Fist* again and told they were to be taken to Gehenna.

Then, finally, they were imprisoned together. And despite the reverberations of battle, and the prospect of Gehenna, they were with Gelasaar again, whose eyes shone with visionary intensity when he said, the moment they were locked in a small cell together: *Brandon is alive.*

The lights in their cell had then dimmed to the night setting, and in the gloom they had talked, quickly.

"The Gnostor Davidiah Jones once said that the power of symbols resides in their ambiguity," Gelasaar had murmured.

Padraic then rumbled in his native Ikraini, "I read a commentary on that passage, by the Angus of Macadoo, where she noted that the hand that too readily wields a sword cannot grasp the symbols behind the words."

Matilde had whispered, "The Sanctus Gabriel said that words were the first gift of Telos:

"The Hand of Telos has five fingers
Forth from the first came first the word
The echo of that act still lingers
Yet to the proud a sound unheard."

Fingers, word, lingers, unheard. Shifts of posture among the others had indicated understanding, and that had begun their pattern: to begin a discussion, usually about history or philosophy, ranging freely among several languages. At some point the real conversation would begin, conducted through isolated words indicated by finger movements.

That night, Gelasaar had revealed his goal: the education of Anaris, already in progress. To this end, seven of the best minds of the Panarchy would willingly bend their focus. Then, by mutual consent, the conversation had lapsed into pure entertainment.

Now, many days later, Caleb sipped at his caf while three of them carried the discussion. To have a purpose again gave them all a semblance of youth and strength. Caleb, Mortan Kree, and Yosefina Paerakles sat silently, each absorbed in thought.

Caleb thought about Teodric sho-Gessinav, who had committed suicide rather than release Infonetics codes. His death at least had been to a purpose, but Casimir Dantre's had not.

Was it being stripped of our powers and privileges? Or our belongings? Or merely imprisonment? They would never find out; they knew only that he had drowned himself, head down, in the disposer.

"I've always been fascinated by the dirazh'u," said Padraic. "Do the Dol'jharians truly believe a person's fate can be bound up in a knot?"

Caleb abandoned his musings and looked over at Carr. This conversation would proceed along entirely symbolic lines, its subject signaled by the faint emphasis on the word "knot."

For that was a crucial question still unanswered. *Do we reveal the Knot that guards Gehenna, or take the ship and all aboard with us into death?* He shivered slightly. Death might be preferable to whatever awaited those who stumbled into the chaotic fivespace anomaly that warded the Gehenna system.

"Belief is a complex concept," Matilde commented. "Do we 'believe' in the symbols we use to rule?"

"That may well be the difference between Dol'jhar and Arthelion," Gelasaar replied. He smiled. "I believe that it is unlikely Eusabian understands anything by the term as we do. His son, however, was raised among us."

"So does Anaris believe his fate is determined by those knots?" asked Padraic. Caleb sensed interest from Mortan and Yosefina as well now. They were debating the fate of the *Samedi*: unbeknownst to their captors, this unlikely tribunal held the power of life and death over everyone on board.

"If so," said Mortan Kree, suddenly breaking his silence, "there is little to choose between them."

"Perhaps," said Gelasaar, "during our next conversation I can determine the role knots play in Anaris' life."

Or death, thought Caleb.

"Do that," Padraic Carr rumbled. "I'll be interested to hear what you decide."

The others nodded, agreeing that, in the end, it would be the Panarch's decision whether Anaris, and all of them, lived or died.

TWENTY-ONE

GROZNIY

Galen Perriath ducked his head low over his papers as Lieutenant Commander Tessler entered the junior officers' wardroom. Then he smiled. Tessler couldn't see him unless he peeked around the bulkhead into Perriath's little alcove, which was unlikely: Tessler was the type who always expected the best place, and this corner wasn't.

Galen liked retreating here to do his compilation work—it was the only place he could spread out his flimsies. He paused, his stylus poised above the compad, watching the reflections in the shiny steel edging to the bulkhead. When one sat just so, the edging served as a mirror into the rest of the wardroom.

Tessler fiddled with the caf dispenser, drumming his fingers on a table, and then walked out, the door sliding shut behind him sounding suspiciously like a sigh of relief.

The little group of officers over on the senior side of the room relaxed, one of them murmuring something in a low voice and another laughing. Those in Perriath's view looked expectantly toward the door once or twice; Perriath realized they were watching for someone.

Half a minute later Lieutenant Tang came in, her round face flushed from exertion. "Stuffcrotch gone?" she asked.

"Was just here sniffing for traces," Ul-Derak said.

"Then he'll be heading down to roust a petty officer or two, or to inspect disposers or something, so let's have it," said a husky alto voice. Perriath couldn't see the speaker, but he knew the voice: Ensign Wychyrski, from SigInt.

Tang sank into a padded chair with a groan.

"It's a nightmare," she said. "Totokili's on a rampage. Just about blew Ensign Leukady through a bulkhead for transposing two items on a routine status report—like he'd tried to open the engine room to space or something."

"They're all sizzled," a deep male voice said; reflected was tall, red-haired Lieutenant Commander Nilotis. "This mission was thrown together so fast they're still sorting out all the supplies. I'm surprised we're not all living on beans."

"But Totokili's the worst," replied Tang.

"Can you blame him?" came a light soprano with the singsong accent of the High Douloi. *Warrigal.* "Supervising the refit of a *Rifter* ship, fitting it with every techno-toy that gnostor can dream up, as fast as Navaz' cims can turn them out."

"Everybody in Engineering is racked up about it," Tang said. "You should have heard Shiffer trying to whang some weird instrument into one of the sensor nacelles on that old Columbiad."

Ul-Derak chuckled. "I take it the chief was mighty fluent."

"Totokili comes up behind him and asks him what's the matter," Tang explained, "and Shiffer says, 'The chatzing chatzer doesn't chatz, sir!' "

The wardroom rang with laughter—more than the joke warranted, Galen thought. *We all need the release.*

"The Rifters thought it was pretty funny, too," Tang continued. "That little blonde almost fell down laughing."

"Rifters." Ul-Derak was suddenly grim. "You think the chief engineer's hot, you should listen to Krajno. He'd like to space the lot of them and tab the lock control himself."

There was a moment's silence. Krajno's mate had died at the hands of Rifters in the Treymontaigne system, when the *Prabhu Shiva* was ambushed.

"Must make it rough in the Captain's Mess," Wychyrski commented. "Was the Aerenarch himself asked the captain to give them civ privilege on board."

"Had to," Tang said, shrugging. "Those Rifters are going on a run at least as dangerous as this one, and no danger pay."

Wychyrski said plaintively, "What I don't follow is why, after the Jupiter Project was so secret you could be cashiered even dreaming about it, they're sending *Rifters* on the final run."

"That was at Omilov's request," Tang said.

A short silence prevailed. Galen pictured the bulky old fellow with the big ears. A professor, a gnostor, and a Chival, who'd turned out to be a Praerogate. No one had stopped talking about that.

"What've those Rifters got—some kind of codes to get around Eusabian's Rifter fleet, in case they get spotted?" Wychyrski went on. "Eusabian's pulling his fleet over that side of the Rift, that much we know."

Tang sat down with a mug of caf, rolling her head tiredly. "They don't have it pinpointed that close, or they wouldn't need this spy run. It's because of the brainburners, mostly: they have been hinkier than usual, the blonde told me, since they saw the hyperwave. But they can sense something connected to this Urian station Eusabian's found—they and the Kelly and two of the Rifters. But the Eya'a are key, and they want to travel on that Columbiad, it's their hive away from hive. Also, scuttlebutt says that Dol'jharian woman's a hot pilot."

Ul-Derak grunted. "Main thing is: Omilov wanted them, so he gets what he wants. As for others' opinions, Krajno knows how to keep his mouth shut, and the Rifters don't eat with the captain," he finished, then turned to Warrigal. "But you were there last night, I hear. What's he like—the Aerenarch, I mean?"

The sublieutenant shook her head. "He is an Arkad." Her Douloi singsong sounded careful to Galen's ears. "Very much what you would expect of an Arkad. More than that is impossible to say."

No one answered for a moment. Galen wondered if they felt the same bemusement, the fallout of whipsaw emotions, that he did. For the last week they'd listened, and talked, unable to do anything about the remarkable acceleration of events around the Panarch's heir. One day it had seemed he would be superseded; then after a matter of hours, he had with Omilov's unexpected help not only established his authority but also managed to make it clear that he would be part of the rescue mission. Galen felt a visceral thrill of pride at the presence of the heir to the Emerald Throne on the *Grozniy*.

"History chip popped up an interesting fact," Wychyrski put in. "If we pull off this rescue, it'll be the first time in almost four hundred years that a Navy ship has hosted both the ruler of the Thousand Suns and the heir."

"Was it true about his scores?" Ul-Derak turned to Nilotis.

"Captain said it was a shame he could never be commissioned," Nilotis replied.

Somebody whistled. It was not Captain Ng's nature to be lavish with praise.

Ul-Derak shook his head and then laughed. "What days! Rifters, Dol'jharians, an old professor pops up as a Praerogate."

"That one nearly made old Hurli blunge," Nilotis said.

Galen's attention sharpened. Commander Hurli was the chief Infonetics officer on the *Grozniy*; she had an almost symbiotic relationship with the huge ship's computers.

"Hurli?"

"*Grozniy* was hard-linked to the Ares Node when Omilov activated his Praerogacy. The Worm crawled right down the link and took over ship functions, just like Ares. For a while there, that gnostor could have done anything he liked with us—fired the ruptors, shoved the engines into supercrit . . . anything."

They were all silent. Galen tried to imagine having that much power, even for a short time.

"How long does the Overt phase last, anyway?" Warrigal asked. "He isn't still in charge, is he?"

"No." Nilotis stretched and yawned. "There's no set limit, but I understand that in this case as soon as the Aerenarch issued his first commands, Omilov relinquished his authority. And that's it, for him: the Worm will never answer him again."

Ul-Derak snorted. "So Hurli can sleep again. You seen all those Rifters, Tang?"

She nodded. "Have to. The big one who'll run com is a chef and a musician. The little blond drivetech cheats at cards, my middy told me. Watch out." They all laughed. Tang said, "But the young redhead, almost cadet age—" She shook her head. "You should see him talking with the Kelly! I swear, the way he moves and honks you'd think he has three arms."

"The Kelly are fascinating," Wychyrski said. "They're a lot

of fun to talk to. What gives me the shillies is the idea of those little brainburners hinking around our ship."

Perriath's neck was beginning to ache from the uncomfortable angle he had to hold it at to see, but he didn't want to miss any of the officers' expressions. He was rewarded by a theatrical shudder from Ul-Derak.

"Brrrr! You said it. You ever seen the datachips on the Eya'a, what they can do to you?"

"Please, not before lunch," Warrigal said with a smile. "In any case, they stay mostly in their cabin, I hear."

"That Dol'jharian with them is almost as bad." Tang's voice was expressive. "Bad enough she's a tempath, but I've heard that with those aliens she can read minds. Luckily she pretty much keeps to herself."

Nilotis laughed. "Can you blame her? Knowing how most of the people on board feel about Rifters just now, you think mind reading is a particularly comfortable thing for her? And I've never heard that tempaths have much luck shutting down their emotional sensitivity."

"Mzinga said the captain told everyone in Navigation to stay clear of her," Warrigal said suddenly.

"What? Why?" Several of the officers spoke at once.

The young woman shook her head. "Didn't say, but I think it has to do with Gehenna. Senior officers are avoiding her too."

"They're the ones with need-to-know." Tang's voice was somber. Perriath shifted uncomfortably in his seat. Nothing was known of Gehenna, save that no one ever returned from it. Beyond that, all was speculation, all of it unpleasant, and some of it downright horrifying.

"Gehenna," said Nilotis flatly. "You think it's really habitable?"

"Doesn't make sense that they'd ship criminals all this way just to shove them out an airlock."

"You don't think it's worth it, seeing how frightened people are of the place?" Wychyrski seemed almost delighted by the thought of such a bizarre conspiracy. "And you know the other reason Totokili's got his trousers all twisted: they're running the skip at a hundred ten percent—maybe trying to get there before His Majesty goes out that airlock? You think the Dol'jharians know any more about it than we do?"

"Telos, Bali, where do you get those weird ideas?" Tang sounded almost angry.

"You got any better ones?" The lieutenant's tone was challenging.

"Null out, you two," Nilotis said with a lazy laugh. "We'll find out when we find out." He stood up. "Meanwhile, we're all earning the Murphy bonus, and I, for one, intend to be around to spend it." He yawned. "Which I won't if I don't catch some Zs."

With that, the conversation broke up and the officers wandered out. As the door closed behind the last of them, Galen heard Wychyrski's voice: "Pleasant dreams, Mdeino."

The ensign jerked his shoulders, trying to shake of the doomful images of Gehenna now crowding his mind as he returned to his manifests. *Pleasant dreams indeed.*

He doubted it.

GEHENNA

The flagstones underfoot gave way to naked rock; the walls glistened wetly in the light of their torches. Londri shuddered as they passed near a pulsating colony of cave-spiders clinging to the fissured ceiling, their grape-sized bodies flexing up and down on their spindly legs in arachnid unison.

Ahead, Gath-Boru held a stonewood flambeau aloft, his massive body bent nearly double. Next to him, Lazoro walked upright, but without his usual chatter. Stepan limped beside her, leaning on his cane to spare his lamed foot. She felt the comforting bulk of Anya behind her.

No one spoke; the only sound was the shuffle of their feet and the occasional spit of the flames from their torches.

Finally the narrow gut of rock opened up into a cavern half-choked with fallen slabs of stone, mute record of the shock wave of the Skyfall. A path had been cleared among the massive shards; ahead, a dim red light grew.

Londri wrinkled her nose at the vile smell that greeted them as they stepped beneath a fissured arch of stone into another, larger cavern. Ahead, suspended over a chasm in the rocky floor, a twisted stonewood cage jutted from a precarious spear of rock. There was a man in the cage, clothed only in his own hair; longer than his body, it trailed in wispy lengths through the bars beneath his feet, fluttering in the draft from the cavernous vent below. Londri heard a grunt of disgust from Anya; she tried to breathe in shallow gasps through her mouth. As far as she knew, the Oracle never left his cage, although it was not locked; indeed, there was no door, the back was open where it clung to the rock.

They stopped ten paces back from the fissure beneath the cage. Wisps of vapor rose from the depths beneath; around them, oil fires burned in hollows carved in the jumbled rocks of the cavern, only dimly illuminating their surroundings.

Slowly she became aware of movement in the shadows, hints of twisted creatures even more vile than the frog-thing that had summoned her. Rejected even by the people of Gehenna, who valued almost any human life, they found refuge here. Anya moved up next to her and put one big arm around her; Londri leaned into her gratefully.

She looked steadily at the Oracle, more to avoid seeing the shadows more clearly than to discern his features, which were lost behind his matted hair and beard, stiff and yellow with filth and bits of food. He'd been landed in the reign of her great-grandmother. No one now living knew who he was or what his crime had been, only that he had been a Phanist of Desrien who had done something so horrible in the shrine entrusted to him that the Magisterium had commanded his exile.

Finally Londri stepped away from the forgemaster. "I come as summoned, Old One. Tell me what Fate would have me know."

The Oracle motioned with one skinny arm, and several creatures—one of them looked to have too many arms—humped to the edge of the fissure, pushing before them a vast earthenware vessel with a gritty scrape that shivered through Londri's teeth. They tipped it over, releasing a silvery spill of water into the red-glowing depths. A few moments later a billow of steam shot up, and the Oracle began to gasp in deep tearing breaths as he inhaled violently. Then his limbs began to shake as the prophetic fit came upon him and he began to chant in a high, quavering voice:

> "Londri Ironqueen and steel's mistress
> When a new star blazes in the sky,

Ferric House against a fallen fortress
Leads both friend and foe to fate defy.
Great the risk, reward is even greater:
Within your grasp the author of your woe;
Until betrayal shifts against the Crater.
With wartime friend revealed as true foe.
For then the best may be to cede desire
The traitor's triumph forcibly deny
See hope consumed in clouds of hellish fire
And wait another chance to end the lie."

He fell silent, and the echoes of his mantic voice died away in susurrous echoes. Londri waited, but there was nothing more.

No advice about the twins. Just war and betrayal, death and hope lost. But that was merely life on Gehenna.

Suddenly a wave of fatigue threatened to overwhelm her, and she knew that she was in no condition to interpret the prophecy just now. She turned, and leaning even more heavily on Anya Steelhand's warm bulk, retraced her steps. The legates of the Great Houses would be arriving in the morning, Aztlan and Comori among them, and she had a judgment to render.

❋ ❋ ❋

Gnostor Stepan Ruderik, late of the College of Archetype and Ritual, Carossa Node, stood in the Ironqueen's Court and watched the pageantry that he himself had designed. It had been his gift to Sarrera, Londri's mother, whom he had loved, to strengthen her hold on the Lodestone Siege, knowing the Gehennans would be helpless against his knowledge of archetypal semiotics.

Around him the light of the cressets and candles flaring above sparked to life the glittering flecks of mica in the granite pillars and vaulted arches of the Skyfall Chamber. The wall tapestries' faded colors were enriched by the flickering glow; the flayed skins of traitors and failed challengers to the rulers of the Crater stared down with empty eyes that seemed to follow the ceremony below.

But Stepan Ruderik remembered the Mandala and the Tree of Worlds—and Gelasaar hai-Arkad seated there, dispensing justice. Pain seized him, and he tried to banish the memory of the man he'd once called friend.

The legates of the Great Houses and their attendants entered in solemn procession, following the Ironqueen and her honor guard. Each of the vassal Houses was preceded by the standards of their heritage—scythe, sword, griffin, eagle, a star made of bones, a glass flower—all thrust aloft and waving, like a wind-tossed forest of heraldry. The rich garb of the nobles threw back the yellow light in subtle tints; their iron jewelry glinted dully, highlighted here and there with gems or the hypnotically iridescent blue-green pearls of the *gauma*.

Again memory took its toll: Stepan Ruderik remembered the Douloi and their subtle dance of power.

The Ferric Fanfaronade pealed forth from the immense wooden hydraulis behind the Lodestone Siege, ringing from the stone walls in battering echoes that drowned the hum of conversation and the clattering of the boots of the attendant guards.

But Stepan Ruderik remembered the Phoenix Fanfare blazing forth in the bright harmonies of brass; to his ears the present sound was dull and reedy. On Gehenna, metal was for war and the maintenance of political power; no one would squander it on a musical instrument.

With an effort he threw off the memories. The Oracle's messenger and the ensuing visit to that horror deep below House Ferric had upset him deeply. Even after nearly thirty years in Gehenna, there were aspects of the planet he could not adjust to. That he had been a Highdweller merely made it worse.

Sarrera had mocked him affectionately for his refusal to reckon in Gehennan years, his flawless Carossa-accented Uni, and other affectations, as she called them. He had never been able to make her understand that without them, Gehenna would long ago have devoured him. He thought he'd have better luck with her daughter.

My daughter. He clamped down hard on the emotion that had no place in Gehennan life, for the harsh mathematics of infertility here made families matrilineal—a father was no more than an uncle. Londri could not understand the depth of feeling between a father and his offspring that was the norm in the Thousand Suns.

The hydraulis fell silent and the ringing cry of steel pulled from scabbard snapped his attention back to the Skyfall Chamber as the Ironqueen's honor guard drew their weapons. Bright steel, the wealth of the Crater, drew all eyes as Londri Ironqueen mounted the dais and turned to face the assembly.

Behind her crouched the Lodestone Siege, a twisted lump of meteoric iron wrought not by human hands, but by its flaming descent from space in the Skyfall so long ago. Only vaguely throne-like, it was hers alone to sit in. Beside her, the massive figure of Gath-Boru stood rigidly, holding the Sword of Maintenance upright before his face.

"Hear ye, noble Houses of Gehenna and all the realms within the Splash, and all that desire justice of House Ferric here assembled." Londri's high, clear voice rang against the stone walls. "By bright steel and established custom, by the courage that preserves life against heaven's hate, and by the wisdom of our mothers and their mothers' mothers, I declare this court of judgment open to petition."

She seated herself on the Lodestone Siege, her white robes spilling in a graceful fall across its pitted surface; Gath-Boru carefully laid the massive broadsword across her knees. To Stepan's eyes, her face seemed distracted, her motions abrupt. He caught the eye of Lazoro, standing next to him; the dwarf shrugged fractionally, but his expression held worry.

The machinery of justice proceeded with deliberate grace. The legates of Comori and Aztlan stood forward, accompanied by their standards, and presented their cases in measured tones. There was no hint of the passions the case had aroused.

Stepan grimaced. This was the true measure of Gehennan poverty: that a war might be fought over a biological fact that people in the Thousand Suns took for granted. Out there, if you wanted twins, you had twins, a simple task for obstetric technology. In here, no one alive remembered the last time twins had been conceived. Live birth was rare enough.

The legates finished their perorations. Pivoting smartly about, they marched back to their House positions, established by custom and power. Stepan saw Londri's eyes narrow and follow the Comori noble. He looked too, but saw nothing untoward.

Silence fell.

Slowly Londri lowered the point of the Sword of Maintenance to the floor before her and stood up, her hands on the hilt.

"Comori," she said loudly. "Stand forth."

Stepan started, stared at the Ironqueen. This was not what he had expected. Nor had Aztlan: anger contorted his face, while triumph filled that of Comori. Would she give the twins to Comori, after all?

"Draw your sword," Londri commanded.

A hiss of surprise swept through the Skyfall Chamber. This was not according to form. The Aztlan legate's face relaxed into confusion, while Comori hesitated. Stepan saw fear blossom in his features. What was going on?

"Draw your sword," the Ironqueen repeated.

Slowly, with visible reluctance, the legate did so. This time the gasp from the assembly was nearly unanimous, and Stepan understood. A glow of pride filled his chest; truly, she was Steel's Mistress.

The sword was stonewood, not steel: Londri must have seen its lighter swing against the legate's side when he swiveled about. Understanding transformed the face of the Aztlan noble. Stepping forward, he knelt before the Lodestone Siege, unsheathed his sword, and laid it on the floor before Londri. Steel rang against granite.

"It seems," said the Ironqueen slowly, "that Comori has no faith in their plea, nor in the justice of House Ferric."

Comori lowered his sword, sweat springing forth on his forehead. His lord had been unwilling to risk precious steel in the presence of one he had evidently decided to defy if judgment went against him.

A growl of anger arose from the other legates, and from the soldiers ranked along each wall. A tide of movement swelled toward the legate standing alone in the middle of the floor.

"No!" Londri held up one slim hand, the sleeve of her white robe falling back from her sinewy arm. "This is a court of justice, not vengeance."

She bent her gaze upon Comori. "So be it, then. You yourself have rendered judgment; your plea is void. Surrender the second child to Aztlan or face the wrath of the Crater."

The legate sheathed his sword with a nervous thrust. "Comori maintains its right to the divided soul," he stated flatly.

A long silence held the hall suspended. Suddenly Londri gasped, her face contorted with pain. The Sword of Maintenance slipped from her grasp and clanged loudly as it fell to the dais. The Ironqueen fell back onto the Lodestone Siege, clutching at her stomach. Across from him, Stepan saw sudden understanding in Anya Steelhand's face as she ran forward to the young woman, and despair gripped him.

Again. He ran forward, Lazoro at his side, hesitating helplessly beside the throne as Anya supported Londri.

The girl made no sound, biting her lip, but all within the hall saw the sudden stain of red spreading across her robes, and knew that Gehenna had claimed another life before it even began.

Terror transformed the face of the Comori legate even as the shouts began.

"The Hook!"

"He bore wood, give him steel!"

"Give him to the Hook!"

Trembling, Londri raised herself partway up, tried to speak. Tears springing in his eyes, Stepan saw pain and despair take her; she screamed, and all the rage of Exile was in that sound.

The Skyfall Chamber erupted, and the Comori legate's scream echoed the Ironqueen's as the others fell upon him and dragged him out, to be hung by the jaw from the steel hook above the gate of House Ferric. He would be days in the dying; the armies of the Crater would march out to war beneath his twitching body.

But Stepan had eyes only for his daughter, eighteen standard years of age, bleeding out the life of her fifth child: another victim of the polity that had rejected him and all upon this world.

TWENTY-TWO

SAMEDI

Emmet Fasthand snarled a curse and shut down his console.

Nothing.

He got up, stamped over to the dispenser, and punched up something hot and intoxicating. Gulping down the scalding liquid, he retreated to his console again.

No real data whatever on Gehenna above M-class—rumor and conjecture—and he knew he had everything available.

He'd always been a data addict; taught when young that information was power, he had always made certain he had the latest, most extensive info. It was this habit to which he attributed forty years of success in the Rift Brotherhood, a career not known for fostering longevity. Only once, in careless haste, had he failed in this habit, and the memory of the failed Abilard raid in '58 still rankled, despite the destruction he'd wrought there recently for the Lord of Vengeance.

He did not depend on just the RiftNet, good as it was. He had also over the decades accrued secret sources for high-coded info culled from other parts of the DataNet. Immediately on his acceptance into Eusabian's fleet before the attack, he had made a data stop; he'd made extensive purchases of the new influx of data from the war when he was dispatched to Rifthaven to fetch Eusabian's Urian artifact; and just after he'd been given his orders for this present run, he'd made another stop, this time to purchase data on Gehenna.

A lot of what he had was so new, so raw, it had not been sorted and rated yet, but he ran his own searches, patient after years of practice.

He'd always found some nugget of info that his enemies did not have. But this time he could find absolutely nothing about Gehenna. Nothing at all about the planet. Even its location was hidden—that had been given him by that ice-faced chatzer Anaris.

Worse—he got up again and ordered caf this time—the search he'd run on any ships that had tried rescue runs showed a uniform result: every one of them had disappeared, no messages, no traces. *Every* one, going back almost seven hundred years.

Fasthand gulped at the caf, trying to soothe his seething guts. Fear and fury warred in him, and he cursed that logos-loving Barrodagh, who had made this Gehenna run seem a sinecure.

"You are to be congratulated," he'd said in his oily voice. "You have been chosen to convey the Avatar's prisoners to their prison planet, and with you will be Eusabian's heir. Upon your safe return, your reward will be commensurate with the honor. . . ."

Return! What return? The Panarchists didn't care—they knew they were dead, anyway. And as for Anaris . . .

He has no intentions of dying, that one.

Fasthand grimaced, remembering the Dol'jharian corvette sitting in the port landing bay, the access guarded at all hours by a pair of those hulking Tarkans.

It's a matter of honor, that ugly little gargoyle Anaris had as secretary had said in his teeth-grating whine. *His position requires that he travel with it, as with his honor guard, though he does not expect to use either.* And then that weird laugh, like the gollup of a frog.

Fasthand grinned, reminded that the secretary was expecting to see him—on a matter of importance.

Glancing at the chrono, the captain decided enough time had passed. He would not dare to keep Anaris waiting, a fact that enraged him. After all, this was his own ship. So he took his resentments out on the secretary, as much as he could.

What could the ugly little blit be on about? The Panarchists, of course. Fasthand had found out from Tat Ombric what had happened to Moob and Sundiver during his Z-watch. The captain grimaced again, but not without humor; he was a little afraid of the vile-tempered Draco and seldom interfered with her private pursuits. She was a lethally expert scantech, and time and again had kept the *Samedi* safe from predators on both sides of Panarchist law, so he endured her. He hoped that someone had recorded the incident—he'd enjoy watching it.

All right, you nasty crawler. Let's hear what your damned master wants now.

Tat licked her lips, flexing her trembling fingers. Aware of the blood rushing in her ears, she activated her *nark* in the captain's cabin and waited, with sickening expectancy, for some kind of alarm to trigger.

Nothing happened.

She used this nark seldom: only when she felt that she or her cousins were endangered—when it seemed worse not to use it. Lately she had the urge to use it all the time.

She crouched on her pod, knees under her chin, as she watched Morrighon enter Fasthand's barbarically splendid cabin.

It was strange, and not at all pleasant, to watch someone who was unmistakably a Bori move with the arrogance of a Dol'jharian. Though Morrighon had none of the grace of the heavy-worlders, he still commanded—and expected—more than his share of personal space, just as his overlords did.

Fasthand dropped back a pace, in his own cabin, then flushed with annoyance. Fasthand did not like being intimidated.

"I'm planning the approach to Gehenna," he said. "Do you or your"—he gestured—"master have any special instructions?"

Morrighon said, "When my lord wishes special instructions given, you may be sure that they will be given." His head tipped sideways, as if he couldn't hold it upright on his scrawny neck. *The grav on Dol'jhar probably twisted him like this,* Tat thought, shuddering. *What's it like in his cabin?* For Morrighon's quarters were in the Dol'jharian portion of the ship, which had been set at a uniform 1.5 gees.

"My lord has given me instructions to pass along to you concerning the well-being of his prisoners," Morrighon went on. "His father, the Avatar, requires them to be set down at their destination in perfect health. This means they are to receive adequate comestibles. . . ." He went on, in his insinuating whine, to outline in precise terms the proper care of the Panarchists, right down to how much laundry they were to be allowed and when it must be renewed. From the first reference to "his prisoners," Fasthand's face had lengthened with annoyance.

Tat bit her lip as the instructions unfolded. Their very detail was an insult, the assumption being that Fasthand was too stupid to know how to look after prisoners. Tat figured that Anaris had not known about the dirty linen or scarce rations, not until Sundiver's trick, even though he'd seen the Panarch several times. *So the Panarch didn't complain, and Anaris didn't ask. Interesting.*

". . . any questions I can convey to Lord Anaris?" Morrighon finished.

"No. Nothing. I hope," Fasthand said with a sneer, "that your own accommodations are not lacking?"

The insult went wide; Morrighon shook his head. "They are adequate for my purposes," he said, and he moved toward the door. Then he turned, and added in a softer voice, "But just in the interests of understanding, you might inform your crew that the Karusch-na Rahali are nearly at hand." He went out.

Fasthand's face was dark with rage and confusion.

Tat knew what was coming next; she did not want to be in her cabin when the summons came. In haste she closed her system down, erasing all traces of the recording, then she skipped out and wandered down a randomly chosen corridor.

Shock panged her in the heart when she nearly ran into Morrighon at an intersection. He was not moving—he might have been waiting. For her.

Blood sang warning in her ears, then subsided as the Bori, exactly her own height, motioned to her. His squinty eyes flickered up and down the empty corridor around them, then he spoke. "You know what the Karusch-na Rahali are," he whispered.

Nothing about spies or coms or anything. Mutely she nodded.

Morrighon's face twisted in a weird smile. "It would do no harm at all," he said, "to let them think they will be the targets." On "them" he thrust a hand out, indicating the Rifter side of the ship. He paused, studying her for a moment as if to gauge her understanding, and then he went on, his walk a peculiar shuffle that made her think of joint disease and broken bones.

Her com burred: summons, to the captain's quarters.

She found Fasthand before his console, the *Starfarer's Handbook* data on Dol'jhar on the screen.

"That stonechatzing wormsucker was in here," he snarled. "What's this Kay-roosh-nuhh . . . something?" He tapped his screen impatiently. "It says something about these brain-bent Dol'jharian logos-spawn duffing each other for sex. What's that got to do with Rifters?" His face changed radically. "Unless he means—they'll go after . . ."

"Us," Tat finished. And as Fasthand began cursing, pouring out heartfelt invective on a rising note, she thought, midway between laughter and despair, *It's going to be a very long trip.*

⁂ ⁂ ⁂

Gelasaar hai-Arkad shuffled along the corridor behind the Bori, feeling the ache of high-gee in every bone of his body. The long incarceration on the *Fist of Dol'jhar* had taken its toll on all of them; the standard gee in the quarters on the *Samedi* was a relief, but healing was slow. These forays into the Dol'jharian part of the ship, and the resumption of heavy grav, as short as they were, did not help.

Morrighon tabbed the annunciator at Anaris' cabin. The door slid open and the Bori motioned Gelasaar through.

As the door hissed shut, Anaris stood up from his console, wiping it clear with a quick motion of one strong hand. He tapped once more at it and turned to face the Panarch; Gelasaar's stomach lurched as the acceleration in the cabin declined to a standard gee. He sighed involuntarily.

The Dol'jharian motioned him to a chair and took up his accustomed position in front of it, the familiar sinuous black shape of his dirazh'u in his fingers. Anaris rarely sat except to work, a characteristic the Panarch remembered from the young man's days on Arthelion.

"Would you prefer a lower gee setting in your quarters?" Anaris asked.

Gelasaar shook his head. "Gehenna pulls one standard gee; there is no sense in getting too comfortable."

If the Dol'jharian heard the irony in his voice he gave no sign of it. "I was astonished at how little information about your prison planet there was in the Palace computer," he remarked. "Little more than its location, the orbit of the Quarantine Monitor, and the landing zone."

"I know little more than that myself," the Panarch replied. "Access is controlled by the Abuffyd family, as established by a decree of Nicolai I. They are closemouthed, and I never had any reason to inquire."

"You know nothing of conditions on its surface aside from its acceleration?"

It is not the surface conditions that matter. "The habitable zone is said to be small."

" 'Ruler of naught,' " quoted Anaris. "But that is not what I wish to discuss."

Nor I, though it is Gehenna that gives me the power to judge you.

"We are running out of time," Anaris said. "Gehenna is less than three days away."

The Panarch felt a shock of—what? Fear? Anticipation? He let nothing of it show as the Dol'jharian continued.

"So I have spent some time trying to sum up our conversations since we left Arthelion. I have decided that there are two aphorisms that encapsulate your philosophy of government. We will spend our remaining time considering them."

Gelasaar made a brief motion with one hand: *I am at your disposal.* Anaris evidently recognized it; there was the faintest gleam of teeth in an almost-smile before he continued.

"The first is the statement carved in the stone over the entrance to the Concordium on Lao Tse."

" 'Do that which consists of no action and order will prevail,' " Gelasaar quoted, amused.

"Yes. I remember my tutors on Arthelion telling me that is a fundamental axiom of your government. I do not understand. If one does not act, how can one govern? Power flows from action."

"Lao Tse did not say not to act. He said to do that which consists of no action."

Anaris merely looked at him.

If I cannot bring you to understand this, you must die, for your partial understanding will make you far more dangerous than your father.

"Do you remember what I said about ritual having no contraries? How hard it is for a participant to conceive of going against the flow of a ritual?"

"Yes."

"So it is with political events. The action which is no action is to discern that flow, which contains within itself all possibilities, and then conform to it . . ."

As Anaris began to question him more closely, Gelasaar found his thoughts splitting along two tracks: one the philosophical argument he was building, the other a consideration of all he had learned about Anaris since the first meeting in the Chamber of the Mysteries on the *Fist of Dol'jhar*.

Eusabian's son had changed since leaving Arthelion, of that there was no doubt. He was less aggressively sure of himself now, which meant he had attained enough wisdom to question his own motives as well as others'. Yet the streak of ruthlessness in him that had motivated him to squander hours in trying to annihilate Brandon had matured into a ruthlessness of intent. *Which would be a lot more dangerous if he had not learned to question*, the Panarch thought.

"I see," Anaris said finally in response to an explanation. "Then the corollary is that the fewer orders given, the fewer opportunities for defiance."

"Exactly. As Lao Tse also said, 'When frying small fish, don't stir.' "

To his great surprise, Anaris suddenly laughed. "Whereas the Dol'jharian approach is to use a ruptor on them."

"Which leaves you with little more than a nasty smell," the Panarch agreed, "and still hungry."

Anaris nodded thoughtfully, then frowned. "But I am not yet convinced that your model of government is not due to the lack of control imposed upon you by interstellar distances."

Perhaps I have reached him, then.

"Ah. Control. We return to that again," Gelasaar said. "Your emphasis on that is not surprising, as a scion of such an uncontrollable planetary environment." He paused, and when Anaris merely looked a question at him, continued. "Was that perhaps the subject of the other aphorism you mentioned?"

Anaris nodded, then turned away and walked over to the data console. He laid one hand lightly on the keyboard, not activating it, and spoke without turning around.

"Yes. It is the same one we have discussed many times:

'Ruler of all, ruler of naught, power unlimited, a prison unsought.' " He turned back to the Panarch. "Your son Semion did not accept that, did he?"

Mingled grief and surprise seized Gelasaar; the abrupt change of subject unsettled him and he took a moment to reply. "I do not think so now," he said at last.

"In fact," Anaris continued, "there have been many Panarchs who did not."

"If you know your history that well, then you also know that they were also, almost always, the least successful of my line. The worst of them was literally obliterated; to this day there is a phage running in the DataNet that holds the only surviving record of his face or name—for the sole purpose of eradicating any memory of him that may still exist. Like my son, he forgot that the more power one possesses, the less one can use it."

Anaris began to speak, but Gelasaar held up his hand.

"I grow tired, and would ask that we defer completion of this discussion until tomorrow. But think on this, Anaris achreash-Eusabian. Your father may already have shattered the Thousand Suns beyond recovery: it may be your hands that mend it, or complete its destruction. To decide which it is to be, I suggest you mediate upon the Jaspran Unalterables, which have made us so much what we are. They are the subject of the second Polarity: 'Seek not control, nor multiply laws; the cracks in the system are blessings, not flaws.' "

Anaris stared at him for a long beat, then nodded. "Very well. We will speak again—after the Karusch-na Rahali."

Something of Gelasaar's surprise must have shown, for again Anaris smiled with sardonic amusement as he touched his console. The door hissed open, revealing the Bori secretary, Morrighon.

"For that is a Dol'jharian Unalterable, which has made us what *we* are."

"It's tomorrow," Tat said.

Moob threw back her head and howled with laughter. Tat looked away from those terrible red-dyed teeth.

"They want a fight, isn't that what you said?" Kedr Five lounged over to the galley access. "What happens if you don't fight? If you play dead?"

Half the crew snickered, the other half made leering remarks.

Tat shrugged and shook her head. "Don't know. Look it up yourself. I saw my last Dol'jharian when I was four."

"I'll duff Dhestaer," Hestik said, making obscene gestures.

Tat pictured the tall, slant-eyed Tarkan woman and thought: *She'll probably duff you, stupid blit.*

"She's mine." Kedr Five smirked. "You couldn't hold off these Bori."

They all roared. Tat hid her annoyance, glancing sideways at her cousin Larghior, who went right on with his game.

Sundiver thrust her long hands through her bright hair. "Take any of those stonebacks you want, just leave Anaris to me."

Howls of derision rent the thick air in the rec room.

"You gonna put a sign on your door?" Moob poked at the silver-haired woman. "Or you goin' down to heavy grav to smoke him out?"

"He wants the best, he'll find me," Sundiver said, and again the derisive howls, though they lacked conviction. Sundiver could have anyone she wanted on the ship—and often did. Problem was, Tat thought narrowly, watching Sundiver admire her own reflection in a polished section of steel inlay, she seemed to have more fun playing her lovers off against one another.

"Hope Anaris crushes her," Larghior muttered.

Only Tat heard. For the most part, everyone ignored the three Bori—unless they wanted things done. Or wanted victims that couldn't fight back. She said nothing, as usual.

Larghior continued playing Phalanx with Daug, the tough, mustache-chewing old engineer, until the game was done. Tat stood with a couple of other crew members, watching, and tried to ignore the speculations that went on and on.

She was uncomfortable with the acuity of Morrighon's insight into the crew. He did not know them, at least he'd scarcely spoken more than a few sentences with any of them. Yet with a mere suggestion he had gotten almost the entire crew so busy anticipating the Dol'jharian attack, they had little time for their usual skiptime pursuits.

Another harsh swell of laughter jolted her attention back to the rest of the crew.

"Think of it," Moob sneered. "Tarkans chatzing those old withered nick logos-chatzers. Won't that be niffy to watch?"

"Ah, they'll be off-limits. You wait," Hestik grumped.

"What I want to know," Sundiver said, still watching her reflection, "is if that ugly little gug Morrighon will get any."

Tat felt a cold chill. Morrighon was a Bori—from him to the Bori in the crew was a predictable connection.

Unexpectedly Daug spoke up and deflected the subject: "He warned us. Could have kept his tongue fused."

"Probably used to it," Griffic said from across the room.

"Used to what?" Kedr Five leered.

As they started again with speculations on sexual variations likely to be preferred by the big-boned, heavy Tarkans, Larghior finished his game and gathered Tat with a quick glance.

They slipped out of the rec room, Tat experiencing a strong sense of relief. She hated spending rec time with the others in the primary crew, but they were likely to get hinky if they thought someone was standoffish. And if she was there, it was slightly less likely she'd find herself a victim of the games they contrived when bored.

"Have to check com," she said to her cousin, who nodded and vanished into the transtube.

Tat took another route to her cabin. She was too tired to listen to the recordings from the captain's telltales in the Panarchist cabin, so she ran a quick search on the various words the captain had expressed interest in. From the size of the files the Panarchists had talked and talked, which was as usual. From the lack of any of even simple key words (war; Eusabian; Infonetics; Fleet) they discussed little of any interest. *Probably more of their endless philosophy,* she thought, clearing the system. Then, throwing her clothes on the bed she never slept in, she pulled on her nightshirt and left.

Larghior and Demeragh were in Larghior's cabin, Dem already asleep. Lar looked from Dem's face to Tat, then he sighed, sitting down to pull off his boots.

"Will he be safe?" Tat asked, worried.

Lar gave her a sour smile. "From Tarkan stonebones, sure. He's double safe: he's only a Bori, and there's the head wound. Stonebones want a fight first."

Tat winced, looking down at the livid purple scar marring the side of Dem's head. Hit when the brothers' first ship was attacked, Dem had moved and spoken as if in a dream ever since. Luckily he was as deft as ever in the galley, and no captain minded a quiet, well-behaved slub.

"How about us?" Tat asked. "This isn't home for them, it's ship."

Lar nodded. Raised on a Bori refuge, he'd been steeped all his life in history. He even knew some of the Dol'jharian language. "We're just weak, small Bori, so we'll be safe," he said. "Though we stay away from crew." He grinned. "Ever think you'd live to be glad you were considered beneath contempt?"

Tat laughed as they got into bed.

There was no discussion; the brothers sensed that she was tense, so she got the middle, Dem moving sleepily to the back of the bed. Soon, sandwiched between her cousins, Dem's arm draped over her shoulder and Lar's soft hair nestled against her cheek, their legs all atangle so her feet rested on warm flesh, Tat felt some of her fears drain out.

She lay silent for a time, then, hearing from Lar's breathing that he was not asleep, either, she whispered, "What makes them like it?"

Dem muttered sleepily, "What makes who like what?"

"Go back to sleep, Demeragh," Tat said.

Dem relaxed obediently, his breathing deepening. Tat stroked the inside of his wrist, her affection for her cousins acute. "I just hope Lutavaen and Pap are all right," she muttered. "Do you think Dol'jharians retook Bori?"

"Don't know," Lar whispered.

"I wish they'd never gone back," Tat whispered fiercely.

Lar's fingers twined in hers. "I miss Lutavaen too. And your pap."

Tat wished, as she had for a year, that her sister hadn't felt it necessary to go back with their father. But he'd decided he was too old for the Riftskip, and of course he couldn't go home alone. Bori never went anywhere alone if they could help it.

A new, chilling thought occurred. "I think I know why Morrighon sleeps with his feet on the wall." Sundiver and the others had screamed with laughter when they found it out, just after the Dol'jharians came on board.

"Of course," Lar murmured, surprised she hadn't figured it out already.

Tat contemplated what it must be like for a Bori to sleep alone—and what the Dol'jharians must have done to wrench him out of centuries of habit. To be totally alone at night, with nothing but cold sheets, and no family around one!

She winced, remembering the Panarchists' occasional mentions of Barrodagh, and the things he'd done to them according to reports over the hyperwave. *Morrighon's all twisted in his body, and Barrodagh all twisted in his mind. What can their lives be like?* "Why doesn't he just leave them? He doesn't seem to be a prisoner."

"Power," Lar said, his voice sleep-husky.

"But they don't all have it," Tat protested. "Not just Last Generation—how about stonebones? Ones at the top might like that life. But most are at bottom. Why don't *they* just leave?"

Lar didn't turn his head, but she could hear his grin in his voice. "Some do leave. A few even live to make it. Most of them seem to like it."

Her mind on the impending Karusch-na Rahali, she burst out, "Why? It doesn't make any sense!"

"Not to us. We're hive people, Mam told me. Our strength is in our numbers, all working together. Stonebones, they fight for place. Grow up angry. Strength is single survival. Anger and fighting are close to sex for some, certainly for them." He looked back over his shoulder and grinned. "Don't have to risk being turned down. Just take who they want."

Tat grimaced. It made a kind of sense; she knew she was certainly too timid to make overtures to any outsider she felt attracted to, so she'd always kept her sex play within the family. "Mmm," she said. "But bunny is fun for us. Can't be fun when you're breaking arms and legs."

"Oh, I imagine it's not always a fight to the death," Lar said, snorting a laugh. "Bet you: ones that want to be taken get into the path of the hunter—just like crew uplevel. Heh. You want to talk more on that, go find Moob and Hestik."

"Urrrgh," Tat muttered, knuckling the back of his head. "I'm asleep." She made a face. "But why'd Fasthand have to get greedy? I want this over. Go back to raiding data."

Lar sighed, but didn't answer.

TWENTY-THREE

GROZNIY

Vi'ya stepped into the chilly cabin and looked down at the two small balls of white fur. Her breath clouded as the temperature dropped; the Eya'a were entering hibernation again. Their thoughts were far away now, and she sighed, feeling a sense of slight release, as if a vise loosened its grip on her skull.

At the same moment, all the other voices crowded into her head: the weird threefold thought of the Kelly, too complex to comprehend; Ivard's happy memory-laced concentration on a difficult vector problem. Markham's voice, from old memory, flickered from Ivard to Vi'ya across the kilometer of distance between her cabin and the classroom where Ivard sat with the cruiser's midshipmen. The voice sparked a pang of grief, which was not quite drowned out by one other entity: far away on the other side of the ship, like a star moving through the void, she felt the distinctive psychic signature of Brandon vlith-Arkad.

He was thinking of her—she decided it was time to face him. Danger sang along her nerves, but she dismissed the warning: it was too late. There was no going back.

She opened her eyes, and when her balance had steadied, she crossed her cabin to the door.

Marim's voice came, sleepy with protest: "Where you going? Anything fun?"

Vi'ya's lips twitched. "Just going to see what Omilov has had done to *Telvarna*. You can come, if you like." And, as expected, Marim sank back into the bed, looking disappointed.

Vi'ya added, "Haven't you already fleeced every slub on this ship?"

Marim propped her tousled head on one small hand and grinned unrepentantly. "I think of it as getting some of our own back."

Vi'ya said, "Their perspective is different: it was Rifters who blew up a lot of their homes. You might keep that in mind."

"Blunge!" Marim buried her head under her covers.

Vi'ya went out, walking down the narrow corridor past the civilian cabins. Most of these were empty: this mission was a military one, except for her crew and the few people involved with Sebastian Omilov's Jupiter Project.

And Manderian, the High Phanist's representative, the only other person outside of Ivard and herself who communicated with the Eya'a. She had not spoken to him, except for the merest commonplace, since he and Omilov appeared at Detention Five with the surprising request that she fly the gnostòr on his mission to the heart of the Rift.

Vi'ya stepped into the transtube and tabbed the key, bracing against the acceleration of the module.

She sensed the busy focus of the thousands of minds aboard the mighty ship. Fighting against a sharp longing to see its bridge, and witness for herself the tremendous capabilities of a battlecruiser, she composed herself for the meeting ahead.

❋ ❋ ❋

Manderian studied the two Marines before him. Both young, both sober and intelligent, both focused, despite physical tiredness that he could sense like a drug in his own system.

"No," he said in answer to a question, "we have not established any semblance of tense in the gestural semiotics. I don't know yet whether the Eya'a perceive time as we do: perhaps the captain will discuss this more fully with you."

Something tugged at the edges of his awareness, as if someone stood just behind his shoulder. He knew it was not a physical presence, and the proximity was relative: Vi'ya was on her way.

A silhouette appeared in the open hatch in the ship; Sebastian Omilov came down the ramp, his step booming softly.

"Well, that's one more thing complete," he said, rubbing his hands. He turned to survey the ordered litter of equipment on the deckplates of the hangar bay, waiting to be carried into the Columbiad for installation and stowing. Then he nodded pleasantly to the two Marines who had been chosen to accompany his mission. "That's enough for this shift, don't you think? I know I'm ready for some rest."

The Marines both sketched salutes, then moved out.

When they were gone, Omilov said, "How are they doing?"

"Well enough," Manderian said. "Solarch sho-Rethven has a degree in xenosemiotics; I think, if Vi'ya is willing, he might substantially add to our sign-pool."

"Which is somewhat superficial," Omilov added. "Or so the High Phanist was lamenting just before our departure."

Omilov looked back at the *Telvarna* reflectively. Manderian waited, observing the changes in the man. It was inevitable that his status would be forever altered. Everywhere he went, respect, deference, and even fear marked people's reactions to him. He did not seem to notice—his focus was entirely on the project at hand. Yet he seemed somehow decades younger than he had, and although everyone was tired after almost seventy-two hours of unremitting effort, his eyes were clear and his step firm.

His emergence as Praerogate Overt has restored his sense of purpose.

"Shall we wrap up for now? I'm for some caf—or even coffee, if we can cadge it," Omilov suggested.

Manderian nodded, then said, "Vi'ya is on her way."

Almost at that moment the transtube lights signaled an arrival and hissed open. The tall woman stepped out, her black eyes surveying the hangar before focusing on the two men.

"Captain Vi'ya," Omilov said in welcome, making no reference to her sudden appearance, or to the late hour. "I thought you might want to order the disposition of these supplies here. You'll find a compilation on the compad. I can have them stowed tomorrow—or what serves for tomorrow on this floating city."

She nodded, her black eyes brushing Manderian's, her manner cool and slightly wary as she passed by and ascended the ramp into her ship.

With a spurt of amusement that he kept strictly hidden, Manderian remembered the date in Dol'jharian terms: the

Karusch-na Rahali, the Star-Tides of Progeny. Though Dol'jhar and its system were far distant, the symbolic pull of its four moons was difficult for expatriates to shut out of their lives; it had taken some twenty years before his subconscious had given over calculating the next alignment. *She knows,* he thought, putting energy into shielding his thoughts as best he could, *and she hates the knowing.*

He still could not guess the range of her psi abilities, but he knew it was great. He wondered if she had withdrawn to her ship to pass the night, far as it was from the sleeping quarters.

"Let's go find that caf, shall we, Gnostor?" he suggested.

Omilov straightened up from examining the contents of a crate and sighed. "Yes, yes, let's."

As they waited for the transtube, once again that sense of someone at his shoulder tweaked at his mind. It took some thought to recognize the aura, but when he did, it surprised him.

But he did not look around, and wisely he said nothing, as he followed Omilov into the module and tabbed the location key.

* * *

The landing bay was entirely empty when Vi'ya sensed Brandon's presence. He emerged from the shadows on the far side, having apparently located a little-used mechanics' adit.

She waited at the top of the ramp while he walked across the deck. They had not spoken since he left her at Tate Kaga's home at the spin axis on Ares. It was the Prophetae who, after keeping her there for some hours, had told her what had transpired in Nyberg's office, and then saw to it that she was conveyed, without witnesses, back to Detention Five.

In the flurry over the Eya'a's withdrawal, and of the news that propagated like a shock wave through the station, she had arrived entirely unnoticed. Scarcely four hours later Omilov himself came seeking her, to make his startling request.

Brandon arrived at the ramp and paused, looking up. He grinned suddenly. "Permission to come aboard, Captain?"

Humor in the quarry pits of mainland Dol'jhar had been confined to the humiliation of one's enemies. It was Markham who had taught her how to joke—with Brandon's sense of the ridiculous.

"No," she said, watching his face. "You'll have to blast your way in."

And there it was, the laughter in his eyes, his emotional

spectrum impacting her like dropping into a pool at the peak of a summer's day.

"Duel to the death," he said, mounting the ramp with leisurely steps. "High-velocity custard flingers at forty paces."

The reminder of his inspired defense against Eusabian's forces in the underground kitchens of his Palace Minor made her smile. "I wonder," she said, "how the Tarkans explained that to Eusabian."

"Barrodagh will have lied, of course," Brandon said. "Said they were some kind of arcane Panarchist secret weapon. And he probably has teams of experts busy replicating them for defense against us when we do go back to retake the planet."

"Then you will have to develop anticustard shields," she said, touching the stylus to the compad Omilov had left waiting.

They walked into the *Telvarna*'s rec room, and Brandon moved to the comestibles console, bringing it to life. "Hmmm," he said, scanning the list as Vi'ya's gaze went from the compad to his face. "Must be Sebastian's new status: they've put real coffee in the stores."

"It's probably yours," she said.

"Then I believe I'll help myself. And add a liberal dose of Montrose's brandy. Want some?"

"No," she said, writing rapidly with the stylus as the aromatic scent of coffee filled the still air.

When she looked up again, he had relaxed into one of the deep chairs, both hands wrapped around the steaming mug. "This is the first break I've had," he said.

"Briefings?"

"Not briefings." He smiled wryly. "Inspections, tours, luncheons, more inspections. Keeping me so busy I won't notice the lack."

She said, "I thought this Captain Ng was your partisan."

"Very much so," he replied. "Which is why I'm cooperatively not noticing the lack." He grinned, inviting her to share the joke.

"I don't understand."

"My status is a legal nightmare," he said. "Ng, Nyberg, Ares, even Eusabian, all know who I am, but as far as the DataNet is concerned, I am still Krysarch Brandon nyr-Arkad, until someone with a higher level releases certain codes into the system. Until then, there is information I cannot access, and despite their most ardent wish, they cannot access it for me. One of those areas is Gehenna. Suppose," he said, gesturing with his mug, "I force my way into one of those briefings. They tap up certain files, which require retinal scans; as soon as I enter the room, the system freezes." He shrugged.

Vi'ya had come with three questions. Two, it appeared, might be answered. "Why did you not stay on Ares, then? Was it not a risk, to establish your position and then disappear so quickly?"

Brandon frowned down into his coffee. "Aside from my own inclinations, my absence seemed the best gift I could give Nyberg. He now has clear orders to act on, the same that I believe my father would issue were he there: recall the Fleet, and prepare for a full-scale attack on the Suneater. My presence—my anomalous legal status—would be exponentially more a hindrance there than here. Ares now has a single goal, hopefully one to unite it. Those orders will not be sullied by any further ones, if I am not there to make them, that might run counter to what my father would wish when he returns to Ares."

"So here, there is only one question, this approach to Gehenna, which will be resolved when we reach it."

"Correct. So, you know that much, do you?" He grinned.

Vi'ya returned his smile. "I know that Captain Ng has expressly ordered her bridge crew and senior officers to stay away from me. I have tried to make it easier for them to do that by staying clear of them."

"But you hear things, anyway," he said.

She shrugged. "When the Eya'a are awake I do, for they are curious, and afraid. But your captain and her staff will take no harm of me."

"Therefore what they don't know can't hurt 'em? Well, I won't tell," he said.

And so we approach my second question. The first has been answered: he will stay with the Panarchists, his days of the Riftskip are over.

"If we are too late?" she asked.

He looked up, his blue eyes intense. "Jaim asked me that," he said finally. "No one else has quite dared. And I can't answer it, except to say that we *must* get my father back. He has never been more needed than he is now." His gaze went distant.

Vi'ya sat quietly, trying without success to block the vertiginous divarication of his emotional spectrum. Foremost in her own mind was the memory of his having cornered her at the splatball tourney; at the time she thought it accidental that he managed it when Jaim was not near, but she had long since suspected that he had always known of the telltale in Jaim, even though Jaim himself had not known

Will you take me to rescue my father? he had asked.

Which meant he knew, *somehow*, about her secret escape plans. At the time, he was still veering between the two paths; now, it appeared, he had chosen his father's course.

So what about her plans? To ask directly might force him to take official notice. It was too early, anyway, for there were two dangerous missions first, and she had to return to Ares to get Lokri free.

And then . . . and then . . .

And then I find out the answer to my third question.

He said suddenly, "No one knows this, either, but during one of those interminable nights after I took the nav tests, I released a worm into the Ares DataNet. If it gets past the scavengers and phages, and the safeguards my trusting brother undoubtedly built around those already extant protecting the Aerenarch's prerogatives, it might clear up some of the anomaly. And incidentally afford me some freedom of action."

She already knew that he was adept at questioning, and answering, obliquely. *So if he's saying he will contrive my freedom, then he is asking if I will leave.*

She stood up and turned away, her hands finding employment in laying aside Omilov's compad and stylus.

That depends on how you answer me at the last.

But the time was not yet right for speech; it was at once too early and too late.

For he had set aside his drink and stood beside the door, watching. With her back turned she could feel his gaze and his question.

For a suspended time neither spoke. Then he tabbed the command console to life, and closed the outer hatch, and locked it under a quick code. And when she did not gainsay, he stepped aside, and it was she who led the way to her cabin.

They faced one another at last, standing eye-to-eye, their gazes locked and blended. She felt the force of his desire and braced against it, iron fighting an increasingly potent magnetic charge.

Finally he smiled, just a little, and she could breathe again. "You wouldn't make the first move, would you."

It wasn't even a question. With Markham, her mate, the first move had ceased to carry responsibility: the future, they'd thought, belonged to them both.

"No," she said.

And then sensed, in the dizzying alteration of his emotional spectrum, that he somehow knew it.

"A request," he said, his voice so soft she could just hear him. "That holo you made, of the garden on the Mandala."

She dropped her hand to her console without removing her eyes from his steady blue gaze; her fingers touched the keys, familiar through years of work, and tabbed the accept.

The cabin disappeared, replaced by the astounding view of sky-brushing sequoias. Birds trilled, darting from the greenery to the branches overhead. The tianqi changed, sending a loam and pine-scented breeze to ruffle over her heated skin.

He drew in one long, unsteady breath, looking around with eyes that seemed blinded, then took a step, and another.

He reached. She moved past his hands, sheathed her fingers in his curling dark hair, and surrendered to his devouring kiss.

❋ ❋ ❋

A kilometer away, Manderian, once rahal'Khesteli, now simply a follower of the Sanctus Lleddyn, fought back the disturbance in his dreams and woke up.

When he identified the source of the disturbance, he slid out of bed and knelt on the cold deckplates of his cabin, still in the darkness, and slid his hands over his face in silence.

❋ ❋ ❋

SAMEDI

Emmet Fasthand leaned forward, watching in increasingly painful fascination the fight between the half-naked Moob, blood-streaked, teeth bared, knife at the ready, and a ferocious gray-clad Dol'jharian.

The night had started out disappointing; after taking great care to secure the Panarchist telltales to his own code, Fasthand had come to the reluctant realization that the Dol'jharians had no interest in the prisoners as sex partners, unwilling or otherwise. The old and weak, it appeared, held little appeal. He had watched his potential fortune disappear with the realization: Fasthand would not have let Sundiver broadcast the rape of the Panarch over the hyperwave, to entertain the Brotherhood for free, not when a little exclusivity could have afforded riches on Rifthaven.

Then his crew had gotten restless, for none of the Dol'jharians came out of their area. The slow realization that they seemed to prefer their own kind for their savage fun and games had made the twistier members of his crew indignant. Fasthand had feared a general riot for a time, until Hestik apparently conceived the bright idea of foraying into Dol'jharian territory.

So far, only two of the hunters had come back out.

Moob and the gray fought their way down a corridor, each cursing and snarling as they feinted and grappled. Long smears of blood marked the walls; Fasthand shuddered, looking over at his door for the fiftieth time to make certain that the plasma cannon he'd rigged up was still in place.

If worse came to worst, he knew where the three Bori were hiding, and he could sic any attacking Dol'jharian on them, but he really preferred them alive. Tat, at least. She was the only one in the crew capable of breaking into Morrighon's codes.

He watched the Dol'jharian trip Moob and land on top of her, one of his huge hands mashing one of her bare, tattooed breasts. Fasthand shifted uncomfortably on his chair, watching in fascination as she writhed from beneath him, then kneed him in the crotch.

Or tried to. He grasped her ankle and sent her sprawling, then again was on top of her, fighting for dominance. A little groan escaped Fasthand, and he sneaked a slightly guilty look around him, as if he'd be able to see any narks.

He was pretty sure he'd found them all, but he couldn't know. The captain who'd had the *Samedi* before him had not only been extraordinarily suspicious even for a Rifter, he'd also had his own cabin wired for multiple images, to record from various vantages his depravities with wooly, cloven-hooved mammals, apparently to be reviewed when he suffered a dearth of the preferred ruminant.

Fasthand grimaced. After he'd seen those images, he'd bundled up all the blankets and knitted wall hangings in the cabin and spaced them—he was pretty broad-minded, but even Dol'jharians didn't make a practice of killing and eating their sex partners.

It was Tat, shortly after being hired on, who uncovered those code-hidden vids and promptly turned them over to the crew, to their unending delight. It had made her instantly popular with them, or at least popular enough that they refrained, for a considerable time, from tormenting her and her Bori relatives in their usual "initiation" games, which had been somewhat of a relief to Fasthand. He'd gotten tired of having to hire new crew at almost every stop.

But her very competence always made him a little uncomfortable. Where would her abilities end? Would she crack any of his own codes?

He dismissed Tat from his mind: she couldn't be watching him now, even if she had found imagers, for she and the two brothers or cousins or whatever they called themselves (since they all slept together, he found the notion of familial relation repellent) were hiding out somewhere along the kilometer-long catwalk in the missile tube.

He licked his lips, thoroughly enjoying seeing Moob on her gut. Presently he flicked over, checking the other corridors: nothing. Of course Morrighon had disabled all the imagers in the Dol'jharian area. He flicked across the channels again, hoping Sundiver would come running out, pursued by a Tarkan or two.

And what about Hestik?

* * *

With a thrill of anticipation, Sundiver slid through the door into Dol'jharian territory. The heavy grav pulled at her insides, damping her enthusiasm somewhat: being chased in this atmosphere would not be fun, but maybe she could lure her target into her own cabin.

She knew where Anaris' cabin was, and she also knew that two Tarkans stood before it at all times. Except now, she was hoping.

She rounded a corner and heard a series of thumps, then a long, gurgling scream. Blood smeared a wall; her heart hammered, but she forced a grin. The hunt was on!

Anaris slept at the end, in the big cabin, she knew that much. She just hoped he wasn't busy with any of those blungebrained Tarkans. Hestik had promised to sidetrack Dhestaer, the Tarkan second-in-command, and Kedr Five had smugly announced that he'd corner all the rest of them.

She slid past the last corner, straightening her shoulders. The damn grav pulled at her spine, making smooth walking hard.

But when she saw the door unguarded, fresh energy zipped through her and she grinned with fierce pleasure.

We'll have to introduce Karusch-na Rahali as a new fashion at Flauri's on Rifthaven, she thought. Amazing no one had thought of it before—chatzing the way the conquerors liked it. *Bunny with no consent—and no consequences.* The idea was so seductive, she was amazed it was not more widespread. But then, it took someone strong to scorn consequences, to not give in to the attempts to bind one by sentiment that weak lovers resorted to.

Her lip curled in scorn as she approached Anaris' door. *He* would never demean himself with talk of love and mates and trust.

She had come armed with several override codes for forcing doors, but first she tried it—and when it slid open, she gasped at the astounding arrogance of an unlocked door.

A quick glance about showed a neat room, no signs of revelry, and Anaris seated at the console, his height and breadth of back dwarfing a workstation built for someone much smaller.

His head turned sharply. A tingle ran down her spine as the dark eyes appraised her.

"What's the matter?" she taunted, lounging in the doorway. "Why aren't you out having fun? No balls?"

"My father has them mounted on the bridge of his flagship," Anaris said, standing up.

His sheer height was somewhat intimidating; the grav and her racing pulse made blood sing in her head.

The door gouged into her hip, so she shifted her stance, and the door slid shut behind her. She tensed, readying—but he only leaned against the back of his pod and regarded her with pronounced amusement. "Any other questions?"

So she would not be able to provoke him with the usual insults that got men going. It only made him more of a challenge. "Why aren't you out there with the rest of them?" She waved behind, misjudged, and her wrist struck the door, sending sharp pain shooting through her.

"Not every Dol'jharian heeds the old superstitions," he said.

"Superstitions?" she repeated, sucking the back of her wrist. It was already bruising: *damn* the heavy grav!

He lifted one shoulder. "What else would you call a belief that you make stronger children by fighting, or that waiting for lunar alignment will prolong your performance, or that your war skills will improve by remaining celibate betweentimes? Superstition." He smiled, a sardonic smile with an edge of strong white teeth that did not promise a sharing of humor. "I prefer to choose the time, the place. And the partner."

It was a not-quite-veiled insult—the first she'd ever received. A flush of anger mounted to her cheeks, so unfamiliar a sensation she could not fight it. So to deflect attention, she looked past him at his screen, and noticed a starmap, with glowing lights and lines lancing in one direction.

She recognized it immediately: Fasthand had one much like it in his ready room, where he was laboriously plotting what little they'd gleaned of Eusabian's fleet movements. From the looks of it, Anaris had access to far more codes.

He shifted position; for the first time, there was faint interest in his face. He knew she'd recognized it.

But instead of explaining, he lazily reached over and shut down his system. Then he took a step toward her.

Alarm glanced through her, almost as sharp as the throb in her wrist. "I won't say anything to anyone," she burst out.

"No, you won't," he agreed.

The alarm turned into fear as she gazed up into the strong-boned face and saw no hint of warmth, of appeal. She said, with a fair attempt at bravado, "I thought you said you liked to pick the time, the place, and the person?"

Cold amusement in the unblinking black eyes hit her like a blow, and she quailed at last and whirled around, scrabbling for the doorpad.

Or tried. The grav pulled at her joints, sending pangs shooting through her, but her movements were too slow. He was right behind her; his hand flicked the lock.

"They're not ideal." He caught her bruised wrist in a grip that promised no tenderness, and smiled, just a little. "But they are convenient," he said.

TWENTY-FOUR

GROZNIY

As they awaited Commander Totokili, Lieutenant Commander Rom-Sanchez thought he detected suppressed amusement in Captain Ng, as though there were a joke she longed to share but couldn't. He glanced around, unsure if others in the Plot Room had noted it. Certainly Commander Krajno had. Although his craggy face was unrevealing, he'd served under Ng too long not to be able to read her moods. As for Navaz, the armorer, Rom-Sanchez never could tell how much sensitivity she had to others' emotions; her life seemed centered on her cims, the machinery that made the *Grozniy* largely independent of supply centers.

The presence of a mindblur on the table in front of the captain indicated the seriousness of her summons. *She wants to make sure that Dol'jharian doesn't pick up any secrets.* There was no doubt in his mind that this meeting concerned their imminent approach to Gehenna, now less than two days away.

Gehenna. The name possessed a doomful resonance for Rom-Sanchez. Out of curiosity he'd looked up the origin of the word, and wished he hadn't. The illustration, animated with indecent clarity by some artist who should have known better, had haunted his dreams for days: a garbage dump outside the towering walls of some ancient city on Lost Earth, wreathed in stinking smoke and the flames of decomposing trash jetting from cracks in the ground, where the bodies of criminals were dumped, with starveling dogs . . . He shook off the memory. Were there really places like that in the Thousand Suns?

At the outset of their mission they'd been given the coordinates of the planet, nothing more. What made it worse was that there was no other information at all about Gehenna in the naval databanks, even at the levels he had access to. None.

The hatch hissed open, rescuing him from his thoughts as Commander Totokili strode in. As soon as the chief engineer had seated himself, Captain Ng reached forward and tapped the top of the mindblur, which began to emit a whine at the edge of hearing.

"This briefing falls under the protocols of secrecy as outlined in the Articles of War," she began. Her voice was measured, laden with a formality contradicted by the faint trace of a smile deepening the corners of her mouth. "Pursuant to my instructions from Admiral Nyberg, the *Grozniy* now being forty-eight hours from Gehenna, I have brought you here to witness the opening of my sealed orders."

With an automatic gesture, Commander Krajno pushed the data console on its swivel over to the captain. But, instead of entering her personal ID, Ng pushed the console away and reached into her jacket, bringing forth a stiff, buff-colored envelope.

"I have always wanted to do this." And she smiled.

The others watched in astonished silence as she worked a finger under the flap. Rom-Sanchez found the crackling of the parchment envelope mesmerizing; his back tingled. *It's like something out of a historical serial chip.* He had never seen hard-copy orders before. Looking at the others, he guessed none of them had, either.

Finally Ng extracted a single sheet of paper from the envelope and unfolded it. She looked at it and her eyes widened. For a long beat she didn't move. Then, laying the sheet down on the table in front of her, she began to laugh.

Rom-Sanchez craned his neck to look, but could discern nothing of the message's content, except that there was only a single line—in fact, only four words—indited on the page in a strong, looping hand. *Not only hard copy, but handwritten.*

"Brilliant!" she gasped finally. "Absolutely chatzing brilliant!"

Rom-Sanchez sucked in his breath. He had never heard Ng use an emphatic vulgarity before. When her eyes encountered his, she laughed even harder, and he felt his face burn.

"I'm sorry, Commander," she said, wiping her eyes. "You look like you've just seen your mother do a strip dance."

Krajno chortled. "All right, Captain. Give." He held out his hand, but Ng snatched the paper back and folded it up. Totokili looked perplexed; Navaz' face was blank, but her eyes ferreted back and forth between Ng and Krajno.

"No, Perthes. I'm enjoying this too much—and so will you. You must have wondered what the secret of Gehenna is, how it's guarded, and, most of all, how the government has kept that information secret all these years." She looked around the table at all of them. They nodded. "Simple. They never put it into the DataNet. The secret of Gehenna exists only on paper, and in the memory of a few people in the highest levels of government."

"So we're going in blind," said Totokili, looking grim. "I don't think that's very funny." He motioned at the paper. "There can't be much information in that."

"All that's needed," Ng replied. She reached out and pulled the console to her, then tapped rapidly at the keys. After a moment, a hologram condensed over the table. Its form tickled Rom-Sanchez's memory: a shallow hyperbola, with a blue-white sun at its center. The conic section was angry red nearest the asymptotes and faded to invisibility as the distance from the sun increased. Small spheres, and even smaller dots, indicated planets and asteroids. The latter were thickly scattered throughout the system.

"System FF," said Navaz suddenly. "The Knot."

Of course! thought Rom-Sanchez. Every cadet remembered the infamous System FF simulation. It was based on a theoretical construct involving the possible intersection of a fivespace fracture, left over from a more energetic period in the universe's history, and a sun with a mass greater than 1.4 Standard. The result postulated was a system that could only be entered in the plane of the ecliptic, and even there, the fiveskip could be used only in very short skips. It made for a very interesting tactical situation.

The hologram evolved, zooming in on the fourth planet;

Rom-Sanchez suddenly remembered being pinned against that planet in the simulation, unable to skip out before his opponent blew him to plasma. He wondered what the others' experience of the FF simulation had been.

Then his thoughts shattered as the import of what he was seeing finally registered on him. As he opened his mouth to speak, Ng unfolded the order and held it up for all of them to see. There, inscribed in Admiral Nyberg's handwriting, was a single sentence:

"Gehenna is System FF."

The Plot Room rang with mirth in a sudden release of tension. Not only were they not going in blind; every officer on the ship was a veteran of at least one simulated battle in the Gehenna system.

Totokili was shaking his head in wonder. "So the secret is just that link—everything else about Gehenna is in the DataNet."

"Just about," Ng said. "Admiral Nyberg told me when he gave me the orders that we would be the first naval ship to enter the Gehenna system since its discovery over seven hundred years ago.

"How do they get the criminals there?" Krajno asked.

"Evidently there's a single Family charged with the responsibility," Ng replied, tapping at the keys. "They've held it since the reign of Nicolai I."

In the hologram, the planet rotated, and the point of view dipped toward the surface. A crater became visible, scale markers indicating its size: nearly sixteen kilometers across. "If we assume that everything about the FF simulation is accurate, and Admiral Nyberg's message certainly implies that, then that crater is the center of the habitable zone."

"I always wondered why that information was specified," said Navaz. "I just assumed it was a touch of verisimilitude."

"So did we all," Commander Krajno added.

"The point is," said Ng, all the humor suddenly gone from her voice, "that we can expect His Majesty to be landed somewhere within five hundred kilometers of it." She paused. "*If* the Rifter ship makes it through the Knot."

There was abrupt silence.

"But the Dol'jharians don't know about the system. . . ." Krajno's voice trailed off.

"Would His Majesty tell them?" Rom-Sanchez asked.

Ng shrugged fractionally. "I don't know. The only one who might have a clue is one I can't confide in, since he still visits the Rifters from time to time, including the tempath."

The Aerenarch. Rom-Sanchez remembered the briefing they'd received from the exiled Dol'jharian gnostor about the Rifter tempath. *"In combination with the Eya'a, she has transcended tempathy and can read conceptual thought—true telepathy. We do not know her limits."*

There was silence again as they considered the possibility that their mission would be for naught.

Then Navaz spoke. "Is that really a consideration anymore?"

"What?" The interjection was Totokili's; Ng merely looked at the armorer, realization dawning on her face.

Navaz pointed at the hologram. "The strength of that secret—its simplicity—is also its weakness. Once we enter the Gehenna system, especially if we fight a ship-to-ship action with a Rifter destroyer, everyone on the ship will know that Gehenna is System FF."

"That's why no naval ship has ever visited it!" Rom-Sanchez exclaimed.

"Then Gehenna will no longer be protected by secrecy," said Ng. "You're right; I won't go into action without a fully informed crew. You never know who may be called upon to make a command decision."

She straightened up. "So I might as well start at the top. Genz, we will convene at . . . oh eight hundred tomorrow to plan our approach."

Rom-Sanchez rose with the others. He felt an acute disappointment at the dismissal; his mind still raced with questions, and (he admitted to himself) he wanted to hear the briefing of the Aerenarch.

Navaz was looking sober as they filed into the corridor.

Totokili said to her, "Problem?"

"We couldn't rescue the Panarch at Arthelion, but now we will," she said slowly.

"Because we're under orders," Rom-Sanchez put in.

Navaz gave him a distracted glance. "AyKay, the Aerenarch ordered the rescue. It's his duty. But . . . what if the Panarch decided it was *his* duty to not tell the Rifters about the Knot?"

"They'll be dead," Totokili said, snapping his blunt fingers. "But we'll see it."

Rom-Sanchez nodded. That much of their mission would be

standard procedure: on emergence, check the tacponders for traces. They could then observe the Rifter destroyer entering the system by standing out from the Gehenna system a distance equal to the time elapsed between its arrival and theirs.

Krajno grunted softly. "As for the Panarch's 'duty'—how he might perceive it, and how he might react—why do you think she's briefing the Aerenarch alone?"

⁂ ⁂ ⁂

Margo Ng was amused at the way her heartbeat accelerated when the middy on duty sent word of the Aerenarch's arrival at the Plot room. It was the first time she had ever been alone with the young man around whom such a storm of controversy had raged.

Young? she thought as Brandon vlith-Arkad walked in, and she scrutinized him. A pair of intelligent blue eyes met hers in a brief, assessing glance that held no hint of the callow arrogance of youth. The bland contours of childhood had long since been planed from the refined face that presented such a formidably amiable front. Years of control rendered his countenance perfectly balanced; the toll the controversy must have taken on him showed only in the tightness of muscle across his brow and the hint of exhaustion marking the skin beneath his eyes. *He can't be any more than a decade younger than I am. If that.*

The novosti had done a lethally perfect job of maintaining the illusion of his eternal youth—with all its attendant irresponsibility. Conjecture flitted through her mind: a deliberate part of Semion's campaign to discredit his youngest brother?

"Your Highness," she said, bowing. "Please, will you sit down?"

They went on with the ritually prescribed exchange of niceties. She tried to make her part sound as sincere as she could. After all, he had willingly deferred all his prerogatives—he'd come to her, and at once, instead of requiring her to transfer all her data up to the cabin hastily fitted out as the royal suite and then making her wait upon his convenience. *As his brother would have done to an upstart Polloi.*

And then it was time for the real business. She glanced at the steward who had finished pouring out coffee, and he silently withdrew.

As soon as the door closed, she leaned forward. "How much do you know about Gehenna, Your Highness?"

"Nothing," Brandon replied with cooperative readiness.

"As much as any of us had, then," she said, and then held out the parchment paper. "The sealed orders from Admiral Nyberg."

She sat back and watched his expression go from surprise to recognition, to enjoyment—and then to comprehension.

He knows that the secret is lost, whether for good or ill; I don't have to risk offense with speech. How could the Panarch have condoned what happened here? Was he too overworked, too distant from his sons after losing his wife—or did he wish, in some way, to preserve the past by regarding Brandon as a youth?

She gave herself a quick mental shake. Fascinating as it was to speculate about the human beings behind the high titles, this was not the time or place. Brandon's remarkably acute perceptions made such speculation dangerous.

She spoke the one sentence she had planned: "Has Your Highness any idea what we might expect?"

It was a very oblique approach to the delicate question of what he thought might be his father's choice: death for the Rifters and Eusabian's heir as well as for himself and his advisers, or life, and if so, to what end?

The Aerenarch spoke, so quickly she knew immediately that he had been thinking about this at least as long as she had: "If they can stay alive without cost of innocent lives, they will. Suicide might be a quicker death, but not more honorable when they are needed back among us."

"You do not think he might balance their lives against that of Eusabian's heir, then, Your Highness?"

Brandon smiled a little. "Do you mean, is Anaris to be counted so little a threat? To that I can't return a simple answer, except that to underestimate him would be a mistake. But you have to realize . . ." He hesitated, then said, "To my father, Anaris is not just an enemy."

Ng waited, hoping her puzzled expression would prompt him to explain.

For a time it seemed that no explanation would be forthcoming, for the Aerenarch rose and walked the length of the room, his coffee cup forgotten in his fingers. He stood for a time staring at the holographic depiction of the movements of Eusasbian's fleet, then he turned and said, "I don't know if I can make it any clearer, because I don't entirely understand it myself."

"Anything that affords us insight can only aid our planning, Your Highness." She uttered the platitude in her most encouraging voice.

And won a brief grin in response. He said, "My own experience of Anaris was limited to hunt and run: he spent his time trying to kill me, for reasons I did not understand, so I retaliated by making him a butt. This went on for, oh, three years or so, and when it showed no sign of abating, they moved Galen and me to Charvann, ostensibly so Galen could attend the university."

Ng did not know what surprised her more: that the Panarch would permit it go on so long, or that his son would be the one removed, and the hostage the one to stay in the place of the son. *The thinking behind it is quintessential Douloi,* she realized. *The first, a matter of training, and the second of honor.*

". . . so I never really saw them together, but my understanding is that my father stood in some wise as tutor to Anaris."

"Subversion?"

Brandon shook his head, his eyes still distant. "No. Eusabian would have had him gutted as soon as he stepped off the transfer ship if he'd suspected that. Always, always they were enemies, but in opening up our history and thought to Anaris, I think he hoped that—despite the exposure of our weakness, which could be used against us—Anaris would take with him memory of our strengths." He finished, turned to face Ng. "My father never told me any of this—I never saw him often enough to hold any kind of serious converse. But Galen found it out." His smile hardened for a moment. "Semion was violently opposed. It was the only really serious disagreement he had with my father that was not resolved to his satisfaction. It was the primary reason he withdrew to his citadel on Narbon."

I hadn't realized just how intertwined with their lives the Eusabian heir was. She felt a frisson of presentiment. Shaking it off, she said, "Was he the only heir?"

Brandon grinned, and swallowed off his coffee. "No, Eusabian had three sons and two daughters. Anaris was the youngest." He set his cup down with a musical ring. "Is this beginning to sound familiar? They are all dead."

"I see," she said.

And my life is tied up with these people as well. . . . Memory wrenched at her, fending off the attack of Eusabian's flagship, the *Blood of Dol,* while the lances boarded it: handing the Panarch his enemy in defeat. The inevitability of a confrontation between the two heirs gripped at her. It had to happen, it *would* happen, and—though she resisted the idea with every atom of her being—she knew she would be there.

❋ ❋ ❋

SAMEDI

The latest changes downloaded from the hyperwave rippled through the strategic display, and Anaris sat back, drumming his fingers on the console. They had woefully underestimated the cunning of their enemy; of this the evidence was clear, in slashing lines of red and green and the fuzzy blue of relativistic indeterminacy. Despite their handicap, the Panarchists were slowly chivvying his father's forces into a revealing redeployment that pointed straight at the Suneater.

The only questions now were: how long would it take the enemy, despite their slower communications, to see the success of their strategy, and how long then to find the Suneater?

At least it is in one of the worst parts of the Rift, he thought. *Their search will be slow.*

He tapped rapidly at the keys, composing a query to his sources in Juvaszt's chain of command, then stopped and wiped the message header. He grimaced.

These conversations with Gelasaar are eroding my sense of propriety. Of course he could not communicate with the *Fist of Dol'jhar,* even now approaching the Suneater; his first message must be the ritual notification of the completion of his father's paliach.

Anaris shrugged and completed the query, then keyed it to his secretary. Morrighon would handle it. *Observing the letter if not the spirit.* Then he laughed. *A very Panarchist approach.*

He glanced at the chrono. Gelasaar would be arriving momentarily. His mind ranged swiftly over all he had learned in their conversations, focused by the Panarch's strangely intense request, at their last meeting, that he study the Unalterables. Almost unconsciously, he toyed with his dirazh'u, the silken cord mirroring the complexity of his thoughts.

The annunciator chimed.

"Enter," Anaris said. As the door to his quarters hissed open he stood up and tapped the gravitors to standard gee, and then hesitated. This would be their last meeting alone; on a whim, he left the strategic display of the Thousand Suns running on the console. Then, feeling the patient gaze of Gelasaar hai-Arkad on his back, he turned around.

The first thing he noted was that that strange intensity had not lapsed—if anything, he sensed it stronger than before. The second was the Panarch's age. The thought startled Anaris. This was the first time he had consciously noted Gelasaar's age. Why?

He let nothing of this show as he motioned the Panarch to a chair, then stepped aside as, instead, Gelasaar walked toward the console. They studied it in silence for a time, standing side by side.

"You see that communications and control are not, after all, always sufficient," the Panarch said finally.

"That is merely a lack of strategic judgment and insufficient understanding of a new weapon," said Anaris.

"Perhaps," the Panarch replied, turning away and seating himself in his usual place. "Have you reflected on the Unalterables, as I requested?"

"Yes."

"And?"

Something about Gelasaar's demeanor mildly unsettled Anaris. He sensed currents here he could not understand.

"The first thing I discovered is that there are two kinds of Unalterables: the prohibitions and the prescriptions. The former have held up better than the latter."

"Why do you think that is?"

This was almost an interrogation. Anaris hesitated, then decided that he would find out why sooner if he went along with it. A sudden thought tugged at him: *"Ritual has no contrary. . . ."*

"As you suggested," he said, "it has to do with the second Polarity: 'Seek not control, nor multiply laws; the cracks in the system are blessings, not flaws.' "

He stopped. Gelasaar waited patiently.

"At least some of the Unalterables seem to express this Polarity perfectly. For instance, the right of sentients to untraceable monetary exchanges, which mitigates against attempts to control economic relationships."

"Very good," said the Panarch, his voice neutral.

A reflex of pleasure triggered annoyance. *I am not under judgment here.* "But the purpose of the prescriptions is not as clear," Anaris said.

Gelasaar nodded. "They are the same." He spread his hands on his knees. "Consider the oneills, fixed by an Unalterable at a maximum population of fifty thousand. That is a fundamental determinant of the structure of civilization in the Thousand Suns and a powerful limitation on the power of government."

"How?"

"First, fifty thousand is the largest polity that can be governed democratically, as are the Highdwellings under their temenarchs. Second, in so small a polity, in any sort of liberal culture, democracy is almost inevitable; the ease of personal associations guarantees it. And that democratic structure forcibly resists any attempts of my government to micromanage human affairs."

"But planets are far larger," Anaris countered.

"Which is why the Covenant of Anarchy makes the distinction it does." The Panarch's gaze became distant. "And even so, the Covenant was showing signs of strain: Highdwellers and Downsiders growing apart, the loss of planets to Quarantine . . ." He appeared to shake himself out of reverie. "Do you see it, Anaris?" His eyes were shadowed with an unfathomable concern; once again the Dol'jharian felt the sense of judgment suspended.

Now, stronger than ever before, Anaris felt the dichotomy of his spirit. His Dol'jharian heritage rejected fiercely what the Panarch was saying—subjects obey or die, it insisted. But the part of him created in his youth on Arthelion saw the wisdom of the action that is no action, the careful layering of responsibility and anarchy that was Panarchic governance.

He nodded slowly. "Loopholes. Alway leave loopholes. If you arrange them carefully, the flow of government will proceed as planned, unresisted by those who choose escape rather than acquiescence. This leaves you free to apply the power you have constructively, rather than fighting those who disagree."

The smile on Gelasaar's face was like a sunrise. "You have transcended your heritage, Anaris achreash-Arkad."

Of the spirit of Arkad. The shock was almost overwhelming; the more so for its truth, and he almost missed what the Panarch said next.

"And so I give you your life."

"What?" The expostulation was involuntary, so outrageous was the Panarch's bald statement.

Instead of answering him, Gelasaar asked: "How far to Gehenna?"

Anaris stared at him for a moment. "About thirty hours."

The Panarch nodded. "Good. You were astonished, you said, at how little there was in the Palace computers about Gehenna. That is because the key to the Gehenna system has never been committed to the DataNet—it exists only in hard copy and the memories of a very few of us." He motioned to the dirazh'u, now lying limply in Anaris' hands. "It is ironic, the Dol'jharian belief in a destiny determined by knots, for it is the Knot that guards Gehenna."

Anaris heard the capitalization of the noun.

"A fracture in fivespace, some thirty light-minutes in extent, left over from the first few seconds of Creation and somehow anchored by Gehenna's sun. I do not understand the physics of it; I only know the Gehenna system can only be approached along the plane of the ecliptic, and even then, it is extremely dangerous to use the fiveskip. Ships attempting any other approach are never seen again."

The Panarch smiled, and Anaris realized that he must be letting his astonishment show.

"There are no guard ships, no weapons—the orbital monitor is unarmed. The guardian of Gehenna is Totality itself."

Almost blindly Anaris turned back to the strategic display, still running the projection of ship movements throughout the Thousand Suns. Two thoughts rang like tocsins in his mind.

I was *under judgment,* and *Once again, we underestimated the Panarchists.* It could be a trick, but he knew it wasn't; Morrighon had told him how frantically the Rifter captain of the *Samedi* had been seeking data on Gehenna, and how little there was. It all fit together. How lethally simple, to preserve a secret merely by leaving it on paper!

He turned back to Gelesaar. And even though he knew the answer, he asked the question, anyway: "Why are you telling me this?" He tabbed the console to summon Morrighon; he would have to notify Fasthand immediately.

"I told you at the beginning that I thought it likely you would be a better ruler than your father." The Panarch stood up. "Now I am sure of it." He waved at the console. "If, of course, you overcome the Navy, which does not seem as handicapped by your advantage as I warrant you expected."

Then his face became pensive. "I regret only one thing—that this last lesson will make it less likely that you will ever underestimate us again."

As the door slid open, Anaris shook his head, meeting the Panarch's eyes in the last personal contact they would ever have, away from the eyes of others.

"No, Gelasaar. Never again."

"Anaris does not believe a person's destiny can be determined by a knot," the Panarch said. "And he is right."

The others drew in around the table at which Gelasaar sat. *So he decided to spare him,* thought Caleb. *I would have liked to hear that conversation.*

The Panarch spread his hands on the table for a moment, then relaxed them. As he continued speaking, one finger twitched occasionally. "I think *we* all agree, as rational beings *must,* that one cannot *plan* one's destiny, nor *escape* the consequences of one's actions."

His voice was measured, without any emphasis save the normal cadence of Douloi speech; the meaning overladen on his words was carried by the movement of a finger.

"*When* I was young," said Mortan Kree, carrying on the conversation in the same fashion, "I thought I could *best* destiny, but then it seemed I had all the *time* in the world."

Their time together on the *Samedi* had made this mode of communication second nature, so much so that the camouflaging words dropped out of memory almost as soon as uttered. Caleb suppressed a grin at the irony of the situation. This was one benefit of political training he'd never expected: that the ability to effortlessly generate words without meaning would someday be his only means of meaningful discourse. Then he bent his attention to the conversation.

"(On) (the way) (down) (or) (on the surface)," said Carr. "(Can't overcome) (whole) (ship)."

"(I agree). (Short journey); (mixed) (people)," said Gelasaar. They'd already discussed the mixture of Dol'jharians and Rifters on the ship, and decided that Anaris' escort was designed to protect him and control the Rifters, relying on the destroyer's crew for technical know-how in all areas save computing, where the Dol'jharians could not afford to cede control.

"(They) (will) (keep us) (in) (lock), (gravity) (standard)," Matilde Ho replied. It was unlikely that the shuttle had independent gravitors, and the Rifter crew wouldn't stand for heavy gee.

"(Heavy) (ones) (aim) (high)," said Yosefina Paerakles. "(Maybe) (yield) (enough) (time)?" The Dol'jharians, used to a fifty percent higher acceleration, would tend to shoot high under standard gee.

Slowly the plan evolved. They had seen in the eyes of their captors nothing but disdain for their aged prisoners—Gelasaar had told them that of the Dol'jharians probably only Anaris knew of the power of the Ulanshu Kinesics. Soon they had all the elements but one.

"(One) (chance) (only)," said Kree.

"(We need) (surprise)," Carr rumbled, rubbing his chest and wincing. Once again, Caleb wondered what they had done to him; his every movement seemed weighted by pain. "(Use) (captors') (superstition)," he continued, coughing.

The Panarch looked a question at him. Padraic met his gaze squarely. "(Willing) (death) (and words of) (their) (native tongue)." The admiral shook his head at the protest in Gelasaar's face, looked around at all of them.

"(Your) (freedom) (is the) (anodyne) (I seek). (Death) (is a) (longed-for) (friend)." He coughed again, a painful, tearing sound.

The Panarch nodded slowly.

There was nothing more to be said.

TWENTY-FIVE

SAMEDI

Emmet Fasthand stomped onto the bridge and glared at his crew. To his surprise, and grudging satisfaction, no one returned his gaze. Even Moob looked away, uncharacteristically subdued.

Maybe that Karushna-whatsis wasn't such a bad thing, after all. He had made the mistake, long ago, of picking a tough crew, in the hopes of making the big kill. It had been profitable, but they'd turned out too tough, and there'd been no way to get out from under. *But this time the Dol'jharians were tougher.*

He laughed, enjoying the startled looks from the crew, and sat down in the command pod. A costly lesson, perhaps, but now, just maybe, if they survived this voyage, they'd be manageable enough to get him somewhere in the evolving Rifter fleet hierarchy. And if not, after this run he'd be able to afford to hire in a new crew that he could dominate.

A sudden movement from Moob, as if of pain, caught his attention. Her tattooed skin was puffed with lacerations. She'd win rank points on Rifthaven with her Draco clan for her battle—the only one, he figured, to claim anything positive from their taste of Dol'jharian custom. She was one of the lucky ones.

The Rifter grimaced, remembering Hestik lying with broken neck and spine in the corridor outside the Dol'jharian territory, and one of the engine crew stuffed, mangled almost beyond recognition, under a console in the aft rec room. And Sundiver, lying in her bunk, face to the wall, unwilling, or unable, to speak.

Fasthand smiled. *Just wish I'd known so I could get imagers in on the fun.* Then the countdown on the main screen caught his eyes and his enjoyment abruptly evaporated: EMERGENCE MINUS 23:08:40.

Gehenna. His tension returned in full measure. At least that chatzer Anaris and his slimy little Bori hadn't specified an approach. He'd play it safe: twenty light-minutes up and over the fourth planet.

Safe. A bitter laugh bubbled up and he suppressed it. The Panarchists had to know by now, after that hyperwave broadcast—they had spies everywhere. The first thing they would have done would be to dispatch a battlecruiser—maybe *several* cruisers—to the Gehenna system, to lie in wait.

The hatch behind him hissed open, and Morrighon entered. *What is he doing here?* The Bori had always avoided the bridge before. Was this more evidence of the shift in power the Dol'jharian chatzwar had precipitated? Had he participated? The Rifter looked over at Tat; she didn't look bruised or battered. Had Morrighon caught one of her cousins?

Fasthand's speculations died as Anaris' secretary walked up to his pod. Despite his twisted frame, the Bori moved as though he owned the bridge and everyone on it.

"Captain," Morrighon said, "the Lord Anaris has instructions for the approach to Gehenna."

Instantly enraged, Fasthand started to order him off the bridge, but his protest stuck in his throat as the Bori continued. "We have learned that the Gehennan system is warded by a hyperbolic fivespace distortion some thirty light-minutes in extent, which infallibly destroys any ship that approaches, whether in skip or under geeplane. The only safe approach is along the plane of the ecliptic."

Disbelief was Fasthand's first reaction. "What kind of trickery is this?" he snarled.

Morrighon said, "It appears to be the trickery by which the Panarchists have protected this planet for centuries."

The whining voice was in dead earnest. Nausea gripped at Fasthand's insides when he saw the horrified gaze of Lassa, Hestik's replacement at the nav console, as she, too, realized the import of Morrighon's words. *We're set to emerge ten light-minutes inside the killing zone.*

The Bori evidently saw his distress, for he smiled thinly. "You are therefore directed to emerge at plus thirty-five light-minutes, well outside the Knot, and approach the fourth planet along the plane of the ecliptic under geeplane, using your fiveskip only in case of dire emergency. Is that understood?"

Something about what Morrighon had said teased at Fasthand's memory, but the churning in his gut held it at bay; that, and the enjoyment apparent in the Bori's face. He could sense the fear sweeping through the bridge crew. *The twisted little chatzer is doing this on purpose.*

"Is that all you can tell me?" Fasthand countered, desperately trying to salvage something from the situation.

"That is all you need to know," Morrighon replied. "Unless you wish me to inform the Lord Anaris of your dissatisfaction with his orders?" He turned away with palpable disinterest in any reply Fasthand might care to make and left the bridge.

After a brief, shocked silence, the crew erupted in a barrage of curses and horrified speculation, scrambling Fasthand's thoughts as he tried to identify what it was Morrighon had said that seemed so important.

"Shut up! Shut up! Shut up!" he shrieked finally. "You stupid, Shiidra-sucking deviants! This is just what that Bori slug wants."

The uproar subsided.

"Lassa, reprogram for thirty-five out and along," he commanded, noting with a fresh surge of anger that she was already doing so, obeying the Bori rather than waiting for him to issue the order. *I'd like to tie that little chatzer's legs in a knot and finish the job the Dol'jharians started.*

"The Knot." He'd heard the emphasis on that word. That was what his mind had seized on, but why?

He had spoken aloud, and Lassa looked up from her console.

"You like hologames, Captain?" Her voice was conciliatory; she'd apparently realized her error in not waiting for his order.

"Hologames?" The sense of familiarity trembled on the edge of dissolution at the distraction.

"Yeah. There's a real famous battlesim called the Knot, based on a real Naval Academy setup—"

"The Knot!" He shouted the word. "Blunge! It's real. . . ." Fasthand's voice trailed off as he realized, first, where he'd heard the phrase before—not Lassa's game, but in a data dump from the MinervaNet he'd picked up long ago—and second, the chilling, damnable cleverness of the Panarchist government in leaving the secret of Gehenna in plain sight like that, thus ensuring that it would be overlooked for seven hundred years.

"Gehenna is the Knot," he said, his tone resonant with wonder. "It must be." He tapped with a controlled frenzy at the console; the main screen flickered with a dizzying riot of images as the computer searched, then stabilized on an image of a reddish hyperbola with a blue-white sun at its center.

"That's it," said Lassa. "I've played it a lot. Problem is, the Knot's unstable." She stopped, her expression changing. "No way," she said, her voice shaking. "That's worse than hitting radius in skip."

"Shut up, you blunge-eating pult," Moob shouted suddenly, her temper flaring. "It's only a chatzing game." The bravado in her voice was painfully apparent.

"No," said Fasthand wearily, "it's not just a game. It's an incredibly detailed simulation from the Naval Academy that we have to assume *is* the Gehenna system." He looked over at Lassa. At least one thing was going right—against all odds he had a navigator who knew the Gehenna system.

If the chatzing game is accurate. It would be just like the Panarchists to throw some inaccurate—and deadly—details into the game, just in case. But he had the real simulation in the *Samedi*'s databanks.

He looked over at the navigator. "What do you mean, unstable?"

She returned his gaze, her eyes stricken. "It—the game. I mean, the Knot—it's sensitive to gravitational impulses. You *can* use the fiveskip, for short hops; you can fire skipmissiles; if you have a battlecruiser, you can even fire your ruptors." She swallowed and motioned at the screen. "But every time you do, the hyperbola flattens out a little and the transverse axis shortens." She stopped speaking.

"And?" said Fasthand impatiently, scanning his data to

match it against her recollection of the game. So far, the game seemed an accurate rendition of the naval simulation.

"And," continued Lassa, "eventually, the two lobes meet, and you don't come out again." She emitted a semi-hysterical snicker. "The Knot's got some killer animations there—in one of 'em, the Knot pulls your skeleton out through your blungehole."

With a shriek of rage Moob spun around her pod and leapt toward Lassa, a knife materializing in her hand. Fasthand's reaction was instantaneous. He couldn't afford to lose this navigator, not now. He jumped up and palmed his sleevejac; only at the last moment did he lower his aim. He couldn't afford to lose his best scantech, either, not with the prospect of a battlecruiser lying in wait.

The jet of plasma screeched out and scored the deck at Moob's feet, splattering her trousered legs with flecks of white-hot metal. She dropped the knife with a howl of pain and slapped frantically at the smoldering cloth. Then she looked up at the Rifter captain with a snarl of rage on her face that slowly leaked away as she saw his resolve. Fasthand steeled himself and did not look away, knowing that if he did so, he would lose this battle, despite having, at the moment, the upper hand.

Moob shrugged and lowered her eyes. "Stupid suck needed some sense scared into her—no good to us if she goes all jellybag on us. I wouldn't have hurt her bad."

"No," said Fasthand, trying very hard not to let his voice shake. "You wouldn't have." He stood unmoving until Moob returned to her console; she did not attempt to retrieve her knife. Lassa watched, her back stiff, her eyes dark with hatred.

Slowly the atmosphere of the bridge returned to something closer to normal. Fasthand sat down and stared at the Knot, portrayed in chilling clarity on the main screen. What other secrets might there be, waiting, like this one, to blast the unwary with sudden agonizing death? Suddenly Emmet Fasthand felt very old—he'd been on the Riftskip too long, and he feared his luck was running out.

Not yet, it isn't. We found out in time.

This time.

⁂ ⁂ ⁂

Tat approached the ready room cautiously, not knowing what to expect. The captain's summons had been terse.

Everyone who'd gone out for the Karusch-na Rahali and lived through it was in a vile temper, moving stiffly as if with pain. She'd heard about Hestik and the drivetech; she hadn't heard anything about what had happened to Sundiver after she went for Anaris, except the obvious fact she hadn't been seen since. And Moob . . . that scene on the bridge had frightened Tat almost senseless; she'd never seen the Draco so wild, yet the captain had forced her to back down. Tat and her cousins had managed a precarious accommodation to conditions on the *Samedi;* now everything was changing.

The hatch opened and she looked into the ready room. No one was there except Fasthand. He was sitting facing the door, a jac on the table in front of him. He motioned her over.

"I want you to wear your boz'l," the captain said, his long, unlovely face twisted in a peculiar grimace midway between worry and anger. "Even to sleep."

Tat nodded.

Fasthand flickered a look at her face, then away. He never met anyone's eyes if he could possibly avoid it; that was part of what had made his face-down of Moob so startling. But that hadn't lasted long. Now he seemed more ferret-like than ever.

"I don't trust that blunge-eating Morrighon not to somehow rizz our comp," he went on. "You are to work night and day on breaking his codes. We'll put you on sick call—no one's to know."

She nodded again, wondering who would take her place in the already depleted prime bridge crew.

He frowned. "Tell Lar he's got to cover you. Less comment that way."

Tat knew what he meant. *No one can tell one Bori from another.* It wasn't that they looked alike, it was more that no one bothered unless they wanted something. Annoying, but now was not the time to lodge a protest on Lar's behalf.

"Keep me posted on whatever you learn," he said. Then he looked at his chrono and winced. "Twenty hours now."

Tat ducked her head and scudded out the door, relieved to get away from Fasthand. Always tense and strange, he'd been manic since the Karusch-na, and she was afraid the information about Gehenna would push him over the edge.

Hunching her shoulders, Tat sped for the relative safety of her cabin. With her door code-locked, she poured herself into the computer system, exploring with foofbug slowness its perimeter. Patient feelers of code probed at anomalies; at last, she discovered by accident that Morrighon, with a lethal cleverness, had masked most of his data by camouflaging it as scavenged dataspace.

With care—for she found guardian phages zapping back and forth, looking for invaders—she tried to find how he'd managed it. Breaking it would be even harder.

Finally, exhausted almost to the point of recklessness, she forced herself to withdraw and to shut down her system. Her hand moved reluctantly, and her burning eyes stared at the now-blank screen, seeing afterimages flickering there.

If she went back in now, she'd do something foolish and get caught. It was time to try another way.

She turned in her pod, surprised at the ache in her neck. A glance at the chrono shocked her: she'd been at it for nine straight hours. It was 03:45.

She got to her feet, and a huge yawn forced its way up from her insides. One longing glance at her nightclothes, then she rubbed her eyes and marched to the door.

Emergence was nearly on top of them. She shared Fasthand's fears of what the Dol'jharians could do if they controlled the ship's functions. *Not to mention Fasthand—he's crazy bad enough to force me out the lock.*

The spurt of fear gave her a semblance of energy, enough to move her to the rec room, which was completely empty. She called up a mug of hot caf and stood with its warmth cradled in her hands, the steam tickling her nose, as she thought.

It was time to abandon the hunt through electronics and do some foraying in realtime. Only, how to flush Morrighon without him knowing he was being flushed?

The idea of stepping into the Dol'jharian area gave her the shillies. And she didn't dare run a locate—he'd know that immediately, of course. She had long since built safeguards for herself against tracers.

But . . . her tired eyes ranged over the galley console, and she took her underlip between her teeth. There was one other route: find out where he'd been and what he'd ordered.

Some quick tapping, and as a list windowed up, her heart began to hammer painfully.

ID 121-SD; roufou-rice, geel soup, caf/snithi, 03:39.

Bori food.

And—she glanced back to make sure—he'd ordered it from

right where she stood, instead of the rec room nearest the Dol'jharian area.

Which suggested he didn't want to eat it in his room, under the heavy grav, if he didn't have to. And—she was sure—he never ate with his overlords.

So that left the rest of the ship, she thought, as she paced back and forth. Think, think! It would be so easy, so convenient, if he'd just take it down to the hidey that Tat and her cousins used sometimes, with the gees changed so it seemed—

She stopped. Why not? He wasn't in his room, or he'd have gotten the food on the other side of the ship. And he had never been sighted eating in the rec areas, where crew normally ate.

And he is a Bori—of sorts—so he might feel as comfortable as we do in high places.

Not that there were any "high places" on shipboard. But there was one place that, with a little bit of imagination, could be turned into one.

First for cover: she called for some food and dumped half her caf. Then she rushed down to the transtube. As the module accelerated, she wondered for the first time what she would say to him if she did find him. *We're Bori, we're both Bori,* she thought, and from somewhere a weird urge to laugh shook her.

When the module stopped, she leaned against the door, trying to still the hammering of her heart. A few deep breaths, a sip of caf. Still, she wanted to laugh—she was even less adept than Captain Fasthand at skulkery in realtime. *Which is why I'm on this ship in the first place. I just hope I live to get off it.*

The urge to snicker seized her again, and she shut her eyes, fighting down panic. Then, one step, another, another, until she reached the access lock to the long missile tube.

And she knew right away that someone was there—and that he had found, or programmed for himself, the little alteration in the grav that made it possible to sit on the edge of the hatch and feel as if a kilometer-long drop stretched out below one's feet. The access lock hatch was yellow-light, blinking four to the second—quarter gee—and the indicator was overlaid by a moiré pattern, indicating not only a changed acceleration but a shift in orientation.

She tabbed the hatch open, cradling her food tray under one arm, and swung herself through, finding, as expected, that the opposite wall of the lock was now down. She landed lightly across the dogged-open hatch and faced the bent figure of Morrighon. His eyes wary and cold, he sat on the edge of the hatch—what would have been its top in normal gee—with his legs dangling over what the altered gee made appear a kilometer-long drop along the missile tube.

Raising her food containers, she made her dry tongue work and forced her lips to smile. "Company?" she said.

And knew at once that he never ate in company. A strange expression, akin to revulsion, narrowed his already pinched features. A chill of fear roughed the skin on her upper arms, the same reaction she'd had when she realized he slept alone. Bori just didn't do that—sleep alone, eat alone.

"You're prime crew," he said. "Why are you awake?"

She shrugged, and a lie came to her lips as if she'd planned it. "Half of prime crew's on sick list, and some of alternate. Captain got me training for backup." And, before he could say anything, she added, "Watch this."

His features tightened; she wondered suddenly if he carried some kind of nasty weapon as she twisted over and stretched a hand out toward the console inset. Pausing, glancing back doubtfully, she wondered if he would indeed kill her and dump her body right out the nearby lock. *Or he could even try his own version of that Karusch-na biznai.*

But he didn't move, so she tapped out a quick code, and a holojac that Lar had installed came to life. Now, instead of the barren dyplast and metal mesh of the catwalk stretching into dimness below them, they were atop a cliff, watching the sparkle of a waterfall roar past them and fall away into darkness below. The sound was quite good—way in the distance came the muted thunder of the water reaching a river, and the tianqi sent a strong breeze ruffling across their faces, bearing traces of scents from Bori: sweetgrass, oroi, carith-herbflower.

She saw Morrighon suck in a long, slow breath. His face in the false sunlight was strained, as if he were in pain.

"You don't like it?" she exclaimed in astonishment. And she tabbed the control, making the holo disappear.

Morrighon said nothing, but he seemed on the verge of speech. Tat's heartbeat marked quick time, *lump-lump, lump-lump.*

"I've only seen Bori in holos," he said at last, a raspy edge to his thin voice. "I didn't think there were any mountains like that."

"No," Tat said. "Not like that. Rivers through hills. Don't know about desert—left when I was four. All I remember is houses on stilts, and one flood season. Anyway, we like it."

And she reached, looking at him. When he didn't move, she tabbed the holo on again, and for a long time they sat there, while the false waterfall thundered into a false river far below.

She said tentatively, "Never saw Bori realtime?"

"Baby." He seemed to shake himself. His food sat, untouched, on the deck—wall—beside him, but he didn't seem on the verge of flight.

"Go ahead and eat," she suggested, feeling a trifle more confident. Things were, well, a little more *normal*—whatever normal was, when both of them were confined on opposite sides aboard this crazy ship so very far from their birth planet.

Once again the peculiar grimace, like pain, deepened the lines in his face.

Confidence restored, her recklessness also returned. She said, "By the way, we—cousins—thank you. You left us alone—" She waved a hand, meaning the day before, then she gawked in surprise when Morrighon's eyes widened and he gulped on a laugh.

"Eh?" she said.

But he shook his head, snuffling his weird high-pitched giggle. One of his hands flexed convulsively, then he got control of it and drew a long breath.

"What's funny?" she demanded. "*Meant* it."

"Because . . . because." His mouth stretched in a grin like a gigged frog, then he said, "You are ignorant, Ombric."

New horror, unlike anything she'd felt yet, suffused her. "You—you aren't—"

Now his grin was sardonic, and he was back in control. "Geld us before we enter the Catennach, the Service of the Lords."

She gasped, and he grinned, obviously enjoying, in a twisted way, her shock. "But—if they don't want you making families, why not contraceptives? Perm ones?"

"Our choice," he said. "We live through that, it's a measure of our strength."

A measure of your desire for power through the likes of Anaris, she thought, shock abating, and her mind now working rapidly. She had no idea whether this conversation was to any purpose she could use—but he was talking. *And my stupid reaction makes me look stupid in his eyes. All right, I'll be stupid.*

"Euuugh," she said. "Dol'jharians don't believe in weakness like anesthesia, bet?"

He snorted.

She leaned against the wall. "So we were safe, anyway. Nice. But, why you told captain crew would be attacked?"

"So what would happen would happen."

"Doesn't make sense," she said. "What if more of our bridge crew got duffed, how we make it through this Knot? No sense."

"Kept them busy," he said. "Knew most of them wouldn't brave our side."

Sudden suspicion thrust aside her pursuit of Morrighon. "Anaris know Sundiver was coming?"

Morrighon shrugged, and wheezed a laugh. "They got what they came for, didn't they?"

She had to admit the truth of it, but not out loud. Besides, the maliciousness of his tone made her wary again.

But the interview was over; he reached for his food and moved to the transtube. "Emergence coming soon," he said over one twisted shoulder. "You'd best be ready, don't you think?" His tone taunted her, reminding her of her original purpose.

And then he was gone.

She slumped down, staring into the mesmerizing spray of water falling, falling. *And I found out nothing.* Suddenly hungry, she pulled her food over and munched, her eyes on the sparkling water as she thought back through the conversation.

Or was it nothing? She now had a new insight into Morrighon, and Barrodagh as well. They slept alone, they ate alone, they couldn't bunny. *It has to have been trained into them, by pain and threats and the pursuit of power. So they turn into hinky little parodies of Dol'jharians. . . .*

Yes, yes, she was almost onto something, she felt it. Morrighon talked like a Dol'jharian, and he lived kind of like one, but he ordered Bori food. And she remembered that first reaction to her waterfall. Like pain . . . *like release from pain.*

That's it, she thought, scrambling to her feet. Her fingers slapped at the controls, restoring the catwalk to normal, erasing the fact that they had ever been there.

Morrighon—maybe all the Bori servants—lived perforce like their masters, but she was certain that they made little retreats for themselves, in ways they wouldn't be caught. Ways the Dol'jharians would scorn to probe. Even in the computer.

She jumped into the transtube module, sleepiness forgotten.

❋ ❋ ❋

GEHENNA

"Incoming!"

The sentry's hoarse shout galvanized the torchlit courtyard into a scurry of sudden activity; soldiers and menials scattered in all directions. Mindful of his dignity, Napier Ur-Comori stepped unhurriedly behind a stone column as a small object arced through the predawn sky over the high castle wall and thumped into the dust nearby with a wet squelch.

Nothing happened. No subtle, deadly haze of sporetox, no sudden flaming burst of neverquench, not even a maddened swarm of stingflies. Above, from the weapons platforms behind the parapet, Napier heard the creak of the catapults swiveling on their platforms, and then the squeal of their unwinding tendon springs as they discharged, mixed with the dull clatter of the stutterbows.

"Cease fire!" The sergeant's voice echoed into a sudden silence as Napier paced as easily back into the courtyard, crossing slowly toward the fallen projectile. Worried eyes followed him from the walls; someone would pay for letting the forces of Londri Ironqueen and her allies get this close.

The Comori warlord prodded the object fastidiously with one armored foot. It was the head of his legate, Urman of Lissandyr, maggots already swarming in the empty eye sockets and boiling up around the hilt of the broken stonewood sword protruding from his mouth. *At least we still have his Steel; and the loyalty of the Lyssand is now assured—or at least their hatred of the Ironqueen.*

Napier crossed his arms on his chest and looked up at the sky as the first rays of the rising sun seared horizontally through the dusty air above House Comori. The siege had begun. Well, they need hold out only a short time, if the Tasuroi ambassador could be trusted.

As if summoned by the thought, a waft of greasy fetor assaulted his nostrils and he turned to see the stumpy, twisted form of Arglebargle approaching, the feathers and quills in his nose fetish bobbing in front of his rotten-toothed smile. The Tasuroi was barely four thirds of a meter tall, but almost as broad, his soiled robes bulging over powerful muscles and an awesome potbelly that didn't jiggle at all.

Arglebargle looked back and forth between the tall Comori leader and the head in the dust before him. He grinned even wider. "Nice of Ironqueen to deliver appetizer before breakfast."

Napier's stomach heaved, but he nodded pleasantly to the barbarian. He'd learned very early in their negotiations that the Tasuroi enjoyed baiting inhabitants of the Splash any way they could, even in their naming convention. Refusing to reveal their real names to outsiders, they chose instead for themselves outlandish cognomens. The higher the rank, the more ridiculous the name, and the greater their delight in forcing their hosts to pronounce it seriously.

But Arglebargle, whatever his true name, wasn't really joking: the Tasuroi lived far outside the Splash, clustered around small craters left by fragments of the Skyfall where there were sufficient trace metals for human life, and they were cannibals. They boiled their victims in huge iron alloy pots that were the sum total of their wealth, which they never emptied. Napier tried not to think about how five-hundred-year-old human soup tasted—little wonder the Tasuroi smelled so bad.

"I'm sorry, my lord ambassador," the Comori leader replied, "but I fear Urman's mother would object most strenuously."

Arglebargle guffawed, assaulting Napier with a blast of searingly bad breath. "Tell old bitch I give her half the brains."

Napier turned away in relief as a subaltern ran up and saluted. "Captain Arbash reports a small artillery force retreating from the crossroads. He believes they took casualties." Her eyes strayed to the Tasuroi, then back to her House's leader.

"Very well." He prodded the head toward the young woman with his foot, noting the caste mark of sterility on her forehead. "Take this away; give it to Lyssand Urmanmater and tell her I share her grief and her anger."

She saluted, picked up the rotting head gingerly by the fringe of hair at the back, and trotted away, holding her arm out stiffly, leaving a trail of squirming bits of insect life dropped from the relic.

Arglebargle shrugged with exaggerated disappointment. "Too

long away from gourmet cooking, I have been." The elegant term, stuck in the midst of his grunting speech like a gauma-pearl in a midden, reminded Napier again not to underestimate the outwardly absurd barbarian—he had a first-class mind and could speak as well as any legate when he chose to.

"But not to mind," the Tasuroi continued. "One of my chatterbats returned last night; Smegmaniggle and horde will be here in three days, maybe two—then we return the favor, no?" He motioned with his chin toward the wall over which Urman's head had been delivered. "Tasuroi will eat well!"

And the Crater's power will take a blow from which it will never recover. He glanced down as the Tasuroi stumped away, looking around shrewdly at the fortifications. *And there will be a surprise for you as well, my greasy little friend.*

Not only that, but last night the chirurgeon had gleefully told him that the Isolate was expecting again, and this time, too, he thought, it would be twins!

As the actinic rays of Shaitan blasted the top of the wall with brilliant heat, Napier Ur-Comori squinted into the light and breathed in with delight.

Success would be his, he could feel it.

Twenty-six

SAMEDI

"Emergence," Lassa said quietly, her voice barely rising above the bells that duplicated her announcement.

Tat looked up blearily from her console, squinting at the screen relaying from the bridge. The captain had arranged this feed at her suggestion.

"Moob!" Emmet Fasthand snapped. The imager surveyed the rest of the crew over his head, so Tat couldn't see his expression, but his voice was anxious.

"Scanning." The Draco tapped swiftly. "No traces."

Tat sucked in a breath. Her argus had spotted a code-spatter that correlated with emergence. *Morrighon!*

Suddenly energized, she threw a web of code across the addresses the argus pointed to, a gossamer of abstract sensation too fine, she hoped, for detection.

"Primary plus 35.2 light-minutes, 33 mark 75." Lassa's fingers worked. "Navsearch initiated." Tat could hear the twitter of the navigator's console as the navcomp began looking for the fourth planet—even if the Gehenna system had a beacon, they couldn't rely on it.

Meanwhile, her search, at least, triggered no alarms. Another window on her console pulsed with the rhythmic probing of the keyword generator; she had it cross-linked to the Bori history chip Lar had given her when she told him of her supposition.

"Sounds right to me," he'd said, rummaging in his locker and handing her the chip. "No Dol'jharian's going to go snooping into Bori history—Rifters neither." His lip curled. "Not this crew, anyway."

She looked closer at the window: the search was already crossing over into second-order conceptual associations generated by the *neuraimai* cognitive mapping circuits. No results yet.

On the screen, Lassa's console chirped. "Planet located, system mark 2-70. Orbital radius 23 light-minutes."

"Lay in a course for system 2-70 mark zero, plus 35 light-minutes," Fasthand commanded. "And use as many zigs as you need to keep us clear of the Knot. Moob!"

The Draco's voice was surly. "I see anything, you'll be the first to know."

Tat's attention returned to her work. She was barely conscious of the passing time as the *Samedi* made a series of skips that brought it to the point on the plane of the ecliptic, thirty-five light-minutes from the system's sun, that was closest to Gehenna. Her stomach burned from too much long-steeped Alygrian tea, the standard neurobooster for noderunners throughout the Thousand Suns, and her eyes throbbed. But she was close, so close. She could feel Morrighon's presence.

Suddenly her console chattered at her and a window bloomed over her work. A surge of adrenaline brought her upright in her seat: one of her trolling phages had snagged a nonstandard scavenger worm. It had to be one of Morrighon's—he'd camouflaged his workspace by making it look invisible to the system's standard scavengers. But no program could work without reclaiming used space.

Tat tapped eagerly at the keypads. Yes! She'd just caught one of Morrighon's. She threw it into stasis and gingerly began to tease apart its header, wary of suicide code and bitbombs. As it unwound, she linked the bitstream to the neuraimai. Now she'd see something!

The emergence bells chimed again; something on the bridge relay caught her attention. Fasthand was sitting upright in the command pod. From the angle of his head, she could tell he was staring at the main screen.

"Thirty-five out, 2-70 mark zero," Lassa announced. "Course for Gehenna laid in."

"System's real dirty," said Moob. "Over to DeeCee."

At the damage control station Galpurus hunched over the console, his narrow hands incongruous at the ends of his bulky arms as they tapped at the keys. He looked up after a time. "Shields can take maybe point-oh-one cee, or a shimmy more. Beyond that we'll ablate pretty bad, take some heat, even."

The strangeness of their situation pulled Tat away from her task for a moment—the dissection of Morrighon's scavenger was largely automatic, anyway. The *Samedi* would be making a Realtime Run into the Gehenna system at one percent lightspeed, trusting to the shields to protect it from the dirt and ice which, in obedience to the laws of orbital dynamics, were concentrated in the ecliptic. Nobody *ever* voluntarily made a Realtime Run: a ship was just too vulnerable in fourspace, and so slow!

A red rose bloomed in her vision, and Fasthand's voice came to her flatly through the neural link. "You got anything yet?"

"I'm on the edge," she replied, wondering if he could sense her fatigue and excitement over the boz'l. "Soon."

"Better be. It'll take us twenty hours to make the run to Gehenna—if a cruiser shows up, their shields'll take 'em through a hell of a lot faster. I want those Dol'jharian chatzers out of the comp before that."

The link terminated. On the screen Fasthand ordered the fiveskip up to tac-level four. The engines burred harshly, then cut out, hurling them into the Gehenna system, into the jaws of the Knot, at 3,100 kilometers per second. On the main screen Tat could see the shields fluorescing under the impact of stellar dust; flares of light blossomed here and there as larger particles were dissipated by the teslas. She shivered; that was something she could have lived the rest of her life without seeing.

Then she turned her attention back to her console. If she didn't break Morrighon's hold on the computer, Telos only knew what else she'd see before she died.

❋ ❋ ❋

GROZNIY

The alarm burred through the racking jumble of Margot Ng's dreams, and she woke up gratefully. A sense of duty had forced her to grab a few hours' sleep; though it had been a good idea, her body still ached and her mind was still keyed-up.

Shaking off the effects of those high-stress dreams, she rose, ran hot water over herself to clear her head, then pulled on her uniform. With a peculiar sense of unreality she made sure all her tabs were fastened correctly and that no flaw marked the fit of the uniform. Within hours she would either face the Panarch, or else would be conveying the new Panarch.

High Politics. She shook her head, turning away from the mirror. One couldn't get any higher. *Despite one's personal inclination,* she reflected with grim humor as she went out in search of coffee. High Politics was worse than muck—once it stuck to you, you could never be rid of it.

By throwing herself behind the Aerenarch, she had made enemies of some of the most powerful Douloi in the Panarchy. Archon Srivashti, who'd lost his one planet to a rabble. What kind of ruler would he make? And the others were no better.

She sighed, eyeing the breakfast she suddenly found she couldn't eat. Pushing it away, she decided that if she had to be involved in politics, she'd do it right.

Leaning over to tab her com, she said: "Would you inquire if Gnostor Omilov is free for a few moments' consultation?"

Her ensign would scrupulously word it just that way, she knew, avoiding all semblance of a command.

While she forced a few bites down, Krajno briefed her on their progress. All systems were functioning; less than an hour to emergence.

Omilov appeared a few minutes later. The man looked tired but alert; he had changed, she thought as he came in. His eyes, stance, everything indicated a younger man than the one she had grown used to seeing. Interesting: experiences like those they'd shared lately tended to age one quickly, but on Sebastian Omilov they appeared to have had the opposite effect. *The remarkably restorative power of action,* she thought wryly.

"We will soon be emerging into the Gehenna system," she said after greeting him. "Would you like to join us on the bridge?"

His eyelids lifted, betraying surprise and, she thought, pleasure. His lips parted, but then his expression fused into a polite gratitude that indicated second thoughts.

Wondering what he'd been about to say, Ng tried to encourage him. "It'll be a trifle crowded, of course," she said. "As the Aerenarch will also be with us. My first thought had been to open a feed to your cabin, but on consideration I thought if our positions were reversed, I would want to be there." She ended on a faintly apologetic note.

Omilov bowed. "And so I do," he said. "I really am grateful; I had not dared to ask. But . . ."

"But?" she prompted.

He drew a deep breath, then said decisively, "I *had* intended to beg for that feed, and also for the company of . . . certain persons to witness with me whatever will transpire."

Ng laughed. "Not the Rifters."

Omilov answered with a rueful smile. "Well, a couple of them. It was Manderian with whom I discussed this. He expressed a wish that the emerging unity represented by the Kelly, the Eya'a, and two of the Rifters be able to observe, if they wished, what happens when we reach Gehenna."

Ng really was surprised. She'd never heard of such a request being made on what amounted to the grounds of religion. Wondering what else was going on that Omilov was reluctant to talk about, she considered rapidly, then nodded. She owed the man too much: this was a relatively easy payback.

"We'll do it," she said. "But they won't have to squeeze into your cabin. I'll close off one of the classrooms, so they can watch it on one of the big screens. In fact, I'll give the order right now."

Omilov bowed again, this time with unalloyed gratitude.

❋ ❋ ❋

"Emergence," Lieutenant Mzinga said quietly. "Primary plus 37 light-minutes, 40 mark zero. FF data indicates we should be within a light-minute of a tacponder."

Their emergence point was a compromise between the most likely course for the *Samedi* and a reasonable distance from a tacponder. *Now to see if we've gotten lucky,* Ng thought.

"SigInt. Pop the tacponder; see if there's an emergence pulse recorded."

Ensign Wychyrski tapped at her console. "Pulsed."

Except for the almost inaudible sigh of the tianqi, the bridge was silent while they waited for the returning pulse of information. Ng sensed the presence of Brandon vlith-Arkad just behind her right shoulder, though he made no move, no sound.

She blinked tired eyes and forced her attention back on task. Less than two minutes later the SigInt console twittered as data from the tacponder flooded in.

"Emergence pulse recorded 16.4 hours ago at primary plus 35 light-minutes, 33 mark 75, signature matches Alpha-class destroyer. Followed three minutes later by another skip pulse. Subsequent pulses indicate vessel headed for system two-seventy degrees, which correlates with current position of Gehenna."

"Blunge," Krajno rumbled. "They're way ahead of us."

"No further data available," said Wychyrski. "The system's way too dirty to pick up anything until we're a lot closer."

On the other side of her, Rom-Sanchez worked his console. "Since they can't know we're coming, I'd wager they're making a Realtime Run to keep from stirring up the Knot. But with all that dust and ice an Alpha won't do better than about point-oh-one, which puts them at the planet in about an hour. Our shields'll handle about point-oh-three or so. . . ."

"So we'll arrive at Gehenna four hours or so after they land His Majesty," said Krajno. "And then we've got to disable and board them to find out where."

" . . . except that if we tune the teslas up that high, we'll perturb the Knot into a dangerous level of instability," Rom-Sanchez continued. He looked over at Ng. "It might be too unstable to allow us even short tactical skips once we get there—and we can't face those skipmissiles with only geeplane maneuvering."

Ng thought quickly. "Can we safely make a series of short skips instead to get there faster?" she asked.

Rom-Sanchez shook his head. "No. The *Samedi*'ll have its shields maxed out, so they're already shaking things up. We're stuck in realtime." He grimaced. "And don't forget that when they start firing skipmissiles, even if we don't, the Knot'll get even more unstable."

Something nibbled at the edge of Ng's mind, a memory from her Academy days. Not the FF simulation . . . For some reason, she thought of Styrgid Armenhaut, killed at Arthelion. What had brought him to mind?

Then she had it. "Ball-and-chain!" she exclaimed. Armenhaut had tried to use that maneuver against her in a battlesim at the Academy, using his tractors to hold an asteroid behind his radiants to protect the weak spot in his cruiser's shields. She'd beaten him, anyway, earning his lasting enmity and her nickname, Broadside O'Reilly, at the same time.

"What?"

Ng ignored Krajno's interjection. She tapped at her console, windowing up a god's-eye projection of the Gehenna system and engaging eyes-on mode. A flare of light raced across the image and settled on the inmost gas giant, just outside the influence of the Knot. "Navigation, plot a course outside the Knot to the trojan point for Number Six that's closest to Gehenna and engage when computed. On emergence, find me an asteroid about four klicks in diameter and take us to tractor range."

She turned back to Rom-Sanchez. "Commander, what's the maximum safe velocity we can use high-tac to decelerate from when we reach Gehenna?"

His brows knit in perplexity, but he soon had the answer. "A single tac-level five maneuver from point-one cee will probably not perturb the Knot beyond safe levels," he replied, "unless the Rifters are smart enough to shake it up while we're on our way in—in which case we may not be able to stop and fight." He looked up at the main viewscreen for a moment. "You're going to use an asteroid for a shield?"

"Steady-state gravitational energy won't perturb the Knot, right?" Ng countered.

Rom-Sanchez shook his head. "It'll excite it a bit, but the lobes shouldn't shift much." He grinned suddenly. "Going to be a hell of a show from the inner system—it'll look like a supernova heading straight for them."

The fiveskip burred into activity as she replied.

"Good. That'll give them time to worry about what we'll do to them when we catch up. There's no way they can pull off the same stunt, so they can't get away."

She looked up at the screen. "When we're finished, they'll be only too happy to tell us where they landed him."

⁂ ⁂ ⁂

Manderian touched the annunciator outside Vi'ya and

Marim's cabin. He felt the mental tug that indicated his presence being scanned, and then the door slid open. He walked into frigid air.

The only human present was Vi'ya. Relief tickled at the back of his mind, but he suppressed it.

The one-who-hears. The Eya'a semaphored rapidly with him, identifying everyone and their setting. It seemed some sort of game with them; why else would they delight in using the signals to state the obvious? Or was it a way of establishing contact with the physical world?

One of their hangings lay spread over a table. Vi'ya sat near it, her face blank, her mind shielded, but tiredness marked her eyes. The Eya'a pointed at one of the figures woven into it, semaphored something that he did not understand, and then pointed at a bulkhead and signed: *We hear.*

Then sharp displeasure compounded by distrust assailed him from Vi'ya, a powerful enough emotional reaction to make him steady himself against a wall. But then it was shielded, so swiftly it left him feeling oddly off balance.

He looked across at Vi'ya, squelching his own emotional reactions. "Is that their sign for the Aerenarch?" he asked.

"Yes," she said.

The Eya'a chittered softly. Manderian put it together, realized that Vi'ya had been using them to listen, in some fashion, to Brandon vlith-Arkad. Was *he* aware of it?

The complexities of this connection bloomed like fireworks in the back of his mind, then spun away. He would consider the implications later.

Right now, they both knew that she'd been trying to watch through the Aerenarch's eyes and that Vi'ya hated Manderian's knowing. But he had learned patience decades ago. He said only, "The captain set up a bridge feed for us in a classroom. The ship will be emerging into the Gehenna system shortly."

She hesitated; Manderian wondered if her cabin mate had been present, if she would have refused outright. Also something to be considered later.

"Then let's go," she said.

The Eya'a followed them. Vi'ya walked in silence, her countenance wary. Manderian was distracted by the little pair of sentients, who semaphored almost constantly, mostly things they knew, but then making reference to something unseen and unheard by Manderian, which was deeply unsettling.

He tried to comprehend the magnitude of their awareness, and as always, it tugged at his sense of balance. Looking sidewise at his human companion, he wondered how she had managed—and if she would ever talk about what she'd learned.

They stepped off the transtube.

Ivard appeared around a corner suddenly and bolted toward them. "Emergence," he gasped. "We're—"

They all felt the tremor through the ship that indicated the shift to realtime flight. Ivard opened his mouth but Vi'ya forestalled him, saying coolly, "It's only for a moment, so they can pop their transponder."

She was right; after a time, as they walked the rest of the way to the empty classroom, Manderian felt the visceral shiver that indicated reentry into skip. Ivard chattered happily about how impressed he was with the size of the bridge, and with the uniforms, and with Ng and her crew. Manderian did not listen to it all; though he agreed, he was more absorbed, for now, with the observations he was making of those with him.

They crossed the room, past banks of empty consoles, toward a sunken circle of comfortable chairs set below a huge screen. Ivard vaulted over the back of a couch and settled next to the Kelly trinity, who hooted softly, headstalks writhing in a mesmerizing pattern.

A sensation midway between fascination and alarm seized Manderian, as the Eya'a responded, their twiggy fingers flickering in a pattern similar to that just used by the Kelly: the two groups were developing their own signal system.

Meanwhile Vi'ya sat down, still without speaking. Manderian stood back and watched the Eya'a settle near her, their limbs suddenly motionless as they stared up at the screen. Ivard leaned against the Intermittor of the Kelly, his fingers absently stroking her ribbons. Kelly headstalks patted him softly as he, too, watched the screen.

Manderian looked up and was just in time to receive a third and greater pang of reaction as the Aerenarch, standing behind the captain, moved just slightly, his eyes glancing up at the imager and then away.

It was so slight a movement that he almost missed it, and he knew that no one on the bridge would have noticed. But it was clear that he had just signaled his awareness of his watchers.

He knows they're here. He knows Vi'ya is here, he corrected himself, and wished overwhelmingly that Eloatri was present for him to discuss this with.

But he was alone, and consideration would have to wait.

He watched as once again the ship emerged.

⁂ ⁂ ⁂

SAMEDI

The door to the rec room hissed open and all conversation ceased. Lufus Kaniffer turned away from the dispenser and forgot the hot cup of caf in his hand as he saw Morrighon standing in the hatch. The Bori looked around and then walked into the room with a strange, light-footed shuffle, seating himself at a central table. He said nothing.

Muttering transparent excuses, most of the crew exited with more haste than dignity, carefully avoiding eye contact with Anaris' lieutenant.

Kaniffer tried to follow, but before he reached the door, Morrighon spoke. "Lufus Kaniffer. Stay." His voice was unstressed, full of the unspoken expectation of obedience.

Lufus felt shock quiver down his muscles; *He knows nobody's going to challenge him after what they did to Hestik and Soge.*

"And you, Neesach An-Jayvan. Come here."

As the woman crossed the room toward them the remainder of the crew made their getaway, crowding past Oglethorp Bugtul, who stood tentatively in the doorway. Morrighon motioned the little engineer over.

"You have been chosen for a signal honor." Morrighon looked at Lufus. "You will pilot the shuttle that carries the Panarch and what remains of his Privy Council to their final exile on Gehenna." He motioned at the other two. "These will be your crew, along with three Tarkan guards. You will use the shuttle in the starboard bay. We reach orbit in a little over four hours, at which time you will debark."

He stood and walked out without looking back.

The three Rifters looked at each other as the hatch hissed shut. Then Kaniffer snickered, exultation possessing him. *This is the break I've been waiting for!*

"What?" exclaimed Neesach, her shrieky voice scratching Kaniffer's ears. She looked over at the hatch as she spoke.

"That little twister just handed us our ticket off the *Samedi* and a ship of our own," Kaniffer replied promptly. He chortled, rubbing his hands together. "Can you imagine what we can get on Rifthaven for a vid of the Panarch getting torn apart by a bunch of Isolates?"

Neesach's jaw dropped, then a calculating look came into her eyes. "Ya think they'll play with 'em a little?"

"Either before they kill 'em . . ." Bugtul said, licking his wet lips, "or after."

Kaniffer grimaced. He'd seen the nacker-chips Bugtul collected; himself, he preferred his partners still breathing. Then he shrugged. "Just means more sunbursts for us either way."

Bugtul frowned. "But those Gehennans—they a threat to us?"

"Nahhh," Neesach scoffed. "That System FF data says there isn't any metal down here, 'cept in that big crater—they can't have any weapons worth worrying about. Prob'ly just spears and rocks. The shields'll handle that."

"Can you imagine the Panarch getting it with a stone spear?" Bugtul gloated, his momentary fear apparently gone.

They were silent for a time. Kaniffer guessed that like him, they were envisioning a future rich with possibilities. *But we've got to stay downside long enough for the Isolates to find the nicks.*

He looked over at the little engineer. "Buggy, you remember that chip of yours with the nick bitches marooned on the asteroid?" As he spoke, Kaniffer touched his nose and ear in the universal symbol denoting the possible presence of a nark.

"Yeah?" The engineer's voice was puzzled.

" 'Member how they got stuck?" The drivetech in the vid had sabotaged the engines so he could take his time with his victims.

"Yeah," Bugtul replied after a pause.

"Hell of a thing, getting stuck like that. Didn't affect the imagers, though."

"Yeah." Now the engineer's voice held comprehension. "Made a good story. I'll have to check at Rifthaven next time, see if old Scrogger has anything new like that."

"Yeah," said Kaniffer, turning to Neesach. "That's the kind of vid you don't want to be interrupted while you're watching."

He saw comprehension dawn on her face.

"Nacky," she said slowly as Kaniffer stood up. "Real nacky. But I guess we'd better get to the shuttle and check out the systems. Needs some work if I remember right."

Kaniffer nodded and followed the others out.

He could see those sunbursts now.

❋ ❋ ❋

Emmet Fasthand paced the confines of his cabin, biting nervously at a tag of flesh his nails had worried from the corner of his thumb. He should catch some Zs; they were less than four hours from Gehenna, but he couldn't sleep. He felt like he'd snorted a whole pod of Fleegian snow garlic: his nerves thrummed like an engine in overload.

When his path took him near the data console, he tapped at the keys, then wiped the command before completion. *If I keep interrupting Tat, she'll never break through.* It galled him to be so dependant on the little Bori tech; but it was preferable to being at the mercy of the other Bori, Anaris' secretary.

He fiddled again with the tianqi, but decided if he fed in any more tranquilizing scents he'd be a zombie. Then he checked the feed from the bridge: the system trash was getting even thicker. The System FF simulation he'd gotten off the MinervaNet said it was due to asteroids perturbed into the Knot by the system's gas giants, shattering them to gravel and dust. *Just like it'll do to the* Samedi *if we're not careful.* But so far, Moob's scans indicated the Knot was apparently not responding to their presence.

At least there was no sign of a cruiser yet. Not that they'd know. The system was too dirty to detect even a ship that big until it was on top of them.

He spun away from the console and paced across the deck. Maybe the Panarchists didn't know. He hoped not—he'd played the FF simulation several times in the past few hours, and would do so again, but it was painfully apparent that he'd have a hard time up against a Navy captain who'd gone through the FF test at the Academy.

Fasthand started as his cabin annunciator chimed. The look- see revealed the lumpy form of Morrighon standing in the corridor. Fresh anger burned in the Rifter as he realized that Morrighon knew where he was at all times—how else would he have known to come to the cabin rather than the bridge? The crew wouldn't have told the Bori where he was without warning him first.

The captain drew in a deep breath in an attempt to stabilize his fear, and said, "Open." The hatch hissed and Morrighon stepped through, holding a flimsy in one hand.

"We will arrive at Gehenna in less than four hours," the Bori began. "As soon as you are within range, you are to destroy the Quarantine Monitor and then take up synchronous orbit in its place, which is the closest sync point to the center of the habitable zone. At that point you will debark the prisoners in the shuttle now being prepared in the port bay."

Now being prepared? Why hadn't he been told? Having so totally dominated the crew in their chatz games, the Dol'jharians apparently no longer cared for appearances. Or was this a slap by Morrighon, in revenge for the jokes some of the crew had perpetrated on him?

"I have prepared the duty roster for the shuttle." He held out the paper to Fasthand, who merely stared at him, feeling the blood rush to his face. After a moment the Bori smiled thinly and placed it on a nearby table.

"The Tarkans, of course, will be in charge of the prisoners. You need not concern yourself with that. I have selected the shuttle crew from your secondary crew, to lessen the impact on the ship's efficiency should there be an incident."

"Incident?" Fasthand croaked, only slowly regaining control of his voice as the rage engendered by the Bori's effrontery subsided. Did the Bori think those old geezes could overcome even one Tarkan?

"System FF contains no information on the Gehennans' capabilities," Morrighon replied. "You will stand by ready to destroy the shuttle if my Lord Anaris so commands."

So the Bori had even managed to snake out his data on the FF simulation. What else did he know?

"The prisoners will be transferred to the shuttle one hour before arrival. Have your crew ready." The Bori turned and left without awaiting his reply.

The Rifter's hand shook as he picked up the flimsy. He had the sense that there had been layers of meaning within Morrighon's words, but he was too tired and too zizzed to unravel them. He scanned the orders. The names written there made no impression on him except one.

Kaniffer. That chatzer would sell his mother for a cup of caf. He had never let Kaniffer hold any position of responsibility, despite his piloting abilities: he just couldn't resist playing the angles. Fasthand wondered what kind of squeeze Kaniffer would make out of this. *Probably take a vid of the Gehennans grabbing the Panarch if he can.*

But he couldn't change that. He was no longer master of the

Samedi. Emmet Fasthand crumpled the orders in his hand and looked over at the data console. It was all up to Tat now.

* * *

The light on the shuttle bay hatch was flashing yellow, and as he stepped through, Gelasaar's spirits lifted. It was more than just the transition to standard gee after their passage through the Dol'jharian section of the destroyer; it was an almost joyful anticipation. Whatever the outcome of the next few hours, there would be no more waiting and no more helplessness. Once again, perhaps for the last time, the former rulers of the Thousand Suns would determine their own fate.

He glanced over at the others as their captors herded them toward the shuttle and saw distinct signs of much the same feeling in them. Even Padraic Carr, tortured by the racking cough that never left him now, seemed cheerful. He saw Gelasaar's look and his mouth quirked just slightly.

Anaris stood next to the shuttle's ramp, his Bori secretary at his side. Gelasaar dismissed his meditations as the Tarkans stopped them in front of Eusabian's son.

At a motion from Anaris, the two guards pushed the others up the ramp, leaving only the Panarch to face the Dol'jharian and the Bori.

"The completion of my father's paliach is upon you, Gelasaar hai-Arkad," said Anaris. "And the lessons are over."

"Learning ceases only when life does," the Panarch replied, "and the converse, too, is true, that when learning ceases, death is not far away." He looked straight into Anaris' eyes. "I have not ceased my studies."

The faintest trace of a smile deepened the corners of Anaris' mouth. "Nor have I."

He held out one hand. On its palm lay two rings.

The sight of them squeezed Gelasaar's heart with an amalgam of emotions he had never felt before. One was a simple ring of gold, his wedding band; the other, the Phoenix Signet, worn only by the ruling Arkad. Slowly he reached out and took them.

As he fitted them onto their accustomed fingers, he looked up at Anaris. No one else, he thought, could have seen it, but he was sure it was there: ever so faint, a trace of regret.

The least Dol'jharian of all emotions.

Gelasaar smiled and bowed gracefully, the deference of equal to equal, then turned and walked up the ramp.

Eusabian's paliach was complete, but he was not the victor.

✻ ✻ ✻

GEHENNA

Londri Ironqueen watched her scout's hands shake as he took the mug and raised it to his lips. The blood oozing from the ragged arrow-graze across his forehead glinted blackly in the firelight. When he lowered the mug his eyes brightened as the stillwine took effect. There was silence for a time as the others considered his report, broken only by the crackle of the fire and the mournful hooning of a fangbat nearby.

"How long do you estimate before the Tasuroi arrive?" she asked finally.

He wiped his lips. "The ones I ran across were just outriders. If they're following their usual pattern, the main horde will be in in less than thirty hours. Maybe sooner."

"Than you, Larinecht Nulson. You have done well. Tell the quartermaster to give you food and a doss for the night."

The scout saluted and strode away, his pride taking most of the exhausted stagger out of his legs.

The Ironqueen looked around at the others seated by the fire. Her eyes stopped on Tlaloc Ur-Aztlan. "If you have any ideas, my lord Aztlan, now is the time."

"I can't suggest anything that hasn't already been done, Your Majesty," he replied, running his fingers through his bushy black beard. "With the exception of Comori Keep, we hold the high ground, the artillery is well positioned, and our forces are tightly interlocked to prevent any flanking movements."

"Perhaps we should hope for a miracle," said Gath-Boru. "Like the sudden collapse of Comori's walls."

Londri didn't miss the sudden glance of dislike that lanced between Tlaloc and her general. Gath-Boru had vociferously opposed their present deployment; while admitting its strength, he was uncomfortable with the thought of having to guard against a sally from Comori during the coming engagement with the Tasuroi.

I don't think he trusts Aztlan to handle Comori. She'd pointed out that neighbors like Comori and Aztlan usually made the worst enemies, but Gath-Boru was unconvinced.

Londri looked up at the stars far above, Was that, too, a

world of betrayal and deceit? She couldn't believe so, for all that Stepan insisted on it. They had so much in the Thousand Suns; what did they have to fight over?

"At least Alyna Weathernose predicts a windless day tomorrow," said Stepan. He'd apparently seen the glance too. "That'll make the sporetox all the more effective."

The Tasuroi didn't have artillery, making the chemical and bioweapons developed by the inhabitants of the Splash one of the most effective weapons against the barbarians.

"Steel and flesh," said Tlaloc. "You can soften up the enemy with artillery, but it's steel and flesh that decides it."

There was no disagreement.

Londri stood up. The meeting had long ago wound down into repetition; only the scout's report had prolonged it. "We should all retire now, or it won't be steel nor flesh that decides it, but lack of sleep."

As she spoke she was suddenly taken by a racking yawn. She tilted back her head and stretched out her arms, then stiffened in shock as a dazzling light blossomed high in the southern sky. Instantly brighter than any star, it grew in intensity until she had to slit her eyes against it, lighting up the camp as bright as day. Shouts of terror resounded from all around, echoed by harsh shrieks from the trees as roosting *corbae* erupted into the glare-stricken sky. The men and women around the fire jumped to their feet, exclaiming in wonder and fear until the light dimmed, leaving behind a dim blotch in the sky that slowly dissipated.

"The Quarantine Monitor," said Stepan in a tone laden with wonder and hope. "Somebody blew up the Monitor."

"What does it mean?" Londri asked. Was their long imprisonment over?

Stepan looked over at her and shook his head slowly. "I don't know."

> "When a new star blazes in the sky
> Ferric House against a fallen fortress
> Leads both friend and foe to fate defy."

Gath-Boru spoke slowly, his voice almost impossibly deep. He put his hand on the hilt of his sword.

"Now it begins," he said.

TWENTY-SEVEN

The shuttle crossed the terminator into darkness, flying eastward against the fall of night. Lufus Kaniffer rubbed his sweaty hands down his pants. "You see anything yet, Neesach?"

"Prani's Balls, Lufus!" His copilot never seemed to be able to speak in anything less than an irritating shriek. "We aren't within ten thousand klicks of the landing zone yet." She slapped at her console. "We got the coördinates of the infrared concentration from the *Samedi*'s scan. We'll get there."

"Whaddya think it is, 'Niff?" came the voice of Bugtul over the com from the engine compartment.

"Some sort of battle, probably. Don't imagine they got anything else to do, with no metals and no tech," Kaniffer replied shortly.

"This is gonna be great!" the engineer exulted. "Nobody's ever seen a vid like this."

"Shut up, Buggy. Too many ears."

"Naah!" came the reply. "This chatzer doesn't speak Uni."

"You sure?"

Bugtul's voice became distant as he turned away from the com. "Hey, Shiidra-blunge. Bet you need both hands to flip your nacker, eh?" Then his voice came back stronger. "See. No Dol'jharian's gonna put up with that."

"Yeah." But there was no sense taking chances, thought Kaniffer. Who knows what that Morrighon crawler might have rigged. "But that's enough yap, anyway."

The remainder of the flight passed in silence. Kaniffer couldn't stand Neesach's screechy voice, so he wasn't about to offer any conversation, and he guessed that Bugtul, despite his bravado, didn't really feel too talkative with that Tarkan glowering at him in the little engine compartment. What they were planning was dangerous, even if the mods they had hurriedly programmed into the computer held off the Dol'jharians in the lock. He wondered how Bugtul planned to deal with the Tarkan.

He checked occasionally on the imagers he'd set up in the lock. No action there. The Panarchists sat against a bulkhead, talking quietly in those singsong voices of theirs—he couldn't make out half of what they said. A lot of it wasn't even Uni. The two Tarkans barely moved, holding their weapons trained on the geezes like they expected them to sprout jacs out of their noses and start shooting up the ship.

Finally their course took the shuttle over a chain of mountains that the navcomp indicated was one edge of the habitable zone.

"Getting some readings now," said Neesach. "Course three forty-nine. Lotta heat, some high-temp, more body-temp." Her voice whined up the scale with excitement. "Looks like you were right!"

Kaniffer brought the shuttle around to the indicated heading. A few minutes later he could see the glow of campfires on the horizon. There were thousands of them!

Beyond was a gap of darkness again, then more lights, spread out around some big stone building that barely showed up in the IR display. It looked like the first batch of fires belonged to some group heading toward the second. But maybe they were just reinforcements. Then he shrugged. Didn't matter, but if they were enemies, it'd be rich. *This is the place.*

He started bringing the shuttle down, announcing over the com: "Final approach commencing."

The sound of the engines suddenly grew rough, and the little craft bucked. He looked over at Neesach and stabbed his little finger in the air, then leaned back as she tabbed the com to call the *Samedi.*

Everything was going according to plan.

⁕ ⁕ ⁕

Cauldronmaster Strongarm-of-the-Leaning-Rocks, known as Smegmaniggle to the Raw Ones, felt the rhythms of the Dance mount up from his feet, infusing him with the certainty of victory and fresh meat. He stomped even harder, raising his knees high, shouting his courage at the Old Ones watching unblinking from their sky-abode; his warriors echoed him a thousandfold.

His wizard threw another bundle of hateweed on the blazing fire. Strong fumes puffed up; Strongarm inhaled gaspingly. Soon dawn would come and they would pour over the hills onto the hated Raw Ones and consume them. Perhaps they would even overcome the stone house, if Tongue-with-Claws had sufficiently lulled the Comori with his eloquence.

Colors spilled over from inside his head and painted the scene around him in pulsing hues that took their vividness from the pounding of the immense manskin drums. He tore at his arms with his teeth; the hot iron taste of blood maddened him further.

Soon it would be time to lead out the captive to join the Dance and become the feast, the living food of the Tasuroi, lending his courage to the warriors of the Leaning Rock clan. Strongarm hoped this one would die well; no one liked the taste of a coward.

The ground shook beneath his feet.

"Ayah!" he exulted. "The World trembles before the Tasuroi!" he shouted, but the rumble increased, mixed with a whine unlike anything he had ever heard before.

"The Dragon!" screamed the wizard, pointing into the sky. The warriors bellowed in rage, shaking their weapons at the angular creature roaring overhead, trailing a cloud of fire.

But after a moment, as the madness drained out of him, the Tasuroi chieftain knew what it was. "No!" shouted Strongarm. "It's the Skypeople!" He pointed at the receding craft. "If we capture the Fallen One, the Raw Ones of Comori will give us iron and meat!"

And the Fallen One might serve as another lever against their temporary allies.

Shouting with joyful rage, the Tasuroi poured out of their

camp, following the glowing ember as it descended over the hills ahead.

⁂ ⁂ ⁂

Commander Totokili glared at the relay screen from the beta engine compartment as though it were an enemy. He looked, thought Ensign Leukady, like he wanted to reach through and tweak them himself, but no one ever came any closer to the engines than that imager relay while they were operating; their space-straining fields were deadly to anything above the level of a virus.

Ensign Leukady held his breath; the commander's jaw was working, causing the stiff brush of hair running from ear to ear across his head to wiggle. Totokili's hairstyle was the butt of many jokes in the junior officers' wardroom; Leukady didn't find it funny now. When it wiggled like this, someone was going to get their ass swung over the radiants.

Finally the commander exhaled explosively and turned away. Leukady busied himself with his console, but not fast enough.

"Status!" Totokili barked the word.

From the corner of his eye Leukady could see the other officers and enlisted crew in the engineering deck concentrating fiercely on their tasks. "Mass compensation successful, sir. All three engines rebalanced within one minus fifth." He essayed a tentative smile.

"What's there to grin about, Ensign?"

"N-nothing, sir," he stuttered; then, as Totokili raised an eyebrow, he hastened to add, "Except, I mean, we did it, and faster than Captain Ng asked."

The corner of the chief engineer's mouth twitched. "Yes, we did it." He glanced over at the main control bank. "But Telos only knows what'll happen when the fiveskip engages. We've practically doubled the mass of the ship with that lump of rock."

Leukady said nothing. Totokili's pessimism was well known—the more outspoken it was, the more sure the commander was of success.

The commander turned away and tabbed the com. "Engineering to bridge, Totokili here. We're ready, Captain."

"Good work, Commander," came Captain Ng's voice. "Stand by for skip."

Totokili looked up and suddenly roared, "Don't just stand

there mooning at me, you scutbrains! You heard the captain—any of you slip up and we'll have ten-power-twelve tons of rock coming through the forward bulkhead at us. So jump!"

Margot Ng grinned as the first part of Totokili's tirade spilled onto the bridge before the commander remembered to cut the connection.

Krajno chuckled. "Sounds like everything's in order in Engineering."

She nodded. "SigInt. Any traces?"

"No, sir. They're probably using tightbeam and there's too much trash in-system to pick up any leakage."

"Very well. Navigation, take us in, tac-level five, emergence at primary plus 32 at point-one cee."

"Fiveskip engaged."

For the first time in a battlecruiser, whose mass usually damped the sensation, she felt the head-bloating sensation of skip transition. The fiveskip groaned. Ng's back prickled. She'd never heard the drives make such a noise before. The ship shuddered; she felt a mild wash of nausea, gone so quickly she wasn't sure it was real or an empathic response to the protest of the *Grozniy* at the unnatural stress placed upon it. When the ship dropped back into fourspace, the jolt was harsh.

"Velocity point-one cee," reported Mzinga. His voice trailed off; Ng heard a gasp from several of the crew. She couldn't blame them.

The main screen was filled with the dark mass of the asteroid now held firmly in the focus of all three forward ruptor turrets in tractor mode, its edges flaring brightly as stellar dust and ice tore into it at 31,000 kilometers per second. Sun-bright plasma plumed off on all sides, dissipating instantly; it looked like the eclipse of a sun at the moment of totality, only raggedly elliptical rather than perfectly round.

"Ablation within expected parameters," reported Ensign Loftus at one of the engineering consoles.

"Telos!" Rom-Sanchez breathed. "I wonder what it looks like in-system."

" 'The third angel blew his trumpet, and a great star fell from heaven, blazing like a torch. . . . ' " Sebastian Omilov's voice was gravely resonant. As Ng swiveled her pod around, he smiled at her. "Forgive me, Captain. I've been dipping into a book the High Phanist gave to me, and that sentence stuck with me. At the time it didn't seem proleptic."

"That's AyKay, Chival Omilov. It does fit." She felt the tension on the bridge relax a little at the distraction, so she asked, "What's the book about?"

Omilov laughed. "The High Phanist told me people have been arguing about that for five thousand years or so. But this particular part is about the end of the world."

"Very appropriate," Krajno said, smiling grimly.

Omilov quirked an eyebrow. "How is that, Commander?"

He motioned forward. "In about ten minutes, when the wavefront from this 'great star' reaches them, there's a whole shipload of Rifters who will probably feel just about that way."

⁂ ⁂ ⁂

Tat's fingers shook as she picked up the ampule for what must have been the tenth time in the past hour and rolled it between her fingers. The minute red-striped dyplast cylinder glinted in the subdued light of her cabin. She hated using brainsuck for noderunning; not only was it dangerously addictive, but the feeling of isolation from all things human was terrifying for a Bori.

But she might not have any choice. She looked up at the imager relay from the bridge. Even at this remove, she could almost smell the tension and fear. Fasthand was compulsively cracking his knuckles; Tat could see Moob's shoulders jerk at every minor detonation of the captain's joints.

Creote's console bleeped. "It's Neesach."

"What's wrong?" the captain snarled as the shuttle navigator's face windowed up on the main screen.

"We got engine trouble here, Cap'n." The woman's eyes weren't aimed straight at the imager. "Lufus says we'll get it down but we'll need a few hours before we can lift."

"Put Kaniffer on!"

She looked away for a moment, then shook her head as the pilot's voice came through. "Gotta get this thing down."

"Kaniffer, you blungesucking, logos-chatzing son of a Shiidra brood-fouler, if this is one of your chatzing angles . . ."

Fasthand's voice choked off as another window bloomed on the screen, revealing Morrighon's face. "Is there a problem?"

In the other window, Neesach's face blanched.

"Just a little engine trouble," Fasthand replied between his teeth. "Everything's under control."

Morrighon turned away from the screen for a moment; Tat heard some rapid-fire Dol'jharian. He was talking to someone on the shuttle, using a parallel comstream over ship's systems! She stabbed at her console again; another code-splatter, and another! Maybe now she'd have enough to work with. She launched two more sniffers and threw them into the nodespace pointed to by her monitors.

On the bridge, a panicky shout erupted in the background, relayed through the shuttle's bridge from its engine compartment. Tat recognized Bugtul's voice. "What're you doing, you chatzing . . . " His voice choked off; she heard a dull thumping sound, then another voice in heavily accented Uni.

"Shiidra-blunge, you would to say? I use two hands for some things, but only one to deal with you." There was a crunching noise, and the thumping suddenly stopped.

The voice then spoke in Dol'jharian.

Morrighon said a moment later, "Your Rifters sabotaged the engines, hoping to gain time to record the death throes of the Panarchists. The dead tech was only moderately successful; it will require no more than four hours to repair."

On the screen Neesach Kaniffer looked around wildly, then leaned forward. Tat guessed she was desperately keying her console.

"Locking down will do you no good," said Morrighon. "But if you return the shuttle with our people, I will turn you over to your captain for discipline, instead of to the Tarkans." His eyes shifted to Fasthand.

"Captain, ready a missile, surface detonation, twenty megatons. Assuming they do indeed manage a safe landing, if they do not lift off in four hours, destroy the shuttle."

Then he said with a sneer on his twisted features, "Let them make their recording. It may have some value." His window dwindled and vanished.

"Captain! You gotta do something!" Kaniffer's face finally windowed up; his voice was almost a sob.

"I gotta do nothing, Lufus, until you bring that shuttle back." Fasthand slapped the com off.

Tat put the ampule down and turned back to her work. She had more time now; she'd hold the brainsuck until she truly had no choice.

❋ ❋ ❋

The whine of the shuttle engines suddenly changed, growing rougher, and the little craft bucked, provoking another coughing fit from Padraic Carr. Gelasaar held him until the spasm passed; one of the Tarkans tabbed the com and spoke into it without taking his eyes off his prisoners.

Suddenly from the communicator burst a stream of Dol'jharian. Gelasaar cupped his ear to clarify it; what he heard made his heart accelerate. He glanced at the others. They, too, had understood. *Four hours!* The only question was, what would the Dol'jharians do now? Would they be expelled from the shuttle immediately upon landing or at the expiration of the deadline?

"Should be one of the more successful vids in history," Padraic Carr commented. "I wouldn't mind my share of the royalties at all."

"I don't think the Dol'jharians care about vids," Ho said softly.

The Tarkan at the com began pounding at the inner lock controls, cursing.

"The Rifters seem to have locked down," said Kree. "It may not be up to the Tarkans now."

The guard turned away from the lock and motioned with his jac. "To your feet," he said. His heavy accent made the words barely comprehensible.

They all stood slowly, their suddenly heightened alertness conveyed in subtle sign. The time had come.

Kree stepped toward the Tarkan, his hands palms-out. "You want me to take a look at that lock?" He spoke in Dol'jharian.

The Dol'jharian glared at them; the other backed away slightly, his weapon tracking the group.

"I know this type of shuttle," said Kree. "Surely you don't want the Rifters remaining in control?"

The shuttle bucked again, more violently; after a moment the Tarkan nodded and backed away from the lock.

Carr squeezed the Panarch's hand, stepped away from his side, and began coughing painfully. He stopped and put his hands on his knees, breathing heavily as he finally controlled the cough. The Tarkan watching Kree glanced over, while the other looked at Carr dispassionately.

Carr looked up at the big Dol'jharian and the jac trained unwaveringly on him. "Do you know who I am?" he asked.

The Tarkan frowned and jerked the muzzle of his jac upward slightly in a warning gesture. "Yes. You are Carr."

"*Firez-hreach i-Acheront,*" the admiral corrected. "The Soul Eater of Acheront." The Tarkan's eyes widened; Carr smiled. "Oh, yes, that Carr." He stepped deliberately forward. "I ate many souls at Acheront; none of them walk the Halls of Dol. I hear them crying out, at night, but I do not answer them."

The Tarkan's jac wavered, then he raised it, pointing it straight at Carr's chest. The other Tarkan watched, his face blanching; he didn't notice little Matilde Ho inching closer, while Mortan Kree worked noisily at the lock.

Carr slapped his chest. "Yes. They're all in here, *tarku niretor,* and I grow tired of their mewling. Will you let them out for me?"

He opened his mouth wide and emitted a gargling hiss. Gelasaar's scalp prickled: it was a horrifying sound. The Tarkan was very still, until Padraic Carr calmly reached out, as though he had all the time in the world, and grasped the muzzle of the Dol'jharian's jac, pulling it into his chest.

The jac discharged; a spot of light flared in Carr's back. He threw his head back in agony and fell forward. His hand welded to the finned radiants in a sizzle of flesh that was almost lost as the admiral's hiss was converted into an eerie shout forced from him by the explosive boiling of the blood in his lungs. A red spray shot from his mouth, blinding the Tarkan.

The Tarkan staggered back, yanking futilely at his weapon, horror distorting his red-smeared face as the flaming corpse of the Soul Eater stumbled after him. Then Gelasaar moved.

The Ulanshu Kinesic was swift and merciful; the Dol'jharian slumped to the deck with a broken neck even as Mortan Kree turned away from the lock and shouted to distract the other.

Caleb launched Matilde through the air at the guard. She twisted, lithe as an acrobat despite the sling on her arm, slamming one heel into his throat. His jac flew wide as he fell dying, choking on his broken larynx. Kree knelt by the Tarkan, twisted his head quickly; the crack of the vertebrae was loud in the sudden silence.

Gelasaar choked; the stench of roasted flesh was strong. He picked up the Tarkan's jac. It had been so easy. Panicked shouting erupted from the com; it was Uni. Were there other Dol'jharians on board? There must be, but where?

Suddenly he remembered the last words spoken as he boarded the shuttle: "I have not ceased my studies," he had said to Anaris.

"*Nor have I.*"

He whirled around. "Mortan! We've got to get to the engine room, quickly."

Kree didn't waste any time with questions. He raised the jac he'd taken from the Tarkan, adjusted the aperture, and motioned them away from the inner lock. "I hope this is only a computer lockdown," he said. "If it's manual . . ." He triggered a thin thread of plasma, once, twice, three times at widely separated places around the lock. It hissed open.

The Panarch handed his jac to Caleb. "Caleb, guard our rear. All of you, follow me."

They pounded through into the shuttle.

The ship was small; they reached the engine compartment just as the shuttle grounded with a shuddering thump. The compartment door yielded quickly, but a bolt of energy lanced out, spattering against the opposite wall. From inside came an intense whine.

Matilde Ho blanched. "They've thrown the engine into supercrit. We haven't much time to stop it."

She looked over at Kree, who waved them away from the hatch. Then he crouched down, motioning Caleb over to him. "I want you to lie flat, and shoot from the floor at the firestop in the ceiling. On the count of three."

He backed away, resetting his jac. "One."

Caleb began to squirm into position.

"Two." The others backed away from the hatch.

"Three." Caleb rolled onto his back in the hatchway and shot, upside down, at the firestop. A thick spray of foam erupted, and then Kree triggered his jac on wide aperture, converting the spray to scalding steam. There was a scream of agony as a man jumped to his feet, firing his jac wildly, then slumped in charred ruin.

The firestop shut off as the heat source was removed. They ran in, Kree to the engine console, followed by Matilde. As she tapped one-handed at the keys, Gelasaar turned to the others. "Caleb, give me your jac. Go with Yosefina and take the bridge."

They ran out. He turned back to Matilde, who looked up from the console at him.

"Well?"

"More than four hours now," she said quietly.

⁂ ⁂ ⁂

Kaniffer watched Neesach give the manual hatch lock to the bridge an extra twist, and then turned back to his piloting with a sigh of relief that stuck in his throat when she gasped.

He followed her gaze to the secondary screen relaying the image from the lock, and amazement stunned him as he fought to land the shuttle while trying to watch the secondary screen, on which the elderly nicks disposed of the Tarkans in a neatly orchestrated flurry of action.

"Oh, blunge," he breathed. Neesach rushed to her console and switched to a view of the engine room just as the Panarchists blew the inner lock and poured through into the ship.

His heart banging against his ribs, Kaniffer brought the ship down in the clearing he'd chosen, the distraction making the landing a bit rougher than he'd intended.

The action in the engine room was just as rapid, and Kaniffer felt a thrill of terror at the casual competence of the men and women he'd so calmly dismissed as worn-out politicians. He looked over at Neesach, who was frantically tapping at her console.

She looked back at him, and the hollow feeling in the pit of his stomach intensified at the hopeless expression on her face. "They've got everything except life support, the plasma cannon, and the outer lock door," she reported. "And the hatch here."

"Everything? Even communications?"

She nodded. "And the engines and the shields. Everything."

Kaniffer looked up at the screen relaying a view of the clearing in which the ship had landed. There was no sign of the Gehennans yet.

Neesach laughed shrilly. "Oh, and we still got the external imagers, if you can figure out some way of pushing the geezes out the hatch." Her sneering emphasis on the word "geezes" griped at him. "You always were one for the angles," she continued. "I'll be real interested to see how you work this one."

Her screechy voice was almost a sob now, but Kaniffer didn't reply.

He was afraid his voice would sound the same.

* * *

Londri slid off the back of her *drom* and followed Gath-Boru up to the brow of the hill, ducking low to avoid skylining herself against the growing dawn light. They crawled the last few feet and she cautiously poked her head up over a low tangle of oilbrush.

Her heart gave a great thump at the sight of the gleaming machine crouched in the meadow below.

"Look at all that metal," the scout with them breathed, her voice reverent.

"With that in our possession, no one could stand against the Crater," Gath-Boru murmured.

The Ironqueen was silent for a moment. Now she knew what the fallen fortress was that the Oracle had referred to. And it was truly a means to defy fate, to escape the world-sized prison they were condemned to.

"It's more than just metal," she whispered past the lump in her throat. She realized that without Stepan's tutoring, she would have reacted just as the scout had, seeing the flying machine just as a valuable lump of metal, or as in Gath-Boru's eyes, a means to power. "It's freedom."

"It's been there for almost an hour now," said the scout. "They never land that long. I don't think it can fly anymore; Tetri said it came down hard, and she saw a landing once."

"They'll fix it," Gath-Boru said. "We must attack now."

Londri turned as another figure crawled up beside them, breathing heavily: Stepan. "Don't be silly, General," he said. "They've got weapons that can melt steel like ice."

"I know that. But you have also told us, as have other Isolates, that usually those weapons cannot fire below a certain angle. If we get close enough . . ."

"And blind them with smoke," added Londri.

Stepan shook his head. "Maybe, but they have eyes that can see in total darkness, like the sapperwyrm that strikes at the heat of a body. Still, a lot of hot fires, with smoke, might confuse them."

Londri turned to the scout. "Go back to Oberauken Vre-Ktash and have him bring up the First and Fourth Artillery, they're the closest, and two companies of sappers. Have them gather as much oilbrush as they can. . . ." As she continued with her orders, deploying her forces to hold off the Tasuroi and deal with the grounded vessel, she peered back at the machine.

When she was finished, the scout sketched a salute and slithered back down the hill until she could stand up and run back to her drom. Londri turned to Stepan.

"Counselor, I need you to approach Comori under flag of truce. Tell him he can keep the twins in return for his help in capturing the skyvessel."

"Aztlan will be wroth," said Stepan.

"Tell Tlaloc he may have one fertile woman captured from the machine, or two potent men."

A flicker like distant lightning briefly illuminated the clearing. Gath-Boru groaned. "The Weathernose promised a clear day. Rain will bog down the artillery and damp the fires. And it'll make it even harder to deal with the Tasuroi: the sporetox won't work."

They looked up; the eastern sky was paling but there were no clouds anywhere. The flicker came again, then again, not from the horizon, but from overhead. Londri rolled onto her back and gasped; high above, a new star flared, not quite as bright as the first, but steady, and around it vast wings of pale light, trembling on the edge of color, reached out in an immense curve.

Then, for the first time in her life, she understood what Stepan had taught her about the worlds above, and the vast space through which the people of the Thousand Suns strode like gods. Suddenly she felt herself, not lying on the ground, but clinging to a toppling wall, exposed to infinite space as something approached beside which the whole expanse of her hurtling world was but a clod of dirt.

A sudden sound beside her pulled her eyes away from the heavens and the vertigo left her. Stepan was weeping quietly, staring up, unmoving as great tears tracked down his cheeks.

She reached over and touched him; he shook his head.

"Not sorrow, not sorrow," he choked. "That can be only one thing, nothing else could generate so much energy."

"What?" she asked, confused.

"Never mind, daughter," he replied, thus emphasizing his origin and knowledge of things beyond Gehenna. "Do you remember my telling you how the Abuffyds mocked me with the secret of Gehenna when they exiled me, the clever lie that keeps us locked away so securely?"

"Yes."

"Then rejoice: no matter what the outcome of this day, the lie is broken forever."

⁂ ⁂ ⁂

As the Panarch came up behind them, Caleb and Yosefina stood in front of the bridge hatch, radiating frustration.

"We've got the hatch locked down manually," came a shaky voice over the com. The image revealed was of a thin-faced man with the bulging jaw muscles of compulsive bruxism—they gave his face a strange pyramidal look. "You'll use up both jacs maybe burning through, and then we'll zap you."

Caleb looked back at the Panarch and shrugged, tapping off the com as he spoke. "He's right. Unless Kree or Matilde can break through the computer safeguards, we can't get into the bridge."

The Panarch nodded at the com and Caleb switched it back on.

"What is your name?"

"Kaniffer," the Rifter blurted, his eyes shifting back and forth. "Lufus Kaniffer."

"Well, genz Kaniffer, for us there is little to choose between Gehenna and your ship," the Panarch said. "Certainly, if you lift off with us still on board, Anaris will order the shuttle destroyed. And we control the engines."

The Rifter stared at him a moment, something like a mix of fear, anger, and awe in his face.

Archetype and Ritual have a long reach, Gelasaar thought as the pilot spoke. "But we control the main lock, and you can't shut the inner lock anymore. Maybe we'll just ask the Gehennans to clear you out.

"The Gehennans have few metals. This ship represents unimaginable wealth to them. . . ." The Panarch broke off as the Rifter suddenly turned away from the screen. There was a muffled colloquy that he could not discern; in the midst of it Mortan Kree hurried up behind him.

"Matilde reports an immense energy source approaching the inner system," he said. "I think the Navy's caught up with us."

Brandon! The Panarch clamped down on his emotions

ruthlessly—there was no way he could know, but joy and certainty thrilled along his nerves.

Finally Kaniffer turned back to the screen, fear widening his eyes as his jaw muscles bulged.

He thought to turn a profit from our deaths, and now sees his own approaching. That's leverage twice over.

"We will repair the engines," said the Panarch, forestalling whatever the Rifter intended to say. "But you will not lift off until you give us control. As you have seen, there is a battlecruiser even now approaching Gehenna. If we reach it with your help, I will give you both your freedom, ships of your own, and a lifetime stipend to run them. You have my word." Gelasaar slapped the com off. "We'll let him think about it."

"Fear and greed are strongly corrosive of the will," Mortan Kree murmured.

"So I'm hoping," said Gelasaar. "It's up to Matilde now." He looked down the corridor toward the lock. "And the Gehennans."

Twenty-eight

"Captain," Moob said suddenly, her voice shaky. "We got hard rads flooding in, ionization off the scale, and the Knot's flaring up." She tapped a few keys. "On-screen."

"Blunge!" Emmet Fasthand shouted, his voice breaking in panic. "What the chatzing hell is that?"

Tat looked up at the bridge relay and her breath stopped. She tapped to a full-screen view of the main bridge display. A glaring point of light blazed dead center; to either side, vast curving sheets of light reached out and up. It looked like the headlight of some swift deadly machine speeding toward them between the walls of an infinite canyon, and Tat realized she was seeing the usually invisible fivespace fracture guarding the Gehenna system as some incredible source of energy excited it into radiance.

"It's an asteroid, about four klicks in diameter, incoming at point-one cee."

"Asteroid my blungehole," Fasthand yelled. "It's a chatzing battlecruiser, using the chatzing asteroid instead of its chatzing shields! They'll be here in less than two hours at that speed!"

A red blotch bloomed in Tat's vision. (*Tat! What the hell are you doing?)* Even through the link, Fasthand's voice revealed a man on the edge of doing something fatally stupid.

Without answering, Tat stripped off her boz'l, grabbed the ampule, jabbed it up her nose, and triggered it. The jet of brainsuck felt like acid, and she shouted with pain. She heard Morrighon's voice from the bridge relay as a rising tide of color overwhelmed her; she looked down at her console screen and then the drug seized her in inescapable claws and the edges of the display expanded around her as she fell into dataspace.

Canyons of light rose around her, triggering memory of the death fast approaching in realtime. She dismissed the thought, that was outside, unreal now.

Tat flew down the lines, following the argus as it scuttled past node after node of data. The systems of the Samedi *were a ghastly mess: the ship was well over four hundred years old, and the computer had never been flushed. She ignored the mess, flitting past codetangles that would have mired her instantly had she touched them, intent on tracking her opponent, the Bori who was not a Bori.*

The neuraimai sat on her shoulder, chattering in her ears like a demented simian. Ahead, the argus slowed, then screamed in agony as a phageworm darted out and impaled it. Tat raised her arm and flung a dart of code at the intruder. It shriveled and fell away, too late. The argus vanished in a burst of color and a bad smell.

No matter; it had taken her most of the way. Vast obelisks of light rose around her, like a valley of monuments to the dead, inscribed with words. Some she could read, others were garbled, out of focus, or impossible to even look at.

The neuraimai suddenly leapt into the air, flinging itself on glutinous wings toward a distant pylon glowing a virulent shade of pustulent green, with veins of red running through it. The obelisk abruptly opened a fanged mouth, and a glittering tongue of diamond lashed out and wrapped itself in brittle splendor around the little codebeast and drew it in. The mouth snapped shut. It masticated hideously, groaning with delight as it crushed the life out of the neuraimai, not noticing that two of the words on its surface now glowed clearly.

SKULEMAM. SEERASINATCH.

Tat raised the book of Bori history, threw it into the air. Its covers transformed into leathery wings, the words within sprouting from the pages into a plethora of teeth like crystal growth from a supersaturated medium. It lunged at the pylon, now shrinking away, and tore at its surface. Blobs of ichor spurted forth, transformed in their flight into more words.

KULESMAM. NATSARREESITCH. LESMAMKUL. ATCHSEERISAN. MAMSELUK. TCHANISARIS. MAMELUKS.

A trumpet blared, mutating into a brassy voice echoing around her. "Ancient Anglic terms for mercenaries become rulers in medieval Lost Earth. Mamelukes. Janissaries."

The Dol'jharians had been mercenaries to the Bori, until the stonebones released the Red Plague and conquered their onetime masters.

The words fell into her hands, became a pair of heavy bronze keys. She plunged them into the madly glaring eyes of the obelisk and twisted; it screamed in agony and collapsed into a seething pool of slime that rapidly evaporated. Other pylons, close and far, tottered and fell. Tat flung out a web of steel and took command, welding codespace to her will. The clangor of metal stuttered around her.

Then, slowly, the air began to congeal—her time was running out, her strength failing. She looked around. Some pylons still stood, mostly environmental functions; she judged them unimportant. She spoke the words of dismissal and spiraled back to realtime.

Tat turned away from the console, retching uncontrollably. As soon as the spasm subsided she tapped a command with trembling hands. The *Samedi* was in lockdown, the Dol'jharian section now a prison rather than a fortress, and Morrighon no longer had any foothold in the computer. "Captain, the ship is yours. The Dol'jharians are locked up."

She didn't hear his reply as blackness overwhelmed her and she slid out of her chair onto the floor.

❋ ❋ ❋

"Let's get out of here," Fasthand shouted. "Lassa, take us out of orbit. Head in-system, it's cleaner. We'll veer off once we're past the primary. And push it. I don't care if we do ablate—check with Lar for what we can handle and how long. Creote, tell the cruiser the Panarch's down on the surface, maybe they won't come after us."

"Can't get through the ionstorm till they decelerate," Creote protested.

"Spool a repeater, blungebrain, and launch it into orbit!" He slapped his compad, trying to control the shaking of his hands. "Security! Mount heavy jacs at all the hatches into the heavy section. Burn down anyone who comes through. We'll relay some eyes to you."

He turned to Lar at Damage Control. "Give me eyes in there, relay it to the jac teams. We gotta see what they're up to."

Several subsidiary screens lit up with views of corridors and rooms, switching rapidly. Some were blank; no one was visible. "They've blasted some of the imagers."

"Then that's where they are. Security, keep a sharp watch, let me know if you see anything. Lar, open the heavy section to space." He laughed, feeling hysteria nibble at the edge of his mind. "That'll slow 'em down."

Lar tapped at his console. "Can't. That function's still locked out."

"Then boost their gees to max."

"Can't do that, either."

"Tat, you chatzer!" Fasthand shouted. There was no answer. "Then cut them out; can't get much momentum in null-gee."

"Done."

On the main screen the planet swung away and dwindled rapidly.

"Knot's holding," said Moob. "So far." She cocked her head at the Urian hyperwave near the communications console. "What're you gonna tell Eusabian?"

"I'll worry about that when we get away from that cruiser," Fasthand snapped.

"You better," Moob snarled. "I'd almost rather face a ruptor than the Lord of Vengeance if you zap his heir. And you're gonna have to, you know."

Fasthand stared at her, then slammed his fist down on the compad again. "Engineering! Engage start-up on the engines. We may need them."

"That'll take a good twenty hours," came the reply from old Daug. "They're stone-cold."

"Just do it." He cut the connection.

Twenty hours to being able to cut and run, away from this chatzing war, away from Dol'jhar. *I'll take us so far out on the*

Fringes that nobody'll ever hear of us again. It was a good thing he'd kept the fuelpods topped up.

He looked up at one of the secondary screens, at the flaring energy of the Knot and the deadly star waxing in the center.

Just let me outrun that cruiser, the Rifter thought, wondering at the same time whom he was talking to.

Anyone that could get him out of this, he decided. Anyone.

⁂ ⁂ ⁂

Napier Ur-Comori knelt before Londri Ironqueen and offered her his sword. She took it from him and raised it up, savoring the moment. His eyes followed the steel.

Londri stared at him a moment longer, then smiled and tossed the sword in the air, catching it by the blade in one gauntleted hand and presenting it back to him. "I am pleased," she said, "that it is truly steel this time."

He rose to his feet in a fluid movement and sheathed the sword. She could see in his eyes that he was mindful of the massive form of Gath-Boru standing nearby, glaring at him.

Napier bowed. "I am deeply sorry for the distress I have caused House Ferric and its noble scion."

Londri waved her hand. "That is past." She motioned toward the hill that concealed the landing site of the flying machine. "What lies ahead is far more important, to you, to me, and to all upon this world."

She turned and started pacing, partially aware of how her polished leather armor gleamed bloodred in the glaring dappled shade of a tall, spreading twistneedle. "Our task now is two-fold: to capture the sky-machine and to hold off the Tasuroi." She stopped, seeing a sudden brightening in Napier's face. "Yes, my lord Comori?"

"I almost forgot, Your Majesty. I have a gift for you."

She stared at him as he motioned to an aide, who came forward with a leather bag. Napier took it and withdrew the still-dripping head of a Tasuroi highborn, its nose fetish bedraggled and soaked in blood.

"One of the strongest arguments on the side of your generous offer of alliance was the pleasure of killing this disgusting creature."

"Your thoughtful gift is most agreeable," said Londri, wrinkling her nose. They both burst out laughing. She turned to one of her aides. "Take this to Vre-Ktash and have him load it into one of the catapults. It will make a fitting gesture when we open our attack." The aide saluted and ran off with the head.

A scout ran up then. "Majesty, Tlaloc of Aztlan reports his forces in position, and begs your permission to remain there."

Londri nodded, turning to Gath-Boru. "General, are we ready?"

"Yes, Your Majesty." He waved toward the hill. "I have had prepared an observation point that Stepan believes will be safe from the vessel's weapons."

They made their way up the shallow incline to a redoubt carefully dug into the brow of the hill. Peering through the vertical slit carved in the heavy, claylike soil, Londri could see the machine still sitting in the clearing.

As she watched, she heard the crackle of flames, and thick smoke started rolling into the clearing. Soon the form of the ship was all but obscured by greasy rolls of sooty smoke from damped oilbrush fires. A few minutes later, a horn call rang out; from nearby came the squeal-thump of the catapults.

She inhaled sharply in amazement, then sneezed as a tinge of smoke seared her nose. As the first rock hit the vessel, its wall glowed, and the rock flew off at right angles, leaving not a dint in the metal. Likewise with a bolt laden with neverquench; it, too, flew off at right angles to its line of flight and splashed in fiery ruin, kindling a blaze in the dry grass.

"That is what I told you about, Your Majesty." She twisted on her side to look and saw Stepan crouching a few paces back. "The teslas twist space so that the momentum of any projectile is deflected at ninety degrees. It is near-perfect armor."

Londri struggled for a moment with the concept of twisted emptiness. "Near perfect?"

"It doesn't deflect heat or light, and very slow-moving things, sporetox, for instance, may get through." He shook his head at the sudden hope reflected in her face. "They are no doubt sealed against our air now, with all the smoke. But if their engines were damaged, they may be low on power, in which case, if we hit the shields with enough heavy projectiles, it may be possible to break through and force their surrender. In addition, I would recommend throwing bundles of oilbrush and neverquench as close to the hull as possible. It will be difficult for them to dissipate the heat."

"See to it," she said to Gath-Boru. He saluted and crawled

away from the scooped-out bunker and ran crouching down the hill.

Stepan crawled forward and peered past her at the ship. "I wonder who they are, and what happened."

"Perhaps you will have a chance to ask them," Londri said.

Stepan nodded slowly. "Perhaps I will."

⁂ ⁂ ⁂

Morrighon clamped his teeth hard in his lower lip, hoping the pain would prevent another eruption of his stomach; not that there was anything left to come up. This was his first experience of null-gee, and, he hoped fervently, his last.

Nearby, Anaris floated relaxed in midair, watching as three Tarkans labored to anchor themselves on each side of a hatch, readying the assault they would shortly endeavor. Eusabian's son held one of Morrighon's communicators, speaking into it occasionally as he coordinated the efforts of his forces to break out of the trap that had been sprung on them.

He lowered the com and looked over at Morrighon, whose stomach fluttered anew. Anaris' expression was mild, the worst sign possible.

"It was the Bori woman who did this, you said?"

"Yes, lord," Morrighon offered no exculpation; it would do no good.

"And you cannot undo her efforts?"

"Not within the time limit you specified, lord."

Anaris nodded thoughtfully. "It would have gone far worse for us had they more environmental control."

Morrighon seized the opportunity gratefully. "I had that hardwired, lord."

His master looked at him, expressionless. "It is well that you did," he said finally. He looked back down the corridor. "She is quite good, isn't she?"

"Yes, lord," Morrighon said. "Possibly the best noderunner I have ever encountered. Perhaps even Ferrasin's superior."

"Then we will take her with us," said Anaris. "The Rifters will not be able to evade the cruiser; I do not wish them to. They will serve my purpose one more time."

"She will not come without her cousins," Morrighon ventured. It appeared that he would not suffer the consequences of his failure this time.

"I leave that to you," Anaris replied, pushing off from the

wall and launching himself across the corridor, through a hatch. His voice echoed out of the compartment. "The assault is about to begin, the corridor will not be safe."

Morrighon followed him clumsily, feeling his stomach roil again. Anaris touched lightly on the opposite wall, then twisted about to face him. He spoke a command into the communicator. There was a moment of silence, then the blast of shaped charges, the hissing roar of jacs, and the frenzied yells of the Tarkans, mixed with horrified screams from the Rifters outside the hatch.

"And Morrighon," Anaris continued, as though there were nothing happening, "do not fail me again."

❋ ❋ ❋

Larghior Alac-lu-Ombric watched as Emmet Fasthand slumped in defeat and tabbed the hatch open. The Tarkans rushed in, spreading out efficiently, menacing the bridge crew with their jacs. No one moved. Two of the Tarkans went over to Moob and yanked her out of her pod, one of them pinioning her while the other roughly relieved her of her knives. Larghior was mildly astonished at the quantity of weapons she managed to conceal on her person.

When their search was finished, the Tarkan slammed her back in her pod and moved away. She snarled at him wordlessly, but her heart obviously wasn't in it.

They searched the rest of the crew just as efficiently; then the senior Tarkan went back to the hatch. A moment later Anaris achreash-Eusabian strode onto the bridge, followed by Morrighon. Lar saw the Bori's eyes seek him out, and shrank back.

Oh, Tatriman, what have you done?

Anaris' secretary walked over to Creote's console and pushed him out of his pod. Creote scrambled away from the Bori like a spider and retreated to a far bulkhead. Seated himself in his place, Morrighon tapped at the keys. There was a squeal of code, followed by the flickering light of a high-speed playback.

He planted a spytrap, independent of the ship's computer.

After a beat, Morrighon looked up. "They launched a repeater, lord, spooled with a message to the cruiser about the shuttle and the Panarch."

"Can you cancel it?" Anaris asked.

Morrighon touched a key. "Self-destruct signal dispatched." He touched another key; Creote's recorded voice suddenly filled the bridge. ". . . on the planet's surface at latitude 33.7, longitude 358.9, according to System FF simulation coordinates. We are leaving the system—"

The message stopped abruptly.

"They cannot have heard it, lord," said Morrighon, staring at Fasthand with a gloating smile. "The ionstorm will have prevented that."

"Good." Anaris took a step toward Fasthand. "They would not have let you go in any case. You know the secret of Gehenna." He smiled coldly. "So you will fight or die."

Somehow, to Larghior's astonishment, Emmet Fasthand found it in himself to reply, "Fight *and* die, you mean."

Anaris merely stared at him, then raised his hand. As one of the Tarkans came forward, Fasthand gobbled quickly, "We'll fight, we'll fight."

"Then bring this ship about," Anaris replied. "You will have one slight advantage."

Fasthand just looked at him blankly.

"They will try to disable and board you, to find out where the Panarch was landed. You will be under no such restraint."

Lar felt a presence at his side and looked over to find Morrighon standing next to his pod.

"Take me to your cousin, Larghior Alac-lu-Ombric." Anaris' secretary must have seen the mute refusal in his eyes, for he added, "No harm will come to you and yours; I have already sent for your brother. This ship will shortly be destroyed in battle. Do you not wish to live?"

Lar nodded, confused, not moving for a moment. Then, at an impatient gesture from Morrighon, he got up from his console and followed the other off the bridge.

❋ ❋ ❋

Matilde Ho slid tiredly down the wall and squatted on the deckplates. She'd done what she could to undo the damage inflicted on the ship by the Dol'jharian saboteur; now it was up to the self-repair algorithms to finish the job of rerouting control to give them enough power to lift off.

BOOM. Another reverberation shook the ship, echoing up through her aching joints, through her healing arm, into her eyeballs. They'd had to tune the shields down to conserve power; the Gehennans had brought up heavy catapults and were throwing quarter-ton rocks at them.

Rocks! It's like something out of a surreal history chip.

She pressed the heels of her hands against her eyes, as if to push the pain back, and let a bubble of laughter well up inside. It sounded more like a sob when it emerged.

A touch on her knee brought her head up. Gelasaar knelt next to her, blue eyes concerned.

She forced a smile to cracked lips. The heat from the fires set by the Gehennans around the ship was slowly seeping in.

"I'll do," she said. She gestured. "Ironic, isn't it—out in space, rocks are the primary hazard to a ship too."

An answering smile lit his face—but it was genuine. Mischievous, even. "Look what I found," he said, brandishing a small dusty bottle full of liquor dark with age. "Some Rifter's private stash is my guess."

Matilde leaned forward, then gasped. "Napoléone!"

"And it's a century old, if the label can be believed," the Panarch agreed. "Shall we?"

Matilde laughed as the shuttle rocked under another concussion. "Why not?"

With an air of ceremony the Panarch eased the cork out, and then after a toast to their unknown benefactor, took a sip. His eyes closed, and he smiled. "Perfect."

So they sat there, side by side, rank forgotten, all forms of ritual set aside, and passed the bottle back and forth from hand to hand while outside the crash and boom of primitive missiles provided a demented symphony.

Matilde cherished the blue-fire burn of the alcohol down her throat, the warmth in her chest, the glow in her head. At first they conversed little, beyond toasts: Padraic, Teodric, and other fallen comrades; Eusabian's downfall.

Then a thought floated to the surface of Matilde's mind: "To Brandon," she said. "Wherever he is." She drank deeply and passed the bottle.

"He's on his way," Gelasaar said softly, nodding upward, then lifted the bottle. "To Brandon." And drank.

For a moment, a semblance of ritual was back.

Matilde bit her numbing lips, wondering if now—at last—had come the time to speak. During these hours of relative freedom they had all talked, tongues more unguarded than ever before. Past mistakes reexamined, Semion and his likeliest future as Panarch considered; Gelasaar seemed to have relinquished the role of Panarch, and his retrospection seemed to regard his past self in the light of a persona, little known and not much liked.

But one subject he had not brought up and the others had stayed clear of: Brandon, the third son and now heir, who was alive only because he had unaccountably left his own Enkainion minutes before it was to have begun.

How *to* discuss it? Semion at least had played out his games within the rules, and to some factions he'd been hailed as a fine prospect for a ruler, one who had the Thousand-Year Peace at heart. Brandon's unexplained action had no precedent, was seen as an insult to the highest in the land—one made, moreover, as publicly as was possible.

Matilde said carefully, "How do you know it's him out there? Foreknowledge?"

Gelasaar smiled ruefully. "No. Faith." He passed the bottle back, then went on, his gaze pensive, "If I'd really known him, I expect many circumstances would be different." He looked over at Matilde. "But I believe I have, in some measure, come to know him a little in the last weeks—as our ancestors came to know something of then-invisible microparticles by observing where they had been, where they ought to be, and where they were not. I have followed my son's shadow through my conversations with Anaris, and through our own discussions."

Matilde sipped, fighting the burn of tears. *I've drunk too much,* she thought. *I'm maudlin with memory and regret.* And she cursed herself for having brought up a subject that could only cause pain.

But Gelasaar's eyes and hands exhibited no trace of regret as he lifted the bottle. "To Brandon," he said. "And faith."

And with a gesture of deliberate benediction he drank off the rest of the bottle, then threw it against the opposite bulkhead to smash into shards.

⁂ ⁂ ⁂

The course of the fleeing Rifter ship took it inward, into less trashy space, and so the chase accelerated. From time to time Ng commanded the dispatch of a tacponder to check the position of their prey—the asteroid and the ionstorm it generated, even in this relatively cleaner space, prevented direct vision.

Gehenna had dwindled and vanished in the glare of the system's primary, now behind them, when it happened. The asteroid sheltering them from the onrushing junk of the Gehenna system suddenly flared so bright that the screens blanked, coming back to reveal a grinding mass of rubble held in the tractors, the pieces vibrating wildly. Ng's heart hammered, but she kept her eyes steady on the screens, her breathing controlled.

"Skipmissile impact," Ensign Wychyrski at SigInt shouted.

"Weapons, release the asteroid rubble. Now." Ng's voice came out cool and quiet.

The ship lurched as the tractors shut down, and the rocks onscreen started to spread and tumble slowly.

"Navigation, come about twenty degrees mark zero, now!" Ng's hands tightened on her pod arms. The Rifters had turned to fight sooner than she had expected. "Tactical, probable range of enemy skipmissile."

"Skipmissile charged," said Tulin at the main weapons console while Rom-Sanchez calculated, confirming per SOP that the *Grozniy*'s main weapon was ready.

But we can't use it, thought Ng. *We need them alive.*

The port shields flared as the ship's turn exposed them to the tenth-cee system dust.

"Twenty degrees mark zero," Lieutenant Mzinga sang out.

"Probably max range for enemy, eleven light-seconds; we're limited to about six."

"Skip fifteen light-seconds, now!" Ng commanded. "SigInt, slave a console to monitor the Knot," she continued as the fiveskip burped. "Put Ensign Grigorian on it."

"Port shields at one-hundred ten and climbing," Damage Control reported.

"Navigation, bring us about to starboard 180 mark zero and take us down to point-oh-one cee at tac-level five."

The engines groaned as they came about, the starboard shields glaring even brighter than the other side had as the massive ship presented its side to the rocks and ice hitting it at 31,000 kilometers per second.

Ng flicked a glance at her right. Brandon Arkad stood motionless, hands behind his back, his gaze moving rapidly. He was following the action without difficulty; she risked a glance at Sebastian Omilov. His sweat-lined brow was puckered in confusion, but he also did not move or speak.

"Starboard shields at one hundred twenty and rising," said

Damage Control. "Estimate fifteen seconds life for aft shields over radiants."

"Probable ruptor range twenty-five light-seconds, max," Rom-Sanchez added.

After a time measured only in heartbeats and damp-palmed anticipation the fiveskip engaged again, harsher. When they emerged, the shields were dim, flaring here and there as small rocks hit them.

"Emergence at point-oh-one cee."

"Tactical skip, now, tac-level one."

"Captain," Rom-Sanchez said urgently as the fiveskip burped. "The Knot."

"I know, Commander," she replied, "but we won't have to worry about that if they hit us square on with one of those hopped-up skipmissiles." She raised her voice. "SigInt, find that destroyer."

"Search initiated, Captain. The Knot's been excited pretty fiercely—still a lot of ionization. Long EMF's pretty much out. And the system's dirty as hell. Sir." Wychyrski reddened.

A wire-frame model of the Knot popped up on one of the subsidiary screens, simulating the computer's best guess at the lines of force within the complex fracture in spacetime. The hyperbola was vibrating subtly, shimmying waves running through the force lines.

"It's flattening out, sir," said Grigorian, his voice thick. He cleared his throat, went on more clearly. "We've lost about seven percent of our leeway by the last maneuvers—and the skipmissile didn't help things any."

"No help for it," replied Ng. "SigInt, where is he?"

The ensign stabbed at her console. "Got him. Forty-seven mark zero, plus 15 light-seconds, course 25 mark zero, plus point-oh-two cee relative." She squinted at the display. "I think he's coming about to port."

"He's still zeroing on the asteroid," Krajno muttered.

"He'll figure that out soon enough," said Ng. She glanced at the god's-eye of the *Grozniy*. "Weapons, ruptor barrage, half-power, forward beta and gamma, aft beta, medium spread, forty-seven, forty-five, forty-three." They couldn't use full power—they had to take the Rifter ship intact to find where they'd landed the Panarch.

She raised her voice for the entire bridge. "We're going on System FF protocol: you can all assume mark zero for all courses unless I command otherwise. The Knot will force us to fight this battle in two dimensions."

She paused, allowed them a brief reaction. A tiny spurt of amusement flared inside her as one or two glances were sidled the Aerenarch's way, as if to gauge his reaction. But she knew by now that he would show no reaction.

"Weapons, fire ruptors," she said, and her crew returned their focus to their tasks.

The gentle vibration of the ruptors formed a counterpoint to Ng's thoughts as she continued issuing orders. With a perverse delight, she suddenly realized that she was fighting a battle with largely the same limitations as had faced Nelson, confined to the two-dimensional surface of Lost Earth's watery skin.

But against Eusabian's skipmissiles, the Grozniy *is far more fragile than Britain's "wooden walls."*

She dismissed the thought and turned her full attention to the battle. Winning it was only one more step in this endeavor.

* * *

"Skipmissile away," said Kedr Five at the weapons console. "Skipmissile charging." Eight seconds later a gout of light erupted, washing out the flaring star that announced the battlecruiser's headlong flight toward them.

"Course 20 mark zero," Fasthand snapped. "Skip five light-seconds on acquisition."

"The asteroid is breaking up," Moob put in. "The next shot'll probably punch right through."

"There won't be anything behind it by then," Fasthand snarled as the fiveskip burped. Then he paused. *Unless that's just what they want me to think.* He cursed silently, feelingly. He hadn't bargained for this kind of fighting when he joined Eusabian's forces. Bad enough facing a cruiser alone; to have to do it in two dimensions . . .

"Ivo! What's happening with the Knot?"

A simulation popped up on a secondary screen. It was vibrating weirdly.

"Flattening out, Cap'n. We've lost about five percent of the margin, what with the skipmissile and all."

"Skipmissile charged," Kedr Five said.

Fasthand gnawed at his thumb. He couldn't take the chance. "Bring it about and fire at the asteroid. Might still be there."

The stars, those visible through the flaring shields and the flickering lightning like discharges of the Knot, swung across the screen. A targeting cross sprung up and centered on the asteroid rubble, now spreading out. The red wakepulse of a skipmissile washed over it; four seconds later the blob of light flared brightly and exploded outward, dissipating into separate points of light like fireworks in atmosphere.

"No cruiser."

"Tactical skip, now." The fiveskip burred again. "Course 270 mark zero . . ."

Fasthand looked up, continuing his orders. The two Tarkans Anaris had left behind still stood to either side of the hatch, their jacs ready.

The Rifter snarled noiselessly. No choice. Never had been, he decided, once he signed onto Dol'jhar's Rifter fleet.

The squeal-rumble of a near-miss ruptor bolt snatched his attention back to the battle, and he forgot Anaris, forgot the Dol'jharians, forgot everything except the fact that he was going to die, and soon.

* * *

Mortan Kree felt his stomach clench at the expression on Matilde Ho's face when the tiny woman looked up from the engineering console.

"The core regeneration is slowing down; the shields and refrigeration units are drawing too much power."

Kree glanced at the others, seeing in their faces the same understanding now flooding his mind. There was silence for a moment, broken only by the mutter of the distress signal spooling out over the com. Then another muffled crash resonated through the ship. On the screen the sun glared through wreaths of oily smoke, which opened up momentarily to reveal burned ground and shattered trees.

"We can't cut refrigeration," Caleb murmured finally. "It's already almost forty-five degrees in here."

"We certainly can't cut the shields," Yosefina put in.

"That's exactly what we have to do," Matilde said. She held up her hand, forestalling their objections. "Correct me if I'm wrong, Mortan, but the hull metal will stand up to at least a few impacts even from five-hundred-kilo rocks?"

Mortan thought for a moment. He'd been a Centripetal Gnostor, one of only thirteen in the Thousand Suns, for over fifty years now; but nothing had ever stressed the fund of general knowledge that was his calling like their present situation. "I would say so; the center of gravity of this type of shuttle is too low for there to be any risk of tipping over. But that's not the worst that could happen."

Gelasaar laughed suddenly. "No, I'm sure it's not."

Mortan smiled. "I assume, Matilde, that you propose cutting the shields to give us sufficient power to lift off."

She nodded and tapped her console. Moments later the screen switched to a diagram, which Kree studied for a moment. "That will expose the outer lock door to direct assault." He motioned at the screen. "From that, I'd say it'll take about an hour to lift after the shields power down."

"That's my estimate."

Mortan shook his head. "Iffy. Very iffy. If they damage the lock sufficiently, the loss of streamlining, in the absence of shields, will doom us."

"Do you think you can regain control of the lock?"

Kree felt a thrill of excitement and fear at what that question portended. "We can certainly crack it manually, but doing so will make it impossible to reengage the hatch motors."

"In other words," said the Panarch, "we can open it, but we can't close it again and hold it against a determined assault."

Mortan nodded.

"We've no choice," said Gelasaar. "If the damage makes it necessary, we'll have to open the lock and let them do their damage inside until we can lift off. But I'm guessing that they'll want the ship intact."

"Whoever possessed it would rule this world," Mortan replied. "But the interior hatch won't hold anywhere near as long; they'll undoubtedly use some sort of battering ram."

"That's no problem," said Caleb. "Two people with jacs can hold the corridor once the hatch fails. There are some breathing masks in the locker."

"This all assumes we can convince the Rifters to cooperate," said Yosefina.

"They can't prevent me from shutting down the shields," said Matilde. She grinned. "And maybe it will hurry their surrender." She looked over at the Panarch, who nodded.

"Do it."

✻ ✻ ✻

Tat opened her eyes and shrank back against the deck as she saw Morrighon bending over her, his hands on his knees. Then her eyes came into fuller focus and she saw Lar and Dem looking anxiously at her over his shoulders.

He's going to have all of us killed.

Morrighon straightened up and stepped back. Lar knelt beside her and lifted her head. "You all right, Tat?"

She levered herself up on her elbows, watching Morrighon's twisted smile warily, and groaned as the cabin seemed to lurch. The last remnants of the brainsuck in her system lent the scene an aura of unreality; she kept expecting Morrighon's teeth to fly out of his head at her, or Dem's head to flit away like a deflating balloon.

Lar murmured, "It's all right, Tat. We won't be punished."

Morrighon added, "Your cleverness has saved all your lives."

Suddenly the deck seemed to cant and the air rang with a squealing rumble. Morrighon set his feet more firmly and continued. "This ship is presently engaged in battle with a Panarchist battlecruiser. It will be destroyed shortly." He turned away and walked to the hatch, speaking over his shoulder. "Come. Now. We are preparing to debark."

Lar and Dem lifted Tat to her feet and she staggered out of her cabin and down the corridor after Morrighon and the two gray-clad guards with him. He took them to the port landing bay; they saw no other crew on the way.

As they stepped through the hatch, Tat heard the whining rumble of engines warming up, emanating from the deadly, thorn-studded shape of a small warship that practically filled the bay. Morrighon hurried them up the ramp, which began to retract even as they turned toward the bridge.

Tat's heart squeezed her throat when Morrighon pushed her through the hatch ahead of him onto the bridge, and Anaris swiveled around in the command pod to transfix her with an unwinking gaze of cold appraisal. She glanced to either side, but her cousins were no longer with her.

Morrighon grabbed her arm and pulled her over to a console as Anaris swiveled back and raised his head to watch the main screen. It was slaved to the bridge of the *Samedi;* Tat saw the wake of a skipmissile dissipating in the midst of a flaring chaos of energy. The blacked-out limb of the system's primary loomed huge to one side. Anaris tapped at his console; another screen lit, showing the bridge of the *Samedi*. Even from here, Tat could see that Fasthand was almost out of control—and the rest of the crew very little better.

"This console is linked to the *Samedi*'s computer," said the Bori secretary, pulling her attention away from the fearful chaos on the bridge. "We do not wish to give Fasthand warning of the exact moment of our departure, lest he bring weapons to bear, despite the presence of two Tarkans on the bridge. Can you momentarily cut the ship's shields from here?"

"Think so. Will take a moment to check." She queried the system, listening with half an ear to the feed from the bridge.

"Captain," said Cefas on screen, who'd taken Lar's position at Damage Control. "That corvette in the port bay is warming up."

Fasthand looked over his shoulder to address someone Tat couldn't see—the Tarkans, she guessed. "You hear that? Your master's leaving you to die."

A voice replied in surprisingly clear Uni, "That is our function and our honor." It added with a twist of irony, "You are fortunate that we are here to ensure that you, too, die with honor."

Fasthand turned back to the main screen with a wordless snarl, as Tat's console bleeped.

"I can do it," she reported.

"I set a tractor to restrain this ship," Anaris said. "Release it at the same time." The sound of the engines rose to a grumbling scream. "On my mark, then," he continued. The main screen switched to a view out the bay lock; one of the secondary displays showed the interior of the bay, its fittings now melting and boiling away as the radiants of the ship blasted sun-hot plasma into its interior. "Three. Two. One. Mark."

Tat slapped the go-pad on her console, canceling the ship's shields for a few seconds and cutting the tractor beam.

The edges of the bay abruptly vanished as the warship exploded from the doomed destroyer; the head-bloating lurch of skip transition followed almost instantaneously.

Tat let her breath out in a gusting sigh as Anaris dropped the ship back into realtime and brought it about with sure motions of his hands. Then she watched in amazement as, rather than setting course out of the system, he merely pulled them back behind some stellar debris and began to watch the battle. She risked a glance at Morrighon, whose face showed nothing.

Tat crouched back in her pod, ignored by all on the bridge. Only one of the Last Generation Bori, she decided, could understand the Dol'jharian mind, and for that knowledge, the price was far too high.

Twenty-nine

Neesach An-Jayvan watched horrified as Kaniffer pounded on the console, his eyes bulging. "You're bugchatz crazy!" he screamed. "Those rocks'll tear the ship apart!"

The reasoned reply of the little nick woman didn't make any impression on the pilot; he slapped the com off and spun around to face her. "Why didn't you hardwire the shields, you stinking blit?" he yelled. Sweat dripped from his scanty hair.

"It's not like that Morrighon chatzer left me a lot of time," Neesach screamed back, noting with satisfaction how Kaniffer winced. She'd always hated her voice, but it made a fine weapon at times like this. "I worked on the stuff we'd need to be safe from the Tarkans. How was I supposed to know . . ."

A shattering bang stopped her. The ship rocked: the shields were down. They stared at each other, dreading the next impact. When it came, it was worse than she had expected. "We can't take this, no matter what those chatzing nicks say. If they punch through and that spore-blunge the sensors detected gets in . . ." She shuddered. They didn't have any breathing masks on the bridge; the Panarchists had them all.

Resolution hardened Kaniffer's face. "We've still got the outer lock, right?"

"Yeah, but . . ."

Kaniffer waved her to silence. "Set up the image feed from the engine room to the external holojac." He turned away and set the com to external sonic broadcast.

"We'll make a deal with you out there," he said. "We've got something you'll want even more than the ship. . . ."

⁂ ⁂ ⁂

A runner pounded up beside Londri and flung himself flat next to her, tear tracks marking pale paths down his soot-coated face. "Aztlan reports he's holding the Tasuroi; his elite guard is in position for an assault on the ship in concert with Gath-Boru and the Ferric Guard."

She nodded—that was the last of the forces she needed—then snapped her head back as something caught her attention. She watched carefully as another massive rock hit the shuttle.

"Stepan!" she shouted. "The rocks aren't bouncing anymore!" This was what they had hoped and prepared for.

He wriggled up beside her, and they both squinted through the haze of smoke. A short time later another massive rock smashed into the ship; a shallow dent appeared in the hull.

"Have them stop the heavy artillery," he said urgently. "They'll damage it beyond repair. And have them aim for the cannon with the light artillery before you begin the assault."

Londri dispatched a runner and motioned a herald over. He listened to her instructions and then raised the war horn to his lips. A glissade of notes ripped out of the wooden bell.

The battlefield quieted. She could clearly hear the crackle of flames and the distant shouts of the battle with the Tasuroi. Londri felt the sweat trickle down her back inside her armor; the long summer day was waning, but it would be hours before the air began to cool—it would be far worse for those inside the ship.

Then, nearby, she could hear the creaking of a light catapult being made ready. Their lighter payload would necessitate a flatter trajectory to inflict meaningful damage—they would have to be exposed to return fire. Fresh billows of smoke began to roll toward the ship as the returning horn calls began to signal the readiness of the other artillery.

She was rehearsing her next orders in her mind when a booming voice from the grounded ship shattered her thoughts.

"We'll make a deal with you out there. We've got something you'll want even more than the ship, and we'll give them to you if you'll let us go."

Londri stared as a wavering image began to take shape in the smoke wreathing the shuttle. Like ghosts wakened to the light of day, she saw, indistinct, the shapes of several elderly people clustered about some incomprehensible shapes, a world's ransom in metal gleaming around them.

Beside her she heard a gasp. She glanced over at Stepan. His eyes were wide, his mouth gaping open, working as though he were trying to speak. He gestured at the image, his hand shaking, but the ship spoke first.

"This is the Panarch of the Thousand Suns, overthrown and exiled to Gehenna by order of the Avatar. If you cease your attack we will give him and his Privy Council to you; if you do not, we will kill him and deprive you of the revenge you never thought you'd have."

Londri's breath stopped. *"Within your grasp the author of your woe."* Would it truly fall to her to revenge the centuries of suffering imposed upon the people of Gehenna by the Panarchy? She looked over at Stepan again.

He nodded, struggled to speak. "It is. It is the Panarch. And some of his council. But they are armed."

She looked again, more closely, saw angular metal objects cradled in the arms of two of the Panarchists.

Then how can they kill them? It is a lie, like everything else they do and say.

She stood up then, heedless of any danger from the ship, feeling a measureless anger well up from some dark fortress deep within her soul. It was as though every one of her mothers, clear back to the arrival of humanity in the merciless prison of Gehenna, shouted with rage.

Whirling about, she seized the war horn from the herald and blew furiously into it, and, as though impelled by one mind, the men and women of the armies of Gehenna poured into the clearing, screaming furiously, flinging a hail of rocks and fire and smoke.

❋ ❋ ❋

"The *Samedi* has launched a ship," Ensign Wychyrski reported. "It appears to be corvette-class. It skipped."

"Probably half the crew has mutinied and is jumping ship," Krajno said, grim satisfaction in his voice.

"I can't match the signature," Wychyrski continued.

"Try the Dol'jharian section of the registry," said the Aerenarch. It was the first time he had spoken.

Ng looked over at him as Wychyrski pursed her lips.

"It's Anaris," the Aerenarch went on, his voice light and nearly dispassionate.

"Confirmed," said the ensign after a time. "Dol'jharian *Lakku*-class corvette."

"No threat to us," Rom-Sanchez added.

Wychyrski looked startled suddenly. "That's odd. Emergence at plus twenty-five light-seconds. He's staying to watch."

In response to Ng's questioning look, the Aerenarch shrugged, then smiled slightly. "When we were young, I could predict his actions fairly well—I had to. Now . . ." He turned his hands palms-up.

"*Samedi* skipped," said Rom-Sanchez.

"Tactical skip, now," Ng commanded, putting the matter out of her mind. The fiveskip burped.

The Rifter ship fought with the desperation of a cornered rat. To her surprise, Ng found that the removal of the third dimension of spatial warfare was an equalizing factor, a fact underscored sometime later by the smash of a skipmissile impact.

The bridge canted for a moment as the ship shuddered.

"Skipmissile hit, aft alpha ruptor turret not reporting, shields oscillating."

"Tactical skip. Now." The fiveskip burped. "Bring us about, thirty-five degrees, skip ten light-seconds on acquisition."

On the main screen the Knot flickered angrily in stuttering vividness, like two curving walls of light closing in to crush the *Grozniy* and its opponent.

"Knot status."

"Lobe closure accelerating. Margin thirty-four percent and falling."

We've got to finish them, and fast, before FF finishes us both. But the restraint imposed upon them by the need to interrogate the Rifters about the Panarch was telling on them—the Rifter, with no such inhibition, fought more violently with every pass of the deadly dance taking place in the Gehenna system, taking them further and further from the planet.

Suddenly Wychyrski stiffened, tapped frantically at her console. "I'm picking up a distress call; trying to clean it up."

A few seconds later the bridge com crackled to life; Ng listened with part of her attention as she conned the ship.

". . . SHUTTLE GROUNDED . . . ENGINES . . . ATTACK BY PLANETARY . . . OFF . . ."

A sudden intake of breath next to her pulled Ng's head around for a moment: the Aerenarch's blue eyes were wide and intense. "That is my father's voice," he said.

The signal faded and vanished back into noise.

"Then they left the shuttle on the surface?" asked Rom-Sanchez.

"They must have overcome the crew," the Aerenarch said.

"Skipmissile status," Ng snapped. "This changes things entirely."

"Skipmissile charge at ninety percent." The oscillating plasma had been held too long; their first shot might not tell.

"The second one will," said Krajno, notifying Ng that she had spoken aloud, but she didn't pause.

"Navigation, bring us about, two-ninety degrees. It's time for the kill."

* * *

"Over there!" screeched Neesach, gesturing wildly. Kaniffer squinted into the setting sun, swiveled the cannon around, and tabbed the fire button, snarling with satisfaction as a catapult exploded into flaming pieces. Then he swiveled it back and swept the beam of plasma along a line of attackers, exulting as they exploded into bloody smoke.

Neesach reached over his shoulder, stabbing at the fire-control screen and leaving a greasy mark on it. "Shoot there!"

"Get away from me, you logos-licker! This isn't a chatzing vidgame!" Kannifer yelled even as he directed the cannon toward the clot of Gehennans she'd indicated, but he caught only some stragglers as a group of the attackers ran up against the hull where he couldn't see them. Moments later a rhythmic thudding commenced.

"You missed 'em, genz I'll-take-the-cannon! Now what're ya gonna do?" she shrieked.

Kaniffer winced, wondering when his ears would start bleeding as he elevated the cannon and picked off another catapult, then another.

"If you'd stop yelling in my ear with that whiny Shiidra-orgasm voice of yours . . . Owww!"

Neesach slapped his face hard; Kaniffer turned around and shoved her violently backward. She fell over a console, screaming furiously, and Kaniffer laughed—just as a catapult bolt hurtled straight at the cannon and jammed its vertical traverse. He jerked at the control, cursing loudly. . . .

⁂ ⁂ ⁂

Londri watched, horrified despite her anger, as a finger of sun-bright flame, like a straight lightning bolt and as loud, reached out from the top of the ship. Where it touched, warriors vanished, their bodies exploding into a red fog.

But still the attackers came on. She saw several squads fanning out in a self-sacrificial effort to distract the fire-thrower from the sapper teams with the rams, while the light catapults thrummed and creaked. The flame reached out with terrifying ease, tracing a path of ruin and agony among her people. Now the ever-present smoke bore the stench of burned flesh.

Then the weapon's barrel hesitated, as if unsure of what target should be next, lifted, and the finger lanced out again. A catapult disintegrated, the stored tension of its cords flinging bits of crossarms high into the air as the rest flamed into smoke and shattered embers, flinging the bodies of its crew in all directions.

But the distraction had accomplished its purpose. A ram team ran forward, under the maximum depression of the fire-thrower, and began battering at the lock, while the rest of the assaulting force fell back. The artillery kept up its fire. Two more catapults disintegrated, then one scored a hit on the ship's weapon. Its barrel swiveled wildly for a moment; it seemed unable to depress as far as before. Another bolt hit it. There was a flash of light and then a shocking detonation as the fire-shooter disintegrated.

Yelling in triumph, the attackers surrounded the shuttle, battering at it in a frenzy of triumphant hate.

⁂ ⁂ ⁂

The end came suddenly. One moment the *Samedi* gleamed sleekly in the light of the FF primary, its radiants flaring, then, as Morrighon watched with satisfaction, a painfully bright point of light blossomed over the destroyer's bridge, caving in the hull like the blow of an angry god's fist.

"Apparently they lost patience with our Rifter allies," Anaris said with a smile.

For a beat, nothing further happened. Then the *Samedi*'s shields flickered, bits of hull plating flew off, and the missile tube twisted drastically and spun away.

Ruptor strike, Morrighon thought, his tension increasing. But he would not suggest their leaving: Anaris manipulated the screens with rapidity, indicating his fascination with the situation. It would only annoy him to point out their increased risk.

Morrighon turned his gaze back to the disintegrating ship. Now there was nothing but an expanding ball of plasma where the *Samedi* had been. Beyond, the full crescent of the system's fifth planet gleamed whitely; two of its moons were also visible, with a third speck that was the *Grozniy*.

"They wouldn't have done that if they didn't feel certain of finding the Panarch," Morrighon ventured.

"Of course," Anaris replied, still intent on the screen. "A battlecruiser's sensors are far better than ours. I would guess they heard a distress call." He smiled. "That will serve our purposes as well as theirs." He tapped at his console, then smiled faintly, as though some thought had just occurred to him.

"Communications."

"Sir."

"Hail the battlecruiser."

The standard recording squealed out; then Anaris brought the ship about and engaged the fiveskip.

When they emerged, the fifth planet loomed large ahead, one of its moons off to their port side. Anaris blipped the fiveskip twice more.

"Communications."

"Sir."

"Deploy a relay around the moon."

There was a barely perceptible whoosh as the relay launched; Morrighon caught a brief glimpse of it streaking away. He wondered what would happen when the cruiser replied—and what did Anaris expect, that he would take this chance?

❋ ❋ ❋

"We can't take much more of this," said Mortan Kree, turning away from the screen as the fire from the plasma cannon ceased. "And now there's nothing to stop multiple assaults."

Matilde Ho nodded. "That ram they're using is amazingly effective. If they bring up a couple more—"

"Listen," said the Panarch.

They fell silent. Timed with the battering impacts of the ram, Mortan could hear a savage chant: "Arrr-KAD *(BOOM)* . . . Arrr-KAD *(BOOM)* . . . Arrr-KAD *(BOOM)* . . ."

Then the rhythm changed.

"ARRR *(BOOM)* KAD *(BOOM)* ARRR *(BOOM)* KAD *(BOOM)* . . ."

"They've brought up another ram," said Caleb.

"How much more time do we need?" Gelasaar asked.

"About an hour or so," Matilde replied.

"Can the lock hold that long?" The Panarch's voice was light, unstressed, as though he were asking about the weather.

Matilde glanced over at Kree; he shook his head wordlessly.

The Panarch nodded. "Then that makes it simple."

"No!" said Yosefina; the word seemed impelled from her involuntarily. Kree felt a chill of horror. The savage chant of their attackers left no doubt of Gelasaar's fate if he stepped outside the ship.

But the man before them had somehow altered, every line of his slight form, the steady light gaze, all evoked the majesty of the Emerald Throne. The Panarch had decided.

"Hear now the words of power, my friends, for in your hands must lie the succession." He held up his hand to prevent further objections; Kree felt his gesture as an almost physical blow. "The Gehennans will be satisfied with nothing less, and their rage is so great I doubt I'll have any time to regret my decision. In the meantime, the Navy approaches, and my son still lives. I bind you all to this: bring him these words, that he may wield that which is his."

With that, Gelasaar hai-Arkad, forty-seventh of his line, began to speak the words never shared before with those not of the lineage of Jaspar Arkad, and Mortan Kree felt them descend on him with a mystical force. He could not look away from that ardent face, but he sensed in the attitudes of the others about him that they felt the same weight.

Then the Panarch ceased speaking and gestured toward the corridor to the lock. "Let us endeavor," he said.

* * *

As the Dol'jharian relay came out of the EM shadow of the moon, the relayed image of the battlecruiser bloomed on the corvette's screen.

"Five-light-second delay," Communications announced. "Reply incoming."

The com hissed for a moment, then a woman's voice filled the bridge. "This is His Majesty's battlecruiser *Grozniy*, Captain Margot O'Reilly Ng commanding."

Anaris sat back and laughed. With a return of his earlier nausea, Morrighon realized that this was the ship that had fought so fiercely at Arthelion. There was now no chance Anaris would do the sensible thing and leave.

An image bloomed on-screen, replacing the stars with the interior of a Panarchist battlecruiser. A small, trim woman sat in the command pod, her naval uniform impeccable. A sudden smile of delight lit up Anaris' face.

Cold terror pooled in Morrighon's churning guts.

Standing behind the captain was a tall, slim man with curling dark hair, blue eyes, and a bone structure instantly familiar. Morrighon stared at Brandon vlith-Arkad, now heir to his father's throne. The young man seemed to gaze right back at him, brows quirked. But he did not speak.

The Panarchist captain said neutrally, "I take it you are Anaris, heir to Eusabian of Dol'jhar?"

"That was a splendid battle over Arthelion, Captain," Anaris said. "Juvaszt and the others are still picking apart your tactics."

Morrighon counted his heartbeats during the long-seeming delay. *Too many.*

"As we are theirs," the captain returned, her voice still neutral.

"It seems a shame that so much effort—so much entertainment—went for nothing," Anaris went on.

After the delay, the captain lifted one shoulder in a slight shrug. "So goes war," she said. One of her hands moved on her chair arm: a command, Morrighon knew. There was no reaction to be seen in the scarcely visible faces of the Navy monitors; Brandon vlith-Arkad stood motionless, hands behind him.

Anaris lifted his head a little. "Still no naval commission, Brandon?"

After five seconds, the Panarch's heir said with mendacious regret: "I've so little free time."

Anaris smiled, his voice edged like monothread: "Allow me to congratulate you on your accession."

Morrighon tried to stifle a snort of laughter, and his nose burned. *A jab at the dead brothers—no! A jab at the Panarch!*

But after the delay, Brandon's mouth smiled, carefree and young, but his eyes stayed cold, clear, and unblinking. "Did you want to swear fealty?"

Anaris laughed and cut the connection.

⁂ ⁂ ⁂

"He skipped," Wychyrski said.

"Knot status," Ng demanded.

"Margin eighteen percent and falling. Still flattening."

"He can make far better speed than we can under these conditions," said Rom-Sanchez.

"Does that class vessel have orbit-to-ground weapons?" Ng asked, leaning forward.

"No, sir."

"Then we have to get there before the Panarch lifts off. SigInt, grab that signal back, see if you can punch through a response."

Wychyrski tried, then shrugged. "Not from here."

"Keep trying, each emergence. Navigation, plot me a minimum perturbation course, to arrive at Gehenna with minimal relative velocity." System FF imposed a delicate balance between the less destabilizing effect of low-frequency, high-tac-level skip, with the high real velocity it imparted, and the more destabilizing effects of low-tac, with its lower real velocity that would leave them able to rendezvous more easily with the shuttle.

She looked at the Aerenarch. "We'll do everything we can."

He nodded, and the fiveskip engaged, hurling them back toward Gehenna.

The sun had set and the light was fading swiftly when the sky suddenly flared again; high overhead another star bloomed, faded, and was gone, leaving only the mysterious, ever-brighter wings of light, fluttering like the banners of an army. Londri looked up, rubbing her gritty eyes and wondering what it meant, then looked down into the clearing as the booming of the ram on the metal doors of the ship ceased. The smoke from the fires banked around the shuttle made it hard to see.

She stepped over the brow of the hill, careless of danger from the ship now that its fire-shooter was ruined. The ram crew was drawing back warily as the doors slid open slightly. A white cloth flapped in the opening until an arrow carried it away.

"Make them stop," Stepan hissed urgently. "That is the symbol for a parley."

Londri gestured at the herald, who raised his horn to his lips and blew a brief glissade. Again, the battlefield grew silent save for the crackle of fires, the screams of the wounded, and the ever-closer pandemonium of the battle with the Tasuroi. The soldiers around the shuttle drew away from the line of fire from the slightly opened doors, taking up flanking positions.

Then a voice came from the ship—not booming like the first, unmagnified by the arts of the enemy. "I wish to discuss the terms of my surrender." The voice carried a ring of authority despite its faintness, along with a slight singsong tone.

Next to her she heard Stepan's breath gust out. "That is his voice," he whispered.

"Can we trust them?"

Stepan frowned, then nodded. "Whatever else one may say of him, he was always a man of his word."

Londri strode forward then, followed by Stepan. The soldiers around the shuttle kindled torches from the dying oilbrush fires; their flickering light painted the shuttle in tones of blood. She stopped before the machine, awed despite herself by the mass of metallic wealth looming above her.

"I am Londri Ironqueen," she said, addressing the unseen listeners within the machine. "Lord of the Kingdoms of Gehenna and all the lands within the Splash." She drew her sword and held it before her face. "By the bright steel that is my birthright, by the courage that has sustained us for seven hundred years against your hate, and by the wisdom of our mothers and their mothers' mothers, I demand to see you face-to-face." She pointed at the partly opened door with her sword. "I will not speak to a crack in a door."

There was the ghost of a chuckle from within. A moment

later the doors opened a bit more and a man emerged, jumping gracefully to the ground despite his age. His outline was blurred by wreaths of smoke; Londri stared and lowered her sword. This was the Panarch of the Thousand Suns? Absolute ruler of more people than there were grains of sand in the deserts beyond the mountains?

The man she saw was slight in stature, and silver-haired. Old. Older than Stepan. But with the eyes of a ruler herself, she discerned the lines that the exercise of power and responsibility had graven in his face.

He walked up to her between the ranks of soldiers drawn up to either side, and stood within reach of her steel. He returned her stare gravely, seemingly oblivious to the host all around. They seemed to realize this; she heard a rising growl of anger and, glancing about, saw their rage intensify. For the first time in her life, she felt the helplessness of a leader who has used the emotions of her followers all too well. Next to her, Gath-Boru flexed his massive hands; she heard his breath rasping in his throat.

But the man looked only at her as he bowed, with the courtesy of one sovereign to another. There was no trace of fear in his demeanor, no intimation that his fate depended on anyone but her.

Then, at her side, Stepan moved. The Panarch glanced his way, then he looked back, his eyes widening with shock. "Stepan? Stepan Ruderik? What are *you* doing here?" he said.

Stepan Ruderik felt the words like a blow to his heart.

How dare he mock me! He took a step forward, then stopped, his anger faltering at the sincerity evident in Gelasaar's eyes. The Panarch reached out to grasp his hands, then stopped, dropped his arms, and shook his head, pain and confusion on his face. "I don't understand, Stepan. I never signed a Warrant of Isolation for you. How . . . ?"

That voice, never forgotten, brought back full force the memories of Arthelion so long ago, and Stepan remembered that, whatever else might have happened without his knowledge, Gelasaar had never lied to him—had never, he was sure, lied to anyone.

And then the truth crashed in on him, the reality behind the sneering hints his Abuffyd jailers had dropped on the long journey to isolation here, their mocking revelation of the secret of

Gehenna, and he knew that, no matter that he had transgressed politically, so long ago, it was not Gelasaar who had summarily condemned him to this hell. Whether it had been Semion or a different enemy, it didn't matter. What mattered was that the man he had sworn fealty to had not forfeited his love and respect. Stepan stumbled forward, weeping, and embraced the man he had never truly been able to hate.

After a time Gelasaar held him out at arm's length and looked searchingly at him. "But why are you here?"

Stepan shook his head, conscious of Londri's anger and impatience, and the ever-growing clamor of the Tasuroi—it sounded like Comori's forces were being driven back upon the clearing.

"There's no time, Gelasaar." He half turned toward the Ironqueen, with Gath-Boru looming at her side. "You must speak for your life now."

The Panarch looked at Londri, his face again composed. "Will you accept my life for theirs?" he asked, gesturing behind him at the shuttle. He nodded skyward. "My son approaches, and I would have them carry to him the means of his inheritance, and the rescue of my subjects from an evil greater than any you can imagine."

The Ironqueen was silent for a time; and Stepan felt a shiver of awe as the wings of the numinous brushed him. Under a flaming sky, ringed by flickering torches, a young woman in bloodred armor faced an old man in prison gray, but to his eyes, they were sacraments of the archetypal energies of Totality, bridging the gap of seven hundred years of isolation, uniting two sundered branches of humanity too long held apart.

He held his breath as the Ironqueen raised her sword and pointed it at the Panarch's throat.

Her voice was quiet, as controlled as the man she faced. "I can imagine no greater evil than the one you and your forebears have committed, condemning those who never transgressed your laws to this hell." She stepped back, waved her sword in a half-circle parallel to the ground, taking in all who stood around, watching.

"Look around you, Gelasaar hai-Arkad, and see how the hand of your justice rests upon my people."

The man's eyes moved in obedience to her command, and despite the Douloi mask, Stepan saw realization in the Panarch's eyes, subtle but unmistakable; he wondered if Londri could detect it. He knew the impact of what Gelasaar was seeing—long inured to it himself, for a moment he saw again through new eyes the twisted limbs, distorted features, skin cancers, cataracts, and all the panoply of the genetic struggle against a world not made for humankind.

"Revenge is a kind of wild justice," said the Panarch finally. He spread his hands, exposing his body even more fully to her sword. "This is little enough to satisfy such an indictment, but it is yours, if you will but permit me to fulfill my last responsibility to my subjects."

"And what of my responsibilities?" replied Londri. "What if I claim more than mere revenge and take wergild as well for the lives you have wasted? She raised her sword and pointed past him at the shuttle. "With that we can escape your prison."

The Panarch shook his head. "No, you cannot. This vessel cannot fly between the stars; you would merely exchange this prison for a slightly larger one." He turned his head toward the shuttle. "My people there will not give you even that; rather than surrender the vessel, they will trigger the engines to destruction."

"Then," said the Ironqueen, "at least I will deny your son his inheritance and obtain your death, and the metals of the ship as well."

"No," said Stepan, suddenly realizing that he was the only one present able to bridge the gap of understanding between the two rulers. "Your pardon, Majesty," he said to Londri, "but the engines of this vessel dispose the energies that light the stars. There would be nothing left for leagues around; Comori Keep itself might not survive."

There was a murmur from the listeners, and some of the soldiers glanced nervously at the shuttle. Stepan heard a flurry of horn calls from beyond the hill that hid the battle with the Tasuroi; next to him Gath-Boru listened intently, frowning, then motioned a herald over. But Londri and the Panarch faced each other, unmoving, as though alone on the battlefield.

"Listen to me, Your Majesties," Stepan continued. "My College insists that there are no accidents when the Archetypes move among us. You two have been brought together." He turned to the Panarch. "My presence here clearly shows that isolation has too long served not your justice, but others' private ends." He gestured upward. "And the secret of Gehenna is broken forever. Will you not end it, in exchange for your life and your son's inheritance?"

Around them there was movement and the clatter of weapons, and the herald next to Gath-Boru blew a long interrogative on his war horn, but Stepan paid it no mind. He turned to the Ironqueen. "It lies in your hands to culminate your mothers' long-held dream and end the isolation of your people. Will you forgo revenge and obtain true justice instead?"

There was a long pause. The light from the sky flared on the faces of two sovereigns and those around them, dimming the torchlight.

Then the Ironqueen spoke. " 'For then the best may be to cede desire.' " She sheathed her sword. "So be it. I give you your life and your succession. Will you give me justice?"

"There will be no more Isolates," said the Panarch, "and Gehenna will join the worlds of the Thousand Suns in full equality. I pledge it on the honor of the Phoenix House." He stepped forward and held out his hand. Londri gripped it for a long moment.

And Stepan's exultation turned to abject horror as, almost in the same moment, a horn call rang out and a wood-fletched arrow sprouted in the Panarch's shoulder. *Tasuroi!*

Then the clearing dissolved into fighting as the Elite Guard of House Aztlan suddenly turned on their erstwhile allies, and the Tasuroi cannibals poured into the clearing. Gath-Boru shouted commands as he threw himself forward and picked the Panarch up in one massive arm. He started toward the shuttle with a small detachment, carrying the wounded ruler of the Thousand Suns, while the Ferric Guard coalesced around the Ironqueen and Stepan and began to fight its way back to the main body.

" 'The traitor's triumph forcibly deny!' " the huge general shouted as the fighting carried him away from his Queen. "We will hold the sky machine until it can launch." He slashed at a Tasuroi who lunged at him, cleaving his head in two.

"And we will be free!"

⁂ ⁂ ⁂

Anaris' corvette scudded low over the planet, laying its deadly cargo. "Sneak-missiles discharged," reported Weapons.

In the main screen, just coming into view over the limb of Gehenna, Morrighon could see the crater near which the

Panarch had been landed, a minute pockmark slipping into the shadow of night. The matte-black missiles vanished as they fell away from the ship, awaiting the signal that would wake them to deadly life, nearly indetectable until then.

Anaris lifted the ship away from the planet, arcing away toward the nearest moon. From the communications console the recorded voice of the Panarch repeated its dispassionate message, reporting the position of the shuttle and its condition.

"Communications," said Anaris. "We'll take up station behind the moon. Stand by to deploy a relay."

He looked over at Morrighon, his eyes bright with an unfamiliar glint. "It should be a touching reunion," he said.

Thirty

Gath-Boru carefully set the old man down against a wall and turned back to lend his strength to closing the doors.

"We can't hold the outer hatch shut against a determined assault," said one of the Panarchists, a short, dark brown man. "And we still have the Rifters to deal with."

As if to underline his words, the little metal room resounded to an impact on the doors. Gath-Boru motioned the guards with him to help hold it closed.

The Panarch looked up from where he sat, wincing as a small woman carefully cut through the arrow shaft in his shoulder with some sort of metal tool. Gath-Boru stared; it cut the tough ironwood shaft as though it were a reed.

"I don't think they'll be a problem. Our friend here brought along some of that bioweapon they use—" He looked up at the general. "What do you call that dust that kills?"

"Sporetox."

"Their sensors will have revealed its toxicity; it only needs a small hole through the hatch, which they know they can't prevent." The old man smiled at Gath-Boru. "Even without it, one look at you would probably convince them to surrender."

The general smiled back, uncertain how to respond.

"It missed the major vessels and nerves," said the little woman. "If you're careful, you should be AyKay."

Evidently seeing Gath-Boru's expression of incomprehension, the sky-lord explained the situation to him. The ship's control was held by enemies. Once they were overcome, the ship could lift off, if they could hold the lock against the Tasuroi.

"And if you cannot?" asked Gath-Boru. He remembered what the old man had said to the Ironqueen about the engines.

The Panarch comprehended instantly. "We will not allow this vessel to fall into the hands of your enemies." The old man's smile was grim. "Is it your custom to burn your dead?" he asked.

Gath-Boru hesitated at the oddity of the question. "Yes."

"Then, if we fail, your pyre will consume your enemies in thousands."

"We won't fail," said a tall, thin man, addressing the Panarch. "You and Matilde can run the lift-off from the bridge. The rest of us can hold the lock—the Rifters have a couple more jacs, and there are enough breathing masks in the locker for us and our new allies."

He turned from Gelasaar to Gath-Boru. "We should be able to hold the lock long enough to lift off."

Watching the Panarch's face, Gath-Boru saw comprehension, then sorrow, then gratitude, and he understood. It was unlikely anyone in the lock would survive.

"Until death take me, or the world end," said the other Panarchist woman in the room, smiling. The words expressed, in different words, the oath he himself had taken to the Ironqueen, and with a rush of some emotion that he couldn't identify, Gath-Boru realized that these men and women from beyond the sky knew loyalty and love just as he did.

"This is a good company to die in," he said, and their responding smiles were all the answer he needed.

Londri's forces stopped the Tasuroi at the breastworks at the crest of the hill from which they had attacked the shuttle that afternoon. The cannibals fell back, decimated by determined archery and a squad of artillerists armed with sporetox—fortunately the wind favored its use.

Londri dispatched runners, but war-horn interrogatives brought back grim news. Comori had fallen, and reinforcements would not reach them anytime soon. It would be all they could do to hold this position. They could only harass them with archery, and their arrow supply was low. The two heavy catapults left from her own assault had fallen to the Tasuroi before the Ferric Guard threw them back; at least the crews had cut the cords before fleeing, rendering them useless.

But the Tasuroi had lost interest in them, turning instead to assault the ship; she could do nothing to stop them. She cursed under her breath as the hordes gave way to allow a company of Aztlan soldiers to bring up sporetox and neverquench, while the cannibals pried at the doors to the grounded vessel.

After a time, they succeeded in levering them open and jamming them with a log. A thread of fire lanced out of the crack they'd forced and speared a Tasuroi who had not backed away fast enough; his head exploded in a flare of bloody smoke, the body flopping in senseless spasms to the burned and ashy ground.

A hail of arrows clattered uselessly against the doors and surrounding hull. Several flew through the opening. Another line of fire lanced out.

Londri watched as a light catapult took aim. The sporetox bolt flew true against the doors, bursting in a deadly haze through the slit between the two halves.

The Tasuroi ran forward again, accompanied by Aztlan soldiers, only to be met once more by the fire weapon: two bolts lanced out, swinging from side to side in a deadly scythe that tore through flesh and armor with equal ease.

"They are no doubt wearing masks against toxic substances," said Stepan from behind her. "Neverquench will do little more, except perhaps from firetubes."

"How long will it take for them to be able to fly?" she asked.

"I don't know," he replied. "We can only hope it's less time than it takes the Tasuroi and Aztlan to overcome the lock party."

"And if not?"

Stepan shook his head. "Then they will trigger the engines, and we will all die."

⁂ ⁂ ⁂

"Bridge secured," Yosefina said, grinning tiredly, and she listened at the com again.

Mortan Kree felt his heart leap. Maybe—despite impossible odds—they would win free, after all.

"The Rifters surrendered," Yosefina continued. "Matilde estimates ten minutes to lift-off. Wants to know how we're holding up."

Mortan Kree stepped forward, laughing. "Tell him we'll make it—"

He jerked, clutched his shoulder where an arrow suddenly sprouted, but he did not drop his jac. Yosefina Paerakles turned away from the com and checked the power on her weapon.

Mortan started to check his jac, but stopped as a burning sensation flared in his shoulder. He looked down and was horrified to see a brownish-red fuzz erupting from the arrow wound. *Sporetox.* He turned to the massive Gehennan general. "Do you have an antidote to this?"

The big man shook his head. "It can't be used on living flesh. Fire sometimes works."

Kree motioned Caleb over and indicated his jac. "Try setting that to wide dispersion, lowest power setting. Let's see if cautery will slow it down."

Caleb grimaced, but did as suggested. The Gehennans looked on dispassionately. Kree guessed they were used to much worse.

The pain of the burn was excruciating, but it did seem to slow the spread of the fungus, or whatever it was.

More arrows clattered against the back wall. Yosefina stepped forward and fired back, drawing a scream of agony. She grinned over at them; without warning a thin tube was thrust through the crack and a stream of liquid arched over and drenched her. Her clothes smoldered for a second, and then she shrieked as she erupted in a column of flame, her skin cracking open and peeling away.

The firestop in the bulkhead foamed her, too late. Somehow, fumbling with fingers burned to the bone, she reset her jac, stumbled forward, and released the entire remaining charge in the weapon at full aperture, provoking a whole chorus of screams as she took her killers into death with her. Then she toppled through the doors and was gone.

Mortan Kree felt weakness spreading through his arm, reaching into his chest. He dialed his jac to the same setting Yosefina had used and stepped forward, waiting to one side of the doors. He grinned at Caleb and Gath-Boru, feeling one side of his mouth droop as the toxin mounted toward his brain.

"My turn now," he said.

❋ ❋ ❋

"Core regeneration complete," said Matilde. "Lift-off in three minutes. Radiant flush cycle initiated." She poked her little finger in the air. "We'll even have a little left over for shielding, so it won't matter that the lock is jammed open."

The Panarch smiled at her. Outside, evening was falling. High above, a star flickered, growing in brightness against the lightning-like discharges of the Knot.

"There he is," he said, jutting his chin at the screen. "We'll meet him halfway."

❋ ❋ ❋

Gath-Boru watched as the Panarchist stepped into the opening of the doors, the sporetox already blooming around his shoulders and head, and triggered his weapon. A flare of light accompanied by agonized screams announced the death of countless more attackers. Then an arrow lanced into his throat and he fell bonelessly out of the ship.

Moments later the doors began to grind apart. The last remaining Panarchist fired carefully at the ends of the wooden levers, but he could only delay the inevitable. The doors opened wide and the Tasuroi poured in.

The sky-weapon charred the first wave of attackers, exploding bodies in a bloody fog; then the beam of power from it faltered and died. The next wave of attackers rolled over the Panarchist; the man tried to counter a blow with his weapon, but the weight of the Tasuroi's club bore the weapon back against him and crushed his skull.

Motioning his soldiers back around him, Gath-Boru backed up against the inner door, meeting the onslaught with the steel that had given the Crater hegemony over the kingdoms of Gehenna, and soon the metal room was splashed with blood.

And then the floor quivered.

❋ ❋ ❋

Another wash of fire blared out of the doors of the shuttle, charring a host of Tasuroi; a moment later a man's body followed it. As the cannibals began levering at the doors with long, thick wooden poles, Londri looked past and saw Aztlan directing the assault on the ship. "Damn the traitor!"

Flares of light struck at the ends of the poles wielded by the Tasuroi, but to no effect. The doors were forced open and the enemy streamed in.

Then a puff of steam lifted lazily from beneath the machine.

"I believe they are preparing to lift off," said Stepan.

* * *

One by one the remaining Ferric Guard fell to the clubs of the Tasuroi until Gath-Boru alone was left. He had always known his huge body had condemned him to an early death from heart failure: it was the mark of his line, so he did not fear death. He feared only failure, but that was the specter that haunted him now as the Tasuroi pressed ever inward, disregarding the scything sweep of his sword. The door behind him was locked, but it would fall all too soon to the battering rams of Aztlan if he fell.

His arms grew heavy, but he knew if he faltered they would overwhelm him in a moment.

There was a coughing roar outside, like the great sabercat of the Surimasi Mountains, and a flare of light, accompanied by a chorus of shrieks that died away instantly. The Tasuroi fell back; emboldened, he pushed forward, slashing at them, and suddenly the room was empty of aught but the dead. The roar repeated, and this time he felt a wave of heat.

The attackers had fallen back at last, but there was something strange about the sounds outside: it sounded like a wind had come up. He cautiously peered around the door and his breath stopped momentarily.

Far below, he could see heaps of burned bodies around a shallow, glassy crater; and around that, the scattered forces of the two armies. Momentarily he caught a glimpse of a pale face upturned, above gleaming red armor, but then the ground was too far away to be sure.

Gath-Boru watched, fascinated, as the battlefield dwindled into insignificance and vanished. Soon the horizon took on a definite curve; he squinted as the sun rose again, but the sky darkened. He gasped for air, but did not move away from the door—he realized that something was keeping the wind of their flight away from him.

His nose began to bleed, and his vision blurred. As the world became a vast blue-white bowl beneath him, his last thought was that he had done what Londri had always wanted: first of all those born upon Gehenna, he had escaped.

Gath-Boru smiled, and then the darkness rose up behind his eyes and carried him away.

Ng leaned forward in her command pod, as if she could impel the *Grozniy* to greater speed. In the main screen the Knot flared with actinic brightness, great sheets of lightning-like discharges sweeping through canyon walls of light. The huge ship could no longer safely skip, and the bright point of light ahead that was Gehenna grew with painful slowness.

"I have a visual, sir," said Wychyrski.

The screen blanked, filled with static, then cleared enough for her to make out the cramped bridge of a standard shuttle with four people, two seated at the consoles and two standing in the background. Ng felt a tremendous surge of emotion as she recognized the dapper bearded figure in the center—the Panarch—and then a pang of alarm when she saw a bloody wooden shaft protruding from his shoulder.

"Your Majesty," she said, rising.

Belatedly, a measure of the stunning sight of their ruler in realtime, her crew also rose.

The famous blue-gray eyes smiled across the distance between them. "No time for niceties, Captain: well done." Then, apparently seeing her alarm, he touched his wound. "This is not as serious as it looks."

Ng bowed again as the crew sat down slowly. "Status, Your Majesty?"

Gelasaar hai-Arkad turned to the soot-smeared figure at his right. Ng recognized Matilde Ho, Gnostor of Energetics, only by her voice as she said crisply, "We'll clear atmosphere in three minutes."

Below Ng, Lieutenant Mzinga turned to her. "Tractor range in four minutes."

The Panarch looked past Ng to Brandon, still standing silently behind the captain's pod.

"My son," the Panarch said, joy changing the timbre of his voice.

Ng felt her throat catch. At the edge of her peripheral vision she saw Brandon give a profound bow. Then he said, "Are you well, Father?"

"I am, my son. The time for reflection granted me has sharpened my vision. And you?"

Nothing. Ng thought, midway between tears and laughter, *not even danger and the threat of death, can eradicate that inbred Douloi singsong.*

"My travels seem to have led me full circle," Brandon said.

"Ah, yes, the Mandala," the Panarch replied. "I heard a little of that. How fares our home?"

He means the raid, Ng thought, but Brandon's answer was completely unexpected.

"On the eighteenth, I left the Hall of Mirrors," he said, his voice so light it was nearly inaudible. The Panarch watched intently.

"No sign of the corvette," said Wychyrski.

But he's got to be out there. Ng nodded. *Eighteenth—the Enkainion! But wasn't that in the Ivory Hall?* Then all her assumptions splintered: she realized they were talking not in code, but so elliptically only they could understand one another.

And they do, she realized. *They both know Anaris has to be listening, and that everything said here will be hashed over by millions, for years and years.*

A burst of static lit the screen, then resolved into a muddier view of the Panarch, who stepped closer to the imager. ". . . It was Jaspar's path, was it not?"

Brandon did not answer, but again made a profound bow. Ng realized that—somehow—Brandon had explained himself, and his father not only understood but concurred. *Hall of Mirrors—repetition—Jaspar . . . Brandon left to escape Semion, but he meant to come back,* she realized. *To create a new system, if he saw his brother ruining the old.* The insight made her almost dizzy.

"Come on, come on . . ." Ng realized she was gripping the pod arms so hard her hands ached.

"Three minutes to tractor range," said Mzinga.

❋ ❋ ❋

Aboard the corvette, Morrighon watched his lord watching the Panarch and his son talk. Most of it was Panarchic silliness, but Anaris listened, his profile intent.

A murmur on the bridge, too low through the static, made

Morrighon sit up. He swallowed once, twice, then spoke: "I believe the cruiser is almost in range."

Anaris waved his hand negligently.

Morrighon sat back, wondering if he'd gone mad. Why didn't he just blow the shuttle up and have done? Reluctantly he returned his eyes to the screen.

The Panarch said, "There is so much I want to tell you, son, but words are not enough. First, though, I must discharge a debt of honor. The first decree from the Emerald Throne must be to end the Isolation of Gehenna and bring the planet fully into the Thousand Suns."

Brandon bowed a third time.

The Panarch's eyes shifted. "Sebastian! Do you remember the poem you taught Brandon about words?"

Morrighon heard a voice, hesitant with surprise:

"The Hand of Telos has five fingers
Forth from the first came first the word
The echo of that act still lingers
Yet to the proud a sound unheard."

Surprised, Morrighon felt a flicker of recognition.

"That's it," said the Panarch, gesturing with one hand. "So much of your teaching was more than words."

Morrighon watched, fascinated, as the talk wandered off into abstruse philosophy. He would never understand the Douloi. Wasn't this exactly what the prisoners had done every night on the *Samedi?*

He felt an even more urgent tug of memory, then grabbed his compad, nearly spilling it onto the deck in his haste. He *had* heard those words before. Moments later the pad delivered up the same verse, from a transcript of the prisoners' talk.

He looked up at the screen. The gestures weren't just graceful punctuation! He turned to Anaris. "Lord, the Panarch is talking in code!"

Anaris' head turned sharply, eyes narrowed. Morrighon held up his compad to Anaris, who scanned rapidly, then motioned to the Tarkan at the weapons console. "Destroy that shuttle, now."

"Sneak-missiles triggered," reported Weapons. "Homing." There was a pause. "Hit."

⁕ ⁕ ⁕

"EMF burst from inner moon," Wychyrski said.

The image of the Panarch smeared out in a static burst and vanished.

Ng heard a harsh gasp from Omilov.

Then: "Missile strike on shuttle." Wychyrski's voice was strained. "Severe damage to stern, possible engine loss."

"I have a vector on the corvette," said Rom-Sanchez. "He's pulling away from the inner moon, heading for skip radius." He grimaced. "He's out of ruptor range."

Ng's first reaction was to chase and destroy the corvette, but then she could not save the shuttle. Fighting down her rage, she said coldly: "Let him go. Time to tractor range?"

"Seventy-five seconds."

She glanced at the Aerenarch. His face was stony with suppressed emotion; sweat lined his brow.

The screen cleared, revealing the shuttle's bridge now filling with smoke.

"We're almost there, Father." Brandon's hand grasped the back of the command pod.

"Sixty seconds to tractor range." A secondary screen showed the shuttle, tiny against the blue-white limb of Gehenna, the Knot flaring violently behind it.

From off-screen Matilde Ho said something Ng couldn't quite catch. The Panarch nodded, not taking his eyes off Brandon.

"There's not enough time, son. The engine is going critical."

"Fifty seconds, Father, just fifty seconds."

The Panarch's image wavered. He held up the Phoenix Signet, distorted into greater size by its proximity to the imager.

"I cannot give this to you now, but it is yours nevertheless." He coughed; the smoke was growing thicker. "Remember the Oath of Fealty: 'in life and in dying, until death take me or the world end.' It is your oath too—"

The screen went blank, then flickered to a view of the planet. Above it a stunning sphere of light bloomed, beautiful in its symmetry, its intricate internal detail slowly fading as it dissipated.

No one spoke, no one moved for what seemed an endless moment. Then the silence was broken by the voice of Sebastian Omilov, choked with grief.

"Out of light were we born, and to light shall we return. The Light-bearer receive him."

Ng clenched her jaw against the tide of reaction, fighting for control as she realized that everyone on the bridge was waiting for her next words.

Slowly she stood up and turned around. Forcing her tired body to obey, she bowed deeply, the same bow she had made once before, twenty years ago in the Palace Major on Arthelion.

Then she spoke.

"Your Majesty, what are your orders?"